Collected Fiction: 1905–1925

H. P. LOVECRAFT

Collected Fiction

A VARIORUM EDITION

VOLUME 1: 1905–1925

Edited by S. T. Joshi

Hippocampus Press

New York

First Paperback Edition.

Published by Hippocampus Press
P.O. Box 641, New York, NY 10156.
http://www.hippocampuspress.com

Cover design and cover artwork by Fergal Fitzpatrick. For the cover of
volume one, Mr. Fitzpatrick has used *the strange and the fantastic* as his
conceptual departure.

"I should describe mine own nature as tripartite, my interests consisting of
three parallel and dissociated groups—(a) Love of the strange and the
fantastic. (b) Love of the abstract truth and of scientific logick. (c) Love of
the ancient and the permanent. Sundry combinations of these three strains
will probably account for all my odd tastes and eccentricities."
                    —H. P. Lovecraft to Rheinhart Kleiner (7 March 1920)

Cover design and cover artwork by Fergal Fitzpatrick.
Portrait of H. P. Lovecraft, 1915.
Photo of S. T. Joshi by Emily Marija Kurmis.

Hippocampus Press logo designed by Anastasia Damianakos.

1 3 5 7 9 8 6 4 2

ISBN: 978-1-61498-109-1

Contents

Introduction

In the winter of 1976, shortly after I entered Brown University as an undergraduate, I began the task of examining the textual status of H. P. Lovecraft's stories, comparing the Arkham House editions of the period (released in 1963–65) with the manuscripts and early printed appearances that were housed in the John Hay Library. The task of preparing corrected versions of the Lovecraft fiction took nearly the entirety of my stay at Brown as an undergraduate and graduate student (1976–82) and eventually led to the publication of these corrected texts in three volumes by Arkham House: *The Dunwich Horror and Others* (1984), *At the Mountains of Madness and Other Novels* (1985), and *Dagon and Other Macabre Tales* (1986). Later, I prepared corrected versions of Lovecraft's revisions (*The Horror in the Museum and Other Revisions*, 1989) and included a small batch of his remaining fiction in *Miscellaneous Writings* (1995).

The Arkham House editions ultimately led to the publication of three annotated editions by Penguin Classics (*The Call of Cthulhu and Other Weird Stories*, 1999; *The Thing on the Doorstep and Other Weird Stories*, 2001; *The Dreams in the Witch House and Other Weird Stories*, 2004), which in turn led to Peter Straub's edition of Lovecraft's *Tales* (2005) for the Library of America, which used my texts. Because of various legal concerns, I was unable to present the stories in chronological order in the Arkham House editions, but this defect was remedied in my edition of Lovecraft's *Complete Fiction* (2008) for Barnes & Noble. Because of a proofreading snafu, the first printing of that edition was full of errors; but a corrected edition appeared in 2011 and to date constitutes the most accurate edition of Lovecraft's collected fiction.

I have, however, now undertaken a renewed investigation of the textual status of Lovecraft's stories, re-examining my textual notes and refining my decisions as to the best textual sources for the stories as well as of Lovecraft's preferences in regard to spelling, punctuation, and other details. I also wished to present these textual variants for interested readers, since there has on occasion been confusion as to the sources of the corrections I made in my previous editions. I have now presented these variegated results in this variorum edition, which lists all the textual variants in important publications of each Lovecraft story.

The end result is a series of slight but on occasion significant revisions of my previous texts so that, in my judgment, the texts presented here are now more in line with Lovecraft's habitual usages. As I was working on my initial corrected editions for Arkham House, I received valuable advice from the publisher's managing editor, James Turner, whose meticulousness in matters of orthography, punctuation, and other matters was unparalleled; but I have now determined that some of the decisions we made in regard to these and other matters are erroneous and need to be revised. I have also determined that, in several texts, such as "Dagon" and "The Rats in the Walls," Lovecraft made slight revisions of his stories when they first appeared in *Weird Tales* or were reprinted in that magazine.

We are fortunate that so many of Lovecraft's manuscripts are still extant. Even though Lovecraft himself stated that he would habitually destroy a manuscript or typescript when any printed version, however inadequate, was available, he in fact preserved many typescripts after they had appeared in print. He did not, it is true, preserve many of his original handwritten drafts, but the existence of a typescript prepared by himself (as opposed to some other hand) is a valuable clue to his textual preferences. In cases where autograph manuscripts are extant, I have at times printed in the textual notes passages that he excised in the course of composition. These excised passages provide important hints as to the direction and focus of the tales.

Many of his early tales were first published in amateur journals. When these tales were republished in *Weird Tales* or other professional magazines (or even in fan magazines such as the *Fantasy Fan*), Lovecraft took occasion to revise the texts slightly. Several extant typescripts in fact embody these revisions; in other cases the revisions must be inferred from subsequent printed appearances.

Lovecraft did not live to see a collection of his tales appear from a major publisher or even a small press; in his lifetime, the stillborn edition of *The Shunned House* (W. Paul Cook/The Recluse Press, 1928), R. H. Barlow's edition of *The Cats of Ulthar* (Dragon-Fly Press, 1935), and William L. Crawford's edition of *The Shadow over Innsmouth* (Visionary Press, 1936) constitute the only separate publications of his fiction. (Several of his tales did appear in anthologies during his lifetime, but these are usually of no textual significance.) When August Derleth and Donald Wandrei founded the firm of Arkham House, they were determined to preserve as much of Lovecraft's work—fiction, essays, poetry, letters—within hard covers as they could; but they were not authorities in textual scholarship and customarily made poor decisions in selecting a "copy-text" (the best extant text of a given work, whether it be a manuscript or a printed source) for use in their early editions, *The Outsider and Others* (1939) and *Beyond the Wall of Sleep* (1943). All apart from textual errors, these and subsequent Arkham House editions are marred by many typographical errors. Regrettably, these editions in turn served as the sources for the numerous paperback editions of Lovecraft's work, beginning with the Bartholomew House edition of *The Weird Shadow over Innsmouth and Other Stories of the Supernatural* (1944) and proceeding on through the editions by Avon, Lancer, Beagle/Ballantine, and others.

My editor's notes to each story in this edition recount in brief compass the textual history of the tale, specify the manuscript and printed sources for it, and identify the copy-text I have chosen. I should here like to outline some broader orthographic and stylistic decisions I have made in the preparation of this edition. On occasion—especially in the absence of a manuscript—I have been compelled to emend the text slightly in accordance with my understanding of Lovecraft's habitual stylistic preferences. I have been somewhat conservative in this procedure, making only such emendations as are virtually certain to have been made by Lovecraft himself as gauged by the sum total of his fictional output. My own decisions can be grouped under the following rubrics:

British Spellings

It is well known that Lovecraft preferred British spellings (words ending in -*our* [for -*or*], -*ise* [for -*ize*], -*re* [for -*er*, as in *theatre* or *centre*], -*ce* [for -*se*, as in *pretence* or *defence*]. and the like). He always used -*ll*- in such words as *travelled* and *jewellery* (for the American *traveled* and *jewelry*), and uniformly used such British variants as *connexion* (for *connection*), *plough* (for *plow*), and *programme* (for *program*). He is generally consistent in using *ae* in such usages as *encyclopaedia, palaeontology, archaeology,* and the like; less consistent with *daemon* and *daemoniac,* but I have systematised these usages. He is generally consistent in using *oe* in *foetor* and a few other words. I had previously altered Lovecraft's *centreing* to *centring*, but *centreing* is listed as a legitimate variant in the *Oxford English Dictionary,* so I have restored it.

The serial comma is more common in British usage than American, and Lovecraft generally adheres to it, although with numerous slips. I have systematised this usage. Lovecraft occasionally uses *an* before a word beginning in *h,* as many British writers up to the present day do; but the usage *an hundred* is far less common than *a hundred,* so I have uniformly printed the latter.

The British *shew* for *show* is nearly universal in Lovecraft's autograph manuscripts; but in later typescripts he begins to use *show.* My feeling is that, as he noticed that *Weird Tales* and other pulp magazines were uniformly changing *shew* to *show,* he decided to accommodate his publishers. I believe, however, his preference was always for *shew,* so I have printed it even when a manuscript or typescript reads *show.*

There are some British spellings and usages that Lovecraft eschewed. Among these are: *practice* as a verb (for the British *practise*); *toward* (for *towards* [this variant appears occasionally in Lovecraft's rendering of New England dialect]); *story* (for *storey*); *inquiry* (for *enquiry*); the period after such abbreviations as *Mr.* or *Dr.; judgment* (for *judgement*).

Other Stylistic Usages

One of the more significant changes I have made in this edition is my decision to render book titles in double quotation marks without italics. Lovecraft is quite consistent in this usage in his earlier tales, but in his later manuscripts he begins to use italics without quotation marks. As with *shew/show,* I believe this was a decision by Lovecraft to accommodate magazine publishers, who uniformly printed book titles in italics. But Lovecraft's letters, from the beginning to the end of his life, print such titles in quotation marks without italics, and this usage was indeed common in his day (H. L. Mencken [1880–1956] followed the usage throughout his lifetime). It is therefore my belief that Lovecraft would have preferred using quotation marks for book titles.

Lovecraft was not entirely consistent in omitting the hyphen in adverb-adjective compounds (e.g., *queerly proportioned*), but he more often omitted it than included it, so I have removed it throughout his texts. (This rule does not apply to *well* when used in conjunction with an adjective.)

On occasion Lovecraft did make errors in spelling and other usages. Among the words he habitually misspelled were *Portugese* (for *Portuguese*) and *accomodate* (for *accommodate*). I have corrected Lovecraft's errors in these cases, as all previous editors have done. I have, however, not corrected Lovecraft's erroneous use of *data* in the singular; nor have I corrected his occasionally lax use of foreign terms (e.g., *facade* without the cedilla; *melange* without the acute accent over the first *e;* some errors in rendering German).

In terms of individual usages, one can make note of the following: Lovecraft used *eery* (not *eerie*) uniformly; he much more often used *for ever* than *forever;* he generally lower-cased *heaven* and *hell;* he used the quasi-British *pandaemoniac* but also preferred the spelling *pandemonium;* he generally lower-cased *colonial,* although the form *Colonial* is found in many of his early texts; he used *motor-car* but also *motor coach* and *motor truck;* he generally used the hyphen for compounds in *-like,* with the exception of certain very common words (e.g., *godlike, lifelike, warlike*); he almost never used a hyphen in compounds with the prefix *over-,* but generally did use the hyphen in most compounds with the prefixes *pre-, trans-, post-, half-, ultra-, extra-, sub-,* and *semi-* (except for *semicircle*). He is rather inconsistent in capitalising *Nature* when the term is personified, but I have systematised this usage.

With regard to usages pertaining to time and date, Lovecraft generally preferred *11* [not *eleven*] *a.m./p.m.* (these abbreviations never written in small capitals), but *eleven* [not *11*] *o'clock; February 7(th)* but *the seventh of February.*

This edition presents Lovecraft's stories in chronological order by their presumed order of composition, not publication. In some cases, the exact date of composition is not known, but evidence from various sources—e.g., several chronologies of his stories prepared at various times by Lovecraft himself—can at least help to ascertain the proper sequence of his tales. No revisions or collaborations are included with the exception of "Under the Pyramids" (1924) and "Through the Gates of the Silver Key" (1932–33); the former because it is as close to original composition as any of his ghostwritten tales are, and the latter because it is a direct sequel to "The Silver Key" and also presents interesting textual variants both in the surviving manuscripts and in the printed texts.

I have presented textual collations from all relevant texts of a given story published in Lovecraft's lifetime. In most cases, this excludes several printings such as anthology appearances or reprints in *Weird Tales*. For the Arkham House editions, I have not felt it necessary in every instance to collate *The Outsider and Others* or other early editions, but have focused on the editions of the 1960s, which remained in print for decades and which I myself revised in the 1980s. My own editions, whether for Arkham House or other publishers, have not been collated. In my editor's notes I have generally indicated when a given text is textually irrelevant.

In most cases, I have not felt the need to present textual variants for section headings or other typographical elements that are largely irrelevant to the textual status of a tale. For example, *Weird Tales* habitually altered Lovecraft's Roman numerals for section divisions into Arabic numerals, but these variants are not recorded.

In this edition, any end-of-line hyphens are Lovecraft's own hyphens. We have deliberately not introduced hyphens in other words, to prevent confusion on this point. As a result, there occasionally may be loose lines, but we feel this is a small imperfection if it eliminates ambiguity on this point.

Abbreviations used in this edition are as follows:

A.Ms.   autograph manuscript

ES   *Essential Solitude: The Letters of H. P. Lovecraft and August Derleth* (2008)

JHL   John Hay Library, Brown University (Providence, RI)

OFF   *O Fortunate Floridian: H. P. Lovecraft's Letters to R. H. Barlow* (2007)

om.   omitted

SL   *Selected Letters* (1965–76; 5 vols.)

T.Ms.   typed manuscript

In my textual work, I have over the years benefited from the valuable advice and encouragement of such scholars as R. Boerem, Donald R. Burleson, Scott Connors, Steven J. Mariconda, Marc A. Michaud, Dirk W. Mosig, Robert M. Price, Juha-Matti Rajala, and David E. Schultz. For the preparation of this edition, I have been assisted by Kory Callaway, Stefan Dziemianowicz, Graham Holroyd, and Kenneth W. Faig, Jr. I am deeply indebted to David E. Schultz for his skill and sensitivity in designing this edition; and also to my publisher, Derrick Hussey of Hippocampus Press, for his exhaustive and detailed proofreading, which has saved me from many errors. For decades I have worked closely with Robert C. Harrall, Administrator of the Estate of H. P. Lovecraft, in arranging for numerous editions of my corrected texts, and he is to be thanked for supporting this most recent—and, I trust, my last—edition.

—S. T. JOSHI

Collected Fiction: 1908–1925

The Beast in the Cave

The horrible conclusion which had been gradually obtruding itself upon my confused and reluctant mind was now an awful certainty. I was lost,[a] completely, hopelessly lost in the vast and labyrinthine recesses[b] of the Mammoth Cave. Turn as I might, in no direction could my straining vision seize on any object capable of serving as a guidepost to set me on the outward path. That nevermore should I behold the blessed light of day, or scan the pleasant hills and dales of the beautiful world outside, my reason could no longer entertain the slightest unbelief. Hope had departed. Yet, indoctrinated as I was by a life of philosophical study, I derived no small measure of satisfaction from my unimpassioned demeanour;[c] for although I had frequently read of the wild frenzies into which were thrown the victims of similar situations,[d] I experienced none of these, but stood quiet as soon as I clearly realised[e] the loss of my bearings.

Nor did the thought that I had probably wandered beyond the utmost limits of an ordinary search cause me to abandon my composure even for a moment. If I must die, I reflected, then was this terrible yet

Editor's Note: HPL's A.Ms. (dated 21 April 1905) survives (JHL). The story was first published in the *Vagrant* (June 1918), edited by W. Paul Cook. This text appears to embody some deliberate revisions by HPL. R. H. Barlow prepared a T.Ms. in the 1930s (JHL), presumably from the A.Ms.; this contains a few handwritten revisions by HPL. I have decided, however, to present the text of the A.Ms. unchanged, without taking note of HPL's later revisions, to exhibit HPL's early prose style. The Arkham House editions follow the T.Ms., making the usual array of errors or alterations.

Texts: A = A.Ms.; B = *Vagrant* No. 7 (June 1918): 113–20; C = T.Ms.; D = *Dagon and Other Macabre Tales* (Arkham House, 1965), 302–8. Copy-text: A.

[a] lost,] lost— B
[b] recesses] recess D
[c] demeanour;] demeanor; B
[d] situations,] situation, D
[e] realised] realized B

majestic cavern as welcome a sepulchre as that which any churchyard might afford;[a] a conception which carried with it more of tranquillity than of despair.

Starving would prove my ultimate fate;[b] of this I was certain. Some, I knew, had gone mad under circumstances such as these,[c] but I felt that this end would not be mine. My disaster was the result of no fault save my own, since unbeknown[d] to the guide I had separated myself from the regular party of sightseers; and,[e] wandering for over an hour in forbidden avenues of the cave, had found myself unable to retrace the devious windings which I had pursued since forsaking my companions.

Already my torch had begun to expire; soon I would be enveloped by the total and almost palpable blackness of the bowels of the earth. As I stood in the waning, unsteady[f] light, I idly wondered over the exact circumstances of my coming end. I remembered the accounts which I had heard of the colony of consumptives, who, taking their residence in the[g] gigantic grotto to find health from the apparently salubrious air of the underground world, with its steady, uniform temperature, pure air, and peaceful quiet,[h] had found, instead, death in strange and ghastly form. I had seen the sad remains of their ill made[i] cottages as I passed them by with the party, and had wondered what unnatural influence a long sojourn in this immense and silent cavern would exert upon one as healthy and as[j] vigorous as I. Now, I grimly told myself, my opportunity for settling this point had arrived,[k] provided that want of food should not bring me too speedy a departure from this life.

As the last fitful rays of my torch faded into obscurity, I resolved to

[a] afford;] afford, D
[b] fate;] fate— B
[c] these,] these; B
[d] unbeknown] unknown C, D
[e] and,] and B
[f] waning, unsteady] waning and unsteady B
[g] the] A, B, C; this D [*changed to* this *in C by HPL*]
[h] quiet,] quiet; B
[i] ill made] ill-made B, D
[j] as] *om.* B, C, D
[k] arrived,] arrived; B

leave no stone unturned, no possible means of escape neglected, so[a] summoning all the powers possessed by my lungs, I set up a series of loud shoutings,[b] in the vain hope of attracting the attention of the guide by my clamour, yet,[c] as I called,[d] I believed in my heart that my cries were to no purpose, and that my voice, magnified and reflected by the numberless ramparts of the black maze about me, fell upon no ears save my own.[e] All at once, however, my attention was fixed with a start as I fancied that I heard the sound of soft approaching steps on the rocky floor of the cavern.[f] Was my deliverance about to be accomplished so soon? Had, then, all my horrible apprehensions been for naught, and was the guide, having marked my unwarranted absence from the party, following my course and seeking me out in this limestone labyrinth? Whilst these joyful queries arose in my brain, I was on the point of renewing my cries, in order that my discovery might come the sooner, when in an instant my delight was turned to horror as I listened; for my ever acute ear, now sharpened in even greater degree by the complete silence of the cave, bore to my benumbed understanding the unexpected and dreadful knowledge that these footfalls were *not like those of any mortal man.* In the unearthly stillness of this subterranean region,[g] the tread of the booted guide would have sounded like a series of sharp and incisive blows. These impacts were soft, and stealthy, as of the padded[h] paws of some feline.[i] Besides, *at times,* [j] when I listened carefully, I seemed to trace the falls of *four* instead of *two* [k] feet.

I was now convinced that I had by my[l] cries aroused and attracted some wild beast, perhaps a mountain lion which had accidentally strayed

---

[a] unturned, . . . neglected, so] A, C [*changed to* neglected; so *by HPL*]; unturned— . . . neglected—so B; unturned, . . . neglected; so, D

[b] shoutings,] shoutings B

[c] clamour, yet,] A, C [*changed to* clamour. Yet, *by HPL*]; clamor; yet, B; clamour. Yet, D

[d] called,] called B

[e] own.] own. ¶ C, D

[f] cavern.] cavern. ¶ C, D

[g] region,] region B

[h] padded] *om.* C, D

[i] some feline.] some monstrous feline. B

[j] *at times,*] *om.* C, D

[k] *four . . . two*] *four, . . . two,* B

[l] my] my own D

within the cave. Perhaps, I considered, the Almighty had chosen for me a swifter and more merciful death than that of hunger. Yet[a] the instinct of self-preservation, never wholly dormant, was stirred in my breast,[b] and though escape from the oncoming[c] peril might but spare me for a sterner and more lingering end, I determined nevertheless to part with my life at as high a price as I could command. Strange as it may seem, my mind conceived of no intent on the part of the visitor save that of hostility.[d] Accordingly, I became very quiet, in the hope that the unknown beast would, in the absence of a guiding sound, lose its direction as had I, and thus pass me by. But this hope was not destined for realisation,[e] for the strange footfalls steadily advanced,[f] the animal evidently having obtained my scent, which in an atmosphere so absolutely free from all distracting influences as is that of the cave, could doubtless be followed at great distance.

Seeing therefore[g] that I must be armed for defence[h] against an uncanny and unseen attack in the dark, I grouped[i] about me the largest of the fragments of rock which were strewn[j] upon all parts of the floor of the cavern in the vicinity, and,[k] grasping one in each hand for immediate use, awaited with resignation the inevitable result.[l] Meanwhile the hideous pattering of the paws drew near. Certainly, the conduct of the creature was exceedingly strange. Most of the time,[m] the tread seemed to be that of a quadruped, walking with a singular *lack of unison* betwixt hind and fore feet,[n] yet at brief and infrequent intervals I fancied that but two feet were engaged in the process of locomotion. I wondered

[a] hunger. Yet] hunger. yet C [*changed to* hunger; yet *by HPL*]; hunger; yet D
[b] breast,] breast; B
[c] oncoming] on-coming D
[d] hostility.] hostility. ¶ B
[e] realisation,] realization, B
[f] advanced,] advanced; B
[g] Seeing therefore] Seeing, therefore, B
[h] defence] defense D
[i] grouped] groped C [*changed to* grouped *by HPL*], D
[j] strewn] strown B
[k] vicinity, and,] vicinity; and, B; vicinity, and D
[l] result.] result. ¶ B
[m] time,] time B
[n] feet,] feet; B

what species of animal was to confront me; it must, I thought, be some unfortunate beast who had paid for its curiosity to investigate one of the entrances of the fearful grotto with a lifelong confinement in its interminable recesses. It doubtless obtained as food the eyeless fish, bats,[a] and rats of the cave, as well as some of the ordinary fish that are wafted in at every freshet of Green River,[b] which communicates in some occult manner with the waters of the cave. I occupied my terrible vigil with grotesque conjectures of what alterations[c] cave life might have wrought in the physical structure of the beast, remembering the awful appearances ascribed by local tradition to the consumptives who had died after long residence in the cavern.[d] Then I remembered with a start that, even should I succeed in killing[e] my antagonist, I should *never behold its form,*[f] as my torch had long since been extinct, and I was entirely unprovided with matches.[g] The tension on my brain now became frightful. My disordered fancy conjured up hideous and fearsome shapes from the sinister darkness that surrounded me, and that actually seemed[h] to *press* upon my body. Nearer, nearer, the dreadful footfalls approached. It seemed that I must give vent to a piercing scream,[i] yet had I been sufficiently irresolute to attempt such a thing, my voice could scarce have responded. I was petrified,[j] rooted to the spot. I doubted if my right arm would allow me to hurl its missile at the oncoming thing[k] when the crucial moment should arrive.[l] Now the steady *pat, pat,*[m] of the steps was close at hand; now,[n] *very* close. I could

[a] bats,] bats C, D
[b] River,] river, B
[c] alterations] A, C [*changed to* alteration *by HPL*]; alteration D
[d] cavern.] cave. C, D
[e] killing] felling C, D
[f] *form,] form;* B
[g] matches.] matches. ¶ B
[h] actually seemed] seemed actually B
[i] scream,] scream— B
[j] petrified,] petrified— B
[k] thing] *thing* B
[l] arrive.] arrive. ¶ B
[m] *pat, pat,] pat, pat, pat* B
[n] now,] now C, D

hear the laboured[a] breathing of the animal, and terror-struck as I was, I realised[b] that it must have come from a considerable distance, and was correspondingly[c] fatigued. Suddenly the spell broke. My right hand, guided by my ever trustworthy sense of hearing, threw with full force the sharp-angled bit of limestone which it contained, toward that point in the darkness from which emanated the breathing and pattering, and,[d] wonderful to relate, it nearly reached its goal,[e] for I heard the thing[f] jump, landing at a distance away, where it seemed to pause.

Having readjusted my aim, I discharged my second missile, this time most effectively,[g] for with a flood of joy I listened as the creature fell in what sounded like a complete collapse, and evidently remained prone and unmoving. Almost overpowered by the great relief which rushed over me, I reeled back against the wall. The breathing continued, in heavy, gasping inhalations and expirations,[h] whence I realised[i] that I had no more than wounded the creature.[j] And now all desire to examine the *thing* ceased. At last something allied to groundless, superstitious,[k] fear had entered my brain,[l] and I did not approach the body, nor did I continue to cast stones at it in order to complete the extinction of its life. Instead, I ran at full speed in what was, as nearly as I could estimate in my frenzied condition, the direction from which I had come.[m] Suddenly I heard a sound, or rather, a regular succession of sounds. In another instant they had resolved themselves into a series of sharp, metallic clicks. This time there was no doubt. *It was the guide.*[n] And then I shouted, yelled, screamed, even shrieked with joy as

---

[a] laboured] labored B
[b] realised] realized B
[c] and was correspondingly] it being obviously much B
[d] pattering, and,] pattering—and B
[e] goal,] goal; B
[f] thing] *thing* B
[g] effectively,] effectively; B
[h] expirations,] exhalations, B
[i] realised] realized B
[j] creature.] creature. ¶ B
[k] superstitious,] superstitious B, D
[l] brain,] brain; B
[m] come.] come. ¶ B
[n] *guide.*] *guide.* ¶ B

I beheld in the vaulted arches above the faint and glimmering effulgence which I knew to be the reflected light of an approaching torch. I ran to meet the flare, and before I could completely understand what had occurred, was lying upon the ground[a] at the feet of the guide, embracing his boots,[b] and gibbering, despite my boasted reserve, in a most meaningless and idiotic manner,[c] pouring out my terrible story,[d] and at the same time overwhelming my auditor with protestations of gratitude. At length[e] I awoke to something like my normal consciousness. The guide had noted my absence upon the arrival of the party at the entrance of the cave, and had, from his own intuitive sense of direction, proceeded to make a thorough canvass of the[f] by-passages just ahead of where he had last spoken to me,[g] locating my whereabouts after a quest of about four hours.

By the time he had related this to me, I, emboldened by his torch and his company, began to reflect upon the strange beast which I had wounded but a short distance back in the darkness, and suggested that we ascertain, by the rushlight's aid,[h] what manner of creature was my victim. Accordingly I retraced my steps, this time with a courage born of companionship, to the scene of my terrible experience. Soon we descried a white object upon the floor, an object whiter even than the gleaming limestone itself. Cautiously advancing, we gave vent to a simultaneous ejaculation of wonderment,[i] for of all the unnatural monsters either of us had in our lifetimes beheld, this was in surpassing degree the strangest.[j] It appeared to be an anthropoid ape of large proportions,[k] escaped, perhaps, from some itinerant menagerie. Its hair was snow-white, a thing

[a] ground] path B
[b] boots,] boots B, C, D
[c] manner,] manner— B
[d] story,] story B
[e] length] length, D
[f] the] *om.* D
[g] me,] me; B
[h] ascertain, ... rushlight's aid,] ascertain ... rushlight's aid B; ascertain, ... flashlight's aid, D
[i] wonderment,] wonderment; B
[j] strangest.] strangest. ¶ B
[k] proportions,] proportions; B

due no doubt to the bleaching action of a long existence within the inky confines of the cave,[a] but it was also surprisingly thin, being indeed largely absent save on the head, where it was of such length and abundance that it fell over the shoulders in considerable profusion. The face was turned away from us, as the creature[b] lay almost directly upon it. The inclination of the limbs was very singular,[c] explaining, however, the alternation in their use which I had before noted, whereby the beast used sometimes all four, and on other occasions but two for its progress. From the tips of the fingers or toes[d] long nail-like[e] claws extended. The hands or feet were not prehensile, a fact that I ascribed to that long residence in the cave which, as I before mentioned, seemed evident from the all-pervading and almost unearthly *whiteness* [f] so characteristic of the whole anatomy. No tail seemed to be present.

The respiration had now grown very feeble, and the guide had drawn his pistol with the evident intent[g] of despatching the creature, when a sudden *sound* emitted by the latter caused the weapon to fall unused. The sound was of a nature difficult to describe. It was not like the normal note of any known species of simian, and I wondered if this unnatural quality were not the result of a long continued[h] and complete silence, broken by the sensations produced by the advent of the light,[i] a thing which the beast could not have seen since its first entrance into the cave. The sound, which I might feebly attempt to classify as a kind of deep toned[j] chattering,[k] was faintly continued.[l] All at once a fleeting spasm of energy seemed to pass through the frame of the beast. The paws went through a convulsive motion,[m] and the limbs

---

[a] cave,] cave; B
[b] creature] creaturo B
[c] singular,] singular; B
[d] toes] toes, B, D
[e] nail-like] rat-like C, D
[f] *whiteness*] whiteness D
[g] intent] intention B
[h] long continued] long-continued B
[i] light,] light— B
[j] deep toned] A, C [*changed to* deep-toned *by HPL*]; deep-toned D
[k] chattering,] *chattering,* B
[l] continued.] continued. ¶ B, C, D
[m] convulsive motion,] series of convulsive motions, B

contracted. With a jerk, the white body rolled over so that its face was turned in our direction. For a moment I was so struck with horror at the eyes thus revealed[a] that I noted nothing else. They were black, those eyes, deep, jetty black,[b] in hideous contrast to the snow-white hair and flesh. Like those of other cave denizens, they were deeply sunken in their orbits, and were entirely destitute of iris. As I looked more closely, I saw that they were set in a face less prognathous than that of the average ape, and infinitely more[c] hairy. The nose was quite distinct.[d]

As we gazed upon the uncanny sight presented to our vision, the thick lips opened, and several *sounds* issued from them,[e] after which the *thing* relaxed in death.

The guide clutched my coat-sleeve[f] and trembled so violently that the light shook fitfully, casting weird,[g] moving shadows on the walls about us.[h]

I made no motion, but stood rigidly still,[i] my horrified eyes fixed upon the floor ahead.

Then[j] fear left, and wonder, awe, compassion, and reverence succeeded in its place,[k] for the *sounds* uttered by the stricken figure that lay stretched out on the limestone had told us the awesome truth. The creature I had killed,[l] the strange beast of the unfathomed cave[m] was, or had at one time been,[n] a **MAN!!!**[o]

---

[a] revealed] revealed, B
[b] deep, jetty black,] deep, jetty black; B; deep jetty black, C, D
[c] more] less C, D
[d] distinct. ¶] distinct. C, D
[e] them,] them; B
[f] coat-sleeve] coatsleeve D
[g] weird,] weird D
[h] walls about us. ¶] A?; walls about us. B; walls. ¶ C, D [*A is torn here, and the final two words are illegible; but the B reading is plausible.*]
[i] still,] still; B
[j] Then] The D
[k] place,] place; B
[l] killed,] killed; B
[m] cave] dave; B; cave, C, D
[n] been,] been D
[o] **MAN!!!**] A, C [triple-underscore]; *man.* B; MAN!!! D

The Alchemist

High up, crowning the grassy summit of a swelling mound[a] whose sides are wooded near the base with the gnarled trees of the primeval forest,[b] stands the old chateau of my ancestors. For centuries its lofty battlements have frowned down upon the wild and rugged countryside about, serving as a home and stronghold for the proud house whose honoured[c] line is older even than the moss-grown castle walls. These ancient turrets, stained by the storms of generations and crumbling under the slow yet mighty pressure of time, formed in the ages of feudalism one of the most dreaded and formidable fortresses in all France. From its machicolated parapets and mounted battlements Barons, Counts, and even Kings had been defied, yet never had its spacious halls resounded to the footsteps of the invader.

But since those glorious years[d] all is changed. A poverty but little above the level of dire want, together with a pride of name that forbids its alleviation by the pursuits of commercial life, have prevented the scions of our line from maintaining their estates in pristine splendour; and the falling stones of the walls, the overgrown vegetation in the parks, the dry and dusty moat, the ill-paved courtyards, and toppling

Editor's Note: The only version of this story published in HPL's lifetime was in the *United Amateur* (November 1916). It is likely that this text presents some revisions from the presumed A.Ms. of 1908. The first Arkham House edition (*The Shuttered Room and Other Pieces*, 1959) made some errors and alterations in reprinting the *United Amateur* text, and the second Arkham House edition (*Dagon and Other Macabre Tales*, 1965) made additional errors and alterations.

Texts: A = *United Amateur* 16, No. 4 (November 1916): 53–57; B = *The Shuttered Room and Other Pieces* (Arkham House, 1959), 54–63; C = *Dagon and Other Macabre Tales* (Arkham House, 1965), 308–16. Copy-text: A.

[a] mound] mount B, C
[b] forest,] forest B, C
[c] honoured] honored B, C
[d] years] years, B, C

towers without, as well as the sagging floors, the worm-eaten
wainscots, and the faded tapestries within, all tell a gloomy tale of
fallen grandeur. As the ages passed, first one, then another of the four
great turrets were left to ruin, until at last but a single tower housed the
sadly reduced descendants of the once mighty lords of the estate.

It was in one of the vast and gloomy chambers of this remaining
tower that I, Antoine, last of the unhappy and accursed Comtes[a] de
C——, first saw the light of day, ninety long years ago. Within these
walls,[b] and amongst the dark and shadowy forests, the wild ravines and
grottoes[c] of the hillside below, were spent the first years of my
troubled life. My parents I never knew. My father had been killed at
the age of thirty-two, a month before I was born, by the fall of a stone
somehow dislodged from one of the deserted parapets of the castle;
and[d] my mother having died at my birth, my care and education
devolved solely upon one remaining servitor, an old and trusted man
of considerable intelligence, whose name I remember as Pierre. I was
an only child,[e] and the lack of companionship which this fact entailed
upon me was augmented by the strange care exercised by my aged
guardian[f] in excluding me from the society of the peasant children
whose abodes were scattered here and there upon the plains that
surround the base of the hill. At the[g] time, Pierre said that this
restriction was imposed upon me because my noble birth placed me
above association with such plebeian company. Now I know that its
real object was to keep from my ears the idle tales of the dread curse
upon our line,[h] that were nightly told and magnified by the simple
tenantry as they conversed in hushed accents in the glow of their
cottage hearths.

Thus isolated, and thrown upon my own resources, I spent the
hours of my childhood in poring over the ancient tomes that filled the

---

[a] Comtes] Counts C
[b] walls,] walls B, C
[c] grottoes] grottos B, C
[d] castle; and] castle, and A; castle. And B, C
[e] child,] child B, C
[f] guardian] guardian, B, C
[g] the] that B, C
[h] line,] line B, C

shadow-haunted library of the chateau, and in roaming without aim or purpose through the perpetual dusk[a] of the spectral wood that clothes the side of the hill near its foot. It was perhaps an effect of such surroundings that my mind early acquired a shade of melancholy. Those studies and pursuits which partake of the dark and occult in Nature[b] most strongly claimed my attention.

Of my own race I was permitted to learn singularly little, yet what small knowledge of it I was able to gain,[c] seemed to depress me much. Perhaps it was at first only the manifest reluctance of my old preceptor to discuss with me my paternal ancestry that gave rise to the terror which I ever felt at the mention of my great house;[d] yet as I grew out of childhood, I was able to piece together disconnected fragments of discourse, let slip from the unwilling tongue which had begun to falter in approaching senility, that had a sort of relation to a certain circumstance which I had always deemed strange, but which now became dimly terrible. The circumstance to which I allude is the early age at which all the Comtes[e] of my line had met their end. Whilst I had hitherto considered this but a natural attribute of a family of short-lived men, I afterward pondered long upon these premature deaths, and began to connect them with the wanderings of the old man, who often spoke of a curse which for centuries had prevented the lives of the holders of my title from much exceeding the span of thirty-two years. Upon my twenty-first birthday, the aged Pierre gave to me a family document which he said had for many generations been handed down from father to son, and continued by each possessor. Its contents were of the most startling nature, and its perusal confirmed the gravest of my apprehensions. At this time, my belief in the supernatural was firm and deep-seated, else I should have dismissed with scorn the incredible narrative unfolded before my eyes.

The paper carried me back to the days of the thirteenth century, when the old castle in which I sat had been a feared and impregnable

---

[a] dusk] dust B, C

[b] Nature] nature A, B, C

[c] gain,] gain B, C

[d] house;] house, A, B, C

[e] Comtes] Counts C

fortress. It told of a certain ancient man who had once dwelt[a] on our estates, a person of no small accomplishments, though little above the rank of peasant;[b] by name, Michel, usually designated by the surname of Mauvais, the Evil, on account of his sinister reputation. He had studied beyond the custom of his kind, seeking such things as the Philosopher's Stone,[c] or the Elixir of Eternal Life, and was reputed wise in the terrible secrets of Black Magic and Alchemy. Michel Mauvais had one son, named Charles, a youth as proficient as himself in the hidden arts, and[d] who had therefore been called Le Sorcier, or the Wizard. This pair, shunned by all honest folk, were suspected of the most hideous practices. Old Michel was said to have burnt his wife alive as a sacrifice to the Devil, and the unaccountable disappearances of many small peasant children were[e] laid at the dreaded door of these two. Yet through the dark natures of the father and the[f] son ran one redeeming ray of humanity; the evil old man loved his offspring with fierce intensity, whilst the youth had for his parent a more than filial affection.

One night the castle on the hill was thrown into the wildest confusion by the vanishment of young Godfrey,[g] son to Henri the Comte.[h] A searching party, headed by the frantic father, invaded the cottage of the sorcerers and there came upon old Michel Mauvais, busy over a huge and violently boiling cauldron. Without certain cause, in the ungoverned madness of fury and despair, the Comte[i] laid hands on the aged wizard, and ere he released his murderous hold[j] his victim was no more. Meanwhile[k] joyful servants were proclaiming the finding of young Godfrey in a distant and unused chamber of the great edifice, telling too

[a] dwelt] dwelled B, C
[b] peasant;] peasant, B, C
[c] Stone,] Stone B, C
[d] and] *om.* B, C
[e] disappearances . . . were] disappearance . . . was B, C
[f] the] *om.* B, C
[g] Godfrey,] Godfrey A
[h] Henri the Comte.] Henri, the Comte. B; Henri, the Count. C
[i] Comte] Count C
[j] hold] hold, B, C
[k] Meanwhile] Meanwhile, B, C

late that poor Michel had been killed in vain. As the Comte[a] and his associates turned away from the lowly abode of the alchemists,[b] the form of Charles Le Sorcier appeared through the trees. The excited chatter of the menials standing about told him what had occurred, yet he seemed at first unmoved at his father's fate. Then, slowly advancing to meet the Comte,[c] he pronounced in dull yet terrible accents the curse that ever afterward haunted the house of C——.

"May ne'er a noble of thy murd'rous line
Survive to reach a greater age than thine!"[d]

spake he, when, suddenly leaping backwards into the black wood,[e] he drew from his tunic a phial of colourless liquid which he threw into the face of his father's slayer as he disappeared behind the inky curtain of the night. The Comte[f] died without utterance, and was buried the next day, but little more than two and thirty years from the hour of his birth. No trace of the assassin could be found, though relentless bands of peasants scoured the neighbouring[g] woods and the meadow-land[h] around the hill.

Thus time and the want of a reminder dulled the memory of the curse in the minds of the late Comte's[i] family, so that when Godfrey, innocent cause of the whole tragedy and now bearing the title, was killed by an arrow whilst hunting,[j] at the age of thirty-two, there were no thoughts save those of grief at his demise. But when, years afterward, the next young Comte,[k] Robert by name, was found dead in a nearby field from[l] no apparent cause, the peasants told in whispers that their seigneur had but lately passed his thirty-second birthday

[a] Comte] Count C
[b] alchemists,] alchemist, B, C
[c] Comte,] Count, C
[d] thine!"] thine"! A
[e] wood,] woods, B, C
[f] Comte] Count C
[g] neighbouring] neighboring A, B, C
[h] meadow-land] meadowland B, C
[i] Comte's] Count's C
[j] hunting,] hunting B, C
[k] Comte,] B; Comte A; Count, C
[l] from] of B, C

when surprised by early death. Louis, son to Robert, was found drowned in the moat at the same fateful age, and thus down through the centuries ran the ominous chronicle;[a] Henris, Roberts, Antoines, and Armands snatched from happy and virtuous lives when little below the age of their unfortunate ancestor at his murder.

That I had left at most but eleven years of further existence was made certain to me by the words which I[b] read. My life, previously held at small value, now became dearer to me each day, as I delved deeper and deeper into the mysteries of the hidden world of black magic. Isolated as I was, modern science had produced no impression upon me, and I laboured as in the Middle Ages, as wrapt as had been old Michel and young Charles themselves in the acquisition of daemonological[c] and alchemical learning. Yet read as I might, in no manner could I account for the strange curse upon my line. In unusually rational moments,[d] I would even go so far as to seek a natural explanation, attributing the early deaths of my ancestors to the sinister[e] Charles Le Sorcier and his heirs; yet[f] having found upon careful inquiry that there were no known descendants of the alchemist, I would fall back to occult studies, and once more endeavour[g] to find a spell that would release my house from its terrible burden. Upon one thing I was absolutely resolved. I should never wed, for[h] since no other branches of my family were[i] in existence, I might thus end the curse with myself.

As I drew near the age of thirty, old Pierre was called to the land beyond. Alone I buried him beneath the stones of the courtyard about which he had loved to wander in life. Thus was I left to ponder on myself as the only human creature within the great fortress, and in my utter solitude my mind began to cease its vain protest against the

---

[a] chronicle;] chronicle: B, C

[b] I] I had B, C

[c] daemonological] demonological A, B, C

[d] moments,] moments B, C

[e] sinister] sisister A

[f] yet] yet, B, C

[g] endeavour] endeavor B, C

[h] for] for, B, C

[i] branches . . . were] branch . . . were B; branch . . . was C

impending doom, to become almost reconciled to the fate which so many of my ancestors had met. Much of my time was now occupied in the exploration of the ruined and abandoned halls and towers of the old chateau, which in youth fear had caused me to shun, and some of which, old Pierre had once told me,[a] had not been trodden by human foot for over four centuries. Strange and awesome[b] were many of the objects I encountered. Furniture, covered by the dust of ages and crumbling with the rot of long dampness,[c] met my eyes. Cobwebs in a profusion never before seen by me were spun everywhere, and huge bats flapped their bony and uncanny wings on all sides of the otherwise untenanted gloom.

Of my exact age, even down to days and hours, I kept a most careful record, for each movement of the pendulum of the massive clock in the library told off so much more[d] of my doomed existence. At length I approached that time which I had so long viewed with apprehension. Since most of my ancestors had been seized some little while before they reached the exact age of the Comte[e] Henri at his end, I was every moment on the watch for the coming of the unknown death. In what strange form the curse should overtake me, I knew not; but I was resolved, at least,[f] that it should not find me a cowardly or a passive victim. With new vigour I applied myself to my examination of the old chateau and its contents.

It was upon one of the longest of all my excursions of discovery in the deserted portion of the castle, less than a week before that fatal hour which I felt must mark the utmost limit of my stay on earth,[g] beyond which I could have not even the slightest hope of continuing to draw breath, that I came upon the culminating event of my whole life. I had spent the better part of the morning in climbing up and down half-ruined[h] staircases in one of the most dilapidated of the

---

[a] which, . . . me,] which . . . me, A; which . . . me B, C
[b] awesome] awsome A
[c] dampness,] dampness A, B
[d] more] *om.* B, C
[e] of the Comte] of Count C
[f] resolved, at least,] resolved at least, A; resolved at least B, C
[g] earth,] earth; A
[h] half-ruined] half ruined A, B, C

ancient turrets. As the afternoon progressed, I sought the lower levels, descending into what appeared to be either a mediaeval place of confinement, or a more recently excavated storehouse for gunpowder. As I slowly traversed the nitre-encrusted passageway at the foot of the last staircase, the paving became very damp, and soon I saw by the light of my flickering torch that a blank, water-stained wall impeded my journey. Turning to retrace my steps, my eye fell upon a small trap-door[a] with a ring, which lay directly beneath my feet.[b] Pausing, I succeeded with difficulty in raising it, whereupon there was revealed a black aperture, exhaling noxious fumes which caused my torch to sputter, and disclosing in the unsteady glare the top of a flight of stone steps.[c] As soon as the torch, which I lowered into the repellent depths,[d] burned freely and steadily, I commenced my descent. The steps were many, and led to a narrow stone-flagged passage which I knew must be far underground. The passage proved of great length, and terminated in a massive oaken door, dripping with the moisture of the place, and stoutly resisting all my attempts to open it. Ceasing after a time my efforts in this direction, I had proceeded back some distance toward the steps,[e] when there suddenly fell to my experience one of the most profound and maddening shocks capable of reception by the human mind. Without warning, *I heard the heavy door behind me creak slowly open upon its rusted hinges.*[f] My immediate sensations are[g] incapable of analysis. To be confronted in a place as thoroughly deserted as I had deemed the old castle with evidence of the presence of man or spirit,[h] produced in my brain a horror of the most acute description. When at last I turned and faced the seat of the sound, my eyes must have started from their orbits at the sight that they beheld.[i] There in the ancient Gothic doorway stood a human figure. It was that of a man

[a] trap-door] trapdoor B, C
[b] feet.] foot. B, C
[c] steps.] steps. ¶ B, C
[d] torch, . . . depths,] torch . . . depths B, C
[e] steps,] steps B, C
[f] *I . . . hinges.*] I . . . hinges. B, C
[g] are] were B, C
[h] spirit,] spirit B, C
[i] beheld.] beheld. ¶ B, C

clad in a skull-cap and long mediaeval tunic of dark colour. His long hair and flowing beard were of a terrible and intense black hue, and of incredible profusion. His forehead, high beyond the usual dimensions; his cheeks, deep sunken[a] and heavily lined with wrinkles; and his hands, long, claw-like,[b] and gnarled, were of such a deathly,[c] marble-like whiteness as I have never elsewhere seen in man. His figure, lean to the proportions of a skeleton, was strangely bent and almost lost within the voluminous folds of his peculiar garment. But strangest of all were his eyes;[d] twin caves of abysmal blackness,[e] profound in expression of understanding, yet inhuman in degree of wickedness. These were now fixed upon me, piercing my soul with their hatred, and rooting me to the spot whereon I stood.[f] At last the figure spoke in a rumbling voice that chilled me through with its dull hollowness and latent malevolence. The language in which the discourse was clothed was that debased form of Latin in use amongst the more learned men of the Middle Ages, and made familiar to me by my prolonged researches into the works of the old alchemists and daemonologists.[g] The apparition spoke of the curse which had hovered over my house, told me of my coming end, dwelt on the wrong perpetrated by my ancestor against old Michel Mauvais, and gloated over the revenge of Charles Le Sorcier. He told how the[h] young Charles had[i] escaped into the night, returning in after years to kill Godfrey the heir with an arrow just as he approached the age which had been his father's at his assassination; how he had secretly returned to the estate and established himself, unknown, in the even then deserted subterranean chamber whose doorway now framed the hideous narrator;[j] how he had seized Robert, son of Godfrey,[k] in a

[a] deep sunken] deep-sunken B, C
[b] claw-like,] claw-/like, A
[c] deathly,] deadly B, C
[d] eyes;] eyes, B, C
[e] blackness,] blackness; A
[f] stood.] stood. ¶ B, C
[g] daemonologists.] demonologists. A, B, C
[h] the] *om.* B, C
[i] had] has C
[j] narrator;] narrator, B, C
[k] Godfrey,] Godfry, A

field, forced poison down his throat,[a] and left him to die at the age of thirty-two, thus maintaining the foul provisions of his vengeful curse. At this point I was left to imagine the solution of the greatest mystery of all, how the curse had been fulfilled since that time when Charles Le Sorcier must in the course of Nature[b] have died, for the man digressed into an account of the deep alchemical studies of the two wizards, father and son, speaking most particularly of the researches of Charles Le Sorcier concerning the elixir which should grant to him who partook of it eternal life and youth.

His enthusiasm had seemed for the moment to remove from his terrible eyes the hatred[c] that had at[d] first so haunted them,[e] but suddenly the fiendish glare returned, and[f] with a shocking sound like the hissing of a serpent, the stranger raised a glass phial with the evident intent of ending my life as had Charles Le Sorcier, six hundred years before, ended that of my ancestor. Prompted by some preserving instinct of self-defence,[g] I broke through the spell that had hitherto held me immovable, and flung my now dying torch at the creature who menaced my existence. I heard the phial break harmlessly against the stones of the passage as the tunic of the strange man caught fire and lit the horrid scene with a ghastly radiance. The shriek of fright and impotent malice emitted by the would-be assassin proved too much for my already shaken nerves, and I fell prone upon the slimy floor in a total faint.

When at last my senses returned, all was frightfully dark, and my mind[h] remembering what had occurred, shrank from the idea of beholding more;[i] yet curiosity overmastered all. Who, I asked myself, was this man of evil, and how came he within the castle walls? Why

[a] throat,] throat A
[b] Nature] nature A, B, C
[c] hatred] black malevolence B, C
[d] at] *om.* B, C
[e] them,] me, B, C
[f] returned, and] returned and, B, C
[g] self-defence,] self-defense, A, B, C
[h] mind] mind, B, C
[i] more;] any more; B, C

should he seek to avenge the death of poor[a] Michel Mauvais, and how had the curse been carried on through all the long centuries since the time of Charles Le Sorcier? The dread of years was lifted off my shoulders,[b] for I knew that he whom I had felled was the source of all my danger from the curse; and now that I was free, I burned with the desire to learn more of the sinister thing which had haunted my line for centuries, and made of my own youth one long-continued nightmare. Determined upon further exploration, I felt in my pockets for flint and steel, and lit the unused torch which I had with me.[c] First of all, the[d] new light revealed the distorted and blackened form of the mysterious stranger. The hideous eyes were now closed. Disliking the sight, I turned away and entered the chamber beyond the Gothic door. Here I found what seemed much like an alchemist's laboratory. In one corner was an immense pile of a[e] shining yellow metal that sparkled gorgeously in the light of the torch. It may have been gold, but I did not pause to examine it, for I was strangely affected by that which I had undergone. At the farther end of the apartment was an opening leading out into one of the many wild ravines of the dark hillside forest. Filled with wonder, yet now realising[f] how the man had obtained access to the chateau, I proceeded to return. I had intended to pass by the remains of the stranger with averted face, but[g] as I approached the body, I seemed to hear emanating from it a faint sound, as though life were not yet wholly extinct. Aghast, I tuned to examine the charred and shrivelled figure on the floor.[h] Then all at once the horrible eyes, blacker even than the seared face in which they were set, opened wide with an expression which I was unable to interpret. The cracked lips tried to frame words which I could not well understand. Once I caught the name of Charles Le Sorcier, and again I fancied that the words "years" and "curse" issued from the twisted mouth. Still I was at a loss to gather the purport of his

[a] poor] *om.* B, C

[b] off my shoulders,] from my shoulders, B; from my shoulder, C

[c] me.] me. ¶ B, C

[d] the] *om.* B, C

[e] a] *om.* C

[f] realising] realizing A, B, C

[g] face, but] face but, B, C

[h] floor.] floor. ¶ B, C

disconnected speech. At my evident ignorance of his meaning, the pitchy eyes once more flashed malevolently at me, until, helpless as I saw my opponent to be, I trembled as I watched him.

Suddenly the wretch, animated with his last burst of strength, raised his hideous[a] head from the damp and sunken pavement. Then, as I remained, paralysed[b] with fear, he found his voice and in his dying breath screamed forth those words which have ever afterward haunted my days and my[c] nights. "Fool,"[d] he shrieked, "can[e] you not guess my secret? Have you no brain whereby you may recognise[f] the will which has through six long centuries fulfilled the dreadful curse upon your[g] house? Have I not told you of the great elixir of eternal life? Know you not how the secret of Alchemy was solved? I tell you, it is I! I! *I! that have lived for six hundred years to maintain my revenge,* FOR I AM CHARLES LE SORCIER!"[h]

---

[a] hideous] piteous B, C
[b] paralysed] paralyzed A, B, C
[c] my] *om.* B, C
[d] "Fool,"] "Fool", A; "Fool!" B, C
[e] "can] "Can B, C
[f] recognise] recognize A, B, C
[g] your] the C
[h] *I! that* ... SORCIER!"] I! that have lived for six hundred years to maintain my revenge, for I am Charles Le Sorcier!" B, C

The Tomb

"Sedibus ut saltem placidis in morte quiescam."
—*Virgil.*[a]

I n relating the circumstances which have led to my confinement
within this refuge for the demented, I am aware that my present
position will create a natural doubt of the authenticity of my
narrative. It is an unfortunate fact that the bulk of humanity is too
limited in its mental vision to weigh with patience and intelligence
those isolated phenomena, seen and felt only by a psychologically
sensitive few, which lie outside its common experience. Men of
broader intellect know that there is no sharp distinction betwixt the

---

Editor's Note: In the absence of an A.Ms. or T.Ms., we are reliant on the first two
publications of the story—*Vagrant* (March 1922) and *Weird Tales* (January 1926)—
to establish the text. The *Vagrant* text, typeset by W. Paul Cook, seems on the
whole sound; but the *Weird Tales* text bears evidence of some deliberate revisions
by HPL, so he in all likelihood prepared a revised typescript and sent it on to the
magazine. There is a legitimate debate as to which of the divergences between the
Vagrant and *Weird Tales* texts are the result of errors by the latter or revisions by
HPL; certainly, the *Weird Tales* text contains the usual array of changes that the magazine tended to make in HPL's stories (Americanisation of HPL's British spellings,
paragraphing and punctuational changes, etc.), but other changes (such as the
omission of the word "disastrous" [40.9]) are likely to be HPL's revisions. The
Arkham House texts followed the *Weird Tales* text, making further errors. An
A.Ms. of the untitled poem that appears in the story survives, as part of a fragmentary letter; it is titled "Gaudeamus" (Latin for "let us delight") and presumably predates the story itself. But it appears to be an early draft, and HPL
probably revised it when writing the story; hence its variant readings should not be
incorporated into the text.

    Texts: A = *Vagrant* No. 14 (March 1922): 50–64; B = *Weird Tales* 7, No. 1 (Jan-
uary 1926): 117–23; C = *Dagon and Other Macabre Tales* (Arkham House, 1965), 9–18;
D = A.Ms. of "Gaudeamus" (JHL). Copy-text: A (but with a few readings from B).

[a] "Sedibus . . . / —*Virgil.*] Sedibus ut saltem placidis in morte quiescam.—*Virgil.*
B; *om.* C

real and the unreal; that all things appear as they do only by virtue of the delicate individual physical and mental media through which we are made conscious of them; but the prosaic materialism of the majority condemns as madness the flashes of super-sight[a] which penetrate the common veil of obvious empiricism.

My name is Jervas Dudley, and from earliest childhood I have been a dreamer and a visionary. Wealthy beyond the necessity of a commercial life, and temperamentally unfitted for the formal studies and social recreations[b] of my acquaintances, I have dwelt ever in realms apart from the visible world; spending my youth and adolescence in ancient and little-known[c] books, and in roaming the fields and groves of the region[d] near my ancestral home. I do not think that what I read in these books or saw in these fields and groves was exactly what other boys read and saw there; but of this I must say little, since detailed speech would but confirm those cruel slanders upon my intellect which I sometimes overhear from the whispers of the stealthy attendants around me. It is sufficient for me to relate events without analysing[e] causes.

I have said that I dwelt apart from the visible world, but I have not said that I dwelt alone. This no human creature may do; for lacking the fellowship of the living, he inevitably draws upon the companionship of things that are not, or are no longer, living. Close by my home there lies a singular wooded hollow, in whose twilight deeps I spent most of my time; reading, thinking, and dreaming. Down its moss-covered slopes my first steps of infancy were taken, and around its grotesquely gnarled oak trees my first fancies of boyhood were woven. Well did I come to know the presiding dryads of those trees, and often have I watched their wild dances in the struggling[f] beams of a waning moon—but of these things I must not now speak. I will tell only of the lone tomb in the darkest of the hillside thickets; the deserted tomb of the Hydes, an old and exalted family whose last direct descendant had been laid within its black recesses many decades before my birth.

[a] super-sight] supersight B, C
[b] recreations] recreation C
[c] little-known] little known A, B, C
[d] region] regions A
[e] analysing] analyzing B, C
[f] struggling] struggilng A

The vault to which I refer is of ancient granite, weathered and discoloured[a] by the mists and dampness of generations. Excavated back into the hillside, the structure is visible only at the entrance. The door, a ponderous and forbidding slab of stone, hangs upon rusted iron hinges, and is fastened *ajar*[b] in a queerly sinister way by means of heavy iron chains and padlocks, according to a gruesome fashion of half a century ago. The abode of the race whose scions are here inurned had once crowned the declivity which holds the tomb, but had long since fallen victim to the flames which sprang up from a[c] stroke of lightning. Of the midnight storm which destroyed this gloomy mansion, the older inhabitants of the region sometimes speak in hushed and uneasy voices; alluding to what they call "divine wrath" in a manner that in later years vaguely increased the always strong fascination which I had[d] felt for the forest-darkened sepulchre.[e] One man only had perished in the fire. When the last of the Hydes was buried in this place of shade and stillness, the sad urnful of ashes had come from a distant land;[f] to which the family had repaired when the mansion burned down. No one remains to lay flowers before the granite portal, and few care to brave the depressing shadows which seem to linger strangely about the water-worn stones.

I shall never forget the afternoon when first I stumbled upon the half-hidden house of death. It was in mid-summer, when the alchemy of Nature[g] transmutes the sylvan landscape to one vivid and almost homogeneous mass of green; when the senses are well-nigh intoxicated with the surging seas of moist verdure and the subtly indefinable odours[h] of the soil and the vegetation. In such surroundings the mind loses its perspective; time and space become trivial and unreal, and echoes of a forgotten prehistoric past beat insistently upon the

---

[a] discoloured] discolored B, C
[b] *ajar*] ajar B, C
[c] a] a disastrous A
[d] had] *om.* A
[e] sepulchre.] sepulcher. B, C
[f] land;] land, A, C
[g] Nature] nature B, C
[h] odours] odors B, C

enthralled consciousness.[a] All day I had been wandering through the mystic groves of the hollow; thinking thoughts I need not discuss, and conversing with things I need not name. In years a child of ten, I had seen and heard many wonders unknown to the throng; and was oddly aged in certain respects. When, upon forcing my way between two savage clumps of briers,[b] I suddenly encountered the entrance of the vault, I had no knowledge of what I had discovered. The dark blocks of granite, the door so curiously ajar, and the funereal[c] carvings above the arch, aroused in me no associations of mournful or terrible character. Of graves and tombs I knew and imagined much, but had on account of my peculiar temperament been kept from all personal contact with churchyards and cemeteries. The strange stone house on the woodland slope was to me only a source of interest and speculation; and its cold,[d] damp interior, into which I vainly peered through the aperture so tantalisingly[e] left, contained for me no hint of death or decay. But in that instant of curiosity was born the madly unreasoning desire which has brought me to this hell of confinement. Spurred on by a voice which must have come from the hideous soul of the forest, I resolved to enter the beckoning gloom in spite of the ponderous chains which barred my passage. In the waning light of day I alternately rattled the rusty impediments with a view to throwing wide the stone door, and essayed to squeeze my slight form through the space already provided; but neither plan met with success. At first curious, I was now frantic; and when in the thickening twilight I returned to my home, I had sworn to the hundred gods of the grove that *at any cost*[f] I would some day force an entrance to the black, chilly depths that seemed calling out to me. The physician with the iron-grey[g] beard who comes each day to my room[h] once told a visitor that this

---

[a] consciousness.] consciousness. ¶ B, C

[b] briers,] briars, B, C

[c] funereal] funeral B, C

[d] cold,] cold A

[e] tantalisingly] tantalizingly B, C

[f] *at any cost*] at any cost A

[g] iron-grey] iron-gray B

[h] room] room, B, C

decision marked the beginning of a pitiful monomania; but I will leave final judgment to my readers when they shall have learnt all.

The months following my discovery were spent in futile attempts to force the complicated padlock of the slightly open vault, and in carefully guarded inquiries regarding the nature and history of the structure. With the traditionally receptive ears of the small boy, I learned much; though an habitual secretiveness caused me to tell no one of my information or my resolve. It is perhaps worth mentioning that I was not at all surprised[a] or terrified on learning of the nature of the vault. My rather original ideas regarding life and death had caused me to associate the cold clay with the breathing body in a vague fashion; and I felt that the great and sinister family of the burned-down mansion was in some way represented within the stone space I sought to explore. Mumbled tales of the weird rites and godless revels of bygone years in the ancient hall gave to me a new and potent interest in the tomb, before whose door I would sit for hours at a time each day. Once I thrust a candle within the nearly closed entrance, but could see nothing save a flight of damp stone steps leading downward. The odour[b] of the place repelled yet bewitched me. I felt I had known it before, in a past remote beyond all recollection; beyond even my tenancy of the body I now possess.

The year after I first beheld the tomb, I stumbled upon a worm-eaten translation of Plutarch's "Lives"[c] in the book-filled attic of my home. Reading the life of Theseus, I was much impressed by that passage telling of the great stone beneath which the boyish hero was to find his tokens of destiny whenever he should become old enough to lift its enormous weight. This[d] legend had the effect of dispelling my keenest impatience to enter the vault, for it made me feel that the time was not yet ripe. Later, I told myself, I should grow to a strength and ingenuity which might enable me to unfasten the heavily chained door with ease; but until then I would do better by conforming to what seemed the will of Fate.

[a] surprised] surprized B
[b] odour] odor B, C
[c] "Lives"] *Lives* B, C
[d] This] The C

Accordingly my watches by the dank portal became less persistent, and much of my time was spent in other though equally strange pursuits. I would sometimes rise very quietly in the night, stealing out to walk in those churchyards and places of burial from which I had been kept by my parents. What I did there I may not say, for I am not now sure of the reality of certain things; but I know that on the day after such a nocturnal ramble I would often astonish those about me with my knowledge of topics almost forgotten for many generations. It was after a night like this that I shocked the community with a queer conceit about the burial of the rich and celebrated Squire Brewster, a maker of local history who was interred in 1711, and whose slate headstone,[a] bearing a graven skull and crossbones, was slowly crumbling to powder. In a moment of childish imagination I vowed not only that the undertaker, Goodman Simpson, had stolen the silver-buckled shoes, silken hose, and satin small-clothes of the deceased before burial; but that the Squire himself, not fully inanimate, had turned twice in his mound-covered coffin on the day after interment.

But the idea of entering the tomb never left my thoughts; being indeed stimulated by the unexpected genealogical discovery that my own maternal ancestry possessed at least a slight link with the supposedly extinct family of the Hydes. Last of my paternal race, I was likewise the last of this older and more mysterious line. I began to feel that the tomb was *mine,* and to look forward with hot eagerness to the time when I might pass within that stone door and down those slimy stone[b] steps in the dark. I now[c] formed the habit of *listening* [d] very intently at the slightly open portal, choosing my favourite[e] hours of midnight stillness for the odd vigil. By the time I came of age, I had made a small clearing in the thicket before the mould-stained[f] facade of the hillside, allowing the surrounding vegetation to encircle and overhang the space like the walls and roof of a sylvan bower. This bower was my temple, the fastened door my shrine, and here I would

[a] headstone,] head-/stone, A, C
[b] stone] ston A
[c] now] *om.* A
[d] *listening*] listening B, C
[e] favourite] favorite B, C
[f] mould-stained] mold-stained B, C

lie[a] outstretched on the mossy ground, thinking strange thoughts and dreaming strange dreams.

The night of the first revelation was a sultry one. I must have fallen asleep from fatigue, for it was with a distinct sense of awakening that I heard the *voices*.[b] Of those[c] tones and accents I hesitate to speak; of their *quality*[d] I will not speak; but I may say that they presented certain uncanny differences in vocabulary, pronunciation,[e] and mode of utterance. Every shade of New England dialect, from the uncouth syllables of the Puritan colonists to the precise rhetoric of fifty years ago,[f] seemed represented in that shadowy colloquy, though it was only later that I noticed the fact. At the time, indeed, my attention was distracted from this matter by another phenomenon; a phenomenon so fleeting that I could not take oath upon its reality. I barely fancied that as I awoke, a *light* had been hurriedly extinguished within the sunken sepulchre.[g] I do not think I was either astounded or panic-stricken, but I know that I was greatly and permanently *changed* that night. Upon returning home I went with much directness to a rotting chest in the attic, wherein I found the key which next day unlocked with ease the barrier I had so long stormed in vain.

It was in the soft glow of late afternoon that I first entered the vault on the abandoned slope. A spell was upon me, and my heart leaped with an exultation I can but ill describe. As I closed the door behind me and descended the dripping steps by the light of my lone candle, I seemed to know the way; and though the candle sputtered with the stifling reek of the place, I felt singularly at home in the musty,[h] charnel-house air. Looking about me, I beheld many marble slabs bearing coffins, or the remains of coffins. Some of these were sealed and intact, but others had nearly vanished, leaving the silver handles and plates isolated amidst certain curious heaps of whitish dust. Upon one

---

[a] lie] lit A
[b] *voices.*] voices. B, C
[c] those] these B, C
[d] *quality*] quality B, C
[e] pronunciation,] pronunciation A
[f] dialect, . . . ago,] dialect . . . ago A
[g] sepulchre.] sepulcher. B, C
[h] musty,] musty A

plate I read the name of Sir Geoffrey Hyde, who had come from Sussex in 1640 and died here a few years later. In a conspicuous alcove was one fairly well-preserved[a] and untenanted casket, adorned with a single name which brought to[b] me both a smile and a shudder. An odd impulse caused me to climb upon the broad slab, extinguish my candle, and lie down within the vacant box.

In the grey[c] light of dawn I staggered from the vault and locked the chain of the door behind me. I was no longer a young man, though but twenty-one winters had chilled my bodily frame. Early-rising[d] villagers who observed my homeward progress looked at me strangely, and marvelled[e] at the signs of ribald revelry which they saw in one whose life was known to be sober and solitary. I did not appear before my parents till after a long and refreshing sleep.

Henceforward I haunted the tomb each night; seeing, hearing,[f] and doing things I must never recall.[g] My speech, always susceptible to environmental influences, was the first thing to succumb to the change; and my suddenly acquired archaism of diction was soon remarked upon. Later a queer boldness and recklessness came into my demeanour,[h] till I unconsciously grew to possess the bearing of a man of the world despite my lifelong seclusion. My formerly silent tongue waxed voluble with the easy grace of a Chesterfield or the godless cynicism of a Rochester. I displayed a peculiar erudition utterly unlike the fantastic, monkish lore over which I had pored in youth; and covered the fly-leaves[i] of my books with facile impromptu epigrams which brought up suggestions of Gay, Prior, and the sprightliest of the Augustan wits and rhymesters.[j] One morning at breakfast I came close to disaster by declaiming in palpably liquorish accents an effusion of

[a] well-preserved] well preserved A, B, C
[b] to] *om.* C
[c] grey] gray B, C
[d] Early-rising] Early rising A
[e] marvelled] marveled B, C
[f] hearing,] hearing A
[g] recall.] reveal. A
[h] demeanour,] demeanor, B, C
[i] fly-leaves] fly leaves A; fly-/leaves C
[j] rhymesters.] rimesters. B, C

eighteenth-century Bacchanalian mirth;[a] a bit of Georgian playfulness
never recorded in a book, which ran something like this:

> Come hither, my lads, with your tankards of ale,
> And drink to the present before it shall fail;[b]
> Pile each on your platter a mountain of beef,
> For 'tis[c] eating and drinking that bring us relief:
> > So fill up your glass,[d]
> > For life[e] will soon pass;[f]
> When you're dead ye'll ne'er drink to your king or your lass![g]

> Anacreon had a red nose, so they say;
> But what's a red nose if ye're happy[h] and gay?
> Gad split me![i] I'd rather be red whilst I'm here[j]
> Than white as a lily—and dead half a year!
> > So Betty, my miss,
> > Come give me a kiss;[k]
> In hell[l] there's no innkeeper's daughter like this!

> Young Harry,[m] propp'd up just as straight as he's able,
> Will soon lose his wig and slip under the table;[n]
> But fill up your goblets and pass 'em around—[o]
> Better under the table than under the ground!

---

[a] eighteenth-century ... mirth;] Eighteenth Century bacchanalian mirth B;
Eighteenth Century bacchanalian mirth, C
[b] fail;] fail. D
[c] 'tis] tis D
[d] glass,] glass D
[e] life] Life D
[f] pass;] pass: D
[g] king ... lass!] King ... lass. D
[h] happy] merry D
[i] me!] me, A
[j] here] D; here, A, B, C
[k] kiss;] kiss D
[l] hell] h—l A, D
[m] Harry,] Harry D
[n] table;] table, C; table: D
[o] 'em around—] them around; D

So revel and chaff
As ye thirstily quaff:[a]
Under six feet of dirt 'tis less easy to laugh!

The[b] fiend strike me blue! I'm scarce able to walk,[c]
And damn[d] me if I can stand upright or talk![e]
Here, landlord, bid[f] Betty to summon a chair;
I'll try home for a while, for my wife is not there![g]
So lend me a hand;
I'm not able to stand,
But I'm gay whilst I linger on top of the land![h]

About this time I conceived my present fear of fire and
thunderstorms. Previously indifferent to such things, I had now an
unspeakable horror of them; and would retire to the innermost
recesses of the house whenever the heavens threatened an electrical
display. A favourite[i] haunt of mine during the day was the ruined cellar
of the mansion that had burned down, and in fancy I would picture
the structure as it had been in its prime. On one occasion I startled a
villager by leading him confidently to a shallow sub-cellar,[j] of whose
existence I seemed to know in spite of the fact that it had been unseen
and forgotten for many generations.

At last came that which I had long feared. My parents, alarmed at
the altered manner and appearance of their only son, commenced to
exert over my movements a kindly espionage which threatened to
result in disaster. I had told no one of my visits to the tomb, having
guarded my secret purpose with religious zeal since childhood; but
now I was forced to exercise care in threading the mazes of the

[a] quaff:] quaff, D
[b] The] May the D
[c] walk,] talk, D
[d] damn] d——n A, D
[e] talk!] walk. D
[f] landlord, bid] landlord! Bid A; landlord, tell D
[g] there!] there. D
[h] Come hither, . . . land!] *Come hither, . . . land!* C
[i] favourite] favorite B, C
[j] sub-cellar,] sub-cellar A

wooded hollow, that I might throw off a possible pursuer. My key to the vault I kept suspended from a cord about my neck, its presence known only to me. I never carried out of the sepulchre[a] any of the things I came upon whilst within its walls.

One morning as I emerged from the damp tomb and fastened the chain of the portal with none too steady hand, I beheld in an adjacent thicket the dreaded face of a watcher. Surely the end was near; for my bower was discovered, and the objective of my nocturnal journeys[b] revealed. The man did not accost me, so I hastened home in an effort to overhear what he might report to my careworn father. Were my sojourns beyond the chained door about to be proclaimed to the world? Imagine my delighted astonishment on hearing the spy inform my parent[c] in a cautious whisper *that I had spent the night in the bower outside the tomb;* my sleep-filmed eyes fixed upon the crevice where the padlocked portal stood ajar! By what miracle had the watcher been thus deluded? I was now convinced that a supernatural agency protected me. Made bold by this heaven-sent circumstance, I began to resume perfect openness in going to the vault; confident that no one could witness my entrance. For a week I tasted to the full the[d] joys of that charnel conviviality which I must not describe, when the *thing* happened, and I was borne away to this accursed abode of sorrow and monotony.

I should not have ventured out that night; for the taint of thunder was in the clouds, and a hellish phosphorescence rose from the rank swamp at the bottom of the hollow. The call of the dead, too, was different. Instead of the hillside tomb, it was the charred cellar on the crest of the slope whose presiding daemon[e] beckoned to me with unseen fingers. As I emerged from an intervening grove upon the plain before the ruin, I beheld in the misty moonlight a thing I had always vaguely expected. The mansion, gone for a century, once more reared its stately height to the raptured vision; every window ablaze with the splendour[f] of many candles. Up the long drive rolled the coaches of

---

[a] sepulchre] sepulcher B, C

[b] journeys] journey A

[c] parent] father A

[d] the] *om.* C

[e] daemon] demon B, C

[f] splendour] splendor B, C

the Boston gentry, whilst on foot came a numerous assemblage of powdered exquisites from the neighbouring[a] mansions. With this throng I mingled, though I knew I belonged with the hosts rather than with the guests. Inside the hall were[b] music, laughter, and wine on every hand. Several faces I recognised;[c] though I should have known them better had they been shrivelled[d] or eaten away by death and decomposition. Amidst a wild and reckless throng I was the wildest and most abandoned. Gay blasphemy poured in torrents from my lips, and in my[e] shocking sallies I heeded no law of God, Man, or Nature.[f] Suddenly a peal of thunder, resonant even above the din of the swinish revelry, clave the very roof and laid a hush of fear upon the boisterous company. Red tongues of flame and searing gusts of heat engulfed the house; and the roysterers, struck with terror at the descent of a calamity which seemed to transcend the bounds of unguided Nature,[g] fled shrieking into the night. I alone remained, riveted to my seat by a grovelling[h] fear which I had never felt before. And then a second horror took possession of my soul. Burnt alive to ashes,[i] my body dispersed by the four winds, *I might never lie in the tomb of the Hydes!*[j] Was not my coffin prepared for me? Had I not a right to rest till eternity amongst the descendants of Sir Geoffrey Hyde? Aye! I would claim my heritage of death, even though my soul go seeking through the ages for another corporeal tenement to represent it on that vacant slab in the alcove of the vault. *Jervas Hyde* should never share the sad fate of Palinurus!

As the phantom of the burning house faded, I found myself screaming and struggling madly in the arms of two men, one of whom was the spy who had followed me to the tomb. Rain was pouring down

---

[a] neighbouring] neighboring B, C

[b] were] was A

[c] recognised;] recognized; B, C

[d] shrivelled] shriveled B, C

[e] my] *om.* C

[f] Man, or Nature.] man, or nature. ¶ B, C

[g] Nature,] nature, B, C

[h] grovelling] groveling B, C

[i] ashes,] ashes; A

[j] *Hydes!*] *Hydes.* A

in torrents, and upon the southern horizon were flashes of the[a] lightning that had so lately passed over our heads. My father, his face lined with sorrow, stood by as I shouted my demands to be laid within the tomb;[b] frequently admonishing my captors to treat me as gently as they could. A blackened circle on the floor of the ruined cellar told of a violent stroke from the heavens; and from this spot a group of curious villagers with lanterns were prying a small box of antique workmanship[c] which the thunderbolt had brought to light.[d] Ceasing my futile and now objectless writhing, I watched the spectators as they viewed the treasure-trove, and was permitted to share in their discoveries. The box, whose fastenings were broken by the stroke which had unearthed it, contained many papers and objects of value;[e] but I had eyes for one thing alone. It was the porcelain miniature of a young man in a smartly curled bag-wig, and bore the initials "J. H." The face was such that as I gazed, I might well have been studying my mirror.

On the following day I was brought to this room with the barred windows, but I have been kept informed of certain things through an aged and simple-minded servitor, for whom I bore a fondness in infancy, and who like me[f] loves the churchyard. What I have dared relate of my experiences within the vault has brought me only pitying smiles. My father, who visits me frequently, declares that at no time did I pass the chained portal, and swears that the rusted padlock had not been touched for fifty years when he examined it. He even says that all the village knew of my journeys to the tomb, and that I was often watched as I slept in the bower outside the grim facade, my half-open eyes fixed on the crevice that leads to the interior. Against these assertions I have no tangible proof to offer, since my key to the padlock was lost in the struggle on that night of horrors. The strange things of the past which I learnt[g] during those nocturnal meetings with

---

[a] the] *om.* C
[b] tomb;] tomb, A, C
[c] workmanship] workmanship, B, C
[d] light.] light. ¶ B, C
[e] value;] value, C
[f] who like me] who, like me, B, C
[g] I learnt] I have learned B, C

the dead he dismisses as the fruits of my lifelong and omnivorous[a] browsing amongst the ancient volumes of the family library. Had it not been for my old servant Hiram, I should have by this time become quite convinced of my madness.

But Hiram, loyal to the last, has held faith in me, and has done that which impels me to make public at least a[b] part of my story. A week ago he burst open the lock which chains the door of the tomb perpetually ajar, and descended with a lantern into the murky depths. On a slab in an alcove he found an old but[c] empty coffin whose tarnished plate bears the single word *"Jervas"*.[d] In that coffin and in that vault they have promised me I shall be buried.

---

[a] and omnivorous] *om.* A

[b] a] *om.* C

[c] but] *om.* A

[d] word *"Jervas"*.] word *"Jervas."* A; word: *Jervas.* B, C

Dagon

I am writing this under an appreciable mental strain, since by tonight I shall be no more. Penniless, and at the end of my supply of the drug which alone makes life endurable, I can bear the torture no longer; and shall cast myself from this garret window into the squalid street below. Do not think from my slavery to morphine that I am a weakling or a degenerate. When you have read these hastily scrawled pages you may guess, though never fully realise,[a] why it is that I must have forgetfulness or death.

It was in one of the most open and least frequented parts of the broad[b] Pacific that the packet of which I was supercargo fell a victim to the German sea-raider. The great war was then at its very beginning, and the enemy's navy had not reached its later degree of ruthlessness,[c] so that our vessel was made a legitimate prize, whilst we of her crew were treated with all the fairness and consideration due us as naval prisoners. So liberal, indeed, was the discipline of our captors, that five days after we were taken I managed to escape alone in a small boat

Editor's Note: The story was first published in the *Vagrant* (November 1919), edited and typeset by W. Paul Cook. The surviving T.Ms. (JHL) is one of the single-spaced T.Mss. that HPL sent to *Weird Tales*, where the story appeared in the October 1923 issue. The T.Ms. bears clear revisions from the *Vagrant* appearance; but since HPL was instructed by editor Edwin Baird to submit a double-spaced T.Ms., he appears to have made some further revisions (e.g., at 52.13) in the process. These alterations from the existing T.Ms. are not likely to have been made by *Weird Tales*. Subsequent *Weird Tales* appearances (January 1936, November 1951) are not relevant to the tale's textual history. The Arkham House editions follow the existing T.Ms.

Texts: A = *Vagrant* No. 11 (November 1919): 23–29; B = T.Ms. (JHL); C = *Weird Tales* 2, No. 3 (October 1923): 23–25; D = *Dagon and Other Macabre Tales* (Arkham House, 1965), 3–8. Copy-text: B (but with a few readings from C).

[a] realise,] realize, A, C

[b] broad] *om.* C

[c] enemy's . . . ruthlessness] ocean forces of the Hun [Kaiser A] had not completely sunk to their later degradation; A, B, D

with water and provisions for a good length of time.

When I finally found myself adrift and free, I had but little idea of my surroundings. Never a competent navigator, I could only guess vaguely by the sun and stars that I was somewhat south of the equator. Of the longitude I knew nothing, and no island or coast-line[a] was in sight. The weather kept fair, and for uncounted days I drifted aimlessly beneath the scorching[b] sun; waiting either for some passing ship, or to be cast on[c] the shores of some habitable land. But neither ship nor land appeared, and I began to despair in my solitude upon the heaving vastnesses of unbroken blue.

The change happened whilst I slept. Its details I shall never know; for my slumber, though troubled and dream-infested, was continuous.[d] When at last I awaked, it was to discover myself half sucked into a slimy expanse of hellish black mire which extended about me in monotonous undulations as far as I could see, and in which my boat lay grounded some distance away.

Though one might well imagine that my first sensation would be of wonder at so prodigious and unexpected a transformation of scenery, I was in reality more horrified than astonished;[e] for there was in the air and in the rotting soil a sinister[f] quality which chilled me to the very core. The region was putrid with the carcasses of decaying fish, and of other less describable things which I saw protruding from the nasty mud of the unending plain. Perhaps I should not hope to convey in mere words the unutterable hideousness that can dwell in absolute silence and barren immensity. There was nothing within hearing, and nothing in sight save a vast reach of black slime; yet the very completeness of the stillness and the homogeneity of the landscape oppressed me with a nauseating fear.

The sun was blazing down from a sky which seemed to me almost black in its cloudless cruelty; as though reflecting the inky marsh beneath

[a] coast-line] coastline D
[b] scorching] sorching D
[c] on] upon A
[d] continuous.] unbroken. A
[e] astonished;] astonished, C
[f] sinister] strange and sinister A

my feet. As I crawled into the stranded boat I realised[a] that only one
theory could explain my position. Through some unprecedented volcanic
upheaval, a portion of the ocean floor must have been thrown to the
surface, exposing regions which for innumerable millions of years had
lain hidden under unfathomable watery depths. So great was the extent
of the new land which had risen beneath[b] me, that I could not detect
the faintest noise of the surging ocean, strain my ears as I might. Nor
were there any sea-fowl to prey upon the dead things.

For several hours I sat thinking or brooding in the boat, which lay
upon its side and afforded a slight shade as the sun moved across the
heavens. As the day progressed, the ground lost some of its stickiness,
and seemed likely to dry sufficiently for travelling[c] purposes in a short
time. That night I slept but little, and the next day I made for myself a
pack containing food and water, preparatory to an overland journey in
search of the vanished sea and possible rescue.

On the third morning I found the soil dry enough to walk upon with
ease. The odour[d] of the fish was maddening; but I was too much
concerned with graver things to mind so slight an evil, and set out boldly
for an unknown goal. All day I forged steadily westward, guided by a far-
away hummock which rose higher than any other elevation on the rolling
desert. That night I encamped,[e] and on the following day still travelled[f]
toward the hummock, though that object seemed scarcely nearer than
when I had first espied[g] it. By the fourth evening I attained the base of
the mound, which turned out to be much higher than it had appeared
from a distance; an intervening valley setting it out in sharper relief from
the general surface. Too weary to ascend, I slept in the shadow of the hill.

I know not why my dreams were so wild that night; but ere[h] the
waning and fantastically gibbous moon had risen far above the eastern
plain, I was awake in a cold perspiration, determined to sleep no more.

---

[a] realised] realized A, C
[b] beneath] under C
[c] travelling] traveling C
[d] odour] odor A, C
[e] encamped,] camped, C
[f] travelled] traveled C
[g] espied] spied C
[h] night; but ere] night, but before C

Such visions as I had experienced were too much for me to endure again. And in the glow of the moon I saw how unwise I had been to travel by day. Without the glare of the parching sun, my journey would have cost me less energy; indeed, I now felt quite able to perform the ascent which had deterred me[a] at sunset. Picking up my pack, I started for the crest of the eminence.

I have said that the unbroken monotony of the rolling plain was a source of vague horror to me; but I think my horror was greater when I gained the summit of the mound and looked down the other side into an immeasurable pit or canyon, whose black recesses the moon had not yet soared high enough to illumine. I felt myself on the edge of the world; peering over the rim into a fathomless chaos of eternal night. Through my terror ran curious reminiscences of "Paradise Lost",[b] and of[c] Satan's hideous climb through the unfashioned realms of darkness.

As the moon climbed higher in the sky, I began to see that the slopes of the valley were not quite so perpendicular as I had imagined. Ledges and outcroppings of rock afforded fairly easy footholds for a descent, whilst after a drop of a few hundred feet, the declivity became very gradual. Urged on by an impulse which I cannot definitely analyse,[d] I scrambled with difficulty down the rocks and stood on the gentler slope beneath, gazing into the Stygian deeps where no light had yet penetrated.

All at once my attention was captured by a vast and singular object on the opposite slope, which rose steeply about a hundred yards ahead of me; an object that gleamed whitely in the newly bestowed rays of the ascending moon. That it was merely a gigantic piece of stone, I soon assured myself; but I was conscious of a distinct impression that its contour and position were not altogether the work of Nature. A closer scrutiny filled me with sensations I cannot express; for despite its enormous magnitude, and its location[e] in an abyss which had yawned at the bottom of the sea since the world was young, I perceived beyond a doubt that the strange object was a well-shaped

[a] me] m A

[b] "Paradise Lost",] Paradise Lost, A, B, C; *Paradise Lost,* D

[c] of] *om.* D

[d] analyse,] analyze, A, C

[e] location] position A, B, D

monolith whose massive bulk had known[a] the workmanship and perhaps the worship of living and thinking creatures.

Dazed and frightened, yet not without a certain thrill of the scientist's or archaeologist's delight,[b] I examined my surroundings more closely. The moon, now near the zenith, shone weirdly and vividly above the towering steeps that hemmed in the chasm, and revealed the fact that a far-flung body of water flowed at the bottom, winding out of sight in both directions, and almost lapping my feet as I stood on the slope.[c] Across the chasm, the wavelets washed the base of the Cyclopean monolith;[d] on whose surface I could now trace both inscriptions and crude sculptures. The writing was in a system of hieroglyphics[e] unknown to me, and unlike anything I had ever seen in books;[f] consisting for the most part of conventionalised[g] aquatic symbols such as fishes, eels, octopi, crustaceans, molluscs, whales,[h] and the like. Several characters obviously represented marine things which are unknown to the modern world, but whose decomposing forms I had observed on the ocean-risen plain.

It was the pictorial carving, however, that did most to hold me spellbound. Plainly visible across[i] the intervening water on account of their enormous size, were[j] an array of bas-reliefs whose subjects would have excited the envy of a Doré.[k] I think that these things were supposed to depict men—at least, a certain sort of men; though the creatures were shewn[l] disporting like fishes in the waters of some marine grotto, or paying homage at some monolithic shrine which appeared to be under the waves as well. Of their faces and forms I dare not speak in detail; for the mere remembrance makes me grow faint. Grotesque beyond the imagination of a Poe or a Bulwer, they

[a] known] know C
[b] delight,] delight. A
[c] slope.] slope. ¶ C
[d] monolith;] monolith, D
[e] hieroglyphics] heiroglyphics A
[f] books;] books, D
[g] conventionalised] conventionalized C
[h] whales,] whales B, D
[i] across] acorss A
[j] size, were] size was D
[k] a Doré.] Dore. A
[l] shewn] shown A, B, C, D

were damnably human in general outline despite webbed hands and feet, shockingly wide and flabby lips, glassy, bulging eyes, and other features less pleasant to recall. Curiously enough, they seemed to have been chiselled[a] badly out of proportion with their scenic background; for one of the creatures was shewn[b] in the act of killing a whale represented as but little larger than himself.[c] I remarked, as I say, their grotesqueness and strange size; but in a moment decided that they were merely the imaginary gods of some primitive fishing or seafaring tribe; some tribe whose last descendant had perished eras before the first ancestor of the Piltdown[d] or Neanderthal Man[e] was born. Awestruck at this unexpected glimpse into a past beyond the conception of the most daring anthropologist, I stood musing[f] whilst the moon cast queer reflections on the silent channel before me.

Then suddenly I saw it. With only a slight churning to mark its rise to the surface, the thing slid into view above the dark waters. Vast, Polyphemus-like,[g] and loathsome, it darted like a stupendous monster of nightmares to the monolith, about which[h] it flung its gigantic scaly arms, the while it bowed its hideous head and gave vent to certain measured sounds. I think I went mad then.

Of my frantic ascent of the slope and cliff, and of my delirious journey back to the stranded boat, I remember little. I believe I sang a great deal, and laughed oddly when I was unable to sing. I have indistinct recollections of a great storm some time after I reached the boat; at any rate, I know that I heard peals of thunder and other tones which Nature[i] utters only in wild and terrible[j] moods.

When I came out of the shadows I was in a San Francisco hospital; brought thither by the captain of the American ship which had picked

---

[a] chiselled] chiseled C
[b] shewn] shown A, B, C, D
[c] himself.] himself. ¶ C
[d] Piltdown] Pitdown A
[e] Man] man C
[f] musing] musing, C
[g] Polyphemus-like,] Polyphemuslike, C
[h] which] *om.* A
[i] Nature] nature A
[j] wild and terrible] her wildest A, B, D

up my boat in mid-ocean. In my delirium I had said much, but found that my words had been given scant attention. Of any land upheaval in the Pacific, my rescuers knew nothing;[a] nor did I deem it necessary to insist upon a thing[b] which I knew they could not believe. Once I sought out a celebrated ethnologist, and amused him with peculiar questions regarding the ancient Philistine legend of[c] Dagon, the Fish-God; but[d] soon perceiving that he was hopelessly conventional, I did not press my inquiries.

It is at night, especially when the moon is gibbous and waning, that I see the thing. I tried morphine;[e] but the drug has[f] given only transient surcease, and has drawn me into its clutches as a hopeless slave. So now I am going to end matters,[g] having written a full account for the information or the contemptuous amusement of my fellow-men. Often I ask myself if it could not all have been a pure phantasm—a mere freak[h] of fever as I lay sun-stricken and raving in the open boat after my escape from the German man-of-war.[i] This I ask myself, but ever does there come before me a hideously vivid vision in reply. I cannot think of the deep sea without shuddering at the nameless things that may at this very moment be crawling and floundering on its slimy bed, worshipping their ancient stone idols and carving their own detestable likenesses on submarine obelisks of water-soaked granite. I dream of a day when they may rise above the billows to drag down in their reeking talons the remnants of puny, war-exhausted[j] mankind—of a day when the land shall sink, and the dark ocean floor shall ascend amidst universal pandemonium.

The end is near. I hear a noise at the door, as of some immense slippery body lumbering against it. It shall not find me. God, *that hand!* The window! The window!

[a] nothing;] nothing, A
[b] thing] thing, A
[c] of] or D
[d] but] but, C
[e] morphine;] morphine, C
[f] has] had A
[g] going to end matters,] to end it all, A, B, D
[h] freak] fraek A
[i] man-of-war.] man-of-war. ¶ C
[j] war-exhausted] war-torn A

A Reminiscence of Dr. Samuel Johnson

The Privilege of Reminiscence, however rambling or tiresome, is one generally allow'd to the very aged; indeed, 'tis frequently by means of such Recollections that the obscure occurrences[a] of History, and the lesser Anecdotes of the Great, are transmitted to Posterity.

Tho' many of my readers have at times observ'd and remark'd a Sort of antique Flow in my Stile of Writing, it hath pleased me to pass amongst the Members of this Generation as a young Man, giving out the Fiction that I was born in 1890, in *America.* I am now, however, resolv'd to unburthen myself of a secret which I have hitherto kept thro' Dread of Incredulity; and to impart to the Publick a true knowledge of my long years, in order to gratifie their taste for authentick Information of an Age with whose famous Personages I was on familiar Terms. Be it then known that I was born on the family Estate in *Devonshire,* of the 10th[b] day of August, 1690, (or in the new *Gregorian* Stile of Reckoning, the 20th of August) being therefore now in my 228th year. Coming early to *London,* I saw as a Child many of the celebrated Men of King *William's* Reign, including the lamented Mr. *Dryden,* who sat much at the Tables of *Will's* Coffee-House. With Mr. *Addison* and Dr. *Swift* I later became very well acquainted, and was an even more familiar Friend to Mr. *Pope,* whom I knew and respected till

Editor's Note: There is only a single text of this story: its first and only appearance, *United Amateur* (November 1917). HPL has clearly written the story in a generally authentic version of late seventeenth- and early eighteenth-century style, although not consistently so (not all nouns are capitalised). As the story was typeset by W. Paul Cook (Official Publisher of the UAPA for the 1917–18 term), one can assume that the text has been printed accurately. (In that appearance, boldface was used for emphasis; italics have been substituted here.)

Text: A = *United Amateur* 17, No. 2 (November 1917): 21–24.

[a] occurrences] ocurrences A
[b] of the 10th] *of the 10th* A

the Day of his Death. But since it is of my more recent Associate, the late Dr. *Johnson,* that I am at this time desir'd to write; I will pass over my Youth for the present.

I had first Knowledge of the Doctor in May of the year 1738, tho' I did not at that Time meet him. Mr. *Pope* had just compleated his Epilogue to his *Satires,* (the Piece beginning: "Not twice a Twelvemonth[a] you appear in Print.") and had arrang'd for its Publication. On the very Day it appear'd, there was also publish'd a Satire in Imitation of *Juvenal,* intitul'd *"London",*[b] by the then unknown *Johnson;* and this so struck the Town, that many Gentlemen of Taste declared, it was the Work of a greater Poet than Mr. *Pope.* Notwithstanding what some Detractors have said of Mr. *Pope's* petty Jealousy, he gave the Verses of his new Rival no small Praise; and having learnt thro' Mr. *Richardson* who the Poet was, told me 'that Mr. *Johnson* wou'd soon be *deterré.'*[c]

I had no personal Acquaintance with the Doctor till 1763, when I was presented to him at the *Mitre* Tavern by Mr. *James Boswell,* a young *Scotchman* of excellent Family and great Learning, but small Wit, whose metrical Effusions I had sometimes revis'd.

Dr. *Johnson,* as I beheld him, was a full, pursy Man, very ill drest, and of slovenly Aspect. I recall him to have worn a bushy Bob-Wig, untyed and without Powder, and much too small for his Head. His cloaths were of rusty brown, much wrinkled, and with more than one Button missing. His Face, too full to be handsom, was likewise marred by the Effects of some scrofulous Disorder; and his Head was continually rolling about in a sort of convulsive way. Of this Infirmity, indeed, I had known before; having heard of it from Mr. *Pope,* who took the Trouble to make particular Inquiries.

Being nearly seventy-three, full nineteen Years older than Dr. *Johnson,* (I say Doctor, tho' his Degree came not till two Years afterward) I naturally expected him to have some Regard for my Age; and was therefore not in that Fear of him, which others confess'd. On my asking him what he thought of my favourable Notice of his Dictionary in *The Londoner,* my periodical Paper, he said: "Sir, I possess

[a] Twelvemonth] Twelve-/month A
[b] *"London",*] *"London,"* A
[c] *deterré.'*] *deterre.'* A

no Recollection of having perus'd your Paper, and have not a great Interest in the Opinions of the less thoughtful Part of Mankind." Being more than a little piqued at the Incivility of one whose Celebrity made me solicitous of his Approbation, I ventur'd to retaliate in kind, and told him, I was surpris'd that a Man of Sense shou'd judge the Thoughtfulness of one whose Productions he admitted never having read. "Why, Sir," reply'd *Johnson*, "I do not require to become familiar with a Man's Writings in order to estimate the Superficiality of his Attainments, when he plainly shews it by his Eagerness to mention his own Productions in the first Question he puts to me." Having thus become Friends, we convers'd on many Matters. When, to agree with him, I said I was distrustful of the Authenticity of *Ossian's* Poems, Mr. *Johnson* said: "That, Sir, does not do your Understanding particular Credit; for what all the Town is sensible of, is no great Discovery for a *Grub-Street* Critick to make. You might as well say, you have a strong Suspicion that *Milton* wrote 'Paradise Lost'!"[a]

I thereafter saw *Johnson* very frequently, most often at Meetings of THE LITERARY CLUB, which was founded the next Year by the Doctor, together with Mr. *Burke,* the parliamentary Orator, Mr. *Beauclerk,* a Gentleman of Fashion, Mr. *Langton,* a pious Man and Captain of Militia, Sir J. *Reynolds,* the widely known Painter, Dr. *Goldsmith,* the prose[b] and poetick Writer, Dr. *Nugent,* father-in-law to Mr. *Burke,* Sir *John Hawkins,* Mr. *Anthony Chamier,* and my self. We assembled generally at seven o'clock of an Evening, once a Week, at the *Turk's-Head,* in *Gerrard-Street, Soho,* till that Tavern was sold and made into a private Dwelling; after which Event we mov'd our Gatherings successively to *Prince's* in *Sackville-Street, Le Tellier's* in *Dover-Street,* and *Parsloe's* and The[c] *Thatched House* in *St. James's-Street.* In these Meetings we preserv'd a remarkable Degree of Amity and Tranquillity, which contrasts very favourably with some of the Dissensions and Disruptions I observe in the literary and amateur Press Associations of today. This Tranquillity was the more remarkable, because we had amongst us Gentlemen of very opposed Opinions. Dr. *Johnson* and I, as well as many others, were

[a] Lost'!"] Lost!'" A
[b] prose] Prose A
[c] *The*] The A

high Tories; whilst Mr. *Burke* was a *Whig*, and against the *American* War, many of his Speeches on that Subject having been widely publish'd. The least congenial Member was one of the Founders, Sir *John Hawkins*, who hath since written many misrepresentations of our Society. Sir *John*, an eccentrick Fellow, once declin'd to pay his part of the Reckoning for Supper, because 'twas his Custom at Home to eat no Supper. Later he insulted Mr. *Burke* in so intolerable a Manner, that we all took Pains to shew our Disapproval; after which Incident he came no more to our Meetings. However, he never openly fell out with the Doctor, and was the Executor of his Will; tho' Mr. *Boswell* and others have Reason to question the genuineness of his Attachment. Other and later Members of the CLUB were Mr. *David Garrick*, the Actor and early Friend of Dr. *Johnson*, Messieurs *Tho.* and *Jos. Warton*, Dr. *Adam Smith*, Dr. *Percy*, Author of the "Reliques",[a] Mr. *Edw. Gibbon*, the Historian, Dr. *Burney*, the Musician, Mr. *Malone*, the Critick, and Mr. *Boswell*. Mr. *Garrick* obtain'd Admittance only with Difficulty; for the Doctor, notwithstanding his great Friendship, was for ever affecting to decry the Stage and all Things connected with it. *Johnson*, indeed, had a most singular Habit of speaking for *Davy* when others were against him, and of arguing against him, when others were for him. I have no Doubt but that he sincerely lov'd Mr. *Garrick*, for he never alluded to him as he did to *Foote*, who was a very coarse Fellow despite his comick Genius. Mr. *Gibbon* was none too well lik'd, for he had an odious sneering Way which offended even those of us who most admir'd his historical Productions. Mr. *Goldsmith*, a little Man very vain of his Dress and very deficient in Brilliancy of Conversation, was my particular Favourite; since I was equally unable to shine in the Discourse. He was vastly jealous of Dr. *Johnson*, tho' none the less liking and respecting him. I remember that once a Foreigner, a *German*, I think, was in our Company; and that whilst *Goldsmith* was speaking, he observ'd the Doctor preparing to utter something. Unconsciously looking upon *Goldsmith* as a meer Encumbrance when compar'd to the greater Man, the Foreigner bluntly interrupted him and incurr'd his lasting Hostility by crying, "Hush, Toctor *Shonson* iss going to speak!"

In this luminous Company I was tolerated more because of my

[a] "Reliques",] "Reliques," A

Years than for my Wit or Learning; being no Match at all for the rest. My Friendship for the celebrated Monsieur *Voltaire* was ever a Cause of Annoyance to the Doctor; who was deeply orthodox, and who us'd to say of the *French* Philosopher: "Vir est acerrimi Ingenii et paucarum Literarum."

Mr. *Boswell*, a little teazing Fellow whom I had known for some Time previously, us'd to make Sport of my aukward Manners and old-fashion'd Wig and Cloaths. Once coming in a little the worse for Wine (to which he was addicted) he endeavour'd to lampoon me by means of an Impromptu in verse, writ on the Surface of the Table; but lacking the Aid he usually had in his Composition, he made a bad grammatical Blunder. I told him, he shou'd not try to pasquinade the Source of his Poesy. At another time *Bozzy* (as we us'd to call him) complain'd of my Harshness toward new Writers in the Articles I prepar'd for *The Monthly Review*.[a] He said, I push'd every Aspirant off the Slopes of Parnassus. "Sir," I reply'd, "you are mistaken. They who lose their Hold do so from their own Want of Strength; but desiring to conceal their Weakness, they attribute the Absence[b] of Success to the first Critick that mentions them." I am glad to recall that Dr. *Johnson* upheld me in this Matter.

Dr. *Johnson* was second to no Man in the Pains he took to revise the bad Verses of others; indeed, 'tis[c] said that in the book of poor blind old Mrs. Williams, there are scarce two lines which are not the Doctor's. At one Time *Johnson* recited to me some lines by a Servant to the Duke of *Leeds*, which had so amus'd him, that he had got them by Heart. They are on the Duke's Wedding, and so much resemble in Quality the Work of other and more recent poetick Dunces, that I cannot forbear copying them:

> "When the Duke of *Leeds* shall marry'd be
> To a fine young Lady of high Quality
> How happy will that Gentlewoman be
> In his Grace of *Leeds'* good Company."

I ask'd the Doctor, if he had ever try'd making Sense of this Piece;

---

[a] *The Monthly Review.*] The Monthly Review. A
[b] Absence] absence A
[c] 'tis] tis A

and upon his saying he had not, I amus'd myself with the following Amendment of it:

> When Gallant LEEDS auspiciously shall wed
> The virtuous Fair, of antient Lineage bred,
> How must the Maid rejoice with conscious Pride
> To win so great an Husband to her Side!

On shewing this to Dr. *Johnson,* he said, "Sir, you have straightened out the Feet, but you have put neither Wit nor Poetry into the Lines."

It wou'd afford me Gratification to tell more of my Experiences with Dr. *Johnson* and his circle of Wits; but I am an old Man, and easily fatigued. I seem to ramble along without much Logick or Continuity when I endeavour to recall the Past; and fear I light upon but few Incidents which others have not before discuss'd. Shou'd my present Recollections meet with Favour, I might later set down some further Anecdotes of old Times of which I am the only Survivor. I recall many Things of *Sam Johnson* and his Club, having kept up my Membership in the Latter long after the Doctor's Death, at which I sincerely mourn'd. I remember how *John Burgoyne,* Esq., the General, whose Dramatick and Poetical Works were printed after his Death, was blackballed by three Votes; probably because of his unfortunate Defeat in the *American* War, at *Saratoga.* Poor *John!* His Son fared better, I think, and was made a Baronet. But I am very tired. I am old, very old, and[a] it is Time for my Afternoon Nap.

---

[a] and] *om.* A

Polaris

Into the north window[a] of my chamber glows the Pole Star with uncanny light. All through the long hellish hours of blackness it shines there. And in the autumn of the year, when the winds from the north curse and whine, and the red-leaved trees of the swamp mutter things to one another[b] in the small hours of the morning under the horned waning moon, I sit by the casement and watch that star. Down from the heights reels the glittering Cassiopeia as the hours wear on, while Charles' Wain lumbers up from behind the vapour-soaked swamp trees that sway in the night-wind.[c] Just before dawn Arcturus winks ruddily from above the cemetery on the low hillock, and Coma Berenices shimmers weirdly afar off in the mysterious east; but still the Pole Star leers down from the same place in the black vault, winking hideously like an insane watching eye which strives to convey some strange message, yet recalls nothing save that it once had a message to convey. Sometimes, when it is cloudy, I can sleep.

Editor's Note: The story was first published in the *Philosopher* (December 1920). HPL apparently made slight revisions in the story for the next appearance, *National Amateur* (May 1926), although the T.Ms. in which these revisions were made does not survive. It is unclear whether HPL provided a T.Ms. or a clipping of the *National Amateur* appearance for the next publication, *Fantasy Fan* (February 1934); I suspect the latter, since HPL was in the habit of discarding his T.Mss. when any published version had appeared. The *Fantasy Fan* appearance made a number of errors; there is no evidence that this text has been revised from the *National Amateur* appearance. Arkham House editions follow the *Fantasy Fan* text.

Texts: A = *Philosopher* 1, No. 1 (December 1920): 3–5; B = *National Amateur* 48, No. 5 (May 1926): 48–49; C = *Fantasy Fan* 1, No. 6 (February 1934): 83–85; D = *Dagon and Other Macabre Tales* (Arkham House, 1965), 19–22. Copy-text: B.

[a] north window] North Window D
[b] one another] each other A
[c] night-wind.] night wind. A, B, C, D

Well do I remember the night of the great Aurora, when over the swamp played the shocking coruscations[a] of the daemon-light.[b] After the beams[c] came clouds, and then I slept.

And it was under a horned waning moon that I saw the city for the first time. Still and somnolent did it lie, on a strange plateau in a hollow betwixt strange peaks. Of ghastly marble were its walls and its towers, its columns, domes, and pavements. In the marble streets were marble pillars, the upper parts of which were carven into the images of grave bearded men. The air was warm and stirred not. And overhead, scarce ten degrees from the zenith, glowed that watching Pole Star. Long did I gaze on the city, but the day came not. When the red Aldebaran, which blinked low in the sky but never set, had crawled a quarter of the way around the horizon, I saw light and motion in the houses and the streets. Forms strangely robed, but at once noble and familiar, walked abroad,[d] and under the horned waning moon men talked wisdom in a tongue which I understood, though it was unlike any language I had ever known. And when the red Aldebaran had crawled more than half way[e] around the horizon, there were again darkness and silence.

When I awaked, I was not as I had been. Upon my memory was graven the vision of the city, and within my soul had arisen another and vaguer recollection, of whose nature I was not then certain. Thereafter, on the cloudy nights when I could sleep, I saw the city often; sometimes under that horned waning moon,[f] and sometimes[g] under the hot[h] yellow rays of a sun which did not set, but which wheeled low around the horizon. And on the clear nights the Pole Star leered as never before.

Gradually I came to wonder what might be my place in that city on the strange plateau betwixt strange peaks. At first content to view the scene as an all-observant uncorporeal[i] presence, I now desired to define

---

[a] coruscations] corruscations C
[b] daemon-light.] demon-light. A; deamon-/light. B; daemon light. C, D
[c] beams] beam C, D
[d] abroad,] abroad C, D
[e] half way] halfway C; half-way D
[f] moon,] moon B; *om.* D [*see below*]
[g] under that horned waning moon, and sometimes] *om.* D
[h] hot] hot, D
[i] uncorporeal] uncorpreal B

my relation to it, and to speak my mind amongst the grave men who conversed each day in the public squares. I said to myself, "This[a] is no dream, for by what means can I prove the greater reality of that other life in the house of stone and brick south of the sinister swamp and the cemetery on the low hillock, where the Pole Star peers[b] into my north window each night?"

One night as I listened to the discourse in the large square containing many statues, I felt a change; and perceived that I had at last a bodily form. Nor was I[c] a stranger in the streets of Olathoë,[d] which lies on the plateau of Sarkis,[e] betwixt the peaks Noton and Kadiphonek. It was my friend Alos who spoke, and his speech was one that pleased my soul, for it was the speech of a true man and patriot. That night had the news come of Daikos' fall, and of the advance of the Inutos;[f] squat, hellish,[g] yellow fiends who five years ago had appeared out of the unknown west to ravage the confines of our kingdom, and finally to besiege[h] our towns. Having taken the fortified places at the foot of the mountains, their way now lay open to the plateau, unless every citizen could resist with the strength of ten men. For the squat creatures were mighty in the arts of war, and knew not the scruples of honour which held back our tall, grey-eyed men of Lomar from ruthless conquest.

Alos, my friend, was commander of all the forces on the plateau, and in him lay the last hope of our country. On this occasion he spoke of the perils to be faced,[i] and exhorted the men of Olathoë,[j] bravest of the Lomarians, to sustain the traditions of their ancestors, who when forced to move southward from Zobna before the advance of the great ice-sheet (even as our descendants must some day flee from the

---

[a] "This] "this A, B
[b] peers] peeps C, D
[c] I] *om.* C
[d] Olathoë,] Olathoe, A, B, C, D
[e] Sarkis,] Sarkia, D
[f] Inutos;] Inutos, A, B
[g] hellish,] hellish B, C, D
[h] kingdom, and finally to besiege] kingdom and finally to beseige C; kingdom, and to besiege many of D
[i] faced,] faced C, D
[j] Olathoë,] Olathoe, A, B, C, D

land of Lomar),[a] valiantly and victoriously swept aside the hairy, long-armed, cannibal Gnophkehs that stood in their way. To me Alos denied a warrior's part, for I was feeble and given to strange faintings when subjected to stress and hardships. But my eyes were the keenest in the city, despite the long hours I gave each day to the study of the Pnakotic[b] manuscripts and the wisdom of the Zobnarian Fathers; so my friend, desiring not to doom me to inaction, rewarded me with that duty which was second to nothing in importance. To the watch-tower[c] of Thapnen he sent me, there to serve as the eyes of our army. Should the Inutos attempt to gain the citadel by the narrow pass behind the peak Noton,[d] and thereby surprise the garrison, I was to give the signal of fire which would warn the waiting soldiers and save the town from immediate disaster.

Alone I mounted the tower, for every man of stout body was needed in the passes below. My brain was sore dazed with excitement and fatigue, for I had not slept in many days; yet was my purpose firm, for I loved my native land of Lomar, and the marble city of Olathoë[e] that lies betwixt the peaks of Noton and Kadiphonek.

But as I stood in the tower's topmost chamber, I beheld the horned waning moon, red and sinister, quivering through the vapours that hovered over the distant valley of Banof. And through an opening in the roof glittered the pale Pole Star, fluttering as if alive, and leering like a fiend and tempter. Methought its spirit whispered evil counsel, soothing me to traitorous somnolence with a damnable rhythmical promise which it repeated over and over:

> "Slumber, watcher, till the spheres[f]
> Six and twenty thousand years
> Have revolv'd, and I return
> To the spot where now I burn.
> Other stars anon shall rise

---

[a] ice-sheet (. . .),] ice-sheet, (. . .) A, C; ice-sheet (. . .) B; ice sheet (. . .) D
[b] Pnakotic] Dnakotic C
[c] watch-tower] watch-/tower C; watchtower D
[d] Noton,] Noton C, D
[e] of Olathoë] of Olathoe A; Olathoe B, C, D
[f] spheres] spheres, C, D

> To the axis of the skies;
> Stars that soothe and stars that bless
> With a sweet forgetfulness:[a]
> Only when my round is o'er
> Shall the past disturb thy door."[b]

Vainly[c] did[d] I struggle with my drowsiness, seeking to connect these strange words with some lore of the skies which I had learnt from the Pnakotic manuscripts. My head, heavy and reeling, drooped to my breast, and when next I looked up it was in a dream;[e] with the Pole Star grinning at me through a window from over the horrible swaying trees of a dream-swamp.[f] And I am still dreaming.

In my shame and despair I sometimes scream frantically, begging the dream-creatures around me to waken me ere the Inutos steal up the pass behind the peak Noton and take the citadel by surprise; but these creatures are daemons,[g] for they laugh at me and tell me I am not dreaming. They mock me whilst I sleep, and whilst the squat yellow foe may be creeping silently upon[h] us. I have failed in my duty and betrayed the marble city of Olathoë;[i] I have proven false to Alos, my friend and commander. But still these shadows of my dream[j] deride me. They say[k] there is no land of Lomar, save in my nocturnal imaginings;[l] that in those[m] realms where the Pole Star[n] shines high[o] and

[a] forgetfulness:] forgetfulness; B
[b] Only when ... door."] Only when my round is through / Shall the past come back to you." A
[c] ¶ Vainly] Vainly A, C
[d] did] dld C
[e] dream;] dream, D
[f] dream-swamp.] dream swamp. D
[g] daemons,] demons, A
[h] upon] upou C
[i] Olathoë;] Olathoe; A, B, C, D
[j] dream] dreams C, D
[k] say] _ay C [*type failed to print*]
[l] imaginings;] imagings; C, D
[m] those] these D
[n] Pole Star] Pole-Star A
[o] high] high, B, C, D

red Aldebaran crawls low around the horizon, there has been naught save ice and snow for thousands of years,[a] and never a man[b] save squat[c] yellow creatures,[d] blighted by the cold, whom they call "Esquimaux".[e]

And as I writhe in my guilty agony, frantic to save the city whose peril[f] every moment grows, and vainly striving to shake off this unnatural dream of a house of stone and brick south of a sinister swamp and a cemetery on a low hillock;[g] the Pole Star, evil and monstrous, leers down from the black vault, winking hideously like an insane watching eye which strives to convey some strange[h] message, yet recalls nothing save that it once had a message to convey.

[a] years,] year, B
[b] a man] __man C [*type failed to print*]
[c] squat] squat, C, D
[d] creatures,] creatures; B
[e] "Esquimaux".] "Esquimaux." A, B, C, D
[f] peril] perii C
[g] hillock;] hillock, D
[h] strange] *om.* B, C, D

Beyond the Wall of Sleep

"I have an exposition of sleep come upon me."
—*Shakespeare.*[a]

I have frequently[b] wondered if the majority of mankind ever pause to reflect upon the occasionally titanic significance of dreams, and of the obscure world to which they belong. Whilst the greater number of our nocturnal visions are perhaps no more than faint and fantastic reflections of our waking experiences—Freud to the contrary with his puerile symbolism—there[c] are still a certain remainder whose immundane and ethereal character permits[d] of no ordinary interpretation, and whose vaguely exciting and disquieting effect suggests possible minute glimpses into a sphere of mental existence no less

Editor's Note: The story was first published in *Pine Cones* (October 1919). At a subsequent date, HPL prepared a new T.Ms. incorporating some revisions in the tale; evidence suggests that it was prepared around 1925. This typescript was presumably sent to the *Fantasy Fan*, where the story was printed in the October 1934 issue. There are a number of divergences between the T.Ms. and the *Fantasy Fan* appearance; it is possible that some of these are deliberate revisions by HPL (e.g., the third word of the story), but I consider that possibility remote: we would have to assume that HPL prepared a new T.Ms. or wrote the revisions into the T.Ms. submitted to the magazine. Given that the *Fantasy Fan* made many clear errors in printing the text, I believe the divergences are also textual errors. The *Fantasy Fan* text was then used for the posthumous appearance in *Weird Tales* (March 1938), where other errors and alterations occurred. The Arkham House texts are based on the *Weird Tales* text.

Texts: A = *Pine Cones* 1, No. 6 (October 1919): 2–10; B = T.Ms. (JHL); C = *Fantasy Fan* 2, No. 2 (October 1934): 25–32; D = *Weird Tales* 31, No. 3 (March 1938): 331–38; E = *Beyond the Wall of Sleep* (Arkham House, 1943), 33–39; F = *Dagon and Other Macabre Tales* (Arkham House, 1965), 22–33. Copy-text: B.

[a] "I ... me." / —*Shakespeare.*] "I ... me". / SHAKESPEARE. A; *'I ... me"*— Shakespeare C; *om.* D, E, F

[b] frequently] often C, D, E, F

[c] experiences—. . .—there] experiences, there A

[d] permits] permit E, F

important than physical life, yet separated[a] from that life by an all but impassable barrier. From my experience I cannot doubt[b] but that man, when lost to terrestrial consciousness, is indeed sojourning in another and uncorporeal life of far different nature from the life we know;[c] and of which only the slightest and most indistinct memories linger after waking. From those blurred and fragmentary memories we may infer much, yet prove little. We may guess that in dreams life, matter, and vitality, as the earth knows such things, are not necessarily constant; and that time and space do not exist as our waking selves comprehend them. Sometimes I believe that this less material life is our truer life, and that our vain presence on the terraqueous globe is itself the secondary or merely virtual phenomenon.

It was from a youthful reverie[d] filled with speculations of this sort that I arose one afternoon in the winter of 1900–1901,[e] when to the state psychopathic institution in which I served as an interne was brought the man whose case has ever since haunted me so unceasingly. His name, as given on the records, was Joe Slater, or Slaader, and his appearance was that of the typical denizen of the Catskill Mountain region; one of those strange, repellent scions of a primitive colonial[f] peasant stock whose isolation for nearly three centuries in the hilly fastnesses of a little-travelled[g] countryside has caused them to sink to a kind of barbaric degeneracy, rather than advance with their more fortunately placed brethren of the thickly settled districts. Among these odd folk, who correspond exactly to the decadent element of "white trash" in the South,[h] law and morals are non-existent;[i] and their general mental status is probably below that of any other section of the[j] native American people.

Joe Slater, who came to the institution in the vigilant custody of

[a] separated] seperated C

[b] doubt] donbt C

[c] know;] know, D, E, F

[d] reverie] revery D, E, F

[e] 1900–1901,] 1900–01, C, D, E, F

[f] colonial] Colonial A, B, C, D, E, F

[g] little-travelled] little travelled A, B; litile travelled C; little traveled D; little-traveled E, F

[h] South,] south, C

[i] non-existent;] non-/existent; B, C

[j] the] *om.* F

four state[a] policemen, and who was described as a highly dangerous character, certainly presented no evidence of his perilous disposition when first I[b] beheld him. Though well above the middle stature, and of somewhat brawny frame, he was given an absurd appearance of harmless stupidity by the pale, sleepy blueness of his small watery eyes, the scantiness of his neglected and never-shaven growth of yellow beard, and the listless drooping of his heavy nether lip. His age was unknown, since among his kind neither family records nor permanent family ties exist; but from the baldness of his head in front, and from the decayed condition of his teeth, the head surgeon wrote him down as a man of about forty.

From the medical and court documents we learned all that could be gathered of his case. This[c] man, a vagabond, hunter,[d] and trapper, had always been strange in the eyes of his primitive associates. He had habitually slept at night beyond the ordinary time, and upon waking would often talk of unknown things in a manner so bizarre as to inspire fear even in the hearts of an unimaginative populace. Not that his form of language was at all unusual, for he never spoke save in the debased patois of his environment; but the tone and tenor of his utterances were of such[e] mysterious wildness, that none might listen without apprehension. He himself was generally as terrified and baffled as his auditors, and within an hour after awakening would forget all that he had said, or at least all that had caused him to say what he did; relapsing into a bovine, half-amiable normality like that of the other hill-dwellers.[f]

As Slater grew older, it appeared, his matutinal aberrations had gradually increased in frequency and violence; till about a month before his arrival at the institution had occurred the shocking tragedy which caused his arrest by the authorities. One day near noon, after a profound sleep begun in a whiskey[g] debauch at about five of the

---

[a] state] *om.* A
[b] first I] I first C, D, E, F
[c] case. This] case: This C, D, E; case: this F
[d] hunter,] hunter D, E, F
[e] such] snch C
[f] hill-dwellers.] hill dwellers. A; hill-/dwellers. B
[g] whiskey] whisky D

previous afternoon, the man had roused himself most suddenly;[a] with ululations so horrible and unearthly that they brought several neighbours[b] to his cabin—a filthy sty where he dwelt with a family as indescribable as himself. Rushing out into the snow, he had flung his arms aloft and commenced a series of leaps directly upward[c] in the air; the while shouting his determination to reach some 'big, big cabin with brightness in the roof and walls and floor,[d] and the loud queer music far away'.[e] As two men of moderate size sought to restrain him, he had struggled with maniacal force and fury, screaming of his desire and need to find and kill a certain 'thing that shines and shakes and laughs'.[f] At length, after temporarily felling one of his detainers with a sudden blow, he had flung himself upon the other in a daemoniac[g] ecstasy[h] of bloodthirstiness,[i] shrieking fiendishly that he would 'jump high in the air and burn his way[j] through anything that stopped him'.[k] Family and neighbours[l] had now fled in a panic, and when the more courageous of them returned, Slater was gone, leaving behind an unrecognisable[m] pulp-like thing that had been a living man but an hour before. None of the[n] mountaineers had dared to pursue him, and it is likely that they would have welcomed his death from the cold; but when several mornings later they heard his screams from a distant ravine,[o] they realised[p] that he had somehow managed to survive, and that his removal in one way or another would be necessary. Then had followed

[a] suddenly;] suddenly, D, E, F

[b] neighbours] neighbors A, D, E, F

[c] upward] upwards A

[d] floor,] floor C, D, E, F

[e] 'big . . . away'.] 'big . . . away.' A, B; "big . . . away." C, D, E, F

[f] 'thing . . . laughs'.] 'thing . . . laughs.' A; "thing . . . laughs". C; "thing . . . laughs." D, E, F

[g] daemoniac] demoniac A, D, E, F

[h] ecstasy] ecstacy A, E

[i] bloodthirstiness,] blood-thirstiness, C, D, E, F

[j] way] was C

[k] 'jump . . . him'.] 'jump . . . him.' A, B; "jump . . . him." C; "jump . . . him." ¶ D, E, F

[l] neighbours] neighbors C, D, E, F

[m] unrecognisable] unrecognizable D, E, F

[n] the] om. C

[o] ravine,] ravine C, D, E, F

[p] realised] realized D, E, F

an armed searching party,[a] whose purpose (whatever it may have been originally) became that of a sheriff's posse after one of the seldom popular state troopers had by accident observed, then questioned, and finally joined the seekers.

On the third day Slater was found unconscious in the hollow of a tree, and taken to the nearest gaol;[b] where alienists from Albany examined him as soon as his senses returned. To them he told a simple story. He had, he said, gone to sleep one afternoon about sundown after drinking much liquor. He had awaked[c] to find himself standing bloody-handed in the snow before his cabin, the mangled corpse of his neighbour[d] Peter Slader at his feet. Horrified, he had taken to the woods in a vague effort to escape from the scene of what must have been his crime. Beyond these things he seemed to know nothing, nor could the expert questioning of his interrogators bring out a single additional fact.[e] That night Slater slept quietly, and the next morning he wakened[f] with no singular feature save a certain alteration of expression. Dr. Barnard,[g] who had been watching the patient, thought he noticed[h] in the pale blue eyes a certain gleam of peculiar quality;[i] and in the flaccid lips an all but imperceptible tightening, as if of intelligent determination. But when questioned, Slater relapsed into the habitual vacancy of the mountaineer, and only reiterated what he had said on the preceding day.

On the third morning occurred the first of the man's mental attacks. After some show of uneasiness in sleep, he burst forth into a frenzy so powerful that the combined efforts of four men were needed to bind him in a strait-jacket.[j] The alienists listened with[k] keen attention

[a] searching party,] searching-party, D, E, F

[b] gaol;] jail; D, E, F

[c] awaked] awakened E, F

[d] neighbour] neighbor A, D, E, F

[e] fact.] fact. ¶ D, E, F

[f] wakened] awakened E, F

[g] Dr. Barnard,] Dr. B——, A; Doctor Barnard, D, E, F

[h] noticed] noted A

[i] quality;] quality, D, E, F

[j] strait-jacket.] straitjacket. D; straightjacket. E, F

[k] listened with] lis / with C [*hyphen failed to print, rest of word omitted*]

to his words, since their curiosity had been aroused to a high pitch by
the suggestive yet mostly conflicting and incoherent stories of his
family and neighbours.[a] Slater raved for upward of fifteen minutes,
babbling in his backwoods dialect of great[b] edifices of light, oceans of
space, strange music, and shadowy mountains and valleys.[c] But most
of all did he dwell upon some mysterious blazing entity that shook and
laughed and mocked at him. This vast, vague personality seemed to
have done him a terrible wrong, and to kill it in triumphant revenge
was his paramount desire. In order to reach it, he said, he would soar
through abysses of emptiness, *burning* every obstacle that stood in his
way. Thus ran his discourse, until with the greatest suddenness he
ceased. The fire of madness died from his eyes, and in dull wonder he
looked at his questioners and asked why he was bound. Dr. Barnard[d]
unbuckled the leathern[e] harness and did not restore it till night, when
he succeeded in persuading Slater to don it of his own volition, for his
own good. The man had now admitted that he sometimes talked
queerly, though he knew not why.

Within a week two more attacks appeared, but from them the
doctors learned little. On the *source* of Slater's visions they speculated at
length, for since he could neither read nor write, and had apparently
never heard a legend or fairy tale,[f] his gorgeous imagery was quite
inexplicable. That it could not come from any known myth or
romance was made especially clear by the fact that the unfortunate
lunatic expressed himself only in his own simple manner. He raved of
things he did not understand and could not interpret; things which he
claimed to have experienced, but which he could not have learned
through any normal or connected narration. The alienists soon agreed
that abnormal dreams were the foundation of the trouble; dreams
whose vividness could for a time completely dominate the waking
mind of this basically inferior man. With due formality Slater was tried

[a] neighbours.] neighbors. A, D, E, F
[b] great] green C, D, E, F
[c] valleys.] vallies. A
[d] Dr. Barnard] Dr. B——— A; R. Barnard C, D
[e] leathern] leather C, D, E, F
[f] fairy tale,] fairy-tale, A, D, E, F

for murder, acquitted on the ground of insanity, and committed to the institution wherein I held so humble a post.

I have said that I am a constant speculator concerning dream life,[a] and from this you may judge of the eagerness with which I applied myself to the study of the new patient as soon as I had fully ascertained the facts of his case. He seemed to sense a certain friendliness in me;[b] born no doubt of the interest I could not conceal, and the gentle manner in which I questioned him. Not that he ever recognised[c] me during his attacks, when I hung breathlessly upon his chaotic but cosmic word-pictures; but he knew me in his quiet hours, when he would sit by his barred window weaving baskets of straw and willow, and perhaps pining for the mountain freedom he could never enjoy again.[d] His family never called to see him; probably it had found another temporary head, after the manner of decadent mountain folk.

By degrees I commenced to feel an overwhelming wonder at the mad and fantastic conceptions of Joe Slater. The man himself was pitiably inferior in mentality and language alike; but his glowing, titanic visions, though described in a barbarous and[e] disjointed jargon, were assuredly things which only a superior or even exceptional brain could conceive. How, I often asked myself, could the stolid imagination of a Catskill degenerate conjure up sights whose very possession argued a lurking spark of genius? How could any backwoods dullard have gained so much as an idea of those glittering realms of supernal radiance and space about which Slater ranted in his furious delirium? More and more I inclined to the belief that in the pitiful personality who cringed before me lay the disordered nucleus of something beyond my comprehension; something infinitely beyond the comprehension of my more experienced but less imaginative medical and scientific colleagues.

And yet I could extract nothing definite from the man. The sum of all my investigation was, that in a kind of semi-uncorporeal[f] dream life[g]

[a] dream life,] dream-life, D, E, F

[b] me;] me, C, D, E, F

[c] recognised] recognized D, E, F

[d] enjoy again.] again enjoy. C, D, E, F

[e] and] *om.* D, E, F

[f] semi-uncorporeal] semi-corporeal C, D, E, F

[g] dream life] dream-life D, E, F

Slater wandered or floated through resplendent and prodigious valleys,[a] meadows, gardens, cities, and palaces of light;[b] in a region unbounded and unknown to man. That[c] there he was no peasant or degenerate, but a[d] creature of importance and vivid life;[e] moving proudly and dominantly, and checked only by a certain deadly enemy, who seemed to be a being of visible yet ethereal structure, and who did not appear to be of human shape, since Slater never referred to it as a *man,* or as aught save a *thing.* This *thing* had done Slater some hideous but unnamed wrong, which the maniac (if maniac he were) yearned to avenge.[f] From the manner in which Slater alluded to their dealings, I judged that he and the luminous *thing* had met on equal terms; that in his dream existence the man was himself a luminous *thing* of the same race as his enemy. This impression was sustained by his frequent references to *flying through space* and *burning* all that impeded his progress. Yet these conceptions were formulated in rustic words wholly inadequate to convey them, a circumstance which drove me to the conclusion that if a true[g] dream-world[h] indeed existed, oral language was not its medium for the transmission of thought. Could it be that the dream-soul[i] inhabiting this inferior body was desperately struggling to speak things which the simple and halting tongue of dulness[j] could not utter? Could it be that I was face to face with intellectual emanations which would explain the mystery if I could but learn to discover and read them? I did not tell the older physicians of these things, for middle age is sceptical,[k] cynical, and disinclined to accept[l] new ideas. Besides, the head of the[m] institution had but lately warned me in his paternal way

[a] valleys,] vallies, A

[b] light;] light, D, E, F

[c] man. That] man; that D, E, F

[d] a] *om.* C

[e] life;] life, D, E, F

[f] avenge.] avenge. ¶ D, E, F

[g] true] *om.* F

[h] dream-world] dream world A, B, C, D, E, F

[i] dream-soul] dream soul C, D, E, F

[j] dulness] dullness C, D, E, F

[k] sceptical,] skeptical, A, D, E, F

[l] accept] aceppt C

[m] the] *om.* C

that I was overworking; that my mind needed a rest.

It had long been my belief that human thought consists basically of atomic or molecular motion, convertible into ether waves of[a] radiant energy like heat, light,[b] and electricity. This belief had early led me to contemplate the possibility of telepathy or mental communication by means of suitable apparatus, and I had in my college days prepared a set of transmitting and receiving instruments somewhat similar to the cumbrous devices employed in wireless telegraphy at that crude, pre-radio period.[c] These I had tested with a fellow-student;[d] but achieving no result, had soon packed them away with other scientific odds and ends for possible future use.[e] Now, in my intense desire to probe into the dream life[f] of Joe Slater, I sought these instruments again;[g] and spent several days in repairing them for action.[h] When they were complete once more I missed no opportunity for their trial. At each outburst of Slater's violence, I would fit the transmitter to his forehead and the receiver to my own;[i] constantly making delicate adjustments for various hypothetical wave-lengths of intellectual energy. I had but little notion of how the thought-impressions would, if successfully conveyed, arouse an intelligent response[j] in my brain;[k] but I felt certain that I could detect and interpret them. Accordingly I continued my experiments, though informing no one of their nature.[l]

It was on the twenty-first of February, 1901, that the thing finally[m] occurred. As I look back across the years I realise[n] how unreal it

---

[a] of] or E, F
[b] light,] light D, E, F
[c] similar to . . . period.] similar to those employed in wireless telegraphy. A
[d] fellow-student;] fellow-student, D, E, F
[e] use.] use. ¶ D, E, F
[f] dream life] dream-life D, E, F
[g] again;] again, D, E, F
[h] action.] use. A
[i] own;] own, D, E, F
[j] response] reaction A
[k] brain;] brain, D, E, F
[l] nature. <*line space*>] nature. <*no line space*> E, F
[m] finally] *om.* C, D, E, F
[n] realise] realize D, E, F

seems;[a] and sometimes half wonder[b] if old Dr. Fenton[c] was not right when he charged it all to my excited imagination. I recall that he listened with great kindness and patience when I told him, but afterward gave me a nerve-powder[d] and arranged for the half-year's[e] vacation on which I departed the next week.[f] That fateful night I was wildly agitated and perturbed, for despite the excellent care he had received, Joe Slater was unmistakably dying. Perhaps it was his mountain freedom[g] that he missed, or perhaps the turmoil in his brain had grown too acute for his rather sluggish physique; but at all events the flame of vitality flickered low in the decadent body. He was drowsy near the end, and as darkness fell he dropped off into a troubled sleep.[h] I did not strap on the strait-jacket[i] as[j] was customary when he slept, since I saw that he was too feeble to be dangerous, even if he woke in mental disorder once more before passing away. But I did place upon his head and mine the two ends of my cosmic "radio";[k] hoping against hope for a first and last message from the dream-world[l] in the brief time remaining. In the cell with us was one nurse, a mediocre fellow who did not understand the purpose of the apparatus, or think to inquire into my course. As the hours wore on I saw his head droop awkwardly in sleep, but I did not disturb him. I myself, lulled by the rhythmical breathing of the healthy and the dying man, must have nodded a little later.

The sound of weird lyric melody was what aroused me. Chords, vibrations, and harmonic ecstasies[m] echoed passionately on every hand;[n] while on my ravished sight burst the stupendous spectacle of ultimate

---

[a] seems;] seems, D, E, F
[b] half wonder] half-wonder A, B, C; wonder F
[c] Dr. Fenton] Dr. F—— A; Doctor Fenton D, E, F
[d] nerve-powder] nerve powder A
[e] half-year's] half year's A
[f] week.] week. ¶ D, E, F
[g] freedom] freedom free-/dom C
[h] sleep.] sleep. ¶ D, E, F
[i] strait-jacket] strait jacket C; straitjacket D; straightjacket E, F
[j] as] was A
[k] cosmic "radio";] ether-wave apparatus; A; cosmic "radio" C; cosmic "radio," D, E, F
[l] dream-world] dream world A, B, C, D, E, F
[m] ecstasies] ecstacies A
[n] hand;] hand, D, E, F

beauty. Walls, columns, and architraves of living fire blazed effulgently around the spot where I seemed to float in air;[a] extending upward to an infinitely high vaulted dome of indescribable splendour.[b] Blending with this display of palatial magnificence, or rather, supplanting it at times in kaleidoscopic rotation, were glimpses of wide plains and graceful valleys, high mountains and inviting grottoes;[c] covered with every lovely attribute of scenery which my delighted eye[d] could conceive of, yet formed wholly of some glowing, ethereal,[e] plastic entity, which in consistency partook as much of spirit as of matter. As I gazed, I perceived that my own brain held the key to these enchanting metamorphoses; for each vista which appeared to me,[f] was the one my changing mind most wished to behold. Amidst this elysian realm I dwelt not as a stranger, for each sight and sound was familiar to me; just as it had been for uncounted aeons[g] of eternity before, and would be for like eternities to come.

Then the resplendent aura of my brother of light drew near and held colloquy with me, soul to soul, with silent and perfect interchange of thought. The hour was one of approaching triumph, for was not my fellow-being escaping at last from a degrading periodic bondage; escaping for ever,[h] and preparing to follow the accursed oppressor even unto the uttermost fields of ether,[i] that upon it might be wrought a flaming cosmic vengeance which would shake the spheres? We floated thus for a little time, when I perceived a slight blurring and fading of the objects around us, as though some force were recalling me to earth—where I least wished to go. The form near me seemed to feel a change also, for it gradually brought its discourse toward a conclusion, and itself prepared to quit the scene;[j] fading from my sight at a rate

[a] air;] air, D, E, F
[b] splendour.] splendor. A, D, E, F
[c] grottoes;] grottoes, D, E, F
[d] eye] eyes D, E, F
[e] ethereal,] ethereal C, D, E, F
[f] me,] me D, E, F
[g] aeons] eons D, E, F
[h] for ever,] forever, A, F
[i] fields of ether,] ether fields, A
[j] scene;] scene, D, E, F

somewhat less rapid than that of the other objects. A few more thoughts were exchanged, and I knew that the luminous one and I were being recalled to bondage, though for my brother of light it would be the last time. The sorry planet-shell[a] being well-nigh[b] spent, in less than an hour my fellow would be free to pursue the oppressor along the Milky Way and past the hither stars to the very confines of infinity.

A well-defined shock separates my final impression of the fading scene of light from[c] my sudden and somewhat shamefaced awakening and straightening up in my chair as I saw the dying figure on the couch move hesitantly. Joe Slater was indeed awaking, though probably for the last time. As I looked more closely, I saw that in the sallow cheeks shone spots of colour[d] which had never before been present. The lips, too, seemed unusual;[e] being tightly compressed, as if by the force of a stronger character than had been Slater's. The whole face finally began to grow tense, and the head turned restlessly with closed eyes.[f] I did not arouse[g] the sleeping nurse, but readjusted the slightly disarranged head-bands[h] of my telepathic "radio",[i] intent to catch any parting message the dreamer might have to deliver. All at once the head turned sharply in my direction and the eyes fell open, causing me to stare in blank amazement at what I beheld. The man who had been Joe Slater, the Catskill decadent, was now[j] gazing at me with a pair of luminous, expanded[k] eyes whose blue seemed subtly to have deepened. Neither mania nor degeneracy was visible in that gaze, and I felt beyond a doubt that I was viewing a face behind which lay an active mind of high order.

At this juncture my brain became[l] aware of a steady external

---

[a] planet-shell] planet shell C, D, E, F
[b] well-nigh] well-night A
[c] light from] light, and A
[d] colour] color D, E, F
[e] unusual;] unusual, D, E, F
[f] eyes.] eyes. ¶ D, E, F
[g] arouse] rouse C, D, E, F
[h] head-bands] head-/bands C, D; headbands E; headband F
[i] "radio",] apparatus, A; "radio" C; "radio," D, E, F
[j] now] om. F
[k] expanded] expanding C, D, E, F
[l] became] beeame C

influence operating upon it. I closed my eyes to concentrate my thoughts more profoundly,[a] and was rewarded by the positive knowledge that *my long-sought mental message had come at last.* Each transmitted idea formed rapidly in my mind, and though no actual language was employed, my habitual association of conception and expression was so great that I seemed to be receiving the message in ordinary English.

"Joe Slater is dead," came the soul-petrifying voice or[b] agency from beyond the wall of sleep. My opened eyes sought the couch of pain in curious horror, but the blue eyes were still calmly gazing, and the countenance was still intelligently animated. "He is better dead, for he was unfit to bear the active intellect of cosmic entity. His gross body could not undergo the needed adjustments between ethereal life and planet life. He was too much of[c] an animal, too little a man; yet it is through his deficiency that you have come to discover me, for the cosmic and planet souls rightly should never meet. He has been my[d] torment and[e] diurnal prison for forty-two of your terrestrial years. I[f] am an entity like that which you yourself become in the freedom of dreamless sleep.[g] I am your brother of light, and have floated with you in the effulgent valleys. It is not permitted me to tell your waking earth-self of your real self, but we are all roamers of vast spaces and travellers[h] in many ages. Next year I may be dwelling in the dark[i] Egypt which you call ancient, or in the cruel empire of Tsan-Chan[j] which is to come three thousand years hence. You and I have drifted to the worlds that reel about the red Arcturus, and dwelt in the bodies of the insect-philosophers that crawl proudly over the fourth moon of Jupiter. How

---

[a] profoundly,] profoundly E, F
[b] or] of an D, E, F
[c] of] *om.* A, D, E, F
[d] my] in my D, E, F
[e] and] and my A
[f] years. I] years. ¶ "I D, E, F
[g] sleep.] sleep, C
[h] travellers] travelers D, E, F
[i] dark] *om.* C, D, E, F
[j] Tsan-Chan] Tsan Chan C, D, E, F

little does the earth-self [a] know of [b] life and its extent! How little, indeed, ought it to know for its own tranquillity! Of [c] the oppressor I cannot speak. You on earth have unwittingly felt its distant presence— you who without knowing [d] idly gave to its [e] blinking beacon the name of *Algol, the Daemon-Star.* [f] It is to meet and conquer the oppressor that I have vainly striven for aeons, [g] held back by bodily encumbrances. Tonight I go as a Nemesis bearing just and blazingly cataclysmic vengeance. *Watch me in the sky close by the Daemon-Star.* I [h] cannot speak longer, for the body of Joe Slater grows cold and rigid, and the coarse brains are ceasing to vibrate as I wish. You have been my friend in the cosmos; you have been my only friend [i] on this planet—the only soul to sense and seek for me within the repellent form which lies on this couch. We shall meet again—perhaps in the shining mists of Orion's Sword, perhaps on a bleak plateau in prehistoric Asia. Perhaps [j] in unremembered dreams tonight; [k] perhaps in some other form an aeon [l] hence, when the solar system shall have been swept away."

At this point the thought-waves abruptly ceased, and the pale eyes of the dreamer—or can I say dead man?—commenced to glaze fishily. In a half-stupor I crossed over to the couch and felt of his wrist, but found it cold, stiff, and pulseless. The sallow cheeks paled again, and the thick lips fell open, disclosing the repulsively rotten fangs of the degenerate Joe Slater. I shivered, pulled a blanket over the hideous face, and awakened the nurse. Then I left the cell and went silently to my room. I had an insistent [m] and unaccountable craving for a sleep whose dreams I should not remember.

[a] earth-self] earth self C, D, E, F

[b] of] *om.* C, D, E, F

[c] tranquillity! Of] tranquillity! ¶ "Of D; tranquility! ¶ "Of E, F

[d] knowing] knowing, A

[e] to its] the C, D, E, F

[f] *Daemon-Star.*] *Daemon Star.* A; *Demon-Star.* D, E, F

[g] aeons,] aeons; B; eons, D, E, F

[h] *Daemon-Star.* I] *Daemon Star.* I A; *Demon-Star.* ¶ "I D, E, F

[i] friend . . . friend] only friend D, E, F

[j] Asia. Perhaps] Asia. Perhnps C; Asia, perhaps D, E, F

[k] tonight;] tonight, D, E, F

[l] aeon] eon D, E, F

[m] insistent] instant C, D, E, F

The climax? What plain tale of science can boast of such a rhetorical effect? I have merely set down certain things appealing to me as facts, allowing you to construe them as you will. As I have already admitted, my superior, old Dr. Fenton,[a] denies the reality of everything I have related. He vows that I was broken down with nervous strain, and badly in need of the[b] long vacation on full pay which he so generously gave me. He assures me on his professional honour[c] that Joe Slater was but a low-grade paranoiac,[d] whose fantastic notions must have come from the crude hereditary folk-tales which circulate[e] in even the most decadent of communities. All this he tells me—yet I cannot forget what I saw in the sky on the night after Slater died. Lest you think me a biased witness, another's[f] pen must add this final testimony, which may perhaps supply the climax you expect. I will quote the following account of the star *Nova Persei* verbatim from the pages of that eminent astronomical authority, Prof.[g] Garrett P. Serviss:

"On February 22, 1901, a marvellous[h] new star was discovered by Dr.[i] Anderson of Edinburgh, *not very far from Algol.* No star had been visible at that point before. Within twenty-four[j] hours the stranger had become so bright that it outshone Capella. In a week or two it had visibly faded, and in the course of a few months it was hardly discernible with the naked eye."[k]

---

[a] Dr. Fenton,] Dr. F——, B; Doctor Fenton, D, E, F
[b] the] a E, F
[c] honour] honor D, E, F
[d] paranoiac,] paranoic, C
[e] circulate] circulated D, E, F
[f] another's] another C, D, E, F
[g] Prof.] Professor C, D, E, F
[h] marvellous] marvelous C, D, E, F
[i] Dr.] Doctor D, E, F
[j] twenty-four] 24 A, B, C
[k] eye."] eye". B

Memory

In the valley of Nis the accursed waning moon shines thinly, tearing a path for its light with feeble horns through the lethal foliage of a great upas-tree. And within the depths of the valley, where the light reaches not, move forms not meet[a] to be beheld. Rank is the herbage on each slope, where evil vines and creeping plants crawl amidst the stones of ruined palaces, twining tightly about broken columns and strange monoliths, and heaving up marble pavements laid by forgotten hands. And in trees that grow gigantic in crumbling courtyards leap little apes, while in and out of deep treasure-vaults writhe poison serpents and scaly things without a name.

Vast are the stones which sleep beneath coverlets of dank moss, and mighty were the walls from which they fell. For all time did their builders erect them, and in sooth they yet serve nobly, for beneath them the grey toad makes his habitation.

At the very bottom of the valley lies the river Than, whose waters are slimy and filled with weeds. From hidden springs it rises, and to subterranean grottoes it flows, so that the Daemon of the Valley knows not why its waters are red, nor whither they are bound.

The Genie that haunts the moonbeams spake to the Daemon of the Valley, saying, "I am old, and forget much. Tell me the deeds and aspect and name of them who built these things of stone."[b] And the Daemon replied, "I am Memory, and am wise in lore of the past, but I

Editor's Note: There is only one text of relevance for this prose-poem: its first and only appearance in HPL's lifetime, in the *United Co-operative* (June 1919). The text seems to have been printed accurately enough.

Texts: A = *United Co-operative* 1, No. 2 (June 1919): 8; B = *Beyond the Wall of Sleep* (Arkham House, 1943), 3. Copy-text: A.

[a] meet] meant B
[b] stone."] Stone." B

too am old. These beings were like the waters of the river Than, not to be understood. Their deeds I recall not, for they were but of the moment. Their aspect I recall dimly, for[a] it was like to that of the little apes in the trees. Their name I recall clearly, for it rhymed with that of the river. These beings of yesterday were called Man."

So the Genie flew back to the thin horned moon, and the Daemon looked intently at a little ape in a tree that grew in a crumbling courtyard.

---

[a] for] *om.* A, B

Old Bugs

AN EXTEMPORANEOUS SOB STORY
by Marcus Lollius, Proconsul of Gaul

Sheehan's Pool Room, which adorns one of the lesser alleys in the heart of Chicago's stockyard district, is not a nice place. Its air, freighted with a thousand odours such as Coleridge may have found at Cologne, too seldom knows the purifying rays of the sun; but fights for space with the acrid fumes of unnumbered cheap cigars and cigarettes which dangle from the coarse lips of unnumbered human animals that haunt the place day and night. But the popularity of Sheehan's remains unimpaired; and for this there is a reason—a reason obvious to anyone who will take the trouble to analyse the mixed stenches prevailing there. Over and above the fumes and sickening closeness rises an aroma once familiar throughout the land, but now happily banished to the back streets of life by the edict of a benevolent government—the aroma of strong, wicked[a] whiskey—a precious kind of forbidden fruit indeed in this year of grace 1950.

Sheehan's is the acknowledged centre of[b] Chicago's subterranean traffic in liquor and narcotics, and as such has a certain dignity which extends even to the unkempt attachés[c] of the place; but there was until lately one who lay outside the pale of that dignity—one who shared the squalor and filth, but not the importance, of Sheehan's. He was called "Old Bugs", and was the most disreputable object in a disreputable environment. What he had once been, many tried to guess; for his language and mode of utterance when intoxicated to a certain degree were such as to excite wonderment;[d] but what he *was*,

Editor's Note: A recently found T.Ms. prepared by HPL indicates—aside from irregularities in punctuation—that the first publication in *The Shuttered Room and Other Pieces and Other Pieces* (Arkham House, 1959) altered the paragraphing and other elements.

Texts: A = T. Ms.; B = *The Shuttered Room,* 76–84. Copy-text: A.

[a] wicked] wicked, A
[b] of] to B
[c] attachés] attaches A
[d] wonderment;] wonderment B

presented less difficulty—for "Old Bugs", in superlative degree, epitomised the pathetic species known as the "bum" or the "down-and-outer". Whence he had come, no one could tell. One night he had burst wildly into Sheehan's, foaming at the mouth and screaming for whiskey and hasheesh; and having been supplied in exchange for a promise to perform odd jobs, had hung about ever since, mopping floors, cleaning cuspidors and glasses, and attending to a hundred similar menial duties in exchange for the drink and drugs which were necessary to keep him alive and sane.[a] He talked but little, and usually in the common jargon of the underworld; but occasionally, when inflamed by an unusually generous dose of crude whiskey, would burst forth into strings of incomprehensible polysyllables and snatches of sonorous prose and verse which led certain habitués[b] to conjecture that he had seen better days. One steady patron—a bank defaulter under cover—came to converse with him quite regularly, and from the tone of his discourse ventured the opinion that he had been a writer or professor in his day. But the only tangible clue to Old Bugs' past was a faded photograph which he constantly carried about with him—the photograph of a young woman of noble and beautiful features. This he would sometimes draw from his tattered pocket, carefully unwrap from its covering of tissue paper, and gaze upon for hours with an expression of ineffable sadness and tenderness. It was not the portrait of one whom an underworld denizen would be likely to know, but of a lady of breeding and quality, garbed in the quaint attire of thirty years before. Old Bugs himself seemed also to belong to the past, for his nondescript clothing bore every hallmark[c] of antiquity. He was a man of immense height, probably more than six feet, though his stooping shoulders sometimes belied this fact. His hair, a dirty white and falling out in patches, was never combed; and over his lean face grew a mangy stubble of coarse beard which seemed always to remain at the bristling stage—never shaven,[d] yet never long enough to form a respectable set of whiskers. His features had perhaps been noble once, but were now seamed with the ghastly effects of terrible dissipation. At one time—probably in middle life—he had evidently been grossly fat; but now he was horribly lean, the purple flesh hanging in loose pouches under his bleary eyes and upon his cheeks. Altogether, Old Bugs was not pleasing to look upon.

The disposition of Old Bugs was as odd as his aspect. Ordinarily he was true to the derelict type—ready to do anything for a nickel or a dose of

---

[a] sane.] sane. ¶ B
[b] habitués] habitues A
[c] hallmark] hall-mark A, B
[d] shaven,] shaven— B

whiskey or hasheesh—but at rare intervals he shewed[a] the traits which earned him his name. Then he would try to straighten up, and a certain fire would creep into the sunken eyes. His demeanour would assume an unwonted grace and even dignity; and the sodden creatures around him would sense something of superiority—something which made them less ready to give the usual kicks and cuffs to the poor butt and drudge. At these times he would shew[b] a sardonic humour and make remarks which the folk of Sheehan's deemed foolish and irrational. But the spells would soon pass, and once more Old Bugs would resume his eternal floor-scrubbing and cuspidor-cleaning. But for one thing Old Bugs would have been an ideal slave to the establishment—and that one thing was his conduct when young men were introduced for their first drink. The old man would then rise from the floor in anger and excitement, muttering threats and warnings, and seeking to dissuade the novices from embarking upon their course of "seeing life as it is". He would sputter and fume, exploding into sesquipedalian admonitions and strange oaths, and animated by a frightful earnestness which brought a shudder to more than one drug-racked mind in the crowded room. But after a time his alcohol-enfeebled brain would wander from the subject, and with a foolish grin he would turn once more to his mop or cleaning-rag.

I do not think that many of Sheehan's regular patrons will ever forget the day that young Alfred Trever came. He was rather a "find"—a rich and high-spirited youth who would "go the limit" in anything he undertook—at least, that was the verdict of Pete Schultz, Sheehan's "runner", who had come across the boy at Lawrence College, in the small town of Appleton, Wisconsin. Trever was the son of prominent parents in Appleton. His father, Karl Trever, was an attorney and citizen of distinction, whilst his mother had made an enviable reputation as a poetess under her maiden name of Eleanor Wing. Alfred was himself a scholar and poet of distinction, though cursed with a certain childish irresponsibility which made him an ideal prey for Sheehan's runner. He was blond, handsome, and spoiled; vivacious,[c] and eager to taste the several forms of dissipation about which he had read and heard. At Lawrence he had been prominent in the mock-fraternity of "Tappa Tappa Keg", where he was the wildest and merriest of the wild and merry young roysterers; but this immature, collegiate frivolity did not satisfy him. He knew deeper vices through books, and he now longed to know them at first hand. Perhaps this tendency

---

[a] shewed] showed A, B
[b] shew] show A, B
[c] vivacious,] vivacious A, B

toward wildness had been stimulated somewhat by the repression to which he had been subjected at home; for Mrs. Trever had particular reason for training her only child with rigid severity. She had, in her own youth, been deeply and permanently impressed with the horror of dissipation by the case of one to whom she had for a time been engaged.[a] Alfred Galpin, Jr.,[b] the fiancé[c] in question, had been one of Appleton's most remarkable sons. Attaining distinction as a boy through his wonderful mentality, he won vast fame at the University of Wisconsin, and at the age of twenty-three[d] returned to Appleton to take up a professorship at Lawrence and to slip a diamond upon the finger of Appleton's fairest and most brilliant daughter. For a season all went happily, till without warning the storm burst. Evil habits, dating from a first drink taken years before in woodland seclusion, made themselves manifest in the young professor; and only by a hurried resignation did he escape a nasty prosecution for injury to the habits and morals of the pupils under his charge. His engagement broken, Galpin moved east[e] to begin life anew; but before long[f] Appletonians heard of his dismissal in disgrace from New York University, where he had obtained an instructorship in English. Galpin now devoted his time to the library and lecture platform, preparing volumes and speeches on various subjects connected with belles lettres,[g] and always shewing[h] a genius so remarkable that it seemed as if the public must some time pardon him for his past mistakes. His impassioned lectures in defence of Villon, Poe, Verlaine, and Oscar Wilde were applied to himself as well, and in the short Indian summer[i] of his glory there was talk of a renewed engagement at a certain cultured home on Park Avenue. But then the blow fell. A final disgrace, compared to which the others had been as nothing, shattered the illusions of those who had come to believe in Galpin's reform; and the young man abandoned his name and disappeared from public view. Rumour now and then associated him with a certain "Consul Hasting" whose work for the stage and for motion-picture companies attracted a certain degree of attention because of its scholarly breadth and depth; but Hasting soon disappeared from the

[a] engaged.] engaged. ¶ B
[b] Alfred Galpin, Jr.,] Young Galpin, B
[c] fiancé] fiance A
[d] twenty-three] 23 A, B
[e] east] East A, B
[f] long] long, B
[g] belles lettres,] *belles lettres,* B
[h] shewing] showing A, B
[i] summer] Summer B

public eye, and Alfred[a] Galpin became only a name for parents to quote in warning accents. Eleanor Wing soon celebrated her marriage to Karl Trever, a rising young lawyer, and of her former admirer retained only enough memory to dictate the naming of her only son, and the moral guidance of that handsome and headstrong youth. Now, in spite of all that guidance, Alfred Trever was at Sheehan's and about to take his first drink.

"Boss,"[b] cried Schultz, as he entered the vile-smelling room with his young victim, "meet my friend Al Trever, bes' li'l' sport up at Lawrence—thas' 'n Appleton, Wis., y' know. Some[c] swell guy, too—'s father's a big corp'ration lawyer up in his burg, 'n' 's mother's some lit'ry genius. He[d] wants to see life as she is—wants to know what the real lightnin' juice tastes like—so jus' remember he's me friend an' treat 'im right."

As the names[e] Trever, Lawrence, and Appleton fell on the air, the loafers seemed to sense something unusual. Perhaps it was only some sound connected with the clicking balls of the pool tables or the rattling glasses that were brought from the cryptic regions in the rear—perhaps only that, plus some strange rustling of the dirty draperies at the one dingy window—but many thought that someone in the room had gritted his teeth and drawn a very sharp breath.

"Glad to know you, Sheehan,"[f] said Trever in a quiet, well-bred tone. "This is my first experience in a place like this, but I am a student of life, and don't want to miss any experience. There's[g] poetry in this sort of thing, you know—or perhaps you don't know, but it's all the same."

"Young feller,"[h] responded the proprietor, "ya come tuh th' right place tuh see life. We got all kinds here—reel life an' a good time. The[i] damn[j] government can try tuh make folks good ef it wants tuh, but it can't stop a feller from hittin' 'er up when he feels like it. Whaddya[k] want, feller—booze, coke, or some other sorta dope? Yuh[l] can't ask for nothin' we ain't got."

---

[a] Alfred] *om.* B
[b] "Boss,"] "Boss", A
[c] Some] "Some A
[d] He] "He A
[e] names] names, B
[f] Sheehan,"] Sheehan", A
[g] There's] "There's A
[h] feller,"] feller", A
[i] The] "The A
[j] damn] damn' B
[k] Whaddya] "Whaddya A
[l] Yuh] "Yuh A

Habitués[a] say that it was at this point they noticed a cessation in the regular, monotonous strokes of the mop.

"I want whiskey—good old-fashioned[b] rye!" exclaimed Trever enthusiastically. "I'll tell you, I'm good and tired of water after reading of the merry bouts fellows used to have in the old days. I[c] can't read an Anacreontic without watering at the mouth—and it's something a lot stronger than water that my mouth waters for!"

"Anacreontic—what 'n hell's that?" several hangers-on looked up as the young man went slightly beyond their depth. But the bank defaulter under cover explained to them that Anacreon was a gay old dog who lived many years ago and wrote about the fun he had when all the world was just like Sheehan's.

"Let me see, Trever,"[d] continued the defaulter. "Didn't[e] Schultz say your mother is a literary person, too?"

"Yes, damn it,"[f] replied Trever, "but nothing like the old Teian! She's[g] one of those dull, eternal moralisers that try to take all the joy out of life. Namby-pamby[h] sort—ever heard of her? She writes under her maiden name of Eleanor Wing."

Here it was that Old Bugs dropped his mop.

"Well, here's yer stuff,"[i] announced Sheehan jovially as a tray of bottles and glasses was wheeled into the room. "Good old rye, an' as fiery as ya kin find anyw'eres in Chi'."

The youth's eyes glistened and his nostrils curled at the fumes of the brownish fluid which an attendant was pouring out for him. It repelled him horribly, and revolted all his inherited delicacy; but his determination to taste life to the full remained with him, and he maintained a bold front. But before his resolution was put to the test, the unexpected intervened. Old Bugs, springing up from the crouching position in which he had hitherto been, leaped at the youth and dashed from his hand[j] the uplifted glass;[k]

---

[a] Habitués] Habitues A, B
[b] old-fashioned] old fashioned A, B
[c] I] "I A
[d] Trever,"] Trever", A
[e] defaulter. "Didn't] defaulter. "didn't A; defaulter, "didn't B
[f] it,"] it", A
[g] She's] "She's A
[h] Namby-pamby] "Namby-pamby A
[i] stuff,"] stuff", A
[j] hand] hands B
[k] glass;] glass, B

almost simultaneously attacking the tray of bottles and glasses with his mop, and scattering the contents upon the floor in a confusion of odoriferous fluid and broken bottles and tumblers. Numbers of men, or things which had been men, dropped to the floor and began lapping at the puddles of spilled liquor, but most remained immovable, watching the unprecedented actions of the barroom drudge and derelict. Old Bugs straightened up before the astonished Trever, and in a mild and cultivated voice said, "Do not do this thing. I was like you once, and I did it. Now I am like—this."

"What do you mean, you damned old fool?" shouted Trever. "What do you mean by interfering with a gentleman in his pleasures?"

Sheehan, now recovering from his astonishment, advanced and laid a heavy hand on the old waif's shoulder.

"This is the last time for you, old bird!" he exclaimed furiously. "When a gen'l'man wants tuh take a drink here, by[a] God, he shall, without you interferin'. Now get th' hell outa here afore I kick hell outa ya."

But Sheehan had reckoned without scientific knowledge of abnormal psychology and the effects of nervous stimulus. Old Bugs, obtaining a firmer hold on his mop, began to wield it like the javelin of a Macedonian hoplite, and soon cleared a considerable space around himself, meanwhile shouting various disconnected bits of quotation, among which was prominently repeated

"———the sons
of Belial, blown with insolence and wine."[b]

The[c] room became pandemonium, and men screamed and howled in fright at the sinister being they had aroused. Trever seemed dazed in the confusion, and shrank to the wall as the strife thickened. "He shall not drink—he[d] shall not drink!" Thus roared Old Bugs as he seemed to run out of—or rise above—quotations. Policemen appeared at the door, attracted by the noise, but for a time they made no move to intervene. Trever, now thoroughly terrified and cured for ever[e] of his desire to see life via the vice route, edged closer to the blue-coated[f] newcomers. Could he but escape and catch a train for Appleton, he reflected, he would consider his education in dissipation quite complete.

[a] by] By A
[b] repeated . . . wine."] repeated, ". . . the sons of Belial, blown with insolence and wine." B
[c] The] ¶ The B
[d] drink—he] drink—He A; drink! He B
[e] for ever] forever A, B
[f] blue-coated] blue coated A

Then suddenly Old Bugs ceased to wield his javelin and stopped still—drawing himself up more erectly than any denizen of the place had ever seen him before. "Ave, Caesar, Moriturus te saluto!"[a] he shouted, and dropped to the whiskey-reeking floor, never to rise again.[b]

Subsequent impressions will never leave the mind of young Trever. The picture is blurred, but ineradicable. Policemen ploughed a way through the crowd, questioning everyone closely both about the incident and about the dead figure on the floor. Sheehan especially did they ply with inquiries, yet without eliciting any information of value concerning Old Bugs. Then the bank defaulter remembered the picture, and suggested that it be viewed and filed for identification at police headquarters. An officer bent reluctantly over the loathsome glassy-eyed form and found the tissue-wrapped cardboard, which he passed around among the others.

"Some chicken!"[c] leered a drunken man as he viewed the beautiful face, but those who were sober did not leer, looking with respect and abashment at the delicate and spiritual features. No one seemed able to place the subject, and all wondered that the drug-degraded derelict should have such a portrait in his possession—that is, all but the bank defaulter, who was meanwhile eyeing the intruding bluecoats rather uneasily. *He* had seen a little deeper beneath Old Bugs' mask of utter degradation.

Then the picture was passed to Trever, and a change came over the youth. After the first start, he replaced the tissue wrapping around the portrait, as if to shield it from the sordidness of the place. Then he gazed long and searchingly at the figure on the floor, noting its great height, and the aristocratic cast of features which seemed to appear now that the wretched flame of life had flickered out. No, he said hastily, as the question was put to him, he did not know the subject of the picture. It was so old, he added, that no one now could be expected to recognise[d] it.

But Alfred Trever did not speak the truth, as many guessed when he offered to take charge of the body and secure its interment in Appleton. Over the library mantel in his home hung the exact replica of that picture, and all his life he had known and loved its original.

For the gentle and noble features were those of his own mother.

---

[a] "Ave . . . saluto!"] *"Ave . . . saluto!"* B
[b] again.] again. [*no line space*] B
[c] chicken!"] Chicken!" A
[d] recognise] recognize B

The Transition of Juan Romero

O f the events which took place at the Norton Mine on October 18th and 19th, 1894,[a] I have no desire to speak. A sense of duty to science is all that impels me to recall, in these[b] last years of my life, scenes and happenings fraught with a terror doubly acute because I cannot wholly define it. But I believe that before I die I should tell what I know of the—shall I say transition[c]—of Juan Romero.

My name and origin need not be related to posterity; in fact, I fancy it is better that they should not be, for when a man suddenly migrates to the States or the Colonies, he leaves his past behind him. Besides, what I once was is not in the least relevant to my narrative; save perhaps the fact that during my service in India I was more at home amongst white-bearded native teachers than amongst my brother-officers. I had delved not a little into odd Eastern lore when overtaken by the calamities which brought about my new life in America's vast West—a life wherein I found it well to accept a name— my present one—which is very common and carries no meaning.

In the summer and autumn of 1894 I dwelt in the drear expanses of the Cactus Mountains, employed as a common labourer at the celebrated

Editor's Note: The A.Ms. of the story survives—it is HPL's original pencil draft, dated 16 September 1919. The T.Ms. was prepared in 1932 by R. H. Barlow (see *OFF* 31); it bears some handwritten corrections by HPL in pen, but not at the places where the T.Ms. diverges from the A.Ms. The story was not published in HPL's lifetime, but appeared first only in *Marginalia* (1944). All Arkham House editions follow the T.Ms.

Texts: A = A.Ms. (JHL); B = T.Ms. (JHL); C = *Marginalia* (Arkham House, 1944), 276–84; D = *Dagon and Other Macabre Tales* (Arkham House, 1965), 327–34. Copy-text: A.

[a] 18th and 19th,] eighteenth and nineteenth, B, C, D
[b] these] the B, C, D
[c] transition] *transition* D

Norton Mine;[a] whose discovery by an aged prospector some years before had turned the surrounding region from a nearly unpeopled waste to a seething cauldron of sordid life. A cavern of gold, lying deep below[b] a mountain lake, had enriched its venerable finder beyond his wildest dreams, and now formed the seat of extensive tunnelling[c] operations on the part of the corporation to which it had finally been sold. Additional grottoes had been found, and the yield of yellow metal was exceedingly great; so that a mighty and heterogeneous army of miners toiled day and night in the numerous passages and rock hollows. The Superintendent, a Mr. Arthur, often discussed the singularity of the local geological formations; speculating on the probable extent of the chain of caves, and estimating the future of the titanic mining enterprise.[d] He considered the auriferous cavities the result of the action of water, and believed the last of them would soon be opened.

It was not long after my arrival and employment that Juan Romero came to the Norton Mine. One of a large herd of unkempt Mexicans attracted thither from the neighbouring[e] country, he at first commanded[f] attention only because of his features; which though plainly of the Red Indian type, were yet remarkable for their light colour and refined conformation, being vastly unlike those of the average "Greaser"[g] or Piute of the locality. It is curious that although he differed so widely from the mass of Hispanicised and tribal Indians, Romero gave not the least impression of Caucasian blood. It was not the Castilian conquistador or the American pioneer, but the ancient and noble Aztec, whom imagination called to view when the silent peon would rise in the early morning and gaze in fascination at the sun as it crept above the eastern hills, meanwhile stretching out his arms to the orb as if in the performance of some rite whose nature he did not himself comprehend. But save for his face, Romero was not in any way suggestive of nobility. Ignorant and dirty, he was at home amongst the

---

[a] Mine;] Mine, D
[b] below] beneath B, C, D
[c] tunnelling] tunneling B, C, D
[d] enterprise.] enterprises. C, D
[e] neighbouring] neighboring B, C, D
[f] commanded] attracted B, C, D
[g] "Greaser"] greaser B, C, D

other brown-skinned Mexicans; having come (so I was afterward told) from the very lowest sort of surroundings. He had been found as a child in a crude mountain hut, the only survivor of an epidemic which had stalked lethally by. Near the hut, close to a rather unusual rock fissure, had lain two skeletons, newly picked by vultures, and presumably forming the sole remains of his parents. No one recalled their identity, and they were soon forgotten by the many. Indeed, the crumbling of the adobe hut and the closing of the rock fissure[a] by a subsequent avalanche had helped to efface even the scene from recollection. Reared by a Mexican cattle-thief who had given him his name, Juan differed little from his fellows.

The attachment which Romero manifested toward me was undoubtedly commenced through the quaint and ancient Hindoo ring which I wore when not engaged in active labour. Of its nature, and manner of coming into my possession, I cannot speak. It was my last link with a chapter of[b] life for ever[c] closed, and I valued it highly. Soon I observed that the odd-looking Mexican was likewise interested; eyeing it with an expression that banished all suspicion of mere covetousness. Its hoary hieroglyphs seemed to stir some faint recollection in his untutored but active mind, though he could not possibly have beheld their like before. Within a few weeks after his advent, Romero was like a faithful servant to me; this notwithstanding the fact that I was myself but an ordinary miner. Our conversation was necessarily limited. He knew but a few words of English, while I found my Oxonian Spanish was something quite different from the patois of the peon of New Spain.

The event which I am about to relate was unheralded by long premonitions. Though the man Romero had interested me, and though my ring had affected him peculiarly, I think that neither of us had any expectation of what was to follow when the great blast was set off. Geological considerations had dictated an extension of the mine directly downward from the deepest part of the subterranean area; and the belief of the Superintendent that only solid rock would be encountered, had led to the placing of a prodigious charge of dynamite. With this work

---

[a] rock fissure] rock-fissure B, D

[b] of] of my B, C, D

[c] for ever] forever A, B, C, D

Romero and I were not connected, wherefore our first knowledge of extraordinary conditions came from others. The charge, heavier perhaps than had been estimated, had seemed to shake the entire mountain. Windows in shanties on the slope outside were shattered by the shock, whilst miners throughout the nearer passages were knocked from their feet. Jewel Lake, which lay above the scene of action, heaved as in a tempest. Upon investigation it was seen that a new abyss yawned indefinitely below the seat of the blast; an abyss so monstrous that no handy line might fathom it, nor any lamp illuminate it. Baffled, the excavators sought a conference with the Superintendent, who ordered great lengths of rope to be taken to the pit, and spliced and lowered without cessation till a bottom might be discovered.

Shortly afterward the pale-faced workmen apprised the Superintendent of their failure. Firmly though respectfully[a] they signified their refusal to revisit the chasm,[b] or indeed to work further in the mine until it might be sealed. Something beyond their experience was evidently confronting them, for so far as they could ascertain, the void below was infinite. The Superintendent did not reproach them. Instead, he pondered deeply, and made many[c] plans for the following day. The night shift did not go on that evening.

At two in the morning a lone coyote on the mountain began to howl dismally. From somewhere within the works a dog barked in[d] answer; either to the coyote—or to something else. A storm was gathering around the peaks of the range, and weirdly shaped clouds scudded horribly across the blurred patch of celestial light which marked a gibbous moon's* attempts to shine through many layers of cirro-stratus vapours. It was Romero's voice, coming from the bunk

---

*AUTHOR'S NOTE: Here is a lesson in scientific accuracy for fiction writers. I have just looked up the moon's phases for October, 1894, to find when a gibbous moon was visible at 2 a.m., and have changed the dates to fit!! [*om.* D]

[a] respectfully] respectfully, C, D
[b] chasm,] chasm B, C, D
[c] many] *om.* C, D
[d] in] an B, C, D

above, that awakened me;[a] a voice excited[b] and tense with some vague expectation I could not understand:

"*¡Madre de Dios!—el*[c] *sonido—ese sonido—¡oiga*[d] *Vd! ¿lo oye*[e] *Vd?— Señor,*[f] THAT SOUND!"

I listened, wondering what sound he meant. The coyote, the dog, the storm, all were audible; the last named now gaining ascendancy as the wind shrieked more and more frantically. Flashes of lightning were visible through the bunk-house window. I questioned the nervous Mexican, repeating the sounds I had heard:

"*¿El coyote?—¿el perro?—¿el viento?*"

But Romero did not reply. Then he commenced whispering as in awe:

"*El ritmo, Señor*[g]*—el ritmo de la tierra*—THAT THROB DOWN IN THE GROUND!"

And now I also heard; heard and shivered[h] without knowing why. Deep, deep, below me was a sound—a rhythm, just as the peon had said—which, though exceedingly faint, yet dominated even the dog, the coyote, and the increasing tempest. To seek to describe it were useless—for it was such that no description is possible. Perhaps it was like the pulsing of the engines far down in a great liner, as sensed from the deck, yet it was not so mechanical; not so devoid of the element of life and consciousness. Of all its qualities, *remoteness* in the earth most impressed me. To my mind rushed fragments of a passage in Joseph Glanvill[i] which Poe has quoted with tremendous effect*—

> "—the vastness, profundity, and unsearchableness of His works, *which have a depth in them greater than the well of Democritus.*"

---

*Motto of "A Descent into the Maelstrom" [*A Descent into the Maelstrom* C, D]

[a] me;] me, C, D
[b] excited] exicted D
[c] *el*] *El*/B, C, D
[d] *oiga*] *orga* B, C, D
[e] *¿lo oye*] *¿lo oyte* B, C; *¡lo oyte* D
[f] *Señor,*] *Sēnor,* C; *Sēnor* D
[g] *Señor*] *Senor* B; *Sēnor* D
[h] shivered] shivered and D
[i] Glanvill] Glanvil D

Suddenly Romero leaped from his bunk;[a] pausing before me to gaze at the strange ring on my hand, which glistened queerly in every flash of lightning, and then staring intently in the direction of the mine shaft. I also rose, and both stood motionless for a time, straining our ears as the uncanny rhythm seemed more and more to take on a vital quality. Then without apparent volition we began to move toward the door, whose rattling in the gale held a comforting suggestion of earthly reality. The chanting in the depths—for such the sound now seemed to be—[b]grew in volume and distinctness; and we felt irresistibly urged out into the storm and thence to the gaping blackness of the shaft.

We encountered no living creature, for the men of the night shift had been released from duty, and were doubtless at the Dry Gulch settlement pouring sinister rumours into the ear of some drowsy bartender. From the watchman's cabin, however, gleamed a small square of yellow light like a guardian eye. I dimly wondered how the rhythmic sound had affected the watchman; but Romero was moving more swiftly now, and I followed without pausing.

As we descended the shaft, the sound beneath grew definitely composite. It struck me as horribly like a sort of Oriental ceremony, with beating of drums and chanting of many voices. I have, as you are aware, been much in India. Romero and I moved without material hesitancy through drifts and down ladders; ever toward the thing that allured us, yet ever with a pitifully helpless fear and reluctance. At one time I fancied I had gone mad—this was when, on wondering how our way was lighted in the absence of lamp or candle, I realised[c] that the ancient ring on my finger was glowing with eery radiance, diffusing a pallid lustre through the damp, heavy air around.

It was without warning that Romero, after clambering down one of the many rude[d] ladders, broke into a run and left me alone. Some new and wild note in the drumming[e] and chanting, perceptible but slightly to me, had acted on him in[f] startling fashion; and with a wild

---

[a] bunk;] bunk, C, D
[b] depths— . . . be—] depths— . . . be,— A; depths,— . . . be,— B
[c] realised] realized D
[d] rude] wide B, C, D
[e] drumming] drummning D
[f] in] in a B, C, D

outcry he forged ahead unguided in the cavern's gloom. I heard his repeated shrieks before me, as he stumbled awkwardly along the level places and scrambled madly down the rickety ladders. And frightened as I was, I yet retained enough of[a] perception to note that his speech, when articulate, was not of any sort known to me. Harsh but impressive polysyllables had replaced the customary mixture of bad Spanish and worse English, and of these[b] only the oft repeated cry *"Huitzilopotchli"* seemed in the least familiar. Later I definitely placed that word in the works of a great historian*[c]—and shuddered when the association came to me.

The climax of that awful night was composite but fairly brief, beginning just as I reached the final cavern of the journey. Out of the darkness immediately ahead burst a final shriek from the Mexican, which was joined by such a chorus of uncouth sound as I could never hear again and survive. In that moment it seemed as if all the hidden terrors and monstrosities of earth had become articulate in an effort to overwhelm the human race. Simultaneously the light from my ring was extinguished, and I saw a new light glimmering from lower space but a few yards ahead of me. I had arrived at the abyss, which was now redly aglow, and which had evidently swallowed up the unfortunate Romero. Advancing, I peered over the edge of that chasm which no line could fathom, and which was now a pandemonium[d] of flickering flame and hideous uproar. At first I beheld nothing but a seething blur of luminosity; but then shapes, all infinitely distant, began to detach themselves from the confusion, and I saw—was it Juan Romero?—*but God! I dare not tell you what I saw! . . .* Some power from heaven, coming to my aid, obliterated both sights and sounds in such a crash as may be heard when two universes collide in space. Chaos supervened, and I knew the peace of oblivion.

I hardly know how to continue, since conditions so singular are involved; but I will do my best, not even trying to differentiate betwixt

---

*Prescott, "Conquest of Mexico" [*Conquest of Mexico.* C; *Conquest of Mexico* D]

[a] of] of my B, C, D
[b] these] these, C, D
[c] historian] historian, A, B
[d] pandemonium] pandaemonium A, B, C, D

the real and the apparent. When I awaked,[a] I was safe in my bunk and the red glow of dawn was visible at the window. Some distance away the lifeless body of Juan Romero lay upon a table, surrounded by a group of men, including the camp doctor. The men were discussing the strange death of the Mexican as he lay asleep; a death seemingly connected in some way with the terrible bolt of lightning which had struck and shaken the mountain. No direct cause was evident, and an autopsy failed to shew[b] any reason why Romero should not be living. Snatches of conversation indicated beyond a doubt that neither Romero nor I had left the bunk-house during the night; that neither had been awake during the frightful storm which had passed over the Cactus range. That storm, said men who had ventured down the mine shaft,[c] had caused extensive caving in,[d] and had completely closed the deep abyss which had created so much apprehension the day before. When I asked the watchman what sounds he had heard prior to the mighty thunderbolt,[e] he mentioned a coyote, a dog, and the snarling mountain wind—nothing more. Nor do I doubt his word.

Upon the resumption of work[f] Superintendent Arthur called on[g] some especially dependable men to make a few investigations around the spot where the gulf had appeared. Though hardly eager, they obeyed;[h] and a deep boring was made. Results were very curious. The roof of the void, as seen whilst[i] it was open, was not by any means thick; yet now the drills of the investigators met what appeared to be a limitless extent of solid rock. Finding nothing else, not even gold, the Superintendent abandoned his attempts; but a perplexed look occasionally steals over his countenance as he sits thinking at his desk.

One other thing is curious. Shortly after waking on that morning after the storm, I noticed the unaccountable absence of my Hindoo

---

[a] awaked,] awakened, B, C, D
[b] shew] show B, C, D
[c] mine shaft,] mine-shaft, B, C, D
[d] caving in,] caving-in, B, C, D
[e] thunderbolt,] thunder-bolt, B; thunder-bolt; C, D
[f] work] work, D
[g] on] upon B, C, D
[h] obeyed;] obeyed, D
[i] whilst] when B, C, D

ring from my finger. I had prized it greatly, yet nevertheless felt a sensation of relief at its disappearance. If one of my fellow-miners appropriated it, he must have been quite clever in disposing of his booty, for despite advertisements and a police search the ring was never seen again. Somehow I doubt if it was stolen by mortal hands, for many strange things were taught me in India.

My opinion of my whole experience varies from time to time. In broad daylight, and at most seasons I am apt to think the greater part of it a mere dream; but sometimes in the autumn, about two in the morning when[a] winds and animals howl dismally, there comes from inconceivable depths below a damnable suggestion of rhythmical throbbing . . . and I feel that the transition of Juan Romero was a terrible one indeed.

[a] when] when the B, C, D

The White Ship

I am Basil Elton, keeper of the North Point light that my father and grandfather kept before me. Far from the shore stands the grey[a] lighthouse, above sunken slimy rocks that are seen when the tide is low, but unseen when the tide is high. Past that beacon for a century have swept the majestic barques of the seven seas. In the days of my grandfather there were many; in the days of my father not so many; and now there are so few that I sometimes feel strangely alone, as though I were the last man on our planet.

From far shores came those white-sailed argosies of old; from far Eastern shores where warm suns shine and sweet odours[b] linger about strange gardens and gay temples. The old captains of the sea came often to my grandfather and told him of these things,[c] which in turn he told to my father, and my father told to me in the long autumn evenings when the wind howled eerily from the East. And I have read more of these things, and of many things besides, in the books men gave me when I was young and filled with wonder.

Editor's Note: The story was first published in the *United Amateur* (November 1919), typeset by W. Paul Cook; it is virtually identical to the surviving T.Ms., one of the single-spaced T.Mss. sent to *Weird Tales* in 1923. The *Weird Tales* (March 1927) appearance derives from the T.Ms., and the Arkham House editions derive from the *Weird Tales* text. An A.Ms. surfaced in the 1970s. It is a fair copy prepared for Alvin Earl Perry on 5 September 1934. Aside from one or two apparent slips of the pen, it appears to embody deliberate revisions from the T.Ms., and these have been incorporated into the present text.

Texts: A = T.Ms. (JHL); B = *United Amateur* 19, No. 2 (November 1919): 30–33; C = *Weird Tales* 9, No. 3 (March 1927): 386–89; D = A.Ms. (published in facsimile in *Whispers* 1, No. 4 [July 1974]: [32–40]); E = *Dagon and Other Macabre Tales* (Arkham House, 1965), 41–46. Copy-text: D.

[a] grey] gray C, E
[b] odours] odors C, E
[c] things,] things C, E

But more wonderful than the lore of old men and the lore of books is the secret lore of ocean. Blue, green, grey,[a] white,[b] or black; smooth, ruffled, or mountainous; that ocean is not silent. All my days have I watched it and listened to it, and I know it well. At first it told to me only the plain little tales of calm beaches and near ports, but with the years it grew more friendly and spoke of other things; of things more strange and more distant in space and in time. Sometimes at twilight the grey vapours[c] of the horizon have parted to grant me glimpses of the[d] ways beyond; and sometimes[e] at night the deep waters of the sea have grown clear and phosphorescent, to grant me glimpses of the ways beneath. And these glimpses have been as often of the ways that were and the ways that might be, as of the ways that are; for ocean is more ancient than the mountains, and freighted with the memories and the dreams of Time.

Out of the South it was that the White Ship used to come when the moon was full and high in the heavens. Out of the South it would glide very smoothly and silently over the sea. And whether the sea was rough or calm, and whether the wind was friendly or adverse, it would always glide smoothly and silently, its sails distent[f] and its long strange tiers of oars moving rhythmically. One night I espied upon the deck a man, bearded and robed, and he seemed to beckon me to embark for fair[g] unknown shores. Many times afterward I saw him under the full moon, and ever did he beckon me.

Very brightly did the moon shine on the night I answered the call, and I walked out over the waters to the White Ship on a bridge of moonbeams. The man who had beckoned now spoke a welcome to me in a soft language I seemed to know well, and the hours were filled with soft songs of the oarsmen as we glided away into a mysterious South, golden with the glow of that full, mellow moon.

And when the day dawned, rosy and effulgent, I beheld the green

[a] grey,] gray, C, E
[b] white,] white A, B, C, E
[c] grey vapours] gray vapors C, E
[d] the] *om.* D
[e] sometimes] some times E
[f] distent] distant C, E
[g] fair] far E

shore of far lands, bright and beautiful, and to me unknown. Up from the sea rose lordly terraces of verdure, tree-studded, and shewing here and there the gleaming white roofs and colonnades of strange temples. As we drew nearer the green shore the bearded man told me of that land, the Land[a] of Zar, where dwell all the dreams and thoughts of beauty that come to men once and then are forgotten. And when I looked upon the terraces again I saw that what he said was true, for among the sights before me were many things I had once seen through the mists beyond the horizon and in the phosphorescent depths of ocean. There too were forms and fantasies more splendid than any[b] I had ever known; the visions of young poets who died in want before the world could learn of what they had seen and dreamed. But we did not set foot upon the sloping meadows of Zar, for it is told that he who treads them may nevermore return to his native place.[c]

As the White Ship sailed silently away from the templed terraces of Zar, we beheld on the distant horizon ahead the spires of a mighty city; and the bearded man said to me, "This is Thalarion, the City of a Thousand Wonders, wherein reside all those mysteries that man has striven in vain to fathom." And I looked again, at closer range, and saw that the city was greater than any city I had known or dreamed of before. Into the sky the spires of its temples reached, so that no man might behold their peaks; and far back beyond the horizon stretched the grim, grey[d] walls, over which one might spy only a few roofs, weird and ominous, yet adorned with rich friezes and alluring sculptures. I yearned mightily to enter this fascinating yet repellent city, and besought[e] the bearded man to land me at the stone[f] pier by the huge carven gate Akariel; but he gently denied my wish, saying:[g] "Into Thalarion, the City of a Thousand Wonders, many have passed but none returned. Therein walk only daemons and mad things that are no longer men, and the streets are white with the unburied bones of those

[a] Land] land E
[b] any] *om.* B
[c] place.] shore. A, B, C, E
[d] grey] gray C, E
[e] besought] beseeched B
[f] stone] shone E
[g] saying:] saying, A, B, C, E

who have looked upon the eidolon Lathi, that reigns over the city." So the White Ship sailed on past the walls of Thalarion, and followed for many days a southward-flying bird, whose glossy plumage matched the sky out of which it had appeared.

Then came we to a pleasant coast gay with blossoms of every hue, where as far inland as we could see basked lovely groves and radiant arbours[a] beneath a meridian sun. From bowers beyond our view came bursts of song and snatches of lyric harmony, interspersed with faint laughter so delicious that I urged the rowers onward in my eagerness to reach the scene. And the bearded man spoke no word, but watched me as we approached the lily-lined shore. Suddenly a wind blowing from over the flowery meadows and leafy woods brought a scent at which I trembled. The wind grew stronger, and the air was filled with the lethal, charnel odour[b] of plague-stricken towns and uncovered cemeteries. And as we sailed madly away from that damnable coast the bearded man spoke at last, saying:[c] "This is Xura, the Land of Pleasures Unattained."

So once more the White Ship followed the bird of heaven, over warm blessed seas fanned by caressing, aromatic breezes. Day after day and night after night did we sail, and when the moon was full we would listen to soft songs of the oarsmen, sweet as on that distant night when we sailed away from my[d] native land. And it was by moonlight that we anchored at last in the harbour[e] of Sona-Nyl, which is guarded by twin headlands of crystal that rise from the sea and meet in a resplendent arch. This is the Land of Fancy, and we walked to the verdant shore upon a golden bridge of moonbeams.

In the Land of Sona-Nyl there is neither time nor space,[f] neither suffering nor death; and there I dwelt for many aeons. Green are the groves and pastures, bright and fragrant the flowers, blue and musical the streams, clear and cool the fountains, and stately and gorgeous the temples, castles, and cities of Sona-Nyl. Of that land there is no bound, for beyond each vista of beauty rises another more beautiful. Over the

[a] arbours] arbors C, E
[b] odour] odor C, E
[c] saying:] saying, A, B, C, E
[d] my] my far A, B, C, E
[e] harbour] harbor C, E
[f] space,] space; D

countryside and amidst the splendour[a] of cities rove[b] at will the happy folk, of whom all are gifted with unmarred grace and unalloyed happiness. For the aeons that I dwelt there I wandered blissfully through gardens where quaint pagodas peep from pleasing clumps of bushes, and where the white walks are bordered with delicate blossoms. I climbed gentle hills from whose summits I could see entrancing panoramas of loveliness, with steepled towns nestling in verdant valleys, and with the golden domes of gigantic cities glittering on the infinitely distant horizon. And I viewed by moonlight the sparkling sea, the crystal headlands, and the placid harbour[c] wherein lay anchored the White Ship.

It was against the full moon one night in the immemorial year of Tharp that I saw outlined the beckoning form of the celestial bird, and felt the first stirrings of unrest. Then I spoke with the bearded man, and told him of my new yearning[d] to depart for remote Cathuria, which no man hath seen, but which all believe to lie beyond the basalt pillars of the West. It is the Land of Hope, and in it shine the perfect ideals of all that we know elsewhere; or at least so men relate. But the bearded man said to me:[e] "Beware of those perilous seas wherein men say Cathuria lies. In Sona-Nyl there is no pain nor[f] death, but who can tell what lies beyond the basalt pillars of the West?" Natheless at the next full moon I boarded the White Ship, and with the reluctant bearded man left the happy harbour[g] for untravelled[h] seas.

And the bird of heaven flew before, and led us toward the basalt pillars of the West, but this time the oarsmen sang no soft songs under the full moon. In my mind I would often picture the unknown Land of Cathuria with its splendid groves and palaces, and would wonder what new delights there awaited me. "Cathuria," I would say to myself, "is the abode of gods and the land of unnumbered cities of gold. Its forests are of aloe and sandalwood, even as the fragrant groves of

[a] splendour] splendor C, E
[b] rove] can move A, B, C, E
[c] harbour] harbor C, E
[d] yearning] yearnings C, E
[e] me:] me, A, B, C, E
[f] nor] or E
[g] harbour] harbor C, E
[h] untravelled] untraveled C, E

Camorin, and among the trees flutter gay birds sweet with song. On the green and flowery mountains of Cathuria stand temples of pink marble[a] rich with carven and painted glories, and having in their courtyards cool fountains of silver, where purl[b] with ravishing music the scented waters that come from the grotto-born river Narg. And the cities of Cathuria are cinctured with golden walls, and their pavements are also[c] of gold. In the gardens of these cities are strange orchids, and perfumed lakes whose beds are of coral and amber. At night the streets and the gardens are lit with gay lanthorns fashioned from the three-coloured[d] shell of the tortoise, and here resound the soft notes of the singer and the lutanist. And the houses of the cities of Cathuria are all palaces, each built over a fragrant canal bearing the waters of the sacred Narg. Of marble and porphyry are the houses, and roofed with glittering gold that reflects the rays of the sun and enhances the splendour[e] of the cities as blissful gods view them from the distant peaks. Fairest of all is the palace of the great monarch Dorieb, whom some say to be a demigod[f] and others a god. High is the palace of Dorieb, and many are the turrets of marble upon its walls. In its wide halls may[g] multitudes assemble, and here hang the trophies of the ages. And the roof is of pure gold, set upon tall pillars of ruby and azure, and having such carven figures of gods and heroes that he who looks up to those heights seems[h] to gaze upon the living Olympus. And the floor[i] is of glass, under which flow the cunningly lighted waters of the Narg, gay with gaudy fish not known beyond the bounds of lovely Cathuria."

Thus would I speak to myself of Cathuria, but ever would the bearded man warn me to turn back to the happy shores of Sona-Nyl; for Sona-Nyl is known of men, while none hath ever beheld Cathuria.

---

[a] marble] marble, A, B, C, E
[b] purl] purr E
[c] are also] also are A, C, E
[d] three-coloured] three-colored C, E
[e] splendour] splendor C, E
[f] demigod] demi-/god C; demi-god E
[g] may] many E
[h] seems] seem B
[i] floor] floor of the palace A, B, C, E

And on the thirty-first day that we followed the bird, we beheld the basalt pillars of the West. Shrouded in mist they were, so that no man might peer beyond them or see their summits—which indeed some say reach even to the heavens. And the bearded man again implored me to turn back, but I heeded him not; for from the mists beyond the basalt pillars I fancied there came the notes of singer and lutanist;[a] sweeter than the sweetest songs of Sona-Nyl, and sounding mine own praises; the praises of me, who had voyaged far under[b] the full moon and dwelt in the Land of Fancy.[c]

So to the sound of melody the White Ship sailed into the mist betwixt the basalt pillars of the West. And when the music ceased and the mist lifted, we beheld not the Land of Cathuria, but a swift-rushing resistless sea, over which our helpless barque was borne toward some unknown goal. Soon to our ears came the distant thunder of falling waters, and to our eyes appeared on the far horizon ahead the titanic spray of a monstrous cataract, wherein the oceans of the world drop down to abysmal nothingness. Then did the bearded man say to me[d] with tears on his cheek, "We have rejected the beautiful Land of Sona-Nyl, which we may never behold again. The gods are greater than men, and they have conquered." And I closed my eyes before the crash that I knew would come, shutting out the sight of the celestial bird which flapped its mocking blue wings over the brink of the torrent.

Out of that crash came darkness, and I heard the shrieking of men and of things which were not men. From the East tempestuous winds arose, and chilled me as I crouched on the slab of damp stone which had risen beneath my feet. Then as I heard another crash I opened my eyes and beheld myself upon the platform of that lighthouse from[e] whence I had sailed so many aeons ago. In the darkness below there loomed the vast blurred outlines of a vessel breaking up on the cruel rocks, and as I glanced out over the waste I saw that the light had failed for the first time since my grandfather had assumed its care.

[a] singer and lutanist;] singers and lutanists; E
[b] under] from E
[c] Fancy. ¶] Fancy. E
[d] me] me, C, E
[e] from] *om.* C, E

And in the later watches of the night, when I went within the tower, I saw on the wall a calendar which still remained as when I had left it at the hour I sailed away. With the dawn I descended the tower and looked for wreckage upon the rocks, but what I found was only this: a strange dead bird whose hue was as of the azure sky, and a single shattered spar, of a whiteness greater than that of the wave-tips or of the mountain snow.

And thereafter the ocean told me its secrets no more; and though many times since has the moon shone full and high in the heavens, the White Ship from the South came never again.

The Street

There be those who say that things and places have souls, and there be those who say they have not; I dare not say, myself, but I will tell of The[a] Street.

Men of strength and honour fashioned that Street; good,[b] valiant men of our blood who had come from the Blessed Isles across the sea. At first it was but a path trodden by bearers of water from the woodland spring to the cluster of houses by the beach. Then,[c] as more men came to the growing cluster of houses and looked about for places to dwell, they built cabins along the north side;[d] cabins of stout oaken logs with masonry on the side toward the forest, for many Indians lurked there with fire-arrows. And in a few years more, men built cabins on the south side of The Street.

Up and down The Street walked grave men in conical hats, who most of the time carried muskets or fowling pieces. And there were also their bonneted[e] wives and sober children. In the evening these

Editor's Note: There is no manuscript for this story, so we are reliant on the two published appearances in HPL's lifetime, both in amateur journals: *Wolverine* (December 1920) and *National Amateur* (January 1922). The latter does not appear to bear any significant revisions from the former. The first reprint of the story after HPL's death occurred in George T. Wetzel's *The Lovecraft Collectors Library* (1952–55), but this reprint—derived from the *National Amateur* text—was full of errors, including dropped lines of text. The Arkham House editions followed the Wetzel text, making makeshift corrections of the garbled passages.

Texts: A = *Wolverine* No. 8 (December 1920): 2–12; B = *National Amateur* 44, No. 3 (January 1922): 25–27; C = *Lovecraft Collectors Library: Volume Two* (North Tonawanda, NY: SSR Publications, 1953), 4–8; D = *The Shuttered Room and Other Pieces* (Arkham House, 1959), 70–75; E = *Dagon and Other Macabre Tales* (Arkham House, 1965), 322–27. Copy-text: A.

[a] The] the D, E [*and so on throughout text*]
[b] Street; good,] Street: good D, E
[c] Then,] Then A, B; Than C
[d] side;] side, C, D, E
[e] bonneted] binneted A

men with their wives and children would sit about gigantic hearths and read and speak. Very simple were the things of which they read and spoke, yet things which gave[a] them courage and goodness and helped them by day to subdue the forest and till the fields. And the children would listen,[b] and learn of the laws and deeds of old, and of that dear England which they had never seen,[c] or could not remember.

There was war, and thereafter no more Indians troubled The Street. The men, busy with labour,[d] waxed prosperous and as happy as they knew how to be. And the children grew up comfortably,[e] and more families came from the Mother Land to dwell on The Street. And the children's children, and the newcomers'[f] children, grew up. The town was now a city, and one by one the cabins gave place to houses:[g] simple, beautiful houses of brick and wood, with stone steps and iron railings and fanlights over the doors. No flimsy creations were these houses, for they were made to serve many a generation. Within there were carven mantels and graceful stairs, and sensible, pleasing furniture, china, and[h] silver, brought from the Mother Land.

So The Street drank in the dreams of a young people,[i] and rejoiced as its dwellers became more graceful and happy. Where once had been only strength and honour, taste and learning now abode as well. Books[j] and paintings and music came to the houses, and the young men went to the university which rose above the plain to the north. In the place of conical hats and muskets there were three-cornered hats and small-swords, and[k] lace and snowy periwigs. And[l] there were cobblestones[m]

---

[a] gave] agve A
[b] listen,] listen D, E
[c] seen,] seen D, E
[d] labour,] labor, A, B, C
[e] comfortably,] comfortable, C, D, E
[f] newcomers'] newcomer's B, C
[g] houses;] houses, C, D; houses— E
[h] and] an E
[i] people,] people D, E
[j] Books] Books, A, B, C
[k] and muskets . . . and] and small-swords, of C, D, E
[l] periwigs. And] periwigs, C, D, E
[m] cobblestones] cobble-stones A, C

over which clattered many a blooded horse and rumbled many a gilded coach; and brick sidewalks with horse blocks and hitching-posts.

There were in that Street many trees; elms[a] and oaks and maples of dignity; so that in the summer[b] the scene was all soft verdure and twittering bird-song. And behind the houses were walled rose-gardens with hedged paths and sundials, where at evening the moon and stars would shine bewitchingly while fragrant blossoms glistened with dew.

So The Street dreamed on, past wars, calamities, and changes.[c] Once most of the young men went away, and some never came back. That was when they furled the Old Flag[d] and put up a new Banner of Stripes and Stars.[e] But though men talked of great changes, The Street felt them not;[f] for its folk[g] were still the same, speaking of the old familiar things in the old familiar accents.[h] And the trees still sheltered singing birds, and at evening the moon and stars looked down upon dewy blossoms in the walled rose-gardens.

In time there were no more swords, three-cornered[i] hats, or periwigs in The Street. How strange seemed the denizens[j] with their walking-sticks, tall beavers, and cropped heads! New sounds came from the distance—first strange puffings and shrieks from the river a mile away,[k] and many years later[l] strange puffings and shrieks and rumblings from other directions. The air was not quite so pure as before, but the spirit of the place had not changed. The blood and soul of the people were as the blood and soul[m] of their ancestors who[n] had fashioned The Street. Nor did the spirit change when they tore open the earth to lay

[a] trees; elms] trees: elms B; trees: elm D, E
[b] summer] summer, C, D, E
[c] changes.] change. D, E
[d] Old Flag] old flag D, E
[e] Banner . . . Stars.] banner of stripes and stars. D, E
[f] not;] not, B, C, D, E
[g] folk] folks A, B, C
[h] accents.] accounts. D, E
[i] three-cornered] three-corner C
[j] denizens] inhabitants D, E
[k] away,] away C
[l] and many . . . later] and then, many . . . later, C, D, E
[m] of the people . . . soul] *om.* C, D, E
[n] who] *om.* C, D, E

down strange pipes, or when they set up tall posts bearing weird wires. There was so much ancient lore in that Street, that the past could not easily be forgotten.

Then came days of evil, when many who had known The Street of old knew it no more;[a] and many knew it,[b] who had not known it before. And those who came were never as those who went away;[c] for their accents were coarse and strident, and their mien[d] and faces unpleasing. Their thoughts, too, fought with the wise,[e] just spirit of The Street. So[f] The Street pined silently as its houses fell into decay, and its trees died one by one, and its rose-gardens grew rank with weeds and waste. But it felt a stir of pride one day when again[g] marched forth young men, some of whom never came back. These young men were clad in blue.

With the years[h] worse fortune came to The Street. Its trees were all gone now, and its rose-gardens were displaced by the backs of cheap,[i] ugly new buildings on parallel streets. Yet the houses remained, despite[j] the ravages of the years and the storms and worms, for they had been made to serve many a generation. New kinds of faces appeared in The Street;[k] swarthy, sinister faces with furtive eyes and odd features, whose owners spoke unfamiliar words and placed signs in known and unknown characters upon most of the musty houses. Push-carts[l] crowded the gutters. A sordid, undefinable stench settled over the place, and the ancient spirit slept.

Great excitement once came to The Street. War and revolution were raging across the seas; a dynasty had collapsed, and its degenerate subjects were flocking with dubious intent to the Western Land. Many

[a] more;] more B, C; more, D, E

[b] it,] it D, E

[c] before. And . . . away;] before. And went away; C; before, and went away, D, E

[d] mien] mein C

[e] wise,] wise D, E

[f] Street. So] Street, so that D, E

[g] again] again, C

[h] years] years, D, E

[i] cheap,] cheap C

[j] despite] dispite C

[k] The Street;] The Street: B; the Street, D, E

[l] Push-carts] Push-/carts A

of these took lodgings in the battered houses that had once known the song[a] of birds and the scent of roses. Then the Western Land itself awoke,[b] and joined the Mother Land in her titanic struggle for civilisation.[c] Over the cities once more floated the Old Flag,[d] companioned by the New Flag[e] and by a plainer[f] yet glorious Tri-colour.[g] But not many flags floated over The Street, for therein brooded only fear and ignorance. Again young men went forth, but not quite as did the young men of those other days. Something was lacking. And the sons of those young men of other days, who did indeed go forth in olive-drab with the true spirit[h] of their ancestors, went from distant places and knew not The Street and its ancient spirit.[i]

Over the seas there was a great victory, and in triumph most of the young men returned. Those who had lacked something lacked it no longer, yet did fear and hatred and ignorance still brood over The Street; for many had stayed behind, and many strangers had come from distant places to the ancient houses. And the young men who had returned[j] dwelt there no longer. Swarthy and sinister were most of the strangers, yet among them one might find a few faces like those who fashioned The Street and moulded its spirit. Like and yet unlike, for there was in the eyes of all a weird, unhealthy glitter as of greed, ambition, vindictiveness, or misguided zeal. Unrest and treason were abroad amongst an evil few who plotted to strike the Western Land its death-blow,[k] that they might mount to power over its ruins;[l] even as assassins had mounted in that unhappy[m] frozen land from whence most of them had come. And the heart of that plotting was in The

[a] song] songs D, E
[b] awoke,] awoke D, E
[c] civilisation.] civilization. A, B, C, D, E
[d] Old Flag,] old flag, D, E
[e] New Flag] new flag, D, E
[f] plainer] plainer, D, E
[g] Tri-colour.] tri-colour. D, E
[h] spirit] spirits C
[i] spirit.] spirits. C
[j] returned] returned, C
[k] death-blow,] death blow, D, E
[l] ruins;] ruins, D, E
[m] unhappy] unhappy, C, D, E

Street, whose crumbling houses teemed with alien makers of discord and echoed with the plans and speeches of those who yearned for the appointed day of blood, flame,[a] and crime.

Of the various odd assemblages in The Street, the law said much but could prove little. With great diligence did men of hidden badges[b] linger and listen about such places as Petrovitch's Bakery, the squalid Rifkin School of Modern Economics, the Circle Social Club, and the Liberty Cafe.[c] There congregated sinister men in great numbers, yet always was their speech guarded or in a foreign tongue. And still the old houses stood, with their forgotten lore of nobler, departed centuries; of sturdy colonial[d] tenants and dewy rose-gardens in the moonlight. Sometimes a lone poet or traveller[e] would come to view them,[f] and would try to picture them in their vanished glory; yet of such travellers[g] and poets there were not many.

The rumour[h] now spread widely that these houses contained the leaders of a vast band of terrorists, who on a designated day were to launch an orgy of slaughter for the extermination of America[i] and of all the fine old traditions which The Street had loved. Handbills and papers fluttered about filthy gutters; handbills and papers printed in many tongues and in many characters, yet all bearing messages of crime and rebellion. In these writings the people were urged to tear down the laws and virtues that our fathers had exalted;[j] to stamp out the soul of the old America—the soul that was bequeathed through a thousand and a half years of Anglo-Saxon freedom, justice,[k] and moderation. It was said that the swart men who dwelt in The Street and congregated in its rotting

---

[a] flame,] flame D, E
[b] badges] badges, C
[c] Cafe.] Club. A, B, C, D; Café. E
[d] colonial] Colonial A, B, D, E, F
[e] traveller] travellor A; traveler B, C, D, E
[f] them,] The Street C
[g] travellers] travellors A; travelers B, C, D, E
[h] rumour] rumor C
[i] America] America, C
[j] exalted;] exalted, D, E
[k] justice,] justice C

edifices were the brains of a hideous revolution;[a] that at their word of command many millions of brainless, besotted beasts would stretch forth their noisome talons from the slums of a thousand cities, burning, slaying, and destroying till the land of our fathers should be no more. All this was said and repeated, and many looked forward in dread to the fourth day of July,[b] about which the strange writings hinted much; yet could nothing be found to place the guilt. None could tell just whose arrest might cut off the damnable plotting at its source. Many times came bands of blue-coated police[c] to search the shaky houses, though[d] at last they ceased to come; for they too had grown tired of law and order, and had abandoned all the city to its fate. Then men in olive-drab came, bearing muskets;[e] till it seemed as if in its sad sleep[f] The Street must have some haunting dreams of those other days,[g] when musket-bearing[h] men in conical hats walked along it from the woodland spring to the cluster of houses by the beach. Yet could no act be performed to check the impending cataclysm, for the swart,[i] sinister men were old in cunning.

So The Street slept uneasily on, till one night there gathered in Petrovitch's Bakery and the Rifkin School of Modern Economics, and the Circle Social Club, and Liberty Cafe,[j] and in other places[k] as well, vast hordes[l] of men whose eyes were big with horrible triumph and expectation. Over hidden wires strange messages travelled,[m] and much was said of still stranger messages yet to travel; but most of this was not guessed till afterward, when the Western Land was safe from the

---

[a] revolution;] revolution, D, E
[b] July,] July C
[c] came . . . police] bands of blue-coated police came C
[d] though] tho A
[e] muskets;] muskets, D, E
[f] sleep] sleep to C
[g] days,] day, A
[h] musket-bearing] musket bearing A, B, C
[i] swart,] swart A, B
[j] Cafe,] Café, D, E
[k] places] places, C
[l] hordes] hoards C
[m] travelled,] traveled C

peril. The men in olive-drab could not tell what was happening,[a] or what they ought to do; for the swart,[b] sinister men were skilled in subtlety and concealment.

And yet the men in olive-drab will always remember that night, and will speak of The Street as they tell of it to their grandchildren; for many of them were sent there toward morning on a mission unlike that which they had expected. It was known that this nest of anarchy was old, and that the houses were tottering from the ravages of the years and the storms and the[c] worms; yet was the happening of that summer night a surprise because of its very queer uniformity. It was, indeed, an exceedingly singular happening;[d] though after all[e] a simple one. For without warning, in one of the small hours beyond midnight,[f] all the ravages of the years and the storms and the worms came to a tremendous climax; and after the[g] crash there was nothing left standing in The Street save two ancient chimneys and part of a stout brick wall. Nor did anything[h] that had been alive come alive from the ruins.[i]

A poet and a traveller,[j] who came with the mighty crowd that sought the scene, tell odd stories. The poet says that all through the hours before dawn he beheld sordid ruins but[k] indistinctly in the glare of the arc-lights;[l] that there loomed above the wreckage another picture wherein he could descry[m] moonlight and fair houses and elms and oaks and maples of dignity. And the traveller[n] declares that instead of the place's wonted stench there lingered a delicate fragrance as of roses in

[a] happening,] happening C

[b] swart,] swart A, B, C

[c] the] *om.* A, B, C, D, E

[d] happening;] happening, D, E

[e] all] all, D, E

[f] warning, . . . midnight,] warning . . . midnight C

[g] after the] afterthe A

[h] anything] an / anything A

[i] ruins. ¶] ruins. B, C, D, E

[j] traveller,] travellor, A; traveler, B, C, D, E

[k] but] *om.* E

[l] arc-lights;] arc lights; A, B, C

[m] could descry] described C; could describe B, D, E

[n] traveller] travellor A; traveler B, C, D, E

full bloom. But are not the dreams of poets and the tales of travellers[a] notoriously false?

There be those who say that things and places have souls, and there be those who say they have not; I dare not say, myself, but I have told you of The Street.

---

[a] travellers] travellors A; travelers B, C, D, E

The Doom That Came to Sarnath

There is in the land of Mnar a vast[a] still lake that is fed by no stream[b] and out of which no stream flows. Ten thousand years ago there stood by its shore the mighty city of Sarnath, but Sarnath stands there no more.

It is told that in the immemorial[c] years when the world was young, before ever the men of Sarnath came to the land of Mnar, another city stood beside the lake; the grey[d] stone city of Ib, which was old as the lake itself, and peopled with beings not pleasing to behold. Very odd and ugly were these beings, as indeed are most beings of a world yet inchoate and rudely fashioned. It is written on the brick cylinders of Kadatheron that the beings of Ib were in hue as green as the lake and the mists that rise above it; that they had bulging eyes, pouting, flabby lips, and curious ears, and were without voice. It is also written that they descended one night from the moon in a mist; they and the vast still lake and grey[e] stone city Ib. However this may be, it is certain that

Editor's Note: An A.Ms. of the story survives, but it is a fair copy that must date after the first appearance—*Scot* (June 1920)—as it incorporates some revisions from that text. The T.Ms. was prepared by R. H. Barlow (see *OFF* 21) and was sent to *Marvel Tales*, where the story appeared in the March–April 1935 issue. This text was the basis of the posthumous appearance in *Weird Tales* (June 1938), which in turn served as the basis of the Arkham House edition. Each appearance introduced its own errors, so that the Arkham House text was very poor.

Texts: A = *Scot* No. 44 (June 1920): 90–98; B = A.Ms. (JHL); C = T.Ms. (JHL); D = *Marvel Tales of Science and Fantasy* 1, No. 4 (March–April 1935): 157–63; E = *Weird Tales* 31, No. 6 (June 1938): 742–46 (as "The Doom that Came to Sarnath"); F = *Dagon and Other Macabre Tales* (Arkham House, 1965), 34–40. Copy-text: B.

[a] vast] vast, B
[b] stream] stream, C, D, E, F
[c] immemorial] memorial D
[d] grey] gray E, F
[e] grey] gray E, F

they worshipped a sea-green stone idol chiselled[a] in the likeness of
Bokrug, the great water-lizard;[b] before which they danced horribly
when the moon was gibbous. And it is written in the papyrus of
Ilarnek, that they one day discovered fire, and thereafter kindled flames
on many ceremonial occasions. But not much is written of these
beings, because they lived in very ancient times, and man is young, and
knows but little of the very ancient living things.

After many aeons[c] men came to the land of Mnar;[d] dark shepherd
folk with their fleecy flocks, who built Thraa, Ilarnek, and Kadatheron
on the winding river Ai. And certain tribes, more hardy than the rest,
pushed on to the border of the lake and built Sarnath at a spot where
precious metals were found in the earth.

Not far from the grey[e] city of Ib did the wandering tribes lay the
first stones of Sarnath, and at the beings of Ib they marvelled[f] greatly.
But with their marvelling[g] was mixed hate, for they thought it not meet
that beings of such aspect should walk about the world of men at dusk.
Nor did they like the strange sculptures upon the grey[h] monoliths of Ib,
for those sculptures were terrible with great[i] antiquity. Why the beings
and the[j] sculptures lingered so late in the world, even until the coming
of men,[k] none can tell; unless it was because the land of Mnar is very
still, and remote from most other lands[l] both of waking and of
dream.[m]

As the men of Sarnath beheld more of the beings of Ib their hate
grew, and it was not less because they found the beings weak, and soft

[a] chiselled] chiseled E, F
[b] water-lizard;] water lizard; A
[c] aeons] eons E, F
[d] Mnar;] Mnar, E, F
[e] grey] gray E, F
[f] marvelled] marveled E, F
[g] marvelling] marveling E, F
[h] grey] gray E, F
[i] great] *om.* E, F [*see below*]
[j] sculptures were . . . and the] *om.* F
[k] men,] man, A
[l] lands] lands, C, D, E, F
[m] dream.] D, E, F; dreams. A, B, C. [dreams *changed to* dream *by HPL in B.*]

as jelly to the touch of stones and spears[a] and arrows. So one day the young warriors, the slingers and the spearmen and the bowmen, marched against Ib and slew all the inhabitants thereof, pushing the queer bodies into the lake with long spears, because they did not wish to touch them. And because they did not like the grey[b] sculptured monoliths of Ib they cast these also into the lake; wondering from the greatness of the labour[c] how ever the stones were brought from afar, as they must have been, since there is naught like them in all[d] the land of Mnar or in the lands adjacent.

Thus of the very ancient city of Ib was nothing spared[e] save the sea-green stone idol chiselled[f] in the likeness of Bokrug, the[g] water-lizard. This the young warriors took back with them to Sarnath[h] as a symbol of conquest over the old gods and beings of Ib, and a[i] sign of leadership in Mnar. But on the night after it was set up in the temple[j] a terrible thing must have happened, for weird lights were seen over the lake, and in the morning the people found the idol gone,[k] and the high-priest Taran-Ish lying dead, as from some fear unspeakable. And before he died, Taran-Ish had scrawled upon the altar of chrysolite[l] with coarse shaky strokes the sign of DOOM.

After Taran-Ish there were many high-priests in Sarnath, but never was the sea-green stone idol found. And many centuries came and went, wherein Sarnath prospered exceedingly, so that only priests and old women remembered what Taran-Ish had scrawled upon the altar of chrysolite. Betwixt Sarnath and the city of Ilarnek arose a caravan route, and the precious metals from the earth were exchanged for

[a] and spears] *om.* C, D, E, F
[b] grey] gray E, F
[c] labour] labor E, F
[d] all] *om.* C, D, E, F
[e] spared] spared, C, D, E, F
[f] chiselled] chiseled E, F
[g] the] the great A
[h] to Sarnath] *om.* D, E, F
[i] a] as a C, D, E, F
[j] temple] temple, E, F
[k] gone,] gone E, F
[l] chrysolite] chrysolilte D

other metals and rare cloths and jewels and books and tools for artificers[a] and all things of luxury that are known to the people who dwell along the winding river Ai and beyond. So Sarnath waxed mighty and learned and beautiful, and sent forth conquering armies to subdue the neighbouring[b] cities; and in time there sate upon a throne in Sarnath the kings of all the land of Mnar and of many lands adjacent.

The wonder of the world and the pride of all mankind was Sarnath the magnificent. Of polished desert-quarried marble were its[c] walls, in height three hundred cubits and in breadth seventy-five, so that chariots might pass each other as men drave[d] them along the top. For full five hundred stadia did they run, being open only on the side toward the lake;[e] where a green stone sea-wall kept back the waves that rose oddly once a year at the festival of the destroying of Ib. In Sarnath were fifty streets from the lake to the gates of the caravans, and fifty more intersecting them. With onyx were they paved, save those whereon the horses and camels and elephants trod, which were paved with granite. And the gates of Sarnath were as many as the landward ends of the streets, each of bronze, and flanked by the figures of lions and elephants carven from some stone no longer known among men. The houses of Sarnath were of glazed brick and chalcedony, each having its walled garden and crystal lakelet. With strange art were they builded, for no other city had houses like them; and travellers[f] from Thraa and Ilarnek and Kadatheron marvelled[g] at the shining domes wherewith[h] they were surmounted.

But more marvellous[i] still were the palaces and the temples, and the gardens made by Zokkar the olden[j] king. There were many palaces,

[a] artificers] artificere D
[b] neighbouring] neighboring C, D, E, F
[c] its] the A, B. [the *erased in B*, its *inserted*]
[d] drave] drove C, D, E, F
[e] lake;] lake D, E, F
[f] travellers] travelers E, F
[g] marvelled] marveled E, F
[h] wherewith] where with F
[i] marvellous] marvelous E, F
[j] olden] elden D

the least[a] of which were mightier than any in Thraa or Ilarnek or Kadatheron. So high were they that one within might sometimes fancy himself beneath only the sky; yet when lighted with torches dipt in the oil of Dothur[b] their walls shewed[c] vast paintings of kings and armies, of a splendour[d] at once inspiring and stupefying to the beholder. Many were the pillars of the palaces, all of tinted marble, and carven into designs of surpassing beauty. And in most of the palaces[e] the floors were mosaics of beryl and lapis-lazuli[f] and sardonyx and carbuncle and other choice materials, so disposed that the beholder might fancy himself walking over beds of the rarest flowers. And there were likewise fountains, which cast scented waters about in pleasing jets arranged with cunning art. Outshining all others was the palace of the kings of Mnar and of the lands adjacent. On a pair of golden crouching lions rested the throne, many steps above the gleaming floor. And it was wrought of one piece of ivory, though no man lives who knows whence so vast a piece could have come. In that palace there were also many galleries, and many amphitheatres[g] where lions and men and elephants battled at the pleasure of the kings. Sometimes the amphitheatres[h] were flooded with water conveyed from the lake in mighty aqueducts, and then were enacted stirring sea-fights, or combats betwixt swimmers and deadly marine things.

Lofty and amazing were the seventeen tower-like temples of Sarnath, fashioned of a bright multi-coloured[i] stone not known elsewhere. A full thousand cubits high stood the greatest among them, wherein the high-priests dwelt with a magnificence scarce less than that of the kings. On the ground were halls as vast and splendid as those of the palaces; where gathered throngs in worship of Zo-Kalar

---

[a] least] last E, F
[b] Dothur] Dother D, E, F
[c] shewed] showed E, F
[d] splendour] splendor E, F
[e] palaces] places E
[f] lapis-lazuli] lapis lazuli E, F
[g] amphitheatres] amphitheaters D, E, F
[h] amphitheatres] amphitheaters E, F
[i] multi-coloured] multi-colored E, F

and Tamash and Lobon,[a] the chief gods of Sarnath, whose incense-enveloped shrines were as the thrones of monarchs. Not like the eikons of other gods were those of Zo-Kalar and Tamash and Lobon, for[b] so close to life were they that one might swear the graceful bearded gods themselves sate on the ivory thrones. And up unending steps of shining[c] zircon was the tower-chamber, wherefrom the high-priests looked out over the city and the plains and the lake by day; and at the cryptic moon and significant stars and planets, and their reflections in the lake, by[d] night. Here was done the very secret and ancient rite in detestation of Bokrug, the water-lizard, and here rested the altar of chrysolite which bore the DOOM-scrawl[e] of Taran-Ish.

Wonderful likewise were the gardens made by Zokkar the olden king. In the centre[f] of Sarnath they lay, covering a great space and encircled by a high wall. And they were surmounted by a mighty dome of glass, through which shone the sun and moon and stars[g] and planets when it was clear, and from which were hung fulgent images of the sun and moon and stars and planets when it was not clear. In summer the gardens were cooled with fresh odorous breezes skilfully[h] wafted by fans, and in winter they were heated with concealed fires,[i] so that in those gardens it was always spring. There ran little streams over bright pebbles, dividing meads of green and gardens of many hues, and spanned by a multitude of bridges. Many were the waterfalls in their courses, and many were the lilied lakelets into which they expanded. Over the streams and lakelets rode white swans, whilst the music of rare birds chimed in with the melody of the waters. In ordered terraces rose the green banks, adorned here and there with bowers of vines and sweet blossoms, and seats and benches of marble and porphyry. And

[a] Lobon,] Labon, A

[b] Lobon, for] Labon, for A; Lobon. For D, E, F

[c] shining] *om.* C, D, E, F

[d] by] at D, E, F

[e] DOOM-scrawl] Doom-scrawl E, F

[f] centre] center E, F

[g] and stars] *om.* D, E, F

[h] skilfully] skillfully B, D

[i] fires,] fires; A

there were many small shrines and temples where one might rest or pray to small gods.

Each year there was celebrated in Sarnath the feast of the destroying of Ib, at which time wine, song, dancing,[a] and merriment of every kind abounded. Great honours[b] were then paid to the shades of those who had annihilated the odd ancient beings, and the memory of those beings and of their elder gods was derided by dancers and lutanists crowned with roses from the gardens of Zokkar. And the kings would look out over the lake and curse the bones of the dead that lay beneath it.[c] At first the high-priests liked not these festivals, for there had descended amongst[d] them queer tales of how the sea-green eikon had vanished, and how Taran-Ish had died from fear and left a warning. And they said that from their high tower they sometimes saw lights beneath the waters of the lake. But as many years passed without calamity[e] even the priests laughed and cursed[f] and joined in the orgies of the feasters. Indeed, had they not themselves, in their high tower, often performed the very ancient and secret rite in detestation of Bokrug, the water-lizard? And a thousand years of riches and delight passed over Sarnath,[g] wonder of the world and pride of all mankind.[h]

Gorgeous beyond thought was the feast of the thousandth year of the destroying of Ib. For a decade had it been talked of in the land of Mnar, and as it drew nigh there came to Sarnath on horses and camels and elephants men from Thraa, Ilarnek, and Kadatheron, and all the cities of Mnar and the lands beyond.[i] Before the marble walls on the appointed night were pitched the pavilions[j] of princes and the tents of travellers, and all the shore resounded with the song of happy revellers.[k]

[a] dancing,] dancing C, D, E, F
[b] honours] honors E, F
[c] it.] it. ¶ E, F
[d] amongst] among A
[e] calamity] calamity, A
[f] cursed] cursed, A
[g] over Sarnath,] over the blessed and magnificent city of Sarnath, A
[h] world . . . mankind.] world. D, E, F
[i] beyond.] beyond D
[j] pavilions] Pavilions A
[k] travellers . . . revellers.] travellers. C, D; travelers. E, F

Within his banquet-hall reclined Nargis-Hei, the king, drunken with ancient wine from the vaults of conquered Pnoth, and surrounded by feasting nobles and hurrying slaves. There were eaten many strange delicacies at that feast; peacocks from the isles of Nariel in the Middle Ocean, young goats from the distant[a] hills of Implan, heels of camels from the Bnazic[b] desert, nuts and spices from Cydathrian[c] groves, and pearls from wave-washed Mtal[d] dissolved in the vinegar of Thraa. Of sauces there were an untold number, prepared by the subtlest cooks in all Mnar, and suited to the palate of every feaster. But most prized of all the viands were the great fishes from the lake, each of vast size, and served up on[e] golden platters set with rubies and diamonds.

Whilst the king and his nobles feasted within the palace, and viewed the crowning dish as it awaited them on golden platters, others feasted elsewhere. In the tower of the great temple the priests held revels,[f] and in pavilions without the walls the princes of neighbouring lands[g] made merry. And it was the high-priest Gnai-Kah who first saw the shadows that descended from the gibbous moon into the lake, and the damnable green mists that arose from the lake to meet the moon and to shroud in a sinister haze the towers and the domes of fated Sarnath. Thereafter those in the towers and without the walls beheld strange lights on the water, and saw that the grey[h] rock Akurion, which was wont to rear high above it near the shore, was almost submerged. And fear grew vaguely yet swiftly, so that the princes of Ilarnek and of far Rokol took down and folded their tents and pavilions and departed for the river Ai,[i] though they scarce knew the reason for their departing.

Then, close to the hour of midnight, all the bronze gates of Sarnath burst open and emptied forth a frenzied throng that blackened

[a] peacocks . . . distant] peacocks from the distant E, F
[b] Bnazic] Rnazic A
[c] Cydathrian] Sydathrian F
[d] Mtal] Mtal, A
[e] up on] upon D, E, F
[f] revels,] ravels, A
[g] neighbouring lands] neighbouring lands, D; neighboring lands E, F
[h] grey] gray E, F
[i] departed . . . Ai,] departed, D, E, F

the plain, so that all the visiting princes and travellers[a] fled away in fright. For on the faces of this throng was writ a madness born of horror unendurable, and on their tongues were words so[b] terrible that no hearer[c] paused for proof. Men whose eyes were wild with fear shrieked aloud of the sight within the king's banquet-hall, where through the windows were seen no longer the forms of Nargis-Hei and his nobles and slaves, but a horde of indescribable green voiceless things with bulging eyes, pouting,[d] flabby lips, and curious ears; things which danced horribly, bearing in their paws golden platters set with rubies and diamonds and containing uncouth flames.[e] And the princes and travellers,[f] as they fled from the doomed city of Sarnath on horses and camels and elephants, looked again upon the mist-begetting lake and saw the grey[g] rock Akurion was quite submerged.[h]

Through all the land of Mnar and the lands[i] adjacent spread the tales of those who had fled from Sarnath, and caravans sought that accursed city and its precious metals no more. It was long ere any traveller[j] went thither, and even then only the brave and adventurous young men of distant Falona dared make the journey; adventurous young men of yellow[k] hair and blue eyes, who are no kin to the men of Mnar. These men indeed went to the lake to view Sarnath; but though they found the vast still lake itself, and the grey[l] rock Akurion which rears high above it near the shore, they beheld not the wonder of the world and pride of all mankind. Where once had risen walls of three hundred cubits and towers yet higher, now stretched only the marshy shore, and where once had dwelt fifty millions[m] of men now crawled

[a] travellers] travelers E, F

[b] so] to A

[c] hearer] hearers A

[d] pouting,] pouting A

[e] flames.] flames, A

[f] travellers,] travelers, E, F

[g] grey] gray E, F

[h] submerged. ¶] submerged. E, F

[i] lands] land F

[j] traveller] travellers C, D; travelers E, F

[k] men of distant . . . yellow] men of yellow D, E, F

[l] grey] gray E, F

[m] millions] million D, E, F

only[a] the detestable green[b] water-lizard. Not even the mines of precious metal remained, for[c] DOOM had come to Sarnath.

But half buried in the rushes was spied a curious green idol of stone;[d] an exceedingly[e] ancient idol coated with seaweed and chiselled[f] in the likeness of Bokrug, the great water-lizard. That idol, enshrined in the high temple at Ilarnek, was subsequently worshipped beneath the gibbous moon throughout the land of Mnar.

[a] only] *om.* F
[b] green] *om.* D, E, F
[c] remained, for] remained. D, E, F
[d] idol of stone;] idol; D, E, F
[e] exceedingly] exceeding E
[f] idol coated . . . chiselled] idol, coated with seaweed and chiselled A; idol chiseled D, E, F

The Statement of Randolph Carter

I repeat to you, gentlemen, that your inquisition is fruitless. Detain me here for ever[a] if you will; confine or execute me if you must have a victim to propitiate the illusion you call justice; but I can say no more than I have said already. Everything that I can remember, I have told[b] with perfect candour.[c] Nothing has been distorted or concealed, and if anything remains vague, it is only because of the dark cloud which has come over my mind—that cloud and the nebulous nature of the horrors which brought it upon me.

Again I say, I do not know what has become of Harley Warren,[d] though I think—almost hope—that he is in peaceful oblivion, if there be anywhere so blessed a thing. It is true that I have for five years been his closest friend, and a partial sharer of his terrible researches into the unknown. I will not deny, though my memory is uncertain and

---

Editor's Note: An A.Ms. (a fair copy) exists, but it must date before the existing T.Ms., as the latter appears to incorporate some revisions from that text. The first published appearance in the *Vagrant* (May 1920), edited by W. Paul Cook, follows the T.Ms. This T.Ms. (single-spaced) was sent to *Weird Tales* in mid-1923. It is possible that some of the divergences between it and the *Weird Tales* (February 1925) appearance—especially in the matter of the italicisation of Harley Warren's utterances—are the result of revisions that HPL made when preparing a double-spaced T.Ms.; but I regard that possibility as too remote to justify overturning the readings of the existing A.Ms. and T.Ms. The Arkham House editions followed the first *Weird Tales* text; the second *Weird Tales* text (August 1937) is of no relevance to the tale's textual history.

Texts: A = A.Ms. (private hands), published by R. Alain Everts (Madison, WI: Strange Co., 1976); B = T.Ms. (JHL); C = *Vagrant* No. 13 (May 1920): 41–48; D = *Weird Tales* 5, No. 2 (February 1925): 149–53; E = *At the Mountains of Madness and Other Novels* (Arkham House, 1964), 284–89. Copy-text: B.

[a] for ever] forever A, C, D, E
[b] told] told you E
[c] candour.] candor. D, E
[d] Warren,] Warren; A

---

indistinct, that this witness of yours may have seen us together as he says, on the Gainsville pike, walking toward Big Cypress Swamp, at half past eleven[a] on that awful night. That we bore electric lanterns, spades, and a curious coil of wire with attached instruments, I will even affirm; for these things all played a part in the single hideous scene which remains burned into my shaken recollection. But of what followed, and of the reason I was found alone and dazed on the edge of the swamp next morning, I must insist that I know nothing save what I have told you over and over again. You say to me that there is nothing in the swamp or near it which could form the setting of that frightful episode. I reply that I know[b] nothing beyond what I saw. Vision or nightmare it may have been—vision or nightmare I fervently hope it was—yet it is all that my mind retains of what took place in those shocking hours after we left the sight of men. And why Harley Warren did not return, he or his shade—or some nameless *thing*[c] I cannot describe—alone can tell.

As I have said before, the weird studies of Harley Warren were well known to me, and to some extent shared by me. Of his vast collection of strange, rare books on forbidden subjects I have read all that are written in the languages of which I am master; but these are few as compared with those in languages I cannot understand. Most, I believe, are in Arabic; and the fiend-inspired book which brought on the end—the book which he carried in his pocket out of the world—was written in characters whose like I never saw elsewhere. Warren would never tell me just what was in that book. As to the nature of our studies—must I say again that I no longer retain full comprehension? It seems to me rather merciful that I do not, for they were terrible studies, which I pursued more through reluctant fascination than through actual inclination. Warren always dominated me, and sometimes I feared him. I remember how I shuddered at his facial expression on the night before the awful happening, when he talked so incessantly of his theory, *why certain corpses never decay, but rest firm and fat in*

---

[a] eleven] 11 D, E
[b] know] knew D, E
[c] *thing*] thing E

their tombs for a thousand years.[a] But I do not fear him now, for I suspect that he has known horrors beyond my ken. Now I fear *for*[b] him.

Once more I say that I have no clear idea of our object on that night. Certainly, it had much to do with something in the book which Warren carried with him—that ancient book in undecipherable characters which had come to him from India a month before—but I swear I do not know what it was that we expected to find. Your witness says he saw us at half past eleven[c] on the Gainsville pike, headed for Big Cypress Swamp. This is probably true, but I have no distinct memory of it. The picture seared into my soul is of one scene only, and the hour must have been long after midnight; for a waning crescent moon was high in the vaporous heavens.

The place was an ancient cemetery; so ancient that I trembled at the manifold signs of immemorial years. It was in a deep, damp hollow, overgrown with rank grass, moss, and curious creeping weeds, and filled with a vague stench which my idle fancy associated absurdly with rotting stone. On every hand were the signs of neglect and decrepitude, and I seemed haunted by the notion that Warren and I were the first living creatures to invade a lethal silence of centuries. Over the valley's rim a wan, waning crescent moon peered through the noisome vapours[d] that seemed to emanate from unheard-of[e] catacombs, and by its feeble, wavering beams I could distinguish a repellent array of antique slabs, urns, cenotaphs, and mausolean[f] facades;[g] all crumbling, moss-grown, and moisture-stained, and partly concealed by the gross luxuriance of the unhealthy vegetation.[h] My first vivid impression of my own presence in this terrible necropolis concerns the act of pausing with Warren before a certain half-obliterated[i] sepulchre,[j] and of throwing down some

[a] *why . . . years.*] why . . . years. D, E
[b] *for*] for E
[c] eleven] 11 D, E
[d] vapours] vapors D, E
[e] unheard-of] unheard of E
[f] mausolean] mausoleum E
[g] facades;] façades; D
[h] vegetation.] vegetation. ¶ D, E
[i] half-obliterated] *om.* A
[j] sepulchre,] sepulcher, D; sepulcher E

burdens which we seemed to have been carrying. I now observed that I had with me an electric lantern and two spades, whilst my companion was supplied with a similar lantern and a portable telephone outfit. No word was uttered, for the spot and the task seemed known to us; and without delay we seized our spades and commenced to clear away the grass, weeds, and drifted earth from the flat, archaic mortuary. After uncovering the entire surface, which consisted of three immense granite slabs, we stepped back some distance to survey the charnel scene; and Warren appeared to make some mental calculations. Then he returned to the sepulchre,[a] and using his spade as a lever,[b] sought to pry up the slab lying nearest to a stony ruin which may have been a monument in its day. He did not succeed, and motioned to me to come to his assistance. Finally our combined strength loosened the stone, which we raised and tipped to one side.

The removal of the slab revealed a black aperture, from which rushed an effluence of miasmal gases so nauseous that we started back in horror. After an interval, however, we approached the pit again, and found the exhalations less unbearable. Our lanterns disclosed the top of a flight of stone steps, dripping with some detestable ichor of the inner earth, and bordered by moist walls encrusted with nitre.[c] And now for the first time my memory records verbal discourse, Warren addressing me at length in his mellow tenor voice; a voice singularly unperturbed by our awesome surroundings.

"I'm sorry to have to ask you to stay on the surface," he said, "but it would be a crime to let anyone with your frail nerves go down there. You can't imagine, even from what you have read and from what I've told you, the things I shall have to see and do. It's fiendish work, Carter, and I doubt if any man without ironclad sensibilities could ever see it through and come up alive and sane. I don't wish to offend you, and heaven[d] knows I'd be glad enough to have you with me; but the responsibility is in a certain sense mine, and I couldn't drag a bundle of

---

[a] sepulchre,] sepulcher, D, E
[b] lever,] [*A seems to indicate an underscore (and is so read by Everts), but it appears to be a stray mark.*]
[c] nitre.] niter. D, E
[d] sane . . . heaven] sane. Heaven A; sane . . . Heaven B, C, D, E

nerves like you down to probable death or madness. I tell you, you can't imagine what the thing is really like! But I promise to keep you informed over the telephone of every move—you see I've enough wire here to reach to the centre[a] of the earth and back!'"

I can still hear, in memory, those coolly spoken words; and I can still remember my remonstrances. I seemed desperately anxious to accompany my friend into those sepulchral depths, yet he proved inflexibly obdurate. At one time he threatened to abandon the expedition if I remained insistent; a threat which proved effective, since he alone held the key to the *thing*.[b] All this I can still remember, though I no longer know what manner of *thing*[c] we sought. After he had secured[d] my reluctant acquiescence in his design, Warren picked up the reel of wire and adjusted the instruments. At his nod I took one of the latter and seated myself upon an aged, discoloured[e] gravestone close by the newly uncovered aperture. Then he shook my hand, shouldered the coil of wire, and[f] disappeared within that indescribable ossuary.[g] For a moment[h] I kept sight of the glow of[i] his lantern, and heard the rustle of the wire as he laid it down after him; but the glow soon disappeared abruptly, as if a turn in the stone staircase had been encountered, and the sound died away almost as quickly. I was alone, yet bound to the unknown depths by those magic strands whose insulated surface lay green beneath the struggling beams of that waning crescent moon.

In the lone silence of that hoary and deserted city of the dead, my mind conceived the most ghastly phantasies[j] and illusions; and the grotesque shrines and monoliths seemed to assume a hideous personality—a half-sentience. Amorphous shadows seemed to lurk in the darker recesses of the weed-choked hollow and to flit as in some blasphemous

[a] centre] center D, E
[b] *thing*.] thing. E
[c] *thing*] thing E
[d] secured] obtained D, E
[e] aged, discoloured] aged discoloured B, C; aged, discolored D, E
[f] and] and silently A
[g] ossuary.] ossuary. ¶ D, E
[h] moment] minute D, E
[i] of] from A
[j] phantasies] fantasies A, C, D; *om.* E [*see below*]

ceremonial procession past the portals of the mouldering[a] tombs in the hillside; shadows which could not have been cast by that pallid, peering crescent moon.[b] I constantly consulted my watch by the light of my electric lantern, and listened with feverish anxiety at the receiver of the telephone; but for more than a quarter of an hour heard nothing. Then a faint clicking came from the instrument, and I called down to my friend in a tense voice. Apprehensive as I was, I was nevertheless unprepared for the words which came up from that uncanny vault in accents more alarmed and quivering than any I had heard before from Harley Warren. He who had so calmly left me a little while previously, now called from below in a shaky whisper more portentous[c] than the loudest shriek:

"God! If you could see what I am seeing!"[d]

I could not answer. Speechless, I could only wait. Then came the frenzied tones again:

"Carter, it's terrible—monstrous[e]*—unbelievable!"*[f]

This time my voice did not fail me, and I poured into the transmitter a flood of excited questions. Terrified, I continued to repeat, "Warren, what is it? What is it?"

Once more came the voice of my friend, still hoarse with fear, and now apparently tinged with despair:

"I can't tell you, Carter! It's too utterly beyond thought—I dare not tell you— no man could know it and live—Great God! I never dreamed of THIS!"[g] Stillness again, save for my now incoherent torrent of shuddering inquiry. Then the voice of Warren in a pitch of wilder consternation:

"Carter! for the love of God, put back the slab and get out of this if you can! Quick!—leave everything else and make for the outside—it's your only chance! Do as I say, and don't ask me to explain!"[h]

I heard, yet was able only to repeat my frantic questions. Around me

---

[a] mouldering] moldering D; *om.* E [*see below*]
[b] In . . . moon.] In . . . moon. ¶ D; *om.* E
[c] portentous] portentious A, B, C
[d] *"God! . . . seeing!"*] "God! . . . seeing!" D, E
[e] *monstrous*] *monstruous* C, E
[f] *"Carter, . . . unbelievable!"*] "Carter, . . . unbelievable!" D, E
[g] *"I can't . . . THIS!"*] "I can't . . . *this!"* ¶ D; "I can't . . . this!" ¶ E
[h] *"Carter! . . . explain!"*] "Carter! . . . explain!" D, E

were the tombs and the darkness and the shadows; below me, some peril beyond the radius of the human imagination. But my friend was in greater danger than I, and through my fear I felt a vague resentment that he should deem me capable of deserting him under such circumstances. More clicking, and after a pause a piteous cry from Warren:

"*Beat it! For God's sake,*[a] *put back the slab and beat it, Carter!*"[b]

Something in the boyish slang of my evidently stricken companion unleashed my faculties. I formed and shouted a resolution,[c] "Warren, brace up! I'm coming down!" But at this offer the tone of my auditor changed to a scream of utter despair:

"*Don't! You can't understand! It's too late—and my own fault. Put back the slab and run—there's nothing else you or anyone can do now!*"[d] The tone changed again, this time acquiring a softer quality, as of hopeless resignation. Yet[e] it remained tense through anxiety for me.

"*Quick—before it's too late!*"[f] I tried not to heed him; tried to break through the paralysis which held me, and to fulfil my vow to rush down to his aid. But his next whisper found me still held inert in the chains of stark horror.[g]

"*Carter—hurry! It's no use—you must go—better one than two—the slab—*"[h] A pause,[i] more clicking, then the faint voice of Warren:

"*Nearly over now—don't make it harder—cover up those damned steps and run for your life—you're losing time— So long, Carter—won't see you again.*"[j] Here Warren's whisper swelled into a cry; a cry that gradually rose to a shriek fraught with all the horror of the ages—

"*Curse these hellish things—legions— My God! Beat it! Beat it! Beat it!*"[k]

<hr />

[a] *sake,*] *sake* A

[b] "*Beat . . . Carter!*"] "Beat . . . Carter!" D, E

[c] resolution,] resolution: A

[d] "*Don't! . . . now!*"] "Don't! . . . now!" ¶ D, E

[e] resignation. Yet] resignation, yet A

[f] "*Quick . . . late!*"] "Quick . . . late!" ¶ D, E

[g] horror.] horror: A

[h] "*Carter . . . slab—*"] "Carter . . . slab—" ¶ D, E

[i] pause,] pause; A

[j] "*Nearly . . . So . . . again.*"] "Nearly . . . so . . . again." ¶ D, E

[k] "*Curse . . . Beat it! Beat it! Beat it!*"] "Curse . . . Beat it! *Beat it!* BEAT IT!" D; "Curse . . . Beat it! Beat it! BEAT IT!" E

After that was silence. I know not how many interminable aeons[a] I sat stupefied; whispering, muttering, calling, screaming into that telephone. Over and over again through those aeons[b] I whispered and muttered, called, shouted, and screamed, "Warren! Warren! Answer me—are you there?"

And then there came to me the crowning horror of all—the unbelievable, unthinkable, almost unmentionable thing. I have said that aeons[c] seemed to elapse after Warren shrieked forth his last despairing warning, and that only my own cries now broke the hideous silence. But after a while there was a further clicking in the receiver, and I strained my ears to listen. Again I called down, "Warren, are you there?",[d] and in answer heard the *thing*[e] which has brought this cloud over my mind. I do not try, gentlemen, to account for that *thing*[f]—that voice—nor can I venture to describe it in detail, since the first words took away my consciousness and created a mental blank which reaches to the time of my awakening in the hospital. Shall I say that the voice was deep; hollow; gelatinous; remote; unearthly; inhuman; disembodied? What shall I say? It was the end of my experience, and is the end of my story. I heard it, and knew no more. Heard[g] it as I sat petrified in that unknown cemetery in the hollow, amidst the crumbling stones and the falling tombs, the[h] rank vegetation and the miasmal vapours. Heard[i] it well up from the innermost depths of that damnable open sepulchre[j] as I watched amorphous, necrophagous shadows dance beneath an accursed waning moon.[k] And this is what it said:

"*YOU FOOL, WARREN IS DEAD!*"[l]

[a] aeons] eons D, E
[b] aeons] eons D, E
[c] aeons] eons D, E
[d] there?",] there?" D, E
[e] *thing*] thing E
[f] *thing*] thing E
[g] more. Heard] more—heard D, E
[h] tombs, the] tombs and the A
[i] vapours. Heard] vapors—heard D, E
[j] sepulchre] sepulcher D, E
[k] moon.] moon. ¶ D, E
[l] "*YOU ... DEAD!*"] "*You fool, Warren is DEAD!*" D; "You fool, Warren is DEAD!" E

The Terrible Old Man

I t was the design of Angelo Ricci and Joe Czanek and Manuel Silva to call on the Terrible Old Man. This old man dwells all alone in a very ancient house in[a] Water Street near the sea, and is reputed to be both exceedingly rich and exceedingly[b] feeble; which forms a situation very attractive to men of the profession of Messrs.[c] Ricci, Czanek,[d] and Silva,[e] for that profession was nothing less dignified than[f] robbery.

The inhabitants of Kingsport say and think many things about the Terrible Old Man which generally keep[g] him safe from the attentions[h] of gentlemen like Mr. Ricci and his colleagues, despite the almost certain fact that he hides a fortune of indefinite magnitude somewhere about his musty and venerable abode. He is, in truth, a very strange person, believed to have been a captain of East India clipper ships in his day; so old that no one can remember when he was young, and so taciturn that few know his real name. Among the gnarled trees in the

Editor's Note: An A.Ms. exists, but it is a fair copy and must date to after the first appearance: *Tryout* (July 1921), as it incorporates some revisions from that text. HPL presumably prepared a T.Ms. for *Weird Tales*, where the story appeared in the August 1926 issue. I now believe that a few slight variants between the A.Ms. and the *Weird Tales* text are the result of deliberate revisions that HPL made in the hypothetical T.Ms. The Arkham House editions followed the *Weird Tales* text.

Texts: A = *Tryout* 7, No. 4 (July 1921): [10–14]; B = A.Ms. (JHL); C = *Weird Tales* 8, No. 2 (July 1926): 191–92; D = *The Dunwich Horror and Others* (Arkham House, 1963), 278–80. Copy-text: B (with some readings from C).

[a] in] on A, B
[b] exceedingly] *om.* A
[c] Messrs.] Messrs A
[d] Czanek,] Czanek C, D
[e] Silva,] Silva A
[f] dignified than] than dignified A
[g] keep] kept A
[h] attentions] attention A, B

front yard of his aged and neglected place he maintains a strange collection of large stones, oddly grouped and painted so that they resemble the idols in some obscure Eastern temple. This collection frightens away most of the small boys who love to taunt the Terrible Old Man about his long white hair and beard, or to break the small-paned windows of his dwelling with wicked missiles; but there are other things which frighten[a] the older and more curious folk who sometimes steal up to the house to peer in through the dusty panes. These folk say that on a table in a bare room on the ground floor are many peculiar bottles, in each a small piece of lead suspended pendulum-wise from a string. And they say that the Terrible Old Man talks to these bottles, addressing them by such names as Jack, Scar-Face, Long Tom, Spanish Joe, Peters,[b] and Mate Ellis, and that whenever he speaks to a bottle the little lead pendulum within makes certain definite vibrations as if in answer. Those who have watched the tall, lean, Terrible Old Man in these peculiar conversations[c] do not watch him again. But Angelo Ricci and Joe Czanek and Manuel Silva were not of Kingsport blood; they were of that new and heterogeneous alien stock which lies outside the charmed circle of New-England[d] life and traditions,[e] and they saw in the Terrible Old Man merely a tottering, almost helpless greybeard,[f] who could not walk without the aid of his knotted cane,[g] and whose thin,[h] weak hands shook pitifully. They were really quite sorry in their way for the lonely,[i] unpopular old fellow, whom everybody shunned, and at whom all the dogs barked singularly. But business is business, and to a[j] robber whose soul is in his profession, there is a lure and a challenge about a very old and very feeble man who has no account at the bank, and

[a] frighten] frightens A
[b] Peters,] Peters. A; Peters C, D
[c] conversations] conversations, B
[d] New-England] New England A, C, D
[e] traditions,] traditions. A
[f] greybeard,] gray-/beard, C; grey-beard, D
[g] cane,] cane A, C, D
[h] thin,] *om.* A
[i] lonely,] lonely A
[j] a] the A

who pays for his few necessities at the village store with Spanish gold and silver minted two centuries ago.

Messrs.[a] Ricci, Czanek, and Silva selected the night of April 11th[b] for their call. Mr. Ricci and Mr. Silva were to interview the poor old gentleman, whilst Mr. Czanek waited for them[c] and their presumable[d] metallic burden with a covered motor-car[e] in Ship Street, by the gate in the tall rear wall of their host's grounds. Desire to avoid needless explanations in[f] case of unexpected police intrusions prompted these plans for a quiet and unostentatious departure.

As prearranged, the three adventurers started out separately in order to prevent any evil-minded suspicions afterward.[g] Messrs.[h] Ricci and Silva met in Water Street by the old man's front gate, and although they did not like the way the moon shone down upon the painted stones through the budding branches of the gnarled trees, they had more important things to think about than mere idle superstition. They feared it might be unpleasant work making the Terrible Old Man loquacious concerning his hoarded gold and silver, for aged sea-captains are notably stubborn and perverse. Still, he was very old and very feeble, and there were two visitors. Messrs.[i] Ricci and Silva were experienced in the art of making unwilling persons voluble, and the screams of a weak and exceptionally venerable man can be easily muffled. So they moved up to the one lighted window and heard the Terrible Old Man talking childishly to his bottles with pendulums. Then they donned masks and knocked politely at the weather-stained oaken door.[j]

[a] Messrs.] Messrs A
[b] 11th] eleventh A, B, C, D
[c] them] the men A
[d] presumable] presumably C, D
[e] motor-car] motor car A, C, D
[f] explanations in] explanationins A
[g] afterward.] afterwards. A, B
[h] Messrs.] Messrs A
[i] Messrs.] Messrs A
[j] door. ¶] door. A

Waiting seemed very long to Mr. Czanek[a] as he fidgeted restlessly in the covered motor-car[b] by the Terrible Old Man's back gate in Ship Street. He was more than ordinarily tender-hearted,[c] and he did not like the hideous screams he had heard in the ancient house just after the hour appointed for the deed. Had he not told his colleagues to be as gentle[d] as possible with the pathetic old sea-captain? Very nervously he watched that narrow oaken gate in the high and ivy-clad stone wall. Frequently he consulted his watch, and wondered at the delay. Had the old man died before revealing where his treasure was hidden, and had a thorough search become necessary? Mr. Czanek did not like to wait so long in the dark in such a place.[e] Then he sensed a soft tread or tapping on the walk inside the gate,[f] heard a gentle fumbling at the rusty latch, and saw the narrow, heavy door swing inward. And in the pallid glow of the single dim street-lamp[g] he strained his eyes to see what his colleagues had brought out of that[h] sinister house which loomed so close behind. But when he looked,[i] he did not see what he had expected; for his[j] colleagues were not there at all, but only the Terrible Old Man leaning quietly on his knotted cane and smiling hideously. Mr. Czanek had never before noticed the colour[k] of that man's eyes; now[l] he saw that they were yellow.

Little things make considerable excitement in little towns, which is the reason that Kingsport people talked all that spring and summer about the three unidentifiable bodies, horribly slashed as with many cutlasses, and horribly mangled as by the tread of many cruel boot-heels, which the tide washed in. And some people even spoke of things as

---

[a] Mr. Czanek] Mr.Czanek A

[b] motor-car] motor car A, C, D

[c] ordinarily tender-hearted,] ordinary tenderh-earted, A

[d] gentle] gentley A

[e] place.] place. ¶ A

[f] gate,] gate. A

[g] street-lamp] street lamp A, C, D

[h] that] the A

[i] looked,] looked A

[j] for his] forhis A

[k] colour] color C, D

[l] now] now; A

trivial as the deserted motor-car[a] found in Ship Street, or certain especially[b] inhuman cries, probably of a stray animal or migratory bird, heard in the night by wakeful citizens.[c] But in this idle village gossip the Terrible Old Man took no interest at all. He was by nature reserved, and when one is aged and feeble one's reserve is doubly strong. Besides, so ancient a sea-captain must have witnessed scores of things much more stirring in the far-off days of his unremembered youth.

---

[a] motor-car] motor car A, C, D
[b] certain especially] certaine pecially A
[c] citizens.] citizens. ¶ A

The Tree

"Fata viam invenient."[a]

O n a verdant slope of Mount Maenalus, in Arcadia, there
stands an olive grove about the ruins of a villa. Close by is a
tomb, once beautiful with the sublimest sculptures, but now
fallen into as great decay as the house. At one end of that tomb, its
curious roots displacing the time-stained blocks of Pentelic marble,
grows an unnaturally large olive tree of oddly repellent shape; so like to
some grotesque man, or death-distorted body of a man, that the
country folk fear to pass it at night when the moon shines faintly
through the crooked boughs. Mount Maenalus is a chosen haunt of
dreaded Pan, whose queer companions are[b] many, and simple swains
believe that the tree must have some hideous kinship to these weird
Panisci; but an old bee-keeper who lives in the neighbouring[c] cottage
told me a different story.

Many years ago, when the hillside villa was new and resplendent,
there dwelt within it the two sculptors Kalos and Musides. From

Editor's Note: The T.Ms. is single-spaced (although not one of those sent to *Weird Tales* in 1923) and was prepared by HPL. It was presumably followed by the *Tryout* (October 1921), but many errors occurred there. In his copy of the issue, HPL has corrected most of the errors. It appears that this corrected copy was followed in the Arkham House editions, for those editions duplicate the errors in the *Tryout* text that HPL did not correct. The posthumous *Weird Tales* appearance (August 1938) is irrelevant to the tale's textual history.

Texts: A = T.Ms. (JHL); B = *Tryout* 7, No. 7 (October 1921): [3–10] (with corrections by HPL [copy at JHL]) (*nc* = not corrected by HPL); C = *Dagon and Other Macabre Tales* (Arkham House, 1965), 86–90. Copy-text: A.

[a] "Fata . . . invenient."] *om.* C
[b] companions are] companionsare B
[c] neighbouring] neighboring B, C

Lydia[a] to Neapolis the beauty of their work was praised, and none dared say that the one excelled the other in skill. The Hermes of[b] Kalos stood in a[c] marble shrine in Corinth, and the Pallas of Musides surmounted[d] a pillar[e] in Athens,[f] near the Parthenon. All men paid homage to Kalos and Musides, and marvelled that no shadow of artistic jealousy cooled the warmth of their brotherly friendship.

But though Kalos and Musides dwelt in unbroken harmony, their natures were not alike. Whilst Musides revelled by night amidst the urban gaieties of Tegea,[g] Kalos would remain at home; stealing away from the sight of his slaves into the cool recesses of the olive grove. There he would meditate upon the visions that filled his mind, and there devise the forms of beauty which later became immortal in breathing marble. Idle folk, indeed, said that Kalos conversed with the spirits of the[h] grove, and that his statues were but images of the fauns and dryads he met there—for he patterned his work after no living model.

So famous were Kalos and Musides, that none wondered when the Tyrant of Syracuse[i] sent to them deputies to speak of the costly statue of Tyché[j] which he had planned for his city. Of great size and cunning workmanship must the statue be, for it was to form a wonder of nations and a goal of travellers. Exalted beyond thought would be he whose work should gain acceptance, and for this honour[k] Kalos and Musides were invited to compete. Their brotherly love was well known,[l] and the crafty Tyrant surmised that each, instead of concealing his work from the other, would offer aid and advice; this charity

---

[a] Lydia] Lyda B
[b] of] and B
[c] a] *om.* B
[d] surmounted] surrounded B
[e] pillar] pillow B
[f] Athens,] Athens B, C, D
[g] Tegea,] Tagea, B
[h] the] *om.* B
[i] Syracuse] Syarcuse B
[j] Tyché] Tyche B, C
[k] honour] honor B [*nc*], C
[l] known,] known B

producing two images of unheard-of[a] beauty, the lovelier[b] of which would eclipse even the dreams of poets.

With joy the sculptors hailed the Tyrant's offer, so that in the days that followed their slaves heard the ceaseless blows of chisels. Not from each other did Kalos and Musides conceal their work, but the sight was for them alone. Saving theirs, no eyes beheld the two divine figures released by skilful blows from the rough blocks that had imprisoned them since the world began.

At night, as of yore, Musides sought the banquet halls of Tegea[c] whilst Kalos[d] wandered alone in the olive grove. But as time passed, men observed a want of gaiety[e] in the once sparkling Musides. It was strange, they said amongst themselves, that depression[f] should thus seize one with so great a chance to win art's loftiest reward. Many months passed, yet in the sour face of Musides came nothing of the sharp expectancy which the situation should arouse.

Then one day Musides spoke of the illness of Kalos,[g] after which none marvelled again at his sadness, since the sculptors' attachment[h] was known to be deep and sacred. Subsequently many went to visit Kalos, and indeed noticed the pallor of his face; but there was about him a happy serenity which made his glance more magical than the glance of Musides—who was clearly distracted with anxiety,[i] and who pushed aside all the slaves in his eagerness to feed and wait upon his friend with his own hands. Hidden behind heavy curtains stood the two unfinished figures of Tyché,[j] little touched of late by the sick man and his faithful attendant.

[a] unheard-of] unheard of B [*nc*], C
[b] lovelier] lovelieer B
[c] Tegea] Thgea B
[d] Kalos] Calos B
[e] gaiety] gaity B
[f] depression] drepression B
[g] Kalos,] Calos, B
[h] attachment] atatchment B
[i] anxiety,] anxiety B [*nc*], C
[j] Tyché,] Tyche, B [*nc*], C

As Kalos grew inexplicably weaker and weaker despite the ministrations of puzzled physicians and of his assiduous friend,[a] he desired to be carried often to the grove which he so loved. There he would ask to be left alone, as if wishing to speak with unseen things. Musides ever granted his requests, though his eyes filled with visible tears at the thought that Kalos should care more for the fauns and the dryads than for him. At last the end drew near, and Kalos discoursed of things beyond this life. Musides, weeping, promised him a sepulchre more lovely than the tomb of Mausolus; but Kalos bade him speak no more of marble glories. Only one wish now haunted the mind of the dying man; that twigs from certain olive trees in the grove be buried by his resting-place[b]—close to his head. And one night, sitting alone in the darkness of the olive grove, Kalos died.

Beautiful beyond words was the marble sepulchre which stricken Musides carved for his beloved friend. None but Kalos himself could have fashioned such bas-reliefs, wherein were displayed all the splendours of Elysium. Nor did Musides fail to bury close to Kalos' head the olive twigs from the grove.

As the first violence of Musides' grief gave place to resignation, he laboured[c] with diligence upon his figure of Tyché.[d] All honour was now his, since the Tyrant of Syracuse would have the work of none save him or Kalos. His task proved a vent for his emotion,[e] and he toiled more steadily each day, shunning the gaieties he once had relished. Meanwhile his evenings were spent beside the tomb of his friend, where a young olive tree had sprung up near the sleeper's head. So swift was the growth of this tree, and so strange was its form, that all who beheld it exclaimed in surprise; and Musides seemed at once fascinated and repelled.

Three years after the death of Kalos, Musides despatched a messenger to the Tyrant, and it was whispered in the agora at Tegea that the mighty statue was finished. By this time the tree by the tomb

---

[a] friend,] friend B

[b] resting-place] resting place B [nc], C

[c] laboured] labored B [nc], C

[d] Tyché.] Tyche. B [nc], C

[e] emotion,] emotion B [nc], C

had attained amazing proportions, exceeding all other trees of its kind, and sending out a singularly heavy branch above the apartment in which Musides laboured.[a] As many visitors came to view the prodigious tree, as to admire the art of the sculptor, so that Musides was seldom alone. But he did not mind his multitude of guests; indeed, he seemed to dread being alone now that his absorbing work was done. The bleak mountain wind, sighing through the olive grove and the tomb-tree, had an uncanny way of forming vaguely articulate sounds.

The sky was dark on the evening that the Tyrant's emissaries came to Tegea. It was definitely known that they had come to bear away the great image of Tyché[b] and bring eternal honour to Musides, so their reception by the proxenoi was of great warmth. As the night wore on,[c] a violent storm of wind broke over the crest of Maenalus, and the men from far Syracuse were glad that they rested snugly in the town. They talked of their illustrious Tyrant, and of the splendour of his capital;[d] and exulted in the glory of the statue which Musides had wrought for him. And then the men of Tegea spoke of the goodness of Musides, and of his heavy grief for his friend; and how not even the coming laurels of art could console him in the absence of Kalos, who might have worn those laurels instead. Of the tree which grew by the tomb, near the head of Kalos, they also spoke. The wind shrieked more horribly, and both the Syracusans and the Arcadians prayed to Aiolos.

In the sunshine of the morning the proxenoi led the Tyrant's messengers up the slope to the abode of the sculptor, but the night-wind[e] had done strange things. Slaves' cries ascended from a scene of desolation, and no more amidst[f] the olive grove rose the gleaming colonnades of that vast hall wherein Musides had dreamed and toiled. Lone and shaken mourned the humble courts and the lower walls, for upon[g] the sumptuous greater peristyle had fallen squarely the heavy[h]

---

[a] laboured.] labored. B [*nc*], C
[b] Tyché] Tyche B [*nc*], C
[c] on,] on B [*nc*], C
[d] capital;] capatil; B capital C
[e] night-wind] night wind A, B, C, D
[f] amidst] admidst B
[g] for upon] forupon B
[h] the heavy] theheavy B [*nc*]

1 overhanging bough of the strange new tree, reducing the stately poem in
2 marble with odd completeness to a mound of unsightly ruins.
3 Strangers and Tegeans stood aghast, looking from the wreckage to the
4 great, sinister tree whose aspect was so weirdly human and whose
5 roots reached so queerly into the sculptured sepulchre of Kalos. And
6 their fear and dismay increased when they searched the fallen
7 apartment;[a] for of the gentle Musides, and of the marvellously
8 fashioned image of Tyché,[b] no trace could be discovered. Amidst[c] such
9 stupendous ruin[d] only chaos dwelt, and the representatives of two[e]
10 cities left disappointed; Syracusans that they had no statue to bear home,
11 Tegeans that they had no artist to crown. However, the Syracusans
12 obtained after a while a very splendid statue in Athens, and the
13 Tegeans consoled themselves by erecting in the agora a marble temple
14 commemorating the gifts, virtues, and brotherly piety of Musides.

15   But the olive grove still stands, as does the tree growing out of the
16 tomb of Kalos, and the old bee-keeper told me that sometimes the
17 boughs whisper to one another in the night-wind,[f] saying over and
18 over again, "Οἶδα! Οἶδα!—*I know! I know!*"[g]

---

[a] apartment;] apartment, C
[b] Tyché,] Tyche, B [*nc*], C
[c] Amidst] Admist B
[d] ruin] ruins B
[e] two] the two B
[f] night-wind,] night wind, A, B, C
[g] "Οἶδα! Οἶδα!—*I know! I know!*"] *"Oida! Oida!—I know! I know!"* A, B; "Oida! Oida!—I know! I know!" C

The Cats of Ulthar

It is said that in Ulthar, which lies beyond the river Skai, no man may kill a cat; and this I can verily believe as I gaze upon him who sitteth purring before the fire. For the cat is cryptic, and close to strange things which men cannot see. He is the soul of antique Ægyptus,[a] and bearer of tales from forgotten cities in Meroë[b] and Ophir. He is the kin of the jungle's lords, and heir to the secrets of hoary and sinister Africa. The Sphinx is his cousin, and he speaks her language; but he is more ancient than the Sphinx, and remembers that which she hath forgotten.

In Ulthar, before ever the burgesses forbade the killing of cats, there dwelt an old cotter and his wife who delighted to trap and slay the cats of their neighbours.[c] Why they did this I know not; save that many hate the voice of the cat in the night, and take it ill that cats should run stealthily about yards and gardens at twilight. But whatever the reason, this old man and woman took pleasure in trapping and slaying every cat which came near to their hovel; and from some of the sounds heard after dark, many villagers fancied that the manner of

Editor's Note: In the absence of a manuscript, we are reliant on the published appearances of the story to establish the text. The first appearance (*Tryout*, November 1920) is surprisingly accurate for that usually error-riddled amateur journal. HPL appears to have revised the text very slightly for subsequent appearances, changing only a few proper names and a phrase or two. The first *Weird Tales* text (February 1926) embodies these revisions, and it was followed by the Arkham House editions. Neither the second *Weird Tales* text (February 1933) nor R. H. Barlow's separate publication (Cassia, FL: Dragon-Fly Press, 1935), derived from the first *Weird Tales* appearance, is relevant to the tale's textual history.

Texts: A = *Tryout* 6, No. 11 (November 1920): [3–9]; B = *Weird Tales* 7, No. 2 (February 1926): 252–54; C = *Dagon and Other Macabre Tales* (Arkham House, 1965), 56–59. Copy-text: B (with some readings from A).

[a] Ægyptus,] Aegyptus, A, C
[b] Meroë] Meroe A, C
[c] neighbours.] neighbors. B, C

slaying was exceedingly peculiar. But the villagers did not discuss such things with the old man and his wife; because of the habitual expression on the withered faces of the two, and because their cottage was so small and so darkly hidden under spreading oaks at the back of a neglected yard. In truth, much as the owners of cats hated these odd folk, they feared them more; and instead of berating them as brutal assassins, merely took care that no cherished pet or mouser should stray toward the remote hovel under the dark trees. When through some unavoidable oversight a cat was missed, and sounds heard after dark, the loser would lament impotently;[a] or console himself by thanking Fate that it was not one of his children who had thus vanished. For the people of Ulthar were simple, and knew not whence it is[b] all cats first came.

One day a caravan of strange wanderers from the South entered the narrow cobbled streets of Ulthar. Dark wanderers they were, and unlike the other roving folk who passed through the village twice every year. In the market-place they told fortunes for silver, and bought gay beads from the merchants. What was the land of these wanderers none could tell; but it was seen that they were given to strange prayers, and that they had painted on the sides of their wagons strange figures with human bodies and the heads of cats, hawks, rams,[c] and lions. And the leader of the caravan wore a head-dress[d] with two horns and a curious disc[e] betwixt the horns.

There was in this singular caravan a little boy with no father or mother, but only a tiny black kitten to cherish. The plague had not been kind to him, yet had left him this small furry thing to mitigate his sorrow; and when one is very young, one can find great relief in the lively antics of a black kitten. So the boy whom the dark people called Menes smiled more often than he wept as he sate[f] playing with his graceful kitten on the steps of an oddly painted wagon.

On the third morning of the wanderers' stay in Ulthar, Menes could not find his kitten; and as he sobbed aloud in the market-place

<hr />

[a] impotently;] impotently, A
[b] is] is that B
[c] rams,] rams A, C
[d] head-dress] headdress C
[e] disc] disk B, C
[f] sate] sat C

certain villagers told him of the old man and his wife, and of sounds heard in the night. And when he heard these things his sobbing gave place to meditation, and finally to prayer. He stretched out his arms toward the sun and prayed in a tongue no villager could understand; though indeed the villagers did not try very hard to understand, since their attention was mostly taken up by the sky and the odd shapes the clouds were assuming. It was very peculiar, but as the little boy uttered his petition there seemed to form overhead the shadowy, nebulous figures of exotic things; of hybrid creatures crowned with horn-flanked discs.[a] Nature is full of such illusions to impress the imaginative.

That night the wanderers left Ulthar, and were never seen again. And the householders were troubled when they noticed that in all the village there was not a cat to be found. From each hearth the familiar cat had vanished; cats large and small, black, grey,[b] striped, yellow,[c] and white.[d] Old Kranon, the burgomaster, swore that the dark folk had taken the cats away in revenge for the killing of Menes' kitten; and cursed the caravan and the little boy. But Nith,[e] the lean notary, declared that the old cotter and his wife were more likely persons to suspect; for their hatred of cats was notorious and increasingly bold. Still, no one durst complain to the sinister couple; even when little Atal, the innkeeper's son, vowed that he had at twilight seen all the cats of Ulthar in that accursed yard under the trees,[f] pacing very slowly and solemnly in a circle around the cottage, two abreast, as if in performance of some unheard-of rite of beasts. The villagers did not know how much to believe from so small a boy; and though they feared that the evil pair had charmed the cats to their death, they preferred not to chide the old cotter till they met him outside his dark and repellent yard.

So Ulthar went to sleep in vain anger; and when the people awaked[g] at dawn—behold! every cat was back at his accustomed

---

[a] discs.] disks. B, C
[b] grey,] gray, A, B
[c] yellow,] yellow A, B, C
[d] white.] white, A
[e] Nith,] Nath, A
[f] trees,] trees A
[g] awaked] awakened C

hearth! Large and small, black, grey,[a] striped, yellow,[b] and white, none was missing. Very sleek and fat did the cats appear, and sonorous with purring content. The citizens talked with one another of the affair, and marvelled[c] not a little. Old Kranon again insisted that it was the dark folk who had taken them, since cats did not return alive from the cottage of the ancient man and his wife. But all agreed on one thing;[d] that the refusal of all the cats to eat their portions of meat or drink their saucers of milk was exceedingly curious. And for two whole days the sleek, lazy cats of Ulthar would touch no food, but only doze by the fire or in the sun.

It was fully a week before the villagers noticed that no lights were appearing at dusk in the windows of the cottage under the trees. Then the lean Nith[e] remarked that no one had seen the old man or his wife since the night the cats were away. In another week the burgomaster decided to overcome his fears and call at the strangely silent dwelling as a matter of duty, though in doing so[f] he was careful to take with him Shang the blacksmith and Thul the cutter of stone as witnesses. And when they had broken down the frail door they found only this: two cleanly picked human[g] skeletons on the earthen floor, and a number of singular beetles crawling in the shadowy corners.

There was subsequently much talk among[h] the burgesses of Ulthar. Zath,[i] the coroner, disputed at length with Nith, the lean notary;[j] and Kranon and Shang and Thul were overwhelmed with questions. Even little Atal, the innkeeper's son, was closely questioned and given a sweetmeat as reward. They talked of the old cotter and his wife, of the caravan of dark wanderers, of small Menes and his black kitten, of the prayer of Menes and of the sky during that prayer, of the

[a] grey,] gray, B
[b] yellow,] yellow A, B, C
[c] marvelled] marveled B, C
[d] thing;] thing: C
[e] Nith] Nath A
[f] doing so] so doing C
[g] human] om. A
[h] among] amongst A, B
[i] Zath,] Zith, A
[j] Nith, . . . notary;] Nath, . . . notary, A

doings of the cats on the night the caravan left, and of what was later found in the cottage under the dark trees in the repellent yard.

And in the end the burgesses passed that remarkable law which is told of by traders in Hatheg and discussed by travellers[a] in Nir; namely, that in Ulthar no man may kill a cat.

---

[a] travellers] travelers B, C

The Temple

(Manuscript found on the coast of Yucatan.)[a]

O n August 20, 1917, I, Karl Heinrich, Graf von Altberg-Ehrenstein, Lieutenant-Commander in the Imperial German Navy and in charge of the submarine U-29, deposit this bottle and record in the Atlantic Ocean at a point to me unknown but probably about N. Latitude 20°, W. Longitude 35°,[b] where my ship lies disabled on the ocean floor. I do so because of my desire to set certain unusual facts before the public; a thing I shall not in all probability survive to accomplish in person, since the circumstances surrounding me are as menacing as they are extraordinary, and involve not only the hopeless crippling of the U-29, but the impairment of my iron German will in a manner most disastrous.

On the afternoon of June 18, as reported by wireless to the U-61, bound for Kiel, we torpedoed the British freighter *Victory*, New York to Liverpool, in N. Latitude 45° 16´, W. Longitude 28° 34´;[c] permitting the crew to leave in boats in order to obtain a good cinema view for the admiralty records. The ship sank quite picturesquely, bow first, the stern rising high out of the water whilst the hull shot down perpendicularly to the bottom of the sea. Our camera missed nothing,

Editor's Note: In the absence of a manuscript, we are reliant on the first publication, *Weird Tales* (September 1925). This text appears relatively sound and does not seem to bear some of the alterations (especially in paragraphing) that *Weird Tales* customarily made. A second *Weird Tales* appearance (February 1936), is not relevant to the textual history of the tale, as the Arkham House editions follow the first appearance.

Texts: A = *Weird Tales* 6, No. 3 (September 1925): 329–36, 429–31; B = *Dagon and Other Macabre Tales* (Arkham House, 1965), 73–85. Copy-text: A.

[a] (Manuscript . . . Yucatan.)] [*Manuscript . . . Yucatan.*] A
[b] 20°, . . . 35°,] 20 degrees, . . . 35 degrees, A, B
[c] 45° 16´, . . . 28° 34´;] 45 degrees 16 minutes, . . . 28 degrees 34 minutes; A, B

and I regret that so fine a reel of film should never reach Berlin. After that we sank the lifeboats with our guns and submerged.

When we rose to the surface about sunset a seaman's body was found on the deck, hands gripping the railing in curious fashion. The poor fellow was young, rather dark, and very handsome; probably an Italian or Greek, and undoubtedly of the *Victory's* crew. He had evidently sought refuge on the very ship which had been forced to destroy his own—one more victim of the unjust war of aggression which the English pig-dogs are waging upon the Fatherland. Our men searched him for souvenirs, and found in his coat pocket a very odd bit of ivory carved to represent a youth's head crowned with laurel. My fellow-officer, Lieut.[a] Klenze, believed that the thing was of great age and artistic value, so took it from the men for himself. How it had ever come into the possession of a common sailor,[b] neither he nor I could imagine.

As the dead man was thrown overboard there occurred two incidents which created much disturbance amongst the crew. The fellow's eyes had been closed; but in the dragging of his body to the rail they were jarred open, and many seemed to entertain a queer delusion that they gazed steadily and mockingly at Schmidt and Zimmer, who were bent over the corpse. The Boatswain Müller, an elderly man who would have known better had he not been a superstitious Alsatian swine, became so excited by this impression that he watched the body in the water; and swore that after it sank a little it drew its limbs into a swimming position and sped away to the south under the waves. Klenze and I did not like these displays of peasant ignorance, and severely reprimanded the men, particularly Müller.

The next day a very troublesome situation was created by the indisposition of some of the crew. They were evidently suffering from the nervous strain of our long voyage, and had had bad dreams. Several seemed quite dazed and stupid; and after satisfying myself that they were not feigning their weakness, I excused them from their duties. The sea was rather rough, so we descended to a depth where the waves were less troublesome. Here we were comparatively calm, despite a somewhat puzzling southward current which we could not

[a] Lieut.] Lieutenant A, B
[b] sailor,] sailor A, B

identify from our oceanographic charts. The moans of the sick men were decidedly annoying; but since they did not appear to demoralise[a] the rest of the crew, we did not resort to extreme measures. It was our plan to remain where we were and intercept the liner *Dacia,* mentioned in information from agents in New York.

In the early evening we rose to the surface, and found the sea less heavy. The smoke of a battleship was on the northern horizon, but our distance and ability to submerge made us safe. What worried us more was the talk of Boatswain Müller, which grew wilder as night came on. He was in a detestably childish state, and babbled of some illusion of dead bodies drifting past the undersea portholes; bodies which looked at him intensely, and which he recognised[b] in spite of bloating as having seen dying during some of our victorious German exploits. And he said that the young man we had found and tossed overboard was their leader. This was very gruesome and abnormal, so we confined Müller in irons and had him soundly whipped. The men were not pleased at his punishment, but discipline was necessary. We also denied the request of a delegation headed by Seaman Zimmer, that the curious carved ivory head be cast into the sea.

On June 20, Seamen[c] Bohm and Schmidt, who had been ill the day before, became violently insane. I regretted that no physician was included in our complement of officers, since German lives are precious; but the constant ravings of the two concerning a terrible curse were most subversive of discipline, so drastic steps were taken. The crew accepted the event in a sullen fashion, but it seemed to quiet Müller; who thereafter gave us no trouble. In the evening we released him, and he went about his duties silently.

In the week that followed we were all very nervous, watching for the *Dacia.* The tension was aggravated by the disappearance of Müller and Zimmer, who undoubtedly committed suicide as a result of the fears which had seemed to harass them, though they were not observed in the act of jumping overboard. I was rather glad to be rid of Müller, for

---

[a] demoralise] demoralize A, B
[b] recognised] recognized A, B
[c] Seamen] Seaman B

even his silence had unfavourably[a] affected the crew. Everyone seemed inclined to be silent now, as though holding a secret fear. Many were ill, but none made a disturbance. Lieut.[b] Klenze chafed under the strain, and was annoyed by the merest trifles—such as the school of dolphins which gathered about the U-29 in increasing numbers, and the growing intensity of that southward current which was not on our chart.

It at length became apparent that we had missed the *Dacia* altogether. Such failures are not uncommon, and we were more pleased than disappointed; since our return to Wilhelmshaven was now in order. At noon June 28 we turned northeastward, and despite some rather comical entanglements with the unusual masses of dolphins were soon under way.

The explosion in the engine room at 2 p.m.[c] was wholly a surprise.[d] No defect in the machinery or carelessness in the men had been noticed, yet without warning the ship was racked from end to end with a colossal shock. Lieut.[e] Klenze hurried to the engine room, finding the fuel-tank and most of the mechanism shattered, and Engineers Raabe and Schneider instantly killed. Our situation had suddenly become grave indeed; for though the chemical air regenerators were intact, and though we could use the devices for raising and submerging the ship and opening the hatches as long as compressed air and storage batteries might hold out, we were powerless to propel or guide the submarine. To seek rescue in the lifeboats[f] would be to deliver ourselves into the hands of enemies unreasonably embittered against our great German nation, and our wireless had failed ever since the *Victory* affair to put us in touch with a fellow U-boat of the Imperial Navy.

From the hour of the accident till July 2 we drifted constantly to the south, almost without plans and encountering no vessel. Dolphins still encircled the U-29, a somewhat remarkable circumstance considering the distance we had covered. On the morning of July 2 we

---

[a] unfavourably] unfavorably A, B

[b] Lieut.] Lieutenant A, B

[c] p.m.] P. M. A; A.M. B

[d] surprise.] surprize. A

[e] Lieut.] Lieutenant A, B

[f] lifeboats] life-/boats A; life-boats B

sighted a warship[a] flying American colours,[b] and the men became very restless in their desire to surrender. Finally Lieut.[c] Klenze had to shoot a seaman named Traube, who urged this un-German act with especial violence. This quieted the crew for the time, and we submerged unseen.

The next afternoon a dense flock of sea-birds appeared from the south, and the ocean began to heave ominously. Closing our hatches, we awaited developments until we realised[d] that we must either submerge or be swamped in the mounting waves. Our air pressure and electricity were diminishing, and we wished to avoid all unnecessary use of our slender mechanical resources; but in this case there was no choice. We did not descend far, and when after several hours the sea was calmer, we decided to return to the surface. Here, however, a new trouble developed; for the ship failed to respond to our direction in spite of all that the mechanics could do. As the men grew more frightened at this undersea imprisonment, some of them began to mutter again about Lieut.[e] Klenze's ivory image, but the sight of an automatic pistol calmed them. We kept the poor devils as busy as we could, tinkering at the machinery even when we knew it was useless.

Klenze and I usually slept at different times; and it was during my sleep, about 5 a.m.,[f] July 4, that the general mutiny broke loose. The six remaining pigs of seamen, suspecting that we were lost, had suddenly burst into a mad fury at our refusal to surrender to the Yankee battleship two days before; and were in a delirium of cursing and destruction. They roared like the animals they were, and broke instruments and furniture indiscriminately; screaming about such nonsense as the curse of the ivory image and the dark dead youth who looked at them and swam away. Lieut.[g] Klenze seemed paralysed[h] and inefficient, as one might expect of a soft, womanish Rhinelander. I shot all six men, for it was necessary, and made sure that none remained alive.

[a] warship] war-/ship A, B
[b] colours,] colors, A, B
[c] Lieut.] Lieutenant A, B
[d] realised] realized A, B
[e] Lieut.] Lieutenant A, B
[f] a.m.,] A. M., A; A.M., B
[g] Lieut.] Lieutenant A, B
[h] paralysed] paralyzed A, B

We expelled the bodies through the double hatches and were alone in the U-29. Klenze seemed very nervous, and drank heavily. It was decided that we remain alive as long as possible, using the large stock of provisions and chemical supply of oxygen, none of which had suffered from the crazy antics of those swine-hound seamen. Our compasses, depth gauges,[a] and other delicate instruments were ruined; so that henceforth our only reckoning would be guesswork,[b] based on our watches, the calendar, and our apparent drift as judged by any objects we might spy through the portholes or from the conning tower. Fortunately we had storage batteries still capable of long use, both for interior lighting and for the searchlight.[c] We often cast a beam around the ship, but saw only dolphins, swimming parallel to our own drifting course. I was scientifically interested in those dolphins; for though the ordinary *Delphinus delphis* is a cetacean mammal, unable to subsist without air, I watched one of the swimmers closely for two hours, and did not see him alter his submerged condition.

With the passage of time Klenze and I decided that we were still drifting south, meanwhile sinking deeper and deeper. We noted the marine fauna and flora, and read much on the subject in the books I had carried with me for spare moments. I could not help observing, however, the inferior scientific knowledge of my companion. His mind was not Prussian, but given to imaginings and speculations which have no value. The fact of our coming death affected him curiously, and he would frequently pray in remorse over the men, women, and children we had sent to the bottom; forgetting that all things are noble which serve the German state. After a time he became noticeably unbalanced, gazing for hours at his ivory image and weaving fanciful stories of the lost and forgotten things under the sea. Sometimes, as a psychological experiment, I would lead him on in these[d] wanderings, and listen to his endless poetical quotations and tales of sunken ships. I was very sorry for him, for I dislike to see a German suffer; but he was not a good man to die with. For myself I was proud, knowing how the Fatherland

---

[a] gauges,] gages, A
[b] guesswork,] guess-work, A; guess work, B
[c] searchlight.] search-/light. A; search-light. B
[d] these] the B

would revere my memory and how my sons would be taught to be men like me.

On August 9, we espied the ocean floor, and sent a powerful beam from the searchlight over it. It was a vast undulating plain, mostly covered with seaweed, and strown with the shells of small molluscs.[a] Here and there were slimy objects of puzzling contour, draped with weeds and encrusted with barnacles, which Klenze declared must be ancient ships lying in their graves. He was puzzled by one thing, a peak of solid matter, protruding above the ocean bed nearly four feet at its apex; about two feet thick, with flat sides and smooth upper surfaces which met at a very obtuse angle. I called the peak a bit of outcropping rock, but Klenze thought he saw carvings on it. After a while he began to shudder, and turned away from the scene as if frightened; yet could give no explanation save that he was overcome with the vastness, darkness, remoteness, antiquity, and mystery of the oceanic abysses. His mind was tired, but I am always a German, and was quick to notice two things: that the U-29 was standing the deep-sea pressure splendidly, and that the peculiar dolphins were still about us, even at a depth where the existence of high organisms is considered impossible by most naturalists. That I had previously overestimated our depth, I was sure; but none the less we must still be deep enough to make these phenomena remarkable. Our southward speed, as gauged[b] by the ocean floor, was about as I had estimated from the organisms passed at higher levels.

It was at 3:15 p.m.,[c] August 12, that poor Klenze went wholly mad. He had been in the conning tower using the searchlight when I saw him bound into the library compartment where I sat reading, and his face at once betrayed him. I will repeat here what he said, underlining the words he emphasised:[d] *"He* is calling! *He*[e] is calling! I hear him! We must go!"* As he spoke he took his ivory image from the table, pocketed it, and seized my arm in an effort to drag me up the companionway to the deck. In a moment I understood that he meant

[a] molluscs.] mollusks. A, B
[b] gauged] gaged A
[c] p.m.,] P. M., A; P.M., B
[d] emphasised:] emphasized: A, B
[e] *He . . . He*] *He . . . He* B

to open the hatch and plunge with me into the water outside, a vagary of suicidal and homicidal mania for which I was scarcely prepared. As I hung back and attempted to soothe him he grew more violent, saying: "Come now[a]—do not wait until later; it is better to repent and be forgiven than to[b] defy and be condemned." Then I tried the opposite of the soothing plan, and told him he was mad—pitifully demented. But he was unmoved, and cried: "If I am mad, it is mercy! May the gods pity the man who in his callousness can remain sane to the hideous end! Come and be mad whilst *he* still calls with mercy!"

This outburst seemed to relieve a pressure in his brain; for as he finished he grew much milder, asking me to let him depart alone if I would not accompany him. My course at once became clear. He was a German, but only a Rhinelander and a commoner; and he was now a potentially dangerous madman. By complying with his suicidal request I could immediately free myself from one who was no longer a companion but a menace. I asked him to give me the ivory image before he went, but this request brought from him[c] such uncanny laughter that I did not repeat it. Then I asked him if he wished to leave any keepsake or lock of hair for his family in Germany in case I should be rescued, but again he gave me that strange laugh. So as he climbed the ladder I went to the levers,[d] and allowing proper time-intervals operated the machinery which sent him to his death. After I saw that he was no longer in the boat I threw the searchlight around the water in an effort to obtain a last glimpse of him; since I wished to ascertain whether the water-pressure would flatten him as it theoretically should, or whether the body would be unaffected, like those extraordinary dolphins. I did not, however, succeed in finding my late companion, for the dolphins were massed thickly and obscuringly about the conning tower.

That evening I regretted that I had not taken the ivory image surreptitiously from poor Klenze's pocket as he left, for the memory of it fascinated me. I could not forget the youthful, beautiful head with its leafy crown, though I am not by nature an artist. I was also sorry

[a] now] *now* B
[b] to] do B
[c] him] his B
[d] levers,] levers A, B

that I had no one with whom to converse. Klenze, though not my mental equal, was much better than no one. I did not sleep well that night, and wondered exactly when the end would come. Surely, I had little enough chance of rescue.

The next day I ascended to the conning tower and commenced the customary searchlight explorations. Northward the view was much the same as it had been all the four days since we had sighted the bottom, but I perceived that the drifting of the U-29 was less rapid. As I swung the beam around to the south, I noticed that the ocean floor ahead fell away in a marked declivity, and bore curiously regular blocks of stone in certain places, disposed as if in accordance with definite patterns. The boat did not at once descend to match the greater ocean depth, so I was soon forced to adjust the searchlight to cast a sharply downward beam. Owing to the abruptness of the change a wire was disconnected, which necessitated a delay of many minutes for repairs; but at length the light streamed on again, flooding the marine valley below me.

I am not given to emotion of any kind, but my amazement was very great when I saw what lay revealed in that electrical glow. And yet as one reared in the best *Kultur* of Prussia[a] I should not have been amazed, for geology and tradition alike tell us of great transpositions in oceanic and continental areas. What I saw was an extended and elaborate array of ruined edifices; all of magnificent though unclassified architecture, and in various stages of preservation. Most appeared to be of marble, gleaming whitely in the rays of the searchlight, and the general plan was of a large city at the bottom of a narrow valley, with numerous isolated temples and villas on the steep slopes above. Roofs were fallen and columns were broken, but there still remained an air of immemorially ancient splendour[b] which nothing could efface.

Confronted at last with the Atlantis I had formerly deemed largely a myth, I was the most eager of explorers. At the bottom of that valley a river once had flowed; for as I examined the scene more closely I beheld the remains of stone and marble bridges and sea-walls, and terraces and embankments once verdant and beautiful. In my enthusiasm I became nearly as idiotic and sentimental as poor Klenze,

[a] *Kultur* of Prussia] *kultur* of Prussia A; *Kultur* of Prussia, B
[b] splendour] splendor A, B

and was very tardy in noticing that the southward current had ceased at last, allowing the U-29 to settle slowly down upon the sunken city as an aëroplane[a] settles upon a town of the upper earth. I was slow, too, in realising[b] that the school of unusual dolphins had vanished.

In about two hours the boat rested in a paved plaza close to the rocky wall of the valley. On one side I could view the entire city as it sloped from the plaza down to the old river-bank;[c] on the other side, in startling proximity, I was confronted by the richly ornate and perfectly preserved facade[d] of a great building, evidently a temple, hollowed from the solid rock. Of the original workmanship of this titanic thing I can only make conjectures. The facade,[e] of immense magnitude, apparently covers a continuous hollow recess; for its windows are many and widely distributed. In the centre[f] yawns a great open door, reached by an impressive flight of steps, and surrounded by exquisite carvings like the figures of Bacchanals in relief. Foremost of all are the great columns and frieze, both decorated with sculptures of inexpressible beauty; obviously portraying idealised[g] pastoral scenes and processions of priests and priestesses bearing strange ceremonial devices in adoration of a radiant god. The art is of the most phenomenal perfection, largely Hellenic in idea, yet strangely individual. It imparts an impression of terrible antiquity, as though it were the remotest rather than the immediate ancestor of Greek art. Nor can I doubt that every detail of this massive product was fashioned from the virgin hillside rock of our planet. It is palpably a part of the valley wall, though how the vast interior was ever excavated I cannot imagine. Perhaps a cavern or series of caverns furnished the nucleus. Neither age nor submersion has corroded the pristine grandeur of this awful fane—for fane indeed it must be—and today after thousands of years it rests untarnished and inviolate in the endless night and silence of an ocean chasm.

I cannot reckon the number of hours I spent in gazing at the

[a] aëroplane] airplane A, B
[b] realising] realizing A, B
[c] river-bank;] river-/bank; A
[d] façade] façade A, B
[e] façade,] façade, A, B
[f] centre] center A, B
[g] idealised] idealized A, B

sunken city with its buildings, arches, statues, and bridges, and the colossal temple with its beauty and mystery. Though I knew that death was near, my curiosity was consuming; and I threw the searchlight's beam about in eager quest. The shaft of light permitted me to learn many details, but refused to shew[a] anything within the gaping door of the rock-hewn temple; and after a time I turned off the current, conscious of the need of conserving power. The rays were now perceptibly dimmer than they had been during the weeks of drifting. And as if sharpened by the coming deprivation of light, my desire to explore the watery secrets grew. I, a German, should be the first to tread those aeon-forgotten[b] ways!

I produced and examined a deep-sea diving suit of jointed metal, and experimented with the portable light and air regenerator. Though I should have trouble in managing the double hatches alone, I believed I could overcome all obstacles with my scientific skill and actually walk about the dead city in person.

On August 16 I effected an exit from the U-29, and laboriously made my way through the ruined and mud-choked streets to the ancient river. I found no skeletons or other human remains, but gleaned a wealth of archaeological[c] lore from sculptures and coins. Of this I cannot now speak save to utter my awe at a culture in the full noon of glory when cave-dwellers roamed Europe and the Nile flowed unwatched to the sea. Others, guided by this manuscript if it shall ever be found, must unfold the mysteries at which I can only hint. I returned to the boat as my electric batteries grew feeble, resolved to explore the rock temple on the following day.

On the 17th, as my impulse to search out the mystery of the temple waxed still more insistent, a great disappointment befell me; for I found that the materials needed to replenish the portable light had perished in the mutiny of those pigs in July. My rage was unbounded, yet my German sense forbade me to venture unprepared into an utterly black interior which might prove the lair of some indescribable marine monster or a labyrinth of passages from whose windings I

[a] shew] show A, B
[b] aeon-forgotten] eon-forgotten A, B
[c] archaeological] archeological A, B

could never extricate myself. All I could do was to turn on the waning searchlight of the U-29, and with its aid walk up the temple steps and study the exterior carvings. The shaft of light entered the door at an upward angle, and I peered in to see if I could glimpse anything, but all in vain. Not even the roof was visible; and though I took a step or two inside after testing the floor with[a] a staff, I dared not go farther. Moreover, for the first time in my life I experienced the emotion of dread. I began to realise[b] how some of poor Klenze's moods had arisen, for as the temple drew me more and more, I feared its aqueous abysses with a blind and mounting terror. Returning to the submarine, I turned off the lights and sat thinking in the dark. Electricity must now be saved for emergencies.

Saturday the 18th I spent in total darkness, tormented by thoughts and memories that threatened to overcome my German will. Klenze had gone mad and perished before reaching this sinister remnant of a past unwholesomely remote, and had advised me to go with him. Was, indeed, Fate preserving my reason only to draw me irresistibly to an end more horrible and unthinkable than any man has dreamed of? Clearly, my nerves were sorely taxed, and I must cast off these impressions of weaker men.

I could not sleep Saturday night, and turned on the lights regardless of the future. It was annoying that the electricity should not last out the air and provisions. I revived my thoughts of euthanasia, and examined my automatic pistol. Toward morning I must have dropped asleep with the lights on, for I awoke in darkness yesterday afternoon to find the batteries dead. I struck several matches in succession, and desperately regretted the improvidence which had caused us long ago to use up the few candles we carried.

After the fading of the last match I dared to waste, I sat very quietly without a light. As I considered the inevitable end my mind ran over preceding events, and developed a hitherto dormant impression which would have caused a weaker and more superstitious man to shudder. *The head of the radiant god in the sculptures on the rock temple is the*

[a] with] was B
[b] realise] realize A, B

same as that carven bit of ivory which the dead sailor brought from the sea and which poor Klenze carried back into the sea.

I was a little dazed by this coincidence, but did not become terrified. It is only the inferior thinker who hastens to explain the singular and the complex by the primitive short cut of supernaturalism. The coincidence was strange, but I was too sound a reasoner to connect circumstances which admit of no logical connexion,[a] or to associate in any uncanny fashion the disastrous events which had led from the *Victory* affair to my present plight. Feeling the need of more rest, I took a sedative and secured some more sleep. My nervous condition was reflected in my dreams, for I seemed to hear the cries of drowning persons, and to see dead faces pressing against the portholes of the boat. And among the dead faces was the living, mocking face of the youth with the ivory image.

I must be careful how I record my awaking[b] today, for I am unstrung, and much hallucination is necessarily mixed with fact. Psychologically my case is most interesting, and I regret that it cannot be observed scientifically by a competent German authority. Upon opening my eyes my first sensation was an overmastering desire to visit the rock temple; a desire which grew every instant, yet which I automatically sought to resist through some emotion of fear which operated in the reverse direction. Next there came to me the impression of *light* amidst the darkness of dead batteries, and I seemed to see a sort of phosphorescent glow in the water through the porthole which opened toward the temple. This aroused my curiosity, for I knew of no deep-sea organism capable of emitting such luminosity. But before I could investigate there came a third impression which because of its irrationality caused me to doubt the objectivity of anything my senses might record. It was an aural delusion; a sensation of rhythmic, melodic sound as of some wild yet beautiful chant or choral hymn, coming from the outside through the absolutely sound-proof hull of the U-29. Convinced of my psychological and nervous abnormality, I lighted some matches and poured a stiff dose of sodium bromide solution, which seemed to calm me to the extent of dispelling

[a] connexion,] connection, A, B
[b] awaking] awakening A, B

the illusion of sound. But the phosphorescence remained, and I had difficulty in repressing a childish impulse to go to the porthole and seek its source. It was horribly realistic, and I could soon distinguish by its aid the familiar objects around me, as well as the empty sodium bromide glass of which I had had no former visual impression in its present location. The last circumstance made me ponder, and I crossed the room and touched the glass. It was indeed in the place where I had seemed to see it. Now I knew that the light was either real or part of an hallucination so fixed and consistent that I could not hope to dispel it, so abandoning all resistance I ascended to the conning tower to look for the luminous agency. Might it not actually be another U-boat, offering possibilities of rescue?

It is well that the reader accept nothing which follows as objective truth, for since the events transcend natural law, they are necessarily the subjective and unreal creations of my overtaxed mind. When I attained the conning tower I found the sea in general far less luminous than I had expected. There was no animal or vegetable phosphorescence about, and the city that sloped down to the river was invisible in blackness. What I did see was not spectacular, not grotesque or terrifying, yet it removed my last vestige of trust in my consciousness. *For the door and windows of the undersea temple hewn from the rocky hill were vividly aglow with a flickering radiance, as from a mighty altar-flame far within.*

Later incidents are chaotic. As I stared at the uncannily lighted door and windows, I became subject to the most extravagant visions—visions so extravagant that I cannot even relate them. I fancied that I discerned objects in the temple; objects both stationary and moving; and seemed to hear again the unreal chant that had floated to me when first I awaked. And over all rose thoughts and fears which centred[a] in the youth from the sea and the ivory image whose carving was duplicated on the frieze and columns of the temple before me. I thought of poor Klenze, and wondered where his body rested with the image he had carried back into the sea. He had warned me of something, and I had not heeded—but he was a soft-headed Rhinelander who went mad at troubles a Prussian could bear with ease.

[a] centred] centered A, B

The rest is very simple. My impulse to visit and enter the temple has now become an inexplicable and imperious command which ultimately cannot be denied. My own German will no longer controls my acts, and volition is henceforward possible only in minor matters. Such madness it was which drove Klenze to his death, bareheaded and unprotected in the ocean; but I am a Prussian and[a] man of sense, and will use to the last what little will I have. When first I saw that I must go, I prepared my diving suit, helmet,[b] and air regenerator for instant donning; and immediately commenced to write this hurried chronicle in the hope that it may some day reach the world. I shall seal the manuscript in a bottle and entrust it to the sea as I leave the U-29 for ever.

I have no fear, not even from the prophecies of the madman Klenze. What I have seen cannot be true, and I know that this madness of my own will at most lead only to suffocation when my air is gone. The light in the temple is a sheer delusion, and I shall die calmly, like a German, in the black and forgotten depths. This daemoniac[c] laughter which I hear as I write comes only from my own weakening brain. So I will carefully don my diving[d] suit and walk boldly up the steps into that primal shrine;[e] that silent secret of unfathomed waters and uncounted years.

[a] and] and a B
[b] helmet,] helmet B
[c] daemoniac] demoniac A, B
[d] diving] om. B
[e] shrine;] shrine, B

Facts concerning
the Late Arthur Jermyn and His Family

L ife is a hideous thing, and from the background behind what we know of it peer daemoniacal[a] hints of truth which make it sometimes a thousandfold[b] more hideous. Science, already oppressive with its shocking revelations, will perhaps[c] be the ultimate exterminator of our human species—if separate species we be—for its reserve of unguessed horrors could never be borne by mortal brains if loosed upon the world.[d] If we knew what we are, we should do as Sir Arthur Jermyn did; and Arthur Jermyn soaked himself in oil and set fire to his clothing one night. No one placed the charred fragments in an urn or set a memorial to him who had been; for certain papers and

Editor's Note: The tale was first published in the *Wolverine* (March and June 1921). At some subsequent date, HPL prepared a T.Ms. embodying a few revisions from that text. This T.Ms. is single-spaced, and HPL must have prepared a double-spaced typescript for *Weird Tales*, where the story appeared in the April 1924 issue; but that appearance does not appear to contain any revisions by HPL from the existing T.Ms. In a letter to Farnsworth Wright (21 May 1934; *Lovecraft Annual* No. 8 [2014]: 40), HPL asked to see the proofs of the *Weird Tales* reprint (May 1935), and there appears to be internal evidence that he made some slight revisions, although he failed to correct (or *Weird Tales* refused to correct) some existing errors (chiefly in paragraphing) in the first appearance; and the reprint introduced a number of further errors. The Arkham House editions followed the T.Ms., hence are fairly accurate aside from the title.

Texts: A = *Wolverine* No. 9 (March 1921): 3–11; No. 10 (June 1921): 6–11; B = T.Ms. (JHL); C = *Weird Tales* 3, No. 4 (April 1924): 15–18 (as "The White Ape"); D = *Weird Tales* 25, No. 5 (May 1935): 642–48 (as "Arthur Jermyn"); E = *Dagon and Other Macabre Tales* (Arkham House, 1965), 47–55 (as "Arthur Jermyn"). Copy-text: B (with some readings from D).

[a] daemoniacal] demoniacal A, B, C, D
[b] thousandfold] thousand fold A
[c] revelations, . . . perhaps] revalations, . . . perchance A
[d] world.] world. ¶ C, D

a certain boxed *object* [a] were found,[b] which made men wish to forget. Some who knew him do not admit that he ever existed.

Arthur Jermyn went out on the moor and burned himself after seeing the boxed *object* which had come from Africa. It was this *object*,[c] and not his peculiar personal appearance, which made him end his life.[d] Many would have disliked to live if possessed of the peculiar features of Arthur Jermyn, but he had been a poet and scholar and had not minded. Learning was in his blood, for his great-grandfather, Sir Robert Jermyn, Bart.,[e] had been an anthropologist of note, whilst his great-great-great-grandfather, Sir Wade Jermyn, was one of the earliest explorers of the Congo region, and had written eruditely of its tribes, animals, and supposed antiquities. Indeed, old Sir Wade had possessed an intellectual zeal amounting almost to a mania; his bizarre conjectures on a prehistoric white Congolese civilisation[f] earning him much ridicule when his book, "Observations on the Several Parts of Africa",[g] was published. In 1765[h] this fearless explorer had been placed in a madhouse at Huntingdon.

Madness was in all the Jermyns, and people were glad there were not many of them. The line put forth no branches, and Arthur was the last of it. If he had not been, one cannot[i] say what he would have done when the *object* came.[j] The Jermyns never seemed to look quite right— something was amiss, though Arthur was the worst, and the old family portraits in Jermyn House shewed[k] fine faces enough before Sir Wade's time. Certainly, the madness began with Sir Wade, whose wild stories of Africa were at once the delight and terror of his few friends. It

[a] *object*] object A
[b] found,] found E
[c] *object*,] object C
[d] life.] life. ¶ C, D
[e] Bart.,] Bt., A, B, C, E
[f] civilisation] civilization A, C, D
[g] "Observations . . . Africa",] "Observations . . . Africa," C; *Observations . . . Africa,* D; *Observation . . . Africa,* E
[h] 1765] 1765, C
[i] cannot] can not A, B, C, D, E
[j] came.] came. ¶ C, D
[k] shewed] showed A, B, C, D, E

shewed[a] in his collection of trophies and specimens, which were not such as a normal man would accumulate and preserve, and appeared strikingly in the Oriental seclusion in which he kept his wife. The latter, he had said, was the daughter of a Portuguese[b] trader whom he had met in Africa; and[c] did not like English ways. She, with an infant son born in Africa, had accompanied him back from the second and longest of his trips, and had gone with him on the third and last, never returning.[d] No one had ever seen her closely, not even the servants; for her disposition had been violent and singular. During her brief stay at Jermyn House she occupied a remote wing, and was waited on by her husband alone. Sir Wade was, indeed, most peculiar in his solicitude for his family; for when he returned to Africa he would permit no one to care for his young son save a loathsome black woman from Guinea. Upon coming back, after the death of Lady Jermyn, he himself assumed complete care of the boy.

But it was the talk of Sir Wade, especially when in his cups, which chiefly led his friends to deem him mad. In a rational age like the eighteenth century[e] it was unwise for a man[f] to talk about wild sights and strange scenes under a Congo moon; of the gigantic walls and pillars of a forgotten city, crumbling and vine-grown, and of damp, silent, stone steps leading interminably down into the darkness of abysmal treasure-vaults and inconceivable catacombs. Especially was it unwise to rave of the living things that might haunt such a place; of creatures half of the jungle and half of the impiously aged city—fabulous creatures which even a Pliny might describe with scepticism;[g] things that might have sprung up after the great apes had overrun the dying city with the walls and the pillars, the vaults and the weird carvings.[h] Yet after he came home for the last time Sir Wade would speak of such matters with a shudderingly uncanny zest, mostly after his third glass at the Knight's

---

[a] shewed] showed A, B, C, D, E
[b] Portuguese] Portugese B
[c] and] and she C
[d] returning.] returning. ¶ C, D
[e] eighteenth century] Eighteenth Century D
[f] man] man of learning A, B, E
[g] scepticism;] skepticism; A, D
[h] carvings.] carvings. ¶ C, D

Head; boasting of what he had found in the jungle and of how he had dwelt among terrible ruins known only to him. And finally he had spoken of the living things in such a manner that he was taken to the madhouse.[a] He had shewn[b] little regret when shut into the barred room at Huntingdon, for his mind moved curiously. Ever since his son had commenced to grow out of infancy he had liked his home less and less, till at last he had seemed to dread it. The Knight's Head had been his headquarters, and when he was confined he expressed some vague gratitude as if for protection.[c] Three years later he died.

Wade Jermyn's son Philip[d] was a highly peculiar person. Despite a strong physical resemblance to his father, his appearance and conduct were in many particulars so coarse that he was universally shunned. Though he did not inherit the madness which was feared by some, he was densely stupid and given to brief periods of uncontrollable violence. In frame he was small, but intensely powerful, and was of incredible agility.[e] Twelve years after succeeding to his title he married the daughter of his gamekeeper, a person said to be of gypsy[f] extraction, but before his son was born[g] joined the navy as a common sailor, completing the general disgust which his habits and mesalliance[h] had begun. After the close of the American war he was heard of as a[i] sailor on a merchantman in the African trade, having a kind of reputation for feats of strength and climbing, but finally disappearing one night as his ship lay off the Congo coast.

In the son of Sir Philip Jermyn the now accepted family peculiarity took a strange and fatal turn. Tall and fairly handsome, with a sort of weird Eastern grace despite certain slight oddities of proportion, Robert Jermyn began life as a scholar and investigator. It was he who first studied scientifically the vast collection of relics which his mad

---

[a] madhouse.] madhouse. ¶ C, D
[b] shewn] shown A, B, C, D, E
[c] protection.] protection. ¶ C, D
[d] son Philip] son, Philip, C, D
[e] agility.] agility. ¶ C, D
[f] gypsy] gipsy D
[g] born] born, A; born he C, D
[h] mesalliance] misalliance E
[i] a] *om.* E

grandfather had brought from Africa, and who made the family name as celebrated in ethnology as in exploration.[a] In 1815[b] Sir Robert married a daughter of the seventh Viscount Brightholme and was subsequently blessed with three children, the eldest and youngest of whom were never publicly seen on account of deformities in mind and body. Saddened by these family misfortunes, the scientist sought relief in work, and made two long expeditions in the interior of Africa. In 1849[c] his second son, Nevil, a singularly repellent[d] person who seemed to combine the surliness of Philip Jermyn with the hauteur of the Brightholmes, ran away with a vulgar dancer, but was pardoned upon his return in the following year. He came back to Jermyn House a widower with an infant son, Alfred, who was one day to be the father of Arthur Jermyn.

Friends said that it was this series of griefs which unhinged the mind of Sir Robert Jermyn, yet it was probably merely a bit of African folklore which caused the disaster. The elderly scholar had been collecting legends of the Onga tribes near the field of his grandfather's and his own explorations, hoping in some way to account for Sir Wade's wild tales of a lost city peopled by strange hybrid creatures. A certain consistency in the strange papers of his ancestor suggested that the madman's imagination might have been stimulated by native myths.[e] On October 19, 1852, the explorer Samuel Seaton called at Jermyn House with a manuscript of notes[f] collected among the Ongas, believing that certain legends of a grey[g] city of white apes ruled by a white god might prove valuable to the ethnologist. In his conversation he probably supplied many additional details,[h] the nature of which will never be known, since a hideous series of tragedies suddenly burst into being.[i] When Sir Robert Jermyn emerged from his library he left behind the strangled corpse of the explorer, and before he could be

[a] exploration.] exploration. ¶ C, D
[b] 1815] 1815, C, D
[c] 1849] 1849, C, D
[d] repellent] repellant A
[e] myths.] myths. ¶ C, D
[f] notes] notes, C, D
[g] grey] gray C, D, E
[h] details,] details; A, B, C, E
[i] being.] being. ¶ C, D

restrained, had put an end to all three of his children; the two who were never seen, and the son who had run away. Nevil Jermyn died in the successful defence[a] of his own two-year-old son, who had apparently been included in the old man's madly murderous scheme. Sir Robert himself, after repeated attempts at suicide and a stubborn refusal to utter any[b] articulate sound, died of apoplexy in the second year of his confinement.

Sir Alfred Jermyn was a baronet before his fourth birthday, but his tastes never matched his title. At twenty he had joined a band of music-hall performers, and at thirty-six had deserted his wife and child to travel with an itinerant American circus.[c] His end was very revolting. Among the animals in the exhibition with which he travelled[d] was a huge bull gorilla of lighter colour[e] than the average; a surprisingly[f] tractable beast of much popularity with the performers. With this gorilla Alfred Jermyn was singularly fascinated, and on many occasions the two would eye each other for long periods through the intervening bars.[g] Eventually Jermyn asked and obtained permission to train the animal, astonishing audiences and fellow-performers alike with his success. One morning in Chicago, as the gorilla and Alfred Jermyn were rehearsing an exceedingly clever boxing match, the former delivered a blow of more than[h] usual force, hurting both the body and[i] dignity of the amateur trainer.[j] Of what followed, members of "The Greatest Show on[k] Earth" do not like to speak. They did not expect to hear Sir Alfred Jermyn emit a shrill, inhuman scream, or to see him seize his clumsy antagonist with both hands, dash it to the floor of the cage, and bite fiendishly at its hairy throat. The gorilla was off its guard, but not

[a] defence] defense C, D
[b] any] an E
[c] circus.] circus. ¶ C, D
[d] travelled] traveled C, D
[e] colour] color C
[f] surprisingly] surprizingly D
[g] bars.] bars. ¶ C, D
[h] than] than the E
[i] and] and the A, C, D, E
[j] trainer.] trainer. ¶ C, D
[k] on] On E

for long, and before anything could be done by the regular trainer the body which had belonged to a baronet was past recognition.

II.[a]

Arthur Jermyn was the son of Sir Alfred Jermyn and a music-hall[b] singer of unknown origin. When the husband and father deserted his family, the mother took the child to Jermyn House;[c] where there was none left to object to her presence. She was not without notions of what a nobleman's dignity should be, and saw to it that her son received the best education which limited money could provide.[d] The family resources were now sadly slender, and Jermyn House had fallen into woeful disrepair, but young Arthur loved the old edifice and all its contents. He was not like any other Jermyn who had ever lived, for he was a poet and a dreamer. Some of the neighbouring[e] families who had heard tales of old Sir Wade Jermyn's unseen Portuguese[f] wife[g] declared that her Latin blood must be shewing[h] itself; but most persons merely sneered at his sensitiveness to beauty, attributing it to his music-hall mother, who was socially unrecognised.[i] The poetic delicacy of Arthur Jermyn was the more remarkable because of his uncouth personal appearance. Most of the Jermyns had possessed a subtly odd and repellent cast, but Arthur's case was very striking. It is hard to say just what he resembled, but his expression, his facial angle, and the length of his arms gave a thrill of repulsion to those who met him for the first time.

It was the mind and character of Arthur Jermyn which atoned for his aspect. Gifted and learned, he took highest honours[j] at Oxford and seemed likely to redeem the intellectual fame of his family. Though of

[a] II.] *om.* C, D, E
[b] music-hall] musical-hall A
[c] Jermyn House;] Jermyn, A
[d] provide.] provide. ¶ C, D
[e] neighbouring] neighboring A, C, D
[f] Portuguese] Portugese B
[g] wife] wife, C, D
[h] shewing] showing A, B, C, D, E
[i] unrecognised.] unrecognized. ¶ C, D
[j] honours] honors C, D

poetic rather than scientific temperament, he planned to continue the work of his forefathers in African ethnology and antiquities, utilising[a] the truly wonderful though strange collection of Sir Wade. With his fanciful mind he thought often of the prehistoric civilisation[b] in which the mad explorer had so implicitly believed, and would weave tale after tale about the silent jungle city mentioned in the latter's wilder notes and paragraphs. For the nebulous utterances concerning a nameless, unsuspected race of jungle hybrids he had a peculiar feeling of mingled terror and attraction; speculating on the possible basis of such a fancy, and seeking to obtain light among the more recent data gleaned by his great-grandfather and Samuel Seaton amongst the Ongas.

In 1911, after the death of his mother, Sir Arthur Jermyn determined to pursue his investigations to the utmost extent. Selling a portion of his estate to obtain the requisite money, he outfitted an expedition and sailed for the Congo. Arranging with the Belgian authorities for a party of guides, he spent a year in the Onga and Kaliri country, finding data beyond the highest of his expectations. Among the Kaliris was an aged chief called Mwanu, who possessed not only a highly retentive memory, but a singular degree of intelligence and interest in old legends. This ancient confirmed every tale which Jermyn had heard, adding his own account of the stone city and the white apes as it had been told to him.

According to Mwanu, the grey[c] city and the hybrid creatures were no more, having been annihilated by the warlike[d] N'bangus many years ago. This tribe, after destroying most of the edifices and killing the live beings, had carried off the stuffed goddess[e] which had been the object of their quest; the white ape-goddess[f] which the strange beings worshipped,[g] and which was held by Congo tradition to be the form of one who had reigned as a princess among those[h] beings. Just what the

---

[a] utilising] utilizing C, D
[b] civilisation] civilization C, D
[c] grey] gray C, D, E
[d] warlike] war-like D
[e] stuffed goddess] Stuffed Goddess D
[f] white ape-goddess] white-ape goddess C
[g] worshipped,] worshiped, C
[h] those] these E

white ape-like[a] creatures could have been, Mwanu had no idea, but he thought they were the builders of the ruined city. Jermyn could form no conjecture, but by close questioning obtained a very picturesque legend of the stuffed goddess.[b]

The ape-princess, it was said, became the consort of a great white god who had come out of the West. For a long time they had reigned over the city together, but when they had a son all three went away. Later the god and the[c] princess had returned, and upon the death of the princess her divine husband had mummified the body and enshrined it in a vast house of stone, where it was worshipped.[d] Then he had departed alone.[e] The legend here seemed to present three variants. According to one story nothing further happened save[f] that the stuffed goddess became a symbol of supremacy for whatever tribe might possess it. It was for this reason that the N'bangus carried it off. A second story told of the[g] god's return and death at the feet of his enshrined wife. A third told of the return of the son, grown to manhood—or apehood or godhood, as the case might be—yet unconscious of his identity. Surely the imaginative blacks had made the most of whatever events might lie behind the extravagant legendry.

Of the reality of the jungle city described by old[h] Sir Wade, Arthur Jermyn had no further doubt; and was hardly astonished when,[i] early in 1912,[j] he came upon what was left of it. Its size must have been exaggerated, yet the stones lying about proved that it was no mere negro[k] village. Unfortunately[l] no carvings could be found, and the small size of the expedition prevented operations toward clearing the

---

[a] ape-like] apelike C, D
[b] stuffed goddess.] Stuffed Goddess. D
[c] the] *om.* A, E
[d] worshipped.] worshiped. C
[e] alone.] alone. ¶ C, D
[f] save] except A
[g] the] a E
[h] jungle . . . old] old jungle city described by C, D
[i] when,] when A, B, C, E
[j] 1912,] 1912 A, B, E
[k] negro] Negro A, D, E
[l] Unfortunately] Unfortunately, C, D

one visible passageway that seemed to lead down into the system of vaults which Sir Wade had mentioned. The white apes and the stuffed goddess[a] were discussed with all the native chiefs of the region, but it remained for a European to improve on the data offered by old Mwanu. M. Verhaeren, Belgian agent at a trading-post on the Congo, believed that he could not only locate but obtain the stuffed goddess,[b] of which he had vaguely heard; since the once mighty N'bangus were now the submissive servants of King Albert's government, and with but little persuasion could be induced to part with the gruesome deity[c] they had carried off.[d] When Jermyn sailed for England, therefore, it was with the exultant probability that he would within a few months receive a priceless ethnological relic confirming the wildest of his great-great-great-grandfather's narratives—that is, the wildest which he had ever heard. Countrymen near Jermyn House had perhaps heard wilder tales handed down from ancestors who had listened to Sir Wade around the tables of the Knight's Head.

Arthur Jermyn waited very patiently for the expected box from M. Verhaeren, meanwhile studying with increased diligence the manuscripts left by his mad ancestor. He began to feel closely akin to Sir Wade, and to seek relics of the latter's personal life in England as well as of his African exploits. Oral accounts of the mysterious and secluded wife had been numerous, but no tangible relic of her stay at Jermyn House remained. Jermyn wondered what circumstance had prompted or permitted such an effacement, and decided that the husband's insanity was the prime cause.[e] His great-great-great-grandmother,[f] he recalled, was said to have been the daughter of a Portuguese[g] trader in Africa. No doubt her practical heritage and superficial knowledge of the Dark Continent had caused her to flout Sir Wade's tales of the interior, a thing which such a man would not be[h] likely to forgive. She had died

[a] stuffed goddess] Stuffed Goddess D
[b] stuffed goddess,] Stuffed Goddess, D
[c] deity] diety A
[d] off.] off. ¶ C, D
[e] cause.] cause. ¶ C, D
[f] great-great-great-grandmother,] great-great-great grandmother, A
[g] Portuguese] Portugese B
[h] would not be] was not A

in Africa, perhaps dragged thither by a husband determined to prove what he had told. But as Jermyn indulged in these reflections he could not but smile at their futility, a century and a half after the death of both of[a] his strange progenitors.

In June, 1913, a letter arrived from M. Verhaeren, telling of the finding of the stuffed goddess.[b] It was, the Belgian averred, a most extraordinary object; an object quite beyond the power of a layman to classify. Whether it was human or simian only a scientist could determine, and the process of determination would be greatly hampered by its imperfect condition. Time and the Congo climate are not kind to mummies; especially when their preparation is as amateurish as seemed to be the case here. Around the creature's neck had been found a golden chain bearing an empty locket on which were armorial designs; no doubt some hapless traveller's[c] keepsake, taken by the N'bangus and hung upon the goddess as a charm. In commenting on the contour of the mummy's face, M. Verhaeren suggested a whimsical comparison; or rather,[d] expressed a humorous wonder just how it would strike his correspondent, but was too much interested scientifically to waste many words in levity. The stuffed goddess,[e] he wrote, would arrive duly packed[f] about a month after receipt of the letter.

The boxed object was delivered at Jermyn House on the afternoon of August 3, 1913, being conveyed immediately to the large chamber which housed the collection of African specimens as arranged by Sir Robert and Arthur. What ensued can best be gathered from the tales of servants and from things and papers later examined. Of the various tales[g] that of aged Soames, the family butler, is most ample and coherent. According to this trustworthy man, Sir Arthur Jermyn dismissed everyone from the room before opening the box, though the instant sound of hammer and chisel shewed[h] that he did not delay the

---

[a] of] *om.* E
[b] stuffed goddess.] Stuffed Goddess. D
[c] traveller's] traveler's C, D
[d] rather,] rather A
[e] stuffed goddess,] Stuffed Goddess, D
[f] arrive . . . packed] arrive, duly packed, C, D
[g] tales] tales, C, D
[h] shewed] showed A, B, C, D, E

operation. Nothing was heard for some time; just how long Soames cannot exactly estimate,[a] but it was certainly less than a quarter of an hour later that the horrible scream, undoubtedly in Jermyn's voice, was heard.[b] Immediately afterward Jermyn emerged from the room, rushing frantically toward the front of the house as if pursued by some hideous enemy. The expression on his face, a face ghastly enough in repose, was beyond description. When near the front door he seemed to think of something, and turned back in his flight, finally disappearing down the stairs to the cellar. The servants were utterly dumbfounded,[c] and watched at the head of the stairs, but their master did not return. A smell of oil was all that came up from the regions below.[d] After dark a rattling was heard at the door leading from the cellar into the courtyard; and a stable-boy saw Arthur Jermyn, glistening from head to foot with oil and redolent of that fluid, steal furtively out and vanish on the black moor surrounding the house. Then, in an exaltation of supreme horror, everyone saw the end. A spark appeared on the moor, a flame arose, and a pillar of human fire reached to the heavens. The house[e] of Jermyn no longer existed.

The reason why Arthur Jermyn's charred[f] fragments were not collected and buried lies in what was found afterward;[g] principally the thing in the box. The stuffed goddess[h] was a nauseous sight, withered and eaten away, but it was clearly a mummified white ape of some unknown species, less hairy than any recorded variety, and infinitely nearer mankind—quite shockingly so.[i] Detailed description would be rather unpleasant, but two salient particulars must be told, for they fit in revoltingly with certain notes of Sir Wade Jermyn's African expeditions and with the Congolese legends of the white god and the ape-princess.

[a] estimate,] estimate; A, B, C, E
[b] heard.] heard. ¶ C, D
[c] dumbfounded,] dumfounded, C, D
[d] below.] below. ¶ C, D
[e] house] House A, C, D
[f] charred] *om.* C, D
[g] afterward;] afterward, A, B, C, E
[h] stuffed goddess] Stuffed Goddess D
[i] so.] so. ¶ C, D

The two particulars in question are these: the[a] arms on the golden locket about the creature's neck were the Jermyn arms, and the jocose suggestion of M. Verhaeren about a[b] certain resemblance as connected with the shrivelled[c] face applied with vivid, ghastly, and unnatural horror to none other than the sensitive Arthur Jermyn, great-great-great-grandson of Sir Wade Jermyn and an unknown wife.[d] Members of the Royal Anthropological Institute burned the thing and threw the locket into a well, and some of them do not admit that Arthur Jermyn ever existed.

[a] the] The C, D
[b] a] *om.* E
[c] shrivelled] shriveled C, D
[d] wife.] wife. ¶ C, D

Celephaïs

In a dream Kuranes saw the city in the valley, and the seacoast[a] beyond, and the snowy peak overlooking the sea, and the gaily painted galleys that sail out of the harbour toward distant regions where the sea meets the sky. In a dream it was also[b] that he came by his name of Kuranes, for when awake he was called by another name. Perhaps it was natural for him to dream a new name; for he was the last of his family, and alone among the indifferent millions of London, so there were not many to speak to him and[c] remind him who he had been. His money and lands were gone, and he did not care for the ways of[d] people about him, but preferred to dream and write of his dreams. What he wrote was laughed at by those to whom he shewed[e] it, so that after a time he kept his writings to himself, and finally ceased

Editor's Note: The story first appeared in the *Rainbow* (May 1922). A surviving T.Ms. must date after the *Rainbow* appearance, as it bears slight revisions from that text; it was not prepared by HPL, and may have been prepared by Donald Wandrei (although preparation of the T.Ms. is not mentioned in their correspondence). The T.Ms. bears the diaeresis over the *i* of the title. The T.Ms. was presumably followed (with many errors) by *Marvel Tales* (May 1934). It is unlikely that the divergences between the T.Ms. and the *Marvel Tales* text are the result of deliberate revisions by HPL, for that would imply that a new T.Ms. was prepared; and the nature of the divergences in virtually every instance suggests printing errors by *Marvel Tales*. The *Marvel Tales* text was used as the basis of the Arkham House editions. The posthumous *Weird Tales* appearance (June–July 1939) is not relevant to the tale's textual history.

Texts: A = *Rainbow* No. 2 (May 1922): 10–12; B = T.Ms. (JHL); C = *Marvel Tales* 1, No. 1 (May 1934): 26, 28–32; D = *Dagon and Other Macabre Tales* (Arkham House, 1965), 60–65. (All published appearances as "Celephais.") Copy-text: B.

[a] seacoast] sea-coast A, B; sea-/coast C
[b] was also] also was A
[c] and] and to C, D
[d] of] of the C, D
[e] shewed] showed C, D

184

to write. The more he withdrew from the world about him, the more wonderful became his dreams; and it would have been quite futile to try to describe them on paper. Kuranes was not modern, and did not think like others[a] who wrote. Whilst they strove to strip from life its embroidered robes of myth,[b] and to shew[c] in naked ugliness the foul thing that is reality, Kuranes sought for beauty alone.[d] When truth and experience failed to reveal it, he sought it in fancy and illusion, and found it on his very doorstep, amid the nebulous memories of childhood tales and dreams.

There are not many persons who know what wonders are opened to them in the stories and visions of their youth; for when as children we listen and dream, we think but half-formed thoughts, and when as men we try to remember, we are dulled and prosaic with the poison of life. But some of us awake in the night with strange phantasms of enchanted hills and gardens, of fountains that sing in the sun, of golden cliffs overhanging murmuring seas, of plains that stretch down to sleeping cities of bronze and stone, and of shadowy companies of heroes[e] that ride caparisoned[f] white horses along the edges of thick forests; and then we know that we have looked back through the ivory gates into that world of wonder which was ours before we were wise and unhappy.

Kuranes came very suddenly upon his old world of childhood. He had been dreaming of the house where he was[g] born; the great stone house covered with ivy, where thirteen generations of his ancestors had lived, and where he had hoped to die. It was moonlight, and he had stolen out into the fragrant summer night, through the gardens, down the terraces, past the great oaks of the park, and along the long white road to the village. The village seemed very old, eaten away at the edge like the moon which had commenced to wane, and Kuranes wondered whether the peaked roofs of the small houses hid sleep or death. In the streets were spears of long grass, and the window-panes

[a] others] other C
[b] myth,] myth C, D
[c] shew] show C, D
[d] alone.] alone_ C [*type failed to print*]
[e] heroes] hereos A
[f] caparisoned] caparison C
[g] was] had been C, D

on either side were either[a] broken or filmily staring. Kuranes had not lingered, but had plodded on as though summoned toward some goal. He dared not disobey the summons for fear it might prove an illusion like the urges and aspirations of waking life, which do not lead to any goal. Then he had been drawn down a lane that led off from the village street toward the channel cliffs, and had come to the end of things—to the precipice and the abyss where all the village and all the world fell abruptly away[b] into the unechoing emptiness of infinity, and where even the sky ahead was empty and unlit by the crumbling moon and the peering stars. Faith had urged him on, over the precipice and into the gulf, where he had floated down, down, down; past dark, shapeless, undreamed dreams, faintly glowing spheres that may have been partly dreamed dreams, and laughing winged things that seemed to mock the dreamers of all the worlds. Then a rift seemed to open in the darkness before him, and he saw the city of the valley, glistening radiantly far, far below, with a background of sea and sky, and a snow-capped mountain near the shore.

Kuranes[c] had awaked the very moment he beheld the city, yet he knew from his brief glance that it was none other than Celephaïs,[d] in the Valley of Ooth-Nargai[e] beyond the Tanarian Hills,[f] where his spirit had dwelt all the eternity of an hour one summer afternoon very long ago, when he had slipt away from his nurse and let the warm sea-breeze lull him to sleep as he watched the clouds from the cliff near the village. He had protested then, when they had found him, waked him, and carried him home, for just as he was aroused[g] he had been about to sail in a golden galley for those alluring regions where the sea meets the sky. And now he was equally resentful of awaking, for he had found his fabulous city after forty weary years.

[a] were either] *om.* C, D

[b] away] *om.* C, D

[c] Kuranes] Knranes C

[d] Celephaïs,] Celephais, A, C, D

[e] Ooth-Nargai] Oooth-Nargai A

[f] Hills,] Hills D

[g] aroused] arroused C

But three nights afterward Kuranes came again to Celephaïs.[a] As before, he dreamed first of the village that was asleep or dead, and of the abyss down which one must float silently; then the rift appeared again, and he beheld the glittering minarets[b] of the city, and saw the graceful galleys riding at anchor in the blue harbour, and watched the gingko trees of Mount Aran swaying in the sea-breeze. But this time he was not snatched away, and like a winged being settled gradually over a grassy hillside till finally his feet rested gently on the turf. He had indeed come back to the Valley[c] of Ooth-Nargai and the splendid city of Celephaïs.[d]

Down the hill amid scented grasses and brilliant flowers walked Kuranes, over the bubbling Naraxa on the small wooden bridge where he had carved his name so many years ago, and through the whispering grove to the great stone bridge by the city gate. All was as of old, nor were the marble walls discoloured, nor the polished bronze statues upon them tarnished. And Kuranes saw that he need not tremble lest[e] the things he knew be vanished; for even the sentries on the ramparts were the same, and still as young as he remembered them. When he entered the city, past the bronze gates and over the onyx pavements, the merchants and camel-drivers greeted him as if he had never been away; and it was the same at the turquoise temple of Nath-Horthath, where the orchid-wreathed priests told him that there is no time in Ooth-Nargai, but only perpetual youth. Then Kuranes walked through the Street of Pillars to the seaward wall, where gathered the traders and sailors, and strange men from the regions where the sea meets the sky. There he stayed long, gazing out over the bright harbour where the ripples sparkled beneath an unknown sun, and where rode lightly the galleys from far places over the water. And he gazed also upon Mount Aran rising regally from the shore, its lower slopes green with swaying trees and its white summit touching the sky.

[a] Celephaïs.] Celephais. A, C, D
[b] minarets] minerets C
[c] Valley] valley C, D
[d] Celephaïs.] Celephais. A, C, D
[e] lest] less C

More than ever Kuranes wished to sail in a galley to the far places of which he had heard so many strange tales, and he sought again the captain who had agreed to carry him so long ago. He found the man, Athib, sitting on the same chest of spices[a] he had sat upon before, and Athib seemed not to realise[b] that any time had passed. Then the two rowed to a galley in the harbour, and giving orders to the oarsmen,[c] commenced to sail out into the billowy Cerenarian Sea that leads to the sky. For several days they glided undulatingly over the water, till finally they came to the horizon, where the sea meets the sky. Here the galley paused not at all, but floated easily in the blue of the sky among fleecy clouds tinted with rose. And far beneath the keel Kuranes could see strange lands and rivers and cities of surpassing beauty, spread indolently in the sunshine which seemed never to lessen or disappear. At length Athib told him that their journey was near its end, and that they would soon enter the harbour of Serannian, the pink marble city of the clouds, which is built on that ethereal coast where the west wind flows into the sky; but as the highest of the city's carven towers came into sight there was a sound somewhere in space, and Kuranes awaked in his London garret.

For many months after that Kuranes sought the marvellous[d] city of Celephaïs[e] and its sky-bound galleys in vain; and though his dreams carried him to many gorgeous and unheard-of places, no one whom he met could tell him how to find Ooth-Nargai,[f] beyond the Tanarian Hills. One night he went flying over dark mountains where there were faint, lone campfires at great distances apart, and strange, shaggy herds with tinkling bells on the leaders;[g] and in the wildest part of this hilly country, so remote that few men could ever have seen it, he found a hideously ancient wall or causeway of stone zigzagging along the ridges and valleys; too gigantic ever to have risen by human hands, and of such a length that neither end of it could be seen. Beyond that wall in

[a] spices] spice C, D
[b] realise] realize A, D
[c] oarsmen,] oarmen, C, D
[d] marvellous] marvelous A
[e] Celephaïs] Celephais A, C, D
[f] Ooth-Nargai,] Ooth-Nargai C, D
[g] leaders;] leaders, C, D

the grey[a] dawn he came to a land of quaint gardens and cherry trees, and when the sun rose he beheld such beauty of red and white flowers, green foliage and lawns, white paths, diamond brooks, blue lakelets, carven bridges, and red-roofed pagodas, that he for a moment forgot Celephaïs[b] in sheer delight. But he remembered it again when he walked down a white path toward a red-roofed pagoda, and would have questioned the people of that[c] land about it, had he not found that there were no people there, but only birds and bees and butterflies. On another night Kuranes walked up a damp stone spiral stairway endlessly, and came to a tower window overlooking a mighty plain and river lit by the full moon; and in the silent city that spread away from the river-bank[d] he thought he beheld some feature or arrangement which he had known before. He would have descended and asked the way to Ooth-Nargai had not a fearsome aurora sputtered up from some remote place beyond the horizon, shewing[e] the ruin and antiquity of the city, and the stagnation of the reedy river, and the death lying[f] upon that land, as it had lain since King Kynaratholis came home from his conquests to find the vengeance of the gods.

So Kuranes sought fruitlessly for the marvellous city of Celephaïs[g] and its galleys that sail to Serannian in the sky, meanwhile seeing many wonders and once barely escaping from the high-priest not to be described, which wears a yellow silken mask over its face and dwells all alone in a prehistoric stone monastery on[h] the cold desert plateau of Leng. In time he grew so impatient of the bleak intervals of day that he began buying drugs in order to increase his periods of sleep. Hasheesh helped a great deal, and once sent him to a part of space where form does not exist, but where glowing gases study the secrets of existence. And a violet-coloured gas told him that this part of space was outside what he had called infinity. The gas had not heard of planets and

[a] grey] gray C, D
[b] Celephaïs] Celephais A, C, D
[c] that] this C, D
[d] river-bank] river bank A, B, C, D
[e] shewing] showing C, D
[f] lying] laying C
[g] Celephaïs] Celephais A, C, D
[h] on] in C, D

organisms before, but identified Kuranes merely as one from the infinity where matter, energy, and gravitation exist. Kuranes was now very anxious to return to minaret-studded Celephaïs,[a] and increased his doses of drugs; but eventually he had no more money left, and could buy no drugs. Then one summer day he was turned out of his garret, and wandered aimlessly through the streets, drifting over a bridge to a place where the houses grew thinner and thinner. And it was there that fulfilment[b] came, and he met the cortege of knights come from Celephaïs[c] to bear him thither for ever.[d]

Handsome knights they were, astride roan horses and clad in shining armour with tabards of cloth-of-gold curiously emblazoned. So numerous were they, that Kuranes almost mistook them for an army, but their leader told him[e] they were sent in his honour; since it was he who had created Ooth-Nargai in his dreams, on which account he was now to be appointed its chief god for evermore. Then they gave Kuranes a horse and placed him at the head of the cavalcade, and all rode majestically through the downs of Surrey and onward toward the region where Kuranes and his ancestors were born. It was very strange, but as the riders went on they seemed to gallop back through Time; for whenever they passed through a village in the twilight they saw only such houses and villagers[f] as Chaucer or men before him might have seen, and sometimes they saw knights on horseback with small companies of retainers. When it grew dark they travelled more swiftly, till soon they were flying uncannily as if in the air. In the dim dawn they came upon the village which Kuranes had seen alive in his childhood, and asleep or dead in his dreams. It was alive now, and early villagers courtesied[g] as the horsemen clattered down the street and turned off into the lane that ends in the abyss of dream.[h] Kuranes had previously entered that abyss only at night, and wondered what it

[a] Celephaïs,] Celephais, C, D
[b] fulfilment] fulfillment D
[c] Celephaïs] Celephais A, C, D
[d] for ever.] forever. D
[e] their leader told him] *om.* C, D
[f] villagers] villages A
[g] courtesied] curtsied D
[h] dream.] dreams. C, D

would look like by day; so he watched anxiously as the column approached its brink. Just as they galloped up the rising ground to the precipice a golden glare came somewhere out of the east[a] and hid all the landscape in its[b] effulgent draperies. The abyss was now[c] a seething chaos of roseate and cerulean splendour, and invisible[d] voices sang exultantly as the knightly entourage plunged over the edge and floated gracefully down past glittering clouds and silvery coruscations. Endlessly down the horsemen floated, their chargers pawing the aether as if galloping over golden sands; and then the luminous vapours spread apart to reveal a greater brightness, the brightness of the city Celephaïs,[e] and the seacoast[f] beyond, and the snowy peak overlooking the sea, and the gaily painted galleys that sail out of the harbour toward distant regions where the sea meets the sky.

And Kuranes reigned thereafter over Ooth-Nargai and all the neighbouring[g] regions of dream, and held his court alternately in Celephaïs[h] and in the cloud-fashioned[i] Serannian. He reigns there still, and will reign happily for ever, though below the cliffs at Innsmouth the channel tides played mockingly with the body of a tramp who had stumbled through the half-deserted village at dawn; played mockingly, and cast it upon the rocks by ivy-covered Trevor Towers, where a notably fat and especially offensive millionaire brewer enjoys the purchased atmosphere of extinct nobility.

---

[a] east] west C, D
[b] its] *om.* C, D
[c] now] *om.* C, D
[d] invisible] invisable C
[e] Celephaïs,] Celephais, A, C, D
[f] seacoast] sea coast A, B, C, D
[g] neighbouring] neighboring D
[h] Celephaïs] Celephais A, C, D
[i] cloud-fashioned] cloud fashioned C, D

From Beyond

Horrible beyond conception was the change which had taken place in my best friend, Crawford Tillinghast.[a] I had not seen him since that day, two months and a half before, when he had[b] told me toward what goal his physical and metaphysical researches were leading; when he had answered my awed and almost frightened remonstrances by driving me from his laboratory and his house in a burst of fanatical rage.[c] I had known that he now remained mostly shut in the attic laboratory with that accursed electrical machine, eating little and excluding even the servants, but I had not thought that a brief period of ten weeks could so alter and disfigure

Editor's Note: The A.Ms. is HPL's original draft, written on the back of correspondence to him. No T.Ms. has come to light, but one must have prepared for the tale's first appearance (*Fantasy Fan,* June 1934). That appearance contains certain important divergences from the A.Ms. (particularly in paragraphing) that are probably not printing errors but revisions made in the hypothetical T.Ms. It appears, however, that HPL may not have prepared the T.Ms. himself: although the *Fantasy Fan* appearance contains some phrases not in the A.Ms. (which might easily have been added on the T.Ms. by hand), there are other omissions and errors in the appearance that may be attributed more to its derivation from a faulty T.Ms. than from errors of its own. Moreover, the A.Ms. contains certain marks and annotations by HPL (e.g., the fact that the central character's name is to be changed from "Henry Annesley" to "Crawford Tillinghast") that would be superfluous unless HPL were making instructions for someone else preparing the T.Ms. Nevertheless, some of the divergences between the A.Ms. and the *Fantasy Fan* appearance are surely due to wilful revisions by HPL. The Arkham House editions followed the *Fantasy Fan* text. The posthumous *Weird Tales* appearance (February 1938) is not relevant to the tale's textual history.

Texts: A = A.Ms.; B = *Fantasy Fan* 1, No. 10 (June 1934): 147–51; C = *Beyond the Wall of Sleep* (Arkham House, 1943), 28–32; D = *Dagon and Other Macabre Tales* (Arkham House, 1965), 66–72. Copy-text: A (with some readings from B).

[a] Crawford Tillinghast.] Henry Annesley. A [*and so on throughout text*]
[b] had] *om.* C, D
[c] rage.] rage, B, C, D

any human creature. It is not pleasant to see a stout man suddenly grown thin, and it is even worse when the baggy skin becomes yellowed or greyed, the eyes sunken, circled, and uncannily glowing, the forehead veined and corrugated, and the hands tremulous and twitching. And if added to this there be a repellent unkemptness;[a] a wild disorder of dress, a bushiness of dark hair white at the roots, and an unchecked growth of pure[b] white beard on a face once clean-shaven, the cumulative effect is quite shocking. But such was the aspect of Crawford Tillinghast on the night his half-coherent[c] message brought me to his door after my weeks of exile; such[d] the spectre that trembled as it admitted me, candle in hand, and glanced furtively over its shoulder as if fearful of unseen things in the ancient, lonely house set back from Benevolent Street.[e]

That Crawford Tillinghast should ever have studied science and philosophy was a mistake. These things should be left to the frigid and impersonal investigator,[f] for they offer two equally tragic alternatives to the man of feeling and action; despair[g] if he fail in his quest, and terrors unutterable and unimaginable if he succeed. Tillinghast had once been the prey of failure, solitary and melancholy; but now I knew, with nauseating fears of my own, that he was the prey of success. I had indeed warned him ten weeks before, when he burst forth with his tale of what he felt himself about to discover. He had been flushed and excited then, talking in a high and unnatural, though always pedantic, voice.[h]

"What do we know,"[i] he had said, "of the world and the universe about us? Our means of receiving impressions are absurdly few, and our notions of surrounding objects infinitely narrow. We see things only as we are constructed to see them, and can gain no idea of their absolute nature. With five feeble senses we pretend to comprehend the

---

[a] repellent unkemptness;] repellant unkemptness; B; repellent unkemptness, C D
[b] pure] *om.* B, C, D
[c] half-coherent] half coherent B, C, D
[d] such] such was B, C, D
[e] house . . . Street.] house. A
[f] investigator,] investigator B, C, D
[g] despair] despair, B, C, D
[h] voice. ¶] voice. A
[i] know,"] know", A

boundlessly complex cosmos, yet other beings with a wider, stronger, or different range of senses might not only see very differently the things we see, but might see and study whole worlds of matter, energy, and life which lie close at hand yet can never be detected with the senses we have. I have always believed that such strange, inaccessible worlds exist at our very elbows, *and now I believe I have found a way to break down the barriers.* I am not joking. Within twenty-four hours that machine near the table will generate waves acting on unrecognised[a] sense-organs that exist in us as atrophied or rudimentary vestiges. Those waves will open up to us many vistas unknown to man, and several unknown to anything we consider organic life. We shall see that at which dogs howl in the dark, and that at which cats prick up their ears after midnight. We shall see these things, and other things which no breathing creature has yet seen. We shall overleap time, space, and dimensions, and without bodily motion peer to the bottom of creation."

When Tillinghast said these things I remonstrated, for I knew him well enough to be frightened rather than amused; but he was a fanatic, and drove me from the house. Now he was no less a fanatic, but his desire to speak had conquered his resentment, and he had written me imperatively in a hand I could scarcely recognise.[b] As I entered the abode of the friend so suddenly metamorphosed to a shivering gargoyle, I became infected with the terror which seemed stalking in all the shadows. The words and beliefs expressed ten weeks before seemed bodied forth in the darkness beyond the small circle of candle light, and I sickened at the hollow, altered voice of my host. I wished the servants were about, and did not like it when he said they had all left three days previously. It seemed strange that old Gregory, at least, should desert his master without telling as tried a friend as I. It was he who had given me all the information I had of Tillinghast after I was repulsed in rage.[c]

---

[a] unrecognised] unrecognized B, C, D

[b] recognise.] recognize. B, C, D

[c] rage.] rage. ¶ Up two flights of stairs I followed the bobbing candle held by the shaking parody on a man. Annesley muttered, but evidently not to me. We entered the laboratory, where the electrical machine stood silently, emitting a violet glow; and my companion started a gasoline engine to generate power. This was necessary, since the rambling, antiquated house was not wired for electricity.

Yet I soon subordinated all my fears to my growing curiosity and fascination. Just what Crawford Tillinghast[a] now wished of me I could only guess, but that he had some stupendous secret or discovery to impart, I could not doubt. Before I had protested at his unnatural pryings into the unthinkable; now that he had evidently succeeded to some degree I almost shared his spirit, terrible though the cost of victory appeared. Up through the dark emptiness of the house I followed the bobbing candle in the hand of this shaking parody on man. The electricity seemed to be turned off, and when I asked my guide he said it was for a definite reason.[b]

"It would be too much. . . . I would not dare,"[c] he continued to mutter. I especially noted his new habit of muttering, for it was not like him to talk to himself. We entered the laboratory in the attic, and I observed that detestable electrical machine, glowing with a sickly, sinister,[d] violet luminosity. It was connected with a powerful chemical battery, but seemed to be receiving no current; for I recalled that in its experimental stage it had sputtered and purred when in action. In reply to my question Tillinghast mumbled that this permanent glow was not electrical in any sense that I could understand.

He now seated me near the machine, so that it was on my right, and turned a switch somewhere below the crowning cluster of glass bulbs. The usual sputtering began, turned to a whine, and terminated in a drone so soft as to suggest a return to silence. Meanwhile the luminosity increased, waned again, then assumed a pale, outré[e] colour or blend of colours which I could neither place nor describe. Tillinghast had been watching me, and noted my puzzled expression.

I wondered at the glow, but Annesley told me that it was not electrical in any sense that I could understand. He now directed me to sit near the machine, while he connected some wires with a rheostat which he held in his hands. After that he took a _____ the range of the human senses, according to your original theory?" A [*excised*]

[a] Tillinghast] Tillinghart B

[b] reason. ¶] reason. A

[c] dare,"] dare", A

[d] sinister,] sinister B, C, D

[e] outré] outre A, B

"Do you know what that is?" he whispered. "*That*[a] *is ultra-violet.*"[b] He chuckled oddly at my surprise. "You thought ultra-violet was invisible, and so it is—but you can see that and many other invisible things *now*.

"Listen to me! The waves from that thing are waking a thousand sleeping senses in us; senses which we inherit from aeons of evolution from the state of detached electrons to the state of organic humanity. I have seen[c] *truth*, and I intend to shew[d] it to you. Do you wonder how it will seem? I will tell you." Here Tillinghast seated himself directly opposite me, blowing out his candle and staring hideously into my eyes. "Your existing sense-organs[e]—ears first, I think—will pick up many of the impressions, for they are closely connected with the dormant organs. Then there will be others. You have heard of the pineal gland? I laugh at the shallow endocrinologist, fellow-dupe and fellow-parvenu of the Freudian.[f] That gland is the great sense-organ[g] of organs—*I have found out.*[h] It is like sight in the end, and transmits visual pictures to the brain. If you are normal, that is the way you ought to get most of it . . . I mean get most of the evidence from[i] *beyond.*"

I looked about the immense attic room with the sloping south wall, dimly lit by rays which the every-day eye cannot see. The far corners were all shadows, and the whole place took on a hazy unreality which obscured its nature and invited the imagination to symbolism and phantasm. During the interval that Tillinghast was silent I fancied myself in some vast and[j] incredible temple of long-dead gods; some vague edifice of innumerable black stone columns reaching up from a floor of damp slabs to a cloudy height beyond the range of my vision. The picture was very vivid for a while, but gradually gave way to a

---

[a] whispered. "*That*] whispered, "*That* A; whispered, "*that* B, C, D
[b] *ultra-violet.*"] *ultr-violet.*" B
[c] seen] seen the D
[d] shew] show A, B, C, D
[e] sense-organs] sense organs A
[f] I laugh . . . Freudian.] *om.* A
[g] sense-organ] sense organ A, B, C, D
[h] organs—*I . . . out.*] organs. A
[i] from] *from* B, C, D
[j] and] *om.* D

more horrible conception; that of utter, absolute solitude in infinite, sightless, soundless[a] space. There seemed to be a void, and nothing more, and I felt a childish fear which prompted me to draw from my hip pocket the revolver I always carried after dark since the night I was held up in East Providence.[b] Then, from the farthermost regions of remoteness, the *sound* softly glided into existence. It was infinitely faint, subtly vibrant, and unmistakably musical, but held a quality of surpassing wildness which made its impact feel like a delicate torture of my whole body. I felt sensations like those one feels when accidentally scratching ground glass. Simultaneously there developed something like a cold draught, which apparently swept past me from the direction of the distant sound. As I waited breathlessly I perceived that both sound and wind were increasing; the effect being to give me an odd notion of myself as tied to a pair of rails in the path of a gigantic approaching locomotive. I began to speak to Tillinghast, and as I did so all the unusual impressions abruptly vanished. I saw only the man, the glowing machine,[c] and the dim apartment. Tillinghast was grinning repulsively at the revolver which I had almost unconsciously drawn, but from his expression I was sure he had seen and heard as much as I, if not a great deal more. I whispered what I had experienced,[d] and he bade me[e] remain as quiet and receptive as possible.[f]

"Don't move," he cautioned, "for in these rays *we are able to be seen as well as to see.* I told you the servants left, but I didn't tell you *how.* It was that thick-witted housekeeper[g]—she turned on the lights downstairs after I had warned her not to, and the wires picked up sympathetic vibrations. It must have been frightful—I could hear the screams up here in spite of all I was seeing and hearing from another direction, and later it was rather awful to find those empty heaps of clothes around the house. Mrs. Updike's clothes were close to the front hall switch—that's how I know she did it. It got them all. But so

[a] soundless] soundless, A; soundiess, B
[b] after . . . Providence.] at night. A; after . . . Provirence. B
[c] machine,] machines, C, D
[d] experienced,] experienced B, C, D
[e] me] me to D
[f] possible. ¶] possible. A
[g] housekeeper] house-/keeper C; house-keeper D

long as we don't move we're fairly safe. Remember we're dealing with a hideous world in which we are practically helpless. . . . *Keep still!"*

The combined shock of the revelation and of the abrupt command gave me a kind of paralysis, and in my terror my mind again opened to the impressions coming from what Tillinghast called[a] *"beyond".*[b] I was now in a vortex of sound and motion, with confused pictures before my eyes. I saw the blurred outlines of the room, but from some point in space there seemed to be pouring a seething column of unrecognisable[c] shapes or clouds, penetrating the solid roof at a point ahead and to the right of me. Then I glimpsed the temple-like effect again, but this time the pillars reached up into an aërial[d] ocean of light, which sent down one blinding beam along the path of the cloudy column I had seen before. After that the scene was almost wholly kaleidoscopic, and in the jumble of sights, sounds, and unidentified sense-impressions I felt that I was about to dissolve or in some way lose the solid form. One definite flash I shall always remember. I seemed for an instant to behold a patch of strange night sky filled with shining, revolving spheres, and as it receded I saw that the glowing suns formed a constellation or galaxy of settled shape; this shape being the distorted face of Crawford Tillinghast. At another time I felt[e] huge animate things brushing past me and occasionally *walking or drifting through my supposedly solid body,* and thought I saw Tillinghast look at them as though his better trained senses could catch them visually. I recalled what he had said of the pineal gland, and wondered what he saw with this preternatural[f] eye.

Suddenly I myself became possessed of a kind of augmented sight. Over and above the luminous and shadowy chaos arose a picture which, though vague, held the elements of consistency and permanence.[g] It was indeed somewhat familiar, for the unusual part

[a] called] cailed B

[b] *"beyond".*] *"beyond."* B, C, D

[c] unrecognisable] unrecognizable B, C, D

[d] aërial] aerial A, B, C, D

[e] felt] felt the D

[f] preternatural] preternaturl B

[g] permanence.] per-/mance. B

was superimposed upon the usual terrestrial[a] scene much as a cinema view may be thrown upon the painted curtain of a theatre.[b] I saw the attic laboratory, the electrical[c] machine, and the unsightly form of Tillinghast opposite me; but of all the space unoccupied by familiar material[d] objects not one particle was vacant. Indescribable shapes both alive and otherwise were mixed in disgusting disarray, and close to every known thing were whole worlds of alien, unknown entities. It likewise seemed that all the known things entered into the composition of other unknown things, and vice versa. Foremost among the living objects were great[e] inky, jellyish monstrosities which flabbily quivered in harmony with the vibrations from the machine. They were present in loathsome profusion, and I saw to my horror that they *overlapped;* that they were semi-fluid and capable of passing through one another and through what we know as solids. These things were never still, but seemed ever floating about with some malignant purpose. Sometimes they appeared to devour one another, the attacker launching itself at its victim and instantaneously obliterating the latter from sight. Shudderingly I felt that I knew what had obliterated the unfortunate servants, and could not exclude the things from my mind as I strove to observe other properties of the newly visible world that lies unseen around us. But Tillinghast had been watching me, and was speaking.

"You see them? You see them? You see the things that float and flop about you and through you every moment of your life? You see the creatures that form what men call the pure air and the blue sky? Have I not succeeded in breaking down the barrier; have I not shewn[f] you worlds that no other living men have seen?" I heard him[g] scream through the horrible chaos, and looked at the wild face thrust so offensively close to mine. His eyes were pits of flame, and they glared at me with what I now saw was overwhelming hatred. The machine droned detestably.

---

[a] terrestrial] tereestrial B
[b] theatre.] theater. B, C, D
[c] electrical] elrctrical B
[d] material] *om.* B, C, D
[e] great] *om.* B, C, D
[f] shewn] shown A, B, C, D
[g] him] his B, C, D

"You think those floundering things wiped out the servants? Fool, they are harmless! But the servants *are* gone, aren't they? You tried to stop me; you discouraged me when I needed every drop of encouragement I could get; you were afraid of the cosmic truth, you damned coward, but now I've got you! What swept up the servants? What made them scream so loud? . . . Don't know, eh?[a] You'll know soon enough![b] Look at me—listen to what I say—do you suppose there are really any such things as time and magnitude?[c] Do you fancy there are such things as form or matter?[d] I tell you, I have struck depths that your little brain can't picture![e] I have seen beyond the bounds of infinity and drawn down daemons[f] from the stars. . . . I have harnessed the shadows that stride from world to world to sow death and madness. . . . Space belongs to me, do you hear? Things are hunting[g] me now—the things that devour and dissolve—but I know how to elude them. It is you they will get, as they got the servants. . . . [h] Stirring, dear sir? I told you it was dangerous to move.[i] I have saved you so far by telling you to keep still—saved you to see more sights and to listen to me. If you had moved, they would have been at you long ago. Don't worry, they won't *hurt* you. They didn't hurt the servants—it was[j] *seeing* that made the poor devils scream so. My pets are not pretty, for they come out of places where aesthetic standards are—*very different.* Disintegration is quite painless, I assure you—but[k] *I want you to see them.* I almost saw them, but I knew how to stop. You are not[l] curious? I always knew you were no scientist![m] Trembling, eh?[n] Trembling with

---

[a] eh?] eh! B, C, D
[b] enough!] enough. B, C, D
[c] magnitude?] magnitude. B
[d] matter?] matter. B
[e] picture!] picture. B, C, D
[f] daemons] demons B
[g] hunting] hunthing B
[h] servants. . . .] servants. A
[i] move.] move, B, C, D
[j] was] was the B, C, D
[k] but] *but* B, C, D
[l] not] *om.* D
[m] scientist!] scientist. B, C, D
[n] eh?] eh. B, C, D

anxiety to see the ultimate things I have discovered?[a] Why don't you move, then? Tired? Well, don't worry, my friend, *for they are coming*.[b] . . . Look! Look,[c] curse you, look![d] . . . It's just over your left shoulder. . . ."

What remains to be told is very brief, and may be familiar to you from the newspaper accounts. The police heard a shot in the old Tillinghast house and found us there—Tillinghast dead and me unconscious. They arrested me because the revolver was in my hand, but released me in three hours, after they found it was apoplexy which had finished Tillinghast and saw that my shot had been directed at the noxious machine which now lay hopelessly shattered on the laboratory floor. I did not tell very much of what I had seen, for I feared the coroner would be sceptical;[e] but from the evasive outline I did give, the doctor told me that I had undoubtedly been hypnotised by the vindictive and homicidal madman.

I wish I could believe that doctor. It would help my shaky nerves if I could dismiss what I now have to think of the air and the sky about and above me. I never feel alone or comfortable, and a hideous sense of pursuit sometimes comes chillingly on me when I am weary. What prevents me from believing the doctor is this one simple fact—that the police never found the bodies of those servants whom they say Crawford Tillinghast murdered.

[a] discovered?] discovered. B, C, D
[b] *coming*.] *coming*. Anxious to go? You can't, dear sir, whilst I am looking at you. No—it will do you no good to attack me, for *my friends are already on the way*. A [*excised*]
[c] Look! Look,] Look, look, B, C, D
[d] look!] look. B, C, D
[e] sceptical;] skeptical; B, C, D

Nyarlathotep

Nyarlathotep . . . the crawling chaos . . . I am the last . . . I will tell the audient void. . . .

I do not recall distinctly when it began, but it was months ago. The general tension was horrible. To a season of political and social upheaval was added a strange and brooding apprehension of hideous physical danger; a danger widespread and all-embracing, such a danger as may be imagined only in the most terrible phantasms of[a] the night. I recall that the people went about with pale and worried faces, and whispered warnings and prophecies[b] which no one dared consciously repeat or acknowledge to himself that he had heard. A sense of monstrous guilt was upon the land, and out of the abysses between the stars swept chill currents that made men shiver in dark and lonely places. There was a daemoniac[c] alteration in the sequence of the seasons—the autumn heat lingered fearsomely, and everyone felt that the world and perhaps the universe had passed from the control of known gods or forces to that of gods or[d] forces which were unknown.

Editor's Note: In the absence of a manuscript, we are reliant on the first appearance, in the *United Amateur* (November 1920). This was typeset by E. E. Ericson, the Official Printer of the UAPA for the 1920–21 term, and appears to be reasonably accurate. It was presumably the basis for the reprint in the *National Amateur* (July 1926); the divergences between the two texts appear to be the result of printing errors rather than deliberate revisions by HPL. The Arkham House edition (there is only one) follows the *United Amateur* text.

Texts: A = *United Amateur* 20, No. 2 (November 1920): 19–21; B = *National Amateur* 48, No. 6 (July 1926): 53–54; C = *Beyond the Wall of Sleep* (Arkham House, 1943), 6–7. Copy-text: A.

[a] of] fo B
[b] prophecies] prophesies B
[c] daemoniac] demoniac A, B, C
[d] or] and A, B

And it was then that Nyarlathotep came out of Egypt. Who he was,[a] none could tell, but he was of the old native blood and looked like a Pharaoh. The fellahin knelt when they saw him, yet could not say why. He said he had risen up out of the blackness of twenty-seven centuries,[b] and that he had heard messages from places not on this planet. Into the lands of civilisation[c] came Nyarlathotep, swarthy, slender, and sinister, always buying strange instruments of glass and metal and combining them into instruments yet stranger. He spoke much of the sciences—of electricity and psychology—[d]and gave exhibitions of power which sent his spectators away speechless,[e] yet which swelled his fame to exceeding magnitude. Men advised one another to see Nyarlathotep, and shuddered. And where Nyarlathotep went, rest vanished;[f] for the small hours were rent with the screams of nightmare. Never before had the screams of nightmare been such a public problem; now the wise men almost wished they could forbid sleep in the small hours, that the shrieks of cities might less horribly disturb the pale, pitying moon as it glimmered on green waters gliding under bridges, and old steeples crumbling against a sickly sky.

I remember when Nyarlathotep came to my city—the great, the old, the terrible city of unnumbered crimes. My friend had told me of him, and of the impelling fascination and allurement of his revelations, and I burned with eagerness to explore his uttermost mysteries. My friend said they were horrible and impressive beyond my most fevered imaginings; that what was thrown on a screen in the darkened room prophesied things none but Nyarlathotep dared prophesy, and that[g] in the sputter of his sparks there was taken from men that which had never been taken before yet which shewed only in the eyes. And I heard it hinted abroad that those who knew Nyarlathotep looked on sights which others saw not.

It was in the hot autumn that I went through the night with the

---

[a] was,] was B
[b] centuries,] centuries B
[c] civilisation] civilization B
[d] psychology—] psychology C
[e] speechless,] speechless B
[f] vanished;] vanished, C
[g] that] *om.* C

restless crowds to see Nyarlathotep; through the stifling night and up the endless stairs into the choking room. And shadowed on a screen,[a] I saw hooded forms amidst ruins, and yellow evil faces peering from behind fallen monuments. And I saw the world battling against blackness; against the waves of destruction from ultimate space; whirling, churning;[b] struggling around the dimming, cooling sun. Then the sparks played amazingly around the heads of the spectators, and hair stood up on end whilst shadows more grotesque than I can tell came out and squatted on the heads. And when I, who was colder and more scientific than the rest, mumbled a trembling protest about "imposture" and "static electricity",[c] Nyarlathotep drave[d] us all out, down the dizzy stairs into the damp, hot, deserted midnight streets. I screamed aloud that I was *not*[e] afraid; that I never could be afraid; and others screamed with me for solace. We sware[f] to one another that the city *was*[g] exactly the same, and still alive; and when the electric lights began to fade we cursed the company over and over again, and laughed at the queer faces we made.

I believe we felt something coming down from the greenish moon, for when we began to depend on its light we drifted into curious involuntary marching formations and seemed to know our destinations though we dared not think of them. Once we looked at the pavement and found the blocks loose and displaced by grass, with scarce a line of rusted metal to shew[h] where the tramways had run. And again we saw a tram-car, lone, windowless, dilapidated, and almost on its side. When we gazed around the horizon,[i] we could not find the third tower by the river, and noticed that the silhouette of the second tower was ragged at the top. Then we split up into narrow columns, each of which seemed drawn in a different direction. One disappeared in a narrow alley to the

[a] screen,] screen B
[b] churning;] churning, C
[c] electricity",] electricity," A, C
[d] drave] drove C
[e] *not*] not B
[f] sware] swore C
[g] *was*] was B
[h] shew] show A
[i] horizon,] horizon B

left, leaving only the echo of a shocking moan. Another filed down a weed-choked subway entrance,[a] howling with a laughter that was mad. My own column was sucked toward the open country, and presently[b] felt a chill which was not of the hot autumn; for as we stalked out on the dark moor,[c] we beheld around us the hellish moon-glitter of evil snows. Trackless, inexplicable snows, swept asunder in one direction only, where lay a gulf all the blacker for its glittering walls. The column seemed very thin indeed as it plodded dreamily into the gulf. I lingered behind, for the black rift in the green-litten[d] snow was frightful, and I thought I had heard the reverberations of a disquieting wail as my companions vanished; but my power to linger was slight. As if beckoned by those who had gone before,[e] I half floated[f] between the titanic snowdrifts, quivering and afraid, into the sightless vortex of the unimaginable.

Screamingly sentient, dumbly delirious, only the gods that were can tell. A sickened, sensitive shadow writhing in[g] hands that are not hands,[h] and whirled blindly past ghastly midnights of rotting creation, corpses of dead worlds with sores that were cities, charnel winds that brush the pallid stars and make them flicker low. Beyond the worlds vague ghosts of monstrous things; half-seen columns of unsanctified temples that rest on nameless rocks beneath space and reach up to dizzy vacua above the spheres of light and darkness. And through this revolting graveyard of the universe the muffled, maddening beating of drums, and thin, monotonous whine of blasphemous flutes from inconceivable, unlighted chambers beyond Time; the detestable pounding and piping whereunto dance slowly, awkwardly, and absurdly the gigantic, tenebrous ultimate gods—the blind, voiceless, mindless gargoyles whose soul is Nyarlathotep.

---

[a] entrance,] entrance B
[b] presently] presently I C
[c] moor,] moor B
[d] green-litten] greenlitten B
[e] before,] before B
[f] half floated] half-floated A, B, C
[g] in] in the B
[h] hands,] hands B

The Picture in the House

Searchers after horror haunt strange, far places. For them are the catacombs of Ptolemais,[a] and the carven mausolea of the nightmare countries. They climb to the moonlit towers of ruined Rhine castles, and falter down black cobwebbed steps beneath the scattered stones of forgotten cities in Asia. The haunted wood and the desolate mountain are their shrines, and they linger around the sinister monoliths on uninhabited islands. But the true epicure in the terrible, to whom a new thrill of unutterable ghastliness is the chief end and justification of existence, esteems most of all the ancient, lonely farmhouses of backwoods New England; for there the dark elements of strength, solitude, grotesqueness,[b] and ignorance combine to form the perfection of the hideous.

Editor's Note: The story was first published in the *National Amateur* ("July 1919"), although that issue probably did not appear until the spring or summer of 1921. (The story was written in December 1920.) At some later date HPL must have prepared a new T.Ms., as the next appearance—*Weird Tales* (January 1924)—contains significant revisions. There is a surviving T.Ms., but it is in an unrecognisable typeface and may have been prepared by E. Hoffmann Price for an anthology he was contemplating in the 1930s (see *SL* 4.112). This T.Ms.—probably derived from the *Weird Tales* text—is very inaccurate and contains numerous corrections by HPL, although he probably proofread it without consultation of any existing text; it also contains some apparently deliberate revisions by HPL. Because of its inaccuracy, the readings of this T.Ms. probably need to be augmented and corrected by readings from the first two published appearances that appear to embody HPL's stylistic and spelling preferences. The Arkham House editions followed Price's T.Ms. The second *Weird Tales* appearance (March 1937) is not relevant to the tale's textual history.

Texts: A = *National Amateur* 41, No. 6 (July 1919): 246–49; B = *Weird Tales* 3, No. 1 (January 1924): 40–42; C = T.Ms. (JHL); D = *The Dunwich Horror and Others* (Arkham House, 1963), 121–29. Copy-text: C (with corrections and revisions from A and B).

[a] Ptolemais,] Ptolemais A
[b] grotesqueness,] grotesqueness A, B, D

Most horrible of all sights are the little unpainted wooden houses remote from travelled[a] ways, usually squatted upon some damp, grassy slope or leaning against some gigantic outcropping of[b] rock. Two hundred years and more[c] they have leaned or squatted there, while the vines have crawled and the trees have swelled and spread. They are almost hidden now in lawless luxuriances of green and guardian shrouds of shadow; but the small-paned windows still stare shockingly, as if blinking through a lethal stupor which wards off madness by dulling the memory of unutterable things.

In such houses have dwelt generations of strange people, whose like the world has never seen. Seized with a gloomy and fanatical belief which exiled them from their kind, their ancestors sought the wilderness for freedom. There the scions of a conquering race indeed flourished[d] free from the restrictions of their fellows, but cowered in an appalling slavery to the dismal phantasms of their own minds.[e] Divorced from the enlightenment of civilisation,[f] the strength of these Puritans turned into singular channels; and in their isolation, morbid self-repression, and struggle for life with relentless Nature, there came to them dark furtive traits from the prehistoric depths of their cold Northern heritage. By necessity practical and by philosophy stern, these folk[g] were not beautiful in their sins. Erring as all mortals must, they were forced by their rigid code to seek concealment above all else; so that they came to use less and less taste in what they concealed. Only the silent, sleepy, staring houses in the backwoods can tell all that has lain hidden since the early days;[h] and they are not communicative, being loath to shake off the drowsiness which helps them forget. Sometimes one feels that it would be merciful to tear down these houses, for they must often dream.

[a] travelled] traveled B
[b] of] *om.* A, B
[c] and more] *om.* A
[d] flourished] flourished, B
[e] minds.] minds. ¶ B
[f] civilisation,] civilization, A, B, D
[g] folk] folks D
[h] days;] days, C, D

It was to a time-battered edifice of this description that I was driven one afternoon in November, 1896, by a rain of such chilling copiousness that any shelter was preferable to exposure. I had been travelling[a] for some time amongst the people of the Miskatonic Valley in quest of certain genealogical data;[b] and from the remote, devious, and problematical[c] nature of my course, had deemed it convenient to employ a bicycle despite the lateness of the season. Now I found myself upon an apparently abandoned road which I had chosen as the shortest cut to Arkham;[d] overtaken by the storm at a point far from any town, and confronted with no refuge save the antique and repellent wooden building which blinked with bleared windows from between two huge leafless elms[e] near the foot of a rocky hill.[f] Distant though it was[g] from the remnant of a road, the house none the less impressed me unfavourably[h] the very moment I espied it. Honest, wholesome structures do not stare at travellers[i] so slyly and hauntingly, and in my genealogical researches I had encountered legends of a century before which biased[j] me against places of this kind. Yet the force of the elements was such as to overcome my scruples, and I did not hesitate to wheel my machine up the weedy rise to the closed door which seemed at once so suggestive and secretive.

I had somehow taken it for granted that the house was abandoned, yet as I approached it I was not so sure;[k] for though the walks were indeed overgrown with weeds, they seemed to retain their nature a little too well to argue complete desertion. Therefore instead of trying the door I knocked, feeling as I did so a trepidation I could scarcely

---

[a] travelling] traveling B
[b] data;] data, A, C [*corrected by HPL*]
[c] problematical] uncertain A
[d] Arkham;] Arkham, C, D
[e] elms] oaks A, B
[f] hill.] hill. ¶ B
[g] was] is D
[h] unfavourably] unfavorably A, B, C, D
[i] travellers] travelers B
[j] biased] biassed C
[k] sure;] sure, C, D

explain.[a] As I waited on the rough,[b] mossy rock which served as a doorstep,[c] I glanced at the neighbouring[d] windows and the panes of the transom[e] above me, and noticed that although old, rattling, and almost opaque with dirt, they were not broken. The building, then, must still be inhabited, despite its isolation and general neglect.[f] However, my rapping evoked no response, so after repeating the summons I tried the rusty latch and found the door unfastened. Inside was a little vestibule with walls from which the plaster was falling, and through the doorway came a faint but peculiarly hateful odour.[g] I entered, carrying my bicycle, and closed the door behind me. Ahead rose a narrow staircase, flanked by a small door probably leading to the cellar, while to the left and right were closed doors leading to rooms on the ground floor.

Leaning my cycle against the wall I opened the door at the left, and crossed into a small low-ceiled chamber but dimly lighted by its two dusty windows and furnished in the barest and most primitive possible way. It appeared to be a kind of sitting-room, for it had a table and several chairs, and an immense fireplace above which ticked an antique clock on a mantel. Books and papers were very few, and in the prevailing gloom I could not readily discern the titles. What interested me was the uniform air of archaism as displayed in every visible detail. Most of the houses in this region I had found rich in relics of the past, but here the antiquity was curiously complete; for in all the room I could not discover a single article of definitely post-revolutionary[h] date. Had the furnishings been less humble, the place would have been[i] a collector's paradise.

As I surveyed this quaint apartment, I felt an increase in that aversion first excited by the bleak exterior of the house. Just what it was

---

[a] explain.] explain. ¶ B
[b] rough,] rough A
[c] doorstep,] door-step, C, D
[d] neighbouring] neighboring B, C, D
[e] transom] fanlight A, B
[f] neglect.] neglect. ¶ B
[g] odour.] odor. B, C, D
[h] post-revolutionary] post-Revolutionary A, B
[i] been] formed A

that I feared or loathed, I could by no means define;[a] but something in the whole atmosphere seemed redolent of unhallowed age, of unpleasant crudeness, and of secrets which should be forgotten.[b] I felt disinclined to sit down, and wandered about[c] examining the various articles which I had noticed. The first object of my curiosity was a book of medium size lying upon the table and presenting such an antediluvian aspect[d] that I marvelled[e] at beholding it outside a museum or library. It was bound in leather with metal fittings, and was in an excellent state of preservation; being altogether an unusual sort of volume to encounter in an abode so lowly. When I opened it to the title page my wonder grew even greater, for it proved to be nothing less rare than Pigafetta's account of the Congo region, written in Latin from the notes of the sailor Lopez[f] and printed at Frankfort in 1598. I had often heard of this work, with its curious illustrations by the brothers De Bry, hence for a moment forgot my uneasiness in my desire to turn the pages before me. The engravings were indeed interesting, drawn wholly from imagination and careless descriptions, and represented negroes with white skins and Caucasian features; nor would I soon have closed the book had not an exceedingly trivial circumstance upset my tired nerves and revived my sensation of disquiet.[g] What annoyed me was merely the persistent way in which the volume tended to fall open of[h] itself at Plate XII, which represented in gruesome detail a butcher's shop of the cannibal Anziques. I experienced some shame at my susceptibility to so slight a thing, but the drawing nevertheless disturbed me, especially in connexion[i] with some adjacent passages descriptive of Anzique gastronomy.

[a] define;] define, A
[b] forgotten.] forgotten. ¶ B
[c] about] about, B
[d] antediluvian aspect] aspect of antiquity A
[e] marvelled] marveled B
[f] Lopez] Lopex D
[g] disquiet.] disquiet. ¶ B
[h] of] to B
[i] connexion] connection B, C, D

I had turned[a] to a neighbouring[b] shelf and was examining its meagre literary contents—an eighteenth-century[c] Bible, a "Pilgrim's Progress" of like period, illustrated with grotesque woodcuts and printed by the almanack-maker Isaiah Thomas, the rotting bulk of Cotton Mather's "Magnalia Christi Americana",[d] and a few other books of evidently equal age—when my attention was aroused by the unmistakable sound of walking in the room overhead.[e] At first astonished and startled, considering the lack of response to my recent knocking at the door, I immediately afterward concluded that the walker had[f] just awaked from a sound sleep;[g] and listened with less surprise as the footsteps[h] sounded on the creaking stairs. The tread was heavy,[i] yet seemed to contain a curious quality of cautiousness; a quality which I disliked the more because the tread was heavy.[j] When I had entered the room I had shut the door behind me. Now, after a moment of silence during which the walker may have been inspecting my bicycle in the hall, I heard a fumbling at the latch and saw the panelled[k] portal swing open again.

In the doorway stood a person of such[l] singular appearance that I should have exclaimed aloud but for the restraints of good breeding. Old,[m] white-bearded, and ragged, my host possessed a countenance and physique which inspired equal wonder and respect. His height could not have been less than six feet, and despite a general air of age and poverty he was stout and powerful in proportion.[n] His face, almost hidden by a

[a] turned] turend A
[b] neighbouring] neighboring A, B, C, D
[c] eighteenth-century] 18th century A; eighteenth century B, C, D
[d] "Magnalia . . . Americana",] "Magnalia . . . Americana," B, D
[e] overhead.] overhead. ¶ B
[f] had] hed A
[g] sleep;] sleep, C, D
[h] footsteps] footseps A
[i] heavy,] heavy A
[j] heavy.] heavy. ¶ B
[k] panelled] paneled B, C, D
[l] such] sush A
[m] Old,] Old A
[n] proportion.] paoportion. A; proportion. ¶ B

long[a] beard which grew high on the cheeks, seemed abnormally ruddy and less wrinkled than one might expect; while over a high forehead fell a shock of white hair little thinned by the years. His blue eyes, though a trifle bloodshot, seemed inexplicably keen and burning. But for his horrible unkemptness[b] the man would have been as distinguished-looking as he was impressive. This unkemptness, however, made him offensive despite his face and figure. Of what his clothing consisted I could hardly tell,[c] for it seemed to me no more than a mass of tatters surmounting a pair of high, heavy boots; and his lack of cleanliness surpassed description.[d]

The appearance of this man, and the instinctive[e] fear he inspired, prepared me for something like enmity;[f] so that I almost shuddered through surprise and a sense of uncanny incongruity when he motioned me to a chair and addressed me in a thin, weak voice full of fawning respect and ingratiating hospitality. His speech was very curious, an extreme form of Yankee dialect I had thought long extinct; and I studied it closely as he sat down opposite me for conversation.

"Ketched in the rain, be ye?" he greeted. "Glad[g] ye was nigh the haouse en[h] hed the sense ta come right in. I calc'late I was asleep, else I'd a heerd ye—I ain't as young as I uster be, an' I need a paowerful sight o' naps naowadays. Trav'lin' fur? I hain't seed many folks 'long this rud sence[i] they tuk[j] off the Arkham stage."

I replied that I was going to Arkham, and apologised[k] for my rude entry into his domicile, whereupon he continued.

[a] long] *om.* A
[b] unkemptness] unkemptness, A, B
[c] tell,] tel,l A
[d] description.] description. On a beard which might have been patriarchal were unsightly stains, some of them disgustingly suggestive of blood. A
[e] instinctive] instructive A
[f] enmity;] enmity, A
[g] greeted. "Glad] greeted, "glad A, B, C
[h] en'] an' A
[i] sence] sense C
[j] tuk] took A
[k] apologised] apologized B, C, D

"Glad[a] ta see ye, young[b] Sir—new faces is scurce arount here, an' I hain't got much ta cheer me up these days. Guess yew hail from Bosting, don't ye? I never ben thar, but I kin tell a taown[c] man when I see 'im—we hed[d] one fer deestrick schoolmaster in 'eighty-four, but he quit suddent an' no one never heerd on 'im sence—" Here[e] the old man lapsed into a kind of chuckle, and made no explanation when I questioned him. He seemed to be in an aboundingly good humour,[f] yet to possess those eccentricities which one might guess from his grooming. For some time he rambled on with an almost feverish geniality, when it struck me to ask him how he came by so rare a book as Pigafetta's "Regnum Congo".[g] The effect of this volume had not left me, and I felt a certain hesitancy in speaking of it;[h] but curiosity overmastered[i] all the vague fears which had steadily accumulated since my first glimpse of the house. To my relief, the question did not seem an awkward one;[j] for the old man answered freely and volubly.

"Oh, thet[k] Afriky book? Cap'n Ebenezer Holt traded me thet in 'sixty-eight—him as was kilt in the war."[l] Something about the name of Ebenezer Holt caused me to look up sharply. I had encountered it in my genealogical work, but not in any record since the Revolution. I wondered if my host could help me in the task at which I was labouring,[m] and resolved to ask him about it later on. He continued.[n]

---

[a] continued.] continued, "Glad A; continued: ¶ "Glad B
[b] young] *om.* A
[c] taown] city A
[d] 'im . . . hed] him . . . had A
[e] sence—" Here] sence—" here A, C, D; sence—" ¶ Here B
[f] humour,] humor, B, C, D
[g] Congo".] Congo." A, B, D
[h] it;] it, A, C, D
[i] overmastered] over mastered A
[j] one;] one, C, D
[k] thet] that D
[l] war."] war." ¶ B
[m] labouring,] laboring, B, C, D
[n] continued.] continued: A, B

"Ebenezer was on a Salem[a] merchantman for[b] years, an' picked up a sight o' queer stuff in every port. He got this in London, I guess—he uster like ter buy things at the shops. I was up ta his haouse onct, on the hill, tradin' hosses, when I see this book. I relished[c] the picters, so he give it in on a swap.[d] 'Tis a queer book—here, leave[e] me git on my spectacles—"[f] The old man fumbled among his rags, producing a pair of dirty and amazingly antique glasses with small octagonal lenses and steel bows. Donning these, he reached for the volume on the table and turned the pages lovingly.

"Ebenezer cud read a leetle o' this—'tis Latin—but I can't. I hed[g] two er three schoolmasters read me a bit, and Passon[h] Clark, him they say got draownded[i] in the pond—kin yew make anything outen it?"[j] I told him that I could, and translated for his benefit a paragraph near the beginning. If I erred, he was not scholar enough to correct me; for he seemed childishly pleased at my English version. His proximity was becoming rather obnoxious, yet I saw no way to escape without offending him. I was amused at the childish fondness of this ignorant old man for the pictures in a book he could not read, and wondered how much better he could read the few books in English which adorned the room. This revelation of simplicity[k] removed much of the ill-defined apprehension I had felt, and I smiled as my host rambled on:

"Queer haow picters kin set a body thinkin'. Take this un[l] here near the front. Hev yew ever seed trees like thet, with big leaves a-floppin' over an' daown? And them men—them can't be niggers—they dew beat all!"[m]

---

[a] Salem] Plymouth A
[b] for] fer B
[c] relished] liked A
[d] swap.] trade. A
[e] leave] let A
[f] spectacles—"] spectacles—" ¶ B
[g] hed] had C, D
[h] Passon] Parson A
[i] draownded] drownded A
[j] it?"] it?" ¶ B
[k] simplicity] simpic-/ity A
[l] un] 'un A
[m] all!] all. C, D

Kinder like Injuns, I guess, even ef[a] they be in Afriky. Some o' these here[b] critters looks like monkeys, or half monkeys an' half men, but I never heerd o' nothing like this un."[c] Here he pointed to a fabulous creature of the artist, which one might describe as a sort of dragon with the head of an alligator.

"But naow I'll shew ye the best un[d]—over here nigh the middle—" The old man's speech grew a trifle thicker and his eyes assumed a brighter glow; but his fumbling hands, though seemingly clumsier than before, were entirely adequate to their mission. The book fell open, almost of its own accord and as if from frequent consultation at this place, to the repellent twelfth plate shewing[e] a butcher's shop amongst the Anzique cannibals. My sense of restlessness returned, though I did not exhibit it. The especially bizarre thing was that the artist had made his Africans look like white men—the limbs and quarters hanging about the walls of the shop were ghastly, while the butcher with his axe was hideously incongruous. But my host seemed to relish the view as much as I disliked it.

"What d'ye think o' this—ain't never see the like hereabouts, eh?[f] When I see this I told Eb Holt, 'Thar's[g] suthin' ta stir ye up an' make yer blood tickle!'[h] When I read in Scripter about slayin'—like them Midianites was slew—I kinder think things, but I ain't got no[i] picter of it. Here a body kin see all they is to it—I s'pose 'tis sinful, but ain't we all born an' livin' in sin?—Thet feller bein' chopped up gives me a tickle every time I look at 'im—I hev ta keep lookin' at 'im—see whar[j] the butcher cut off his feet? Thar's his[k] head on thet bench, with one

<hr />

[a] ef] if A

[b] here] *om.* A

[c] un."] 'un." A

[d] un] 'un A

[e] shewing] showing B, C, D

[f] eh?] eh A

[g] 'Thar's] 'Thar's A; 'That's C, D

[h] tickle!'] tickle! A; tickle.' C, D

[i] no] a B

[j] whar] where A

[k] his] 'is A

arm side of[a] it, an' t'other[b] arm's on the graound[c] side o' the meat block."

As[d] the man mumbled on in his shocking ecstasy the expression on his hairy,[e] spectacled face became[f] indescribable, but his voice sank rather than mounted. My own sensations can scarcely be recorded. All the terror I had dimly felt before rushed upon me actively and vividly, and I knew that I loathed the ancient and abhorrent creature so near me with an infinite intensity. His madness, or at least his partial perversion, seemed beyond dispute. He was almost whispering now, with a huskiness more terrible than a scream, and I trembled as I listened.

"As I says, 'tis queer haow picters sets ye thinkin'. D'ye know, young Sir, I'm right sot on this un[g] here. Arter[h] I got the book off Eb I uster look at it a lot, especial when I'd heerd Passon[i] Clark rant o' Sundays in his big wig. Onct I tried suthin' funny—here, young Sir, don't git skeert—all I done was ter[j] look at the picter afore I kilt the sheep for market—killin' sheep was kinder more fun arter lookin' at it—"[k] The tone of the old man now sank very low, sometimes becoming so faint that his words were hardly audible. I listened to the rain, and to the rattling of the bleared,[l] small-paned windows, and marked a rumbling of approaching thunder quite unusual for the season. Once a terrific flash and peal shook the frail house to its foundations, but the whisperer seemed not to notice it.

"Killin' sheep was kinder more fun—but[m] d'ye know, 'twan't quite *satisfyin'*. Queer haow a *cravin*[n] gits a holt on ye— As ye love the

[a] side of] beside A

[b] t'other] t'oter B

[c] graound] ground A; other C, D [other *in C is crossed out,* graound *written over it*]

[d] block." ¶ As] block." As A

[e] hairy,] hairy A

[f] became] become A

[g] un] 'un A

[h] Arter] After A

[i] Passon] Parson A

[j] ter] ta A

[k] it—"] it—" ¶ B

[l] bleared,] *om.* A

[m] but] but, A

[n] *cravin*] cravin' C, D

Almighty, young man, don't tell nobody, but I swar ter[a] Gawd thet picter begun[b] ta make me *hungry fer victuals I couldn't raise nor buy*—here, set still, what's ailin' ye?—I didn't do nothin', only I wondered haow 'twud be ef I *did*— They say meat makes blood an' flesh, an' gives ye new life, so I wondered ef 'twudn't make a man live longer an' longer ef 'twas *more the same*—"[c] But the whisperer never continued. The interruption was not produced by my fright, nor by[d] the rapidly increasing storm amidst whose fury I was presently to open my eyes on a smoky solitude of blackened ruins. It was produced by[e] a very simple though somewhat unusual happening.

The open book lay flat between us, with the picture staring repulsively upward. As the old man whispered the words *"more the same"* a tiny spattering[f] impact was heard, and something shewed[g] on the yellowed paper of the upturned volume. I thought of the rain and of a leaky roof, but rain is not red. On the butcher's shop of the Anzique cannibals a small red spattering glistened picturesquely, lending vividness to the horror of the engraving. The old man saw it, and stopped whispering even before my expression of horror made it necessary; saw it and glanced quickly toward the floor of the room he had left an hour before. I followed his glance, and beheld just above us on the loose plaster of the ancient ceiling a large irregular spot of wet crimson which seemed to spread even as I viewed it. I did not shriek or move, but merely shut my eyes.[h] A moment later came the titanic thunderbolt of thunderbolts; blasting that[i] accursed house of unutterable secrets and bringing the oblivion which alone saved my mind.

[a] ter] to A
[b] begun] began A
[c] *same—"*] *same—"* ¶ B
[d] produced by . . . by] due to . . . to A, B, C [*corrected*]
[e] produced by] due to A, B, C [*corrected*]
[f] spattering] splattering C [*corrected*], D
[g] shewed] showed B, C, D
[h] eyes.] eyes. ¶ B
[i] thunderbolts; blasting that] thunderbolts, striking the A, B, C [*corrected*]

Ex Oblivione

When the last days were upon me, and the ugly trifles of existence began to drive me to madness like the small drops of water that torturers let fall ceaselessly upon one spot of their victim's body, I loved the irradiate refuge of sleep. In my dreams I found a little of the beauty I had vainly sought in life, and wandered through old gardens and enchanted woods.

Once when the wind was soft and scented I heard the south calling, and sailed endlessly and languorously under strange stars.

Once when the gentle rain fell I glided in a barge down a sunless stream under the earth till I reached another world of purple twilight, iridescent arbours,[a] and undying roses.

And once I walked through a golden valley that led to shadowy groves and ruins, and ended in a mighty wall green with antique vines, and pierced by a little gate of bronze.

Many times I walked through that valley, and longer and longer would I pause in the spectral half-light where the giant trees squirmed and twisted grotesquely, and the grey ground stretched damply from trunk to trunk, sometimes disclosing the mould-stained stones of buried temples. And always the goal of my fancies was the mighty vine-grown wall with the little gate of bronze therein.

Editor's Note: In the absence of a manuscript, we are reliant on two texts published in or soon after HPL's lifetime. The prose-poem was first published in the *United Amateur* (March 1921), typeset by E. E. Ericson. It was reprinted in the *Phantagraph* (July 1937). It is unclear whether the editor, Donald A. Wollheim, received a T.Ms. from HPL or worked from the *United Amateur* appearance; I suspect the former, in which case some readings in the *Phantagraph* text may reflect HPL's wishes. The Arkham House text appears to follow the *Phantagraph* appearance.

Texts: A = *United Amateur* 20, No. 4 (March 1921): 59–60; B = *Phantagraph* 6, No. 3 (July 1937): 2–4; C = *Beyond the Wall of Sleep* (Arkham House, 1943), 8–9. Copy-text: A (with some readings from B).

[a] arbours,] arbours A

After a while, as the days of waking became less and less bearable from their greyness and sameness, I would often drift in opiate peace through the valley and the shadowy groves, and wonder how I might seize them for my eternal dwelling-place, so that I need no more crawl back to a dull world stript of interest and new colours. And as I looked upon the little gate in the mighty wall, I felt that beyond it lay a dream-country from which, once it was entered, there would be no return.

So each night in sleep I strove to find the hidden latch of the gate in the ivied antique wall, though it was exceedingly well hidden.[a] And I would tell myself that the realm beyond the wall was not more lasting merely, but more lovely and radiant as well.

Then one night in the dream city[b] of Zakarion I found a yellowed papyrus filled with the thoughts of dream-sages who dwelt of old in that city, and who were too wise ever to be born in the waking world. Therein were written many things concerning the world of dream, and among them was lore of a golden valley and a sacred grove with temples, and a high wall pierced by a little bronze gate. When I saw this lore, I knew that it touched on the scenes I had haunted, and I therefore read long in the yellowed papyrus.

Some of the dream-sages wrote gorgeously of the wonders beyond the irrepassable gate, but others told of horror and disappointment. I knew not which to believe, yet longed more and more to cross for ever[c] into the unknown land; for doubt and secrecy are the lure of lures, and no new horror can be more terrible than the daily torture of the commonplace. So when I learned of the drug which would unlock the gate and drive me through, I resolved to take it when next I awaked.

Last night I swallowed the drug and floated dreamily into the golden valley and the shadowy groves; and when I came this time to the antique wall, I saw that the small gate of bronze was ajar. From beyond came a glow that weirdly[d] lit the giant twisted trees and[e] tops

---

[a] well hidden.] well-hidden. A, B

[b] dream city] dream-city C

[c] for ever] forever A

[d] that weirdly] thet wierdly B

[e] and] and the C

of the buried temples, and I drifted on songfully, expectant of the glories of the land from whence I should never return.

But as the gate swung wider and the sorcery of[a] drug and dream pushed me through, I knew that all sights and glories were at an end; for in that new realm was neither land nor sea, but only the white void of unpeopled and illimitable space. So, happier than I had ever dared hoped to be, I dissolved again into that native infinity of crystal oblivion from which the daemon Life had called me for one brief and desolate hour.

---

[a] of] of the B, C

Sweet Ermengarde;
or, The Heart of a Country Girl

By Percy Simple

Chapter I.
A Simple Rustic Maid[a]

Ermengarde Stubbs was the beauteous blonde daughter of Hiram Stubbs, a poor but honest farmer-bootlegger of Hogton, Vt. Her name was originally Ethyl Ermengarde, but her father persuaded her to drop the praenomen after the passage of the 18th[b] Amendment, averring that it made him thirsty by reminding him of ethyl[c] alcohol, C_2H_5OH.[d] His own products contained mostly methyl or wood alcohol, CH_3OH. Ermengarde confessed to sixteen[e] summers, and branded as mendacious all reports to the effect that she was thirty.[f] She had large black eyes, a prominent Roman nose, light hair which was never dark at the roots except when the local drug store was short

---

Editor's Note: This story has been placed here for want of a better place: its exact date of writing has not been determined, and all that can be said is that it must have been written after the onset of Prohibition (July 1919). The original A.Ms. survives and served as the basis of the first publication, in *Beyond the Wall of Sleep* (1943). This appearance diverged in some particulars from the A.Ms., although the latter contains some irregularities in typographical matters (e.g., quotation marks) that need correction in any authoritative text.

Texts: A = A.Ms. (JHL); B = *Beyond the Wall of Sleep* (Arkham House, 1943), 349–53. Copy-text: A.

[a] Chapter I. / *A . . . Maid*] I. A . . . MAID B
[b] 18th] Eighteenth B
[c] ethyl] Ethyl B
[d] C_2H_5OH.] C_2H_8OH. B
[e] sixteen] 16 A
[f] thirty.] 30. A

on supplies, and a beautiful but inexpensive complexion. She was about 5[ft] 5.33...[in] [a] tall, weighed 115.47 lbs.[b] on her father's copy scales—also off them—and was adjudged most lovely by all the village swains who admired her father's farm and liked his liquid crops.

Ermengarde's hand was sought in matrimony by two ardent lovers. 'Squire Hardman, who had a mortgage on the old home, was very rich and elderly. He was dark and cruelly handsome, and always rode horseback and carried a riding-crop. Long had he sought the radiant Ermengarde, and now his ardour was fanned to fever heat by a secret known to him alone—for upon the humble acres of Farmer Stubbs he had discovered a vein of rich GOLD!![c] "Aha!"[d] said he, "I will win the maiden ere her parent knows of his unsuspected wealth, and join to my fortune a greater fortune still!" And so he began to call twice a week instead of once as before.

But alas for the sinister designs of a villain—'Squire Hardman was not the only suitor for the fair one. Close by the village dwelt another— the handsome Jack Manly, whose curly yellow hair had won the sweet Ermengarde's affection when both were toddling youngsters at the village school. Jack had long been too bashful to declare his passion, but one day while strolling along a shady lane by the old mill with Ermengarde, he had found courage to utter that which was within his heart.

"O light of my life,"[e] said he, "my soul is so overburdened that I must speak! Ermengarde,[f] my ideal [he pronounced it i-deel!], life[g] has become an empty thing without you. Beloved[h] of my spirit, behold a suppliant kneeling in the dust before thee. Ermengarde—oh, Ermengarde, raise me to an heaven of joy and say that you will some day be mine! It is true that I am poor, but have I not youth and strength to fight my way to fame? This I can do only for you, dear Ethyl—pardon me, Ermengarde—my only, my most precious—" but here he paused

[a] 5[ft] 5.33...[in]] five feet 5.33 inches B
[b] 115.47 lbs.] 115.57 pounds B
[c] GOLD!!] *gold!!* B [*A has double underscore*]
[d] "Aha!"] "Aha!", A
[e] life,"] life", A
[f] speak! Ermengarde,] speak!" "Ermengarde, A
[g] ideal [. . .], life] ideal, [. . .] life A; ideal," (. . .) "life B
[h] Beloved] "Beloved A

to wipe his eyes and mop his brow, and the fair responded:

"Jack—my angel—at last—I mean, this is so unexpected and quite unprecedented! I had never dreamed that you entertained sentiments of affection in connexion[a] with one so lowly as Farmer Stubbs' child—for I am still but a child! Such is your natural nobility that I had feared—I mean thought—you would be blind to such slight charms as I possess, and that you would seek your fortune in the great city; there meeting and wedding one of those more comely damsels whose splendour we observe in fashion books.

"But, Jack, since it is really I whom you adore, let us waive all needless circumlocution. Jack—my darling—my heart has long been susceptible to your manly graces. I cherish an affection for thee—consider me thine own and be sure to buy the ring at Perkins' hardware store where they have such nice imitation diamonds in the window."

"Ermengarde, me[b] love!"

"Jack—my precious!"

"My darling!"

"My own!"

"My Gawd!"

[Curtain][c]

Chapter II.
And the Villain Still Pursued Her[d]

But these tender passages, sacred though their fervour, did not pass unobserved by profane eyes; for crouched in the bushes and gritting his teeth was the dastardly 'Squire Hardman! When the lovers had finally strolled away he leapt out into the lane, viciously twirling his moustache and riding-crop, and kicking an unquestionably innocent cat who was also out strolling.

"Curses!" he cried—Hardman, not the cat—"I am foiled in my plot to get the farm and the girl! But Jack Manly shall never succeed! I am a man of power—and we shall see!"

[a] connexion] connection B
[b] me] my B
[c] [Curtain]] [curtain] A; (Curtain) B
[d] Chapter II. / *And . . . Her*] II. AND . . . HER B

Thereupon he repaired to the humble Stubbs' cottage, where he found the fond father in the still-cellar washing bottles under the supervision of the gentle wife and mother, Hannah Stubbs. Coming directly to the point, the villain spoke:

"Farmer Stubbs, I cherish a tender affection of long standing for your lovely offspring, Ethyl Ermengarde. I am consumed with love, and wish her hand in matrimony. Always a man of few words, I will not descend to euphemism. Give me the girl or I will foreclose the mortgage and take the old home!"

"But, Sir," pleaded the distracted Stubbs while his stricken spouse merely glowered, "I am sure the child's affections are elsewhere placed."

"She must be mine!" sternly snapped the sinister 'Squire. "I will make her love me—none shall resist my will! Either she becomes muh wife or the old homestead goes!"

And with a sneer and flick of his riding-crop 'Squire Hardman strode out into the night.

Scarce had he departed, when there entered by the back door the radiant lovers, eager to tell the senior Stubbses of their new-found happiness. Imagine the universal consternation which reigned when all was known! Tears flowed like white mule,[a] till suddenly Jack remembered he was the hero and raised his head, declaiming in appropriately virile accents:

"Never shall the fair Ermengarde be offered up to this beast as a sacrifice while I live! I shall protect her—she is mine, mine, mine—and then some! Fear not, dear father and mother to be—I will defend you all! You shall have the old home still [adverb, not noun—although Jack was by no means out of sympathy with Stubbs' kind of farm produce] and[b] I shall lead to the altar the beauteous Ermengarde, loveliest of her sex! To perdition with the crool 'Squire[c] and his ill-gotten gold—the right shall always win, and a hero is always in the right! I will go to the great city and there make a fortune to save you all ere the mortgage fall due! Farewell, my love—I leave you now in tears, but I shall return to pay off the mortgage and claim you as my bride!"

[a] mule,] ale, B
[b] still [. . .] and] still" (. . .) "and B
[c] 'Squire] squire A, B

"Jack, my protector!"

"Ermie, my sweet roll!"[a]

"Dearest!"

"Darling!—and don't forget that ring at Perkins'."

"Oh!"

"Ah!"

[Curtain][b]

Chapter III.
A Dastardly Act[c]

But the resourceful 'Squire Hardman was not so easily to be foiled. Close by the village lay a disreputable settlement of unkempt shacks, populated by a shiftless scum who lived by thieving and other odd jobs. Here the devilish villain secured two accomplices—ill-favoured fellows who were very clearly no gentlemen. And in the night the evil three broke into the Stubbs[d] cottage and abducted the fair Ermengarde, taking her to a wretched hovel in the settlement and placing her under the charge of Mother Maria, a hideous old hag. Farmer Stubbs was quite distracted, and would have advertised in the papers if the cost had been less than a cent a word for each insertion. Ermengarde was firm, and never wavered in her refusal to wed the villain.

"Aha, my proud beauty," quoth he, "I have ye in me power, and sooner or later I will break that will of thine! Meanwhile think of your poor old father and mother as turned out of hearth and home and wandering helpless through the meadows!"

"Oh, spare them, spare them!" said the maiden.

"Neverr . . . ha ha ha ha!" leered the brute.

And so the cruel days sped on, while all in ignorance young Jack Manly was seeking fame and fortune in the great city.[e]

---

[a] sweet roll!"] sweetest!" B

[b] [Curtain]] [curtain] A; (Curtain) B

[c] Chapter III. / *A . . . Act*] III. A . . . ACT B

[d] Stubbs] Stubbs' B

[e] city.] city. / (Curtain) B

Chapter IV.
Subtle Villainy[a]

One day as 'Squire Hardman sat in the front parlour of his expensive and palatial home, indulging in his favourite[b] pastime of gnashing his teeth and swishing his riding-crop, a great thought came to him; and he cursed aloud at the statue of Satan on the onyx mantelpiece.

"Fool that I am!" he cried. "Why did I ever waste all this trouble on the girl when I can get the farm by simply foreclosing? I never thought of that! I will let the girl go, take the farm, and be free to wed some fair city maid like the leading lady of that burlesque troupe which played last week at the Town Hall!"

And so he went down to the settlement, apologised to Ermengarde, let her go home, and went home himself to plot new crimes and invent new modes of villainy.

The days wore on, and the Stubbses grew very sad over the coming loss of their home and still but nobody seemed able to do anything about it. One day a party of hunters from the city chanced to stray over the old farm, and one of them found the gold!! Hiding his discovery from his companions, he feigned rattlesnake-bite and went to the Stubbs' cottage for aid of the usual kind. Ermengarde opened the door and saw him. He also saw her, and in that moment resolved to win her and the gold. "For my old mother's sake I must"—he cried loudly to himself.[c] "No sacrifice is too great!"[d]

Chapter V.
The City Chap[e]

Algernon Reginald Jones was a polished man of the world from the great city, and in his sophisticated hands our poor little Ermengarde was as a mere child. One could almost believe that sixteen-year-old[f] stuff. Algy was a fast worker, but never crude. He could have taught

[a] Chapter IV. / *Subtle Villainy*] IV. SUBTLE VILLAINY B
[b] favourite] favorite B
[c] himself.] himself, A
[d] great!"] great!" / (Curtain) B
[e] Chapter V. / *The City Chap*] V. THE CITY CHAP B
[f] sixteen-year-old] 16-year-old A

Hardman a thing or two about finesse in sheiking. Thus only a week after his advent to the Stubbs family circle, where he lurked like the vile serpent that he was, he had persuaded the heroine to elope! It was in the night that she went leaving a note for her parents, sniffing the familiar mash for the last time, and kissing the cat goodbye—touching stuff! On the train Algernon became sleepy and slumped down in his seat, allowing a paper to fall out of his pocket by accident. Ermengarde, taking advantage of her supposed position as a bride-elect, picked up the folded sheet and read its perfumed expanse— when lo! she almost fainted! It was a love letter from another woman!!

"Perfidious deceiver!" she whispered at the sleeping Algernon, "so this is all that your boasted fidelity amounts to! I am done with you for all eternity!"

So saying, she pushed him out the window and settled down for a much needed rest.[a]

Chapter VI.
Alone in the Great City[b]

When the noisy train pulled into the dark station at the city, poor helpless Ermengarde was all alone without the money to get back to Hogton. "Oh why,"[c] she sighed in innocent regret, "didn't I take his pocketbook before I pushed him out? Oh[d] well, I should worry![e] He told me all about the city so I can easily earn enough to get home if not to pay off the mortgage!"

But alas for our little heroine—work is not easy for a greenhorn to secure, so for a week she was forced to sleep on park benches and obtain food from the bread-line. Once a wily and wicked person, perceiving her helplessness, offered her a position as dish-washer in a fashionable and depraved cabaret; but our heroine was true to her rustic ideals and refused to work in such a gilded and glittering palace of

---

[a] rest.] rest. / (Curtain) B
[b] Chapter VI. / *Alone . . . City*] VI. ALONE . . . CITY B
[c] "Oh why,"] "Oh why", A; "Oh, why," B
[d] out? Oh] out?" "Oh A; out?" "Oh, B
[e] worry!] worry!" A

frivolity—especially since she was offered only $3.00[a] per week with meals but no board. She tried to look up Jack Manly, her one-time lover, but he was nowhere to be found. Perchance, too, he would not have known her; for in her poverty she had perforce become a brunette again, and Jack had not beheld her in that state since school days. One day she found a neat but costly purse in the park; and after seeing that there was not much in it, took it to the rich lady whose card proclaimed her ownership. Delighted beyond words at the honesty of this forlorn waif, the aristocratic Mrs. Van Itty adopted Ermengarde to replace the little one who had been stolen from her so many years ago. "How like my precious Maude,"[b] she sighed, as she watched the fair brunette return to blondeness. And so several weeks passed, with the old folks at home tearing their hair and the wicked 'Squire Hardman chuckling devilishly.[c]

Chapter VII.
Happy Ever Afterward[d]

One day the wealthy heiress Ermengarde S. Van Itty hired a new second assistant chauffeur. Struck by something familiar in his face, she looked again and gasped. Lo! it was none other than the perfidious Algernon Reginald Jones, whom she had pushed from a car window on that fateful day! He had survived—this much was almost immediately evident. Also, he had wed the other woman, who had run away with the milkman and all the money in the house. Now wholly humbled, he asked forgiveness of our heroine, and confided to her the whole tale of the gold on her father's farm. Moved beyond words, she raised his salary a dollar a month and resolved to gratify at last that always unquenchable anxiety to relieve the worry of the old folks. So one bright day Ermengarde motored back to Hogton and arrived at the farm just as 'Squire Hardman was foreclosing the mortgage and ordering the old folks out.

[a] $3.00] three dollars B
[b] Maude,"] Maude", A
[c] devilishly.] devilishly. / (Curtain) B
[d] Chapter VII. / *Happy . . . Afterward*] VII. HAPPY . . . AFTERWARD B

"Stay, villain!" she cried, flashing a colossal roll of bills. "You are foiled at last![a] Here is your money—now go, and never darken our humble door again!"

Then followed a joyous reunion, whilst the 'Squire twisted his moustache and riding-crop in bafflement and dismay. But hark! What is this? Footsteps sound on the old gravel walk, and who should appear but our hero, Jack Manly—worn and seedy, but radiant of face. Seeking at once the downcast villain, he said:

"'Squire—lend me a ten-spot, will you? I have just come back from the city with my beauteous bride, the fair Bridget Goldstein, and need something to start things on the old farm." Then turning to the Stubbses, he apologised for his inability to pay off the mortgage as agreed.[b]

"Don't mention it," said Ermengarde, "prosperity has come to us, and I will consider it sufficient payment if you will forget for ever[c] the foolish fancies of our childhood."

All this time Mrs. Van Itty had been sitting in the motor waiting for Ermengarde; but as she lazily eyed the sharp-faced Hannah Stubbs a vague memory started from the back of her brain. Then it all came to her, and she shrieked accusingly at the agrestic matron.

"You—you—Hannah Smith—I know you now! Twenty-eight years ago you were my baby Maude's nurse and stole her from the cradle!! Where, oh, where is my child?" Then a thought came as the lightning in a murky sky. "*Ermengarde*—you say she is *your* daughter. . . . She is mine! Fate has restored to me my old chee-ild[d]—my tiny Maudie!—Ermengarde—Maude—come to your mother's loving arms!!!"[e]

But Ermengarde was doing some tall thinking. How could she get away with the sixteen-year-old[f] stuff if she had been stolen twenty-eight[g] years ago? And if she was not Stubbs' daughter the gold would never be hers. Mrs. Van Itty was rich, but 'Squire Hardman was richer.

---

[a] last!] last!" A
[b] agreed. ¶] agreed. A
[c] for ever] forever A, B
[d] chee-ild] che-ild B
[e] arms!!!"] arms!!! A, B
[f] sixteen-year-old] 16-year-old A
[g] twenty-eight] 28 A

So, approaching the dejected villain, she inflicted upon him the last terrible punishment.

"'Squire, dear," she murmured, "I have reconsidered all. I love you and your naive strength. Marry me at once or I will have you prosecuted for that kidnapping last year. Foreclose your mortgage and enjoy with me the gold your cleverness discovered. Come, dear!" And the poor dub did.

THE END.[a]

---

[a] THE END.] (Curtain) B

The Nameless City

When I drew nigh the nameless city I knew it was accursed. I was travelling[a] in a parched and terrible valley under the moon, and afar I saw it protruding uncannily above the sands as parts of a corpse may protrude from an ill-made grave. Fear spoke from the age-worn stones of this hoary survivor of the deluge, this great-grandmother of the eldest pyramid; and a viewless aura repelled me and bade me retreat from antique and sinister secrets that no man should see, and no man else had ever dared to see.

Remote in the desert of Araby lies the nameless city, crumbling and inarticulate, its low walls nearly hidden by the sands of uncounted ages. It must have been thus before the first stones of Memphis were laid, and while the bricks of Babylon were yet unbaked. There is no legend so old as to give it a name, or to recall that it was ever alive; but it is told of in whispers around campfires and muttered about by

Editor's Note: The story was first published in the *Wolverine* (November 1921). At some later date HPL prepared a new T.Ms. bearing slight but significant revisions from that text. HPL speaks in letters of his many failed attempts to land the story in various pulp markets. He presumably sent the existing T.Ms. to *Fanciful Tales* (ed. Donald A. Wollheim and Wilson Shepherd), where it appeared in the Fall 1936 issue. HPL complained to numerous correspondents (although not to Derleth or Wandrei) about the many "misprints" in this appearance, which suggests that the divergences between the T.Ms. and the *Fanciful Tales* text are the result of printing errors and not of deliberate revision by HPL (which would presumably have necessitated the preparation of a new T.Ms., for which there is no evidence). The Arkham House editions unfortunately followed the *Fanciful Tales* text; indeed, the 1965 edition made numerous errors even from the text it had printed in 1939.

Texts: A = *Wolverine* No. 11 (November 1921): 3–15; B = T.Ms. (JHL); C = *Fanciful Tales* 1, No. 1 (Fall 1936): 5–18; D = *The Outsider and Others* (Arkham House, 1939), 234–41; E = *Dagon and Other Macabre Tales* (Arkham House, 1965), 99–110. Copy-text: B.

[a] travelling] traveling E

grandams[a] in the tents of sheiks,[b] so that all the tribes shun it without wholly knowing why. It was of this place that Abdul Alhazred the mad poet dreamed on the night before he sang his unexplainable couplet:

> "That is not dead which can eternal[c] lie,
>   And with strange aeons even[d] death may die."[e]

I should have known that the Arabs had good reason for shunning the nameless city, the city told of in strange tales but seen by no living man, yet I defied them and went into the untrodden waste with my camel. I alone have seen it, and that is why no other face bears such hideous lines of fear as mine; why no other man shivers so horribly when the night-wind[f] rattles the windows. When I came upon it in the ghastly stillness of unending sleep it looked at me, chilly from the rays of a cold moon amidst the desert's heat. And as I returned its look I forgot my triumph at finding it, and stopped still with my camel to wait for the dawn.

For hours I waited, till the east grew grey and the stars faded, and the grey turned to roseal[g] light edged with gold. I heard a moaning and saw a storm of sand stirring among the antique stones though the sky was clear and the vast reaches of the[h] desert still. Then suddenly above the desert's far rim came the blazing edge of the sun, seen through the tiny sandstorm which was passing away, and in my fevered state I fancied that from some remote depth there came a crash of musical metal to hail the fiery disc as Memnon hails it from the banks of the Nile. My ears rang and my imagination seethed as I led[i] my camel slowly across the sand to that unvocal stone place; that place too old for Egypt and Meroë[j] to remember;[k] that place[l] which I alone of living men had seen.

[a] grandams] grandmas D
[b] sheiks,] sheiks C, D, E
[c] eternal] eteral C
[d] even] *om.* E
[e] die."] die". A; die.' C
[f] night-wind] night wind A, B, C, D, E
[g] roseal] roseate D, E
[h] the] *om.* E
[i] led] lead D
[j] Meroë] Meroe C, D; *om.* E [*see below*]
[k] remember;] remember: C; *om.* E [*see below*]
[l] stone . . . place] place; that place E

In and out amongst the shapeless foundations of houses and palaces[a] I wandered, finding never a carving or inscription to tell of those[b] men, if men they were, who built the[c] city and dwelt therein so long ago. The antiquity of the spot was unwholesome, and I longed to encounter some sign or device to prove that the city was indeed fashioned by mankind. There were certain *proportions* and *dimensions* in the ruins which I did not like. I had with me many tools, and dug much within the walls of the obliterated edifices; but progress was slow, and nothing significant was revealed. When night and the moon returned I felt a chill wind which brought new fear, so that I did not dare to remain in the city. And as I went outside the antique walls to sleep, a small sighing sandstorm gathered behind me, blowing over the grey stones though the moon was bright and most of the desert still.

I awaked just at dawn from a pageant of horrible dreams, my ears ringing as from some metallic peal. I saw the sun peering redly through the last gusts of a little sandstorm that hovered over the nameless city, and marked the quietness of the rest of the landscape. Once more I ventured within those brooding ruins that swelled beneath the sand like an ogre under a coverlet, and again dug vainly for relics of the forgotten race. At noon I rested, and in the afternoon I spent much time tracing the walls, and the[d] bygone streets, and the outlines of the nearly vanished buildings. I saw that the city had been mighty indeed, and wondered at the sources of its greatness. To myself I pictured all the splendours of an age so distant that Chaldaea[e] could not recall it, and thought of Sarnath the Doomed, that stood in the land of Mnar when mankind was young, and of Ib, that was carven of grey[f] stone before mankind existed.

All at once I came upon a place where the bed-rock[g] rose stark through the sand and formed a low cliff; and here I saw with joy what seemed to promise further traces of the antediluvian people. Hewn

[a] palaces] places D, E
[b] those] these C, D, E
[c] the] this C, D, E
[d] walls, and the] walls and the C; walls and D, E
[e] Chaldaea] Chaldea A
[f] grey] gray C, D
[g] bed-rock] bed rock A, B, C, D, E

rudely on the face of the cliff were the unmistakable facades[a] of several small, squat rock houses or temples; whose interiors might preserve many secrets of ages too remote for calculation, though sandstorms had long since effaced any carvings which may have been outside.

Very low and sand-choked were all of[b] the dark apertures near me, but I cleared one with my spade and crawled through it, carrying a torch to reveal whatever[c] mysteries it might hold. When I was inside I saw that the cavern was indeed a temple, and beheld plain signs of the race that had lived and worshipped before the desert was a desert. Primitive altars, pillars, and niches, all curiously low, were not absent; and though I saw no sculptures nor[d] frescoes, there were many singular stones clearly shaped into symbols by artificial means. The lowness of the chiselled[e] chamber was very strange, for I could hardly more than[f] kneel upright; but the area was so great that my torch shewed[g] only part[h] at a time. I shuddered oddly in some of the far corners; for certain altars and stones suggested forgotten rites of terrible, revolting, and inexplicable nature,[i] and made me wonder what manner of men could have made and frequented such a temple. When I had seen all that the place contained, I crawled out again, avid to find what the other[j] temples might yield.

Night had now approached, yet the tangible things I had seen made curiosity stronger than fear, so that I did not flee from the long moon-cast shadows that had daunted me when first I saw the nameless city. In the twilight I cleared another aperture and with a new torch crawled into it, finding more vague stones and symbols, though nothing more definite than the other temple had contained. The room was just as low, but much less broad, ending in a very narrow passage

---

[a] facades] façades D, E

[b] of] *om.* E

[c] whatever] what ever C, D

[d] nor] or A, B, E [*revised in B by HPL*]

[e] chiselled] chiseled A

[f] more than] *om.* D, E

[g] shewed] showed E

[h] part] part of it C, D, E

[i] nature,] nature C, D, E

[j] other] *om.* E

crowded with obscure and cryptical shrines. About these shrines I was prying when the noise of a wind and of[a] my camel outside broke through the stillness and drew me forth to see what could have frightened the beast.

The moon was gleaming vividly over the primeval[b] ruins, lighting a dense cloud of sand that seemed blown by a strong but decreasing wind from some point along the cliff ahead of me. I knew it was this chilly, sandy wind which had disturbed the camel,[c] and was about to lead him to a place of better shelter when I chanced to glance up and saw that there was no wind atop the cliff. This astonished me and made me fearful again, but I immediately recalled the sudden local winds[d] I had seen and heard before at sunrise and sunset, and judged it was a normal thing. I decided that[e] it came from some rock fissure leading to a cave, and watched the troubled sand to trace it to its source; soon perceiving[f] that it came from the black orifice of a temple a long distance south of me, almost out of sight. Against the choking sand-cloud I plodded toward this temple, which as I neared it loomed larger than the rest, and shewed a doorway far less clogged with caked sand.[g] I would have entered had not the terrific force of the icy wind almost quenched my torch. It poured madly out of the dark door, sighing uncannily as it ruffled the sand and spread about[h] the weird ruins. Soon it grew fainter and the sand grew more and more still, till finally all was at rest again; but a presence seemed stalking among the spectral stones of the city, and when I glanced at the moon it seemed to quiver as though mirrored in unquiet waters. I was more afraid than I could explain, but not enough to dull my thirst for wonder; so as soon as the wind was quite gone I crossed into the dark chamber from which it had come.

---

[a] of] *om.* E
[b] primeval] primitive C, D, E
[c] camel,] camel D, E
[d] winds] winds that C, D, E
[e] that] *om.* C, D, E
[f] perceiving] I perceived A; perceaving C
[g] sand.] sand, C
[h] about] among D, E

This temple, as I had fancied from the outside, was larger than either of those I had visited before; and was presumably a natural cavern,[a] since it bore winds from some region beyond. Here I could stand quite upright, but saw that the stones and altars were as[b] low as those in the other temples. On the walls and roof I beheld for the first time some traces of the pictorial art of the ancient race, curious curling streaks of paint that had almost faded or crumbled away; and on two of the altars I saw with rising excitement a maze of well-fashioned[c] curvilinear carvings. As I held my torch aloft it seemed to me that the shape of the roof was too regular to be natural, and I wondered what the prehistoric[d] cutters of stone had first worked upon. Their engineering skill must have been vast.

Then a brighter flare of the fantastic flame shewed me[e] that for which I had been seeking, the opening to those remoter abysses whence the sudden wind had blown; and I grew faint when I saw that it was a small and plainly *artificial*[f] door chiselled in the solid rock. I thrust my torch within, beholding a black tunnel with the roof arching low over a rough flight of very small, numerous,[g] and steeply descending steps. I shall always see those steps in my dreams, for I came to learn what they meant. At the time I hardly knew whether to call them steps or mere footholds in a precipitous descent. My mind was whirling with mad thoughts,[h] and the words and warnings of Arab prophets seemed to float across the desert from the[i] lands that men know to the nameless city that men dare not know. Yet I hesitated only[j] a moment before advancing through the portal and commencing to climb cautiously down the steep passage, feet first, as though on a ladder.

It is only in the terrible phantasms of drugs or delirium that any

---

[a] cavern,] cavern A, B, C, D, E
[b] as] an C
[c] well-fashioned] well fashioned C
[d] prehistoric] pre-historic C, D
[e] shewed me] showed me C; showed D, E
[f] *artificial*] artificial A, D, E
[g] numerous,] numerous E
[h] thoughts,] thoughs, C
[i] the] the / the C
[j] only] only for E

other man can have had[a] such a descent as mine. The narrow passage led infinitely down like some hideous haunted well, and the torch I held above my head could not light the unknown depths toward which I was crawling. I lost track of the hours and forgot to consult my watch, though I was frightened when I thought of the distance I must be traversing. There were changes of direction and of steepness,[b] and once I came to a long, low, level passage where I had to wriggle[c] feet first along the rocky floor, holding my[d] torch at arm's length beyond my head. The place was not high enough for kneeling. After that were more of the steep steps, and I was still scrambling down interminably when my failing torch died out. I do not think I noticed it at the time, for when I did notice it[e] I was still holding it high[f] above me as if it were ablaze. I was quite unbalanced with that instinct for the strange and the unknown which has[g] made me a wanderer upon earth and a haunter of far, ancient, and forbidden places.

In the darkness there flashed before my mind fragments of my cherished treasury[h] of daemoniac lore; sentences from Alhazred the mad Arab, paragraphs from the apocryphal nightmares[i] of Damascius, and infamous lines from the delirious "Image du Monde"[j] of Gauthier de Metz.[k] I repeated queer extracts, and muttered of Afrasiab and the daemons that floated with him down the Oxus; later chanting[l] over and over again a phrase from one of Lord Dunsany's tales—"the[m] unreverberate blackness of the abyss".[n] Once when the descent grew

[a] had] *om.* C, D, E
[b] steepness,] steepness; C, D, E
[c] wriggle] wriggle my E
[d] my] *om.* C, D, E
[e] it] it, A
[f] high] *om.* C, D, E
[g] has] had A, C, D, E
[h] treasury] *bijouterie* A, B [*revised by HPL*]
[i] apocryphal nightmares] apoeryphal mightmares C
[j] "Image du Monde"] *Image du Monde* E
[k] the apocryphal . . . Metz.] Poe and Beaudelaire [Baudelaire B], and thoughts from the venerable Ambrose Bierce. A, B [*revised by HPL*]
[l] chanting] chaunting A, C, D
[m] tales—"the] Tales—"the A; Tales—"The D; tales—"The E
[n] abyss".] abyss." A, C, D, E

amazingly steep I recited something in sing-song[a] from Thomas Moore until I feared to recite more:[b]

> "A reservoir of darkness, black
>   As witches' cauldrons[c] are, when fill'd
> With moon-drugs in th' eclipse distill'd.
> Leaning to look if foot might pass
> Down thro' that chasm, I saw, beneath,
> As far as vision could explore,
> The jetty sides as smooth as glass,
> Looking as if just varnish'd o'er
> With that dark pitch the Sea[d] of Death
> Throws out upon its slimy shore."

Time had quite ceased to exist when my feet again felt a level floor, and I found myself in a place slightly higher than the rooms in the two smaller temples now so incalculably far above my head. I could not quite stand, but could kneel upright, and in the dark I shuffled and crept hither and thither at random. I soon knew that I was in a narrow passage whose walls were lined with cases of wood having glass fronts. As in that palaeozoic[e] and abysmal place I felt of such things as polished wood and glass I shuddered at the possible implications. The cases were apparently ranged along each side of the passage at regular intervals, and were oblong and horizontal, hideously like coffins in shape and size. When I tried to move two or three for further examination, I found[f] they were firmly fastened.

I saw that the passage was a long one, so floundered ahead rapidly in a creeping run that would have seemed horrible had any eye watched me in the blackness; crossing from side to side occasionally[g] to feel of my surroundings and be sure[h] the walls and rows of cases

---

[a] sing-song] singsong D
[b] more:] more— A
[c] cauldrons] caldrons A
[d] Sea] Seat D, E
[e] palaeozoic] palaeozotic A; Palaeozoic D, E
[f] found] found that C, D, E
[g] occasionally] occasionly A
[h] sure] sur C

still stretched on. Man[a] is so used to thinking visually that I almost forgot the darkness and pictured the endless corridor of wood and glass in its low-studded monotony as though I saw it. And then in a moment of indescribable emotion I did see it.

Just when my fancy merged into real sight I cannot tell; but there came a gradual glow ahead, and all at once I knew that I saw the dim outlines of the corridor and the cases, revealed by some unknown subterranean phosphorescence. For a little while all was exactly as I had imagined it, since the glow was very faint; but as I mechanically kept on[b] stumbling ahead into the stronger light I realised that my fancy had been but feeble. This hall was no relic of crudity like the temples in the city above, but a monument of the most magnificent and exotic art. Rich, vivid, and daringly fantastic designs and pictures formed a continuous scheme of mural painting whose lines and colours were beyond description. The cases were of a strange golden wood, with fronts of exquisite glass, and contained[c] the mummified forms of creatures outreaching in grotesqueness the most chaotic dreams of man.

To convey any idea of these monstrosities is impossible. They were of the reptile kind, with body lines suggesting sometimes the crocodile, sometimes the seal, but more often nothing of which either the naturalist or the paleaeontologist ever heard. In size they approximated a small man, and their fore legs[d] bore delicate and evidently flexible[e] feet curiously like human hands and fingers. But strangest of all were their heads, which presented a contour violating all known biological principles. To nothing can such things be well compared—in one flash I thought of comparisons as varied as the cat, the bulldog,[f] the mythic Satyr, and the human being. Not Jove himself had[g] so colossal and protuberant[h] a forehead, yet the horns and the

[a] Man] man C
[b] on] *om.* C, D, E
[c] contained] containing C, D, E
[d] fore legs] fore-legs D, E
[e] evidently flexible] evidently C; evident D, E
[f] bulldog,] bull-dog, A
[g] had] had had C, D, E
[h] protuberant] protruberant D

noselessness and the alligator-like[a] jaw placed the things outside all established categories. I debated for a time on the reality of the mummies, half[b] suspecting they were artificial idols; but soon decided they were indeed some palaeogean species which had lived when the nameless city was alive. To crown their grotesqueness, most of them were gorgeously enrobed in the costliest of fabrics, and lavishly laden with ornaments of gold, jewels, and unknown shining metals.

The importance of these crawling creatures must have been vast, for they held first place among the wild designs on the frescoed walls and ceiling. With matchless skill had the artist drawn them in a world of their own, wherein they had cities and gardens fashioned to suit their dimensions; and I could not[c] but think that their pictured history was allegorical, perhaps shewing the progress of the race that worshipped them. These creatures, I said to myself, were to the men of the nameless city what the she-wolf was to Rome, or some totem-beast is to a tribe of Indians.

Holding this view, I thought[d] I could trace roughly a wonderful epic of the nameless city; the tale of a mighty seacoast metropolis that ruled the world before Africa rose out of the waves, and of[e] its struggles as the sea shrank[f] away, and the desert crept into the fertile valley that held it. I saw its wars and triumphs, its troubles and defeats, and afterward[g] its terrible fight against the desert when thousands of its people—here represented in allegory by the grotesque reptiles—were driven to chisel their way down through the rocks in some marvellous manner to another world whereof their prophets had told them. It was all vividly weird and realistic, and its connexion[h] with the awesome descent I had made was unmistakable. I even recognised[i] the passages.

---

[a] alligator-like] aligator-like A
[b] half] have A
[c] not] not help C, D, E
[d] I thought] *om.* E
[e] of] *om.* A
[f] shrank] shrunk A
[g] afterward] afterwards A
[h] connexion] connection C, D, E
[i] recognised] recognized A, E

As I crept along the corridor toward the brighter light I saw later stages of the painted epic[a]—the leave-taking[b] of the race that had dwelt in the nameless city and the valley around for ten million years; the race whose souls shrank from quitting scenes their bodies had known so long,[c] where they had settled as nomads in the earth's youth, hewing in the virgin rock those primal[d] shrines at which they never[e] ceased to worship. Now that the light was better I studied the pictures more closely,[f] and, remembering that the strange reptiles must represent the unknown men, pondered upon the customs of the nameless city. Many things were peculiar and inexplicable. The civilisation, which included a written alphabet, had seemingly risen to a higher order than those immeasurably later civilisations[g] of Egypt and Chaldaea,[h] yet there were curious omissions.[i] I could, for example, find no pictures to represent deaths or funeral customs, save such as were related to wars, violence, and plagues; and I wondered at the reticence shewn[j] concerning natural death. It was as though an ideal of earthly[k] immortality had been fostered as a cheering illusion.

Still nearer the end of the passage were painted scenes of the utmost picturesqueness and extravagance;[l] contrasted views of the nameless city in its desertion and growing ruin, and of the strange new realm or[m] paradise to which the race had hewed[n] its way through the stone. In these views the city and the desert valley were shewn always by moonlight, a[o] golden nimbus hovering over the fallen walls and half

[a] epic] epopee A, B [*revised by HPL*]
[b] leave-taking] leave taking C
[c] long,] long C, D, E
[d] primal] premal C
[e] never] nevef A; had never C, D, E
[f] closely,] closely C, D, E
[g] later civilisations] latler eivilisations C
[h] Chaldaea,] Chaldeo, A; Chaldea D, E
[i] omissions.] omissions C
[j] shewn] shown D, E
[k] earthly] *om.* C, D, E
[l] extravagance;] extravagance: E
[m] or] of C, D, E
[n] hewed] hewn A
[o] a] *om.* E

revealing[a] the splendid perfection of former times, shewn[b] spectrally[c] and elusively by the artist. The paradisal scenes were almost too extravagant to be believed;[d] portraying a hidden world of eternal day filled with glorious cities and ethereal[e] hills and valleys. At the very last I thought I saw signs of an artistic anticlimax. The paintings were less skilful,[f] and much more bizarre than even the wildest of the earlier scenes. They seemed to record a slow decadence of the ancient stock, coupled with a growing ferocity toward the outside world from which it was driven by the desert. The forms of the people—always represented by the sacred reptiles—appeared to be gradually wasting away, though their spirit as[g] shewn hovering about[h] the ruins by moonlight gained in proportion. Emaciated priests, displayed as reptiles in ornate robes, cursed the upper air and all who breathed it; and one terrible final scene shewed a primitive-looking man, perhaps a pioneer of ancient Irem, the City of Pillars,[i] torn to pieces by members of the elder race. I remembered[j] how the Arabs fear the nameless city,[k] and was glad that beyond this place the grey walls and ceiling were bare.

As I viewed the pageant of mural history I had approached very closely the end of the low-ceiled hall, and was aware of a great[l] gate through which came all of the illuminating phosphorescence. Creeping up to it, I cried aloud in transcendent amazement at what lay beyond; for instead of other and brighter chambers there was only an illimitable void of uniform radiance, such as one might fancy when gazing down from the peak of Mount Everest upon a sea of sunlit mist. Behind me

---

[a] half revealing] half-revealing A, B, C, D, E
[b] shewn] shown E
[c] spectrally] sprectrally A
[d] believed;] believed, E
[e] ethereal] etherial A
[f] skilful,] skillful, E
[g] as] was D
[h] about] above C, D, E
[i] City of Pillars,] city of pillars, A
[j] remembered] remember D, E
[k] city,] sity, E
[l] great] *om.* C, D, E

was a passage so cramped that I could not stand upright in it; before me was an infinity of subterranean effulgence.

Reaching down from the passage into the abyss was the head of a steep flight of steps—small numerous steps like those of the[a] black passages I had traversed—but after a few feet the glowing vapours concealed everything. Swung back open against the left-hand wall of the passage was a massive door of brass, incredibly thick and decorated with fantastic bas-reliefs, which could if closed shut the whole inner world of light away from the vaults and passages of rock. I looked at the steps, and for the nonce dared not try them. I touched the open brass door, and could not move it. Then I sank prone to the stone floor, my mind aflame with prodigious reflections which not even a death-like[b] exhaustion could banish.[c]

As I lay still with closed eyes, free to ponder, many things I had lightly noted[d] in the frescoes came back to me with new and terrible significance—scenes representing the nameless city in its heyday,[e] the vegetation of the valley around it, and the distant lands with which its merchants traded. The allegory of the crawling creatures puzzled me by its universal prominence,[f] and I wondered that it should[g] be so closely followed in a pictured history of such importance.[h] In the frescoes the nameless city had been shewn in proportions fitted to the reptiles. I wondered what its real proportions and magnificence had been, and reflected a moment on certain oddities I had noticed in the ruins. I thought curiously of the lowness of the primal temples and of the underground corridor, which were doubtless hewn thus out of deference to the reptile deities[i] there honoured; though it perforce reduced the worshippers to crawling. Perhaps the very rites had[j]

---

[a] the] *om.* E
[b] death-like] death like A; deathlike B
[c] banish.] banish— C
[d] noted] noted lightly C
[e] heyday,] heyday— D, E
[f] prominence,] prominance, C
[g] should] would D, E
[h] importance.] importane. C
[i] deities] dieties A
[j] had] here C, D, E

involved a crawling in imitation of the creatures. No religious theory, however, could easily[a] explain why the level passage[b] in that awesome descent should be as low as the temples—or lower, since one could not even kneel in it. As I thought of the crawling creatures, whose hideous mummified forms were so close to me, I felt a new throb of fear. Mental associations are curious, and I shrank from the idea that except for the poor primitive man torn to pieces in the last painting, mine was the only human form amidst the many relics and symbols of primordial life.

But as always in my strange and roving existence, wonder soon drove out fear; for the luminous abyss and what it might contain presented a problem worthy of the greatest explorer. That a weird[c] world of mystery lay far down that flight of peculiarly small steps I could not doubt, and I hoped to find there those human memorials which the painted corridor had failed to give. The frescoes had pictured unbelievable cities, hills,[d] and valleys in this lower realm, and my fancy dwelt on the rich and colossal ruins that awaited me.

My fears, indeed, concerned the past rather than the future. Not even the physical horror of my position in that cramped corridor of dead reptiles and antediluvian frescoes, miles below the world I knew and faced by another world of eery light and mist, could match the lethal dread I felt at the abysmal antiquity of the scene and its soul. An ancientness so vast that measurement is feeble seemed to leer down from the primal stones and rock-hewn temples in[e] the nameless city, while the very latest of the astounding maps in the frescoes shewed oceans and continents that man has forgotten, with only here and there some vaguely familiar outline. Of what could have happened in the geological aeons[f] since the paintings ceased and[g] the death-hating race resentfully succumbed to decay, no man might say. Life had once teemed in these caverns and in the luminous realm beyond; now I was

---

[a] easily] *om.* A; easly C
[b] passage] passages C, D, E
[c] weird] wierd A
[d] hills,] *om.* C, D, E
[e] in] of A, C, D, E
[f] aeons] ages C, D, E
[g] and] had C

alone with vivid relics, and I trembled to think of the countless ages through which these relics had kept a silent and[a] deserted vigil.

Suddenly there came another burst of that acute fear which had intermittently seized me ever since I first saw the terrible valley and the nameless city under a cold moon, and despite my exhaustion I found myself starting frantically to a sitting[b] posture and gazing back along the black corridor toward the tunnels that rose to the outer world. My sensations were much[c] like those which had made me shun the nameless city at night, and were as inexplicable as they were poignant. In another moment, however, I received a still greater shock in the form of a definite sound—the first which had broken the utter silence of these tomb-like depths. It was a deep, low moaning, as of a distant throng of condemned spirits, and came from the direction in which I was staring. Its volume rapidly grew, till soon it[d] reverberated frightfully through the low passage, and at the same time I became conscious of an increasing draught of cold air, likewise flowing from the tunnels and the city above. The touch of this air seemed to restore my balance, for I instantly recalled the sudden gusts which had risen around the mouth of the abyss each sunset and sunrise, one of which had indeed served to reveal[e] the hidden tunnels to me. I looked at my watch and saw that sunrise was near, so braced myself to resist the gale which[f] was sweeping down to its cavern home as it had swept forth at evening. My fear again waned low, since a natural phenomenon tends to dispel broodings over the unknown.

More and more madly poured the shrieking, moaning[g] night-wind[h] into that[i] gulf of the inner earth. I dropped prone again and clutched vainly at the floor for fear of being swept bodily through the open gate into the phosphorescent abyss. Such fury I had not expected, and as I

[a] and] *om.* C, D, E
[b] sitting] setting C
[c] much] *om.* C, D, E
[d] soon it] it soon E
[e] served to reveal] revealed C, D, E
[f] which] that C, D, E
[g] shrieking, moaning] shrieking A
[h] night-wind] night wind A, B, C, D, E
[i] that] the E

grew aware of an actual slipping of my form toward the abyss I was beset by a thousand new terrors of apprehension and imagination. The malignancy of the blast awakened incredible fancies; once more I compared myself shudderingly to the only other[a] human image in that frightful corridor, the man who was torn to pieces by the nameless race, for in the fiendish clawing of the swirling currents there seemed to abide a vindictive rage all the stronger because it was largely impotent. I think I screamed frantically near the last—I was almost mad—but if I did so my cries were lost in the hell-born babel of the howling wind-wraiths. I tried to crawl against the murderous invisible torrent, but I could not even hold my own as I was pushed slowly and inexorably toward the unknown world. Finally reason must have wholly snapped,[b] for I fell to babbling over and over that unexplainable[c] couplet of the mad Arab Alhazred, who dreamed of the nameless city:

> "That is not dead which can eternal lie,
> And with strange aeons even death may die."[d]

Only the grim brooding desert gods know what really took place—what indescribable[e] struggles and scrambles in the dark I endured or what Abaddon guided me back to life, where I must always remember and shiver in the night-wind[f] till oblivion—or worse—claims me. Monstrous, unnatural, colossal, was the thing—too far beyond all the ideas of man to be believed except in the silent damnable small hours[g] when one cannot sleep.

I have said that the fury of the rushing blast was infernal—cacodaemoniacal—and that its voices were hideous with the pent-up viciousness of desolate eternities. Presently those[h] voices, while still chaotic before me, seemed to my beating brain to take articulate form

---

[a] other] *om.* C, D, E

[b] snapped,] snapped; C, D, E

[c] unexplainable] inexplainable A

[d] die."] die". A; die" C

[e] indescribable] indescrible C

[f] night-wind] night wind A, B, C, D, E

[g] hours] hours of the morning C, D, E

[h] those] these C, D, E

behind me; and down there in the grave of unnumbered[a] aeon-dead antiquities, leagues below the dawn-lit world of men, I heard the ghastly cursing and snarling of strange-tongued fiends. Turning, I saw outlined against the luminous aether of the abyss what[b] could not be seen against the dusk of the corridor—a nightmare horde of rushing devils; hate-distorted, grotesquely panoplied, half-transparent;[c] devils of a race no man might mistake—the crawling reptiles of the nameless city.

And as the wind died away I was plunged into the ghoul-peopled blackness[d] of earth's bowels; for behind the last of the creatures the great brazen door clanged shut with a deafening peal of metallic music whose reverberations swelled out to the distant world to hail the rising sun as Memnon hails it from the banks of the Nile.

[a] unnumbered] un-numbered C
[b] what] that D, E
[c] half-transparent;] half-transparent C, D, E
[d] ghoul-peopled blackness] ghoul-peoled darkness C; ghoul pooled darkness D; ghoul-pooled darkness E

The Quest of Iranon

Into the granite city of Teloth wandered the youth, vine-crowned, his yellow hair glistening with myrrh and his purple robe torn with briers of the mountain Sidrak that lies across the antique bridge of stone. The men of Teloth are dark and stern, and dwell in square houses, and with frowns they asked the stranger whence he had come and what were his name and fortune. So the youth answered:

"I am Iranon, and come from Aira, a far city that I recall only dimly but seek to find again. I am a singer of songs that I learned in the far city, and my calling is to make beauty with the things remembered of childhood. My wealth is in little memories and dreams, and in hopes that I sing in gardens when the moon is tender and the west wind stirs the lotos-buds."[a]

When the men of Teloth heard these things they whispered to one another; for though in the granite city there is no laughter or song, the stern men sometimes look to the Karthian hills in the spring and think of the lutes of distant Oonai whereof travellers have told. And thinking thus, they bade the stranger stay and sing in the square before the Tower of Mlin, though they liked not the colour of his tattered robe, nor the myrrh in his hair, nor his chaplet of vine-leaves, nor the

Editor's Note: The surviving A.Ms. is HPL's original draft, though not containing a great many revisions; it is written on the back of correspondence to him. A T.Ms. was prepared by Donald Wandrei (see *SL* 2.211) and is quite accurate; it bears a few corrections by HPL in pen. The first appearance—*Galleon* (July–August 1935)—followed the T.Ms., and the Arkham House editions followed the *Galleon* text. The posthumous *Weird Tales* appearance (March 1939) is not relevant to the tale's textual history.

Texts: A = A.Ms. (JHL); B = T.Ms. (JHL); C = *Galleon* 1, No. 1 (July–August 1935): 12–20; D = *Dagon and Other Macabre Tales* (Arkham House, 1965), 116–21. Copy-text: A.

[a] lotos-buds."] lotus-buds." B, C, D

youth in his golden voice. At evening Iranon sang, and while he sang an old man prayed and a blind man said he saw a nimbus over the singer's head. But most of the men of Teloth yawned, and some laughed and some went away[a] to sleep; for Iranon told nothing useful, singing only his memories, his dreams, and his hopes.

"I remember the twilight, the moon, and soft songs, and the window where I was rocked to sleep. And through the window was the street where the golden lights came, and where the shadows danced on houses of marble. I remember the square of moonlight on the floor, that was not like any other light, and the visions that danced in the moonbeams when my mother sang to me. And too, I remember the sun of morning bright above the many-coloured hills in summer, and the sweetness of flowers borne on the south wind that made the trees sing.

"O Aira, city of marble and beryl, how many are thy beauties! How loved I[b] the warm and fragrant groves across the hyaline Nithra, and the falls of the tiny Kra that flowed through the verdant valley! In those groves and in that vale the children wove wreaths for one another, and at dusk I dreamed strange dreams under the yath-trees on the mountain as I saw below me the lights of the city, and the curving Nithra reflecting a ribbon of stars.

"And in the city were palaces of veined and tinted marble, with golden domes and painted walls, and green gardens with cerulean pools and crystal fountains. Often I played in the gardens and waded in the pools, and lay and dreamed among the pale flowers under the trees. And sometimes at sunset I would climb the long hilly street to the citadel and the open place, and look down upon Aira, the magic city of marble and beryl, splendid in a robe of golden flame.

"Long have I missed thee, Aira, for I was but young when we went into exile; but my father was thy King and I shall come again to thee, for it is so decreed of Fate. All through seven lands have I sought thee, and some day shall I reign over thy groves and gardens, thy streets and palaces, and sing to men who shall know whereof I sing, and laugh not nor turn away. For I am Iranon, who was a Prince in Aira."

That night the men of Teloth lodged the stranger in a stable, and

[a] away] *om.* D
[b] loved I] I loved D

in the morning an archon came to him and told him to go to the shop of Athok the cobbler, and be apprenticed to him.

"But I am Iranon, a singer of songs," he said, "and have no heart for the cobbler's trade."

"All in Teloth must toil," replied the archon, "for that is the law." Then said Iranon,[a]

"Wherefore do ye toil; is it not that ye may live and be happy? And if ye toil only that ye may toil more, when shall happiness find you? Ye toil to live, but is not life made of beauty and song? And if ye suffer no singers among you, where shall be the fruits of your toil? Toil without song is like a weary journey without an end. Were not death more pleasing?" But the archon was sullen and did not understand, and rebuked the stranger.

"Thou art a strange youth, and I like not thy face nor[b] thy voice. The words thou speakest are blasphemy, for the gods of Teloth have said that toil is good. Our gods have promised us a haven of light beyond death, where there shall be rest without end, and crystal coldness amidst which none shall vex his mind with thought or his eyes with beauty. Go thou then to Athok the cobbler or be gone out of the city by sunset. All here must serve, and song is folly."

So Iranon went out of the stable and walked over the narrow stone streets between the gloomy square houses[c] of granite, seeking something green in the air of spring. But in Teloth was nothing[d] green, for all was of stone. On the faces of men were frowns, but by the stone embankment along the sluggish river Zuro sate[e] a young boy with sad eyes gazing into the waters to spy green budding branches washed down from the hills by the freshets. And the boy said to him:[f]

"Art thou not indeed he of whom the archons tell, who seekest a far city in a fair land? I am Romnod, and born of the blood of Teloth, but am not old in the ways of the granite city, and yearn daily for the warm groves and the distant lands of beauty and song. Beyond the

[a] Iranon,] Iranon: C, D
[b] nor] or C, D
[c] houses] house D
[d] green in . . . nothing] *om.* D
[e] sate] sat D
[f] him:] him, B

Karthian hills lieth Oonai, the city of lutes and dancing, which men whisper of and say is both lovely and terrible. Thither would I go were I old enough to find the way, and thither shouldst thou go an[a] thou wouldst sing and have men listen to thee. Let us leave the city[b] Teloth and fare together among the hills of spring. Thou shalt shew me the ways of travel and I will attend thy songs at evening when the stars one by one bring dreams to the minds of dreamers. And peradventure it may be that Oonai the city of lutes and dancing is even the fair Aira thou seekest, for it is told that thou hast not known Aira since old days, and a name often changeth. Let us go to Oonai, O Iranon of the golden head, where men shall know our longings and welcome us as brothers, nor ever laugh or frown at what we say." And Iranon answered:

"Be it so, small one; if any in this stone place yearn for beauty he must seek the mountains and beyond, and I would not leave thee to pine by the sluggish Zuro. But think not that delight and understanding dwell just across the Karthian hills, or in any spot thou canst find in a day's, or a year's, or a lustrum's journey. Behold, when I was small like thee I dwelt in the valley of Narthos by the frigid Xari, where none would listen to my dreams; and I told myself that when older I would go to Sinara on the southern slope, and sing to smiling dromedary-men in the market-place.[c] But when I went to Sinara I found the dromedary-men all drunken and ribald, and saw that their songs were not as mine, so I travelled in a barge down the Xari to onyx-walled Jaren. And the soldiers at Jaren laughed at me and drave me out, so that I wandered to many other cities. I have seen Stethelos that is below the great cataract, and have gazed on the marsh where Sarnath once stood. I have been to Thraa, Ilarnek, and Kadatheron on the winding river Ai, and have dwelt long in Olathoë[d] in the land of Lomar. But though I have had listeners sometimes, they have ever been few, and I know that welcome shall wait me only in Aira, the city of marble and beryl where my father once ruled as King. So for Aira shall we seek, though it were well to visit distant and lute-blessed Oonai across the Karthian

---

[a] an] and D
[b] city] city of D
[c] market-place.] market place. A, B, C, D
[d] Olathoë] Olathoe D

hills, which may indeed be Aira, though I think not. Aira's beauty is past imagining, and none can tell of it without rapture, whilst of Oonai the camel-drivers whisper leeringly."

At the sunset Iranon and small Romnod went forth from Teloth, and for long wandered amidst the green hills and cool forests. The way was rough and obscure, and never did they seem nearer to Oonai the city of lutes and dancing; but in the dusk as the stars came out Iranon would sing of Aira and its beauties and Romnod would listen, so that they were both happy after a fashion. They ate plentifully of fruit and red berries, and marked not the passing of time, but many years must have slipped away. Small Romnod was now not so small, and spoke deeply instead of shrilly, though Iranon was always the same, and decked his golden hair with vines and fragrant resins found in the woods. So it came to pass one day that Romnod seemed older than Iranon, though he had been very small when Iranon had found him watching for green budding branches in Teloth beside the sluggish stone-banked Zuro.[a]

Then one night when the moon was full the travellers came to a mountain crest and looked down upon the myriad lights[b] of Oonai. Peasants had told them they were near, and Iranon knew that this was not his native city of Aira. The lights of Oonai were not like those of Aira; for they were harsh and glaring, while the lights of Aira shine as softly and magically as shone the moonlight on the floor by the window where Iranon's mother once rocked him to sleep with song. But Oonai was a city of lutes and dancing, so Iranon and Romnod went down the steep slope that they might find men to whom songs and dreams would bring pleasure. And when they were come into the town they found rose-wreathed revellers bound from house to house and leaning from windows and balconies, who listened to the songs of Iranon and tossed him flowers and applauded when he was done. Then for a moment did Iranon believe he had found those who thought and felt even as he, though the town was not a[c] hundredth as fair as Aira.

---

[a] Zuro.] Zura. C
[b] lights] light D
[c] a] an A, B, C, D

When dawn came Iranon looked about with dismay, for the domes of Oonai were not golden in the sun, but grey and dismal. And the men of Oonai were pale with revelling[a] and dull with wine, and unlike the radiant men of Aira. But because the people had thrown him blossoms and acclaimed his songs Iranon stayed on, and with him Romnod, who liked the revelry of the town and wore in his dark hair roses and myrtle. Often at night Iranon sang to the revellers, but he was always as before, crowned only with the vine of the mountains and remembering the marble streets of Aira and the hyaline Nithra. In the frescoed halls of the Monarch did he sing, upon a crystal dais raised over a floor that was a mirror, and as he sang[b] he brought pictures to his hearers till the floor seemed to reflect old, beautiful, and half-remembered things instead of the wine-reddened feasters who pelted him with roses. And the King bade him put away his tattered purple, and clothed him in satin and cloth-of-gold, with rings of green jade and bracelets of tinted ivory, and lodged him in a gilded and tapestried chamber on a bed of sweet carven wood with canopies and coverlets of flower-embroidered silk. Thus dwelt Iranon in Oonai, the city of lutes and dancing.

It is not known how long Iranon tarried in Oonai, but one day the King brought to the palace some wild whirling dancers from the Liranian desert, and dusky flute-players from Drinen in the East, and after that the revellers threw their roses not so much at Iranon as at the dancers and the[c] flute-players. And day by day that Romnod who had been a small boy in granite Teloth grew coarser and redder with wine, till he dreamed less and less, and listened with less delight to the songs of Iranon. But though Iranon was sad he ceased not to sing, and at evening told again his dreams of Aira, the city of marble and beryl. Then one night the red[d] and fattened Romnod snorted heavily amidst the poppied silks of his banquet-couch and died writhing, whilst Iranon, pale and slender, sang to himself in a far corner. And when

---

[a] revelling] revelling, A, B, C, D [*comma crossed out in A by HPL*]
[b] sang] sang, C, D
[c] the] *om.* D
[d] red] reddened C, D

Iranon had wept over the grave of Romnod and strown[a] it with green budding branches, such as Romnod used to love, he put aside his silks and gauds and went forgotten out of Oonai the city of lutes and dancing clad only in the ragged purple in which he had come, and garlanded with fresh vines from the mountains.

Into the sunset wandered Iranon, seeking still for his native land and for men who would understand and cherish his songs and dreams. In all the cities of Cydathria and in the lands beyond the Bnazic[b] desert gay-faced children laughed at his olden songs and tattered robe of purple; but Iranon stayed ever young, and wore wreaths upon his golden head whilst he sang of Aira, delight of the past and hope of the future.

So came he one night to the squalid cot of an antique shepherd, bent and dirty, who kept lean[c] flocks on a stony slope above a quicksand marsh. To this man Iranon spoke, as to so many others:

"Canst thou tell me where I may find Aira, the city of marble and beryl, where flows the hyaline Nithra and where the falls of the tiny Kra sing to verdant valleys and hills forested with yath trees?" And[d] the shepherd, hearing, looked long and strangely at Iranon, as if recalling something very far away in time, and noted each line of the stranger's face, and his golden hair, and his crown of vine-leaves. But he was old, and shook his head as he replied:

"O stranger, I have indeed heard the name of Aira, and the other names thou hast spoken, but they come to me from afar down the waste of long years. I heard them in my youth from the lips of a playmate, a beggar's boy given to strange dreams, who would weave long tales about the moon and the flowers and the west wind. We used to laugh at him, for we knew him from his birth though he thought himself a King's son. He was comely, even as thou, but full of folly and strangeness; and he ran away when small to find those who would listen gladly to his songs and dreams. How often hath he sung to me of lands that never were, and things that never can be! Of Aira did he speak much; of Aira and the river Nithra, and the falls of the tiny Kra.

---

[a] strown] strewn B, C, D
[b] Bnazic] Bnazie D
[c] lean] *om.* C, D
[d] And] ¶ And B; and D

There would he ever say he once dwelt as a Prince, though here we knew him from his birth. Nor was there ever a marble city of Aira, nor[a] those who could delight in strange songs, save in the dreams of mine old playmate Iranon who is gone."

And in the twilight, as the stars came out one by one and the moon cast on the marsh a radiance like that which a child sees quivering on the floor as he is rocked to sleep at evening, there walked into the lethal quicksands a very old man in tattered purple, crowned with withered vine-leaves and gazing ahead as if upon the golden domes of a fair city where dreams are understood. That night something of youth and beauty died in the elder world.

---

[a] nor] or C, D

The Moon-Bog

Somewhere, to what remote and fearsome region I know not, Denys Barry has gone. I was with him the last night he lived among men, and heard his screams when the thing came to him; but all the peasants and police in County Meath could never find him, or the others, though they searched long and far. And now I shudder when I hear the frogs piping in swamps, or see the moon in lonely places.

I had known Denys Barry well in America, where he had grown rich, and had congratulated him when he bought back the old castle by the bog at sleepy Kilderry. It was from Kilderry that his father had come, and it was there that he wished to enjoy his wealth among ancestral scenes. Men of his blood had once ruled over Kilderry and built and dwelt in the castle, but those days were very remote, so that for generations the castle had been empty and decaying. After he went to Ireland Barry wrote me often, and told me how under his care the grey[a] castle was rising tower by tower to its ancient splendour;[b] how the ivy was climbing slowly over the restored walls as it had climbed so many centuries ago, and how the peasants blessed him for bringing back the old days with his gold from over the sea. But in time there came troubles, and the peasants ceased to bless him, and fled away instead as from a doom. And then he sent a letter and asked me to

Editor's Note: This is one of several tales where no manuscript and no publication in an amateur journal exist. We are therefore reliant on the only publication in HPL's lifetime—*Weird Tales* (June 1926)—which was followed by the Arkham House editions. The text seems on the whole accurately printed, but in the absence of a manuscript it is difficult to tell. My text makes standard emendations in conformity with HPL's customary orthorgraphic and typographical usages.

Texts: A = *Weird Tales* 7, No. 6 (June 1926): 805–10; B = *Dagon and Other Macabre Tales* (Arkham House, 1965), 91–98. Copy-text: A.

[a] grey] gray A, B
[b] splendour;] splendor; A; splendor, B

visit him, for he was lonely in the castle with no one to speak to save the new servants and labourers[a] he had brought from the North.

The bog was the cause of all these troubles, as Barry told me the night I came to the castle. I had reached Kilderry in the[b] summer sunset, as the gold of the sky lighted the green of the hills and groves and the blue of the bog, where on a far islet a strange olden ruin glistened spectrally. That sunset was very beautiful, but the peasants at Ballylough had warned me against it and said that Kilderry had become accursed, so that I almost shuddered to see the high turrets of the castle gilded with fire. Barry's motor had met me at the Ballylough station, for Kilderry is off the railway. The villagers had shunned the car and the driver from the North, but had whispered to me with pale faces when they saw I was going to Kilderry. And that night, after our reunion, Barry told me why.

The peasants had gone from Kilderry because Denys Barry was to drain the great bog. For all his love of Ireland, America had not left him untouched, and he hated the beautiful wasted space where peat might be cut and land opened up. The legends and superstitions of Kilderry did not move him, and he laughed when the peasants first refused to help, and then cursed him and went away to Ballylough with their few belongings as they saw his determination. In their place he sent for labourers[c] from the North, and when the servants left he replaced them likewise. But it was lonely among strangers, so Barry had asked me to come.

When I heard the fears which had driven the people from Kilderry I laughed as loudly as my friend had laughed, for these fears were of the vaguest, wildest, and most absurd character. They had to do with some preposterous legend of the bog, and of a grim guardian spirit that dwelt in the strange olden ruin on the far islet I had seen in the sunset. There were tales of dancing lights in the dark of the moon, and of chill winds when the night was warm; of wraiths in white hovering over the waters, and of an imagined city of stone deep down below the swampy surface. But foremost among the weird fancies, and alone in its absolute unanimity, was that of the curse awaiting him who should dare to touch or drain the vast reddish morass. There were secrets, said

---

[a] labourers] laborers A, B
[b] the] the the B
[c] labourers] laborers A, B

the peasants, which must not be uncovered; secrets that had lain hidden since the plague came to the children of Partholan in the fabulous years beyond history. In the "Book of Invaders"[a] it is told that these sons of the Greeks were all buried at Tallaght, but old men in Kilderry said that one city was overlooked save by its patron moon-goddess; so that only the wooded hills buried it when the men of Nemed swept down from Scythia in their thirty ships.

Such were the idle tales which had made the villagers leave Kilderry, and when I heard them I did not wonder that Denys Barry had refused to listen. He had, however, a great interest in antiquities;[b] and proposed to explore the bog thoroughly when it was drained. The white ruins on the islet he had often visited, but though their age was plainly great, and their contour very little like that of most ruins in Ireland, they were too dilapidated to tell the days of their glory. Now the work of drainage was ready to begin, and the labourers[c] from the North were soon to strip the forbidden bog of its green moss and red heather, and kill the tiny shell-paved streamlets and quiet blue pools fringed with rushes.

After Barry[d] had told me these things I was very drowsy, for the travels of the day had been wearying and my host had talked late into the night. A manservant shewed[e] me to my room, which was in a remote tower overlooking the village, and the plain at the edge of the bog, and the bog itself; so that I could see from my windows in the moonlight the silent roofs from which the peasants had fled and which now sheltered the labourers[f] from the North, and too, the parish church with its antique spire, and far out across the brooding bog the remote olden ruin on the islet gleaming white and spectral. Just as I dropped to sleep I fancied I heard faint sounds from the distance; sounds that were wild and half musical, and stirred me with a weird excitement which coloured[g] my dreams. But when I awaked next morning I felt it had all been a dream, for the visions I had seen were

[a] "Book of Invaders"] *Book of Invaders* A; *Book Of Invaders* B
[b] antiquities;] antiquities, B
[c] labourers] laborers A, B
[d] Barry] Berry B
[e] manservant shewed] man-servant showed A, B
[f] labourers] laborers A, B
[g] coloured] colored A, B

more wonderful than any sound of wild pipes in the night. Influenced by the legends that Barry had related, my mind had in slumber hovered around a stately city in a green valley, where marble streets and statues, villas and temples, carvings and inscriptions, all spoke in certain tones the glory that was Greece. When I told this dream to Barry we both laughed; but I laughed the louder, because he was perplexed about his labourers[a] from the North. For the sixth time they had all overslept, waking very slowly and dazedly, and acting as if they had not rested, although they were known to have gone early to bed the night before.

That morning and afternoon I wandered alone through the sun-gilded village and talked now and then with idle labourers,[b] for Barry was busy with the final plans for beginning his work of drainage. The labourers[c] were not as happy as they might have been;[d] for most of them seemed uneasy over some dream which they had had, yet which they tried in vain to remember. I told them of my dream, but they were not interested till I spoke of the weird sounds I thought I had heard. Then they looked oddly at me, and said that they seemed to remember weird sounds, too.

In the evening Barry dined with me and announced that he would begin the drainage in two days. I was glad, for although I disliked to see the moss and the heather and the little streams and lakes depart, I had a growing wish to discern the ancient secrets the deep-matted peat might hide. And that night my dreams of piping flutes and marble peristyles came to a sudden and disquieting end; for upon the city in the valley I saw a pestilence descend, and then a frightful avalanche of wooded slopes that covered the dead bodies in the streets and left unburied only the temple of Artemis on the high peak, where the aged moon-priestess Cleis lay cold and silent with a crown of ivory on her silver head.

I have said that I awaked suddenly and in alarm. For some time I could not tell whether I was waking or sleeping, for the sound of flutes still rang shrilly in my ears; but when I saw on the floor the icy

---

[a] labourers] laborers A, B
[b] labourers,] laborers, A, B
[c] labourers] laborers A, B
[d] been;] been, A, B

moonbeams and the outlines of a latticed Gothic[a] window I decided I
must be awake and in the castle at[b] Kilderry. Then I heard a clock
from some remote landing below strike the hour of two, and I knew I
was awake. Yet still there came that monotonous piping from afar;
wild, weird airs that made me think of some dance of fauns on distant
Maenalus. It would not let me sleep, and in impatience I sprang up and
paced the floor. Only by chance did I go to the north window and
look out upon the silent village and the plain at the edge of the bog. I
had no wish to gaze abroad, for I wanted to sleep; but the flutes
tormented me, and I had to do or see something. How could I have
suspected the thing I was to behold?

There in the moonlight that flooded the spacious plain was a
spectacle which no mortal, having seen it, could ever forget. To the
sound of reedy pipes that echoed over the bog there glided silently and
eerily a mixed throng of swaying figures, reeling through such a revel as
the Sicilians may have danced to Demeter in the old days under the
harvest moon beside the Cyane. The wide plain, the golden moonlight,
the shadowy moving forms, and above all the shrill monotonous piping,
produced an effect which almost paralysed[c] me; yet I noted amidst my
fear that half of these tireless, mechanical dancers were the labourers[d]
whom I had thought asleep, whilst the other half were strange airy beings
in white, half-indeterminate in nature, but suggesting pale wistful naiads
from the haunted fountains of the bog. I do not know how long I gazed
at this sight from the lonely turret window before I dropped suddenly in
a dreamless swoon, out of which the high sun of morning aroused me.

My first impulse on awaking was to communicate all my fears and
observations to Denys Barry, but as I saw the sunlight glowing
through the latticed east window I became sure that there was no
reality in what I thought I had seen. I am given to strange phantasms,[e]
yet am never weak enough to believe in them; so on this occasion
contented myself with questioning the labourers,[f] who slept very late

[a] Gothic] gothic A, B
[b] at] of B
[c] paralysed] paralyzed A, B
[d] labourers] laborers A, B
[e] phantasms,] fantasms, A, B
[f] labourers,] laborers, A, B

and recalled nothing of the previous night save misty dreams of shrill sounds. This matter of the spectral piping harassed me greatly, and I wondered if the crickets of autumn had come before their time to vex the night and haunt the visions of men. Later in the day I watched Barry in the library poring over his plans for the great work which was to begin on the morrow, and for the first time felt a touch of the same kind of fear that had driven the peasants away. For some unknown reason I dreaded the thought of disturbing the ancient bog and its sunless secrets, and pictured terrible sights lying black under the unmeasured depth of age-old peat. That these secrets should be brought to light seemed injudicious, and I began to wish for an excuse to leave the castle and the village. I went so far as to talk casually to Barry on the subject, but did not dare continue after he gave his resounding laugh. So I was silent when the sun set fulgently over the far hills, and Kilderry blazed all red and gold in a flame that seemed a portent.

Whether the events of that night were of reality or illusion I shall never ascertain. Certainly they transcend anything we dream of in Nature[a] and the universe; yet in no normal fashion can I explain those disappearances which were known to all men after it was over. I retired early and full of dread, and for a long time could not sleep in the uncanny silence of the tower. It was very dark, for although the sky was clear the moon was now well in the wane, and would not rise till the small hours. I thought as I lay there of Denys Barry, and of what would befall that bog when the day came, and found myself almost frantic with an impulse to rush out into the night, take Barry's car, and drive madly to Ballylough out of the menaced lands. But before my fears could crystallise[b] into action I had fallen asleep, and gazed in dreams upon the city in the valley, cold and dead under a shroud of hideous shadow.

Probably it was the shrill piping that awaked me, yet that piping was not what I noticed first when I opened my eyes. I was lying with my back to the east window overlooking the bog, where the waning moon would rise, and therefore expected to see light cast on the opposite wall before me; but I had not looked for such a sight as now appeared. Light indeed glowed on the panels ahead, but it was not any

[a] Nature] nature A, B
[b] crystallise] crystallize A, B

light that the moon gives. Terrible and piercing was the shaft of ruddy refulgence that streamed through the Gothic[a] window, and the whole chamber was brilliant with a splendour[b] intense and unearthly. My immediate actions were peculiar for such a situation, but it is only in tales that a man does the dramatic and foreseen thing. Instead of looking out across the bog toward the source of the new light, I kept my eyes from the window in panic fear, and clumsily drew on my clothing with some dazed idea of escape. I remember seizing my revolver and hat, but before it was over I had lost them both without firing the one or donning the other. After a time the fascination of the red radiance overcame my fright, and I crept to the east window and looked out whilst the maddening, incessant piping whined and reverberated through the castle and over all the village.

Over the bog was a deluge of flaring light, scarlet and sinister, and pouring from the strange olden ruin on the far islet. The aspect of that ruin I cannot[c] describe—I must have been mad, for it seemed to rise majestic and undecayed, splendid and column-cinctured, the flame-reflecting marble of its entablature piercing the sky like the apex of a temple on a mountaintop.[d] Flutes shrieked and drums began to beat, and as I watched in awe and terror I thought I saw dark saltant forms silhouetted grotesquely against the vision of marble and effulgence. The effect was titanic—altogether unthinkable—and I might have stared indefinitely had not the sound of the piping seemed to grow stronger at my left. Trembling with a terror oddly mixed with ecstasy I crossed the circular room to the north window from which I could see the village and the plain at the edge of the bog. There my eyes dilated again with a wild wonder as great as if I had not just turned from a scene beyond the pale of Nature,[e] for on the ghastly red-litten plain was moving a procession of beings in such a manner as none ever saw before save in nightmares.

Half gliding, half floating in the air, the white-clad bog-wraiths

---

were slowly retreating toward the still waters and the island ruin in fantastic formations suggesting some ancient and solemn ceremonial dance. Their waving translucent arms, guided by the detestable piping of those unseen flutes, beckoned in uncanny rhythm to a throng of lurching labourers[a] who followed dog-like[b] with blind, brainless, floundering steps as if dragged by a clumsy but resistless daemon-will.[c] As the naiads neared the bog, without altering their course, a new line of stumbling stragglers zigzagged drunkenly out of the castle from some door far below my window, groped sightlessly across the courtyard and through the intervening bit of village, and joined the floundering column of labourers[d] on the plain. Despite their distance below me I at once knew they were the servants brought from the North, for I recognised[e] the ugly and unwieldy form of the cook, whose very absurdness had now become unutterably tragic. The flutes piped horribly, and again I heard the beating of the drums from the direction of the island ruin. Then silently and gracefully the naiads reached the water and melted one by one into the ancient bog; while the line of followers, never checking their speed, splashed awkwardly after them and vanished amidst a tiny vortex of unwholesome bubbles which I could barely see in the scarlet light. And as the last pathetic straggler, the fat cook, sank heavily out of sight in that sullen pool, the flutes and the drums grew silent, and the blinding red rays from the ruins snapped instantaneously out, leaving the village of doom lone and desolate in the wan beams of a new-risen moon.

My condition was now one of indescribable chaos. Not knowing whether I was mad or sane, sleeping or waking, I was saved only by a merciful numbness. I believe I did ridiculous things such as offering prayers to Artemis, Latona, Demeter, Persephone, and Plouton. All that I recalled of a classic youth came to my lips as the horrors of the situation roused my deepest superstitions. I felt that I had witnessed the death of a whole village, and knew I was alone in the castle with Denys

[a] labourers] laborers A, B
[b] dog-like] doglike A, B
[c] daemon-will.] demon-will. A, B
[d] labourers] laborers A, B
[e] recognised] recognized A, B

Barry, whose boldness had brought down a doom. As I thought of him new terrors convulsed me, and I fell to the floor; not fainting, but physically helpless. Then I felt the icy blast from the east window where the moon had risen, and began to hear the shrieks in the castle far below me. Soon those shrieks had attained a magnitude and quality which cannot[a] be written of, and which make me faint as I think of them. All I can say is that they came from something I had known as a friend.

At some time during this shocking period the cold wind and the screaming must have roused me, for my next impression is of racing madly through inky rooms and corridors and out across the courtyard into the hideous night. They found me at dawn wandering mindless near Ballylough, but what unhinged me utterly was not any of the horrors I had seen or heard before. What I muttered about as I came slowly out of the shadows was a pair of fantastic incidents which occurred in my flight;[b] incidents of no significance, yet which haunt me unceasingly when I am alone in certain marshy places or in the moonlight.

As I fled from that accursed castle along the bog's edge I heard a new sound;[c] common, yet unlike any I had heard before at Kilderry. The stagnant waters, lately quite devoid of animal life, now teemed with a horde of slimy enormous frogs which piped shrilly and incessantly in tones strangely out of keeping with their size. They glistened bloated and green in the moonbeams, and seemed to gaze up at the fount of light. I followed the gaze of one very fat and ugly frog, and saw the second of the things which drove my senses away.

Stretching directly from the strange olden ruin on the far islet to the waning moon, my eyes seemed to trace a beam of faint quivering radiance having no reflection in the waters of the bog. And upward along that pallid path my fevered fancy pictured a thin shadow slowly writhing; a vague contorted shadow struggling as if drawn by unseen daemons.[d] Crazed as I was, I saw in that awful shadow a monstrous resemblance—a nauseous, unbelievable caricature—a blasphemous effigy of him who had been Denys Barry.

---

[a] cannot] can not A, B
[b] flight;] flight: B
[c] sound;] sound: B
[d] daemons.] demons. A, B

The Outsider

That night the Baron dreamt of many a woe;[a]
And all his warrior-guests, with shade and form
Of witch, and demon, and large coffin-worm,
Were long be-nightmared.

—Keats.[b]

U nhappy is he to whom the memories of childhood bring only
fear and sadness. Wretched is he who looks back upon lone
hours in vast and dismal chambers with brown hangings and
maddening rows of antique books, or upon awed watches in twilight
groves of grotesque, gigantic, and vine-encumbered trees that silently
wave twisted branches far aloft. Such a lot the gods gave to me—to
me, the dazed, the disappointed; the barren, the broken. And yet I am
strangely content,[c] and cling desperately to those sere memories, when
my mind momentarily threatens to reach beyond to *the other.*

I know not where I was born, save that the castle was infinitely old

---

Editor's Note: In the absence of a manuscript, we are reliant on the two publications in HPL's lifetime, both in *Weird Tales* (April 1926 and June–July 1931).
The second appearance reveals numerous divergences from the first, but these seem
to be in line with *Weird Tales'* usual emendations of HPL's texts in accordance
with "house style"; they do not appear to constitute deliberate revisions by HPL.
Unfortunately, the Arkham House editions followed the second appearance. Aside
from restoring many readings from the first appearance, I have made other
emendations in conformity with HPL's customary usages.

    Texts: A = *Weird Tales* 7, No. 4 (April 1926): 449–53; B = *Weird Tales* 17, No.
4 (June–July 1931): 566–71; C = *The Dunwich Horror and Others* (Arkham House,
1963), 53–59. Copy-text: A.

[a] woe;] wo; A, B, C
[b] That . . . be-nightmared. / —Keats.] *That . . . be-nightmared.*   —KEATS B
[c] content,] content B, C

and infinitely horrible;[a] full of dark passages and having high ceilings where the eye could find only cobwebs and shadows. The stones in the crumbling corridors seemed always hideously damp, and there was an accursed smell everywhere, as of the piled-up corpses of dead generations. It was never light, so that I used sometimes to light candles and gaze steadily at them for relief;[b] nor was there any sun outdoors, since the terrible trees grew high above the topmost accessible tower. There was one black tower which reached above the trees into the unknown outer sky, but that was partly ruined and could not be ascended save by a well-nigh impossible climb up the sheer wall, stone by stone.

I must have lived years in this place, but I cannot[c] measure the time. Beings must have cared for my needs, yet I cannot[d] recall any person except myself;[e] or anything alive but the noiseless rats and bats and spiders. I think that whoever nursed me must have been shockingly aged, since my first conception of a living person was that of something mockingly like myself, yet distorted, shrivelled,[f] and decaying like the castle. To me there was nothing grotesque in the bones and skeletons that strowed[g] some of the stone crypts deep down among the foundations. I fantastically associated these things with every-day[h] events, and thought them more natural than the coloured[i] pictures of living beings which I found in many of the mouldy[j] books. From such books I learned all that I know. No teacher urged or guided me, and I do not recall hearing any human voice in all those years—not even my own; for although I had read of speech, I had never thought to try to speak aloud. My aspect was a matter equally unthought of, for there were no mirrors in the castle, and I merely regarded myself by instinct

[a] horrible;] horrible, B, C

[b] relief;] relief, B, C

[c] cannot] can not A, B, C

[d] cannot] can not A, B, C

[e] myself;] myself, B, C

[f] shrivelled,] shriveled, A, B, C

[g] strowed] strewed A, B, C

[h] every-day] everyday A, B, C

[i] coloured] colored A, B, C

[j] mouldy] moldy A, B, C

as akin to the youthful figures I saw drawn and painted in the books. I felt conscious of youth because I remembered so little.

Outside, across the putrid moat and under the dark mute trees, I would often lie and dream for hours about what I read in the books; and would longingly picture myself amidst gay crowds in the sunny world beyond the endless forest.[a] Once I tried to escape from the forest, but as I went farther from the castle the shade grew denser and the air more filled with brooding fear; so that I ran frantically back lest I lose my way in a labyrinth of nighted silence.

So through endless twilights I dreamed and waited, though I knew not what I waited for. Then in the shadowy solitude my longing for light grew so frantic that I could rest no more, and I lifted entreating hands to the single black ruined tower that reached above the forest into the unknown outer sky. And at last I resolved to scale that tower, fall though I might; since it were better to glimpse the sky and perish, than to live without ever beholding day.

In the dank twilight I climbed the worn and aged stone stairs till I reached the level where they ceased, and thereafter clung perilously to small footholds leading upward. Ghastly and terrible was that dead, stairless cylinder of rock; black, ruined, and deserted, and sinister with startled bats whose wings made no noise. But more ghastly and terrible still was the slowness of my progress; for climb as I might, the darkness overhead grew no thinner, and a new chill as of haunted and venerable mould[b] assailed me. I shivered as I wondered why I did not reach the light, and would have looked down had I dared. I fancied that night had come suddenly upon me, and vainly groped with one free hand for a window embrasure, that I might peer out and above, and try to judge the height I had attained.

All at once, after an infinity of awesome, sightless crawling up that concave and desperate precipice, I felt my head touch a solid thing, and I knew I must have gained the roof, or at least some kind of floor. In the darkness I raised my free hand and tested the barrier, finding it stone and immovable. Then came a deadly circuit of the tower, clinging to whatever holds the slimy wall could give; till finally my

[a] forest.] forests. C
[b] mould] mold A, B, C

testing hand found the barrier yielding, and I turned upward again, pushing the slab or door with my head as I used both hands in my fearful ascent. There was no light revealed above, and as my hands went higher I knew that my climb was for the nonce ended; since the slab was the trap-door of an aperture leading to a level stone surface of greater circumference than the lower tower, no doubt the floor of some lofty and capacious observation chamber. I crawled through carefully, and tried to prevent the heavy slab from falling back into place;[a] but failed in the latter attempt. As I lay exhausted on the stone floor I heard the eery echoes of its fall, but hoped when necessary to pry it up again.

Believing I was now at a[b] prodigious height, far above the accursed branches of the wood, I dragged myself up from the floor and fumbled about for windows, that I might look for the first time upon the sky, and the moon and stars of which I had read. But on every hand I was disappointed; since all that I found were vast shelves of marble, bearing odious oblong boxes of disturbing size. More and more I reflected, and wondered what hoary secrets might abide in this high apartment so many aeons[c] cut off from the castle below. Then unexpectedly my hands came upon a doorway, where hung a portal of stone, rough with strange chiselling.[d] Trying it, I found it locked; but with a supreme burst of strength I overcame all obstacles and dragged it open inward. As I did so there came to me the purest ecstasy I have ever known; for shining tranquilly through an ornate grating of iron, and down a short stone passageway of steps that ascended from the newly found doorway, was the radiant full moon, which I had never before seen save in dreams and in vague visions I dared not call memories.

Fancying now that I had attained the very pinnacle of the castle, I commenced to rush up the few steps beyond the door; but the sudden veiling of the moon by a cloud caused me to stumble, and I felt my way more slowly in the dark. It was still very dark when I reached the grating—which I tried carefully and found unlocked, but which I did

[a] place;] place, B, C
[b] a] om. C
[c] aeons] eons A, B, C
[d] chiselling.] chiseling. A, B, C

not open for fear of falling from the amazing height to which I had climbed. Then the moon came out.

Most daemoniacal[a] of all shocks is that of the abysmally unexpected and grotesquely unbelievable. Nothing I had before undergone could compare in terror with what I now saw; with the bizarre[b] marvels that sight implied. The sight itself was as simple as it was stupefying, for it was merely this: instead of a dizzying prospect of treetops seen from a lofty eminence, there stretched around me on a[c] level through the grating nothing less than *the solid ground,* decked and diversified by marble slabs and columns, and overshadowed by an ancient stone church, whose ruined spire gleamed spectrally in the moonlight.

Half unconscious, I opened the grating and staggered out upon the white gravel path that stretched away in two directions. My mind, stunned and chaotic as it was, still held the frantic craving for light; and not even the fantastic wonder which had happened could stay my course. I neither knew nor cared whether my experience was insanity, dreaming, or magic; but was determined to gaze on brilliance and gaiety[d] at any cost. I knew not who I was or what I was, or what my surroundings might be; though as I continued to stumble along I became conscious of a kind of fearsome latent memory that made my progress not wholly fortuitous. I passed under an arch out of that region of slabs and columns, and wandered through the open country; sometimes following the visible road, but sometimes leaving it curiously to tread across meadows where only occasional ruins bespoke the ancient presence of a forgotten road. Once I swam across a swift river where crumbling, mossy masonry told of a bridge long vanished.

Over two hours must have passed before I reached what seemed to be my goal, a venerable ivied castle in a thickly wooded park;[e] maddeningly familiar, yet full of perplexing strangeness to me. I saw that the moat was filled in, and that some of the well-known[f] towers were demolished; whilst new wings existed to confuse the beholder.

[a] daemoniacal] demoniacal A, B, C
[b] bizarre] bizzare C
[c] a] the C
[d] gaiety] gayety A, B, C
[e] park;] park, B, C
[f] well-known] well known A

But what I observed with chief interest and delight were the open windows—gorgeously ablaze with light and sending forth sound of the gayest revelry. Advancing to one of these I looked in and saw an oddly dressed company, indeed; making merry, and speaking brightly to one another. I had never, seemingly, heard human speech before;[a] and could guess only vaguely what was said. Some of the faces seemed to hold expressions that brought up incredibly remote recollections;[b] others were utterly alien.

I now stepped through the low window into the brilliantly lighted room, stepping as I did so from my single bright moment of hope to my blackest convulsion of despair and realisation.[c] The nightmare was quick to come;[d] for as I entered, there occurred immediately one of the most terrifying demonstrations I had ever conceived. Scarcely had I crossed the sill when there descended upon the whole company a sudden and unheralded fear of hideous intensity, distorting every face and evoking the most horrible screams from nearly every throat. Flight was universal, and in the clamour[e] and panic several fell in a swoon and were dragged away by their madly fleeing companions. Many covered their eyes with their hands, and plunged blindly and awkwardly in their race to escape;[f] overturning furniture and stumbling against the walls before they managed to reach one of the many doors.

The cries were shocking; and as I stood in the brilliant apartment alone and dazed, listening to their vanishing echoes, I trembled at the thought of what might be lurking near me unseen. At a casual inspection the room seemed deserted, but when I moved toward one of the alcoves I thought I detected a presence there—a hint of motion beyond the golden-arched doorway leading to another and somewhat similar room. As I approached the arch I began to perceive the presence more clearly; and then, with the first and last sound I ever uttered—a ghastly ululation that revolted me almost as poignantly as its noxious cause—I beheld in full, frightful vividness the inconceivable, indescribable, and

[a] before;] before C
[b] recollections;] recollections, B, C
[c] realisation.] realization. A, B, C
[d] come;] come, A, B, C
[e] clamour] clamor A, B, C
[f] escape;] escape, A, B, C

unmentionable monstrosity which had by its simple appearance changed a merry company to a herd of delirious fugitives.

I cannot[a] even hint what it was like, for it was a compound of all that is unclean, uncanny, unwelcome, abnormal, and detestable. It was the ghoulish shade of decay, antiquity, and desolation;[b] the putrid, dripping eidolon of unwholesome revelation;[c] the awful baring of that which the merciful earth should always hide. God knows it was not of this world—or no longer of this world—yet to my horror I saw in its eaten-away and bone-revealing outlines a leering, abhorrent travesty on the human shape; and in its mouldy,[d] disintegrating apparel an unspeakable quality that chilled me even more.

I was almost paralysed,[e] but not too much so to make a feeble effort toward flight; a backward stumble which failed to break the spell in which the nameless, voiceless monster held me. My eyes,[f] bewitched by the glassy orbs which stared loathsomely into them, refused to close; though they were mercifully blurred, and shewed[g] the terrible object but indistinctly after the first shock. I tried to raise my hand to shut out the sight, yet so stunned were my nerves that my arm could not fully obey my will. The attempt, however, was enough to disturb my balance; so that I had to stagger forward several steps to avoid falling. As I did so I became suddenly and agonisingly[h] aware of the *nearness* of the carrion thing, whose hideous hollow breathing I half fancied I could hear. Nearly mad, I found myself yet able to throw out a hand to ward off the foetid[i] apparition which pressed so close; when in one cataclysmic second of cosmic nightmarishness and hellish accident *my fingers touched the rotting outstretched paw of the monster beneath the golden arch.*

I did not shriek, but all the fiendish ghouls that ride the night-wind shrieked for me as in that same second there crashed down upon my

---

[a] cannot] can not A, B, C
[b] desolation;] desolution; C
[c] revelation;] revelation, B, C
[d] mouldy,] moldy, A, B, C
[e] paralysed,] paralyzed, A, B, C
[f] eyes,] eyes C
[g] shewed] showed A, B, C
[h] agonisingly] agonizingly A, B, C
[i] foetid] fetid A, B, C

mind a single and fleeting avalanche of soul-annihilating memory. I knew in that second all that had been; I remembered beyond the frightful castle and the trees, and recognised[a] the altered edifice in which I now stood; I recognised,[b] most terrible of all, the unholy abomination that stood leering before me as I withdrew my sullied fingers from its own.

But in the cosmos there is balm as well as bitterness, and that balm is nepenthe. In the supreme horror of that second I forgot what had horrified me, and the burst of black memory vanished in a chaos of echoing images. In a dream I fled from that haunted and accursed pile, and ran swiftly and silently in the moonlight. When I returned to the churchyard place of marble and went down the steps I found the stone trap-door immovable; but I was not sorry, for I had hated the antique castle and the trees. Now I ride with the mocking and friendly ghouls on the night-wind,[c] and play by day amongst the catacombs of Nephren-Ka in the sealed and unknown valley of Hadoth by the Nile. I know that light is not for me, save that of the moon over the rock tombs of Neb, nor any gaiety[d] save the unnamed[e] feasts of Nitokris beneath the Great Pyramid; yet in my new wildness and freedom I almost welcome the bitterness of alienage.

For although nepenthe has calmed me, I know always that I am an outsider; a stranger in this century and among those who are still men. This I have known ever since I stretched out my fingers to the abomination within that great gilded frame; stretched out my fingers and touched *a cold and unyielding surface of polished glass.*

[a] recognised] recognized A, B, C

[b] recognised,] recognized, A, B, C

[c] night-wind,] night wind, B, C

[d] gaiety] gayety A, B, C

[e] unnamed] unamed C

The Other Gods

Atop the tallest of earth's peaks dwell the gods of earth, and suffer no man to tell that he hath looked upon them. Lesser peaks they once inhabited; but ever the men from the plains would scale the slopes of rock and snow, driving the gods to higher and higher mountains till now only the last remains. When they left their older peaks they took with them all signs of themselves;[a] save once, it is said, when they left a carven image on the face of the mountain which they called Ngranek.

But now they have betaken themselves to unknown Kadath in the cold waste where no man treads, and are grown stern, having no higher peak whereto to flee at the coming of men. They are grown stern, and where once they suffered men to displace them, they now forbid men to come,[b] or coming, to depart. It is well for men that they know not of

Editor's Note: The surviving A.Ms is HPL's original draft, written on the back of correspondence to him. A T.Ms. was apparently prepared by Donald Wandrei; it is quite accurate and is slightly corrected by HPL. The *Fantasy Fan* followed the T.Ms. when it published the tale (November 1933), making some serious errors. The *Weird Tales* appearance (October 1938) derives from the *Fantasy Fan* text, repeating its errors and making the usual alterations. The Arkham House editions derive from the *Weird Tales* text.

On p. 5 of the A.Ms. is found a synopsis of the story: "Barzai thinks he can with his wisdom defeat the gods of earth & witness their conclave. He climbs high & sees—X X X X—Just as Atal is about to see the sight the moon goes into eclipse. Shrieks. Black shapes—Barzai is gone & on the face of the peak are strange coloured characters newly engraved in the stone that make him fear."

Texts: A = A.Ms. (JHL); B = T.Ms. (JHL); C = *Fantasy Fan* 1, No. 3 (November 1933): 35–38; D = *Weird Tales* 32, No. 4 (October 1938): 489–92; E = *Beyond the Wall of Sleep* (Arkham House, 1943), 13–15; F = *Dagon and Other Macabre Tales* (Arkham House, 1965), 111–15. Copy-text: A.

[a] themselves;] themselves, C, D, E, F

[b] come,] come; C, D, E, F

Kadath in the cold waste,[a] else they would seek injudiciously to scale it.

Sometimes when earth's gods are homesick they visit in the still night the peaks where once they dwelt, and weep softly as they try to play in the olden way on remembered slopes. Men have felt the tears of the gods on white-capped Thurai, though they have thought it rain; and have heard the sighs of the gods in the plaintive dawn-winds of Lerion. In cloud-ships the gods are wont to travel, and wise cotters have legends that keep them from certain high peaks at night when it is cloudy, for the gods are not lenient as of old.

In Ulthar, which lies beyond the river Skai, once dwelt an old man avid to behold the gods of earth; a man deeply learned in the seven cryptical books of Hsan,[b] and familiar with the Pnakotic Manuscripts[c] of distant and frozen Lomar. His name was Barzai the Wise, and the villagers tell of how he went up a mountain on the night of the strange eclipse.

Barzai knew so much of the gods that he could tell of their comings and goings, and guessed so many of their secrets that he was deemed half a god himself. It was he who wisely advised the burgesses of Ulthar when they passed their remarkable law against the slaying of cats, and who first told the young priest Atal where it is that black cats go at midnight on St. John's Eve. Barzai was learned in the lore of[d] earth's gods, and had gained a desire to look upon their faces. He believed that his great secret knowledge of gods could shield him from their wrath, so resolved to go up to the summit of high and rocky Hatheg-Kla on a night when he knew the gods would be there.

Hatheg-Kla is far in the stony desert beyond Hatheg, for which it is named, and rises like a rock statue in a silent temple. Around its peak the mists play always mournfully, for mists are the memories of the gods, and the gods loved Hatheg-Kla when they dwelt upon it in the old days. Often the gods of earth visit Hatheg-Kla in their ships of cloud, casting pale vapours[e] over the slopes as they dance reminiscently on

---

[a] waste,] waste B; waste; D, E, F

[b] Hsan,] earth; C, D; earth, E, F

[c] Pnakotic Manuscripts] *Pnakotic Manuscripts* E, F

[d] of] of the F

[e] vapours] vapors D, E, F

the summit under a clear moon. The villagers of Hatheg say it is ill to climb[a] Hatheg-Kla at any time, and deadly to climb it by night when pale vapours[b] hide the summit and the moon; but Barzai heeded them not when he came from neighbouring[c] Ulthar with the young priest Atal, who was his disciple. Atal was only the son of an innkeeper, and was sometimes afraid; but Barzai's father had been a landgrave who dwelt in an ancient castle, so he had no common superstition in his blood, and only laughed at the fearful cotters.

Barzai and Atal went out of Hatheg into the stony desert despite the prayers of peasants, and talked of earth's gods by their campfires at night. Many days they travelled,[d] and from afar saw lofty Hatheg-Kla with his aureole of mournful mist. On the thirteenth day they reached the mountain's lonely base, and Atal spoke of his fears. But Barzai was old and learned and had no fears, so led the way boldly up the slope that no man had scaled since the time of Sansu, who is written of with fright in the mouldy Pnakotic Manuscripts.[e]

The way was rocky, and made perilous by chasms, cliffs, and falling stones. Later it grew cold and snowy; and Barzai and Atal often slipped and fell as they hewed and plodded upward with staves and axes. Finally the air grew thin, and the sky changed colour,[f] and the climbers found it hard to breathe; but[g] still they toiled up and up, marvelling[h] at the strangeness of the scene and thrilling at the thought of what would happen on the summit when the moon was out and the pale vapours[i] spread around. For three days they climbed higher, higher,[j] and higher toward the roof of the world; then they camped to wait for the clouding of the moon.

[a] climb] climb the E, F

[b] vapours] vapors D, E, F

[c] neighbouring] neighboring C, D, E, F

[d] travelled,] traveled, D, E, F

[e] mouldy Pnakotic Manuscripts.] moldy Pnakotic Manuscripts. D; moldy *Pnakotic Manuscripts.* E, F

[f] colour,] color, D, E, F

[g] but] bnt C

[h] marvelling] marveling D, E, F

[i] vapours] vapors D, E, F

[j] higher, higher,] higher, C; higher D, E, F

For four nights no clouds came, and the moon shone down cold through the thin mournful mists around the silent pinnacle. Then on the fifth night, which was the night of the full moon, Barzai saw some dense clouds far to the north, and stayed up with Atal to watch them draw near. Thick and majestic they sailed, slowly and deliberately onward; ranging themselves round the peak high above the watchers, and hiding the moon and the summit from view. For a long hour the watchers gazed, whilst the vapours[a] swirled and the screen of clouds grew thicker and more restless. Barzai was wise in the lore of earth's gods, and listened hard for certain sounds, but Atal felt the chill of the vapours[b] and the awe of the night, and feared much. And when Barzai began to climb higher and beckon eagerly, it was long before Atal would follow.

So thick were the vapours[c] that the way was hard, and though Atal followed on[d] at last, he could scarce see the grey[e] shape of Barzai on the dim slope above in the clouded moonlight. Barzai forged very far ahead, and seemed despite his age to climb more easily than Atal; fearing not the steepness that began to grow too great for any save a strong and dauntless man, nor pausing at wide black chasms that Atal scarce could[f] leap. And so they went up wildly over rocks and gulfs, slipping and stumbling, and sometimes awed at the vastness and horrible silence of bleak ice pinnacles and mute granite steeps.

Very suddenly Barzai went out of Atal's sight, scaling a hideous cliff that seemed to bulge outward and block the path for any climber not inspired of earth's gods. Atal was far below, and planning what he should do when he reached the place, when curiously he noticed that the light had grown strong, as if the cloudless peak and moonlit meeting-place[g] of the gods were very near. And as he scrambled on toward the bulging cliff and litten sky he felt fears more shocking than any he had

[a] vapours] vapors D, E, F
[b] vapours] vapors D, E, F
[c] vapours] vapors D, E, F
[d] on] om. F
[e] grey] gray D, E, F
[f] scarce could] could scarce C, D, E, F
[g] meeting-place] meeting place A

known before. Then through the high mists he heard the voice of unseen[a] Barzai shouting wildly in delight:

"I have heard the gods![b] I have heard earth's gods singing in revelry on Hatheg-Kla! The voices of earth's gods are known to Barzai the Prophet! The mists are thin and the moon is bright, and I shall see the gods dancing wildly on Hatheg-Kla that[c] they loved in youth![d] The wisdom of Barzai hath made him greater than earth's gods, and against his will their spells and barriers are as naught; Barzai will behold the gods, the proud gods, the secret gods, the gods of earth who spurn the sight of men!"[e]

Atal could not hear the voices Barzai heard, but he was now close to the bulging cliff and scanning it for footholds. Then he heard Barzai's voice grow shriller and louder:

"The mists are[f] very thin, and the moon casts shadows on the slope; the voices[g] of earth's gods are high and wild, and they fear the coming of Barzai the Wise, who is greater than they. . . . The moon's light flickers, as earth's gods dance against it; I shall see the dancing forms of the gods that leap and howl in the moonlight. . . . The light is dimmer and the gods are afraid. . . ."

Whilst Barzai was shouting these things Atal felt a spectral change in all the air, as if the laws of earth were bowing to greater laws; for though the way was steeper than ever, the upward path was now grown fearsomely easy, and the bulging cliff proved scarce an obstacle when he reached it and slid perilously up its convex face. The light of the moon had strangely failed, and as Atal plunged upward through the mists he heard Barzai the Wise shrieking in the shadows:

"The moon is dark, and the gods dance in the night; there is terror in the sky, for upon the moon hath sunk an eclipse foretold in no books of men or of earth's gods. . . . There is unknown magic on Hatheg-Kla, for the screams of the frightened gods have turned to laughter, and the

[a] unseen] *om.* F
[b] gods!] gods. F
[c] that] taat C
[d] youth!] youth. C, D, E, F
[e] men!"] man!" C, D, E, F
[f] mists are] mist is C, D, E, F
[g] voices] voice C, D

slopes of ice shoot up endlessly into the black heavens whither I am plunging. . . . Hei! Hei! At last! *In the dim light I behold the gods of earth!*"[a]

And now Atal, slipping dizzily up over inconceivable steeps, heard in the dark a loathsome[b] laughing, mixed with such a cry as no man else ever heard save in the Phlegethon of unrelatable nightmares; a cry wherein reverberated the horror and anguish of a haunted lifetime packed into one atrocious moment:

"The *other* gods! The *other*[c] gods! The gods of the outer hells that guard the feeble gods of earth![d] . . . Look away! . . . Go back![e] . . . Do not see! . . . Do not see! . . .[f] The vengeance of the infinite abysses . . . That cursed, that damnable pit . . . Merciful gods of earth, *I am falling into the sky!*"[g]

And as Atal shut his eyes and stopped his ears[h] and tried to jump downward against the frightful pull from unknown heights, there resounded on Hatheg-Kla that terrible peal of thunder which awaked the good cotters of the plains and the honest burgesses of Hatheg, and Nir,[i] and Ulthar, and caused them to behold through the clouds that strange eclipse of the moon that no book ever predicted. And when the moon came out at last Atal was safe on the lower snows of the mountain without sight of earth's gods, or of the *other*[j] gods.

Now it is told in the mouldy Pnakotic Manuscripts[k] that Sansu found naught but wordless ice and rock when he climbed[l] Hatheg-Kla in the youth of the world. Yet when the men of Ulthar and Nir and Hatheg crushed their fears and scaled that haunted steep by day in search of Barzai the Wise, they found graven in the naked stone of the summit a

[a] *In . . . earth!*"] In . . . earth!" C, D, E, F

[b] loathsome] loathesome C

[c] *other . . . other*] Other . . . Other C; other . . . other D, E, F

[d] earth!] earth C

[e] away! . . . back!] away. . . . back. C, D, E, F

[f] see! . . . Do not see! . . .] see! Do not see! . . . B; see! Do not see! C, D, E, F

[g] *I . . . sky!*"] I . . . sky!" C, D, E, F

[h] ears] eyes and stopped his ears C

[i] Hatheg, and Nir,] Hatheg and Nir B; Hatheg, Nir C, D, E, F

[j] *other*] Other C; other D, E, F

[k] mouldy Pnakotic Manuscripts] moldy Pnakotic Manuscripts D; moldy *Pnakotic Manuscripts* E, F

[l] climbed] did climb C, D, E, F

curious and Cyclopean[a] symbol fifty cubits wide, as if the rock had been riven by some titanic chisel. And the symbol was like to one that learned men have discerned in those frightful parts of the Pnakotic Manuscripts[b] which are[c] too ancient to be read. This they found.

Barzai the Wise they never found, nor could the holy priest Atal ever be persuaded to pray for his soul's repose. Moreover, to this day the people of Ulthar and Nir and Hatheg fear eclipses, and pray by night when pale vapours[d] hide the mountaintop[e] and the moon. And above the mists on Hatheg-Kla[f] earth's gods sometimes dance reminiscently; for they know they are safe, and love to come from unknown Kadath in ships of cloud and play in the olden way, as they did when earth was new and men not given to the climbing of inaccessible places.

[a] Cyclopean] cyclopean D, E, F
[b] Pnakotic Manuscripts] *Pnakotic Manuscripts* E, F
[c] are] were C, D, E, F
[d] vapours] vapors D, E, F
[e] mountaintop] mountain-top A, B, C, D, E, F
[f] Hatheg-Kla] Hatheg-Kla, C, D, E, F

The Music of Erich Zann

I have examined maps of the city with the greatest care, yet have never again found the Rue d'Auseil. These maps have not been modern maps alone, for I know that names change. I have, on the contrary, delved deeply into all the antiquities of the place;[a] and have personally explored every region, of whatever name, which could possibly answer to the street I knew as the Rue d'Auseil. But despite all I have done[b] it remains an humiliating fact that I cannot find the house, the street, or even the locality, where, during the last months of my impoverished life as a student of metaphysics at the University,[c] I heard the music of Erich Zann.

That my memory is broken, I do not wonder; for my health, physical and mental, was gravely disturbed throughout the period of my residence in the Rue d'Auseil, and I recall that I took none of my few acquaintances there. But that I cannot find the place again is both singular and perplexing; for it was within a half-hour's walk of the

Editor's Note: There is no manuscript, so we are reliant on printed appearances in HPL's lifetime. The story first appeared in the *National Amateur* (March 1922). At some later date HPL must have prepared a new T.Ms., for the next appearance—*Weird Tales* (May 1925)—embodies significant revisions from the earlier text, including the addition of several new passages; but it also appears to contain standard alterations in accordance with the magazine's "house style." The Arkham House editions followed the *Weird Tales* text. Other appearances in HPL's lifetime—including Dashiell Hammett's *Creeps by Night* (1931) and other anthologies derived from this appearance, as well as the *Evening Standard* (London) (24 October 1932)—are not relevant to the tale's textual history.

Texts: A = *National Amateur* 44, No. 4 (March 1922): 38–40; B = *Weird Tales* 5, No. 5 (May 1925): 219–24; C = *The Dunwich Horror and Others* (Arkham House, 1963), 89–97. Copy-text: A (with some readings from B).

[a] place;] place, C
[b] done] done, B, C
[c] University,] university, B, C

University[a] and was distinguished by peculiarities which could hardly be forgotten by anyone[b] who had been there. I have never met a person who has seen the Rue d'Auseil.[c]

The Rue d'Auseil lay across a dark river bordered by precipitous brick blear-windowed warehouses and spanned by a ponderous bridge of dark stone. It was always shadowy along that river, as if the smoke of neighbouring[d] factories shut out the sun perpetually. The river was also odorous with evil stenches which I have never smelled elsewhere, and which may some day help me to find it, since I should recognise[e] them at once. Beyond the bridge were narrow cobbled streets with rails; and then came the ascent, at first gradual,[f] but incredibly steep as the Rue d'Auseil was reached.

I have never seen another street as narrow and steep as the Rue d'Auseil. It was almost a cliff, closed to all vehicles, consisting in several places of flights[g] of steps, and ending at the top in a lofty ivied wall. Its paving was irregular, sometimes stone slabs, sometimes cobblestones,[h] and sometimes bare earth with struggling greenish-grey[i] vegetation. The houses were tall, peaked-roofed, incredibly old, and crazily leaning backward, forward, and sidewise. Occasionally an opposite pair, both leaning forward, almost met across the street like an arch; and certainly they kept most of the light from the ground below. There were a few overhead bridges from house to house across the street.

The inhabitants of that street impressed me peculiarly. At first I thought it was because they were all silent and reticent; but later decided it was because they were all very old. I do not know how I came to live on such a street, but I was not myself when I moved there. I had been living in many poor places, always evicted for want of money; until at last I came upon that tottering house in the Rue

[a] University] university B, C
[b] anyone] any one C
[c] d'Auseil.] a'Auseil. A
[d] neighbouring] neighboring A, B, C
[e] recognise] recognize A, B, C
[f] were narrow . . . gradual,] was narrow A
[g] flights] flghts A
[h] cobblestones,] cobble-stones, A
[i] greenish-grey] greenish-gray B

d'Auseil,[a] kept by the paralytic Blandot. It was the third house from
the top of the street, and by far the tallest of them all.

My room was on the fifth story; the only inhabited room there,
since the house was almost empty. On the night I arrived I heard
strange music from the peaked garret overhead, and the next day asked
old Blandot about it. He told me it was an old German viol-player, a
strange dumb man who signed his name as Erich Zann, and who
played evenings in a cheap theatre[b] orchestra; adding that Zann's
desire to play in the night after his return from the theatre[c] was the
reason he had chosen this lofty and isolated garret room, whose single
gable window was the only point on the street from which one could
look over the terminating wall at the declivity and panorama beyond.

Thereafter I heard Zann every night, and although he kept me
awake, I was haunted by the weirdness of his music. Knowing little of
the art myself, I was yet certain that none of his harmonies had any
relation to music I had heard before; and concluded that he was a
composer of highly original genius. The longer I listened, the more I
was fascinated, until after a week I resolved to make the old man's
acquaintance.

One night,[d] as he was returning from his work, I intercepted Zann
in the hallway and told him that I would like to know him and be with
him when he played. He was a small, lean, bent person, with shabby
clothes, blue eyes, grotesque, satyr-like[e] face, and nearly bald head; and
at my first words seemed both angered and frightened. My obvious
friendliness, however, finally melted him; and he grudgingly motioned
to me to follow him up the dark, creaking,[f] and rickety attic stairs. His
room, one of only two in the steeply pitched garret, was on the west
side, toward the high wall that formed the upper end of the street. Its
size was very great, and seemed the greater because of its extraordinary
bareness[g] and neglect. Of furniture there was only a narrow iron

[a] d'Auseil,] d'Auseil C
[b] theatre] theater B, C
[c] theatre] theater B, C
[d] night,] night C
[e] satyr-like] satyrlike B, C
[f] creaking,] creaking C
[g] bareness] barrenness B, C

bedstead, a dingy washstand,[a] a small table, a large bookcase, an iron music-rack, and three old-fashioned chairs. Sheets of music were piled in disorder about the floor. The walls were of bare boards, and had probably never known plaster; whilst the abundance of dust and cobwebs made the place seem more deserted than inhabited. Evidently Erich Zann's world of beauty lay in some far cosmos of the imagination.

Motioning me to sit down, the dumb man closed the door, turned the large wooden bolt, and lighted a candle to augment the one he had brought with him. He now removed his viol from its moth-eaten covering, and taking it, seated himself in the least uncomfortable of the chairs. He did not employ the music-rack, but[b] offering no choice and playing from memory, enchanted me for over an hour with strains I had never heard before; strains which must have been of his own devising. To describe their exact nature is impossible for one unversed in music. They were a kind of fugue, with recurrent passages of the most captivating quality, but to me were notable for the absence of any of the weird notes I had overheard from my room below on other occasions.

Those haunting notes I had remembered, and had often hummed and whistled inaccurately to myself;[c] so when the player at length laid down his bow I asked him if he would render some of them. As I began my request the wrinkled satyr-like[d] face lost the bored placidity it had possessed during the playing, and seemed to shew[e] the same curious mixture of anger and fright which I had noticed when first I accosted the old man. For a moment I was inclined to use persuasion, regarding rather lightly the whims of senility; and even tried to awaken my host's weirder mood by whistling a few of the strains to which I had listened the night before. But I did not pursue this course for more than a moment; for when the dumb musician recognised[f] the whistled air his face grew suddenly distorted with an expression wholly beyond analysis, and his long, cold, bony right hand reached out to stop my mouth and silence the crude imitation. As he did this he

[a] washstand,] wash-stand, C
[b] but] but, B, C
[c] myself;] myself, B, C
[d] satyr-like] satyrlike B, C
[e] shew] show A, B, C
[f] recognised] recognied A; recognized B, C

further demonstrated his eccentricity by casting a startled glance toward the lone curtained window, as if fearful of some intruder;[a] a glance doubly absurd, since the garret stood high and inaccessible above all the adjacent roofs, this window being the only point on the steep street, as the concierge had told me, from which one could see over the wall at the summit.

The old man's glance brought Blandot's remark to my mind, and with a certain capriciousness I felt a wish to look out over the wide and dizzying panorama of moonlit roofs and city lights beyond the hilltop, which of all the dwellers in the Rue d'Auseil only this crabbed musician could see. I moved toward the window and would have drawn aside the nondescript curtains, when with a frightened rage even greater than before[b] the dumb lodger was upon me again; this time motioning with his head toward the door as he nervously strove to drag me thither with both hands. Now thoroughly disgusted with my host, I ordered him to release me, and told him I would go at once. His clutch relaxed, and as he saw my disgust and offence[c] his own anger seemed to subside. He tightened his relaxing grip, but this time in a friendly manner;[d] forcing me into a chair,[e] then with an appearance of wistfulness crossing to the littered table[f] where he wrote many words with a pencil[g] in the laboured[h] French of a foreigner.

The note which he finally handed me was an appeal for tolerance and forgiveness. Zann said that he was old, lonely, and afflicted with strange fears and nervous disorders connected with his music and with other things. He had enjoyed my listening to his music, and wished I would come again and not mind his eccentricities. But he could not play to another his weird harmonies, and could not bear hearing them from another; nor could he bear having anything in his room touched by another. He had not known until our hallway conversation that I

[a] intruder;] intruder— B, C
[b] before] before, B, C
[c] offence] offense, B, C
[d] manner;] manner, B, C
[e] chair,] chair; B, C
[f] table] table, B, C
[g] pencil] pencil, B, C
[h] laboured] labored A, B, C

could overhear his playing in my room, and now asked me if I would arrange with Blandot to take a lower room where I could not hear him in the night. He would, he wrote, defray the difference in rent.

As I sat deciphering the execrable French[a] I felt more lenient toward the old man. He was a victim of physical and nervous suffering, as was I; and my metaphysical studies had taught me kindness. In the silence there came a slight sound from the window—the shutter must have rattled in the night-wind—[b]and for some reason I started almost as violently as did Erich Zann. So when I had finished reading[c] I shook my host by the hand, and departed as a friend.[d] The next day Blandot gave me a more expensive room on the third floor, between the apartments of an aged money-lender and the room of a respectable upholsterer. There was no one on the fourth floor.

It was not long before I found that Zann's eagerness for my company was not as great as it had seemed while he was persuading me to move down from the fifth story. He did not ask me to call on him, and when I did call he appeared uneasy and played listlessly. This was always at night—in the day he slept and would admit no one. My liking for him did not grow, though the attic room and the weird music seemed to hold an odd fascination for me. I had a curious desire to look out of that window, over the wall and down the unseen slope at the glittering roofs and spires which must lie outspread there. Once I went up to the garret during theatre[e] hours, when Zann was away, but the door was locked.

What I did succeed in doing was to overhear the[f] nocturnal playing of the dumb old man. At first I would tiptoe[g] up to my old fifth floor, then I grew bold enough to climb the last creaking staircase to the peaked garret. There in the narrow hall, outside the bolted door with the covered keyhole, I often heard sounds which filled me with an indefinable dread—the dread of vague wonder and brooding mystery.

[a] French] French, B, C
[b] night-wind—] night-wind, B; night wind, C
[c] reading] reading, C
[d] friend.] friend. ¶ B, C
[e] theatre] theater B, C
[f] the] *om.* A
[g] tiptoe] tip-toe C

It was not that the sounds were hideous,[a] for they were not; but that they held vibrations suggesting nothing on this globe of earth, and that at certain intervals they assumed a symphonic quality which I could hardly conceive as produced by one player. Certainly, Erich Zann was a genius of wild power. As the weeks passed, the playing grew wilder, whilst the old musician acquired an increasing haggardness and furtiveness pitiful to behold. He now refused to admit me at any time, and shunned me whenever we met on the stairs.

Then one night as I listened at the door[b] I heard the shrieking viol swell into a chaotic babel of sound; a pandemonium which would have led me to doubt my own shaking sanity had there not come from behind that barred portal a piteous proof that the horror was real—the awful, inarticulate cry which only a mute can utter, and which rises only in moments of the most terrible fear or anguish. I knocked repeatedly at the door, but received no response. Afterward I waited in the black hallway, shivering with cold and fear, till I heard the poor musician's feeble effort to rise from the floor by the aid of a chair. Believing him just conscious after a fainting fit, I renewed my rapping, at the same time calling out my name[c] reassuringly. I heard Zann stumble to the window and close both shutter and sash, then stumble to the door, which he falteringly unfastened to admit me. This time his delight at having me present was real; for his distorted face gleamed with relief,[d] while he clutched at my coat as a child clutches at its mother's skirts.[e]

Shaking pathetically, the old man forced me into a chair whilst he sank into another, beside which his viol and bow lay carelessly on the floor. He sat for some time inactive, nodding oddly, but having a paradoxical suggestion of intense and frightened listening. Subsequently he seemed to be satisfied, and crossing to a chair by the table wrote a brief note, handed it to me, and returned to the table, where he began to write rapidly and incessantly. The note implored me in the name of

[a] hideous,] hideous A
[b] door] door, C
[c] name] *om.* A
[d] relief,] *om.* A [*see below*]; relief C
[e] This time . . . skirts.] *om.* A

mercy, and for the sake of my own curiosity, to wait where I was while he prepared a full account in German of all the marvels and terrors which beset him. I waited, and the dumb man's pencil flew.[a]

It was perhaps an hour later, while I still waited and while the old musician's feverishly written sheets still continued to pile up, that I saw Zann start as from the hint of a horrible shock. Unmistakably he was looking at the curtained window and listening shudderingly. Then I half fancied I heard a sound myself; though it was not a horrible sound,[b] but rather an exquisitely low and infinitely distant musical note, suggesting a player in one of the neighbouring[c] houses, or in some abode beyond the lofty wall over which I had never been able to look. Upon Zann the effect was terrible, for dropping his pencil[d] suddenly he rose, seized his viol, and commenced to rend the night with the wildest playing I had ever heard from his bow save when listening at the barred door.

It would be useless to describe the playing of Erich Zann on that dreadful night. It was more horrible than anything I had ever overheard, because I could now see the expression of his face, and could realise[e] that this time the motive was stark fear. He was trying to make a noise; to ward something off or drown something out—what, I could not imagine, awesome though I felt it must be. The playing grew fantastic, delirious,[f] and hysterical, yet kept to the last the qualities of supreme genius which I know[g] this strange old man possessed. I recognised[h] the air—it was a wild Hungarian dance popular in the theatres,[i] and I reflected for a moment that this was the first time I had ever heard Zann play the work of another composer.

Louder and louder, wilder and wilder, mounted the shrieking and whining of that desperate viol. The player was dripping with an uncanny

[a] The note . . . flew.] *om.* A
[b] sound,] sound A
[c] neighbouring] neighboring A, B, C
[d] for . . . pencil] for, . . . pencil, B, C
[e] realise] realize A, B, C
[f] delirious,] delirous, A
[g] know] knew C
[h] recognised] recognized A, B, C
[i] theatres,] theaters, B, C

perspiration and twisted like a monkey;[a] always looking frantically at the curtained window. In his frenzied strains I could almost see shadowy satyrs and Bacchanals[b] dancing and whirling insanely through seething abysses of clouds and smoke and lightning. And then I thought I heard a shriller, steadier note that was not from the viol; a calm, deliberate, purposeful, mocking note from far away in the west.[c]

At this juncture the shutter began to rattle in a howling night-wind[d] which had sprung up outside as if in answer to the mad playing within. Zann's screaming viol now outdid itself,[e] emitting sounds I had never thought a viol could emit. The shutter rattled more loudly, unfastened,[f] and commenced slamming against the window. Then the glass broke shiveringly under the persistent impacts, and the chill wind rushed in, making the candles sputter and rustling the sheets of paper on the table where Zann had begun to write out his horrible secret. I looked at Zann[g] and saw that he was past conscious observation. His blue eyes were bulging, glassy,[h] and sightless, and the frantic playing had become a blind, mechanical,[i] unrecognisable[j] orgy that no pen could even suggest.

A sudden gust, stronger than the others, caught up the manuscript and bore it toward the window. I followed the flying sheets in desperation, but they were gone before I reached the demolished panes. Then I remembered my old wish to gaze from this window, the only window in the Rue d'Auseil from which one might see the slope beyond the wall, and the city outspread beneath. It was very dark, but the city's lights always burned, and I expected to see them there amidst the rain and wind. Yet when I looked from that highest of all gable windows, looked while the candles sputtered and the insane viol

---

[a] monkey;] monkey, B, C
[b] Bacchanals] bacchanals A, B, C
[c] west.] West. C
[d] night-wind] night wind C
[e] itself,] itself C
[f] unfastened,] unfastened A
[g] Zann] Zann, B, C
[h] glassy,] glassy B, C
[i] mechanical,] mechanical C
[j] unrecognisable] unrecognizable A, B, C

howled with the night-wind, I saw no city spread below, and no friendly lights gleaming[a] from remembered streets, but only the blackness of space illimitable; unimagined space alive with motion and music, and having no semblance to anything on earth. And as I stood there looking in terror, the wind blew out both the candles in that ancient peaked garret, leaving me in savage and impenetrable darkness with chaos and pandemonium before me, and the daemon[b] madness of that night-baying viol behind me.

I staggered back in the dark, without the means of striking a light, crashing against the table, overturning a chair, and finally groping my way to the place where the blackness screamed with shocking music. To save myself and Erich Zann I could at least try, whatever the powers opposed to me. Once I thought some chill thing brushed me, and I screamed, but my scream could not be heard above that hideous viol. Suddenly out of the blackness the madly sawing bow struck me, and I knew I was close to the player. I felt ahead, touched the back of Zann's chair, and then found and shook his shoulder in an effort to bring him to his senses.

He did not respond, and still the viol shrieked on without slackening. I moved my hand to his head, whose mechanical nodding I was able to stop, and shouted in his ear that we must both flee from the unknown things of the night. But he neither answered me nor abated the frenzy of his unutterable music, while all through the garret strange currents of wind seemed to dance in the darkness and babel. When my hand touched his ear I shuddered, though I knew not why—knew[c] not why till I felt of the still face; the ice-cold, stiffened, unbreathing face whose glassy eyes bulged uselessly into the void. And then, by some miracle[d] finding the door and the large wooden bolt, I plunged wildly away from that glassy-eyed thing in the dark, and from the ghoulish howling of that accursed viol whose fury increased even as I plunged.

Leaping, floating, flying down those endless stairs through the dark house; racing mindlessly out into the narrow, steep, and ancient street

---

[a] gleaming] gleamed B, C
[b] daemon] demon B, C
[c] why—knew] why. Knew A
[d] miracle] miracle, C

of steps and tottering houses; clattering down steps and over cobbles to the lower streets and the[a] putrid canyon-walled river; panting across the great dark bridge to the broader, healthier streets and boulevards we know; all these are terrible impressions that linger with me. And I recall that there was no wind, and that the moon was out, and that all the lights of the city twinkled.

Despite my most careful searches and investigations, I have never since been able to find the Rue d'Auseil. But I am not wholly sorry; either for this or for the loss in undreamable abysses of the closely written[b] sheets which alone could have explained the music of Erich Zann.

---

[a] the] *om.* A
[b] closely written] closely-written A, B, C

Herbert West—Reanimator

I. From the Dark

Of Herbert West, who was my friend in college[a] and in after[b] life, I can speak only with extreme terror. This terror is not due altogether to the sinister manner of his recent disappearance, but was engendered by the whole nature of his life-work, and first gained its acute form more than seventeen years ago, when we were in the third year of our course at the Miskatonic University Medical School[c] in Arkham. While he was with me, the wonder and diabolism of his experiments fascinated me utterly, and I was his closest companion. Now that he is gone and the spell is broken, the actual fear is greater. Memories and possibilities are ever more hideous than realities.

The first horrible incident of our acquaintance was the greatest shock I ever experienced, and it is only with reluctance that I repeat it. As I have said, it happened when we were in the[d] medical school, where

Editor's Note: A T.Ms. survives; it is single-spaced and each of the six episodes is numbered separately. It is likely that HPL sent each episode separately for the serialisation in *Home Brew* (February–July 1922). There is no indication that HPL retyped the T.Ms. double-spaced, so that the divergences between it and the *Home Brew* appearance are almost certainly the result of printing errors. The Arkham House editions followed the T.Ms., hence are comparatively accurate aside from some curious errors.

Texts: A = T.Ms. (JHL); B = *Home Brew* 1, No. 1 (February 1922): 19–25; 1, No. 2 (March 1922): 45–50; 1, No. 3 (April 1922): 21–26; 1, No. 4 (May 1922): 53–58; 1, No. 5 (June 1922): 45–50; 1, No. 6 (July 1922): 57–62 (as "Grewsome Tales"); C = *Dagon and Other Macabre Tales* (Arkham House, 1965), 123–51. Copy-text: A.

[a] college] college, B
[b] after] other C
[c] Medical School] medical school A, C
[d] the] *om.* C

West had already made himself notorious through his wild theories on the nature of death and the possibility of overcoming it artificially. His views, which were widely ridiculed by the faculty and by his fellow-students, hinged on the essentially mechanistic nature of life; and concerned means for operating the organic machinery of mankind by calculated chemical action after the failure of natural processes. In his experiments with various animating solutions he had killed and treated immense numbers of rabbits, guinea-pigs, cats, dogs, and monkeys, till he had become the prime nuisance of the college. Several times he had actually obtained signs of life in animals supposedly dead; in many cases violent signs; but he soon saw that the perfection of this process, if indeed possible, would necessarily involve a lifetime of research. It likewise became clear that, since the same solution never worked alike on different organic species, he would require human subjects for further and more specialised[a] progress. It was here that he first came into conflict with the college authorities, and was debarred from future experiments by no less a dignitary than the dean of the medical school himself—the learned and benevolent Dr. Allan Halsey, whose work in behalf of the stricken is recalled by every old resident of Arkham.

I had always been exceptionally tolerant of West's pursuits, and we frequently discussed his theories, whose ramifications and corollaries were almost infinite. Holding with Haeckel that all life is a chemical and physical process, and that the so-called "soul" is a myth, my friend believed that artificial reanimation of the dead can depend only on the condition of the tissues; and that unless actual decomposition has set in, a corpse fully equipped with organs may with suitable measures be set going again in the peculiar fashion known as life. That the psychic or intellectual life might be impaired by the slight deterioration of sensitive brain-cells which even a short period of death would be apt to cause, West fully realised.[b] It had at[c] first been his hope to find a reagent which would restore vitality before the actual advent of death, and only repeated failures on animals had shewn[d] him that the natural

---

[a] specialised] specialized B
[b] realised.] realized. B
[c] at] *om.* B
[d] shewn] shown A, B, C

and artificial life-motions were incompatible. He then sought extreme freshness in his specimens, injecting his solutions into the blood immediately after the extinction of life. It was this circumstance which made the professors so carelessly sceptical,[a] for they felt that true death had not occurred in any case. They did not stop to view the matter closely and reasoningly.

It was not long after the faculty had interdicted his work that West confided to me his resolution to get fresh human[b] bodies in some manner, and continue in secret the experiments he could no longer perform openly. To hear him discussing ways and means was rather ghastly, for at the college we had never procured anatomical specimens ourselves. Whenever the morgue proved inadequate, two local negroes attended to this matter, and they were seldom questioned. West was then a small, slender, spectacled youth with delicate features, yellow hair, pale blue eyes, and a soft voice, and it was uncanny to hear him dwelling on the relative merits of Christchurch[c] Cemetery and the potter's field. We finally decided on the potter's field,[d] because practically every body in Christchurch[e] was embalmed; a thing of course ruinous to West's researches.

I was by this time his active and enthralled assistant, and helped him make all his decisions, not only concerning the source of bodies but concerning a suitable place for our loathsome work. It was I who thought of the deserted Chapman farmhouse beyond Meadow Hill, where we fitted up on the ground floor an operating room and a laboratory, each with dark curtains to conceal our midnight doings. The place was far from any road, and in sight of no other house, yet precautions were none the less necessary; since rumours[f] of strange lights, started by chance nocturnal roamers, would soon bring disaster on our enterprise. It was agreed to call the whole thing a chemical laboratory if discovery should occur. Gradually we equipped our sinister haunt of science with materials either purchased in Boston or

[a] sceptical,] skeptical, B, C

[b] human] *om.* C

[c] Christchurch] Christ Church B, C

[d] field. . . . field,] field, C

[e] Christchurch] Christ Church B, C

[f] rumours] rumors B

quietly borrowed from the college—materials carefully made unrecognisable[a] save to expert eyes—and provided spades and picks for the many burials we should have to make in the cellar. At the college we used an incinerator, but the apparatus was too costly for our unauthorised[b] laboratory. Bodies were always a nuisance—even the small guinea-pig bodies from the slight clandestine experiments in West's room at the boarding-house.

We followed the local death-notices like ghouls, for our specimens demanded particular qualities. What we wanted were corpses interred soon after death and without artificial preservation; preferably free from malforming disease, and certainly with all organs present. Accident victims were our best hope. Not for many weeks did we hear of anything suitable; though we talked with morgue and hospital authorities, ostensibly in the college's interest, as often as we could without exciting suspicion. We found that the college had first choice in every case, so that it might be necessary to remain in Arkham during the summer, when only the limited summer-school classes were held. In the end, though, luck favoured[c] us; for one day we heard of an almost ideal case in the potter's field; a brawny young workman drowned only the morning before in Sumner's[d] Pond, and buried at the town's expense without delay or embalming. That afternoon we found the new grave, and determined to begin work soon after midnight.

It was a repulsive task that we undertook in the black small hours, even though we lacked at that time the special horror of graveyards which later experiences brought to us. We carried spades and oil dark lanterns, for although electric torches were then manufactured, they were not as satisfactory as the tungsten contrivances of today. The process of unearthing was slow and sordid—it might have been gruesomely poetical if we had been artists instead of scientists—and we were glad when our spades struck wood. When the pine box was fully uncovered West scrambled down and removed the lid, dragging out and propping up the contents. I reached down and hauled the

---

[a] unrecognisable] unrecognizable B, C
[b] unauthorised] unauthorized B, C
[c] favoured] favored B
[d] Sumner's] Summer's C

contents out of the grave, and then both toiled hard to restore the spot to its former appearance. The affair made us rather nervous, especially the stiff form and vacant face of our first trophy, but we managed to remove all traces of our visit. When we had patted down the last shovelful of earth we put the specimen in a canvas sack and set out for the old Chapman place beyond Meadow Hill.

On an improvised dissecting-table in the old farmhouse, by the light of a powerful acetylene lamp, the specimen was not very spectral looking. It had been a sturdy and apparently unimaginative youth of wholesome plebeian type—large-framed, grey-eyed, and brown-haired—a sound animal without psychological subtleties, and probably having vital processes of the simplest and healthiest sort. Now, with the eyes closed, it looked more asleep than dead; though the expert test of my friend soon left no doubt on that[a] score. We had at last what West had always longed for—a real dead man of the ideal kind, ready for the solution as prepared according to the most careful calculations and theories for human use. The tension on our part became very great. We knew that there was scarcely a chance for anything like complete success, and could not avoid hideous fears at possible grotesque results of partial animation. Especially were we apprehensive concerning the mind and impulses of the creature, since in the space following death some of the more delicate cerebral cells might well have suffered deterioration. I, myself, still held some curious notions about the traditional "soul" of man, and felt an awe at the secrets that might be told by one returning from the dead. I wondered what sights this placid youth might have seen in inaccessible spheres, and what he could relate if fully restored to life. But my wonder was not overwhelming, since for the most part I shared the materialism of my friend. He was calmer than I as he forced a large quantity of his fluid into a vein of the body's arm, immediately binding the incision securely.

The waiting was gruesome, but West never faltered. Every now and then he applied his stethoscope to the specimen, and bore the negative results philosophically. After about three-quarters of an hour without the least sign of life he disappointedly pronounced the solution inadequate, but determined to make the most of his opportunity and

---

[a] that] the C

try one change in the formula before disposing of his ghastly prize. We had that afternoon dug a grave in the cellar, and would have to fill it by dawn—for although we had fixed a lock on the house we wished to shun even the remotest risk of a ghoulish discovery. Besides, the body would not be even approximately fresh the next night. So taking the solitary acetylene lamp into the adjacent laboratory, we left our silent guest on the slab in the dark, and bent every energy to the mixing of a new solution; the weighing and measuring supervised by West with an almost fanatical care.

The awful event was very sudden, and wholly unexpected. I was pouring something from one test-tube to another, and West was busy over the alcohol blast-lamp which had to answer for a Bunsen burner in this gasless edifice, when from the pitch-black room we had left there burst the most appalling and daemoniac[a] succession of cries that either of us had ever heard. Not more unutterable could have been the chaos of hellish sound if the pit itself had opened to release the agony of the damned, for in one inconceivable cacophony was centred[b] all the supernal terror and unnatural despair of animate nature. Human it could not have been—it is not in man to make such sounds—and without a thought of our late employment or its possible discovery both West and I leaped to the nearest window like stricken animals; overturning tubes, lamp, and retorts, and vaulting madly into the starred abyss of the rural night. I think we screamed ourselves as we stumbled frantically toward the town, though as we reached the outskirts we put on a semblance of restraint—just enough to seem like belated revellers staggering home from a debauch.

We did not separate, but managed to get to West's room, where we whispered with the gas up until dawn. By then we had calmed ourselves a little with rational theories and plans for investigation, so that we could sleep through the day—classes being disregarded. But that evening two items in the paper, wholly unrelated, made it again impossible for us to sleep. The old deserted Chapman house had inexplicably burned to an amorphous heap of ashes; that we could understand because of the upset lamp. Also, an attempt had been

[a] daemoniac] demoniac A, B, C
[b] centred] centered B

made to disturb a new grave in the potter's field, as if by futile and spadeless clawing at the earth. That we could not understand, for we had patted down the mould very carefully.

And for seventeen years after that West would look frequently over his shoulder, and complain of fancied footsteps behind him. Now he has disappeared.

II. THE PLAGUE-DAEMON

I shall never forget that hideous summer sixteen years ago, when like a noxious afrite from the halls of Eblis[a] typhoid stalked leeringly[b] through Arkham. It is by that satanic scourge that most recall the year, for truly terror brooded with bat-wings over the piles of coffins in the tombs of Christchurch[c] Cemetery; yet for me there is a greater horror in that time—a horror known to me alone now that Herbert West has disappeared.

West and I were doing post-graduate work in summer classes at the medical school of Miskatonic University, and my friend had attained a wide notoriety because of his experiments leading toward the revivification of the dead. After the scientific slaughter of uncounted small animals the freakish work had ostensibly stopped by order of our sceptical dean, Dr. Allan Halsey; though West had continued to perform certain secret tests in his dingy boarding-house room, and had on one terrible and unforgettable occasion taken a human body from its grave in the potter's field to a deserted farmhouse[d] beyond Meadow Hill.

I was with him on that odious occasion, and saw him inject into the still veins the elixir which he thought would[e] to some extent restore life's chemical and physical processes. It had ended horribly— in a delirium of fear which we gradually came to attribute to our own overwrought nerves—and West had never afterward been able to shake off a maddening sensation of being haunted and hunted. The body had not been quite fresh enough; it is obvious that to restore

[a] Eblis] Elbis B
[b] leeringly] *om.* B
[c] Christchurch] Christ Church B, C
[d] farmhouse] farm-house B
[e] would] could B

normal mental attributes a body must be very fresh indeed; and the burning of the old house had prevented us from burying the thing. It would have been better if we could have known it was underground.[a]

After that experience West had dropped his researches for some time; but as the zeal of the born scientist slowly returned, he again became importunate with the college faculty, pleading for the use of the dissecting-room and of fresh human[b] specimens for the work he regarded as so overwhelmingly important. His pleas, however, were wholly in vain; for the decision of Dr. Halsey was inflexible, and the other professors all endorsed the verdict of their leader. In the radical theory of reanimation they saw nothing but the immature vagaries of a youthful enthusiast whose slight form, yellow hair, spectacled blue eyes,[c] and soft voice gave no hint of the supernormal[d]—almost diabolical—power of the cold brain within. I can see him now as he was then—and I shiver. He grew sterner of face, but never elderly. And now Sefton Asylum[e] has had the mishap and West has vanished.

West clashed disagreeably with Dr. Halsey near the end of our last undergraduate term in a wordy dispute that did less credit to him than to the kindly dean in point of courtesy. He felt that he was needlessly and irrationally retarded in a supremely great work; a work which he could of course conduct to suit himself in later years, but which he wished to begin while still possessed of the exceptional facilities of the university. That the tradition-bound elders should ignore his singular results on animals, and persist in their denial of the possibility of reanimation,[f] was inexpressibly disgusting and almost incomprehensible to a youth of West's logical temperament. Only greater maturity could help him understand the chronic mental limitations of the "professor-doctor" type—the product of generations of pathetic Puritanism;[g] kindly, conscientious, and sometimes gentle and amiable, yet always narrow, intolerant, custom-ridden, and lacking in perspective. Age has more

[a] underground.] under ground. B
[b] human] *om.* B
[c] eyes,] eyes B
[d] supernormal] super-normal C
[e] Asylum] *om.* C
[f] and persist . . . reanimation,] *om.* B
[g] Puritanism;] Puritanism, C

charity for these incomplete yet high-souled characters, whose worst real vice is timidity, and who are ultimately punished by general ridicule for their intellectual sins—sins like Ptolemaism, Calvinism, anti-Darwinisn, anti-Nietzscheism, and every sort of Sabbatarianism and sumptuary legislation. West, young despite his marvellous[a] scientific acquirements, had scant patience with good Dr. Halsey and his erudite colleagues; and nursed an increasing resentment, coupled with a desire to prove his theories to these obtuse worthies in some striking and dramatic fashion. Like most youths, he indulged in elaborate day-dreams of revenge, triumph,[b] and final magnanimous forgiveness.

And then had come the scourge, grinning and lethal, from the nightmare caverns of Tartarus. West and I had graduated about the time of its beginning, but had remained for additional work at the summer school, so that we were in Arkham when it broke with full daemoniac[c] fury upon the town. Though not as yet licenced[d] physicians, we now had our degrees, and were pressed frantically into public service as the numbers of the stricken grew. The situation was almost past management, and deaths ensued too frequently for the local undertakers fully to handle. Burials without embalming were made in rapid succession, and even the Christchurch[e] Cemetery receiving tomb was crammed with coffins of the unembalmed dead. This circumstance was not without effect on West, who thought often of the irony of the situation—so many fresh specimens, yet none for his persecuted researches! We were frightfully overworked, and the terrific mental and nervous strain made my friend brood morbidly.

But West's gentle enemies were no less harassed with prostrating duties. College had all but closed, and every doctor of the medical faculty was helping to fight the typhoid plague. Dr. Halsey in particular had distinguished himself in sacrificing service, applying his extreme skill with whole-hearted energy to cases which many others shunned because of danger or apparent hopelessness. Before a month was over

[a] marvellous] marvelous B, C
[b] triumph,] triumph B
[c] daemoniac] demoniac A, B, C
[d] licenced] licensed B, C
[e] Christchurch] Christ Church B, C

the fearless dean had become a popular hero,[a] though he seemed unconscious of his fame as he struggled to keep from collapsing with physical fatigue and nervous exhaustion. West could not withhold admiration for the fortitude of his foe, but because of this was even more determined to prove to him the truth of his amazing doctrines. Taking advantage of the disorganisation[b] of both college work and municipal health regulations, he managed to get a recently deceased body smuggled into the university dissecting-room[c] one night, and in my presence injected a new modification of his solution. The thing actually opened its eyes, but only stared at the ceiling with a look of soul-petrifying horror before collapsing into an inertness from which nothing could rouse it. West said it was not fresh enough—the hot summer air does not favour[d] corpses. That time we were almost caught before we incinerated the thing, and West doubted the advisability of repeating his daring misuse of the college laboratory.

The peak of the epidemic was reached in August. West and I were almost dead, and Dr. Halsey did die on the 14th.[e] The students all attended the hasty funeral on the 15th,[f] and bought an impressive wreath, though the latter was quite overshadowed by the tributes sent by wealthy Arkham citizens and by the municipality itself. It was almost a public affair, for the dean had surely been a public benefactor. After the entombment we were all somewhat depressed, and spent the afternoon at the bar of the Commercial House; where West, though shaken by the death of his chief opponent, chilled the rest of us with references to his notorious theories. Most of the students went home, or to various duties, as the evening advanced; but West persuaded me to aid him in "making a night of it".[g] West's landlady saw us arrive at his room about two in the morning, with a third man between us; and told her husband that we had all evidently dined and wined rather well.

[a] hero,] hero B
[b] disorganisation] disorganization B, C
[c] dissecting-room] dissecting room B
[d] favour] favor B
[e] 14th.] fourteenth. C
[f] 15th,] fifteenth, C
[g] it".] it." B, C

Apparently this acidulous matron was right; for about 3 a.m.[a] the whole house was aroused by cries coming from West's room, where when they broke down the door they found the two of us unconscious on the blood-stained carpet, beaten, scratched, and mauled, and with the broken remnants of West's bottles and instruments around us. Only an open window told what had become of our assailant, and many wondered how he himself had fared after the terrific leap from the second story to the lawn which he must have made. There were some strange garments in the room, but West upon regaining consciousness[b] said they did not belong to the stranger, but were specimens collected for bacteriological analysis in the course of investigations on the transmission of germ diseases. He ordered them burnt[c] as soon as possible in the capacious fireplace. To the police we both declared ignorance of our late companion's identity. He was, West nervously said, a congenial stranger whom we had met at some downtown bar of uncertain location. We had all been rather jovial, and West and I did not wish to have our pugnacious companion hunted down.

That same night saw the beginning of the second Arkham horror—the horror that to me eclipsed the plague itself. Christchurch[d] Cemetery was the scene of a terrible killing; a watchman having been clawed to death in a manner not only too hideous for description, but raising a doubt as to the human agency of the deed. The victim had been seen alive considerably after midnight—the dawn revealed the unutterable thing. The manager of a circus at the neighbouring[e] town of Bolton was questioned, but he swore that no beast had at any time escaped from its cage. Those who found the body noted a trail of blood leading to the receiving tomb, where a small pool of red lay on the concrete just outside the gate. A fainter trail led away toward the woods, but it soon gave out.

The next night devils danced on the roofs of Arkham, and unnatural madness howled in the wind. Through the fevered town had

---

[a] 3 a.m.] 3 p. m. B; three A. M. C
[b] consciousness] consciousness, B
[c] burnt] burned B
[d] Christchurch] Christ Church B, C
[e] neighbouring] neighboring B

crept a curse which some said was greater than the plague, and which others[a] whispered was the embodied daemon-soul[b] of the plague itself.[c] Eight houses were entered by a nameless thing which strowed[d] red death in its wake—in all, seventeen maimed and shapeless[e] remnants of bodies were left behind by the voiceless, sadistic monster that crept abroad. A few persons had half seen it in the dark, and said it was white and like a malformed ape or anthropomorphic fiend. It had not left behind quite all that it had attacked, for sometimes it had been hungry. The number it had killed was fourteen; three of the bodies had been in stricken homes and had not been alive.

On the third night frantic bands of searchers, led by the police, captured it in a house on Crane Street near the Miskatonic campus. They had organised[f] the quest with care, keeping in touch by means of volunteer telephone stations, and when someone in the college district had reported hearing a scratching at a shuttered window, the net was quickly spread. On account of the general alarm and precautions, there were only two more victims, and the capture was effected without major casualties. The thing was finally stopped by a bullet, though not a fatal one, and was rushed to the local hospital amidst universal excitement and loathing.

For it had been a man. This much was clear despite the nauseous eyes, the voiceless simianism, and the daemoniac[g] savagery. They dressed its[h] wound and carted it to the asylum at Sefton, where it beat its head against the walls of a padded cell for sixteen years—until the recent mishap, when it escaped under circumstances that few like to mention. What had most disgusted the searchers of Arkham was the thing they noticed when the monster's face was cleaned—the mocking, unbelievable resemblance to a learned and self-sacrificing martyr who

---

[a] others] some A, B, C [*revision found in handwritten note in copy of A in possession of L. W. Currey*]

[b] daemon-soul] demon-soul A, C; *om*. B [*see below*]

[c] plague, . . . plague itself.] plague. B

[d] strowed] strewed A, B, C

[e] shapeless] shapelss C

[f] organised] organized B, C

[g] daemoniac] demoniac A, B, C

[h] its] the C

had been entombed but three days before—the late Dr. Allan Halsey, public benefactor and dean of the medical school of Miskatonic University.

To the vanished Herbert West and to me the disgust and horror were supreme. I shudder tonight as I think of it;[a] shudder even more than I did that morning when West muttered through his bandages,

"Damn it, it wasn't *quite*[b] fresh enough!"

III. SIX SHOTS BY MIDNIGHT

It is uncommon to fire all six shots of a revolver with great suddenness when one would probably be sufficient, but many things in the life of Herbert West were uncommon. It is, for instance, not often that a young physician leaving college is obliged to conceal the principles which guide his selection of a home and office, yet that was the case with Herbert West. When he and I obtained our degrees at the medical school of Miskatonic University, and sought to relieve our poverty by setting up as general practitioners, we took great care not to say that we chose our house because it was fairly well isolated, and as near as possible to the potter's field.

Reticence such as this is seldom without a cause, nor indeed was ours; for our requirements were those resulting from a life-work distinctly unpopular. Outwardly we were doctors only, but beneath the surface were aims of far greater and more terrible moment—for the essence of Herbert West's existence was a quest amid black and forbidden realms of the unknown, in which he hoped to uncover the secret of life and restore to perpetual animation the graveyard's cold clay. Such a quest demands strange materials, among them fresh human bodies; and in order to keep supplied with these indispensable things one must live quietly and not far from a place of informal interment.

West and I had met in college, and I had been the only one to sympathise[c] with his hideous experiments. Gradually I had come to be his inseparable assistant, and now that we were out of college we had

---

[a] it;] it, C
[b] *quite*] *om.* B
[c] sympathise] sympathize B, C

to keep together. It was not easy to find a good opening for two doctors in company, but finally the influence of the university secured us a practice in Bolton—a factory town near Arkham, the seat of the college. The Bolton Worsted Mills[a] are the largest in the Miskatonic Valley, and their polyglot employees[b] are never popular as patients with the local physicians. We chose our house with the greatest care, seizing at last on a rather run-down cottage near the end of Pond Street; five numbers from the closest neighbour, and separated from the local potter's field by only a stretch of meadow land, bisected by a narrow neck of the rather dense forest which lies to the north. The distance was greater than we wished, but we could get no nearer house without going on the other side of the field, wholly out of the factory district. We were not much displeased, however, since there were no people between us and our sinister source of supplies. The walk was a trifle long, but we could haul our silent specimens undisturbed.

Our practice was surprisingly large from the very first—large enough to please most young doctors, and large enough to prove a bore and a burden to students whose real interest lay elsewhere. The mill-hands were of somewhat turbulent inclinations; and besides their many natural needs, their frequent clashes and stabbing affrays gave us plenty to do. But what actually absorbed our minds was the secret laboratory we had fitted up in the cellar—the laboratory with the long table under the electric lights, where in the small hours of the morning we often injected West's various solutions into the veins of the things we dragged from the potter's field. West was experimenting madly to find something which would start man's vital motions anew after they had been stopped by the thing we call death, but had encountered the most ghastly obstacles. The solution had to be differently compounded for different types—what would serve for guinea-pigs would not serve for human beings, and different human[c] specimens required large modifications.

The bodies had to be exceedingly fresh, or the slight decomposition of[d] brain tissue would render perfect reanimation

---

[a] Mills] Mills, B
[b] employees] employes B
[c] human] _om._ C
[d] of] of the B

impossible. Indeed, the greatest problem was to get them fresh enough—West had had horrible experiences during his secret college researches[a] with corpses of doubtful vintage. The results of partial or imperfect animation were much more hideous than were the total failures, and we both held fearsome recollections of such things. Ever since our first daemoniac[b] session in the deserted farmhouse[c] on Meadow Hill in Arkham, we had felt a brooding menace; and West, though a calm, blond,[d] blue-eyed scientific automaton in most respects, often confessed to a shuddering sensation of stealthy pursuit. He half felt that he was followed—a[e] psychological delusion of shaken nerves, enhanced by the undeniably disturbing fact that at least one of our reanimated specimens was still alive—a frightful carnivorous thing in a padded cell at Sefton. Then there was another—our first—whose exact fate we had never learned.

We had fair luck with specimens in Bolton—much better than in Arkham. We had not been settled a week before we got an accident victim on the very night of burial, and made it open its eyes with an amazingly rational expression before the solution failed. It had lost an arm—if it had been a perfect body we might have succeeded better. Between then and the next January we secured three more;[f] one total failure, one case of marked muscular motion, and one rather shivery thing—it rose of itself and uttered a sound. Then came a period when luck was poor; interments fell off, and those that did occur were of specimens either too diseased or too maimed for use.[g] We kept track of all the deaths and their circumstances with systematic care.

One March night, however, we unexpectedly obtained a specimen which did not come from the potter's field. In Bolton the prevailing spirit of Puritanism had outlawed the sport of boxing—with the usual result. Surreptitious and ill-conducted bouts among the mill-workers were common, and occasionally professional talent of low grade was

---

[a] researches] researchs C
[b] daemoniac] demoniac A, B, C
[c] farmhouse] farm-house C
[d] blond,] blonde, B
[e] a] *om.* C
[f] more;] more, C
[g] use.] us. C

imported. This late winter night there had been such a match; evidently with disastrous results, since two timorous Poles had come to us with incoherently whispered entreaties to attend to a very secret and desperate case. We followed them to an abandoned barn, where the remnants of a crowd of frightened foreigners were watching a silent black form on the floor.

The match had been between Kid O'Brien—a lubberly and now quaking youth with a most un-Hibernian hooked nose—and Buck Robinson, "The Harlem Smoke".[a] The negro had been knocked out, and a moment's examination shewed[b] us that he would permanently remain so. He was a loathsome, gorilla-like thing, with abnormally long arms which I could not help calling fore legs,[c] and a face that conjured up thoughts of unspeakable Congo secrets and tom-tom poundings under an eery moon. The body must have looked even worse in life— but the world holds many ugly things. Fear was upon the whole pitiful crowd, for they did not know what the law would exact of them if the affair were not hushed up; and they were grateful when West, in spite of my involuntary shudders, offered to get rid of the thing quietly— for[d] a purpose I knew too well.

There was bright moonlight over the snowless landscape, but we dressed the thing and carried it home between us through the deserted streets and meadows, as we had carried a similar thing one horrible night in Arkham. We approached the house from the field in the rear, took the specimen in the back door and down the cellar stairs, and prepared it for the usual experiment. Our fear of the police was absurdly great, though we had timed our trip to avoid the solitary patrolman of that section.

The result was wearily anticlimactic.[e] Ghastly as our prize appeared, it was wholly unresponsive to every solution we injected in its black arm;[f] solutions prepared from experience[g] with white specimens only.

[a] Smoke".] Smoke." B, C
[b] shewed] showed A, B, C
[c] fore legs,] fore-legs, A, B, C
[d] quietly—for] quietly for B
[e] anticlimactic.] anti-climactic. C
[f] arm;] arm, C
[g] experience] experiments B

So as the hour grew dangerously near to dawn, we did as we had done with the others—dragged the thing across the meadows to the neck of woods near the potter's field, and buried it there in the best sort of grave the frozen ground would furnish. The grave was not very deep, but fully as good as that of the previous specimen—the thing which had risen of itself and uttered a sound. In the light of our dark lanterns we carefully covered it with leaves and dead vines, fairly certain that the police would never find it in a forest so dim and dense.

The next day I was increasingly apprehensive about the police, for a patient brought rumours of a suspected fight and death. West had still another source of worry, for he had been called in the afternoon to a case which ended very threateningly. An Italian woman had become hysterical over her missing child—[a]a lad of five who had strayed off early in the morning and failed to appear for dinner—and had developed symptoms highly alarming in view of an always weak heart. It was a very foolish hysteria, for the boy had often run away before; but Italian peasants are exceedingly superstitious, and this woman seemed as much harassed by omens as by facts. About seven o'clock in the evening she had died, and her frantic husband had made a frightful scene in his efforts to kill West, whom he wildly blamed for not saving her life. Friends had held him when he drew a stiletto, but West departed amidst his inhuman shrieks, curses, and oaths of vengeance. In his latest affliction the fellow seemed to have forgotten his child, who was still missing as the night advanced. There was some talk of searching the woods, but most of the family's friends were busy with the dead woman and the screaming man. Altogether, the nervous strain upon West must have been tremendous. Thoughts of the police and of the mad Italian both weighed heavily.

We retired about eleven, but I did not sleep well. Bolton had a surprisingly good police force for so small a town, and I could not help fearing the mess which would ensue if the affair of the night before were ever tracked down. It might mean the end of all our local work—and perhaps prison for both West and me. I did not like those[b] rumours of a fight which were floating about. After the clock had struck three the

---

[a] child—] child, C
[b] those] these B

moon shone in my eyes, but I turned over without rising to pull down the shade. Then came the steady rattling at the back door.

I lay still and somewhat dazed, but before long heard West's rap on my door. He was clad in dressing-gown and slippers, and had in his hands a revolver and an electric flashlight. From the revolver I knew that he was thinking more of the crazed Italian than of the police.

"We'd better both go,"[a] he whispered. "It wouldn't do not to answer it anyway, and it may be a patient—it would be like one of those fools to try the back door."

So we both went down the stairs on tiptoe, with a fear partly justified and partly that which comes only from the soul of the weird small hours. The rattling continued, growing somewhat louder. When we reached the door I cautiously unbolted it and threw it open, and as the moon streamed revealingly down on the form silhouetted there, West did a peculiar thing. Despite the obvious danger of attracting notice and bringing down on our heads the dreaded police investigation—a thing which after all was mercifully averted by the relative isolation of our cottage—my friend suddenly, excitedly, and unnecessarily emptied all six chambers of his revolver into the nocturnal visitor.

For that visitor was neither Italian nor policeman. Looming hideously against the spectral moon was a gigantic misshapen thing not to be imagined save in nightmares—a glassy-eyed, ink-black apparition nearly on all fours, covered with bits of mould, leaves, and vines, foul with caked blood, and having between its glistening teeth a snow-white, terrible, cylindrical object terminating in a tiny hand.

IV. THE SCREAM OF THE DEAD

The scream of a dead man gave to me that acute and added horror of Dr. Herbert West which harassed the latter years of our companionship. It is natural that such a thing as a dead man's scream should give horror, for it is obviously not a pleasing or ordinary occurrence; but I was used to similar experiences, hence suffered on this occasion only because of a particular circumstance. And, as I have implied, it was not of the dead man himself that I became afraid.

[a] go,"] go." A

Herbert West, whose associate and assistant I was, possessed scientific interests far beyond the usual routine of a village physician. That was why, when establishing his practice in Bolton, he had chosen an isolated house near the potter's field. Briefly and brutally stated, West's sole absorbing interest was a secret study of the phenomena of life and its cessation, leading toward the reanimation of the dead through injections of an excitant solution. For this ghastly experimenting it was necessary to have a constant supply of very fresh human bodies; very fresh because even the least decay hopelessly damaged the brain structure, and human because we found that the solution had to be compounded differently for different types of organisms. Scores of rabbits and guinea-pigs had been killed and treated, but their trail was a blind one. West had never fully succeeded because he had never been able to secure a corpse sufficiently fresh. What he wanted were bodies from which vitality had only just departed; bodies with every cell intact and capable of receiving again the impulse toward that mode of motion called life. There was hope that this second and artificial life might be made perpetual by repetitions of the injection, but we had learned that an ordinary natural life would not respond to the action. To establish the artificial motion, natural[a] life must be extinct— the specimens must be very fresh, but genuinely dead.

The awesome quest had begun when West and I were students at the Miskatonic University Medical School[b] in Arkham, vividly conscious for the first time of the thoroughly mechanical nature of life. That was seven years before, but West looked scarcely a day older now—he was small, blond, clean-shaven, soft-voiced,[c] and spectacled, with only an occasional flash of a cold blue eye to tell of the hardening and growing fanaticism of his character under the pressure of his terrible investigations. Our experiences had often been hideous in the extreme; the results of defective reanimation, when lumps of graveyard clay had been galvanised[d] into morbid, unnatural, and brainless motion by various modifications of the vital solution.

---

[a] natural] noctural C
[b] Medical School] medical school C
[c] soft-voiced,] soft voiced, B
[d] galvanised] galvanized B

One thing had uttered a nerve-shattering scream; another had risen violently, beaten us both to unconsciousness, and run amuck in a shocking way before it could be placed behind asylum bars; still another, a loathsome African monstrosity, had clawed out of its shallow grave and done a deed—West had had to shoot that object. We could not get bodies fresh enough to shew[a] any trace of reason when reanimated, so had perforce created nameless horrors. It was disturbing to think that one, perhaps two, of our monsters still lived—that thought haunted us shadowingly, till finally West disappeared under frightful circumstances. But at the time of the scream in the cellar laboratory of the isolated Bolton cottage, our fears were subordinate to our anxiety for extremely fresh specimens. West was more avid than I, so that it almost seemed to me that he looked half-covetously at any very healthy living physique.

It was in July, 1910, that the bad luck regarding specimens began to turn. I had been on a long visit to my parents in Illinois, and upon my return found West in a state of singular elation. He had, he told me excitedly, in all likelihood solved the problem of freshness through an approach from an entirely new angle—that of artificial preservation. I had known that he was working on a new and highly unusual embalming compound, and was not surprised that it had turned out well; but until he explained the details I was rather puzzled as to how such a compound could help in our work, since the objectionable staleness of the specimens was largely due to delay occurring before we secured them. This, I now saw, West had clearly recognised;[b] creating his embalming compound for future rather than immediate use, and trusting to fate to supply again some very recent and unburied corpse, as it had years before when we obtained the negro[c] killed in the Bolton prize-fight. At last fate had been kind, so that on this occasion there lay in the secret cellar laboratory a corpse whose decay could not by any possibility have begun. What would happen on reanimation, and whether we could hope for a revival of mind and reason, West did not venture to predict. The experiment would be a landmark in our

[a] shew] show A, B, C
[b] recognised;] recognized; B, C
[c] negro] Negro C

studies, and he had saved the new body for my return, so that both might share the spectacle in accustomed fashion.

West told me how he had obtained the specimen. It had been a vigorous man; a well-dressed stranger just off the train on his way to transact some business with the Bolton Worsted Mills. The walk through the town had been long, and by the time the traveller paused at our cottage to ask the way to the factories his heart had become greatly overtaxed. He had refused a stimulant, and had suddenly dropped dead only a moment later. The body, as might be expected, seemed to West a heaven-sent gift. In his brief conversation the stranger had made it clear that he was unknown in Bolton, and a search of his pockets subsequently revealed him to be one Robert Leavitt of St. Louis, apparently without a family to make instant[a] inquiries about his disappearance. If this man could not be restored to life, no one would know of our experiment. We buried our materials in a dense strip of woods between the house and the potter's field. If, on the other hand, he could be restored, our fame would be brilliantly and perpetually established. So without delay West had injected into the body's wrist the compound which would hold it fresh for use after my arrival. The matter of the presumably weak heart, which to my mind imperiled the success of our experiment, did not appear to trouble West extensively. He hoped at last to obtain what he had never obtained before—a rekindled spark of reason and perhaps a normal,[b] living creature.

So on the night of July 18, 1910, Herbert West and I stood in the cellar laboratory and gazed at a white, silent figure beneath the dazzling arc-light. The embalming compound had worked uncannily well, for as I stared fascinatedly at the sturdy frame which had lain two weeks without stiffening I was moved to seek West's assurance that the thing was really dead. This assurance he gave readily enough; reminding me that the reanimating solution was never used without careful tests as to life;[c] since it could have no effect if any of the original vitality were present. As West proceeded to take preliminary steps, I was impressed by the vast intricacy of the new experiment; an intricacy so vast that he

[a] instant] *om.* C
[b] normal,] normal B
[c] life;] life, B

could trust no hand less delicate than his own. Forbidding me to touch the body, he first injected a drug in the wrist just beside the place his needle had punctured when injecting the embalming compound. This, he said, was to neutralise[a] the compound and release the system to a normal relaxation so that the reanimating solution might freely work when injected. Slightly later, when a change and a gentle tremor seemed to affect the dead limbs, West stuffed a pillow-like object violently over the twitching face, not withdrawing it until the corpse appeared quiet and ready for our attempt at reanimation. The pale enthusiast now applied some last perfunctory tests for absolute lifelessness, withdrew satisfied, and finally injected into the left arm an accurately measured amount of the vital elixir, prepared during the afternoon with a greater care than we had used since college days, when our feats were new and groping. I cannot express the wild, breathless suspense with which we waited for results on this first really fresh specimen—the first we could reasonably expect to open its lips in rational speech, perhaps to tell of what it had seen beyond the unfathomable abyss.

West was a materialist, believing in no soul and attributing all the working of consciousness to bodily phenomena; consequently he looked for no revelation of hideous secrets from gulfs and caverns beyond death's barrier. I did not wholly disagree with him theoretically, yet held vague instinctive remnants of the primitive faith of my forefathers; so that I could not help eyeing the corpse with a certain amount of awe and terrible expectation. Besides—I could not extract from my memory that hideous,[b] inhuman shriek we heard on the night we tried our first experiment in the deserted farmhouse at Arkham.

Very little time had elapsed before I saw the attempt was not to be a total failure. A touch of colour came to cheeks hitherto chalk-white, and spread out under the curiously ample stubble of sandy beard. West, who had his hand on the pulse of the left wrist, suddenly nodded significantly; and almost simultaneously a mist appeared on the mirror inclined above the body's mouth. There followed a few spasmodic muscular motions, and then an audible breathing and

[a] neutralise] neutralize C
[b] hideous,] hideous B

visible motion of the chest. I looked at the closed eyelids, and thought I detected a quivering. Then the lids opened, shewing[a] eyes which were grey, calm, and alive, but still unintelligent and not even curious.

In a moment of fantastic whim I whispered questions to the reddening ears; questions of other worlds of which the memory might still be present. Subsequent terror drove them from my mind, but I think the last one, which I repeated, was: "Where have you been?" I do not yet know whether I was answered or not, for no sound came from the well-shaped mouth; but I do know that at that moment I firmly thought the thin lips moved silently, forming syllables I would have vocalised as "only now" if that phrase had possessed any sense or relevancy. At that moment, as I say, I was elated with the conviction that the one great goal had been attained; and that for the first time a reanimated corpse had uttered distinct words impelled by actual reason. In the next moment there was no doubt about the triumph; no doubt that the solution had truly accomplished, at least temporarily, its full mission of restoring rational and articulate life to the dead. But in that triumph there came to me the greatest of all horrors—not horror of the thing that spoke, but of the deed that I had witnessed and of the man with whom my professional fortunes were joined.

For that very fresh body, at last writhing into full and terrifying consciousness with eyes dilated at the memory of its last scene on earth, threw out its frantic hands in a life and death struggle with the air; and suddenly collapsing into a second and final dissolution from which there could be no return, screamed out the cry that will ring eternally in my aching brain:

"Help! Keep off, you cursed little tow-head fiend—keep that damned needle away from me!"

V. THE HORROR FROM THE SHADOWS

Many men have related hideous things, not mentioned in print, which happened on the battlefields of the Great War. Some of these things have made me faint, others have convulsed me with devastating nausea, while still others have made me tremble and look behind me in

---

[a] shewing] showing A, B, C

the dark; yet despite the worst of them I believe I can myself[a] relate the most hideous thing of all—the shocking, the unnatural, the unbelievable horror from the shadows.

In 1915 I was a physician with the rank of First Lieutenant in a Canadian regiment in Flanders, one of many Americans to precede the government itself into the gigantic struggle. I had not entered the army on my own[b] initiative, but rather as a natural result of the enlistment of the man whose indispensable assistant I was—the celebrated Boston surgical specialist, Dr. Herbert West. Dr. West had been avid for a chance to serve as surgeon in a great war, and when the chance had come he carried me with him almost against my will. There were reasons why I would have been glad to let the war separate us; reasons why I found the practice of medicine and the companionship of West more and more irritating; but when he had gone to Ottawa and through a colleague's influence secured a medical commission as Major, I could not resist the imperious persuasion of one determined that I should accompany him in my usual capacity.

When I say that Dr. West was avid to serve in battle, I do not mean to imply that he was either naturally warlike or anxious for the safety of civilisation.[c] Always an ice-cold intellectual machine; slight, blond,[d] blue-eyed, and spectacled;[e] I think he secretly sneered at my occasional martial enthusiasms and censures of supine neutrality. There was, however, something he wanted in embattled Flanders; and in order to secure it he had to assume a military exterior. What he wanted was not a thing which many persons want, but something connected with the peculiar branch of medical science which he had chosen quite clandestinely to follow, and in which he had achieved amazing and occasionally hideous results. It was, in fact, nothing more or less than an abundant supply of freshly killed men in every stage of dismemberment.

Herbert West needed fresh bodies because his life-work was the

---

[a] myself] *om.* C

[b] own] *om.* C

[c] civilisation.] civilization. B, C

[d] blond,] blonde, B

[e] machine; . . . spectacled;] machine: . . . spectacled: C

reanimation of the dead. This work was not known to the fashionable clientele who had so swiftly built up his fame after his arrival in Boston; but was only too well known to me, who had been his closest friend and sole assistant since the old days in Miskatonic University Medical School[a] at Arkham. It was in those college days that he had begun his terrible experiments, first on small animals and then on human bodies shockingly obtained. There was a solution which he injected into the veins of dead things, and if they were fresh enough they responded in strange ways. He had had much trouble in discovering the proper formula, for each type of organism was found to need a stimulus especially adapted to it. Terror stalked him when he reflected on his partial failures; nameless things resulting from imperfect solutions or from bodies insufficiently fresh. A certain number of these failures had remained alive—one was in an asylum while others had vanished—and as he thought of conceivable yet virtually impossible eventualities he often shivered beneath his usual stolidity.

West had soon learned that absolute freshness was the prime requisite for useful specimens, and had accordingly resorted to frightful and unnatural expedients in body-snatching. In college, and during our early practice together in the factory town of Bolton, my attitude toward him had been largely one of fascinated admiration; but as his boldness in methods grew, I began to develop a gnawing fear. I did not like the way he looked at healthy living bodies; and then there came a nightmarish session in the cellar laboratory when I learned that a certain specimen had been a living body when he secured it. That was the first time he had ever been able to revive the quality of rational thought in a corpse; and his success, obtained at such a loathsome cost, had completely hardened him.

Of his methods in the intervening five years I dare not speak. I was held to him by sheer force of fear, and witnessed sights that no human tongue could repeat. Gradually I came to find Herbert West himself more horrible than anything he did—that was when it dawned on me that his once normal scientific zeal for prolonging life had subtly degenerated into a mere morbid and ghoulish curiosity and secret sense of charnel picturesqueness. His interest became a hellish

[a] Medical School] medical school C

and perverse addiction to the repellently and fiendishly abnormal; he gloated calmly over artificial monstrosities which would make most healthy men drop dead from fright and disgust; he became, behind his pallid intellectuality, a fastidious Baudelaire of physical experiment—a languid Elagabalus of the tombs.

Dangers he met unflinchingly; crimes he committed unmoved. I think the climax came when he had proved his point that rational life can be restored, and had sought new worlds to conquer by experimenting on the reanimation of detached parts of bodies. He had wild and original ideas on the independent vital properties of organic cells and nerve-tissue[a] separated from natural physiological systems; and achieved some hideous preliminary results in the form of never-dying, artificially nourished tissue obtained from the nearly hatched[b] eggs of an indescribable tropical reptile. Two biological points he was exceedingly anxious to settle—first, whether any amount of consciousness and rational action[c] be possible without the brain, proceeding from the spinal cord and various nerve-centres; and second, whether any kind of ethereal, intangible relation distinct from the material cells may exist to link the surgically separated parts of what has previously been a single living organism. All this research work required a prodigious supply of freshly slaughtered human flesh—and that was why Herbert West had entered the Great War.

The phantasmal, unmentionable thing occurred one midnight late in March, 1915, in a field hospital behind the lines at St. Eloi. I wonder even now if it could have been other than a daemoniac[d] dream of delirium. West had a private laboratory in an east room of the barn-like temporary edifice, assigned him on his plea that he was devising new and radical methods for the treatment of hitherto hopeless cases of maiming. There he worked like a butcher in the midst of his gory wares—I could never get used to the levity with which he handled and classified certain things. At times he actually did perform marvels of surgery for the soldiers; but his chief delights were of a less public and

---

[a] nerve-tissue] nerve tissue C
[b] nearly hatched] nearly-hatched A, B, C
[c] action] action might C
[d] daemoniac] demoniac A, B, C

philanthropic kind, requiring many explanations of sounds which seemed peculiar even amidst that babel of the damned. Among these sounds were frequent revolver-shots[a]—surely not uncommon on a battlefield, but distinctly uncommon in an[b] hospital. Dr. West's reanimated specimens were not meant for long existence or a large audience. Besides human tissue, West employed much of the reptile embryo tissue which he had cultivated with such singular results. It was better than human material for maintaining life in organless fragments, and that was now my friend's chief activity. In a dark corner of the laboratory, over a queer incubating burner, he kept a large covered vat full of this reptilian cell-matter; which multiplied and grew puffily and hideously.

On the night of which I speak we had a splendid new specimen— a man at once physically powerful and of such high mentality that a sensitive nervous system was assured. It was rather ironic, for he was the officer who had helped West to his commission, and who was now to have been our associate. Moreover, he had in the past secretly studied the theory of reanimation to some extent under West. Major Sir Eric Moreland Clapham-Lee, D.S.O., was the greatest surgeon in our division, and had been hastily assigned to the St. Eloi sector when news of the heavy fighting reached headquarters. He had come in an aëroplane[c] piloted by the intrepid Lieut.[d] Ronald Hill, only to be shot down when directly over his destination. The fall had been spectacular and awful; Hill was unrecognisable[e] afterward, but the wreck yielded up the great surgeon in a nearly decapitated but otherwise intact condition. West had greedily seized the lifeless thing which had once been his friend and fellow-scholar; and I shuddered when he finished severing the head, placed it in his hellish vat of pulpy reptile-tissue to preserve it for future experiments, and proceeded to treat the decapitated body on the operating table. He injected new blood, joined certain veins, arteries, and nerves at the headless neck, and closed the

[a] revolver-shots] revolver shots B
[b] an] a C
[c] aëroplane] aeroplane A, B, C
[d] Lieut.] Lieutenant C
[e] unrecognisable] unrecognizable B, C

ghastly aperture with engrafted skin from an unidentified specimen which had borne an officer's uniform. I knew what he wanted—to see if this highly organised[a] body could exhibit, without its head, any of the signs of mental life which had distinguished Sir Eric Moreland Clapham-Lee. Once a student of reanimation, this silent trunk was now gruesomely called upon to exemplify it.

I can still see Herbert West under the sinister electric light as he injected his reanimating solution into the arm of the headless body. The scene I cannot describe—I should faint if I tried it, for there is madness in a room full of classified charnel things, with blood and lesser human debris almost ankle-deep on the slimy floor, and with hideous reptilian abnormalities sprouting, bubbling, and baking over a winking bluish-green spectre of dim flame in a far corner of black shadows.

The specimen, as West repeatedly observed, had a splendid nervous system. Much was expected of it; and as a few twitching motions began to appear, I could see the feverish interest on West's face. He was ready, I think, to see proof of his increasingly strong opinion that consciousness, reason, and personality can exist independently of the brain—that man has no central connective spirit, but is merely a machine of nervous matter, each section more or less complete in itself. In one triumphant demonstration West was about to relegate the mystery of life to the category of myth. The body now twitched more vigorously, and beneath our avid eyes commenced to heave in a frightful way. The arms stirred disquietingly, the legs drew up, and various muscles contracted in a repulsive kind of writhing. Then the headless thing threw out its arms in a gesture which was unmistakably one of desperation—an intelligent desperation apparently sufficient to prove every theory of Herbert West. Certainly, the nerves were recalling the man's last act in life; the struggle to get free of the falling aëroplane.[b]

What followed, I shall never positively know. It may have been wholly an hallucination from the shock caused at that instant by the sudden and complete destruction of the building in a cataclysm of German shell-fire—who can gainsay it, since West and I were the only proved survivors? West liked to think that before his recent

[a] organised] organized B, C
[b] aëroplane.] aeroplane. A, B, C

disappearance, but there were times when he could not; for it was queer that we both had the same hallucination. The hideous occurrence itself was very simple, notable only for what it implied.

The body on the table had risen with a blind and terrible groping, and we had heard a sound. I should not call that sound a voice, for it was too awful. And yet its timbre was not the most awful thing about it. Neither was its message—it had merely screamed, "Jump, Ronald, for God's sake, jump!" The awful thing was its source.

For it had come from the large covered vat in that ghoulish corner of crawling black shadows.

VI. THE TOMB-LEGIONS

When Dr. Herbert West disappeared a year ago, the Boston police questioned me closely. They suspected that I was holding something back, and perhaps suspected graver things; but I could not tell them the truth because they would not have believed it. They knew, indeed, that West had been connected with activities beyond the credence of ordinary men; for his hideous experiments in the reanimation of dead bodies had long been too extensive to admit of perfect secrecy; but the final soul-shattering catastrophe held elements of daemoniac[a] phantasy which make even me doubt the reality of what I saw.

I was West's closest friend and only confidential assistant. We had met years before, in medical school, and from the first I had shared his terrible researches. He had slowly tried to perfect a solution which, injected into the veins of the newly deceased, would restore life; a labour demanding an abundance of fresh corpses and therefore involving the most unnatural actions. Still more shocking were the products of some of the experiments—grisly masses of flesh that had been dead, but that West waked to a blind, brainless, nauseous animation. These were the usual results, for in order to reawaken the mind it was necessary to have specimens so absolutely fresh that no decay could possibly affect the delicate brain-cells.[b]

This need for very fresh corpses had been West's moral undoing.

---

[a] daemoniac] demoniac A, B, C
[b] brain-cells.] brain cells. A, B, C

They were hard to get, and one awful day he had secured his specimen while it was still alive and vigorous. A struggle, a needle, and a powerful alkaloid had transformed it to a very fresh corpse, and the experiment had succeeded for a brief and memorable moment; but West had emerged with a soul calloused and seared, and a hardened eye which sometimes glanced with a kind of hideous and calculating appraisal at men of especially sensitive brain and especially vigorous physique. Toward the last I became acutely afraid of West, for he began to look at me that way. People did not seem to notice his glances, but they noticed my fear; and after his disappearance used that as a basis for some absurd suspicions.

West, in reality, was more afraid than I; for his abominable pursuits entailed a life of furtiveness and dread of every shadow. Partly it was the police he feared; but sometimes his nervousness was deeper and more nebulous, touching on certain indescribable things into which he had injected a morbid life, and from which he had not seen that life depart. He usually finished his experiments with a revolver, but a few times he had not been quick enough. There was that first specimen on whose rifled grave marks of clawing were later seen. There was also that Arkham professor's body which had done cannibal things before it had been captured and thrust unidentified into a madhouse cell at Sefton, where it beat the walls for sixteen years. Most of the other possibly surviving results were things less easy to speak of—for in later years West's scientific zeal had degenerated to an unhealthy and fantastic mania, and he had spent his chief skill in vitalising[a] not entire human bodies but isolated parts of bodies, or parts joined to organic matter other than human. It had become fiendishly disgusting by the time he disappeared; many of the experiments could not even be hinted at in print. The Great War, through which both of us served as surgeons, had intensified this side of West.

In saying that West's fear of his specimens was nebulous, I have in mind particularly its complex nature. Part of it came merely from knowing of the existence of such nameless monsters, while another part arose from apprehension of the bodily harm they might under certain circumstances do him. Their disappearance added horror to the

---

[a] vitalising] vitalizing B, C

situation—of them all West knew the whereabouts of only one, the pitiful asylum thing. Then there was a more subtle fear—a very fantastic sensation resulting from a curious experiment in the Canadian army in 1915. West, in the midst of a severe battle, had reanimated Major Sir Eric Moreland Clapham-Lee, D.S.O., a fellow-physician who knew about his experiments and could have duplicated them. The head had been removed, so that the possibilities of quasi-intelligent life in the trunk might be investigated. Just as the building was wiped out by a German shell, there had been a success. The trunk had moved intelligently; and, unbelievable to relate, we were both sickeningly sure that articulate sounds had come from the detached head as it lay in a shadowy corner of the laboratory. The shell had been merciful, in a way—but West could never feel as certain as he wished, that we two were the only survivors. He used to make shuddering conjectures about the possible actions of a headless physician with the power of reanimating the dead.

West's last quarters were in a venerable house of much elegance, overlooking one of the oldest burying-grounds[a] in Boston. He had chosen the place for purely symbolic and fantastically aesthetic reasons, since most of the interments were of the colonial[b] period and therefore of little use to a scientist seeking very fresh bodies. The laboratory was in a sub-cellar secretly constructed by imported workmen, and contained a huge incinerator for the quiet and complete disposal of such bodies, or fragments and synthetic mockeries of bodies, as might remain from the morbid experiments and unhallowed amusements of the owner. During the excavation of this cellar the workmen had struck some exceedingly ancient masonry; undoubtedly connected with the old burying-ground,[c] yet far too deep to correspond with any known sepulchre therein. After a number of calculations West decided that it represented some secret chamber beneath the tomb of the Averills, where the last interment had been made in 1768. I was with him when he studied the nitrous, dripping walls laid bare by the spades and mattocks of the men, and was prepared for the gruesome thrill which

[a] burying-grounds] burying grounds A, B, C
[b] colonial] Colonial A, B, C
[c] burying-ground,] burying ground, A, B, C

would attend the uncovering of centuried grave-secrets; but for the first time West's new timidity conquered his natural curiosity, and he betrayed his degenerating fibre by ordering the masonry left intact and plastered over. Thus it remained till that final hellish night;[a] part of the walls of the secret laboratory. I speak of West's decadence, but must add that it was a purely mental and intangible thing. Outwardly he was the same to the last—calm, cold, slight, and yellow-haired, with spectacled blue eyes and a general aspect of youth which years and fears seemed never to change. He seemed calm even when he thought of that clawed grave and looked over his shoulder; even when he thought of the carnivorous thing that gnawed and pawed at Sefton bars.

The end of Herbert West began one evening in our joint study when he was dividing his curious glance between the newspaper and me. A strange headline item had struck at him from the crumpled pages, and a nameless titan claw had seemed to reach down through sixteen years. Something fearsome and incredible had happened at Sefton Asylum[b] fifty miles away, stunning the neighbourhood[c] and baffling the police. In the small hours of the morning a body of silent men had entered the grounds and their leader had aroused the attendants. He was a menacing military figure who talked without moving his lips and whose voice seemed almost ventriloquially connected with an immense black case he carried. His expressionless face was handsome to the point of radiant beauty, but had shocked the superintendent when the hall light fell on it—for it was a wax face with eyes of painted glass. Some nameless accident had befallen this man. A larger man guided his steps; a repellent hulk whose bluish face seemed half eaten away by some unknown malady. The speaker had asked for the custody of the cannibal monster committed from Arkham sixteen years before; and upon being refused, gave a signal which precipitated a shocking riot. The fiends had beaten, trampled, and bitten every attendant who did not flee; killing four and finally succeeding in the liberation of the monster. Those[d] victims who could recall the event

---

[a] night;] night, C
[b] Asylum] Asylum, B
[c] neighbourhood] neighborhood C
[d] Those] These C

without hysteria swore that the creatures had acted less like men than like unthinkable automata guided by the wax-faced leader. By the time help could be summoned, every trace of the men and of their mad charge had vanished.

From the hour of reading this item until midnight, West sat almost paralysed.[a] At midnight the doorbell rang, startling him fearfully. All the servants were asleep in the attic, so I answered the bell. As I have told the police, there was no wagon in the street; but only a group of strange-looking figures bearing a large square box which they deposited in the hallway after one of them had grunted in a highly unnatural voice, "Express—prepaid." They filed out of the house with a jerky tread, and as I watched them go I had an odd idea that they were turning toward the ancient cemetery on which the back of the house abutted. When I slammed the door after them West came downstairs and looked at the box. It was about two feet square, and bore West's correct name and present address. It also bore the inscription, "From Eric Moreland Clapham-Lee, St. Eloi, Flanders." Six years before, in Flanders, a shelled hospital had fallen upon the headless reanimated trunk of Dr. Clapham-Lee, and upon the detached head which—perhaps—had uttered articulate sounds.

West was not even excited now. His condition was more ghastly. Quickly he said, "It's the finish—but let's incinerate—this." We carried the thing down to the laboratory—listening. I do not remember many particulars—you can imagine my state of mind—but it is a vicious lie to say it was Herbert West's body which I put into the incinerator. We both inserted the whole unopened wooden[b] box, closed the door, and started the electricity. Nor did any sound come from the box, after all.

It was West who first noticed the falling plaster on that part of the wall where the ancient tomb masonry had been covered up. I was going to run, but he stopped me. Then I saw a small black aperture, felt a ghoulish wind of ice, and smelled the charnel bowels of a putrescent earth. There was no sound, but just then the electric lights went out and I saw outlined against some phosphorescence of the nether world a horde of silent toiling things which only insanity—or

[a] paralysed.] paralyzed. C
[b] wooden] *om.* C

worse—could create. Their outlines were human, semi-human, fractionally human, and not human at all—the horde was grotesquely heterogeneous. They were removing[a] the stones quietly, one by one, from the centuried wall. And then, as the breach became large enough, they came out into the laboratory in[b] single file; led by a stalking thing with a beautiful head made of wax. A sort of mad-eyed monstrosity behind the leader seized on Herbert West. West did not resist or utter a sound. Then they all sprang at him and tore him to pieces before my eyes, bearing the fragments away into that subterranean vault of fabulous abominations. West's head was carried off by the wax-headed leader, who wore a Canadian officer's uniform. As it disappeared I saw that the blue eyes behind the spectacles were hideously blazing with their first touch of frantic, visible emotion.

Servants found me unconscious in the morning. West was gone. The incinerator contained only unidentifiable ashes. Detectives have questioned me, but what can I say? The Sefton tragedy they will not connect with West; not that, nor the men with the box, whose existence they deny. I told them of the vault, and they pointed to the unbroken plaster wall and laughed. So I told them no more. They imply that I am a madman or a murderer—probably I am mad. But I might not be mad if those accursed tomb-legions had not been so silent.

[a] removing] removng B
[b] in] in a C

Hypnos

To S. L.[a]

"Apropos of sleep, that sinister adventure of all our nights, we may say that men go to bed daily with an audacity that would be incomprehensible if we did not know that it is the result of ignorance of the danger."[b]

—Baudelaire.[c]

M ay the merciful gods,[d] if indeed there be such, guard those hours when no power of the will, or drug that the cunning of man devises, can keep me from the chasm of sleep. Death is merciful, for there is no return therefrom,[e] but with him who has come back out of the nethermost chambers of night, haggard and knowing, peace rests nevermore. Fool that I was to plunge with such unsanctioned phrensy into mysteries no man was meant to penetrate;

Editor's Note: A single-spaced T.Ms. surfaced after my first corrected edition of this text (1986). It appears to date prior to the first publication of the story— *National Amateur* (May 1923)—but bears some revisions in HPL's handwriting (including the dedication) that postdate that appearance, and perhaps also the *Weird Tales* (May–June–July 1924) appearance. But HPL must have prepared a double-spaced T.Ms. for *Weird Tales,* and this hypothetical T.Ms. seems to have embodied a few revisions from the existing T.Ms.; but in my judgment, the paragraph divisions introduced in the *Weird Tales* text are the result of editorial tampering, as was the case with other stories published in *Weird Tales* at this time. The Arkham House editions prior to mine follow the *Weird Tales* text.

Texts: A = T.Ms. (private hands); B = *National Amateur* 45, No. 5 (May 1923): 1–3; C = *Weird Tales* 4, No. 2 (May–June–July 1924): 33–35; D = *Dagon and Other Macabre Tales* (Arkham House, 1965), 160–66. Copy-text: A.

[a] To S. L.] *om.* B, C, D [*added in pen in A*]
[b] "Apropos . . . danger."] *"Apropos . . . danger."* C; *Apropos . . . danger.* D
[c] *—Baudelaire.*] —BAUDELAIRE A, B; —*BAUDELAIRE* C; BAUDELAIRE D
[d] gods,] Gods, B
[e] therefrom,] there / from, B

fool or god that *he*[a] was—my only friend, who led me and went before me, and who in the end passed into terrors which[b] may yet be mine.[c]

We met, I recall, in a railway station, where he was the centre[d] of a crowd of the vulgarly curious. He was unconscious, having fallen in a kind of convulsion which imparted to his slight black-clad body a strange rigidity. I think he was then approaching forty years of age, for there were deep lines in the face, wan and hollow-cheeked, but oval and actually *beautiful;*[e] and touches of grey[f] in the thick, waving hair and small full beard which had once been of the deepest raven black. His brow was white as the marble of Pentelicus, and of a height and breadth almost godlike.[g] I said to myself, with all the ardour[h] of a sculptor, that this man was a faun's statue out of antique Hellas, dug from a temple's ruins and brought somehow to life in our stifling age only to feel the chill and pressure of devastating years. And when he opened his immense, sunken, and wildly luminous black eyes I knew he would be thenceforth my only friend—the only friend of one who had never possessed a friend before—for I saw that such eyes must have looked fully upon the grandeur and the terror of realms beyond normal consciousness and reality; realms which I had cherished in fancy, but vainly sought. So as I drove the crowd away I told him he must come home with me and be my teacher and leader in unfathomed mysteries, and he assented without speaking a word. Afterward I found that his voice was music—the music of deep viols and of crystalline spheres. We talked often in the night, and in the day, when I chiselled[i] busts of him,[j] and carved miniature heads in ivory to immortalise[k] his different expressions.

---

[a] *he*] he B, C, D [*underscore added in pen in A*]
[b] which] wihch B
[c] mine.] mine! C, D
[d] centre] center B, C, D
[e] *beautiful;*] beautiful; B, C, D
[f] grey] gray C, D
[g] godlike.] god-/like. ¶ C; god-like. ¶ D
[h] ardour] ardor C, D
[i] chiselled] chiseled C, D
[j] him,] him B
[k] immortalise] immortalize B, C, D

Of our studies it is impossible to speak, since they held so slight a connexion[a] with anything of the world as living men conceive it. They were of that vaster and more appalling universe of dim entity and consciousness which lies deeper than matter, time, and space, and whose existence we suspect only in certain forms of sleep—those rare dreams beyond dreams which come never to common men, and but once or twice in the lifetime of imaginative men. The cosmos of our waking knowledge, born from such an universe as a bubble is born from the pipe of a jester, touches it only as such a bubble may touch its sardonic source when sucked back by the jester's whim. Men of learning suspect it little,[b] and ignore it mostly. Wise men have interpreted dreams, and the gods have laughed. One man with Oriental eyes has said that all time and space are relative, and men have laughed. But even that man with Oriental eyes has done no more than suspect. I had wished and tried to do more than suspect, and my friend had tried and partly succeeded. Then we both tried together, and with exotic drugs courted terrible and forbidden dreams in the tower studio chamber of the old manor-house in hoary Kent.

Among the agonies of these after days is that chief of torments—inarticulateness. What I learned and saw in those hours of impious exploration can never be told—for want of symbols or suggestions in any language. I say this because from first to last our discoveries partook only of the nature of *sensations;*[c] sensations correlated with no impression which the nervous system of normal humanity is capable of receiving. They were sensations, yet within them lay unbelievable elements of time and space—things which at bottom possess no distinct and definite existence. Human utterance can best convey the general character of our experiences by calling them *plungings* or *soarings;*[d] for in every period of revelation some part of our minds broke boldly away from all that is real and present, rushing aërially[e] along shocking, unlighted, and fear-haunted abysses, and occasionally

---

[a] connexion] connection C, D
[b] little,] little D
[c] *sensations;*] sensations; B, C, D [*underscore added in pen in A*]
[d] *plungings* or *soarings;*] plungings or soarings; B, C, D [*underscore added in pen in A*]
[e] aërially] aerially A, B, C, D

tearing[a] through certain well-marked and typical obstacles describable only as viscous, uncouth clouds or[b] vapours.[c] In these black and bodiless flights we were sometimes alone and sometimes together. When we were together, my friend was always far ahead; I could comprehend his presence despite the absence of form by a species of pictorial memory whereby his face appeared to me, golden from a strange light and frightful with its weird beauty, its anomalously youthful cheeks, its burning eyes, its Olympian brow, and its shadowing hair and growth of beard.

Of the progress of time we kept no record, for time had become to us the merest illusion. I know only that there must have been something very singular involved, since we came at length to marvel why we did not grow old. Our discourse was unholy, and always hideously ambitious—no god or daemon could have aspired to discoveries and conquests[d] like those which we planned in whispers. I shiver as I speak of them, and dare not be explicit; though I will say that my friend once wrote on paper a wish which he dared not utter with his tongue, and which made me burn the paper and look affrightedly out of the window at the spangled night sky. I will hint—only hint—that he had designs which involved the rulership of the visible universe and more; designs whereby the earth and the stars would move at his command, and the destinies of all living things be his. I affirm—I swear—that I had no share in these extreme aspirations. Anything my friend may have said or written to the contrary must be erroneous, for I am no man of strength to risk the unmentionable warfare in unmentionable[e] spheres by which alone one might achieve success.

There was a night when winds from unknown spaces whirled us irresistibly into limitless vacua beyond all thought and entity. Perceptions of the most maddeningly untransmissible sort thronged upon us; perceptions of infinity which at the time convulsed us with

---

[a] *tearing*] tearing B, C, D [*underscore added in pen in A*]

[b] or] of B, C, D

[c] vapours.] vapors. ¶ C, D

[d] conquests] conquest D

[e] warfare in unmentionable] *om.* D

joy, yet which are now partly lost to my memory and partly incapable of presentation to others. Viscous obstacles were clawed through in rapid succession, and at length I felt that we had been borne to realms of greater remoteness than any we had previously known.[a] My friend was vastly in advance as we plunged into this awesome ocean of virgin aether, and I could see the sinister exultation on his floating, luminous, too youthful[b] memory-face. Suddenly that face became dim and quickly disappeared, and in a brief space I found myself projected against an obstacle which I could not penetrate. It was like the others, yet incalculably denser; a sticky,[c] clammy mass, if such terms can be applied to analogous qualities in a non-material sphere.

I had, I felt, been halted by a barrier which my friend and leader had successfully passed. Struggling anew, I came to the end of the drug-dream and opened my physical eyes to the tower studio in whose opposite corner reclined the pallid and still unconscious form of my fellow-dreamer,[d] weirdly haggard and wildly beautiful as the moon shed gold-green light on his marble features.[e] Then, after a short interval, the form in the corner stirred; and may pitying heaven keep from my sight and sound[f] another thing like that which took place before me. I cannot tell you how he shrieked, or what vistas of unvisitable hells gleamed for a second in black eyes crazed with fright. I can only say that I fainted, and did not stir till he himself recovered and shook me in his phrensy for someone to keep away the horror and desolation.

That was the end of our voluntary searchings in the caverns of dream. Awed, shaken, and portentous, my friend who had been beyond the barrier warned me that we must never venture within those realms again. What he had seen, he dared not tell me; but he said from his wisdom that we must sleep as little as possible, even if drugs were necessary to keep us awake. That he was right, I soon learned from the unutterable fear which engulfed me whenever consciousness lapsed.[g]

[a] known.] known. ¶ C, D
[b] too youthful] too-youthful C, D
[c] sticky,] sticky D
[d] fellow-dreamer,] fellow dreamer, D
[e] features.] features. ¶ C, D
[f] sound] sounnd B
[g] lapsed.] lapsed. ¶ C, D

After each short and inevitable sleep I seemed older, whilst my friend aged with a rapidity almost shocking. It is hideous to see wrinkles form and hair whiten almost before one's eyes. Our mode of life was now totally altered. Heretofore a recluse so far as I know—his true name and origin never having passed his lips—my friend now became frantic in his fear of solitude. At night he would not be alone, nor would the company of a few persons calm him. His sole relief was obtained in revelry of the most general and boisterous sort; so that few assemblies of the young and the[a] gay were unknown to us.[b] Our appearance and age seemed to excite in most cases a ridicule which I keenly resented, but which my friend considered a lesser evil than solitude. Especially was he afraid to be out of doors alone when the stars were shining, and if forced to this condition he would often glance furtively at the sky as if hunted by some monstrous thing therein. He did not always glance at the same place in the sky—it seemed to be a different place at different times. On spring evenings it would be low in the northeast. In the summer it would be nearly overhead. In the autumn it would be in the northwest. In winter it would be in the east, but mostly if in the small hours of morning.[c] Midwinter evenings seemed least dreadful to him. Only after two years did I connect this fear with anything in particular; but then I began to see that he must be looking at a special spot on the celestial vault whose position at different times corresponded to the direction of his glance—a spot roughly marked by the constellation Corona Borealis.

We now had a studio in London, never separating, but never discussing the days when we had sought to plumb the mysteries of the unreal world. We were aged and weak from our drugs, dissipations, and nervous overstrain, and the thinning hair and beard of my friend had become snow-white. Our freedom from long sleep was surprising, for seldom did we succumb more than an hour or two at a time to the shadow which had now grown so frightful a menace.[d] Then came one January of fog and rain, when money ran low and drugs were hard to

---

[a] the] *om.* C, D
[b] us.] us. ¶ C, D
[c] morning.] morning. ¶ C, D
[d] menace.] menace. ¶ C, D

buy. My statues and ivory heads were all sold, and I had no means to purchase new materials, or energy to fashion them even had I possessed them. We suffered terribly, and on a certain night my friend sank into a deep-breathing sleep from which I could not awaken him. I can recall the scene now—the desolate, pitch-black garret studio under the eaves with the rain beating down; the ticking of our[a] lone clock; the fancied ticking of our watches as they rested on the dressing-table; the creaking of some swaying shutter in a remote part of the house; certain distant city noises muffled by fog and space; and worst of all[b] the deep, steady, sinister breathing of my friend on the couch—a rhythmical breathing which seemed to measure moments of supernal fear and agony for his spirit as it wandered in spheres forbidden, unimagined, and hideously remote.

The tension of my vigil became oppressive, and a wild train of trivial impressions and associations thronged through my almost unhinged mind. I heard a clock strike somewhere—not ours, for that was not a striking clock—and my morbid fancy found in this a new starting-point for idle wanderings. Clocks—time—space—infinity— and then my fancy reverted to the local[c] as I reflected that even now, beyond the roof and the fog and the rain and the atmosphere, Corona Borealis was rising in the northeast. Corona Borealis, which my friend had appeared to dread, and whose scintillant semicircle of stars must even now be glowing unseen through the measureless abysses of aether. All at once my feverishly sensitive ears seemed to detect a new and wholly distinct component in the soft medley of drug-magnified sounds—a low and damnably insistent whine from very far away; droning, clamouring,[d] mocking, calling, *from the northeast.*[e]

But it was not that distant whine which robbed me of my faculties and set upon my soul such a seal of fright as may never in life be removed; not that which drew the shrieks and excited the convulsions which caused lodgers and police to break down the door. It was not

[a] our] the A, B
[b] and . . . all] and, . . . all, C, D
[c] local] locale C, D
[d] clamouring,] clamoring, C, D
[e] *from the northeast.*] from the northeast. B

what I *heard,* but what I *saw;*[a] for in that dark, locked, shuttered, and curtained room there appeared from the black northeast corner a shaft of horrible red-gold light—a shaft which bore with it no glow to disperse the darkness, but which streamed only upon the recumbent head of the troubled sleeper, bringing out in hideous duplication the luminous and strangely youthful memory-face as I had known it in dreams of abysmal space and unshackled time, when my friend had pushed behind the barrier to those secret, innermost,[b] and forbidden caverns of nightmare.

And as I looked, I beheld the head rise, the black, liquid, and deep-sunken eyes open in terror, and the thin, shadowed lips part as if for a scream too frightful to be uttered. There dwelt in that ghastly and inflexible[c] face, as it shone bodiless, luminous, and rejuvenated in the blackness, more of stark, teeming, brain-shattering fear than all the rest of heaven and earth has ever revealed to me.[d] No word was spoken amidst the distant sound that grew nearer and nearer, but as I followed the memory-face's mad stare along that cursed shaft of light to its source, the source whence also the whining came, I too[e] saw for an instant what it saw, and fell with ringing ears in that fit of shrieking and[f] epilepsy which brought the lodgers and the police. Never could I tell, try as I might, what it actually was that I saw; nor could the still face tell, for although it must have seen more than I did, it will never speak again. But always I shall guard against the mocking and insatiate Hypnos, lord of sleep, against the night sky, and against the mad ambitions of knowledge and philosophy.

Just what happened is unknown, for not only was my own mind unseated by the strange and hideous thing, but others were tainted with a forgetfulness which can mean nothing if not madness. They have said, I know not for what reason, that I never had a friend;[g] but that art, philosophy, and insanity had filled all my tragic life. The

[a] *heard, . . . saw;*] heard, . . . saw; B, C, D [*underscore added in pen in A*]

[b] innermost,] innermost A, B, C, D

[c] inflexible] flexible A, B, C, D

[d] me.] me. ¶ C, D

[e] I too] I, too, C, D

[f] and] *om.* C, D

[g] friend;] friend, A, B

lodgers and police on that night soothed me, and the doctor administered something to quiet me, nor did anyone see what a nightmare event had taken place. My stricken friend moved them to no pity, but what they found on the couch in the studio made them give me a praise which sickened me, and now a fame which I spurn in despair as I sit for hours, bald, grey-bearded, shrivelled,[a] palsied, drug-crazed, and broken, adoring and praying to the object they found.

For they deny that I sold the last of my statuary, and point with ecstasy at the thing which the shining[b] shaft of light left cold, petrified, and unvocal. It is all that remains of my friend; the friend who led me on to madness and wreckage; a[c] godlike head of such marble as only old Hellas could yield, young with the youth that is outside time, and with beauteous bearded face, curved,[d] smiling lips, Olympian brow, and dense locks waving and poppy-crowned. They say that that haunting memory-face is modelled[e] from my own, as it was at twenty-five;[f] but upon the marble base is carven a single name in the letters of Attica—ΎΠΝΟΣ.[g]

---

[a] grey-bearded, shrivelled,] grey-beared, shrivelled, B; gray-bearded, shriveled, C, D
[b] shining] whining B, C
[c] a] and C
[d] curved,] curved A, B
[e] modelled] modeled C, D
[f] twenty-five;] twenty-five, A, B
[g] ΎΠΝΟΣ.] ΥΠΝΟΣ. A; HYPNOS. B, C, D

What the Moon Brings

I hate the moon—I am afraid of it—for when it shines on certain scenes familiar and loved[a] it sometimes makes them unfamiliar and hideous.

It was in the spectral summer when the moon shone down on the old garden where I wandered; the spectral summer of narcotic flowers and humid seas of foliage that bring wild and many-coloured dreams. And as I walked by the shallow crystal stream I saw unwonted ripples tipped with yellow light, as if those placid waters were drawn on in resistless currents to strange oceans that are not in the world. Silent and sparkling, bright and baleful, those moon-cursed waters hurried I knew not whither; whilst from the embowered banks white lotos blossoms[b] fluttered one by one in the opiate night-wind and dropped despairingly into the stream, swirling away horribly under the arched, carven bridge, and staring back with the sinister resignation of calm, dead faces.

And as I ran along the shore, crushing sleeping flowers with heedless feet and maddened ever by the fear of unknown things and the lure of the dead faces, I saw that the garden had no end under that moon; for where by day the walls were, there stretched now only new vistas of trees and paths, flowers and shrubs, stone idols and pagodas, and bendings of the yellow-litten stream past grassy banks and under grotesque bridges of marble. And the lips of the dead lotos-faces whispered sadly, and bade me follow, nor did I cease my steps till the

Editor's Note: The surviving A.Ms. is HPL's original draft, written in pencil on the back of correspondence to him. The first appearance (*National Amateur,* May 1923) derives from the A.Ms., as does (surprisingly) the Arkham House edition.

Texts: A = A.Ms. (JHL); B = *National Amateur* 45, No. 5 (May 1923): 9; C = *Beyond the Wall of Sleep* (Arkham House, 1943), 4–5. Copy-text: A.

[a] loved] loved, B
[b] lotos blossoms] lotos-blossoms B, C

stream became a river, and joined amidst marshes of swaying reeds and beaches of gleaming sand the shore of a vast and nameless sea.

Upon that sea the hateful moon shone, and over its unvocal waves weird perfumes brooded.[a] And as I saw therein the lotos-faces vanish, I longed for nets that I might capture them and learn from them the secrets which the moon had brought upon the night. But when the moon went over to the west and the[b] still tide ebbed from the sullen shore, I saw in that light old spires that the waves almost uncovered, and white columns gay with festoons of green seaweed. And knowing that to this sunken place all the dead had come, I trembled and did not wish again to speak with the lotos-faces.

Yet when I saw afar out in the sea[c] a black condor descend from the sky to seek rest on a vast reef, I would fain have questioned him, and asked him of those whom I had known when they were alive. This I would have asked him had he not been so far away, but he was very far, and could not be seen at all when he drew nigh that gigantic reef.

So I watched the tide go out under that sinking moon, and saw gleaming the spires, the towers, and the roofs of that dead, dripping city. And as I watched, my nostrils tried to close against the perfume-conquering stench of the world's dead; for truly, in this unplaced and forgotten spot had all the flesh of the churchyards gathered for puffy sea-worms to gnaw and glut upon.

Over those horrors the evil moon now hung very low, but the puffy worms of the sea need no moon to feed by. And as I watched the ripples that told of the writhing of worms beneath, I felt a new chill from afar out whither the condor had flown, as if my flesh had caught a horror before my eyes had seen it.

Nor had my flesh trembled without cause, for when I raised my eyes I saw that the waters had ebbed very low, shewing much of the vast reef whose rim I had seen before. And when I saw that this[d] reef was but the black basalt crown of a shocking eikon whose monstrous

---

[a] brooded.] breeded. C
[b] moon went . . . and the] *om.* B
[c] saw afar . . . sea] saw, far . . . sea, B
[d] this] the C

forehead now shone[a] in the dim moonlight and whose vile hooves must paw the hellish ooze miles below, I shrieked and shrieked lest the hidden face rise above the waters, and lest the hidden eyes look at me after the slinking away of that leering and treacherous yellow moon.

And to escape this relentless thing I plunged gladly and unhesitatingly[b] into the stinking shallows where amidst weedy walls and sunken streets fat sea-worms feast upon the world's dead.

[a] shone] shown C
[b] unhesitatingly] unhesitantly C

Azathoth

When age fell upon the world, and wonder went out of the minds of men; when grey cities reared to smoky skies tall towers grim and ugly, in whose shadow none might dream of the sun or of spring's[a] flowering meads; when learning stripped earth[b] of her mantle of beauty, and poets sang no more save of twisted phantoms seen with bleared and inward-looking eyes; when these things had come to pass, and childish hopes had gone away for ever, there was a man who travelled out of life on a quest into the spaces whither the world's dreams had fled.

Of the name and abode of this man but little is written, for they were of the waking world only; yet it is said that both were obscure. It is enough to know that he dwelt in a city of high walls where sterile twilight reigned, and that he toiled all day among shadow and turmoil, coming home at evening to a room whose one window opened not on the fields and groves but on a dim court where other windows stared in dull despair. From that casement one might see only walls and windows, except sometimes when one leaned far out and peered aloft at the small stars that passed. And because mere walls and windows must soon drive to madness a man who dreams and reads much, the dweller in that room used night after night to lean out and peer aloft to glimpse some fragment of things beyond the waking world and the greyness of tall cities. After years he began to call the slow-sailing stars

Editor's Note: The surviving A.Ms. is HPL's original draft. It was followed accurately enough in the two posthumous appearances. My text prints some passages that were deleted in the A.Ms.

Texts: A = A.Ms. (JHL); B = *Leaves* No. 2 (1938): 107; C = *Dagon and Other Macabre Tales* (Arkham House, 1965), 335–36. Copy-text: A.

[a] spring's] Spring's B
[b] earth] Earth B

by name, and to follow them in fancy when they glided regretfully out of sight; till at length his vision opened to many secret vistas whose existence no common eye suspects. And one night a mighty gulf was bridged, and the dream-haunted skies swelled down to the lonely watcher's window to merge with the close air of his room and make him a part of their fabulous wonder.[a]

There came to that room wild streams of violet midnight glittering with dust of gold; vortices of dust and fire, swirling out of the ultimate spaces and heavy with perfumes from beyond the worlds. Opiate oceans poured there, litten by suns that the eye may never behold and having in their whirlpools strange dolphins and sea-nymphs of unrememberable deeps. Noiseless infinity eddied around the dreamer and wafted him away without even touching the body that leaned stiffly from the lonely window; and for days not counted in men's calendars the tides of far spheres bare[b] him gently to join the dreams for which he longed; the dreams that men have lost. And in the course of many cycles they tenderly left him sleeping on a green sunrise shore; a green shore fragrant with lotus-blossoms and starred by red camalotes.[c]

---

[a] wonder.] wonder. ¶ Thereafter the nights of the dreamer were spent in strange places, and amidst unheard-of splendours. In boats of darkness he sailed to fortunate isles, and on one of them built a palace where he ruled as Miral, King of the Isles [*deleted*]; ¶ He had been sleeping when space came to claim him. Very suddenly had the skies swelled down, for as the dreamer sat leaning out [*deleted*] A

[b] bare] bore B, C

[c] camalotes.] camalates. C

The Hound

I.[a]

In my tortured ears there sounds unceasingly a nightmare whirring and flapping, and a faint,[b] distant baying as of[c] some gigantic hound. It is not dream—it is not, I fear, even madness—for too much has already happened to give me these merciful doubts.[d] St. John is a mangled corpse; I alone know why, and such is my knowledge that I am about to blow out my brains for fear I shall be mangled in the same way. Down unlit and illimitable corridors of eldritch phantasy sweeps the black, shapeless Nemesis that drives me to self-annihilation.[e]

May heaven forgive the folly and morbidity which led us both to so monstrous a fate! Wearied with the commonplaces of a prosaic world,[f] where even the joys of romance and adventure soon grow stale, St. John and I had followed enthusiastically every aesthetic and intellectual

Editor's Note: The surviving T.Ms. is one of HPL's single-spaced T.Mss. sent to *Weird Tales* in mid-1923. He must have subsequently made slight revisions, as the *Weird Tales* text (February 1924) appears to bear a few deliberate alterations by HPL; but the majority of the divergences between the single-spaced T.Ms. and the *Weird Tales* text are probably the result of alterations in accordance with the magazine's "house style." The Arkham House editions follow the *Weird Tales* text; the 1965 edition makes numerous additional errors. The second *Weird Tales* appearance (September 1929) is not relevant to the textual history of the tale.

Texts: A = T.Ms. (JHL); B = *Weird Tales* 3, No. 2 (February 1924): 50–52, 78; C = *Beyond the Wall of Sleep* (Arkham House, 1943), 45–49; D = *Dagon and Other Macabre Tales* (Arkham House, 1965), 152–59. Copy-text: A (with a few readings from B).

[a] I.] *om.* A, B, C, D
[b] faint,] faint D
[c] of] if B
[d] doubts.] doubts. ¶ B, C, D
[e] self-annihilation.] annihilation. A
[f] world,] world; D

movement which promised respite from our devastating ennui. The enigmas of the symbolists and the ecstasies of the pre-Raphaelites all were ours in their time, but each new mood was drained too soon[a] of its diverting novelty and appeal.[b] Only the sombre philosophy of the decadents could hold[c] us, and this we found potent only by increasing gradually the depth and diabolism of our penetrations. Baudelaire and Huysmans were soon exhausted of thrills, till finally there remained for us only the more direct stimuli of unnatural personal experiences and adventures. It was this frightful emotional need which led us eventually to that detestable course which even in my present fear I mention with shame and timidity—that hideous extremity of human outrage, the abhorred practice of grave-robbing.

I cannot reveal the details of our shocking expeditions, or catalogue even partly the worst of the trophies adorning the nameless museum we prepared in the great stone house where we jointly dwelt, alone and servantless. Our museum was a blasphemous, unthinkable place, where with the satanic taste of neurotic virtuosi we had assembled an universe of terror and decay to excite our jaded sensibilities. It was a secret room, far, far[d] underground; where huge winged daemons carven of basalt and onyx vomited from wide grinning mouths weird green and orange light, and hidden pneumatic pipes ruffled into kaleidoscopic dances of death the lines of red charnel things hand in hand woven in voluminous black hangings. Through these pipes came at will the odours[e] our moods most craved; sometimes the scent of pale funereal lilies,[f] sometimes the narcotic incense[g] of imagined Eastern shrines of the kingly dead, and sometimes—how I shudder to recall it!—the frightful, soul-upheaving stenches of the uncovered grave.

Around the walls of this repellent chamber were cases of antique mummies alternating with comely, lifelike bodies perfectly stuffed and cured by the taxidermist's art, and with headstones snatched from the

---

[a] soon] soon, C, D
[b] appeal.] appeal. ¶ B, C, D
[c] hold] help D
[d] far] far, C, D
[e] odours] odors B, C, D
[f] funereal lilies,] funeral lilies; D
[g] incense] incence D

oldest churchyards of the world. Niches here and there contained skulls of all shapes, and heads preserved in various stages of dissolution. There one might find the rotting, bald pates of famous noblemen, and the fresh and radiantly golden heads of new-buried children.[a] Statues and paintings there were, all of fiendish subjects and some executed by St. John and myself. A locked portfolio, bound in tanned human skin, held certain unknown and unnamable[b] drawings which it was rumoured[c] Goya had perpetrated but dared not acknowledge.[d] There were nauseous musical instruments, stringed, brass, and wood-wind, on which St. John and I sometimes produced dissonances of exquisite morbidity and cacodaemoniacal ghastliness; whilst in a multitude of inlaid ebony cabinets reposed the most incredible and unimaginable variety of tomb-loot ever assembled by human madness and perversity. It is of this loot in particular that I must not speak—thank God I had the courage to destroy it long before I thought of destroying myself![e]

The predatory excursions on which we collected our unmentionable treasures were always artistically memorable events. We were no vulgar ghouls, but worked only under certain conditions of mood, landscape, environment, weather, season, and moonlight. These pastimes were to us the most exquisite form of aesthetic expression, and we gave their details a fastidious technical care. An inappropriate hour, a jarring lighting effect, or a clumsy manipulation of the damp sod, would almost totally destroy for us that ecstatic titillation which followed the exhumation of some ominous, grinning secret of the earth. Our quest for novel scenes and piquant conditions was feverish and insatiate—St. John was always the leader, and he it was who led the way at last to that mocking, that[f] accursed spot which brought us our hideous and inevitable doom.

By what malign fatality were we lured to that terrible Holland churchyard? I think it was the dark rumour[g] and legendry, the tales of

[a] children.] children. ¶ B, C, D
[b] unnamable] unnameable D
[c] rumoured] rumored B, C, D
[d] held ... acknowledge.] held the unknown and unnamable drawings of Clark Ashton Smith. A [*revised in pencil by HPL*]
[e] myself!] myself. A
[f] that] *om.* B, C, D
[g] rumour] rumor B, C, D

one buried for five centuries, who had himself been a ghoul in his time and had stolen a potent thing from a mighty sepulchre. I can recall the scene in these final moments—the pale autumnal moon over the graves, casting long horrible shadows; the grotesque trees, drooping sullenly to meet the neglected grass and the crumbling slabs; the vast legions of strangely colossal bats that flew against the moon; the antique ivied church pointing a huge spectral finger at the livid sky; the phosphorescent insects that danced like death-fires under the yews in a distant corner; the odours[a] of mould, vegetation, and less explicable things that mingled feebly with the night-wind from over far swamps and seas; and[b] worst of all, the faint deep-toned baying of some gigantic hound which we could neither see nor definitely place. As we heard this suggestion of baying we shuddered, remembering the tales of the peasantry; for he whom we sought had centuries before been found in this selfsame spot, torn and mangled by the claws and teeth of some unspeakable beast.

I remembered how we delved in this[c] ghoul's grave with our spades, and how we thrilled at the picture of ourselves, the grave, the pale watching moon, the horrible shadows, the grotesque trees, the titanic bats, the antique church, the dancing death-fires, the sickening odours,[d] the gently moaning night-wind, and the strange, half-heard,[e] directionless baying,[f] of whose objective existence we could scarcely be sure.[g] Then we struck a substance harder than the damp mould, and beheld a rotting oblong box crusted with mineral deposits from the long undisturbed ground. It was incredibly tough and thick, but so old that we finally pried it open and feasted our eyes on what it held.

Much—amazingly much—was left of the object despite the lapse of five hundred years. The skeleton, though crushed in places by the jaws of the thing that had killed it, held together with surprising firmness, and we gloated over the clean white skull and its long, firm teeth and its

[a] odours] odors B, C, D
[b] and] and, B, C, D
[c] this] the D
[d] odours,] odors, B, C, D
[e] half-heard,] half-heard D
[f] baying,] baying D
[g] sure.] sure. ¶ B, C, D

eyeless sockets that once had glowed with a charnel fever like our own. In the coffin lay an amulet of curious and exotic design, which had apparently been worn around the sleeper's neck. It was the oddly conventionalised[a] figure of a crouching winged hound, or sphinx with a semi-canine face, and was exquisitely carved in antique Oriental fashion from a small piece of green jade. The expression on[b] its features was repellent in the extreme, savouring[c] at once of death, bestiality, and malevolence. Around the base was an inscription in characters which neither St. John nor I could identify; and on the bottom, like a maker's seal, was graven a grotesque and formidable skull.

Immediately upon beholding this amulet we knew that we must possess it; that this treasure alone was our logical pelf from the centuried grave. Even had its outlines been unfamiliar we would have desired it, but as we looked more closely we saw that it was not wholly unfamiliar. Alien it indeed was to all art and literature which sane and balanced readers know, but we recognised[d] it as the thing hinted of in the forbidden "Necronomicon"[e] of the mad Arab Abdul Alhazred; the ghastly soul-symbol of the corpse-eating cult of inaccessible Leng, in Central Asia. All too well did we trace the sinister lineaments described by the old Arab daemonologist; lineaments, he wrote, drawn from some obscure supernatural manifestation of the souls of those who vexed and gnawed at the dead.

Seizing the green jade object, we gave a last glance at the bleached and cavern-eyed face of its owner and closed up the grave as we found it. As we hastened from that[f] abhorrent spot, the stolen amulet in St. John's pocket, we thought we saw the bats descend in a body to the earth we had so lately rifled, as if seeking for some cursed and unholy nourishment. But the autumn moon shone weak and pale, and we could not be sure.[g] So, too, as we sailed the next day away from Holland to our home, we thought we heard the faint distant baying of

[a] conventionalised] conventionalized D
[b] on] of D
[c] savouring] savoring B, C, D
[d] recognised] recognized B, C, D
[e] "Necronomicon"] *Necronomicon* D
[f] that] the D
[g] sure.] sure. ¶ B, C, D

some gigantic hound in the background. But the autumn wind moaned sad and wan, and we could not be sure.

II.[a]

Less than a week after our return to England, strange things began to happen. We lived as recluses; devoid of friends, alone, and without servants in a few rooms of an ancient manor-house on a bleak and unfrequented moor; so that our doors were seldom disturbed by the knock of the visitor.[b] Now, however, we were troubled by what seemed to be frequent fumblings[c] in the night, not only around the doors but around the windows also, upper as well as lower. Once we fancied that a large, opaque body darkened the library window when the moon was shining against it, and another time we thought we heard a whirring or flapping sound not far off. On each occasion investigation revealed nothing, and we began to ascribe the occurrences to imagination alone—that same curiously disturbed imagination[d] which still prolonged in our ears the faint far baying we thought we had heard in the Holland churchyard. The jade amulet now reposed in a niche in our museum, and sometimes we burned strangely scented candles[e] before it. We read much in Alhazred's "Necronomicon"[f] about its properties, and about the relation of ghouls'[g] souls to the objects it symbolised;[h] and were disturbed by what we read.[i] Then terror came.

On the night of September 24, 19—, I heard a knock at my chamber door. Fancying it St. John's, I bade the knocker enter, but was answered only by a shrill laugh. There was no one in the corridor. When I aroused St. John from his sleep, he professed entire ignorance of the event, and became as worried as I. It was that[j] night that the

---

[a] II.] *om.* C, D

[b] visitor.] visitor. ¶ B, C, D

[c] frequent fumblings] a frequent fumbling D

[d] alone . . . imagination] *om.* D

[e] strangely . . . candles] a strangely . . . candle D

[f] "Necronomicon"] *Necronomicon* D

[g] ghouls'] ghosts' C, D

[h] symbolised;] symbolized; B, C, D

[i] read.] read. ¶ B, C, D

[j] that] the D

faint, distant baying over the moor became to us a certain and dreaded reality.[a] Four days later, whilst we were both in the hidden museum, there came a low, cautious scratching at the single door which led to the secret library staircase. Our alarm was now divided, for[b] besides our fear of the unknown, we had always entertained a dread that our grisly collection might be discovered. Extinguishing all lights, we proceeded to the door and threw it suddenly open; whereupon we felt an unaccountable rush of air, and heard as if receding far away[c] a queer combination of rustling,[d] tittering, and articulate chatter. Whether we were mad, dreaming, or in our senses, we did not try to determine. We only realised,[e] with the blackest of apprehensions, that the apparently disembodied chatter was beyond a doubt *in the Dutch language.*

After that we lived in growing horror and fascination. Mostly we held to the theory that we were jointly going mad from our life of unnatural excitements, but sometimes it pleased us more to dramatise[f] ourselves as the victims of some creeping and appalling doom. Bizarre manifestations were now too frequent to count. Our lonely house was seemingly alive with the presence of some malign being whose nature we could not guess, and every night that daemoniac baying rolled over the windswept[g] moor, always louder and louder. On October 29 we found in the soft earth underneath the library window a series of footprints utterly impossible to describe. They were as baffling as the hordes of great bats which haunted the old manor-house in unprecedented and increasing numbers.

The horror reached a culmination on November 18, when St. John, walking home after dark from the distant[h] railway station, was seized by some frightful carnivorous thing and torn to ribbons. His screams had reached the house, and I had hastened to the terrible scene in time to hear a whir of wings and see a vague black cloudy

---

[a] reality.] reality. ¶ B, C, D
[b] for] for, B, C, D
[c] heard . . . away] heard, . . . away, B, C, D
[d] rustling,] rusting, D
[e] realised,] realized, B, C, D
[f] dramatise] dramatize B, C, D
[g] windswept] wind-swept A, B, C, D
[h] distant] dismal B, C, D

thing silhouetted against the rising moon.[a] My friend was dying when I spoke to him, and he could not answer coherently. All he could do was to whisper, "The amulet—that damned thing—."[b] Then he collapsed, an inert mass of mangled flesh.

I buried him the next midnight in one of our neglected gardens, and mumbled over his body one of the devilish rituals he had loved in life. And as I pronounced the last daemoniac sentence I heard afar on the moor the faint baying of some gigantic hound. The moon was up, but I dared not look at it. And when I saw on the dim-litten[c] moor a wide nebulous shadow sweeping from mound to mound, I shut my eyes and threw myself face down upon the ground. When I arose[d] trembling, I know not how much later, I staggered into the house and made shocking obeisances[e] before the enshrined amulet of green jade.

Being now afraid to live alone in the ancient house on the moor, I departed on the following day for London, taking with me the amulet after destroying by fire and burial the rest of the impious collection in the museum. But after three nights I heard the baying again, and before a week was over felt strange eyes upon me whenever it was dark. One evening as I strolled on Victoria Embankment for some needed air, I saw a black shape obscure one of the reflections of the lamps in the water. A wind stronger than the night-wind[f] rushed by, and I knew that what had befallen St. John must soon befall me.

The next day I carefully wrapped the green jade amulet and sailed for Holland. What mercy I might gain by returning the thing to its silent, sleeping owner I knew not; but I felt that I must at least[g] try any step conceivably logical. What the hound was, and why it[h] pursued me, were questions still vague; but I had first heard the baying in that ancient churchyard, and every subsequent event including St. John's dying whisper had served to connect the curse with the stealing of the

---

[a] moon.] moon. ¶ B, C, D

[b] thing—."] thing—". A; thing—." ¶ B, C, D

[c] dim-litten] dim-lighted B, C, D

[d] arose] arose, B, C, D

[e] obeisances] obeisance D

[f] wind . . . night-wind] wind, . . . night-wind, B, C, D

[g] at least] *om.* C, D

[h] it] it had B, C, D

amulet. Accordingly I sank into the nethermost abysses of despair when, at an inn in Rotterdam, I discovered that thieves had despoiled me of this sole means of salvation.

The baying was loud that evening, and in the morning I read of a nameless deed in the vilest quarter of the city. The rabble were in terror, for upon an evil tenement had fallen a red death beyond the foulest previous crime of the neighbourhood.[a] In a squalid thieves' den an entire family had been torn to shreds by an unknown thing which left no trace, and those around had heard all night above the usual clamour[b] of drunken voices[c] a faint, deep, insistent note as of a gigantic hound.

So at last I stood again in that[d] unwholesome churchyard where a pale winter moon cast hideous shadows, and leafless trees drooped sullenly to meet the withered, frosty grass and cracking slabs, and the ivied church pointed a jeering finger at the unfriendly sky, and the night-wind howled maniacally from over frozen swamps and frigid seas. The baying was very faint now, and it ceased altogether as I approached the ancient grave I had once violated, and frightened away an abnormally large horde of bats which had been hovering curiously around it.

I know not why I went thither unless to pray, or gibber out insane pleas and apologies to the calm white thing that lay within; but, whatever my reason, I attacked the half-frozen sod with a desperation partly mine and partly that of a dominating will outside myself. Excavation was much easier than I expected, though at one point I encountered a queer interruption; when a lean vulture darted down out of the cold sky and pecked frantically at the grave-earth until I killed him with a blow of my spade. Finally I reached the rotting oblong box and removed the damp nitrous cover. This is the last rational act I ever performed.

For crouched within that centuried coffin, embraced by a close-packed[e] nightmare retinue of huge, sinewy, sleeping bats, was the bony thing my friend and I had robbed; not clean and placid as we had seen it then, but covered with caked blood and shreds of alien flesh and

---

[a] neighbourhood.] neighborhood. B, C, D

[b] clamour] clamor B; *om.* C, D [*see below*]

[c] above . . . voices] *om.* C, D

[d] that] the B, C, D

[e] close-packed] closepacked B, C, D

hair, and leering sentiently at me with phosphorescent sockets and sharp ensanguined fangs yawning twistedly in mockery of my inevitable doom. And when it gave from those grinning jaws a deep, sardonic bay as of some gigantic hound, and I saw that it held in its gory,[a] filthy claw the lost and fateful amulet of green jade, I merely screamed and ran away idiotically, my screams soon dissolving into peals of hysterical laughter.

Madness rides the star-wind ... claws and teeth sharpened on centuries of corpses ... dripping death astride a Bacchanale[b] of bats from night-black ruins of buried temples of Belial. ... Now, as the baying of that dead,[c] fleshless monstrosity grows louder and louder, and the stealthy whirring and flapping of those accursed[d] web-wings circles closer and closer, I shall seek with my revolver the oblivion which is my only refuge from the unnamed and unnamable.[e]

---

[a] gory,] gory C, D
[b] Bacchanale] bacchanale A, B, C, D
[c] dead,] dead C, D
[d] accursed] accused B
[e] unnamable.] unnameable. D

The Lurking Fear

I. THE SHADOW ON THE CHIMNEY

There was thunder in the air on the night I went to the deserted mansion atop Tempest Mountain to find the lurking fear. I was not alone, for foolhardiness was not then mixed with that love of the grotesque and the terrible which has made my[a] career a series of quests for strange horrors in literature and in life. With me were two faithful and muscular men for whom I had sent when the time came; men long associated with me in my ghastly explorations because of their peculiar fitness.

We had started quietly from the village because of the reporters who still lingered about after the eldritch panic of a month before— the nightmare creeping death. Later, I thought, they might aid me; but I did not want them then. Would to God I had let them share the search, that I might not have had to bear the secret alone so long; to bear it alone for fear the world would call me mad or go mad itself at the daemon[b] implications of the thing. Now that I am telling it anyway,

Editor's Note: This is one of the rare instances in which all relevant texts derive from the existing T.Ms.—a single-spaced T.Ms. presumably submitted to *Home Brew*, where the story was serialised in the January–April 1923 issues. HPL may have prepared a double-spaced T.Ms. when submitting the story to *Weird Tales* (where the story appeared in the June 1928 issue), but there is no evidence that HPL revised the tale in the process. The Arkham House editions also derive from the T.Ms. All these texts have made slight errors, including the omission of some words or lines.

Texts: A = T.Ms. (JHL); B = *Home Brew* 2, No. 6 (January 1923): 4–10; 3, No. 1 (February 1923): 18–23; 3, No. 2 (March 1923): 31–37, 44, 48; 3, No. 3 (April 1923): 35–42; C = *Weird Tales* 11, No. 6 (June 1928): 791–804; D = *Dagon and Other Macabre Tales* (Arkham House, 1965), 167–86. Copy-text: A.

[a] my] by D
[b] daemon] demon A, B, C, D

lest the brooding make me a maniac, I wish I had never concealed it. For I, and I only, know what manner of fear lurked on that spectral and desolate mountain.

In a small motor-car we covered the miles of primeval forest and hill until the wooded ascent checked it. The country bore an aspect more than usually sinister as we viewed it by night and without the accustomed[a] crowds of investigators, so that we were often tempted to use the acetylene headlight[b] despite the attention it might attract. It was not a wholesome landscape after dark, and I believe I would have noticed its morbidity even had I been ignorant of the terror that stalked there. Of wild creatures there were none—they are wise when death leers close. The ancient lightning-scarred trees seemed unnaturally large and twisted, and the other vegetation unnaturally thick and feverish, while curious mounds and hummocks in the weedy, fulgurite-pitted earth reminded me of snakes and dead men's skulls swelled to gigantic proportions.

Fear had lurked on Tempest Mountain for more than a century. This I learned at once from newspaper accounts of the catastrophe which first brought the region to the world's notice. The place is a remote, lonely elevation in that part of the Catskills where Dutch civilisation[c] once feebly and transiently penetrated, leaving behind as it receded only a few ruined mansions and a degenerate squatter population inhabiting pitiful hamlets on isolated slopes. Normal beings seldom visited the locality till the state police were formed, and even now only infrequent troopers patrol it. The fear, however, is an old tradition throughout the neighbouring[d] villages;[e] since it is a prime topic in the simple discourse of the poor mongrels who sometimes leave their valleys to trade hand-woven[f] baskets for such primitive necessities as they cannot[g] shoot, raise, or make.

---

[a] accustomed] ac1/customed B
[b] headlight] headlights C
[c] civilisation] civilization B, C
[d] neighbouring] neighboring B, C, D
[e] villages;] villages B
[f] hand-woven] hand-/woven B; handwoven D
[g] cannot] can not C

The lurking fear dwelt in the shunned and deserted Martense mansion, which crowned the high but gradual eminence whose liability to frequent thunderstorms gave it the name of Tempest Mountain. For over a hundred years the antique, grove-circled stone house had been the subject of stories incredibly wild and monstrously hideous; stories of a silent colossal creeping death which stalked abroad in summer. With whimpering insistence the squatters told tales of a daemon[a] which seized lone wayfarers after dark, either carrying them off or leaving them in a frightful state of gnawed dismemberment; while sometimes they whispered of blood-trails[b] toward the distant mansion. Some said the thunder called the lurking fear out of its habitation, while others said the thunder was its voice.

No one outside the backwoods had believed these varying and conflicting stories, with their incoherent, extravagant descriptions of the half-glimpsed fiend; yet not a farmer or villager doubted that the Martense mansion was ghoulishly haunted. Local history forbade such a doubt, although no ghostly evidence was ever found by such investigators as had visited the building after some especially vivid tale[c] of the squatters. Grandmothers told strange myths of the Martense spectre;[d] myths concerning the Martense family itself, its queer hereditary dissimilarity of eyes, its long, unnatural annals, and the murder which had cursed it.

The terror which brought me to the scene was a sudden and portentous confirmation of the mountaineers' wildest legends. One summer night, after a thunderstorm of unprecedented violence, the countryside was aroused by a squatter stampede which no mere delusion could create. The pitiful throngs of natives shrieked and whined of the unnamable horror which had descended upon them, and they were not doubted. They had not seen it, but had heard such cries from one of their hamlets that they knew a creeping death had come.

In the morning citizens and state troopers followed the shuddering mountaineers to the place where they said the death had come. Death

[a] daemon] demon A, B, C, D
[b] blood-trails] bloodtrails D
[c] tale] tales C
[d] spectre;] specter; C

was indeed there. The ground under one of the squatters'[a] villages had caved in after a lightning stroke, destroying several of the malodorous shanties; but upon this property damage was superimposed an organic devastation which paled it to insignificance. Of a possible seventy-five natives who had inhabited this spot, not one living specimen was visible. The disordered earth was covered with blood and human debris bespeaking too vividly the ravages of daemon[b] teeth and talons; yet no visible trail led away from the carnage. That some hideous animal must be the cause, everyone quickly agreed; nor did any tongue now revive the charge that such cryptic deaths formed merely the sordid murders common in decadent communities. That charge was revived only when about twenty-five of the estimated population were found missing from the dead; and even then it was hard to explain the murder of fifty by half that number. But the fact remained that on a summer night a bolt had come out of the heavens and left a dead village whose corpses were horribly mangled, chewed, and clawed.

The excited countryside immediately connected the horror with the haunted Martense mansion, though the localities were over three miles apart. The troopers were more sceptical;[c] including the mansion only casually in their investigations, and dropping it altogether when they found it thoroughly deserted. Country and village people, however, canvassed the place with infinite care; overturning everything in the house, sounding ponds and brooks, beating down bushes, and ransacking the nearby[d] forests. All was in vain; the death that had come had left no trace save destruction itself.

By the second day of the search the affair was fully treated by the newspapers, whose reporters overran Tempest Mountain. They described it in much detail, and with many interviews to elucidate the horror's history as told by local grandams. I followed the accounts languidly at first, for I am a connoisseur in horrors; but after a week I detected an atmosphere which stirred me oddly, so that on August 5th, 1921, I registered among the reporters who crowded the hotel at

---

[a] squatters'] squatter's D

[b] daemon] demon A, B, C, D

[c] sceptical;] skeptical, C; skeptical; D

[d] nearby] near-by C

Lefferts Corners, nearest village to Tempest Mountain and acknowledged headquarters of the searchers. Three weeks more, and the dispersal of the reporters left me free to begin a terrible exploration based on the minute inquiries and surveying with which I had meanwhile busied myself.

So on this summer night, while distant thunder rumbled, I left a silent motor-car and tramped with two armed companions up the last mound-covered reaches of Tempest Mountain, casting the beams of an electric torch on the spectral grey[a] walls that began to appear through the[b] giant oaks ahead. In this morbid night solitude and feeble shifting illumination, the vast box-like[c] pile displayed obscure hints of terror which day could not uncover; yet I did not hesitate, since I had come with fierce resolution to test an idea. I believed that the thunder called the death-daemon[d] out of some fearsome secret place; and be that daemon[e] solid entity or vaporous pestilence, I meant to see it.[f]

I had thoroughly searched the ruin before, hence knew my plan well; choosing as the seat of my vigil the old room of Jan Martense, whose murder looms so great in the rural legends. I felt subtly that the apartment of this ancient victim was best for my purposes. The chamber, measuring about twenty feet square, contained like the other rooms some rubbish which had once been furniture. It lay on the second story, on the southeast corner of the house, and had an immense east window and narrow south window, both devoid of panes or shutters. Opposite the large window was an enormous Dutch fireplace with scriptural tiles representing the prodigal son, and opposite the narrow window was a spacious bed built into the wall.

As the tree-muffled thunder grew louder, I arranged my plan's details. First I fastened side by side to[g] the ledge of the large window three rope ladders which I had brought with me. I knew they reached a suitable spot on the grass outside, for I had tested them. Then the

[a] grey] gray C
[b] the] *om.* D
[c] box-like] boxlike A, B, C, D
[d] death-daemon] death-demon A, B, C, D
[e] daemon] demon A, B, C, D
[f] see it.] see. B
[g] to] on C

three of us dragged from another room a wide four-poster bedstead, crowding it laterally against the window. Having strown[a] it with fir boughs, all now rested on it with drawn automatics, two relaxing while the third watched. From whatever direction the daemon[b] might come, our potential escape was provided. If it came from within the house, we had the window ladders; if from outside,[c] the door and the stairs. We did not think, judging from precedent, that it would pursue us far even at worst.

I watched from midnight to one[d] o'clock, when in spite of the sinister house, the unprotected window, and the approaching thunder and lightning, I felt singularly drowsy. I was between my two companions,[e] George Bennett being toward the window and William Tobey toward the fireplace. Bennett was asleep, having apparently felt the same anomalous drowsiness which affected me, so I designated Tobey for the next watch although even he was nodding. It is curious how intently I had been watching that[f] fireplace.

The increasing thunder must have affected my dreams, for in the brief time I slept there came to me apocalyptic visions. Once I partly awaked, probably because the sleeper toward the window had restlessly flung an arm across my chest. I was not sufficiently awake to see whether Tobey was attending to his duties as sentinel, but felt a distinct anxiety on that score. Never before had the presence of evil so poignantly oppressed me. Later I must have dropped asleep again, for it was out of a phantasmal chaos that my mind leaped when the night grew hideous with shrieks beyond anything in my former experience or imagination.

In that shrieking the inmost soul of human fear and agony clawed hopelessly and insanely at the ebony gates of oblivion. I awoke to red madness and the mockery of diabolism, as farther and farther down inconceivable vistas that phobic and crystalline anguish retreated and reverberated. There was no light, but I knew from the empty space at

---

[a] strown] strewn A, B, C, D

[b] daemon] demon A, B, C, D

[c] outside,] outside D

[d] one] 1 C

[e] companions,] companions. C

[f] that] the D

my right that Tobey was gone, God alone knew whither. Across my chest still lay the heavy arm of the sleeper at my left.

Then came the devastating stroke of lightning which shook the whole mountain, lit the darkest crypts of the hoary grove, and splintered the patriarch of the twisted trees. In the daemon[a] flash of a monstrous fireball the sleeper started up suddenly while the glare from beyond the window threw his shadow vividly upon the chimney above the fireplace from which my eyes had never strayed. That I am still alive and sane, is a marvel I cannot fathom. I cannot[b] fathom it, for the shadow on that[c] chimney was not that of George Bennett or of any other human creature,[d] but a blasphemous abnormality from hell's nethermost craters; a nameless, shapeless abomination which no mind could fully grasp and no pen even partly describe. In another second I was alone in the accursed mansion, shivering and gibbering. George Bennett and William Tobey had left no trace, not even of a struggle. They were never heard of again.

II. A Passer in the Storm

For days after that hideous experience in the forest-swathed mansion I lay nervously exhausted in my hotel room at Lefferts Corners. I do not remember exactly how I managed to reach the motor-car, start it, and slip unobserved back to the village; for I retain no distinct impression save of wild-armed titan trees, daemoniac[e] mutterings of thunder, and Charonian shadows athwart the low mounds that dotted and streaked the region.

As I shivered and brooded on the casting of that brain-blasting shadow, I knew that I had at last pried out one of earth's supreme horrors—one of those nameless blights of outer voids whose faint daemon[f] scratchings we sometimes hear on the farthest rim of space, yet from which our own finite vision has given us a merciful immunity. The

---

[a] daemon] demon A, B, C, D
[b] cannot . . . cannot] can not . . . can not C
[c] that] the B
[d] creature,] creature; C
[e] daemoniac] demoniac A, B, C, D
[f] daemon] demon A, B, C, D

shadow I had seen, I hardly dared to analyse[a] or identify. Something had lain between me and the window that night, but I shuddered whenever I could not cast off the instinct to classify it. If it had only snarled,[b] or bayed, or laughed titteringly—even that would have relieved the abysmal hideousness. But it was so silent. It had rested a heavy arm or fore leg[c] on my chest. . . . Obviously[d] it was organic, or had once been organic. . . . Jan Martense, whose room I had invaded, was buried in the graveyard near the mansion. . . . I must find Bennett and Tobey,[e] if they lived . . . why[f] had it picked them, and left me for the last? . . . Drowsiness is so stifling, and dreams are so horrible. . . .[g]

In a short time I realised[h] that I must tell my story to someone or break down completely. I had already decided not to abandon the quest for the lurking fear, for in my rash ignorance it seemed to me that uncertainty was worse than enlightenment, however terrible the latter might prove to be. Accordingly I resolved in my mind the best course to pursue; whom to select for my confidences, and how to track down the thing which had obliterated two men and cast a nightmare shadow.

My chief acquaintances at Lefferts Corners had been the affable reporters, of whom several[i] still remained to collect final echoes of the tragedy. It was from these that I determined to choose a colleague, and the more I reflected the more my preference inclined toward one Arthur Munroe, a dark, lean man of about thirty-five, whose education, taste, intelligence, and temperament all seemed to mark him as one not bound to conventional ideas and experiences.

On an afternoon in early September[j] Arthur Munroe listened to my story. I saw from the beginning that he was both interested and

[a] analyse] analyze B, C
[b] snarled,] snarled B
[c] fore leg] foreleg A, B, C, D
[d] chest. . . . Obviously] chest . . . obviously B
[e] Tobey,] Tobey; B
[f] why] Why B
[g] horrible. . . .] horrible. B
[h] realised] realized B, C
[i] several] several had D
[j] September] September, D

sympathetic, and when I had finished he analysed[a] and discussed the thing with the greatest shrewdness and judgment.[b] His advice, moreover, was eminently practical; for he recommended a postponement of operations at the Martense mansion until we might become fortified with more detailed historical and geographical data. On his initiative we combed the countryside for information regarding the terrible Martense family, and discovered a man who possessed a marvellously[c] illuminating ancestral diary. We also talked at length with such of the mountain mongrels as had not fled from the terror and confusion to remoter slopes, and arranged to precede our culminating task—the exhaustive and definitive examination of the mansion in the light of its detailed history—with an equally[d] exhaustive and definitive examination of spots associated with the various tragedies of squatter legend.

The results of this examination were not at first very enlightening, though our tabulation of them seemed to reveal a fairly significant trend; namely, that the number of reported horrors was by far the greatest in areas either comparatively near the avoided house or connected with it by stretches of the morbidly overnourished[e] forest. There were, it is true, exceptions; indeed, the horror which had caught the world's ear had happened in a treeless space remote alike from the mansion and from any connecting woods.

As to the nature and appearance of the lurking fear, nothing could be gained from the scared and witless shanty-dwellers. In the same breath they called it a snake and a giant, a thunder-devil and a bat, a vulture and a walking tree. We did, however, deem ourselves justified in assuming that it was a living organism highly susceptible to electrical storms; and although certain of the stories suggested wings, we believed that its aversion for open spaces made land locomotion a more probable theory. The only thing really incompatible with the latter view was the rapidity with which the creature must have travelled[f] in order to perform all the deeds attributed to it.

[a] analysed] analyzed C
[b] judgment.] judgement. D
[c] marvellously] marvelously C
[d] task—the . . . equally] task with the D
[e] overnourished] over-/nourished C; over-nourished D
[f] travelled] traveled C

When we came to know the squatters better, we found them curiously likeable[a] in many ways. Simple animals they were, gently descending the evolutionary scale because of their unfortunate ancestry and stultifying isolation. They feared outsiders, but slowly grew accustomed to us; finally helping vastly when we beat down all the thickets and tore out all the partitions of the mansion in our search for the lurking fear. When we asked them to help us find Bennett and Tobey they were truly distressed; for they wanted to help us, yet knew that these victims had gone as wholly out of the world as their own missing people. That great numbers of them had actually been killed and removed, just as the wild animals had long been exterminated, we were of course thoroughly convinced; and we waited apprehensively for further tragedies to occur.

By the middle of October we were puzzled by our lack of progress. Owing to the clear nights no daemoniac[b] aggressions had taken place, and the completeness of our vain searches of house and country almost drove us to regard the lurking fear as a non-material agency. We feared that the cold weather would come on and halt our explorations, for all agreed that the daemon[c] was generally quiet in winter. Thus there was a kind of haste and desperation in our last daylight canvass of the horror-visited hamlet; a hamlet now deserted because of the squatters' fears.

The ill-fated squatter hamlet had borne no name, but had long stood in a sheltered though treeless cleft between two elevations called respectively Cone Mountain and Maple Hill. It was closer to Maple Hill than to Cone Mountain, some of the crude abodes indeed being dugouts on the side of the former eminence. Geographically it lay about two miles northwest of the base of Tempest Mountain, and three miles from the oak-girt mansion. Of the distance between the hamlet and the mansion, fully two miles and a quarter on the hamlet's side was entirely open country; the plain being of fairly level character[d]

---

[a] likeable] likable C
[b] daemoniac] demoniac A, B, C, D
[c] daemon] demon A, B, C, D
[d] character] character, B

save for some of the low snake-like[a] mounds, and having as vegetation only grass and scattered weeds. Considering this topography, we had finally concluded that the daemon[b] must have come by way of Cone Mountain, a wooded southern prolongation of which ran to within a short distance of the westernmost spur of Tempest Mountain. The upheaval of ground we traced conclusively to a landslide from Maple Hill, a tall lone splintered tree on whose side had been the striking point of the thunderbolt which summoned the fiend.

As for the twentieth time or more Arthur Munroe and I went minutely over every inch of the violated village, we were filled with a certain discouragement coupled with vague and novel fears. It was acutely uncanny, even when frightful and uncanny things were common, to encounter so blankly clueless a scene after such overwhelming occurrences; and we moved about beneath the leaden, darkening sky with that tragic directionless zeal which results from a combined sense of futility and necessity of action. Our care was gravely minute; every cottage was again entered, every hillside dugout again searched for bodies, every thorny foot of adjacent slope again scanned for dens and caves, but all without result. And yet, as I have said, vague new fears hovered menacingly over us; as if giant bat-winged gryphons squatted invisibly on the mountaintops[c] and leered with Abaddon-eyes that had[d] looked on trans-cosmic[e] gulfs.

As the afternoon advanced, it became increasingly difficult to see; and we heard the rumble of a thunderstorm gathering over Tempest Mountain. This sound in such a locality naturally stirred us, though less than it would have done at night. As it was, we hoped desperately that the storm would last until well after dark; and with that hope turned from our aimless hillside searching toward the nearest inhabited hamlet to gather a body of squatters as helpers in the investigation. Timid as they were, a few of the younger men were sufficiently inspired by our protective leadership to promise such help.

---

[a] snake-like] snakelike A, C, D
[b] daemon] demon A, B, C, D
[c] mountaintops] mountain-tops A, B, C; *om.* D [*see below*]
[d] squatted . . . had] *om.* D
[e] trans-cosmic] transcosmic C

We had hardly more than turned, however, when there descended such a blinding sheet of torrential rain that shelter became imperative. The extreme, almost nocturnal darkness of the sky caused us to stumble sadly,[a] but guided by the frequent flashes of lightning and by our minute knowledge of the hamlet we soon reached the least porous cabin of the lot; an heterogeneous combination of logs and boards whose still existing door and single tiny window both faced Maple Hill. Barring the door after us against the fury of the wind and rain, we put in place the crude window shutter which our frequent searches had taught us where to find. It was dismal sitting there on rickety boxes in the pitchy darkness, but we smoked pipes and occasionally flashed our pocket lamps about. Now and then we could see the lightning through cracks in the wall; the afternoon was so incredibly dark that each flash was extremely vivid.

The stormy vigil reminded me shudderingly of my ghastly night on Tempest Mountain. My mind turned to that odd question which had kept recurring ever since the nightmare thing had happened; and again I wondered why the daemon,[b] approaching the three watchers either from the window or the interior, had begun with the men on each side and left the middle man till the last, when the titan fireball had scared it away. Why had it not taken its victims in natural order, with myself second, from whichever direction it had approached? With what manner of far-reaching tentacles did it prey? Or did it know that I was the leader, and save[c] me for a fate worse than that of my companions?

In the midst of these reflections, as if dramatically arranged to intensify them, there fell nearby[d] a terrific bolt of lightning followed by the sound of sliding earth. At the same time the wolfish wind rose to daemoniac crescendoes[e] of ululation. We were sure that the lone[f] tree on Maple Hill had been struck again, and Munroe rose from his box and went to the tiny window to ascertain the damage. When he took down the shutter the wind and rain howled deafeningly in, so that I

[a] sadly,] badly, D
[b] daemon,] demon, A, B, C, D
[c] save] saved D
[d] nearby] near by C
[e] daemoniac crescendoes] demoniac crescendos A, B, C, D
[f] lone] one D

could not hear what he said; but I waited while he leaned out and tried to fathom Nature's[a] pandemonium.

Gradually a calming of the wind and dispersal of the unusual darkness told of the storm's passing. I had hoped it would last into the night to help our quest, but a furtive sunbeam from a knothole behind me removed the likelihood of such a thing. Suggesting to Munroe that we had better get some light even if more showers came, I unbarred and opened the crude door. The ground outside was a singular mass of mud and pools, with fresh heaps of earth from the slight landslide; but I saw nothing to justify the interest which kept my companion silently leaning out the window. Crossing to where he leaned, I touched his shoulder; but he did not move. Then, as I playfully shook him and turned him around, I felt the strangling tendrils of a cancerous horror whose roots reached into illimitable pasts and fathomless abysms of the night that broods beyond time.

For Arthur Munroe was dead. And on what remained of his chewed and gouged head there was no longer a face.

III. What the Red Glare Meant

On the tempest-racked night of November 8,[b] 1921, with a lantern which cast charnel shadows, I stood digging alone and idiotically in the grave of Jan Martense. I had begun to dig in the afternoon, because a thunderstorm was brewing, and now that it was dark and the storm had burst above the maniacally thick foliage I was glad.

I believe that my mind was partly unhinged by events since August 5th; the daemon[c] shadow in the mansion, the general strain and disappointment, and the thing that occurred at the hamlet in an October storm. After that thing[d] I had dug a grave for one whose death I could not understand. I knew that others could not understand either, so let them think Arthur Munroe had wandered away. They searched, but found nothing. The squatters might have understood, but I dared not frighten them more. I myself seemed strangely callous.

[a] Nature's] nature's C
[b] 8,] 8th, C
[c] daemon] demon A, B, C, D
[d] thing] thing, B

That shock at the mansion had done something to my brain, and I could think only of the quest for a horror now grown to cataclysmic stature in my imagination; a quest which the fate of Arthur Munroe made me vow to keep silent and solitary.

The scene of my excavations would alone have been enough to unnerve any ordinary man. Baleful primal trees of unholy size, age, and grotesqueness leered above me like the pillars of some hellish Druidic temple;[a] muffling the thunder, hushing the clawing wind, and admitting but little rain. Beyond the scarred trunks in the background,[b] illumined by faint flashes of filtered lightning, rose the damp ivied stones of the deserted mansion,[c] while somewhat nearer was the abandoned Dutch garden whose walks and beds were polluted by a white, fungous, foetid,[d] overnourished[e] vegetation[f] that never saw full daylight. And nearest of all was the graveyard, where deformed trees tossed insane branches as their roots displaced unhallowed slabs and sucked venom from what lay below. Now and then, beneath the brown pall of leaves that rotted and festered in the antediluvian forest darkness, I could trace the sinister outlines of some of those low mounds which characterised[g] the lightning-pierced region.

History had led me to this archaic grave. History, indeed, was all I had after everything else ended in mocking Satanism. I now believed that the lurking fear was no material thing, but a wolf-fanged ghost that rode the midnight lightning. And I believed, because of the masses of local tradition I had unearthed in my[h] search with Arthur Munroe, that the ghost was that of Jan Martense, who died in 1762. That[i] is why I was digging idiotically in his grave.

The Martense mansion was built in 1670 by Gerrit Martense,

---

[a] temple;] temple, B
[b] background,] background B
[c] mansion,] mansion B
[d] foetid,] fetid, C
[e] overnourished] over-/nourished B, over-nourished D
[f] vegetation] vegitation B
[g] characterised] characterized B, C, D
[h] my] *om.* D
[i] That] This D

a wealthy New-Amsterdam[a] merchant who disliked the changing order under British rule,[b] and had constructed this magnificent domicile on a remote[c] woodland summit whose untrodden solitude and unusual scenery pleased him. The only substantial disappointment encountered in this site was that which concerned the prevalence of violent thunderstorms in summer. When selecting the hill and building his mansion, Mynheer Martense had laid these frequent natural outbursts to some peculiarity of the year; but in time he perceived that the locality was especially liable to such phenomena. At length, having found these storms injurious to his health,[d] he fitted up a cellar into which he could retreat from their wildest pandemonium.

Of Gerrit Martense's descendants less is known than of himself; since they were all reared in hatred of the English civilisation,[e] and trained to shun such of the colonists as accepted it. Their life was exceedingly secluded, and people declared that their isolation had made them heavy of speech and comprehension. In appearance all were marked by a peculiar inherited dissimilarity of eyes; one generally being blue and the other brown. Their social contacts grew fewer and fewer, till at last they took to intermarrying with the numerous menial class about the estate. Many of the crowded family degenerated, moved across the valley, and merged with the mongrel population which was later to produce the pitiful squatters. The rest had stuck sullenly to their ancestral mansion, becoming more and more clannish and taciturn, yet developing a nervous responsiveness to the frequent thunderstorms.

Most of this information reached the outside world through young Jan Martense, who from some kind of restlessness joined the colonial army when news of the Albany Convention reached Tempest Mountain. He was the first of Gerrit's descendants to see much of the world; and when he returned in 1760[f] after six years of campaigning, he was hated as an outsider by his father, uncles, and brothers, in spite of his dissimilar Martense eyes. No longer could he share the

[a] New-Amsterdam] New Amsterdam C
[b] rule,] rule B
[c] remote] remote remote A
[d] health,] head, A, B, C, D
[e] civilisation,] civilization, B, C
[f] 1760] 1760, C

peculiarities and prejudices of the Martenses, while the very mountain thunderstorms failed to intoxicate him as they had before. Instead, his surroundings depressed him; and he frequently wrote to a friend in Albany of plans to leave the paternal roof.

In the spring of 1763 Jonathan Gifford, the Albany friend of Jan Martense, became worried by his correspondent's silence; especially in view of the conditions and quarrels at the Martense mansion. Determined to visit Jan in person, he went into the mountains on horseback. His diary states that he reached Tempest Mountain on September 20,[a] finding the mansion in great decrepitude. The sullen, odd-eyed Martenses, whose unclean animal aspect[b] shocked him, told him in broken gutturals that Jan was dead. He had, they insisted, been struck by lightning the autumn before;[c] and now lay buried behind the neglected sunken gardens. They shewed[d] the visitor the grave, barren and devoid of markers. Something in the Martenses' manner gave Gifford a feeling of repulsion and suspicion, and a week later he returned with spade and mattock to explore the sepulchral spot. He found what he expected—a skull crushed cruelly as if by savage blows—so returning to Albany he openly charged the Martenses with the murder of their kinsman.

Legal evidence was lacking, but the story spread rapidly round[e] the countryside; and from that time the Martenses were ostracised[f] by the world. No one would deal with them, and their distant manor was shunned as an accursed place. Somehow they managed to live on independently by the products[g] of their estate, for occasional lights glimpsed from far-away hills attested their continued presence. These lights were seen as late as 1810, but toward the last they became very infrequent.

Meanwhile there grew up about the mansion and the mountain a body of diabolic legendry. The place was avoided with doubled

[a] September 20,] Sept. 20, B; September 20th, C
[b] unclean animal aspect] unclean, animal-/aspect B
[c] before;] before, C
[d] shewed] showed A, B, C, D
[e] round] around B, C
[f] ostracised] ostracized C
[g] products] product D

assiduousness, and invested with every whispered myth tradition could supply. It remained unvisited till 1816, when the continued absence of lights was noticed by the squatters. At that time a party made investigations, finding the house deserted and partly in ruins.

There were no skeletons about, so that departure rather than death was inferred. The clan seemed to have left several years before, and improvised penthouses shewed[a] how numerous it had grown prior to its migration. Its cultural level had fallen very low, as proved by decaying furniture and scattered silverware which must have been long abandoned when its owners left. But though the dreaded Martenses were gone, the fear of the haunted house continued; and grew very acute when new and strange stories arose among the mountain decadents. There it stood; deserted, feared, and linked with the vengeful ghost of Jan Martense. There it still stood on the night I dug in Jan Martense's[b] grave.

I have described my protracted digging as idiotic, and such it indeed was in object and method. The coffin of Jan Martense had soon been[c] unearthed—it now held only dust and nitre[d]—but in my fury to exhume his ghost I delved irrationally and clumsily down beneath where he had lain. God knows what I expected to find—I only felt that I was digging in the grave of a man whose ghost stalked by night.

It is impossible to say what monstrous depth I had attained when my spade, and soon my feet, broke through the ground beneath. The event, under the circumstances, was tremendous; for in the existence of a subterranean space here, my mad theories had terrible confirmation. My slight fall had extinguished the lantern, but I produced an electric pocket lamp[e] and viewed the small horizontal tunnel which led away indefinitely in both directions. It was amply large enough[f] for a man to wriggle through; and though no sane person would have tried it[g] at that time, I forgot danger, reason, and cleanliness in my single-minded

---

[a] shewed] showed A, B, C, D
[b] Martense's] Martenses's B
[c] soon been] been soon C
[d] nitre] niter C
[e] pocket lamp] pocket-lamp C
[f] enough] *om.* C
[g] it] *om.* D

fever to unearth the lurking fear. Choosing the direction toward the house, I scrambled recklessly into the narrow burrow; squirming ahead blindly and rapidly, and flashing but seldom the lamp I kept before me.

What language can describe the spectacle of a man lost in infinitely abysmal earth; pawing, twisting, wheezing; scrambling madly through sunken convolutions of immemorial blackness without an idea of time, safety, direction, or definite object? There is something hideous in it, but that is what I did. I did it for so long that life faded to a far memory, and I became one with the moles and grubs of nighted depths. Indeed, it was only by accident that after interminable writhings I jarred my forgotten electric lamp alight, so that it shone eerily along the burrow of caked loam that stretched and curved ahead.

I had been scrambling in this way for some time, so that my battery had burned very low, when the passage suddenly inclined sharply upward, altering my mode of progress. And as I raised my glance it was without preparation that I saw glistening in the distance two daemoniac[a] reflections of my expiring lamp; two reflections glowing with a baneful and unmistakable effulgence, and provoking maddeningly nebulous memories. I stopped automatically, though lacking the brain to retreat. The eyes approached, yet of the thing that bore them I could distinguish only a claw. But what a claw! Then far overhead I heard a faint crashing which I recognised.[b] It was the wild thunder of the mountain, raised to hysteric fury—I[c] must have been crawling upward for some time, so that the surface was now quite near. And as the muffled thunder clattered, those eyes still stared with vacuous viciousness.

Thank God I did not then know what it was, else I should have died. But I was saved by the very thunder that had summoned it, for after a hideous wait there burst from the unseen outside sky one of those frequent mountainward bolts whose aftermath I had noticed here and there as gashes of disturbed earth and fulgurites of various sizes. With Cyclopean rage it tore through the soil above that damnable pit, blinding and deafening me, yet not wholly reducing me to a coma.

[a] daemoniac] demoniac A, B, C, D
[b] recognised.] recognized. B, C, D
[c] fury—I] fury. I C

In the chaos of sliding, shifting earth I clawed and floundered helplessly till the rain on my head steadied me and I saw that I had come to the surface in a familiar spot; a steep unforested place on the southwest slope of the mountain. Recurrent sheet lightnings illumed the tumbled ground and the remains of the curious low hummock which had stretched down from the wooded higher slope, but there was nothing in the chaos to shew[a] my place of egress from the lethal catacomb. My brain was as great a chaos as the earth, and as a distant red glare burst on the landscape from the south I hardly realised[b] the horror I had been through.

But when two days later the squatters told me what the red glare meant, I felt more horror than that which the mound-burrow[c] and the claw and eyes had given; more horror because of the overwhelming implications. In a hamlet twenty miles away an orgy of fear had followed the bolt which brought me above ground, and a nameless thing had dropped from an overhanging tree into a weak-roofed cabin. It had done a deed, but the squatters had fired the cabin in frenzy before it could escape. It had been doing that deed at the very moment the earth caved in on the thing with the claw and eyes.

IV. THE HORROR IN THE EYES

There can be nothing normal in the mind of one who, knowing what I knew of the horrors of Tempest Mountain, would seek alone for the fear that lurked there. That at least two of the fear's embodiments were destroyed, formed but a slight guarantee of mental and physical safety in this Acheron[d] of multiform diabolism; yet I continued my quest with even greater zeal as events and revelations became more monstrous.

When, two days after my frightful crawl through that crypt of the eyes and claw, I learned that a thing had malignly hovered twenty miles away at the same instant the eyes were glaring at me, I experienced virtual convulsions of fright. But that fright was so mixed with wonder

[a] shew] show A, B, C, D
[b] realised] realized B, C
[c] mound-burrow] mould-burrow A, B, D; mold-burrow C
[d] Acheron] acheron B

and alluring grotesqueness, that it was almost a pleasant sensation. Sometimes, in the throes of a nightmare[a] when unseen powers whirl one over the roofs of strange dead cities toward the grinning chasm of Nis, it is a relief and even a delight to shriek wildly and throw oneself voluntarily along with the hideous vortex of dream-doom into whatever bottomless gulf may yawn. And so it was with the waking[b] nightmare of Tempest Mountain; the discovery that two monsters had haunted the spot gave me ultimately a mad craving to plunge into the very earth of the accursed region, and with bare hands dig out the death that leered from every inch of the poisonous soil.

As soon as possible I visited the grave of Jan Martense and dug vainly where I had dug before. Some extensive cave-in had obliterated all trace of the underground passage, while the rain had washed so much earth back into the excavation that I could not tell how deeply I had dug that other day. I likewise made a difficult trip to the distant hamlet where the death-creature had been burnt, and was little repaid for my trouble. In the ashes of the fateful cabin I found several bones, but apparently none of the monster's. The squatters said the thing had had only one victim; but in this I judged them inaccurate, since besides the complete skull of a human being,[c] there was another bony fragment which seemed certainly to have belonged to a human skull at some time. Though the rapid drop of the monster had been seen, no one could say just what the creature was like; those who had glimpsed it called it simply a devil. Examining the great tree where it had lurked, I could discern no distinctive marks. I tried to find some trail into the black forest, but on this occasion could not stand the sight of those morbidly large boles,[d] or of those vast serpent-like[e] roots that twisted so malevolently before they sank into the earth.

My next step was to re-examine[f] with microscopic care the deserted hamlet where death had come most abundantly, and where Arthur Munroe had seen something he never lived to describe.

[a] nightmare] nightmare, B
[b] waking] walking D
[c] being,] being B
[d] boles,] boles B
[e] serpent-like] serpentlike C
[f] re-examine] reexamine D

Though my vain previous searches had been exceedingly minute, I now had new data to test; for my horrible grave-crawl convinced me that at least one of the phases of the monstrosity had been an underground creature. This time, on the 14th of November, my quest concerned itself mostly with the slopes of Cone Mountain and Maple Hill where they overlook the unfortunate hamlet, and I gave particular attention to the loose earth of the landslide region on the latter eminence.

The afternoon of my search brought nothing to light, and dusk came as I stood on Maple Hill looking down at the hamlet and across the valley to Tempest Mountain. There had been a gorgeous sunset, and now the moon came up, nearly full and shedding a silver flood over the plain, the distant mountainside, and the curious low mounds that rose here and there. It was a peaceful Arcadian scene, but knowing what it hid I hated it. I hated the mocking moon, the hypocritical plain, the festering mountain, and those sinister mounds. Everything seemed to me tainted with a loathsome contagion, and inspired by a noxious alliance with distorted hidden powers.

Presently, as I gazed abstractedly at the moonlit panorama, my eye became attracted by something singular in the nature and arrangement of a certain topographical element. Without having any exact knowledge of geology, I had from the first been interested in the odd mounds and hummocks of the region. I had noticed that they were pretty widely distributed around Tempest Mountain, though less numerous on the plain than near the hilltop itself, where prehistoric glaciation had doubtless found feebler opposition to its striking and fantastic caprices. Now, in the light of that low moon which cast long weird shadows, it struck me forcibly that the various points and lines of the mound system had a peculiar relation to the summit of Tempest Mountain. That summit was undeniably a centre[a] from which the lines or rows of points radiated indefinitely and irregularly, as if the unwholesome Martense mansion had thrown visible tentacles of terror. The idea of such tentacles gave me an unexplained thrill, and I stopped to analyse[b] my reason for believing these mounds glacial phenomena.

---

[a] centre] center C
[b] analyse] analyze B, C

The more I analysed[a] the less I believed, and against my newly opened mind there began to beat grotesque and horrible analogies based on superficial aspects and upon my experience beneath the earth. Before I knew it I was uttering frenzied and disjointed words to myself:[b] "My God![c] ... Molehills ... the damned place must be honeycombed ... how many ... that[d] night at the mansion ... they took Bennett and Tobey first ... on each side of us. . . ."[e] Then I was digging frantically into the mound which had stretched nearest me; digging desperately, shiveringly, but almost jubilantly; digging and at last shrieking aloud with some unplaced emotion as I came upon a tunnel or burrow just like the one through which I had crawled on that[f] other daemoniac[g] night.

After that I recall running, spade in hand; a hideous run across moon-litten, mound-marked meadows and through diseased,[h] precipitous abysses of haunted hillside forest; leaping, screaming, panting, bounding toward the terrible Martense mansion. I recall digging unreasoningly[i] in all parts of the brier-choked cellar; digging to find the core and centre[j] of that malignant universe of mounds. And then I recall how I laughed when I stumbled on the passageway; the hole at the base of the old chimney, where the thick weeds grew and cast queer shadows in the light of the lone candle I had happened to have with me. What still remained down in that hell-hive, lurking and waiting for the thunder to arouse it, I did not know. Two had been killed; perhaps that had finished it. But still there remained that burning determination to reach the innermost secret of the fear, which I had once more come to deem definite, material, and organic.

---

[a] analysed] analyzed B, C
[b] myself:] myself; A, B, D
[c] God!] God B
[d] that] the B
[e] us. . . ."] us." . . . C
[f] that] the D
[g] daemoniac] demoniac A, B, C, D
[h] diseased,] diseased B
[i] unreasoningly] unreasonably D
[j] centre] center C

My indecisive speculation whether to explore the passage alone and immediately with my pocket-light or to try to assemble a band of squatters for the quest,[a] was interrupted after a time by a sudden rush of wind from outside which blew out the candle and left me in stark blackness. The moon no longer shone through the chinks and apertures above me, and with a sense of fateful alarm I heard the sinister and significant rumble of approaching thunder. A confusion of associated ideas possessed my brain, leading me to grope back toward the farthest corner of the cellar. My eyes,[b] however, never turned away from the horrible opening at the base of the chimney; and I began to get glimpses of the crumbling bricks and unhealthy weeds as faint glows of lightning penetrated the woods[c] outside and illumined the chinks in the upper wall. Every second I was consumed with a mixture of fear and curiosity. What would the storm call forth—or was there anything left for it to call? Guided by a lightning flash I settled myself down behind a dense clump of vegetation, through which I could see the opening without being seen.

If heaven is merciful, it will some day efface from my consciousness the sight that I saw, and let me live my last years in peace. I cannot[d] sleep at night now, and have to take opiates when it thunders. The thing came abruptly and unannounced; a daemon, rat-like[e] scurrying from pits remote and unimaginable, a hellish panting and stifled grunting, and then from that opening beneath the chimney a burst of multitudinous and leprous life—a loathsome night-spawned flood of organic corruption more devastatingly hideous than the blackest conjurations of mortal madness and morbidity. Seething, stewing, surging, bubbling like serpents' slime it rolled up and out of that yawning hole, spreading like a septic contagion and streaming from the cellar at every point of egress—streaming out to scatter through the accursed midnight forests and strew fear, madness, and death.

---

[a] quest,] quest C
[b] eyes,] eyes B
[c] woods] weeds D
[d] cannot] can not C
[e] daemon, rat-like] demon, ratlike A, B, C, D

God knows how many there were—there must have been thousands. To see the stream of them in that faint,[a] intermittent lightning was shocking. When they had thinned out enough to be glimpsed as separate organisms, I saw that they were dwarfed, deformed hairy devils or apes—monstrous and diabolic caricatures of the monkey tribe. They were so hideously silent; there was hardly a squeal when one of the last stragglers turned with the skill of long practice[b] to make a meal in accustomed fashion on a weaker companion. Others snapped up what it left and ate with slavering relish. Then, in spite of my daze of fright and disgust, my morbid curiosity triumphed; and as the last of the monstrosities oozed up alone from that nether world of unknown nightmare, I drew my automatic pistol and shot it under cover of the thunder.

Shrieking, slithering, torrential shadows of red viscous madness chasing one another through endless, ensanguined corridors of purple fulgurous sky . . . formless phantasms and kaleidoscopic mutations of a ghoulish,[c] remembered scene; forests of monstrous overnourished[d] oaks with serpent roots twisting and sucking unnamable juices from an earth verminous with millions of cannibal devils; mound-like[e] tentacles groping from underground nuclei of polypous perversion . . . insane lightning over malignant ivied walls[f] and daemon[g] arcades choked with fungous vegetation. . . . Heaven be thanked for the instinct which led me unconscious to places where men dwell; to the peaceful village that slept under the calm stars of clearing skies.

I had recovered enough in a week to send to Albany for a gang of men to blow up the Martense mansion and the entire top of Tempest Mountain with dynamite, stop up all the discoverable mound-burrows, and destroy certain overnourished[h] trees whose very existence seemed an insult to sanity. I could sleep a little after they had done this, but

[a] faint,] faint D
[b] practice] practise C
[c] ghoulish,] ghoulfish, B
[d] overnourished] over-nourished D
[e] mound-like] moundlike A, C, D
[f] walls] walk B
[g] daemon] demon A, B, C, D
[h] overnourished] over-nourished D

true rest will never come as long as I remember that nameless secret of the lurking fear. The thing will haunt me, for who can say the extermination is complete, and that analogous phenomena do not exist all over the world? Who can, with my knowledge, think of the earth's unknown caverns without a nightmare dread of future possibilities? I cannot[a] see a well or a subway entrance without shuddering . . . why cannot[b] the doctors give me something to make me sleep, or truly calm my brain when it thunders?[c]

What I saw in the glow of my[d] flashlight after I shot the unspeakable straggling object was so simple that almost a minute elapsed before I understood and went delirious. The object was nauseous; a filthy whitish gorilla thing with sharp yellow fangs and matted fur. It was the ultimate product of mammalian degeneration; the frightful outcome of isolated spawning, multiplication, and cannibal nutrition above and below the ground; the embodiment of all the snarling[e] chaos and grinning fear that lurk behind life. It had looked at me as it died, and its eyes had the same odd quality that marked those other eyes which had stared at me underground and excited cloudy recollections. One eye was blue, the other brown. They were the dissimilar Martense eyes of the old legends, and I knew in one inundating cataclysm of voiceless horror what had become of that vanished family; the terrible and thunder-crazed house of Martense.

---

[a] cannot] can not C
[b] cannot] can not C
[c] thunders?] thunders. B
[d] my] *om.* D
[e] snarling] snarling and D

The Rats in the Walls

On July 16, 1923, I moved into Exham Priory after the last workman had finished his labours.[a] The restoration had been a stupendous task, for little had remained of the deserted pile but a shell-like ruin; yet because it had been the seat of my ancestors[b] I let no expense deter me. The place had not been inhabited since the reign of James the First, when a tragedy of intensely hideous, though largely unexplained, nature had struck down the master, five of his children, and several servants; and driven forth under a cloud of suspicion and terror the third son, my lineal progenitor and the only survivor of the abhorred line.[c] With this sole heir denounced as a murderer, the estate had reverted to the crown, nor had the accused man made any attempt to exculpate himself or regain his property. Shaken by some horror greater than that of conscience or the law, and expressing only a frantic wish to exclude the ancient edifice from his sight and memory, Walter de la Poer, eleventh Baron Exham, fled to

Editor's Note: There is no surviving manuscript, so we are reliant on the two published appearances in HPL's lifetime, both in *Weird Tales* (March 1924 and June 1930). There is internal evidence that HPL revised the story for the second appearance, although it is a matter of judgment which divergences between the two texts constitute deliberate revisions by HPL and which are alterations by the *Weird Tales* editors; many changes seem in accordance with the magazine's later "house style," hence must be editorial. The first appearance also appears to feature numerous instances where HPL's long paragraphs were broken down into two or three shorter paragraphs; these paragraphs have been conjecturally restored. The Arkham House editions followed the first *Weird Tales* appearance.

Texts: A = *Weird Tales* 3, No. 3 (March 1924): 25–31; B = *Weird Tales* 15, No. 6 (June 1930): 841–53; C = *The Dunwich Horror and Others* (Arkham House, 1963), 33–52. Copy-text: A (with some readings from B).

[a] labours.] labors. A, B, C
[b] ancestors] ancestors, B
[c] line.] line. ¶ A, B, C

Virginia and there founded the family which by the next century had become known as Delapore.

Exham Priory had remained untenanted, though later allotted to the estates of the Norrys family and much studied because of its peculiarly composite architecture; an architecture involving Gothic towers resting on a Saxon or Romanesque substructure, whose foundation in turn was of a still earlier order or blend of orders—Roman, and even Druidic or native Cymric,[a] if legends speak truly. This foundation was a very singular thing, being merged on one side with the solid limestone of the precipice from whose brink the priory overlooked a desolate valley three miles west of the village of Anchester.[b] Architects and antiquarians loved to examine this strange relic of forgotten centuries, but the country folk hated it. They had hated it hundreds of years before, when my ancestors lived there, and they hated it now, with the moss and mould[c] of abandonment on it. I had not been a day in Anchester before I knew I came of an accursed house. And this week workmen have blown up Exham Priory, and are busy obliterating the traces of its foundations.[d]

The bare statistics of my ancestry I had always known, together with the fact that my first American forbear[e] had come to the colonies under a strange cloud. Of details, however, I had been kept wholly ignorant through the policy of reticence always maintained by the Delapores. Unlike our planter neighbours,[f] we seldom boasted of crusading ancestors or other mediaeval and Renaissance heroes; nor was any kind of tradition handed down except what may have been recorded in the sealed envelope left before the Civil War by every squire to his eldest son for posthumous opening. The glories we cherished were those achieved since the migration; the glories of a proud and honourable,[g] if somewhat reserved and unsocial Virginia line.

During the war our fortunes were extinguished and our whole existence changed by the burning of Carfax, our home on the banks of

[a] Cymric,] Cymric A
[b] Anchester.] Anchester. ¶ A, B, C
[c] mould] mold B
[d] foundations. ¶] foundations. C
[e] forbear] forebear B
[f] neighbours,] neighbors, A, B, C
[g] honourable,] honorable, A, B, C

the James. My grandfather, advanced in years, had perished in that incendiary outrage, and with him the envelope that[a] bound us all to the past. I can recall that fire today as I saw it then at the age of seven, with the Federal soldiers shouting, the women screaming, and the negroes howling and praying. My father was in the army, defending Richmond, and after many formalities my mother and I were passed through the lines to join him.

When the war ended we all moved north, whence my mother had come; and I grew to manhood, middle age, and ultimate wealth as a stolid Yankee. Neither my father nor I ever knew what our hereditary envelope had contained, and as I merged into the greyness[b] of Massachusetts business life I lost all interest in the mysteries which evidently lurked far back in my family tree. Had I suspected their nature, how gladly I would have left Exham Priory to its moss, bats, and cobwebs!

My father died in 1904, but without any message to leave me, or to my only child, Alfred, a motherless boy of ten. It was this boy who reversed the order of family information;[c] for although I could give him only jesting conjectures about the past, he wrote me of some very interesting ancestral legends when the late war took him to England in 1917 as an aviation officer. Apparently the Delapores had a colourful[d] and perhaps sinister history, for a friend of my son's, Capt.[e] Edward Norrys of the Royal Flying Corps, dwelt near the family seat at Anchester and related some peasant superstitions which few novelists could equal for wildness and incredibility. Norrys himself, of course, did not take them[f] seriously; but they amused my son and made good material for his letters to me. It was this legendry which definitely turned my attention to my transatlantic heritage, and made me resolve to purchase and restore the family seat which Norrys shewed[g] to Alfred in its picturesque

[a] that] that had C

[b] greyness] grayness B

[c] information;] information, A, B, C

[d] colourful] colorful A, B, C

[e] Capt.] Captain B

[f] them] them so C

[g] shewed] showed A, B, C

desertion, and offered to get for him at a surprisingly[a] reasonable figure, since his own uncle was the present owner.

I bought Exham Priory in 1918, but was almost immediately distracted from my plans of restoration by the return of my son as a maimed invalid. During the two years that he lived I thought of nothing but his care, having even placed my business under the direction of partners.[b] In 1921, as I found myself bereaved and aimless, a retired manufacturer no longer young, I resolved to divert my remaining years with my new possession. Visiting Anchester in December, I was entertained by Capt.[c] Norrys, a plump, amiable young man who had thought much of my son, and secured his assistance in gathering plans and anecdotes to guide in the coming restoration. Exham Priory itself I saw without emotion, a jumble of tottering mediaeval ruins covered with lichens and honeycombed with rooks' nests, perched perilously upon a precipice, and denuded of floors or other interior features save the stone walls of the separate towers.

As I gradually recovered the image of the edifice as it had been when my ancestor left it over three centuries before, I began to hire workmen for the reconstruction. In every case I was forced to go outside the immediate locality, for the Anchester villagers had an almost unbelievable fear and hatred of the place. This sentiment was so great that it was sometimes communicated to the outside labourers,[d] causing numerous desertions; whilst its scope appeared to include both the priory and its ancient family.

My son had told me that he was somewhat avoided during his visits because he was a de la Poer, and I now found myself subtly ostracised[e] for a like reason until I convinced the peasants how little I knew of my heritage. Even then they sullenly disliked me, so that I had to collect most of the village traditions through the mediation of Norrys. What the people could not forgive, perhaps, was that I had come to restore a symbol so abhorrent to them; for, rationally or not, they viewed

[a] surprisingly] surprizingly B
[b] partners.] partners. ¶ A, B, C
[c] Capt.] Captain B
[d] labourers,] laborers, A, B, C
[e] ostracised] ostracized B

Exham Priory as nothing less than a haunt of fiends and werewolves.

Piecing together the tales which Norrys collected for me, and supplementing them with the accounts of several savants who had studied the ruins, I deduced that Exham Priory stood on the site of a prehistoric temple; a Druidical or ante-Druidical thing which must have been contemporary with Stonehenge. That indescribable rites had been celebrated there, few doubted;[a] and there were unpleasant tales of the transference of these rites into the Cybele-worship which the Romans had introduced.[b] Inscriptions still visible in the sub-cellar[c] bore such unmistakable letters as "DIV . . . OPS . . . MAGNA. MAT . . ." sign of the Magna Mater whose dark worship was once vainly forbidden to Roman citizens. Anchester had been the camp of the third Augustan legion, as many remains attest, and it was said that the temple of Cybele was splendid and thronged with worshippers who performed nameless ceremonies at the bidding of a Phrygian priest. Tales added that the fall of the old religion did not end the orgies at the temple, but that the priests lived on in the new faith without real change. Likewise was it said that the rites did not vanish with the Roman power, and that certain among the Saxons added to what remained of the temple, and gave it the essential outline it subsequently preserved, making it the centre[d] of a cult feared through half the heptarchy. About 1000 A.D. the place is mentioned in a chronicle as being a substantial stone priory housing a strange and powerful monastic order and surrounded by extensive gardens which needed no walls to exclude a frightened populace. It was never destroyed by the Danes, though after the Norman Conquest it must have declined tremendously; since there was no impediment when Henry the Third granted the site to my ancestor, Gilbert de la Poer, First Baron Exham, in 1261.

Of my family before this date there is no evil report, but something strange must have happened then. In one chronicle there is a reference to a de la Poer as "cursed of God" in 1307, whilst village legendry had nothing but evil and frantic fear to tell of the castle that

[a] doubted;] doubted, A, B, C
[b] introduced.] introduced. ¶ A, B, C
[c] sub-cellar] sub-/cellar A, B; subcellar C
[d] centre] center A, B, C

went up on the foundations of the old temple and priory. The fireside tales were of the most grisly description, all the ghastlier because of their frightened reticence and cloudy evasiveness. They represented my ancestors as a race of hereditary daemons beside whom Gilles de Retz and the Marquis de Sade would seem the veriest tyros, and hinted whisperingly at their responsibility for the occasional disappearances of villagers through several generations.

The worst characters, apparently, were the barons and their direct heirs; at least, most was whispered about these. If of healthier inclinations, it was said, an heir would early and mysteriously die to make way for another more typical scion. There seemed to be an inner cult in the family, presided over by the head of the house, and sometimes closed except to a few members. Temperament rather than ancestry was evidently the basis of this cult, for it was entered by several who married into the family. Lady Margaret Trevor from Cornwall, wife of Godfrey, the second son of the fifth baron, became a favourite[a] bane of children all over the countryside, and the daemon heroine of a particularly horrible old ballad not yet extinct near the Welsh border. Preserved in balladry, too, though not illustrating the same point, is the hideous tale of Lady Mary de la Poer, who shortly after her marriage to the Earl of Shrewsfield was killed by him and his mother, both of the slayers being absolved and blessed by the priest to whom they confessed what they dared not repeat to the world.

These myths and ballads, typical as they were of crude superstition, repelled me greatly. Their persistence, and their application to so long a line of my ancestors, were especially annoying; whilst the imputations of monstrous habits proved unpleasantly reminiscent of the one known scandal of my immediate forbears[b]—the case of my cousin, young Randolph Delapore of Carfax, who went among the negroes and became a voodoo priest after he returned from the Mexican War.

I was much less disturbed by the vaguer tales of wails and howlings in the barren, windswept valley beneath the limestone cliff; of the graveyard stenches after the spring rains; of the floundering, squealing white thing on which Sir John Clave's horse had trod one night in a

[a] favourite] favorite A, B, C
[b] forbears] forebears B

lonely field; and of the servant who had gone mad at what he saw in the priory in the full light of day. These things were hackneyed spectral lore, and I was at that time a pronounced sceptic.[a] The accounts of vanished peasants were less to be dismissed, though not especially significant in view of mediaeval custom. Prying curiosity meant death, and more than one severed head had been publicly shewn[b] on the bastions—now effaced—around Exham Priory.

A few of the tales were exceedingly picturesque, and made me wish I had learnt more of[c] comparative mythology in my youth. There was, for instance, the belief that a legion of bat-winged[d] devils kept Witches' Sabbath[e] each night at the priory—a legion whose sustenance might explain the disproportionate abundance of coarse vegetables harvested in the vast gardens. And, most vivid of all, there was the dramatic epic of the rats—the scampering army of obscene vermin which had burst forth from the castle three months after the tragedy that doomed it to desertion—the lean, filthy, ravenous army which had swept all before it and devoured fowl, cats, dogs, hogs, sheep, and even two hapless human beings before its fury was spent. Around that unforgettable rodent army a whole separate cycle of myths revolves, for it scattered among the village homes and brought curses and horrors in its train.

Such was the lore that assailed me as I pushed to completion, with an elderly obstinacy, the work of restoring my ancestral home. It must not be imagined for a moment that these tales formed my principal psychological environment. On the other hand, I was constantly praised and encouraged by Capt.[f] Norrys and the antiquarians who surrounded and aided me. When the task was done, over two years after its commencement, I viewed the great rooms, wainscotted walls, vaulted ceilings, mullioned windows, and broad staircases with a pride which fully compensated for the prodigious expense of the restoration.[g] Every attribute of the Middle Ages was cunningly reproduced, and the new

---

[a] sceptic.] skeptic. A, B, C

[b] shewn] shown A, B, C

[c] of] of the A, C

[d] bat-winged] bat-/winged A; batwinged C

[e] Witches' Sabbath] witches' sabbath A, B, C

[f] Capt.] Captain B

[g] restoration.] restoration. ¶ A, B, C

parts blended perfectly with the original walls and foundations. The seat of my fathers was complete, and I looked forward to redeeming at last the local fame of the line which ended in me. I would reside here permanently, and prove that a de la Poer (for I had adopted again the original spelling of the name) need not be a fiend. My comfort was perhaps augmented by the fact that, although Exham Priory was mediaevally fitted, its interior was in truth wholly new and free from old vermin and old ghosts alike.

As I have said, I moved in on July 16, 1923. My household consisted of seven servants and nine cats, of which latter species I am particularly fond. My eldest cat, "Nigger-Man",[a] was seven years old and had come with me from my home in Bolton, Massachusetts; the others I had accumulated whilst living with Capt.[b] Norrys' family during the restoration of the priory.[c] For five days our routine proceeded with the utmost placidity, my time being spent mostly in the codification of old family data. I had now obtained some very circumstantial accounts of the final tragedy and flight of Walter de la Poer, which I conceived to be the probable contents of the hereditary paper lost in the fire at Carfax. It appeared that my ancestor was accused with much reason of having killed all the other members of his household, except four servant confederates, in their sleep, about two weeks after a shocking discovery which changed his whole demeanour,[d] but which, except by implication, he disclosed to no one save perhaps the servants who assisted him and afterward fled beyond reach.

This deliberate slaughter, which included a father, three brothers, and two sisters, was largely condoned by the villagers, and so slackly treated by the law that its perpetrator escaped honoured,[e] unharmed, and undisguised to Virginia; the general whispered sentiment being that he had purged the land of an[f] immemorial curse. What discovery had prompted an act so terrible, I could scarcely even conjecture. Walter de la Poer must have known for years the sinister tales about his family, so

[a] "Nigger-Man",] "Nigger-Man," A, B, C
[b] Capt.] Captain B
[c] priory.] priory. ¶ A, B, C
[d] demeanour,] demeanor, A, B, C
[e] honoured,] honored, A, B, C
[f] an] *om.* C

that this material could have given him no fresh impulse. Had he, then, witnessed some appalling ancient rite, or stumbled upon some frightful and revealing symbol in the priory or its vicinity? He was reputed to have been a shy, gentle youth in England. In Viriginia he seemed not so much hard or bitter as harassed and apprehensive. He was spoken of in the diary of another gentleman-adventurer,[a] Francis Harley of Bellview, as a man of unexampled justice, honour,[b] and delicacy.

On July 22 occurred the first incident which, though lightly dismissed at the time, takes on a preternatural significance in relation to later events. It was so simple as to be almost negligible, and could not possibly have been noticed under the circumstances; for it must be recalled that since I was in a building practically fresh and new except for the walls, and surrounded by a well-balanced staff of servitors, apprehension would have been absurd despite the locality.[c] What I afterward remembered is merely this—that my old black cat, whose moods I know so well, was undoubtedly alert and anxious to an extent wholly out of keeping with his natural character. He roved from room to room, restless and disturbed, and sniffed constantly about the walls which formed part of the old[d] Gothic structure. I realise[e] how trite this sounds—like the inevitable dog in the ghost story, which always growls before his master sees the sheeted figure—yet I cannot consistently suppress it.

The following day a servant complained of restlessness among all the cats in the house. He came to me in my study, a lofty west room on the second story, with groined arches, black oak panelling,[f] and a triple Gothic window overlooking the limestone cliff and desolate valley; and even as he spoke I saw the jetty form of Nigger-Man creeping along the west wall and scratching at the new panels which overlaid the ancient stone.[g] I told the man that there must be some singular odour[h] or emanation from the old stonework, imperceptible to

---

[a] gentleman-adventurer,] gentleman adventurer, A, B, C
[b] honour,] honor, A, C; honor B
[c] locality.] locality. ¶ A, B, C
[d] old] *om.* C
[e] realise] realize A, B, C
[f] panelling,] paneling, B
[g] stone.] stone. ¶ A, B, C
[h] odour] odor A, B, C

human senses, but affecting the delicate organs of cats even through the new woodwork. This I truly believed, and when the fellow suggested the presence of mice or rats, I mentioned that there had been no rats there for three hundred years, and that even the field mice of the surrounding country could hardly be found in these high walls, where they had never been known to stray. That afternoon I called on Capt.[a] Norrys, and he assured me that it would be quite incredible for field mice to infest the priory in such a sudden and unprecedented fashion.

That night, dispensing as usual with a valet, I retired in the west tower chamber which I had chosen as my own, reached from the study by a stone staircase and short gallery—the former partly ancient, the latter entirely restored. This room was circular, very high, and without wainscotting, being hung with arras which I had myself chosen in London.[b] Seeing that Nigger-Man was with me, I shut the heavy Gothic door and retired by the light of the electric bulbs which so cleverly counterfeited candles, finally switching off the light and sinking on the carved and canopied four-poster, with the venerable cat in his accustomed place across my feet. I did not draw the curtains, but gazed out at the narrow north window which I faced. There was a suspicion of aurora in the sky, and the delicate traceries of the window were pleasantly silhouetted.

At some time I must have fallen quietly asleep, for I recall a distinct sense of leaving strange dreams,[c] when the cat started violently from his placid position. I saw him in the faint auroral glow, head strained forward, fore feet[d] on my ankles, and hind feet stretched behind. He was looking intensely at a point on the wall somewhat west of the window, a point which to my eye had nothing to mark it, but toward which all my attention was now directed.[e] And as I watched, I knew that Nigger-Man was not vainly excited. Whether the arras actually moved I cannot[f] say. I think it did, very slightly. But what I can swear to is that behind it I heard a low, distinct scurrying as of rats or mice. In a moment the cat

[a] Capt.] Captain B
[b] London.] London. ¶ A, B, C
[c] dreams,] dreams B
[d] fore feet] forefeet A, B, C
[e] directed.] directed. ¶ A, B, C
[f] cannot] can not B

had jumped bodily on the screening tapestry, bringing the affected section to the floor with his weight, and exposing a damp, ancient wall of stone; patched here and there by the restorers, and devoid of any trace of rodent prowlers.[a] Nigger-Man raced up and down the floor by this part of the wall, clawing the fallen arras and seemingly trying at times to insert a paw between the wall and the oaken floor. He found nothing, and after a time returned wearily to his place across my feet. I had not moved, but I did not sleep again that night.

In the morning I questioned all the servants, and found that none of them had noticed anything unusual,[b] save that the cook remembered the actions of a cat which had rested on her windowsill.[c] This cat had howled at some unknown hour of the night, awaking the cook in time for her to see him dart purposefully out of the open door down the stairs. I drowsed away the noontime, and in the afternoon called again on Capt.[d] Norrys, who became exceedingly interested in what I told him. The odd incidents—so slight yet so curious—appealed to his sense of the picturesque, and elicited from him a number of reminiscences of local ghostly lore. We were genuinely perplexed at the presence of rats, and Norrys lent me some traps and paris-green,[e] which I had the servants place in strategic localities when I returned.

I retired early, being very sleepy, but was harassed by dreams of the most horrible sort. I seemed to be looking down from an immense height upon a twilit grotto, knee-deep with filth, where a white-bearded daemon swineherd drove about with his staff a flock of fungous, flabby beasts whose appearance filled me with unutterable loathing. Then, as the swineherd paused and nodded over his task, a mighty swarm of rats rained down on the stinking abyss and fell to devouring beasts and man alike.

From this terrific vision I was abruptly awaked by the motions of Nigger-Man, who had been sleeping as usual across my feet. This time I did not have to question the source of his snarls and hisses, and of the

---

[a] prowlers.] prowlers. ¶ A, B, C
[b] unusual,] unusual B
[c] windowsill.] window-sill. B
[d] Capt.] Captain B
[e] paris-green,] Paris green, C

fear which made him sink his claws into my ankle, unconscious of their effect; for on every side of the chamber the walls were alive with nauseous sound—the verminous slithering of ravenous, gigantic rats. There was now no aurora to shew[a] the state of the arras—the fallen section of which had been replaced—but I was not too frightened to switch on the light.

As the bulbs leapt into radiance I saw a hideous shaking all over the tapestry, causing the somewhat peculiar designs to execute a singular dance of death. This motion disappeared almost at once, and the sound with it. Springing out of bed, I poked at the arras with the long handle of a warming-pan that rested near, and lifted one section to see what lay beneath. There was nothing but the patched stone wall, and even the cat had lost his tense realisation[b] of abnormal presences. When I examined the circular trap that had been placed in the room, I found all of the openings sprung, though no trace remained of what had been caught and had escaped.

Further sleep was out of the question, so, lighting a candle, I opened the door and went out in the gallery toward the stairs to my study, Nigger-Man following at my heels. Before we had reached the stone steps, however, the cat darted ahead of me and vanished down the ancient flight. As I descended the stairs myself, I became suddenly aware of sounds in the great room below; sounds of a nature which could not be mistaken.[c] The oak-panelled[d] walls were alive with rats, scampering and milling, whilst Nigger-Man was racing about with the fury of a baffled hunter. Reaching the bottom, I switched on the light, which did not this time cause the noise to subside. The rats continued their riot, stampeding with such force and distinctness that I could finally assign to their motions a definite direction. These creatures, in numbers apparently inexhaustible, were engaged in one stupendous migration from inconceivable heights to some depth conceivably, or inconceivably,[e] below.

I now heard steps in the corridor, and in another moment two

---

[a] shew] show A, B, C
[b] realisation] realization A, B, C
[c] mistaken.] mistaken. ¶ A, B, C
[d] oak-panelled] oak-paneled A, B
[e] conceivably, or inconceivably,] conceivably or inconceivably C

servants pushed open the massive door. They were searching the house for some unknown source of disturbance which had thrown all the cats into a snarling panic and caused them to plunge precipitately down several flights of stairs and squat, yowling, before the closed door to the sub-cellar. I asked them if they had heard the rats, but they replied in the negative. And when I turned to call their attention to the sounds in the panels, I realised[a] that the noise had ceased.[b] With the two men[c] I went down to the door of the sub-cellar, but found the cats already dispersed. Later[d] I resolved to explore the crypt below;[e] but for the present I merely made a round of the traps. All were sprung, yet all were tenantless. Satisfying myself that no one had heard the rats save the felines and me, I sat in my study till morning;[f] thinking profoundly,[g] and recalling every scrap of legend I had unearthed concerning the building I inhabited.

I slept some in the forenoon, leaning back in the one comfortable library chair which my mediaeval plan of furnishing could not banish. Later I telephoned to Capt.[h] Norrys, who came over and helped me explore the sub-cellar.[i] Absolutely nothing untoward was found, although we could not repress a thrill at the knowledge that this vault was built by Roman hands. Every low arch and massive pillar was Roman—not the debased Romanesque of the bungling Saxons, but the severe and harmonious classicism of the age of the Caesars; indeed, the walls abounded with inscriptions familiar to the antiquarians who had repeatedly explored the place—things like "P. GETAE. PROP ... TEMP ... DONA ..." and "L. PRAEC ... VS ... PONTIFI ... ATYS ..."

The reference to Atys made me shiver, for I had read Catullus and knew something of the hideous rites of the Eastern god, whose

---

[a] realised] realized A, B, C
[b] ceased.] ceased. ¶ A, B, C
[c] men] men, A, C
[d] Later] Later, B
[e] below;] below, A, C
[f] morning;] morning, A, B, C
[g] profoundly,] profoundly C
[h] Capt.] Captain B
[i] sub-cellar.] sub-cellar. ¶ A, B, C

worship was so mixed with that of Cybele. Norrys and I, by the light of lanterns, tried to interpret the odd and nearly effaced designs on certain irregularly rectangular blocks of stone generally held to be altars, but could make nothing of them. We remembered that one pattern, a sort of rayed sun, was held by students to imply a non-Roman origin, suggesting that these altars had merely been adopted by the Roman priests from some older and perhaps aboriginal temple on the same site. On one of these blocks were some brown stains which made me wonder. The largest, in the centre[a] of the room, had certain features on the upper surface which indicated its connexion[b] with fire—probably burnt offerings.

Such were the sights in that crypt before whose door the cats had[c] howled, and where Norrys and I now determined to pass the night. Couches were brought down by the servants, who were told not to mind any nocturnal actions of the cats, and Nigger-Man was admitted as much for help as for companionship. We decided to keep the great oak door—a modern reproduction[d] with slits for ventilation—tightly closed; and, with this attended to, we retired with lanterns still burning to await whatever might occur.

The vault was very deep in the foundations of the priory, and undoubtedly far down on the face of the beetling limestone cliff overlooking the waste valley. That it had been the goal of the scuffling and unexplainable rats I could not doubt, though why, I could not tell. As we lay there expectantly, I found my vigil occasionally mixed with half-formed dreams from which the uneasy motions of the cat across my feet would rouse me.[e] These dreams were not wholesome, but horribly like the one I had had the night before. I saw again the twilit grotto, and the swineherd with his unmentionable fungous beasts wallowing in filth, and as I looked at these things they seemed nearer and more distinct—so distinct that I could almost observe their features. Then I did observe the flabby features of one of them—and awaked

[a] centre] center A, B, C

[b] connexion] connection A, B, C

[c] had] *om.* C

[d] reproduction] replica A, C

[e] me.] me. ¶ A, B, C

with such a scream that Nigger-Man started up, whilst Capt.[a] Norrys, who had not slept, laughed considerably. Norrys might have laughed more—or perhaps less—had he known what it was that made me scream. But I did not remember myself till later. Ultimate horror often paralyses[b] memory in a merciful way.

Norrys waked me when the phenomena began. Out of the same frightful dream I was called by his gentle shaking and his urging to listen to the cats. Indeed, there was much to listen to, for beyond the closed door at the head of the stone steps was a veritable nightmare of feline yelling and clawing, whilst Nigger-Man, unmindful of his kindred outside, was running excitedly around the bare stone walls, in which I heard the same babel of scurrying rats that had troubled me the night before.

An acute terror now rose within me, for here were anomalies which nothing normal could well explain. These rats, if not the creatures of a madness which I shared with the cats alone, must be burrowing and sliding in Roman walls I had thought to be of solid limestone blocks . . . unless perhaps the action of water through more than seventeen centuries had eaten winding tunnels which rodent bodies had worn clear and ample. . . . But even so, the spectral horror was no less; for if these were living vermin why did not Norrys hear their disgusting commotion? Why did he urge me to watch Nigger-Man and listen to the cats outside, and why did he guess wildly and vaguely at what could have aroused them?

By the time I had managed to tell him, as rationally as I could, what I thought I was hearing, my ears gave me the last fading impression of the scurrying; which had retreated *still downward,* far underneath this deepest of sub-cellars,[c] till it seemed as if the whole cliff below were riddled with questing rats. Norrys was not as sceptical[d] as I had anticipated, but instead seemed profoundly moved. He motioned to me to notice that the cats at the door had ceased their clamour,[e] as if giving up the rats for lost; whilst Nigger-Man had a

---

[a] Capt.] Captain B

[b] paralyses] paralyzes A, B

[c] sub-cellars,] sub-cellars A, C

[d] sceptical] skeptical A, B, C

[e] clamour,] clamor, A, B, C

burst of renewed restlessness, and was clawing frantically around the bottom of the large stone altar in the centre[a] of the room, which was nearer Norrys' couch than mine.

My fear of the unknown was at this point very great. Something astounding had occurred, and I saw that Capt.[b] Norrys, a younger, stouter, and presumably more naturally materialistic man, was affected fully as much as myself—perhaps because of his lifelong and intimate familiarity with local legend. We could for the moment do nothing but watch the old black cat as he pawed with decreasing fervour[c] at the base of the altar, occasionally looking up and mewing to me in that persuasive manner which he used when he wished me to perform some favour[d] for him.

Norrys now took a lantern close to the altar and examined the place where Nigger-Man was pawing; silently kneeling and scraping away the lichens of[e] centuries which joined the massive pre-Roman block to the tessellated[f] floor. He did not find anything, and was about to abandon his efforts when I noticed a trivial circumstance which made me shudder, even though it implied nothing more than I had already imagined.[g] I told him of it, and we both looked at its almost imperceptible manifestation with the fixedness of fascinated discovery and acknowledgment. It was only this—that the flame of the lantern set down near the altar was slightly but certainly flickering from a draught[h] of air which it had not before received, and which came indubitably from the crevices[i] between floor and altar where Norrys was scraping away the lichens.

We spent the rest of the night in the brilliantly lighted[j] study, nervously discussing what we should do next. The discovery that some vault deeper than the deepest known masonry of the Romans underlay

[a] centre] center A, B, C
[b] Capt.] Captain B
[c] fervour] fervor A, B, C
[d] favour] favor A, B, C
[e] of] of the C
[f] tessellated] tesselated A, B, C
[g] imagined.] imagined. ¶ A, B, C
[h] draught] draft B
[i] crevices] crevice A, C
[j] brilliantly lighted] brilliantly-lighted A, C

this accursed pile—some vault unsuspected by the curious antiquarians of three centuries—[a]would have been sufficient to excite us without any background of the sinister. As it was, the fascination became twofold; and we paused in doubt whether to abandon our search and quit the priory for ever[b] in superstitious caution, or to gratify our sense of adventure and brave whatever horrors might await us in the unknown depths.[c] By morning we had compromised, and decided to go to London to gather a group of archaeologists[d] and scientific men fit to cope with the mystery. It should be mentioned that before leaving the sub-cellar we had vainly tried to move the central altar which we now recognised[e] as the gate to a new pit of nameless fear. What secret would open the gate, wiser men than we would have to find.

During many days in London Capt.[f] Norrys and I presented our facts, conjectures, and legendary[g] anecdotes to five eminent authorities, all men who could be trusted to respect any family disclosures which future explorations might develop. We found most of them little disposed to scoff, but instead[h] intensely interested and sincerely sympathetic. It is hardly necessary to name them all, but I may say that they included Sir William Brinton, whose excavations in the Troad excited most of the world in their day. As we all took the train for Anchester I felt myself poised on the brink of frightful revelations, a sensation symbolised[i] by the air of mourning among the many Americans at the unexpected death of the President on the other side of the world.

On the evening of August 7th[j] we reached Exham Priory, where the servants assured me that nothing unusual had occurred. The cats, even old Nigger-Man, had been perfectly placid; and not a trap in the house had been sprung. We were to begin exploring on the following

---

[a] pile— . . . centuries—] pile; . . . centuries; A, B, C
[b] for ever] forever A, C
[c] depths.] depths. ¶ A, B, C
[d] archaeologists] archeologists B
[e] recognised] recognized A, B, C
[f] Capt.] Captain B
[g] legendary] legendry B
[h] but instead] but, instead, A, B, C
[i] symbolised] symbolized A, B, C
[j] 7th] 7 C

day, awaiting which I assigned well-appointed rooms to all my guests.[a] I myself retired in my own tower chamber, with Nigger-Man across my feet. Sleep came quickly, but hideous dreams assailed me. There was a vision of a Roman feast like that of Trimalchio, with a horror in a covered platter. Then came that damnable, recurrent thing about the swineherd and his filthy drove in the twilit grotto. Yet when I awoke it was full daylight, with normal sounds in the house below. The rats, living or spectral, had not troubled me; and Nigger-Man was still quietly asleep. On going down, I found that the same tranquillity had prevailed elsewhere; a condition which one of the assembled savants—a fellow named Thornton, devoted to the psychic—rather absurdly laid to the fact that I had now been shewn[b] the thing which certain forces had wished to shew[c] me.

All was now ready, and at eleven a.m.[d] our entire group of seven men, bearing powerful electric searchlights and implements of excavation, went down to the sub-cellar and bolted the door behind us. Nigger-Man was with us, for the investigators found no occasion to despise his excitability, and were indeed anxious that he be present in case of obscure rodent manifestations. We noted the Roman inscriptions and unknown altar designs only briefly, for three of the savants had already seen them, and all knew their characteristics. Prime attention was paid to the momentous central altar, and within an hour Sir William Brinton had caused it to tilt backward, balanced by some unknown species of counterweight.

There now lay revealed such a horror as would have overwhelmed us had we not been prepared. Through a nearly square opening in the tiled floor, sprawling on a flight of stone steps so prodigiously worn that it was little more than an inclined plane at the centre,[e] was a ghastly array of human or semi-human bones. Those which retained their collocation as skeletons shewed[f] attitudes of panic fear, and over all were the marks of rodent gnawing. The skulls denoted nothing short of utter idiocy,

[a] guests.] guests. ¶ A, B, C
[b] shewn] shown A, B, C
[c] shew] show A, B, C
[d] eleven a.m.] 11 a. m. A; eleven a. m. B; 11 A.M. C
[e] centre,] center, A, B, C
[f] shewed] showed A, B, C

cretinism, or primitive semi-apedom.[a] Above the hellishly littered steps arched a descending passage seemingly chiselled[b] from the solid rock, and conducting a current of air. This current was not a sudden and noxious rush as from a closed vault, but a cool breeze with something of freshness in it. We did not pause long, but shiveringly began to clear a passage down the steps. It was then that Sir William, examining the hewn walls, made the odd observation that the passage, according to the direction of the strokes, must have been chiselled[c] *from beneath*.

I must be very deliberate now, and choose my words.

After ploughing[d] down a few steps amidst the gnawed bones we saw that there was light ahead; not any mystic phosphorescence, but a filtered daylight which could not come except from unknown fissures in the cliff that overlooked the waste valley. That such fissures had escaped notice from outside was hardly remarkable, for not only is the valley wholly uninhabited, but the cliff is so high and beetling that only an aëronaut[e] could study its face in detail. A few steps more, and our breaths were literally snatched from us by what we saw; so literally that Thornton, the psychic investigator, actually fainted in the arms of the dazed man who stood behind him. Norrys, his plump face utterly white and flabby, simply cried out inarticulately; whilst I think that what I did was to gasp or hiss, and cover my eyes.[f] The man behind me— the only one of the party older than I—croaked the hackneyed "My God!" in the most cracked voice I ever heard. Of seven cultivated men, only Sir William Brinton retained his composure;[g] a thing more to his credit because he led the party and must have seen the sight first.

It was a twilit grotto of enormous height, stretching away farther than any eye could see; a subterranean world of limitless mystery and horrible suggestion. There were buildings and other architectural remains—in one terrified glance I saw a weird pattern of tumuli, a savage circle of monoliths, a low-domed Roman ruin, a sprawling Saxon

[a] semi-apedom.] semi-apedom. ¶ A, B, C

[b] chiselled] chiseled A, B, C

[c] chiselled] chiseled A, B, C

[d] ploughing] plowing B

[e] aëronaut] aeronaut A, B, C

[f] eyes.] eyes. ¶ A, B, C

[g] composure;] composure, A, B, C

pile, and an early English edifice of wood—but all these were dwarfed by the ghoulish spectacle presented by the general surface of the ground. For yards about the steps extended an insane tangle of human bones, or bones at least as human as those on the steps. Like a foamy sea they stretched, some fallen apart, but others wholly or partly articulated as skeletons; these latter invariably in postures of daemoniac frenzy, either fighting off some menace or clutching other forms with cannibal intent.

When Dr. Trask, the anthropologist, stooped[a] to classify the skulls, he found a degraded mixture which utterly baffled him. They were mostly lower than the Piltdown man in the scale of evolution, but in every case definitely human. Many were of higher grade, and a very few were the skulls of supremely and sensitively developed types. All the bones were gnawed, mostly by rats, but somewhat by others of the half-human drove. Mixed with them were many tiny bones of rats—fallen members of the lethal army which closed the ancient epic.

I wonder that any man among us lived and kept his sanity through that hideous day of discovery. Not Hoffmann[b] or Huysmans could conceive a scene more wildly incredible, more frenetically repellent, or more Gothically grotesque than the twilit grotto through which we seven staggered; each stumbling on revelation after revelation, and trying to keep for the nonce from thinking of the events which must have taken place there three hundred, or a thousand, or two thousand, or ten thousand years ago. It was the antechamber of hell, and poor Thornton fainted again when Trask told him that some of the skeleton things must have descended as quadrupeds through the last twenty or more generations.

Horror piled on horror as we began to interpret the architectural remains. The quadruped things—with their occasional recruits from the biped class—had been kept in stone pens, out of which they must have broken in their last delirium of hunger or rat-fear.[c] There had been great herds of them, evidently fattened on the coarse vegetables whose remains could be found as a sort of poisonous ensilage at the bottom of huge stone bins older than Rome. I knew now why my

---

[a] stooped] stopped C
[b] Hoffmann] Hoffman A, C
[c] rat-fear.] rat-fever. B

ancestors had had such excessive gardens—would to heaven I could forget! The purpose of the herds I did not have to ask.

Sir William, standing with his searchlight in the Roman ruin, translated aloud the most shocking ritual I have ever known; and told of the diet of the antediluvian cult which the priests of Cybele found and mingled with their own. Norrys, used as he was to the trenches, could not walk straight when he came out of the English building. It was a butcher shop and kitchen—he had expected that—but it was too much to see familiar English implements in such a place, and to read familiar English *graffiti* there, some as recent as 1610. I could not go in that building—that building whose daemon activities were stopped only by the dagger of my ancestor Walter de la Poer.

What I did venture to enter was the low Saxon building,[a] whose oaken door had fallen, and there I found a terrible row of ten stone cells with rusty bars. Three had tenants, all skeletons of high grade, and on the bony forefinger of one I found a seal ring with my own coat-of-arms. Sir William found a vault with far older cells below the Roman chapel, but these cells were empty. Below them was a low crypt with cases of formally arranged bones, some of them bearing terrible parallel inscriptions carved in Latin, Greek,[b] and the tongue of Phrygia.[c] Meanwhile, Dr. Trask had opened one of the prehistoric tumuli, and brought to light skulls which were slighty more human than a gorilla's,[d] and which bore indescribable[e] ideographic carvings. Through all this horror my cat stalked unperturbed. Once I saw him monstrously perched atop a mountain of bones, and wondered at the secrets[f] that might lie behind his yellow eyes.

Having grasped to some slight degree the frightful revelations of this twilit[g] area—an area so hideously foreshadowed by my recurrent dream—we turned to that apparently boundless depth of midnight cavern where no ray of light from the cliff could penetrate. We shall

[a] building,] building C
[b] Greek,] Greek B
[c] Phrygia.] Phrygia. ¶ A, B, C
[d] gorilla's,] gorilla's B
[e] indescribable] indescribably C
[f] secrets] secret B
[g] twilit] twilight B

never know what sightless Stygian worlds yawn beyond the little distance we went, for it was decided that such secrets are not good for mankind. But there was plenty to engross us close at hand, for we had not gone far before the searchlights shewed[a] that accursed infinity of pits in which the rats had feasted, and whose sudden lack of replenishment had driven the ravenous rodent army first to turn on the living herds of starving things, and then to burst forth from the priory in that historic orgy of devastation which the peasants will never forget.

God! those carrion black pits of sawed, picked bones and opened skulls! Those nightmare chasms choked with the pithecanthropoid, Celtic, Roman, and English bones of countless unhallowed centuries! Some of them were full, and none can say how deep they had once been. Others were still bottomless to our searchlights, and peopled by unnamable fancies. What, I thought, of the hapless rats that stumbled into such traps amidst the blackness of their quests in this grisly Tartarus?

Once my foot slipped near a horribly yawning brink, and I had a moment of ecstatic fear. I must have been musing a long time, for I could not see any of the party but the plump Capt.[b] Norrys. Then there came a sound from that inky, boundless, farther distance that I thought I knew; and I saw my old black cat dart past me like a winged Egyptian god, straight into the illimitable gulf of the unknown. But I was not far behind, for there was no doubt after another second. It was the eldritch scurrying of those fiend-born rats, always questing for new horrors, and determined to lead me on even unto those grinning caverns of earth's centre[c] where Nyarlathotep, the mad faceless god, howls blindly in the darkness to the piping of two amorphous idiot flute-players.

My searchlight expired, but still I ran. I heard voices, and yowls, and echoes, but above all there gently rose that impious, insidious scurrying; gently rising, rising, as a stiff bloated corpse gently rises above an oily river that flows under endless onyx bridges to a black, putrid sea.[d] Something bumped into me—something soft and plump. It must have been the rats; the viscous, gelatinous, ravenous army that feast on

---

[a] shewed] showed A, B, C
[b] Capt.] Captain B
[c] centre] center A, B, C
[d] sea.] sea. ¶ A, B, C

the dead and the living. . . . Why shouldn't rats eat a de la Poer as a de la Poer eats forbidden things? . . . The war ate my boy, damn them all . . . and the Yanks ate Carfax with flames and burnt Grandsire Delapore and the secret. . . . No, no, I tell you, I am *not* that daemon swineherd in the twilit grotto! It was *not* Edward Norrys' fat face on that flabby,[a] fungous thing! Who says I am a de la Poer? He lived, but my boy died! . . . Shall a Norrys hold the lands of a de la Poer? . . . It's voodoo, I tell you . . . that spotted snake . . . Curse you, Thornton, I'll teach you to faint at what my family do! . . . 'Sblood, thou stinkard, I'll learn ye how to gust . . . wolde ye swynke me thilke wys? . . . *Magna Mater! Magna Mater! . . . Atys . . . Dia ad aghaidh 's ad aodann*[b] . . . *agus bas dunach ort! Dhonas 's dholas ort, agus leat-sa! . . . Ungl . . . ungl*[c] . . . *rrrlh*[d] . . . *chchch* . . .

That is what they say I said when they found me in the blackness after three hours; found me crouching in the blackness over the plump, half-eaten body of Capt.[e] Norrys, with my own cat leaping and tearing at my throat. Now they have blown up Exham Priory, taken my Nigger-Man away from me, and shut me into this barred room at Hanwell with fearful whispers about my heredity and experiences.[f] Thornton is in the next room, but they prevent me from talking to him. They are trying, too, to suppress most of the facts concerning the priory. When I speak of poor Norrys they accuse me of a hideous thing, but they must know that I did not do it. They must know it was the rats; the slithering,[g] scurrying rats whose scampering will never let me sleep; the daemon rats that race behind the padding in this room and beckon me down to greater horrors than I have ever known; the rats they can never hear; the rats, the rats in the walls.[h]

[a] flabby,] flabby C
[b] *aodann*] *aodaun* A, B, C
[c] *ungl*] *nngl* A, B
[d] *rrrlh*] *rrlh* C
[e] Capt.] Captain B
[f] experiences.] experience. C
[g] slithering,] slithering C
[h] walls.] walls! A, B

The Unnamable

We were sitting on a dilapidated seventeenth-century tomb in the late afternoon of an autumn day at the old burying-ground[a] in Arkham, and speculating about the unnamable. Looking toward the giant willow in the centre of[b] the cemetery, whose trunk has[c] nearly engulfed an ancient, illegible slab, I had made a fantastic remark about the spectral and unmentionable nourishment which the colossal roots must be sucking in[d] from that hoary, charnel earth; when my friend chided me for such nonsense and told me that since no interments had occurred there for over a century, nothing could possibly exist to nourish the tree in other than an ordinary manner. Besides, he added, my constant talk about "unnamable" and "unmentionable" things was a very puerile device, quite in keeping with my lowly standing as an author. I was too fond of ending my stories with sights or sounds which paralysed[e] my heroes' faculties and left them without courage, words, or associations to tell what they had experienced. We know things, he said, only through our five senses or our religious intuitions; wherefore it is quite impossible to refer to any object or spectacle which cannot be clearly depicted by the solid definitions of fact or the correct doctrines of theology—

Editor's Note: In the absence of a manuscript, we are reliant on the only text published in HPL's lifetime: *Weird Tales* (July 1925). This appearance seems to have followed HPL's presumed T.Ms. accurately enough—more so than later stories published in the magazine. The Arkham House editions follow the *Weird Tales* appearance, making some additional errors.

Texts: A = *Weird Tales* 6, No. 1 (July 1925): 78–82; B = *Dagon and Other Macabre Tales* (Arkham House, 1965), 196–203. Copy-text: A.

[a] burying-ground] burying ground A, B
[b] the centre of] the center of A; *om.* B
[c] has] had B
[d] in] *om.* B
[e] paralysed] paralyzed A, B

preferably those of the Congregationalists, with whatever modifications tradition and Sir Arthur Conan Doyle may supply.

With this friend, Joel Manton, I had often languidly disputed. He was principal of the East High School, born and bred in Boston and sharing New England's self-satisfied deafness to the delicate overtones of life. It was his view that only our normal, objective experiences possess any aesthetic[a] significance, and that it is the province of the artist not so much to rouse strong emotion by action, ecstasy, and astonishment, as to maintain a placid interest and appreciation by accurate, detailed transcripts of every-day[b] affairs. Especially did he object to my preoccupation with the mystical and the unexplained; for although believing in the supernatural much more fully than I, he would not admit that it is sufficiently commonplace for literary treatment. That a mind can find its greatest pleasure in escapes from the daily treadmill, and in original and dramatic re-combinations of images usually thrown by habit and fatigue into the hackneyed patterns of actual existence, was something virtually incredible to his clear, practical, and logical intellect. With him all things and feelings had fixed dimensions, properties, causes, and effects; and although he vaguely knew that the mind sometimes holds visions and sensations of far less geometrical, classifiable, and workable nature, he believed himself justified in drawing an arbitrary line and ruling out of court all that cannot be experienced and understood by the average citizen. Besides, he was almost sure that nothing can be really "unnamable".[c] It didn't sound sensible to him.

Though I well realised[d] the futility of imaginative and metaphysical arguments against the complacency of an orthodox sun-dweller, something in the scene of this afternoon colloquy moved me to more than usual contentiousness. The crumbling slate slabs, the patriarchal trees, and the centuried gambrel roofs of the witch-haunted old town that stretched around, all combined to rouse my spirit in defence[e] of

[a] aesthetic] esthetic A, B
[b] every-day] everyday B
[c] "unnamable".] "unnamable." B
[d] realised] realized A, B
[e] defence] defense A, B

my work; and I was soon carrying my thrusts into the enemy's own country. It was not, indeed, difficult to begin a counter-attack, for I knew that Joel Manton actually half clung to many old-wives' superstitions which sophisticated people had long outgrown; beliefs in the appearance of dying persons at distant places, and in the impressions left by old faces on the windows through which they have[a] gazed all their lives. To credit these whisperings of rural grandmothers, I now insisted, argued a faith in the existence of spectral substances on the earth apart from and subsequent to their material counterparts. It argued a capability of believing in phenomena beyond all normal notions; for if a dead man can transmit his visible or tangible image half across the world, or down the stretch of the centuries, how can it be absurd to suppose that deserted houses are full of queer sentient things, or that old graveyards teem with the terrible, unbodied intelligence of generations? And since spirit, in order to cause all the manifestations attributed to it, cannot be limited by any of the laws of matter; why is it extravagant to imagine psychically living dead things in shapes—or absences of shapes—which must for human spectators be utterly and appallingly "unnamable"? "Common sense" in reflecting on these subjects, I assured my friend with some warmth, is merely a stupid absence of imagination and mental flexibility.

Twilight had now approached, but neither of us felt any wish to cease speaking. Manton seemed unimpressed by my arguments, and eager to refute them, having that confidence in his own opinions which had doubtless caused his success as a teacher; whilst I was too sure of my ground to fear defeat. The dusk fell, and lights faintly gleamed in some of the distant windows, but we did not move. Our seat on the tomb was very comfortable, and I knew that my prosaic friend would not mind the cavernous rift in the ancient, root-disturbed brickwork close behind us, or the utter blackness of the spot brought by the intervention of a tottering, deserted seventeenth-century house between us and the nearest lighted road. There in the dark, upon that riven tomb by the deserted house, we talked on about the "unnamable",[b] and after my friend had finished his scoffing I told him of the awful evidence

[a] have] had B
[b] "unnamable",] "unnamable," B

behind the story at which he had scoffed the most.

My tale had been called "The Attic Window",[a] and appeared in the January, 1922, issue of *Whispers*. In a good many places, especially the South and the Pacific coast, they took the magazines off the stands at the complaints of silly milksops; but New England didn't get the thrill and merely shrugged its shoulders at my extravagance. The thing, it was averred, was biologically impossible to start with; merely another of those crazy country mutterings which Cotton Mather had been gullible enough to dump into his chaotic "Magnalia Christi Americana",[b] and so poorly authenticated that even he had not ventured to name the locality where the horror occurred. And as to the way I amplified the bare jotting of the old mystic—that was quite impossible, and characteristic of a flighty and notional scribbler! Mather had indeed told of the thing as being born, but nobody but a cheap sensationalist would think of having it grow up, look into people's windows at night, and be hidden in the attic of a house, in flesh and in spirit, till someone saw it at the window centuries later and couldn't describe what it was that turned his hair grey.[c] All this was flagrant trashiness, and my friend Manton was not slow to insist on that fact. Then I told him what I had found in an old diary kept between 1706 and 1723, unearthed among family papers not a mile from where we were sitting; that, and the certain reality of the scars on my ancestor's chest and back which the diary described. I told him, too, of the fears of others in that region, and how they were whispered down for generations; and how no mythical madness came to the boy who in 1793 entered an abandoned house to examine certain traces suspected to be there.

It had been an eldritch thing—no wonder sensitive students shudder at the Puritan age in Massachusetts. So little is known of what went on beneath the surface—so little, yet such a ghastly festering as it bubbles up putrescently in occasional ghoulish glimpses. The witchcraft terror is a horrible ray of light on what was stewing in men's crushed brains, but even that is a trifle. There was no beauty;[d] no freedom—we

[a] "The Attic Window",] *The Attic Window,* B

[b] "Magnalia Christi Americana",] *Magnalia Christi Americana,* B

[c] grey.] gray. A, B

[d] beauty;] beauty: B

can see that from the architectural and household remains, and the poisonous sermons of the cramped divines. And inside that rusted iron strait-jacket[a] lurked gibbering hideousness, perversion, and diabolism. Here, truly, was the apotheosis of the unnamable.

Cotton Mather, in that daemoniac[b] sixth book which no one should read after dark, minced no words as he flung forth his anathema. Stern as a Jewish prophet, and laconically unamazed as none since his day could be, he told of the beast that had brought forth what was more than beast but less than man—the thing with the blemished eye—and of the screaming drunken wretch that they hanged for having such an eye. This much he baldly told, yet without a hint of what came after. Perhaps he did not know, or perhaps he knew and did not dare to tell. Others knew, but did not dare to tell—there is no public hint of why they whispered about the lock on the door to the attic stairs in the house of a childless, broken, embittered old man who had put up a blank slate slab by an avoided grave, although one may trace enough evasive legends to curdle the thinnest blood.

It is all in that ancestral diary I found; all the hushed innuendoes and furtive tales of things with a blemished eye seen at windows in the night or in deserted meadows near the woods. Something had caught my ancestor on a dark valley road, leaving him with marks of horns on his chest and of ape-like[c] claws on his back; and when they looked for prints in the trampled dust they found the mixed marks of split hooves and vaguely anthropoid paws. Once a post-rider said he saw an old man chasing and calling to a frightful loping, nameless thing on Meadow Hill in the thinly moonlit hours before dawn, and many believed him. Certainly, there was strange talk one night in 1710 when the childless, broken old man was buried in the crypt behind his own house in sight of the blank slate slab. They never unlocked that attic door, but left the whole house as it was, dreaded and deserted. When noises came from it, they whispered and shivered; and hoped that the lock on that attic door was strong. Then they stopped hoping when the horror occurred at the parsonage, leaving not a soul alive or in one

[a] strait-jacket] straitjacket A, B
[b] daemoniac] demoniac A, B
[c] ape-like] apelike A, B

piece. With the years the legends take on a spectral character—I suppose the thing, if it was a living thing, must have died. The memory had lingered hideously—all the more hideous because it was so secret.

During this narration my friend Manton had become very silent, and I saw that my words had impressed him. He did not laugh as I paused, but asked quite seriously about the boy who went mad in 1793, and who had presumably been the hero of my fiction. I told him why the boy had gone to that shunned, deserted house, and remarked that he ought to be interested, since he believed that windows retained latent images of those who had sat at them. The boy had gone to look at the windows of that horrible attic, because of tales of things seen behind them, and had come back screaming maniacally.

Manton remained thoughtful as I said this, but gradually reverted to his analytical mood. He granted for the sake of argument that some unnatural monster had really existed, but reminded me that even the most morbid perversion of Nature[a] need not be *unnamable* or scientifically indescribable. I admired his clearness and persistence, and added some further revelations I had collected among the old people. Those later spectral legends, I made plain, related to monstrous apparitions more frightful than anything organic could be; apparitions of gigantic bestial forms sometimes visible and sometimes only tangible, which floated about on moonless nights and haunted the old house, the crypt behind it, and the grave where a sapling had sprouted beside an illegible slab. Whether or not such apparitions had ever gored or smothered people to death, as told in uncorroborated traditions, they had produced a strong and consistent impression; and were yet darkly feared by very aged natives, though largely forgotten by the last two generations—perhaps dying for lack of being thought about. Moreover, so far as aesthetic[b] theory was involved, if the psychic emanations of human creatures be grotesque distortions, what coherent representation could express or portray so gibbous and infamous a nebulosity as the spectre[c] of a malign, chaotic perversion,

---

[a] Nature] nature A, B

[b] aesthetic] esthetic A, B

[c] spectre] specter A, B

itself a morbid blasphemy against Nature? Moulded[a] by the dead brain of a hybrid nightmare, would not such a vaporous terror constitute in all loathsome truth the exquisitely, the shriekingly *unnamable?*

The hour must now have grown very late. A singularly noiseless bat brushed by me, and I believe it touched Manton also, for although I could not see him I felt him raise his arm. Presently he spoke.

"But is that house with the attic window still standing and deserted?"

"Yes," I answered. "I have seen it."

"And did you find anything there—in the attic or anywhere else?"

"There were some bones up under the eaves. They may have been what that boy saw—if he was sensitive he wouldn't have needed anything in the window-glass to unhinge him. If they all came from the same object it must have been an hysterical, delirious monstrosity. It would have been blasphemous to leave such bones in the world, so I went back with a sack and took them to the tomb behind the house. There was an opening where I could dump them in. Don't think I was a fool—you ought to have seen that skull. It had four-inch horns, but a face and jaw something like yours and mine."

At last I could feel a real shiver run through Manton, who had moved very near. But his curiosity was undeterred.

"And what about the window-panes?"[b]

"They were all gone. One window had lost its entire frame, and in the other[c] there was not a trace of glass in the little diamond apertures. They were that kind—the old lattice windows that went out of use before 1700. I don't believe they've had any glass for a hundred years or more—maybe the boy broke 'em if he got that far; the legend doesn't say."

Manton was reflecting again.

"I'd like to see that house, Carter. Where is it? Glass or no glass, I must explore it a little. And the tomb where you put those bones, and the other grave without an inscription—the whole thing must be a bit terrible."

[a] Nature? Moulded] nature? Molded A, B
[b] window-panes?"] window-/panes?" A
[c] in the other] in all the others B

"You did see it—until it got dark."

My friend was more wrought upon than I had suspected, for at this touch of harmless theatricalism he started neurotically away from me and actually cried out with a sort of gulping gasp which released a strain of previous repression. It was an odd cry, and all the more terrible because it was answered. For as it was still echoing, I heard a creaking sound through the pitchy blackness, and knew that a lattice window was opening in that accursed old house beside us. And because all the other frames were long since fallen, I knew that it was the grisly glassless frame of that daemoniac[a] attic window.

Then came a noxious rush of noisome, frigid air from that same dreaded direction, followed by a piercing shriek just beside me on that shocking rifted tomb of man and monster. In another instant I was knocked from my gruesome bench by the devilish threshing of some unseen entity of titanic size but undetermined nature; knocked sprawling on the root-clutched mould[b] of that abhorrent graveyard, while from the tomb came such a stifled uproar of gasping and whirring that my fancy peopled the rayless gloom with Miltonic legions of the misshapen damned. There was a vortex of withering, ice-cold wind, and then the rattle of loose bricks and plaster; but I had mercifully fainted before I could learn what it meant.

Manton, though smaller than I, is more resilient; for we opened our eyes at almost the same instant, despite his greater injuries. Our couches were side by side, and we knew in a few seconds that we were in St. Mary's Hospital. Attendants were grouped about in tense curiosity, eager to aid our memory by telling us how we came there, and we soon heard of the farmer who had found us at noon in a lonely field beyond Meadow Hill, a mile from the old burying-ground,[c] on a spot where an ancient slaughterhouse is reputed to have stood. Manton had two malignant wounds in the chest, and some less severe cuts or gougings in the back. I was not so seriously hurt, but was covered with welts and contusions of the most bewildering character, including the print of a split hoof. It was plain that Manton knew more

[a] daemoniac] demoniac A, B
[b] mould] mold A, B
[c] burying-ground,] burying ground, A, B

than I, but he told nothing to the puzzled and interested physicians till he had learned what our injuries were. Then he said we were the victims of a vicious bull—though the animal was a difficult thing to place and account for.

After the doctors and nurses had left, I whispered an awestruck[a] question:

"Good God, Manton, but *what was it?* Those scars—*was it like that?*"

And I was too dazed to exult when he whispered back a thing I had half expected—

"*No*[b]—*it wasn't that way at all.* It was everywhere—a gelatin—a slime—yet it had shapes, a thousand shapes of horror beyond all memory. There were eyes—and a blemish. It was the pit—the maelstrom—the ultimate abomination. Carter, *it was the unnamable!*"

[a] awestruck] awe struck B
[b] "*No*] "No B

The Festival

"Efficiunt Daemones, ut quae non sunt, sic tamen quasi sint, conspicienda hominibus exhibeant."[a]

—Lactantius.[b]

I was far from home, and the spell of the eastern sea was upon me. In the twilight I heard it pounding on the rocks, and I knew it lay just over the hill where the twisting willows writhed against the clearing sky and the first stars of evening. And because my fathers had called me to the old town beyond, I pushed on through the shallow, new-fallen snow along the road that soared lonely up to where Aldebaran twinkled among the trees; on toward the very ancient town I had never seen but often dreamed of.

It was the Yuletide, that men call Christmas[c] though they know in their hearts it is older than Bethlehem and Babylon, older than Memphis and mankind. It was the Yuletide, and I had come at last to the ancient sea town where my people had dwelt and kept festival in the elder time when festival was forbidden; where also they had commanded their

---

Editor's Note: The story was first published in *Weird Tales* (January 1925). At some subsequent date a new T.Ms. was prepared; this T.Ms. was not prepared by HPL, but bears clear revisions from the first *Weird Tales* appearance. These revisions appear in the second *Weird Tales* appearance (October 1933), but it is likely that HPL merely supplied revisions on proofs rather than sending in the T.Ms. (which in fact may even date after the second *Weird Tales* appearance). The Arkham House editions follow the T.Ms. but make a number of errors in the process.

Texts: A = *Weird Tales* 5, No. 1 (January 1925): 169–74; B = T.Ms. (JHL); C = *Weird Tales* 22, No. 4 (October 1933): 519–20, 522–28; D = *Dagon and Other Macabre Tales* (Arkham House, 1965), 187–95. Copy-text: B.

[a] "Efficiunt Daemones, . . . exhibeant."] "Efficiunt daemones, . . . exhibeant." A; *"Efficiunt daemones, . . . exhibeant."* C; *Efficiut Daemones, . . . exhibeant.* D
[b] *—Lactantius.*] —Lactantius. A, C; —LACTANTIUS D
[c] Christmas] Christmas, A, C

sons to keep festival once every century, that the memory of primal secrets might not be forgotten. Mine were an old people, and were[a] old even when this land was settled three hundred years before. And they were strange, because they had come as dark[b] furtive folk from opiate southern gardens of orchids, and spoken another tongue before they learnt the tongue of the blue-eyed fishers. And now they were scattered, and shared only the rituals of mysteries that none living could understand. I was the only one who came back that night to the old fishing town as legend bade, for only the poor and the lonely remember.

Then beyond the hill's crest I saw Kingsport outspread frostily in the gloaming; snowy Kingsport with its ancient vanes and steeples, ridgepoles and chimney-pots,[c] wharves and small bridges, willow-trees[d] and graveyards; endless labyrinths of steep, narrow, crooked streets, and dizzy church-crowned central peak that time durst not touch; ceaseless mazes of colonial houses piled and scattered at all angles and levels like a child's disordered blocks; antiquity hovering on grey[e] wings over winter-whitened gables and gambrel roofs; fanlights and small-paned windows one by one gleaming out in the cold dusk to join Orion and the archaic stars.[f] And against the rotting wharves the sea pounded; the secretive, immemorial sea out of which the people had come in the elder time.

Beside the road at its crest a still higher summit rose, bleak and windswept,[g] and I saw that it was a burying-ground where black gravestones stuck ghoulishly through the snow like the decayed fingernails of a gigantic corpse. The printless road was very lonely, and sometimes I thought I heard a distant horrible creaking as of a gibbet in the wind. They had hanged four kinsmen of mine for witchcraft in 1692, but I did not know just where.

As the road wound down the seaward slope I listened for the merry sounds of a village at evening, but did not hear them. Then I

[a] and were] *om.* A, C
[b] dark] dark, A, C
[c] chimney-pots,] chimneypots, A, C
[d] willow-trees] willow trees A, C
[e] grey] gray A, C
[f] roofs; . . . stars.] roofs. A
[g] windswept,] wind-/swept, A; wind-swept, C

thought of the season, and felt that these old Puritan folk might well have Christmas customs strange to me, and full of silent hearthside prayer. So after that I did not listen for merriment or look for wayfarers, but[a] kept on down past the hushed[b] lighted farmhouses and shadowy stone walls to where the signs of ancient shops and sea-taverns[c] creaked in the salt breeze, and the grotesque knockers of pillared doorways glistened along deserted,[d] unpaved lanes in the light of little, curtained windows.

I had seen maps of the town, and knew where to find the home of my people. It was told that I should be known and welcomed, for village legend lives long; so I hastened through Back Street to Circle Court, and across the fresh snow on the one full flagstone pavement in the town, to where Green Lane leads off behind the Market House. The old maps still held good, and I had no trouble; though at Arkham they must have lied when they said the trolleys ran to this place, since I saw not a wire overhead. Snow would have hid the rails in any case.[e] I was glad I had chosen to walk, for the[f] white village had seemed very beautiful from the hill; and now I was eager to knock at the door of my people, the seventh house on the left in Green Lane, with an ancient peaked roof and jutting second story, all built before 1650.

There were lights inside the house when I came upon it, and I saw from the diamond window-panes that it must have been kept very close to its antique state. The upper part overhung the narrow[g] grass-grown street and nearly met the overhanging[h] part of the house opposite, so that I was almost in a tunnel, with the low stone doorstep wholly free from snow. There was no sidewalk, but many houses had high doors reached by double flights of steps with iron railings. It was an odd scene, and because I was strange to New England I had never known its like before. Though it pleased me, I would have relished it

---

[a] but] *om.* D
[b] hushed] hushed, A, C
[c] sea-taverns] sea taverns A, B, C, D
[d] deserted,] deserted D
[e] The old . . . case.] *om.* A
[f] walk, for the] walk. The A
[g] narrow] narrow, A, C
[h] overhanging] over-hanging D

better if there had been footprints in the snow, and people in the streets, and a few windows without drawn curtains.

When I sounded the archaic iron knocker I was half afraid. Some fear had been gathering in me, perhaps because of the strangeness of my heritage, and the bleakness of the evening, and the queerness of the silence in that aged town of curious customs. And when my knock was answered I was fully afraid, because I had not heard any footsteps before the door creaked open. But I was not afraid long, for the gowned, slippered old man in the doorway had a bland face that reassured me; and though he made signs that he was dumb, he wrote a quaint and ancient welcome with the stylus and wax tablet he carried.

He beckoned me into a low, candle-lit room with massive exposed rafters and dark, stiff, sparse furniture of the seventeenth century.[a] The past was vivid there, for not an attribute was missing. There was a cavernous fireplace and a spinning-wheel at which a bent old woman in loose wrapper and deep poke-bonnet sat back toward me, silently spinning despite the festive season. An indefinite dampness seemed upon the place, and I marvelled[b] that no fire should be blazing. The high-backed settle faced the row of curtained windows at the left, and seemed to be occupied, though I was not sure. I did not like everything about what I saw, and felt again the fear I had had. This fear grew stronger from what had before lessened it, for the more I looked at the old man's bland face[c] the more its very blandness terrified me. The eyes never moved, and the skin was too[d] like wax. Finally I was sure it was not a face at all, but a fiendishly cunning mask. But the flabby hands, curiously gloved, wrote genially on the tablet and told me I must wait a while before I could be led to the place of the[e] festival.

Pointing to a chair, table, and pile of books, the old man now left the room; and when I sat down to read I saw that the books were hoary and mouldy,[f] and that they included old Morryster's wild

---

[a] seventeenth century.] Seventeenth Century. C
[b] marvelled] marveled A, C
[c] face] face, A, C
[d] too] too much D
[e] the] *om.* A, C
[f] mouldy,] moldy, A, C

"Marvells of Science",[a] the terrible "Saducismus Triumphatus"[b] of Joseph Glanvill,[c] published in 1681, the shocking "Daemonolatreia"[d] of Remigius, printed in 1595 at Lyons, and worst of all, the unmentionable "Necronomicon"[e] of the mad Arab Abdul Alhazred, in Olaus Wormius' forbidden Latin translation;[f] a book which I had never seen, but of which I had heard monstrous things whispered. No one spoke to me, but I could hear the creaking of signs in the wind outside, and the whir of the wheel as the bonneted old woman continued her silent spinning, spinning.[g] I thought the room and the books and the people very morbid and disquieting, but because an old tradition of my fathers[h] had summoned me to strange feastings, I resolved to expect queer things. So I tried to read, and soon became tremblingly absorbed by something I found in that accursed "Necronomicon";[i] a thought and a legend too hideous for sanity or consciousness. But[j] I disliked it when I fancied I heard the closing of one of the windows that the settle faced, as if it had been stealthily opened. It had seemed to follow a whirring that was not of the old woman's spinning-wheel. This was not much, though, for the old woman was spinning very hard, and the aged clock had been striking. After that I lost the feeling that there were persons on the settle, and was reading intently and shudderingly when the old man came back booted and dressed in a loose antique costume, and sat down on that very bench, so that I could not see him. It was certainly nervous waiting, and the blasphemous book in my hands made it doubly so. When eleven[k] struck, however, the old man stood up, glided to a

<hr>

[a] "Marvells of Science",] "Marvells of Science," A; *Marvells of Science,* C, D
[b] "Saducismus Triumphatus"] *Saducismus Triumphatus* C, D
[c] Glanvill,] Glanvil, A, C, D
[d] "Daemonolatreia"] *Daemonolatreia* C, D
[e] "Necronomicon"] *Necronomicon* C, D
[f] translation;] translation: A, C
[g] spinning.] spinning. ¶ A, B, C
[h] fathers] father's A, C
[i] "Necronomicon";] *Necronomicon;* C, D
[j] consciousness. But] consciousness, But B; consciousness, but D
[k] eleven] 11 o'clock A

massive carved chest in a corner, and got two hooded cloaks;[a] one of which he donned, and the other of which he draped round the old woman, who was ceasing her monotonous spinning. Then they both started for the outer door; the woman lamely creeping, and the old man, after picking up the very book I had been reading, beckoning me as he drew his hood over that unmoving face or mask.

We went out into the moonless and tortuous network of that incredibly ancient town; went out as the lights in the curtained windows disappeared one by one, and the Dog Star leered at the throng of cowled, cloaked figures that poured silently from every doorway and formed monstrous processions up this street and that, past the creaking signs and antediluvian gables, the thatched roofs and[b] diamond-paned windows; threading precipitous lanes where decaying houses overlapped and crumbled together, gliding across open courts and churchyards where the bobbing lanthorns[c] made eldritch drunken constellations.

Amid these hushed throngs I followed my voiceless guides; jostled by elbows that seemed preternaturally soft, and pressed by chests and stomachs that seemed abnormally pulpy; but seeing never a face and hearing never a word. Up, up, up[d] the eery columns slithered, and I saw that all the travellers[e] were converging as they flowed near a sort of focus of crazy alleys at the top of a high hill in the centre[f] of the town, where perched a great white church. I had seen it from the road's crest when I looked at Kingsport in the new dusk, and it had made me shiver because Aldebaran had seemed to balance itself a moment on the ghostly spire.

There was an open space around the church; partly a churchyard with spectral shafts, and partly a half-paved square swept nearly bare of snow by the wind, and lined with unwholesomely archaic houses having peaked roofs and overhanging gables. Death-fires danced over the tombs, revealing gruesome vistas, though queerly failing to cast any shadows. Past the churchyard, where there were no houses, I could see

[a] cloaks;] cloaks, A, C
[b] and] and the A, C
[c] lanthorns] lanthems A
[d] up] up, A, C, D
[e] travellers] travelers A, C
[f] centre] center A, C

over the hill's summit and watch the glimmer of stars on the harbour,[a] though the town was invisible in the dark. Only once in a while a lanthorn[b] bobbed horribly through serpentine alleys on its way to overtake the throng that was now slipping speechlessly into the church.[c] I waited till the crowd had oozed into the black doorway, and till all the stragglers had followed. The old man was pulling at my sleeve,[d] but I was determined to be the last. Then finally I went, the sinister man and the old spinning woman before me.[e] Crossing the threshold into that[f] swarming temple of unknown darkness, I turned once to look at the outside world as the churchyard phosphorescence cast a sickly glow on the hilltop pavement. And as I did so I shuddered. For though the wind had not left much snow, a few patches did remain on the path near the door; and in that fleeting backward look it seemed to my troubled eyes[g] that they bore no mark of passing feet, not even mine.

The church was scarce lighted by all the lanthorns[h] that had entered it, for most of the throng had already vanished. They had streamed up the aisle between the high white[i] pews to the trap-door[j] of the vaults which yawned loathsomely open just before the pulpit, and were now squirming noiselessly in. I followed dumbly down the footworn[k] steps and into the dank,[l] suffocating crypt. The tail of that sinuous line of night-marchers seemed very horrible, and as I saw them wriggling into a venerable tomb they seemed more horrible still. Then I noticed that the tomb's floor had an aperture down which the throng was sliding, and in a moment we were all descending an

[a] harbour,] harbor, A, C
[b] lanthorn] lanthern A
[c] church.] church. ¶ A, C
[d] sleeve,] seeve, D
[e] Then . . . me.] om. D
[f] that] the D
[g] eyes] eye A, C
[h] lanthorns] lantherns A
[i] white] om. D
[j] trap-door] trapdoor A
[k] footworn] foot-/worn B
[l] dank,] dark, D

ominous staircase of rough-hewn stone; a narrow spiral staircase damp and peculiarly odorous, that wound endlessly down into the bowels of the hill[a] past monotonous walls of dripping stone blocks and crumbling mortar. It was a silent, shocking descent, and I observed after a horrible interval that the walls and steps were changing in nature, as if chiselled[b] out of the solid rock. What mainly troubled me was that the myriad footfalls made no sound and set up no echoes.[c] After more aeons[d] of descent I saw some side passages or burrows leading from unknown recesses of blackness to this shaft of nighted mystery. Soon they became excessively numerous, like impious catacombs of nameless menace; and their pungent odour[e] of decay grew quite unbearable. I knew we must have passed down through the mountain and beneath the earth of Kingsport itself, and I shivered that a town should be so aged and maggoty with subterranean evil.

Then I saw the lurid shimmering of pale light, and heard the insidious lapping of sunless waters. Again I shivered, for I did not like the things that the night had brought, and wished bitterly that no forefather had summoned me to this primal rite. As the steps and the passage grew broader, I heard another sound, the thin, whining mockery of a feeble flute; and suddenly there spread out before me the boundless vista of an inner world—a vast fungous shore litten by a belching column of sick greenish flame and washed by a wide oily river that flowed from abysses frightful and unsuspected to join the blackest gulfs of immemorial ocean.

Fainting and gasping, I looked at that unhallowed Erebus of titan toadstools, leprous fire,[f] and slimy water, and saw the cloaked throngs forming a semicircle around the blazing pillar. It was the Yule-rite, older than man and fated to survive him; the primal rite of the solstice and of spring's promise beyond the snows; the rite of fire and evergreen, light and music. And in that Stygian[g] grotto I saw them do the rite, and

---

[a] hill] hill, A, C
[b] chiselled] chiseled A, C
[c] echoes.] echoes. ¶ A, C
[d] aeons] eons A, C
[e] odour] odor A, C
[f] fire,] fire A, B, C, D
[g] that Stygian] that stygian B; the stygian D

adore the sick pillar of flame, and throw into the water handfuls gouged out of the viscous vegetation which glittered green in the chlorotic glare. I saw this, and I saw something amorphously squatted far away from the light, piping noisomely on a flute; and as the thing piped I thought I heard noxious muffled flutterings in the foetid[a] darkness where I could not see. But what frightened me most was that flaming column; spouting volcanically from depths profound and inconceivable, casting no shadows as healthy flame should, and coating the nitrous stone above[b] with a nasty, venomous verdigris. For in all that seething combustion no warmth lay, but only the clamminess of death and corruption.

The man who had brought me now squirmed to a point directly beside the hideous flame, and made stiff ceremonial motions to the semicircle he faced. At certain stages of the ritual they did grovelling[c] obeisance, especially when he held above his head that abhorrent "Necronomicon"[d] he had taken with him; and I shared all the obeisances because I had been summoned to this festival by the writings of my forefathers. Then the old man made a signal to the half-seen flute-player in the darkness, which player thereupon changed its feeble drone to a scarce louder drone in another key; precipitating as it did so a horror unthinkable and unexpected. At this horror I sank nearly to the lichened earth, transfixed with a dread not of this nor[e] any world, but only of the mad spaces between the stars.

Out of the unimaginable blackness beyond the gangrenous glare of that cold flame, out of the tartarean leagues through which that oily river rolled uncanny, unheard, and unsuspected, there flopped rhythmically a horde of tame, trained, hybrid winged things that no sound eye could ever wholly grasp, or sound brain ever wholly remember. They were not altogether crows, nor moles, nor buzzards, nor ants, nor vampire bats, nor decomposed human beings;[f] but

[a] foetid] fetid A, C

[b] above] *om.* D

[c] grovelling] groveling A, C

[d] "Necronomicon"] *Necronomicon* C, D

[e] nor] or D

[f] beings;] beings, A, C

something I cannot[a] and must not recall. They flopped limply along, half with their webbed feet and half with their membraneous[b] wings; and as they reached the throng of celebrants the cowled figures seized and mounted them, and rode off one by one along the reaches of that unlighted river, into pits and galleries of panic where poison springs feed frightful and undiscoverable cataracts.

The old spinning woman had gone with the throng, and the old man remained only because I had refused when he motioned me to seize an animal and ride like the rest. I saw when I staggered to my feet that the amorphous flute-player had rolled out of sight, but that two of the beasts were patiently standing by. As I hung back, the old man produced his stylus and tablet and wrote that he was the true deputy of my fathers who had founded the Yule worship in this ancient place; that it had been decreed I should come back,[c] and that the most secret mysteries were yet to be performed. He wrote this in a very ancient hand, and when I still hesitated he pulled from his loose robe a seal ring and a watch, both with my family arms, to prove that he was what he said. But it was a hideous proof, because I knew from old papers that that watch had been buried with my great-great-great-great-grandfather in 1698.

Presently the old man drew back his hood and pointed to the family resemblance in his face, but I only shuddered,[d] because I was sure that the face was merely a devilish waxen mask. The flopping animals were now scratching restlessly at the lichens, and I saw that the old man was nearly as restless himself. When one of the things began to waddle and edge away, he turned quickly to stop it; so that the suddenness of his motion dislodged the waxen mask from what should have been his head. And then, because that nightmare's position barred me from the stone staircase down which we had come, I flung myself into the oily underground river that bubbled somewhere to the caves of the sea; flung myself into that putrescent juice of earth's inner

[a] cannot] can not C
[b] membraneous] membranous A, B, C, D
[c] back,] back; A, C
[d] shuddered,] suddered, D

horrors before the madness of my screams could bring down upon me all the charnel legions these pest-gulfs might conceal.

At the hospital they told me I had been found half-frozen in Kingsport Harbour[a] at dawn, clinging to the drifting spar that accident sent to save me. They told me I had taken the wrong fork of the hill road the night before, and fallen over the cliffs at Orange Point;[b] a thing they deduced[c] from prints found in the snow. There was nothing I could say, because everything was wrong. Everything was wrong, with the broad window shewing[d] a sea of roofs in which only about one in five was ancient, and the sound of trolleys and motors in the streets below. They insisted that this was Kingsport, and I could not deny it.[e] When I went delirious at hearing that the hospital stood near the old churchyard on Central Hill, they sent me to St. Mary's Hospital in Arkham, where I could have better care. I liked it there, for the doctors were broad-minded,[f] and even lent me their influence in obtaining the carefully sheltered copy of Alhazred's objectionable "Necronomicon"[g] from the library of Miskatonic University. They said something about a "psychosis",[h] and agreed I had better get any[i] harassing obsessions off my mind.

So I read again[j] that hideous chapter, and shuddered doubly because it was indeed not new to me. I had seen it before, let footprints tell what they might; and where it was I had seen it were best forgotten. There was no one—in waking hours—who could remind me of it; but my dreams are filled with terror, because of phrases I dare not quote. I dare quote only one paragraph, put into such English as I can make from the awkward Low Latin.

---

[a] Harbour] Harbor A, C
[b] Point;] Point— A, C
[c] deduced] deducted A
[d] window shewing] window showing A, B, C; windows showing D
[e] it.] it. ¶ A, C
[f] broad-minded,] broadminded, A
[g] "Necronomicon"] *Necronomicon* C, D
[h] "psychosis",] "psychosis," A
[i] any] my A
[j] again] *om.* D

"The nethermost caverns," wrote the mad Arab, "are not for the fathoming of eyes that see; for their marvels are strange and terrific. Cursed the ground where dead thoughts live new and oddly bodied, and evil the mind that is held by no head. Wisely did Ibn Schacabac say,[a] that happy is the tomb where no wizard hath lain, and happy the town at night whose wizards are all[b] ashes. For it is of old rumour[c] that the soul of the devil-bought hastes not from his charnel clay, but fats and instructs *the very worm that gnaws;* till out of corruption horrid life springs, and the dull scavengers of earth wax crafty to vex it and swell monstrous to plague it. Great holes secretly are digged where earth's pores ought to suffice, and things have learnt to walk that ought to crawl."[d]

[a] Schacabac say,] Schacabac say A; Schacabao say, D
[b] all] all in A, C
[c] rumour] rumor A, C
[d] "The nethermost . . . crawl."] *not printed as indented text in A, C*

Under the Pyramids

(with Harry Houdini)

I.[a]

Mystery attracts mystery. Ever since the wide appearance of my name as a performer of unexplained feats, I have encountered strange narratives and events which my calling has led people to link with my interests and activities. Some of these have been trivial and irrelevant, some deeply dramatic and absorbing, some productive of weird and perilous experiences,[b] and some involving me in extensive scientific and historical research. Many of these matters I have told and shall continue to tell freely; but there is one of which I speak with great reluctance, and which I am now relating only after a session of grilling persuasion from the publishers of this magazine, who had heard vague

---

Editor's Note: HPL's A.Ms. (long in the hands of Samuel Loveman) has recently surfaced and is currently being offered for sale by L. W. Currey; but I have not been able to examine the ms. In its absence, we are reliant on the only publication in HPL's lifetime: *Weird Tales* (May–June–July 1924). Regrettably, the Arkham House editions and all subsequent texts prior to 1986 followed the second *Weird Tales* appearance (June–July 1939), which made a number of alterations, especially in paragraphing. The first appearance also has some readings that are not likely to reflect HPL's usages, so they have been altered in accordance with my usual procedure. The title is taken from HPL's ad in the *Providence Journal* (3 June 1924), noting the loss of the T.Ms. at Union Station.

Texts: A = *Weird Tales* 4, No. 2 (May–June–July 1924): 3–12 (as "Imprisoned with the Pharaohs"; as by "Houdini"); B = *Weird Tales* 34, No. 1 (June–July 1939): 133–50 (as "Imprisoned with the Pharaohs"; as by "Houdini"); C = *Dagon and Other Macabre Tales* (Arkham House, 1965), 204–29 (as "Imprisoned with the Pharaohs"; as "With Harry Houdini"). Copy-text: A.

[a] I.] *om.* A, B, C
[b] experiences,] experiences A, B, C

rumours[a] of it from other members of my family.

The hitherto guarded subject pertains to my non-professional visit to Egypt fourteen years ago, and has been avoided by me for several reasons. For one thing, I am averse to exploiting certain unmistakably actual facts and conditions obviously unknown to the myriad tourists who throng about the pyramids and apparently secreted with much diligence by the authorities at Cairo, who cannot be wholly ignorant of them. For another thing, I dislike to recount an incident in which my own fantastic imagination must have played so great a part. What I saw—or thought I saw—certainly did not take place; but is rather to be viewed as a result of my then recent readings in Egyptology, and of the speculations anent this theme which my environment naturally prompted. These imaginative stimuli, magnified by the excitement of an actual event terrible enough in itself, undoubtedly gave rise to the culminating horror of that grotesque night so long past.

In January, 1910, I had finished a professional engagement in England and signed a contract for a tour of Australian theatres. A liberal time being allowed for the trip, I determined to make the most of it in the sort of travel which chiefly interests me; so accompanied by my wife I drifted pleasantly down the Continent and embarked at Marseilles on the P. & O. Steamer *Malwa*,[b] bound for Port Said. From that point I proposed to visit the principal historical localities of lower Egypt before leaving finally for Australia.

The voyage was an agreeable one, and enlivened by many of the amusing incidents which befall a magical performer apart from his work. I had intended, for the sake of quiet travel, to keep my name a secret; but was goaded into betraying myself by a fellow-magician whose anxiety to astound the passengers with ordinary tricks tempted me to duplicate and exceed his feats in a manner quite destructive of my incognito. I mention this because of its ultimate effect—an effect I should have foreseen before unmasking to a shipload of tourists about to scatter throughout the Nile Valley.[c] What it did was to herald my identity wherever I subsequently went, and deprive my wife and me of all the

[a] rumours] rumors A, B, C
[b] *Malwa*,] "Malwa," A
[c] Valley.] valley. B, C

placid inconspicuousness we had sought. Travelling[a] to seek curiosities, I was often forced to stand inspection as a sort of curiosity myself!

We had come to Egypt in search of the picturesque and the mystically impressive, but found little enough when the ship edged up to Port Said and discharged its passengers in small boats. Low dunes of sand, bobbing buoys in shallow water, and a drearily European small town with nothing of interest save the great De Lesseps statue, made us anxious to get on to something more worth our while. After some discussion we decided to proceed at once to Cairo and the Pyramids, later going to Alexandria for the Australian boat and for whatever Graeco-Roman[b] sights that ancient metropolis might present.

The railway journey was tolerable enough, and consumed only four hours and a half. We saw much of the Suez Canal, whose route we followed as far as Ismailiya,[c] and later had a taste of Old Egypt in our glimpse of the restored fresh-water canal of the Middle Empire. Then at last we saw Cairo glimmering through the growing dusk; a twinkling[d] constellation which became a blaze as we halted at the great Gare Centrale.

But once more disappointment awaited us, for all that we beheld was European save the costumes and the crowds. A prosaic subway led to a square teeming with carriages, taxicabs, and trolley-cars,[e] and gorgeous with electric lights shining on tall buildings; whilst the very theatre where I was vainly requested to play,[f] and which I later attended as a spectator, had recently been renamed the "American Cosmograph".[g] We stopped at Shepherd's[h] Hotel, reached in a taxi that sped along broad, smartly built-up streets; and amidst the perfect service of its restaurant, elevators,[i] and generally Anglo-American luxuries the mysterious East and immemorial past seemed very far away.

[a] Travelling] Traveling A, B, C
[b] Graeco-Roman] Greco-Roman B, C
[c] Ismailiya,] Ismailiya B, C
[d] twinkling] winkling C
[e] trolley-cars,] trolley-cars B, C
[f] play,] play A, B, C
[g] Cosmograph".] Cosmograph." A, B, C
[h] Shepherd's] Shepheard's C
[i] elevators,] elevators B, C

The next day, however, precipitated us delightfully into the heart of the Arabian Nights[a] atmosphere; and in the winding ways and exotic skyline of Cairo, the Bagdad of Haroun-al-Raschid[b] seemed to live again. Guided by our Baedeker, we had struck east past the Ezbekiyeh[c] Gardens along the Mouski in quest of the native quarter, and were soon in the hands of a clamorous cicerone who—notwithstanding later developments—was assuredly a master at his trade.[d] Not until afterward did I see that I should have applied at the hotel for a licenced[e] guide. This man, a shaven, peculiarly hollow-voiced,[f] and relatively cleanly fellow who looked like a Pharaoh and called himself "Abdul Reis el Drogman",[g] appeared to have much power over others of his kind; though subsequently the police professed not to know him, and to suggest that *reis* is merely a name for any person in authority, whilst "Drogman" is obviously no more than a clumsy modification of the word for a leader of tourist parties—*dragoman.*

Abdul led us among such wonders as we had before only read and dreamed of. Old Cairo is itself a story-book and a dream—labyrinths of narrow alleys redolent of aromatic secrets; Arabesque balconies and oriels nearly meeting above the cobbled streets; maelstroms of Oriental traffic with strange cries, cracking whips, rattling carts, jingling money, and braying donkeys; kaleidoscopes of polychrome robes, veils, turbans, and tarbushes; water-carriers and dervishes, dogs and cats, soothsayers and barbers; and over all the whining of blind beggars crouched in alcoves, and the sonorous chanting of muezzins from minarets limned delicately against a sky of deep, unchanging blue.

The roofed, quieter bazaars were hardly less alluring. Spice, perfume, incense,[h] beads, rugs, silks, and brass—old Mahmoud Suleiman squats cross-legged amidst his gummy bottles while chattering youths

[a] Arabian Nights] *Arabian Nights* B, C
[b] Haroun-al-Raschid] Harun-al-Raschid B, C
[c] Ezbekiyeh] Exbekiyeh A
[d] trade.] trade. ¶ B, C
[e] licenced] licensed A, B, C
[f] hollow-voiced,] hollow-voiced B, C
[g] Drogman",] Drogman," A, B, C
[h] incense,] incense B, C

pulverise[a] mustard in the hollowed-out capital of an ancient classic column—a Roman Corinthian, perhaps from neighbouring[b] Heliopolis, where Augustus stationed one of his three Egyptian legions. Antiquity begins to mingle with exoticism. And then the mosques and the museum—we saw them all, and tried not to let our Arabian revel succumb to the darker charm of Pharaonic Egypt which the museum's priceless treasures offered. That was to be our climax, and for the present we concentrated on the mediaeval Saracenic glories of the Caliphs[c] whose magnificent tomb-mosques form a glittering faery necropolis on the edge of the Arabian Desert.

At length Abdul took us along the Sharia Mohammed Ali to the ancient mosque of Sultan Hassan, and the tower-flanked[d] Bab-el-Azab,[e] beyond which climbs the steep-walled pass to the mighty citadel that Saladin himself built with the stones of forgotten pyramids. It was sunset when we scaled that cliff, circled the modern mosque of Mohammed Ali, and looked down from the dizzying parapet over mystic Cairo—mystic Cairo all golden with its carven domes, its ethereal minarets,[f] and its flaming gardens.[g] Far over the city towered the great Roman dome of the new museum; and beyond it—across the cryptic yellow Nile that is the mother of aeons[h] and dynasties—lurked the menacing sands of the Libyan Desert, undulant and iridescent and evil with older arcana.[i] The red sun sank low, bringing the relentless chill of Egyptian dusk; and as it stood poised on the world's rim like that ancient god of Heliopolis—Re-Harakhte, the Horizon-Sun—we saw silhouetted against its vermeil holocaust the black outlines of the Pyramids of Gizeh—the palaeogean tombs there were hoary with a thousand years when Tut-Ankh-Amen mounted his golden throne in distant Thebes. Then we knew that we were done with Saracen Cairo,

[a] pulverise] pulverize A, B, C
[b] neighbouring] neighboring A, B, C
[c] Caliphs] Califs B, C
[d] tower-flanked] towel-flanked A, B
[e] Bab-el-Azab,] Bab-/el-Azab, B; Babel-Azab, C
[f] minarets,] minarets B, C
[g] gardens.] gardens. ¶ B, C
[h] aeons] eons B, C
[i] arcana.] arcana. ¶ B, C

and that we must taste the deeper mysteries of primal Egypt—the black Khem[a] of Re and Amen, Isis and Osiris.

The next morning we visited the Pyramids, riding out in a Victoria across the great Nile bridge with its bronze lions, the[b] island of Ghizereh[c] with its massive lebbakh trees, and the smaller English bridge to the western shore. Down the shore road we drove, between great rows of lebbakhs and past the vast Zoölogical[d] Gardens to the suburb of Gizeh, where a new bridge to Cairo proper has since been built. Then, turning inland along the Sharia-el-Haram, we crossed a region of glassy canals and shabby native villages till before us loomed the objects of our quest, cleaving the mists of dawn and forming inverted replicas in the roadside pools. Forty centuries, as Napoleon had told his campaigners there, indeed looked down upon us.

The road now rose abruptly, till we finally reached our place of transfer between the trolley station and the Mena House Hotel. Abdul Reis, who capably purchased our Pyramid tickets, seemed to have an understanding with the crowding, yelling,[e] and offensive Bedouins who inhabited a squalid mud village some distance away and pestiferously assailed every traveller;[f] for he kept them very decently at bay and secured an excellent pair of camels for us, himself mounting a donkey and assigning the leadership of our animals to a group of men and boys more expensive than useful. The area to be traversed was so small that camels were hardly needed, but we did not regret adding to our experience this troublesome form of desert navigation.

The Pyramids[g] stand on a high rock plateau, this group forming next to the northernmost of the series of regal and aristocratic cemeteries built in the neighbourhood[h] of the extinct capital Memphis, which lay on the same side of the Nile, somewhat south of Gizeh, and which flourished between 3400 and 2000 B.C. The greatest pyramid,

[a] Khem] Kem A, B, C
[b] great . . . the] *om.* C
[c] Ghizereh] Chizereh C
[d] Zoölogical] Zoological A, B, C
[e] yelling,] yelling B, C
[f] traveller;] traveler; A, B, C
[g] Pyramids] pyramids C
[h] neighbourhood] neighborhood A, B, C

which lies nearest the modern road, was built by King Cheops or Khufu about 2800 B.C., and stands more than 450 feet in perpendicular height. In a line southwest from this are successively the Second Pyramid, built a generation later by King Khephren, and though slightly smaller, looking even larger because set on higher ground, and the radically smaller Third Pyramid of King Mycerinus, built about 2700 B.C. Near the edge of the plateau and due east of the Second Pyramid, with a face probably altered to form a colossal portrait of Khephren, its royal restorer, stands the monstrous Sphinx—mute, sardonic, and wise beyond mankind and memory.

Minor pyramids and the traces of ruined minor pyramids are found in several places, and the whole plateau is pitted with the tombs of dignitaries of less than royal rank. These latter were originally marked by *mastabas,* or stone bench-like structures about the deep burial shafts, as found in other Memphian cemeteries and exemplified by Perneb's Tomb in the Metropolitan Museum of New York. At Gizeh, however, all such visible things have been swept away by time and pillage; and only the rock-hewn shafts, either sand-filled or cleared out by archaeologists,[a] remain to attest their former existence. Connected with each tomb was a chapel in which priests and relatives offered food and prayer to the hovering *ka* or vital principle of the deceased. The small tombs have their chapels contained in their stone *mastabas* or superstructures, but the mortuary chapels of the pyramids, where regal Pharaohs lay, were separate temples, each to the east of its corresponding pyramid, and connected by a causeway to a massive gate-chapel or propylon at the edge of the rock plateau.

The gate-chapel leading to the Second Pyramid, nearly buried in the drifting sands, yawns subterraneously southeast[b] of the Sphinx. Persistent tradition dubs it the "Temple of the Sphinx"; and it may perhaps be rightly called such if the Sphinx indeed represents the Second Pyramid's builder Khephren. There are unpleasant tales of the Sphinx before Khephren—but whatever its elder features were, the monarch replaced them with his own that men might look at the

---

[a] archaeologists,] archeologists, B
[b] southeast] south-east C

colossus without fear.[a] It was in the great gateway-temple that the life-size diorite statue of Khephren now in the Cairo Museum[b] was found; a statue before which I stood in awe when I beheld it. Whether the whole edifice is now excavated I am not certain, but in 1910 most of it was below ground, with the entrance heavily barred at night. Germans were in charge of the work, and the war or other things may have stopped them. I would give much, in view of my experience and of certain Bedouin whisperings discredited or unknown in Cairo, to know what has developed in connexion[c] with a certain well in a transverse gallery where statues of the Pharaoh were found in curious juxtaposition to the statues of baboons.

The road, as we traversed it on our camels that morning, curved sharply past the wooden police quarters, post-office,[d] drug store,[e] and shops on the left, and plunged south and east in a complete bend that scaled the rock plateau and brought us face to face with the desert under the lee of the Great Pyramid. Past Cyclopean masonry we rode, rounding the eastern face and looking down ahead into a valley of minor pyramids beyond which the eternal Nile glistened to the east, and the eternal desert shimmered to the west. Very close loomed the three major pyramids, the greatest devoid of outer casing and shewing[f] its bulk of great stones, but the others retaining here and there the neatly fitted covering which had made them smooth and finished in their day.

Presently we descended toward the Sphinx, and sat silent beneath the spell of those terrible unseeing eyes. On the vast stone breast we faintly discerned the emblem of Re-Harakhte, for whose image the Sphinx was mistaken in a late dynasty; and though sand covered the tablet between the great paws, we recalled what Thutmosis IV inscribed thereon, and the dream he had when a prince. It was then that the smile of the Sphinx vaguely displeased us, and made us wonder about the legends of subterranean passages beneath the monstrous creature, leading down, down, to depths none might dare

[a] fear.] fear. ¶ B, C
[b] Museum] museum A, B, C
[c] connexion] connection A, B, C
[d] post-office,] post office, B, C
[e] store,] store B, C
[f] shewing] showing A, B, C

hint at—depths connected with mysteries older than the dynastic Egypt we excavate, and having a sinister relation to the persistence of abnormal, animal-headed gods in the ancient Nilotic pantheon. Then, too, it was I asked myself an idle question whose hideous significance was not to appear for many an hour.

Other tourists now began to overtake us, and we moved on to the sand-choked Temple of the Sphinx, fifty yards to the southeast, which I have previously mentioned as the great gate of the causeway to the Second Pyramid's mortuary chapel on the plateau. Most of it was still underground, and although we dismounted and descended through a modern passageway to its alabaster corridor and pillared hall, I felt that Abdul[a] and the local German attendant had not shewn[b] us all there was to see.[c] After this we made the conventional circuit of the pyramid plateau, examining the Second Pyramid and the peculiar ruins of its mortuary chapel to the east, the Third Pyramid and its miniature southern satellites and ruined eastern chapel, the rock tombs and the honeycombings of the fourth and fifth[d] dynasties, and the famous Campbell's Tomb whose shadowy shaft sinks precipitously for fifty-three feet to a sinister sarcophagus which one of our camel-drivers[e] divested of the cumbering sand after a vertiginous descent by rope.

Cries now assailed us from the Great Pyramid, where Bedouins were besieging a party of tourists with offers of guidance to the top, or of displays of[f] speed in the performance of solitary trips up and down. Seven minutes is said to be the record for such an ascent and descent, but many lusty sheiks and sons of sheiks[g] assured us they could cut it to[h] five if given the requisite impetus of liberal *baksheesh.* They did not get this impetus, though we did let Abdul take us up, thus obtaining a view of unprecedented magnificence which included not only remote

[a] Abdul] Adul C
[b] shewn] shown B, C
[c] see.] see. ¶ B, C
[d] fourth and fifth] Fourth and Fifth B, C
[e] camel-drivers] camel drivers C
[f] guidance . . . displays of] *om.* B, C
[g] sheiks . . . sheiks] shieks . . . shieks C
[h] to] *om.* C

and glittering Cairo with its crowned Citadel and[a] background of gold-violet hills, but all the pyramids of the Memphian district[b] as well, from Abu Roash on the north to the Dashur on the south. The Sakkara step-pyramid, which marks the evolution of the low *mastaba* into the true pyramid, shewed[c] clearly and alluringly in the sandy distance. It is close to this transition-monument that the famed Tomb[d] of Perneb was found—more than 400 miles north of the Theban rock valley where Tut-Ankh-Amen sleeps. Again I was forced to silence through sheer awe. The prospect[e] of such antiquity, and the secrets each hoary monument seemed to hold and brood over, filled me with a reverence and sense of immensity nothing else ever gave me.

Fatigued by our climb, and disgusted with the importunate Bedouins whose actions seemed to defy every rule of taste, we omitted the arduous detail of entering the cramped interior passages of any of the pyramids, though we saw several of the hardiest tourists preparing for the suffocating crawl through Cheops' mightiest memorial. As we dismissed and overpaid our local bodyguard and drove back to Cairo with Abdul Reis under the afternoon sun, we half regretted the omission we had made. Such fascinating things were whispered about lower pyramid passages not in the guide-books;[f] passages whose entrances had been hastily blocked up and concealed by certain uncommunicative archaeologists[g] who had found and begun to explore them.[h] Of course, this whispering was largely baseless on the face of it; but it was curious to reflect how persistently visitors were forbidden to enter the Pyramids at night, or to visit the lowest burrows and crypt of the Great Pyramid. Perhaps in the latter case it was the psychological effect which was feared—the effect on the visitor of feeling himself huddled down beneath a gigantic world of solid masonry; joined to the life he has known by the merest tube, in which

---

[a] Citadel and] citadel and B; citadel C
[b] district] district, A, B
[c] shewed] showed B, C
[d] Tomb] tomb C
[e] prospect] propsect C
[f] guide-books;] guide books; A, B, C
[g] archaeologists] archeologists B
[h] them.] them. ¶ B, C

he may only crawl, and which any accident or evil design might block. The whole subject seemed so weird and alluring that we resolved to pay the pyramid plateau another visit at the earliest possible opportunity. For me this opportunity came much earlier than I expected.

That evening,[a] the members of our party feeling somewhat tired after the strenuous programme[b] of the day, I went alone with Abdul Reis for a walk through the picturesque Arab quarter. Though I had seen it by day, I wished to study the alleys and bazaars in the dusk, when rich shadows and mellow gleams of light would add to their glamour[c] and fantastic illusion. The native crowds were thinning, but were still very noisy and numerous when we came upon a knot of revelling[d] Bedouins in the Suken-Nahhasin, or bazaar[e] of the coppersmiths. Their apparent leader, an insolent youth with heavy features and saucily cocked tarbush, took some notice of us;[f] and evidently recognised[g] with no great friendliness my competent but admittedly supercilious and sneeringly disposed guide.[h] Perhaps, I thought, he resented the odd reproduction of the Sphinx's half-smile[i] which I had often remarked with amused irritation; or perhaps he did not like the hollow and sepulchral resonance of Abdul's voice. At any rate, the exchange of ancestrally opprobrious language became very brisk; and before long Ali Ziz, as I heard the stranger called when called by no worse name, began to pull violently at Abdul's robe, an action quickly reciprocated,[j] and leading to a spirited scuffle in which both combatants lost their sacredly cherished headgear[k] and would have reached an even direr condition had I not intervened and separated them by main force.

My interference, at first seemingly unwelcome on both sides,

---

[a] evening,] evening A
[b] programme] program B, C
[c] glamour] glamor B, C
[d] revelling] reveling B, C
[e] bazaar] bazar B
[f] us;] us, B, C
[g] recognised] recognized A, B, C
[h] guide.] guide. ¶ B, C
[i] half-smile] half smile A
[j] reciprocated,] reciprocated B, C
[k] headgear] head-gear B

succeeded at last in effecting a truce. Sullenly each belligerent composed his wrath and his attire;[a] and with an assumption of dignity as profound as it was sudden, the two formed a curious pact of honour[b] which I soon learned is a custom of great antiquity in Cairo—a pact for the settlement of their difference by means of a nocturnal fist fight atop the Great Pyramid, long after the departure of the last moonlight sightseer. Each duellist was to assemble a party of seconds, and the affair was to begin at midnight, proceeding by rounds in the most civilised[c] possible fashion.[d] In all this planning there was much which excited my interest. The fight itself promised to be unique and spectacular, while the thought of the scene on that hoary pile overlooking the antediluvian plateau of Gizeh under the wan moon of the pallid small hours appealed to every fibre[e] of imagination in me. A request found Abdul exceedingly willing to admit me to his party of seconds; so that all the rest of the early evening I accompanied him to various dens in the most lawless regions of the town—mostly northeast of the Ezbekiyeh—where he gathered one by one a select and formidable band of congenial cutthroats as his pugilistic background.

Shortly after nine our party, mounted on donkeys bearing such royal or tourist-reminiscent names as "Rameses", "Mark Twain", "J. P. Morgan", and "Minnehaha",[f] edged through street labyrinths both Oriental and Occidental, crossed the muddy and mast-forested Nile by the bridge of the bronze lions, and cantered philosophically between the lebbakhs on the road to Gizeh. Slightly over two hours were consumed by the trip, toward the end of which we passed the last of the returning tourists, saluted the last in-bound[g] trolley-car, and were alone with the night and the past and the spectral moon.

Then we saw the vast pyramids at the end of the avenue, ghoulish with a dim atavistical menace which I had not seemed to notice in the

---

[a] attire;] attire, B, C
[b] honour] honor B, C
[c] civilised] civilized A, B, C
[d] fashion.] fashion. ¶ B, C
[e] fibre] fiber A, B, C
[f] "Rameses", . . . "Minnehaha",] "Rameses," "Mark Twain," "J. P. Morgan," and "Minnehaha," A, B, C
[g] in-bound] in-/bound B; inbound C

daytime. Even the smallest of them held a hint of the ghastly—for was it not in this that they had buried Queen Nitokris[a] alive in the Sixth Dynasty; subtle Queen Nitokris,[b] who once invited all her enemies to a feast in a temple below the Nile, and drowned them by opening the water-gates? I recalled that the Arabs whisper things about Nitokris,[c] and shun the Third Pyramid at certain phases of the moon. It must have been over her that Thomas Moore was brooding when he wrote a thing muttered about by Memphian boatmen—[d]

> "The subterranean nymph that dwells
> 'Mid sunless gems and glories hid—
> The lady of the Pyramid!"

Early as we were, Ali Ziz and his party were ahead of us; for we saw their donkeys outlined against the desert plateau at Kafr-el-Haram;[e] toward which squalid Arab settlement, close to the Sphinx, we had diverged instead of following the regular road to the Mena House, where some of the sleepy, inefficient police might have observed and halted us. Here, where filthy Bedouins stabled camels and donkeys in the rock tombs of Khephren's courtiers, we were led up the rocks and over the sand to the Great Pyramid, up whose time-worn sides the Arabs swarmed eagerly,[f] Abdul Reis offering me the assistance I did not need.

As most travellers[g] know, the actual apex of this structure has long been worn away, leaving a reasonably flat platform twelve yards square. On this eery pinnacle a squared circle was formed, and in a few moments the sardonic desert moon leered down upon a battle which, but for the quality of the ringside cries, might well have occurred at some minor athletic club in America. As I watched it, I felt that some of our less desirable institutions were not lacking; for every blow, feint, and defence[h] bespoke "stalling" to my not inexperienced eye. It was

[a] Nitokris] Nitocris A, B, C
[b] Nitokris,] Nitocris, A, B, C
[c] Nitokris,] Nitocris, A, B, C
[d] boatmen—] boatmen: B, C
[e] Kafr-el-Haram;] Kafr-/el-Haram; B; Kafrel-Haram; C
[f] eagerly,] eagerly. B
[g] travellers] travelers A, B, C
[h] defence] defense A, B, C

quickly over, and despite my misgivings as to methods I felt a sort of proprietary pride when Abdul Reis was adjudged the winner.

Reconciliation was phenomenally rapid, and amidst the singing,[a] fraternising,[b] and drinking which followed, I found it difficult to realise[c] that a quarrel had ever occurred. Oddly enough, I myself seemed to be more of[d] a centre[e] of notice than the antagonists; and from my smattering of Arabic I judged that they were discussing my professional performances and escapes from every sort of manacle and confinement, in a manner which indicated not only a surprising knowledge of me, but a distinct hostility and scepticism[f] concerning my feats of escape. It gradually dawned on me that the elder magic of Egypt did not depart without leaving traces, and that fragments of a strange secret lore and priestly cult-practices[g] have survived surreptitiously amongst the fellaheen to such an extent that the prowess of a strange "hahwi"[h] or magician is resented and disputed. I thought of how much my hollow-voiced guide Abdul Reis looked like an old Egyptian priest or Pharaoh or smiling Sphinx . . . and wondered.

Suddenly something happened which in a flash proved the correctness of my reflections and made me curse the denseness whereby I had accepted this night's events as other than the empty and malicious "frameup"[i] they now shewed[j] themselves to be. Without warning, and doubtless in answer to some subtle sign from Abdul, the entire band of Bedouins precipitated itself upon me; and having produced heavy ropes, soon had me bound as securely as I was ever bound in the course of my life, either on the stage or[k] off.[l] I struggled at first, but soon saw that one

---

[a] singing,] singing C
[b] fraternising,] fraternizing A, B, C
[c] realise] realize A, B, C
[d] of] *om.* B, C
[e] centre] center A, B, C
[f] scepticism] skepticism B, C
[g] cult-practices] cult-practises B, C
[h] "hahwi"] *hahwi* B, C
[i] "frameup"] "frame-up" B; "frame-/up" C
[j] shewed] showed A, B, C
[k] or] of C
[l] off.] off. ¶ B, C

man could make no headway against a band of over twenty sinewy
barbarians. My hands were tied behind my back, my knees bent to their
fullest extent, and my wrists and ankles stoutly linked together with
unyielding cords. A stifling gag was forced into my mouth, and a
blindfold fastened tightly over my eyes. Then, as the[a] Arabs bore me
aloft on their shoulders and began a jouncing descent of the pyramid, I
heard the taunts of my late guide Abdul, who mocked and jeered
delightedly in his hollow voice, and assured me that I was soon to have
my "magic powers" put to a supreme test which would quickly remove
any egotism I might have gained through triumphing over all the tests
offered by America and Europe. Egypt, he reminded me, is very old;[b]
and full of inner mysteries and antique powers not even conceivable to
the experts of today, whose devices had so uniformly failed to entrap me.

How far or in what direction I was carried, I cannot tell; for the
circumstances were all against the formation of any accurate judgment.
I know, however, that it could not have been a great distance; since my
bearers at no point hastened beyond a walk, yet kept me aloft a
surprisingly short time. It is this perplexing brevity which makes me
feel almost like shuddering whenever I think of Gizeh and its
plateau—for one is oppressed by hints of the closeness to every-day[c]
tourist routes of what existed then and must exist still.

The evil abnormality I speak of did not become manifest at first.
Setting me down on a surface which I recognised[d] as sand rather than
rock, my captors passed a rope around my chest and dragged me a few
feet to a ragged opening in the ground, into which they presently lowered
me with much rough handling. For apparent aeons[e] I bumped against the
stony irregular sides of a narrow hewn well which I took to be one of the
numerous burial shafts[f] of the plateau until the prodigious, almost
incredible depth of it robbed me of all bases of conjecture.

The horror of the experience deepened with every dragging
second. That any descent through the sheer solid rock could be so vast

---

[a] the] *om.* C
[b] old;] old, B, C
[c] every-day] everyday B, C
[d] recognised] recognized A, B, C
[e] aeons] eons A, B, C
[f] burial shafts] burial-shafts B, C

without reaching the core of the planet itself, or that any rope made by man could be so long as to dangle me in these unholy and seemingly fathomless profundities of nether earth, were beliefs of such grotesqueness that it was easier to doubt my agitated senses than to accept them. Even now I am uncertain, for I know how deceitful the sense of time becomes when one or more of the usual perceptions or conditions of life[a] is removed or distorted. But I am quite sure that I preserved a logical consciousness that far; that at least I did not add any full-grown[b] phantoms of imagination to a picture hideous enough in its reality, and explicable by a type of cerebral illusion vastly short of actual hallucination.

All this was not the cause of my first bit of fainting. The shocking ordeal was cumulative, and the beginning of the later terrors was a very perceptible increase in my rate of descent. They were paying out that infinitely long rope very swiftly now, and I scraped cruelly against the rough and constricted sides of the shaft as I shot madly downward. My clothing was in tatters, and I felt the trickle of blood all over, even above the mounting and excruciating pain. My nostrils, too, were assailed by a scarcely definable menace;[c] a creeping odour[d] of damp and staleness curiously unlike anything I had ever smelt[e] before, and having faint overtones of spice and incense that lent an element of mockery.

Then the mental cataclysm came. It was horrible—hideous beyond all articulate description because it was all of the soul, with nothing of detail to describe. It was the ecstasy of nightmare and the summation of the fiendish. The suddenness of it was apocalyptic and daemoniac[f]— one moment I was plunging agonisedly[g] down that narrow well of million-toothed torture, yet the next moment I was soaring on bat-wings in the gulfs of hell; swinging free and swoopingly through illimitable miles of boundless, musty space; rising dizzily to measureless pinnacles of chilling ether, then diving gaspingly to

[a] or more . . . life] *om.* C
[b] full-grown] fullgrown C
[c] menace;] menace: C
[d] odour] odor A, B, C
[e] smelt] smelled C
[f] daemoniac] demoniac B, C
[g] agonisedly] agonizedly A, B; agonizingly C

sucking nadirs of ravenous, nauseous lower vacua. . . . Thank God for the mercy that shut out in oblivion those clawing Furies of consciousness which half unhinged[a] my faculties, and tore Harpy-like[b] at my spirit! That one respite, short as it was, gave me the strength and sanity to endure those still greater sublimations of cosmic panic that lurked and gibbered on the road ahead.

II.

It was very gradually that I regained my senses after that eldritch flight through Stygian[c] space. The process was infinitely painful, and coloured[d] by fantastic dreams in which my bound and gagged condition found singular embodiment. The precise nature of these dreams was very clear while I was experiencing them, but became blurred in my recollection almost immediately afterward, and was soon reduced to the merest outline by the terrible events—real or imaginary—which followed. I dreamed that I was in the grasp of a great and horrible paw; a yellow, hairy, five-clawed paw which had reached out of the earth to crush and engulf me. And when I stopped to reflect what the paw was, it seemed to me that it was Egypt. In the dream I looked back at the events of the preceding weeks, and saw myself lured and enmeshed little by little, subtly and insidiously, by some hellish ghoul-spirit of the elder Nile sorcery; some spirit that was in Egypt before ever man was, and that will be when man is no more.

I saw the horror and unwholesome antiquity of Egypt, and the grisly alliance it has always had with the tombs and temples of the dead. I saw phantom processions of priests with the heads of bulls, falcons, cats, and ibises; phantom processions marching interminably through subterraneous labyrinths and avenues of titanic propylaea beside which a man is as a fly, and offering unnamable sacrifices[e] to indescribable gods. Stone colossi marched in endless night and drove herds of grinning androsphinxes down to the shores of illimitable

[a] half unhinged] half-unhinged A
[b] Harpy-like] harpy-like B, C
[c] Stygian] stygian A, B, C
[d] coloured] colored A, B, C
[e] sacrifices] sacrifice B, C

stagnant rivers of pitch. And behind it all I saw the ineffable malignity of primordial necromancy, black and amorphous, and fumbling greedily after me in the darkness to choke out the spirit that had dared to mock it by emulation.[a] In my sleeping brain there took shape a melodrama of sinister hatred and pursuit, and I saw the black soul of Egypt singling me out and calling me in inaudible whispers; calling and luring me, leading me on with the glitter and glamour[b] of a Saracenic surface, but ever pulling me down to the age-mad catacombs and horrors of its dead[c] and abysmal pharaonic heart.

Then the dream-faces[d] took on human resemblances, and I saw my guide Abdul Reis in the robes of a king, with the sneer of the Sphinx on his features. And I knew that those features were the features of Khephren the Great, who raised the Second Pyramid, carved over the Sphinx's face in the likeness of his own,[e] and built that titanic gateway temple whose myriad corridors the archaeologists[f] think they have dug out of the cryptical sand and the uninformative rock. And I looked at the long, lean, rigid hand of Khephren; the long, lean, rigid hand as I had seen it on the diorite statue in the Cairo Museum—the statue they had found in the terrible gateway temple— and wondered that I had not shrieked when I saw it on Abdul Reis. . . . That hand! It was hideously cold, and it was crushing me; it was the cold and cramping of the sarcophagus . . . the chill and constriction of unrememberable Egypt. . . . It was nighted, necropolitan Egypt itself . . . that yellow paw . . . and they whisper such things of Khephren. . . .

But at this juncture I began to awake—or at least, to assume a condition less completely that of sleep than the one just preceding. I recalled the fight atop the pyramid, the treacherous Bedouins and their attack, my frightful descent by rope through endless rock depths, and my mad swinging and plunging in a chill void redolent of aromatic putrescence. I perceived that I now lay on a damp rock floor, and that my bonds were still biting into me with unloosened force. It was very

[a] emulation.] emulation. ¶ B, C
[b] glamour] glamor B, C
[c] dead] *dead* B, C
[d] dream-faces] dream faces C
[e] own,] own B, C
[f] archaeologists] archeologists B

cold, and I seemed to detect a faint current of noisome air sweeping across me. The cuts and bruises I had received from the jagged sides of the rock shaft were paining me woefully,[a] their soreness enhanced to a stinging or burning acuteness by some pungent quality in the faint draught,[b] and the mere act of rolling over was enough to set my whole frame throbbing with untold agony.[c] As I turned I felt a tug from above, and concluded that the rope whereby I was lowered still reached to the surface. Whether or not the Arabs still held it, I had no idea; nor had I any idea how far within the earth I was. I knew that the darkness around me was wholly or nearly total, since no ray of moonlight penetrated my blindfold; but I did not trust my senses enough to accept as evidence of extreme depth the sensation of vast duration which had characterised[d] my descent.

Knowing at least that I was in a space of considerable extent reached from the surface directly above by an opening in the rock, I doubtfully conjectured that my prison was perhaps the buried gateway chapel of old Khephren—the Temple of the Sphinx—perhaps some inner corridor which the guides had not shewn[e] me during my morning visit, and from which I might easily escape if I could find my way to the barred entrance. It would be a labyrinthine wandering, but no worse than others out of which I had in the past found my way.[f] The first step was to get free of my bonds, gag, and blindfold; and this I knew would be no great task, since subtler experts than these Arabs had tried every known species of fetter upon me during my long and varied career as an exponent of escape, yet had never succeeded in defeating my methods.

Then it occurred to me that the Arabs might be ready to meet and attack me at the entrance upon any evidence of my probable escape from the binding cords, as would be furnished by any decided agitation of the rope which they probably held. This, of course, was taking for granted that my place of confinement was indeed Khephren's Temple of the Sphinx. The direct opening in the roof, wherever it might lurk,

[a] woefully,] wofully, B
[b] draught,] draft, B, C
[c] agony.] agony. ¶ B, C
[d] characterised] characterized A, B, C
[e] shewn] shown A, B, C
[f] way.] way. ¶ B, C

could not be beyond easy reach of the ordinary modern entrance near the Sphinx; if in truth it were any great distance at all on the surface, since the total area known to visitors is not at all enormous. I had not noticed any such opening during my daytime pilgrimage, but knew that these things are easily overlooked amidst the drifting sands.[a] Thinking these matters over as I lay bent and bound on the rock floor, I nearly forgot the horrors of the[b] abysmal descent and cavernous swinging which had so lately reduced me to a coma. My present thought was only to outwit the Arabs, and I accordingly determined to work myself free as quickly as possible, avoiding any tug on the descending line which might betray an effective or even problematical attempt at freedom.

This, however, was more easily determined than effected. A few preliminary trials made it clear that little could be accomplished without considerable motion; and it did not surprise me when, after one especially energetic struggle, I began to feel the coils of falling rope as they piled up about me and upon me. Obviously, I thought, the Bedouins had felt my movements and released their end of the rope; hastening no doubt to the temple's true entrance to lie murderously in wait for me.[c] The prospect was not pleasing—but I had faced worse in my time without flinching, and would not flinch now. At present I must first of all free myself of bonds, then trust to ingenuity to escape from the temple unharmed. It is curious how implicitly I had come to believe myself in the old temple of Khephren beside the Sphinx, only a short distance below the ground.

That belief was shattered, and every pristine apprehension of preternatural depth and daemoniac[d] mystery revived, by a circumstance which grew in horror and significance even as I formulated my philosophical plan. I have said that the falling rope was piling up about and upon me. Now I saw that it was *continuing to pile*,[e] as no rope of normal length could possibly do. It gained in momentum and became an avalanche of hemp, accumulating mountainously on the floor,[f] and half

[a] sands.] sands. ¶ B, C
[b] the] *om.* A, B, C
[c] me.] me. ¶ B, C
[d] daemoniac] demoniac B, C
[e] *continuing to pile*,] continuing to pile, B, C
[f] floor,] floor B, C

burying[a] me beneath its swiftly multiplying coils. Soon I was completely engulfed and gasping for breath as the increasing convolutions submerged and stifled me.[b] My senses tottered again, and I vainly tried to fight off a menace desperate and ineluctable. It was not merely that I was tortured beyond human endurance—not merely that life and breath seemed to be crushed slowly out of me—it was the knowledge of *what those unnatural lengths of rope implied,*[c] and the consciousness of what unknown and incalculable gulfs of inner earth must at this moment be surrounding me. My endless descent and swinging flight through goblin space, then, must have been real;[d] and even now I must be lying helpless in some nameless cavern world toward the core of the planet. Such a sudden confirmation of ultimate horror was insupportable, and a second time I lapsed into merciful oblivion.

When I say oblivion, I do not imply that I was free from dreams. On the contrary, my absence from the conscious world was marked by visions of the most unutterable hideousness. God! . . . If only I had not read so much Egyptology before coming to this land which is the fount[e] of all darkness and terror! This second spell of fainting filled my sleeping mind anew with shivering realisation[f] of the country and its archaic secrets, and through some damnable chance my dreams turned to the ancient notions of the dead and their sojournings in soul *and body*[g] beyond those mysterious tombs which were more houses than graves. I recalled, in dream-shapes which it is well that I do not remember, the peculiar and elaborate construction of Egyptian sepulchres;[h] and the exceedingly singular and terrific doctrines which determined this construction.

All these people thought of was death and the dead. They[i]

[a] half burying] half-burying B

[b] me.] me. ¶ B, C

[c] *what . . . implied,*] *what those unnatural* / lengths of rope implied, A; what those unnatural lengths of rope implied, B, C

[d] real;] real, B, C

[e] fount] fountain A, B, C

[f] realisation] realization A, B, C

[g] *and body*] and body B, C

[h] sepulchres;] sepulchers; B, C

[i] They] Theey A

conceived of a literal resurrection of the body which made them mummify it with desperate care, and preserve all the vital organs in canopic jars near the corpse; whilst besides the body they believed in two other elements, the soul, which after its weighing and approval by Osiris dwelt in the land of the blest, and the obscure and portentous *ka* or life-principle which wandered about the upper and lower worlds in a horrible way, demanding occasional access to the preserved body, consuming the food offerings brought by priests and pious relatives to the mortuary chapel, and sometimes—as men whispered—taking its body or the wooden double always buried beside it and stalking noxiously abroad on errands peculiarly repellent.

For thousands of years those bodies rested gorgeously encased and staring glassily upward when not visited by the *ka,* awaiting the day when Osiris should restore both *ka* and soul, and lead forth the stiff legions of the dead from the sunken houses of sleep. It was to have been a glorious rebirth—but not all souls were approved, nor were all tombs inviolate, so that certain grotesque *mistakes* and fiendish *abnormalities* were to be looked for. Even today the Arabs murmur of unsanctified convocations and unwholesome worship in forgotten nether abysses, which only winged invisible *kas* and soulless mummies may visit and return unscathed.

Perhaps the most leeringly blood-congealing legends are those which relate to certain perverse products of decadent priestcraft—*composite mummies* made by the artificial union of human trunks and limbs with the heads of animals in imitation of the elder gods. At all stages of history the sacred animals were mummified, so that consecrated bulls, cats, ibises, crocodiles,[a] and the like might return some day to greater glory. But only in the decadence did they mix the human and animal in the same mummy—only in the decadence, when they did not understand the rights and prerogatives of the *ka* and the soul.[b] What happened to those composite mummies is not told of—at least publicly—and it is certain that no Egyptologist ever found one. The whispers of Arabs are very wild, and cannot be relied upon. They

[a] crocodiles,] crocodiles B, C
[b] soul.] soul. ¶ B, C

even hint that old Khephren—he of the Sphinx, the Second Pyramid,[a] and the yawning gateway temple—lives far underground wedded to the ghoul-queen Nitokris[b] and ruling over the mummies that are neither of man nor of beast.

It was of these—of Khephren and his consort and his strange armies of the hybrid dead—that I dreamed, and that is why I am glad the exact dream-shapes have faded from my memory. My most horrible vision was connected with an idle question I had asked myself the day before when looking at the great carven riddle of the desert and wondering with what unknown depths[c] the temple so[d] close to it might be secretly connected. That question, so innocent and whimsical then, assumed in my dream a meaning of frenetic and hysterical madness ... *what huge and loathsome abnormality was the Sphinx originally carven to represent?*

My second awakening—if awakening it was—is a memory of stark hideousness which nothing else in my life—save one thing which came after—can parallel; and that life has been full and adventurous beyond most men's. Remember that I had lost consciousness whilst buried beneath a cascade of falling rope whose immensity revealed the cataclysmic depth of my present position. Now, as perception returned, I felt the entire weight gone; and realised[e] upon rolling over that although I was still tied, gagged,[f] and blindfolded, *some agency had removed completely the suffocating hempen landslide which had overwhelmed me.* The significance of this condition, of course, came to me only gradually; but even so I think it would have brought unconsciousness again had I not by this time reached such a state of emotional exhaustion that no new horror could make much difference. I was alone ... with[g] *what?*

Before I could torture myself with any new reflection, or make any fresh effort to escape from my bonds, an additional circumstance

[a] Pyramid,] Pyramid B, C
[b] Nitokris] Nitocris A, B, C
[c] depths] depth C
[d] so] *om.* B, C
[e] realised] realized A, B, C
[f] gagged,] gagged A, B, C
[g] with] *with* C

became manifest. Pains not formerly felt were racking my arms and legs, and I seemed coated with a profusion of dried blood beyond anything my former cuts and abrasions could furnish. My chest, too, seemed pierced by a[a] hundred wounds, as though some malign, titanic ibis had been pecking at it. Assuredly the agency which had removed the rope was a hostile one, and had begun to wreak terrible injuries upon me when somehow impelled to desist. Yet at the time my sensations were distinctly the reverse of what one might expect. Instead of sinking into a bottomless pit of despair, I was stirred to a new courage and action; for now I felt that the evil forces were physical things which a fearless man might encounter on an even basis.

On the strength of this thought I tugged again at my bonds, and used all the art of a lifetime to free myself as I had so often done amidst the glare of lights and the applause of vast crowds. The familiar details of my escaping process commenced to engross me, and now that the long rope was gone I half regained my belief that the supreme horrors were hallucinations after all, and that there had never been any terrible shaft, measureless[b] abyss,[c] or interminable rope. Was I after all in the gateway temple of Khephren beside the Sphinx, and had the sneaking Arabs stolen in to torture me as I lay helpless there? At any rate, I must be free. Let me stand up unbound, ungagged, and with eyes open to catch any glimmer of light which might come trickling from any source, and I could actually delight in the combat against evil and treacherous foes!

How long I took in shaking off my encumbrances I cannot tell. It must have been longer than in my exhibition performances, because I was wounded, exhausted, and enervated by the experiences I had passed through. When I was finally free, and taking deep breaths of a chill, damp, evilly spiced air all the more horrible when encountered without the screen of gag and blindfold edges, I found that I was too cramped and fatigued to move at once. There I lay, trying to stretch a frame bent and mangled, for an indefinite period, and straining my eyes to catch a glimpse of some ray of light which would give a hint as to my position.

---

[a] a] an A
[b] measureless] measurless A
[c] abyss,] abyss B, C

By degrees my strength and flexibility returned, but my eyes beheld nothing. As I staggered to my feet I peered diligently in every direction, yet met only an ebony blackness as great as that I had known when blindfolded. I tried my legs, blood-encrusted beneath my shredded trousers, and found that I could walk; yet could not decide in what direction to go. Obviously I ought not to walk at random, and perhaps retreat directly from the entrance I sought; so I paused to note the direction of the cold, foetid,[a] natron-scented air-current which I had never ceased to feel. Accepting the point of its source as the possible entrance to the abyss, I strove to keep track of this landmark and to walk consistently toward it.

I had had[b] a match-box[c] with me, and even a small electric flashlight; but of course the pockets of my tossed and tattered clothing were long since emptied of all heavy articles. As I walked cautiously in the blackness, the draught[d] grew stronger and more offensive, till at length I could regard it as nothing less than a tangible stream of detestable vapour[e] pouring out of some aperture like the smoke of the genie from the fisherman's jar in the Eastern tale. The East ... Egypt ... truly, this dark cradle of civilisation[f] was ever the well-spring[g] of horrors and marvels unspeakable![h] The more I reflected on the nature of this cavern wind, the greater my sense of disquiet became; for although despite its odour[i] I had sought its source as at least an indirect clue to the outer world, I now saw plainly that this foul emanation could have no admixture or connexion[j] whatsoever with the clean air of the Libyan Desert, but must be essentially a thing vomited from sinister gulfs still lower down. I had, then, been walking in the wrong direction!

After a moment's reflection I decided not to retrace my steps.

[a] foetid,] fetid, B, C
[b] had had] had B, C
[c] match-box] match box A
[d] draught] draft B, C
[e] vapour] vapor B, C
[f] civilisation] civilization B, C
[g] well-spring] well-/spring B; wellspring C
[h] unspeakable!] unspeakable! ¶ B, C
[i] odour] odor A, B, C
[j] connexion] connection A, B, C

Away from the draught[a] I would have no landmarks, for the roughly level rock floor was devoid of distinctive configurations. If, however, I followed up the strange current, I would undoubtedly arrive at an aperture of some sort, from whose gate I could perhaps work round the walls to the opposite side of this Cyclopean and otherwise unnavigable hall. That I might fail, I well realised.[b] I saw that this was no part of Khephren's gateway temple which tourists know, and it struck me that this particular hall might be unknown even to archaeologists,[c] and merely stumbled upon by the inquisitive and malignant Arabs who had imprisoned me. If so, was there any present gate of escape to the known parts or to the outer air?

What evidence, indeed, did I now possess that this was the gateway temple at all? For a moment all my wildest speculations rushed back upon me, and I thought of that vivid melange of impressions—descent, suspension in space, the rope, my wounds, and the dreams that were frankly dreams. Was this the end of life for me? Or indeed, would it be merciful if this moment *were* the end? I could answer none of my own questions, but merely kept on[d] till Fate for a third time reduced me to oblivion.[e] This time there were no dreams, for the suddenness of the incident shocked me out of all thought either conscious or subconscious. Tripping on an unexpected descending step at a point where the offensive draught[f] became strong enough to offer an actual physical resistance, I was precipitated headlong down a black flight of huge stone stairs into a gulf of hideousness unrelieved.

That I ever breathed again is a tribute to the inherent vitality of the healthy human organism. Often I look back to that night and feel a touch of actual *humour*[g] in those repeated lapses of consciousness; lapses whose succession reminded me at the time of nothing more than the crude cinema melodramas of that period. Of course, it is possible that the repeated lapses never occurred; and that all the

---

[a] draught] draft B, C
[b] realised.] realized. A, B, C
[c] archaeologists,] archeologists, B
[d] on] on, B, C
[e] oblivion.] oblivion. ¶ B, C
[f] draught] draft B, C
[g] *humour*] humor B, C

features of that underground nightmare were merely the dreams of one long coma which began with the shock of my descent into that abyss and ended with the healing balm of the outer air and of the rising sun which found me stretched on the sands of Gizeh before the sardonic and dawn-flushed face of the Great Sphinx.

I prefer to believe this latter explanation as much as I can, hence was glad when the police told me that the barrier to Khephren's gateway temple had been found unfastened, and that a sizeable[a] rift to the surface did actually exist in one corner of the still buried part. I was glad, too, when the doctors pronounced my wounds only those to be expected from my seizure, blindfolding,[b] lowering, struggling with bonds, falling some distance—perhaps into a depression in the temple's inner gallery—dragging myself to the outer barrier and escaping from it, and experiences like that ... a very soothing diagnosis. And yet I know that there must be more than appears on the surface. That extreme descent is too vivid a memory to be dismissed—and it is odd that no one has ever been able to find a man answering the description of my guide[c] Abdul Reis el Drogman—the tomb-throated guide who looked and smiled like King Khephren.

I have digressed from my connected narrative—perhaps in the vain hope of evading the telling of that final incident; that incident which of all is most certainly an hallucination. But I promised to relate it, and[d] do not break promises. When I recovered—or seemed to recover—my senses after that fall down the black stone stairs, I was quite as alone and in darkness as before. The windy stench, bad enough before, was now fiendish; yet I had acquired enough familiarity by this time to bear it stoically. Dazedly I began to crawl away from the place whence the putrid wind came, and with my bleeding hands felt the colossal blocks of a mighty pavement. Once my head struck against a hard object, and when I felt of it I learned that it was the base of a column—a column of unbelievable immensity—whose surface

[a] sizeable] sizable A, B, C
[b] blindfolding,] blinding, A, B
[c] guide] guide, B, C
[d] and] and I B, C

was covered with gigantic chiselled[a] hieroglyphics very perceptible to my touch.[b] Crawling on, I encountered other titan columns at incomprehensible distances apart; when suddenly my attention was captured by the realisation[c] of something which must have been impinging on my subconscious hearing long before the conscious sense was aware of it.

From some still lower chasm in earth's bowels were proceeding certain *sounds,* measured and definite, and like nothing I had ever heard before. That they were very ancient and distinctly ceremonial,[d] I felt almost intuitively; and much reading in Egyptology led me to associate them with the flute, the sambuke, the sistrum, and the tympanum. In their rhythmic piping, droning, rattling,[e] and beating I felt an element of terror beyond all the known terrors of earth—a terror peculiarly dissociated from personal fear, and taking the form of a sort of objective pity for our planet, that it should hold within its depths such horrors as must lie beyond these aegipanic cacophonies. The sounds increased in volume, and I felt that they were approaching. Then—and may all the gods of all pantheons unite to keep the like from my ears again—I began to hear, faintly and afar off, *the morbid and millennial tramping of the marching things.*[f]

It was hideous that footfalls *so dissimilar*[g] should move in such perfect rhythm. The training of unhallowed thousands of years must lie behind that march of earth's inmost monstrosities ... padding, clicking, walking, stalking, rumbling, lumbering, crawling ... and all to the abhorrent discords of those mocking instruments. And then ...[h] God keep the memory of those Arab legends out of my head! The[i] mummies without souls ... the meeting-place[j] of the wandering *kas*

---

[a] chiselled] chiseled A, B, C
[b] touch.] touch. ¶ B, C
[c] realisation] realization A, B, C
[d] ceremonial,] ceremonial C
[e] rattling,] rattling B, C
[f] *the ... things.*] the ... things. B, C
[g] *so dissimilar*] so dissimilar B, C
[h] then ...] then— B, C
[i] head! The] head!—the B, C
[j] meeting-place] meeting place A

... the hordes of the devil-cursed pharaonic dead of forty centuries ... the *composite mummies* led through the uttermost onyx voids by King Khephren and his ghoul-queen Nitokris.[a] ...

The tramping drew nearer—heaven[b] save me from the sound of those feet and paws and hooves and pads and talons as it commenced to acquire detail! Down limitless reaches of sunless pavement a spark of light flickered in the malodorous wind,[c] and I drew behind the enormous circumference of a Cyclopic column that I might escape for a while the horror that was stalking million-footed toward me through gigantic hypostyles of inhuman dread and phobic antiquity. The flickers increased, and the tramping and dissonant rhythm grew sickeningly loud. In the quivering orange light there stood faintly forth a scene of such stony awe that I gasped from a[d] sheer wonder that conquered even fear and repulsion. Bases of columns whose middles were higher than human sight ... mere bases of things that must each dwarf the Eiffel Tower to insignificance ... hieroglyphics carved by unthinkable hands in caverns where daylight can be only a remote legend. ...

I *would not* look at the marching things. That I desperately resolved as I heard their creaking joints and nitrous wheezing above the dead music and the dead tramping. It was merciful that they did not speak ... but God! *their crazy torches began to cast shadows on the surface of those stupendous columns.* Heaven take it away![e] *Hippopotami should not have human hands and carry torches ... men should not[f] have the heads of crocodiles.* ...

I tried to turn away, but the shadows and the sounds and the stench were everywhere. Then I remembered something I used to do in half-conscious nightmares as a boy, and began to repeat to myself, "This[g] is a dream! This is a dream!" But it was of no use, and I could only shut my eyes and pray ... at least, that is what I think I did, for one is never sure in visions—and I know this can have been nothing more. I wondered whether I should ever reach the world again, and at

[a] Nitokris.] Nitocris. A, B, C
[b] heaven] Heaven A, B, C
[c] wind,] wind C
[d] a] *om.* C
[e] Heaven ... away!] *om.* B, C
[f] *men ... not*] men ... not [*end of line*] A
[g] "This] "this A

times would furtively open my eyes to see if I could discern any feature of the place other than the wind of spiced putrefaction, the topless columns, and the thaumatropically grotesque shadows of abnormal horror. The sputtering glare of multiplying torches now shone, and unless this hellish place were wholly without walls, I could not fail to see some boundary or fixed landmark soon. But I had to shut my eyes again when I realised[a] *how many*[b] of the things were assembling—and when I glimpsed a certain object walking solemnly and steadily *without any body above the waist.*

A fiendish and ululant corpse-gurgle or death-rattle now split the very atmosphere—the charnel atmosphere poisonous with naphtha[c] and bitumen blasts—in one concerted chorus from the ghoulish legion of hybrid blasphemies. My eyes, perversely shaken open, gazed for an instant upon a sight which no human creature could even imagine without panic[d] fear and physical exhaustion. The things had filed ceremonially in one direction, the direction of the noisome wind, where the light of their torches shewed[e] their bended heads . . .[f] or the bended heads of such as had heads. . . .[g] They were worshipping[h] before a great black foetor-belching[i] aperture which reached up almost out of sight, and which I could see was flanked at right angles by two giant staircases whose ends were far away in shadow. One of these was indubitably the staircase I had fallen down.

The dimensions of the hole were fully in proportion with those of the columns—an ordinary house would have been lost in it, and any average public building could easily have been moved in and out. It was so vast a surface that only by moving the eye could one trace its boundaries . . . so vast, so hideously black, and so aromatically stinking. . . . Directly in front of this yawning Polyphemus-door the

[a] realised] realized A, B, C
[b] *how many*] how many B, C
[c] naphtha] naftha B, C
[d] panic] panic, C
[e] shewed] showed A, B, C
[f] heads . . .] heads— B, C
[g] heads. . . .] heads. B, C
[h] worshipping] worshiping A
[i] foetor-belching] fetor-belching B, C

things were throwing objects—evidently sacrifices or religious offerings, to judge by their gestures. Khephren was their leader; sneering King Khephren *or the guide Abdul Reis,* crowned with a golden pshent and intoning endless formulae with the hollow voice of the dead. By his side knelt beautiful Queen Nitokris,[a] whom I saw in profile for a moment, noting that the right half of her face was eaten away by rats or other ghouls. And I shut my eyes again when I saw *what*[b] objects were being thrown as offerings to the foetid[c] aperture or its possible local deity.

It occurred to me that[d] judging from the elaborateness of this worship, the concealed deity must be one of considerable importance. Was it Osiris or Isis, Horus or Anubis, or some vast unknown God of the Dead still more central and supreme? There is a legend that terrible altars and colossi were reared to an Unknown One before ever the known gods were worshipped.[e] . . .

And now, as I steeled myself to watch the rapt and sepulchral adorations of those nameless things, a thought of escape flashed upon me. The hall was dim, and the columns heavy with shadow. With every creature of that nightmare throng absorbed in shocking raptures, it might be barely possible for me to creep past to the far-away end of one of the staircases and ascend unseen; trusting to Fate and skill to deliver me from the upper reaches. Where I was, I neither knew nor seriously reflected upon—and for a moment it struck me as amusing to plan a serious escape from that which I knew to be a dream. Was I in some hidden and unsuspected lower realm of Khephren's gateway temple—that temple which generations have persistently called the Temple of the Sphinx? I could not conjecture, but I resolved to ascend to life and consciousness if wit and muscle could carry me.

Wriggling flat on my stomach, I began the anxious journey toward the foot of the left-hand staircase, which seemed the more accessible of the two. I cannot describe the incidents and sensations of that

[a] Nitokris,] Nitocris, A, B, C
[b] *what*] what B, C
[c] foetid] fetid B, C
[d] that] that, B, C
[e] worshipped.] worshiped. A

crawl, but they may be guessed when one reflects on *what I had to watch steadily in that malign, wind-blown torchlight*[a] in order to avoid detection. The bottom of the staircase was, as I have said, far away in shadow;[b] as it had to be to rise without a bend to the dizzy parapeted landing above the titanic aperture. This placed the last stages of my crawl at some distance from the noisome herd, though the spectacle chilled me even when quite remote at my right.

At length I succeeded in reaching the steps and began to climb; keeping close to the wall, on which I observed decorations of the most hideous sort, and relying for safety on the absorbed, ecstatic interest with which the monstrosities watched the foul-breezed aperture and the impious objects of nourishment they had flung on the pavement before it. Though the staircase was huge and steep, fashioned of vast porphyry blocks as if for the feet of a giant, the ascent seemed virtually interminable. Dread of discovery and the pain which renewed exercise had brought to my wounds combined to make that upward crawl a thing of agonising[c] memory. I had intended, on reaching the landing, to climb immediately onward along whatever upper staircase might mount from there; stopping for no last look at the carrion abominations that pawed and genuflected some seventy or eighty feet below—yet a sudden repetition of that thunderous corpse-gurgle and death-rattle chorus, coming as I had nearly gained the top of the flight and shewing[d] by its ceremonial rhythm that it was not an alarm of my discovery, caused me to pause and peer cautiously over the parapet.

The monstrosities were hailing something which had poked itself out of the nauseous aperture to seize the hellish fare proffered it. It was something quite ponderous, even as seen from my height; something yellowish and hairy, and endowed with a sort of nervous motion. It was as large, perhaps, as a good-sized hippopotamus, but very curiously shaped. It seemed to have no neck, but five separate shaggy heads springing in a row from a roughly cylindrical trunk; the first very small, the second good-sized, the third and fourth equal and

---

[a] *what . . . torchlight*] what . . . torchlight B, C
[b] shadow;] shadow, B, C
[c] agonising] agonizing A, B, C
[d] shewing] showing A, B, C

largest of all, and the fifth rather small, though not so small as the first.[a] Out of these heads darted curious rigid tentacles which seized ravenously on the *excessively great* [b] quantities of unmentionable food placed before the aperture. Once in a while the thing would leap up, and occasionally it would retreat into its den in a very odd manner. Its locomotion was so inexplicable that I stared in fascination, wishing it would emerge further from the cavernous lair beneath me.

Then it *did* emerge[c] . . . it *did* emerge, and at the sight I turned and fled into the darkness up the higher staircase that rose behind me; fled unknowingly up incredible steps and ladders and inclined planes to which no human sight or logic guided me, and which I must ever relegate to the world of dreams for want of any confirmation. It must have been[d] dream, or the dawn would never have found me breathing on the sands of Gizeh before the sardonic dawn-flushed face of the Great Sphinx.

The Great Sphinx! God!—that *idle question*[e] I asked myself on that sun-blest morning before . . . *what huge and loathsome abnormality was the Sphinx originally carven to represent?* Accursed is the sight, be it in dream or not, that revealed to me the supreme horror—the Unknown[f] God of the Dead, which licks its colossal chops in the unsuspected abyss, fed hideous morsels by soulless absurdities that should not exist.[g] The five-headed monster that emerged . . . that five-headed monster as large as a hippopotamus . . . the five-headed monster—*and that of which it is the merest fore-paw.*[h] . . .

But I survived, and I know it was only a dream.

---

[a] first.] first. ¶ B, C

[b] *excessively great*] excessively great B, C

[c] emerge] *emerge* B, C

[d] been] been a C

[e] *idle question*] *idle* / question A; idle question B, C

[f] Unknown] unknown B, C

[g] exist.] exist! A

[h] *fore-paw.*] *fore-/paw.* B; *forepaw.* C

The Shunned House

I.

From even the greatest of horrors irony is seldom absent. Sometimes it enters directly into the composition of the events, while sometimes it relates only to their fortuitous position among persons and places. The latter sort is splendidly exemplified by a case in the ancient city of Providence, where in the late 'forties[a] Edgar Allan Poe used to sojourn often during his unsuccessful wooing of the gifted poetess, Mrs. Whitman. Poe generally stopped at the Mansion House in Benefit Street—the renamed Golden Ball Inn whose roof has sheltered Washington, Jefferson, and Lafayette—and his favourite walk led northward along the same street to Mrs. Whitman's home and the neighbouring hillside churchyard of St. John's,[b] whose hidden expanse of eighteenth-century gravestones had for him a peculiar fascination.

Now the irony is this. In this walk, so many times repeated, the world's greatest master of the terrible and the bizarre was obliged to pass a particular house on the eastern side of the street; a dingy,

Editor's Note: A T.Ms. exists at JHL, but it is not by HPL nor in any other recognisable typeface. Although it has not been examined in detail, it probably is not original but derives from W. Paul Cook's abortive pamphlet of 1928. The original A.Ms. was given to Samuel Loveman (see HPL to R. H. Barlow, 12 July 1934; *OFF* 149); and although HPL believed that Loveman had misplaced it, Loveman declared owning the text well after HPL's death (see Samuel Loveman to Winfield Townley Scott, 19 April 1944; ms., JHL). The A.Ms. has now surfaced and is currently being offered for sale by the dealer L. W. Currey. No other ms. of the work has ever come to light. The Cook printing, however, is probably quite accurate. The Arkham House editions follow Cook but make a number of errors, including the dropping of several lines of text.

Texts: A = *The Shunned House* (Athol. MA: W. Paul Cook/The Recluse Press, 1928); B = *At the Mountains of Madness and Other Novels* (Arkham House, 1964), 222–47. Copy-text: A.

[a] 'forties] forties A, B
[b] John's,] John's B

antiquated structure perched on the abruptly rising side-hill,[a] with a great unkempt[b] yard dating from a time when the region was partly open country. It does not appear that he ever wrote or spoke of it, nor is there any evidence that he even noticed it. And yet that house, to the two persons in possession of certain information, equals or outranks in horror the wildest phantasy of the genius who so often passed it unknowingly, and stands starkly leering as a symbol of all that is unutterably hideous.

The house was—and for that matter still is—of a kind to attract the attention of the curious. Originally a farm or semi-farm building, it followed the average New England colonial lines of the middle eighteenth century—the prosperous peaked-roof sort, with two stories and dormerless attic, and with the Georgian doorway and interior panelling dictated by the progress of taste at that time. It faced south, with one gable end[c] buried to the lower windows in the eastward rising hill, and the other exposed to the foundations toward the street. Its construction, over a century and a half ago, had followed the grading and straightening of the road in that especial vicinity; for Benefit Street—at first called Back Street—was laid out as a lane winding amongst the graveyards of the first settlers, and straightened only when the removal of the bodies to the North Burial Ground made it decently possible to cut through the old family plots.

At the start, the western wall had lain some twenty feet up a precipitous lawn from the roadway; but a widening of the street at about the time of the Revolution sheared off most of the intervening space, exposing the foundations so that a brick basement wall had to be made, giving the deep cellar a street frontage with[d] door and two windows above ground, close to the new line of public travel. When the sidewalk was laid out a century ago the last of the intervening space was removed; and Poe in his walks must have seen only a sheer ascent of dull grey brick flush with the sidewalk and surmounted at a height of ten feet by the antique shingled bulk of the house proper.

---

[a] side-hill,] side hill, A, B
[b] unkempt] unkept B
[c] end] and B
[d] with] with the B

The farm-like[a] grounds extended back very deeply up the hill, almost to Wheaton Street. The space south of the house, abutting on Benefit Street, was of course greatly above the existing sidewalk level, forming a terrace bounded by a high bank wall of damp, mossy stone pierced by a steep flight of narrow steps which led inward between canyon-like surfaces to the upper region of mangy lawn, rheumy brick walls, and neglected gardens whose dismantled cement urns, rusted kettles fallen from tripods of knotty sticks, and similar paraphernalia set off the weather-beaten[b] front door with its broken fanlight, rotting Ionic pilasters, and wormy triangular pediment.

What I heard in my youth about the shunned house was merely that people died there in alarmingly great numbers. That, I was told, was why the original owners had moved out some twenty years after building the place. It was plainly unhealthy, perhaps because of the dampness and fungous growth in the cellar, the general sickish smell, the draughts of the hallways, or the quality of the well and pump water. These things were bad enough, and these were all that gained belief among the persons whom I knew. Only the notebooks of my antiquarian uncle, Dr. Elihu Whipple, revealed to me at length the darker, vaguer surmises which formed an undercurrent of folklore among old-time servants and humble folk;[c] surmises which never travelled far, and which were largely forgotten when Providence grew to be a metropolis with a shifting modern population.

The general fact is, that the house was never regarded by the solid part of the community as in any real sense "haunted".[d] There were no widespread tales of rattling chains, cold currents of air, extinguished lights, or faces at the window. Extremists sometimes said the house was "unlucky",[e] but that is as far as even they went. What was really beyond dispute is that a frightful proportion of persons died there; or more accurately, *had* died there, since after some peculiar happenings over sixty years ago the building had become deserted through the

---

[a] farm-like] farmlike A, B
[b] weather-beaten] weatherbeaten B
[c] folk;] folk, B
[d] "haunted".] "haunted." B
[e] "unlucky",] "unlucky," B

sheer impossibility of renting it. These persons were not all cut off suddenly by any one cause; rather did it seem that their vitality was insidiously sapped, so that each one died the sooner from whatever tendency to weakness he may have naturally had. And those who did not die displayed in varying degree a type of anaemia or consumption, and sometimes a decline of the mental faculties, which spoke ill for the salubriousness of the building. Neighbouring houses, it must be added, seemed entirely free from the noxious quality.

This much I knew before my insistent questioning led my uncle to shew[a] me the notes which finally embarked us both on our hideous investigation. In my childhood the shunned house was vacant, with barren, gnarled,[b] and terrible old trees, long, queerly pale grass,[c] and nightmarishly misshapen weeds in the high terraced yard where birds never lingered. We boys used to overrun the place, and I can still recall my youthful terror not only at the morbid strangeness of this sinister vegetation, but at the eldritch atmosphere and odour of the dilapidated house, whose unlocked front door was often entered in quest of shudders. The small-paned windows were largely broken, and a nameless air of desolation hung round the precarious panelling, shaky interior shutters, peeling wall-paper,[d] falling plaster, rickety staircases, and such fragments of battered furniture as still remained. The dust and cobwebs added their touch of the fearful; and brave indeed was the boy who would voluntarily ascend the ladder to the attic, a vast raftered length lighted only by small blinking windows in the gable ends, and filled with a massed wreckage of chests, chairs, and spinning-wheels which infinite years of deposit had shrouded and festooned into monstrous and hellish shapes.

But after all, the attic was not the most terrible part of the house. It was the dank, humid cellar which somehow exerted the strongest repulsion on us, even though it was wholly above ground on the street side, with only a thin door and window-pierced brick wall to separate it from the busy sidewalk. We scarcely knew whether to haunt it in

[a] shew] show A, B
[b] gnarled,] gnarled A, B
[c] grass,] grass A, B
[d] wall-paper,] wallpaper, B

spectral fascination, or to shun it for the sake of our souls and our sanity. For one thing, the bad odour of the house was strongest there; and for another thing, we did not like the white fungous growths which occasionally sprang up in rainy summer weather from the hard earth floor. Those fungi, grotesquely like the vegetation in the yard outside, were truly horrible in their outlines; detestable parodies of toadstools and Indian pipes, whose like we had never seen in any other situation. They rotted quickly, and at one stage became slightly phosphorescent; so that nocturnal passers-by sometimes spoke of witch-fires glowing behind the broken panes of the foetor-spreading windows.

We never—even in our wildest Hallowe'en moods—visited this cellar by night, but in some of our daytime visits could detect the phosphorescence, especially when the day was dark and wet. There was also a subtler thing we often thought we detected—a very strange thing which was, however, merely suggestive at most. I refer to a sort of cloudy whitish pattern on the dirt floor—a vague, shifting deposit of mould or nitre which we sometimes thought we could trace amidst the sparse fungous growths near the huge fireplace of the basement kitchen. Once in a while it struck us that this patch bore an uncanny resemblance to a doubled-up human figure, though generally no such kinship existed, and often there was no whitish deposit whatever. On a certain rainy afternoon when this illusion seemed phenomenally strong, and when, in addition, I had fancied I glimpsed a kind of thin, yellowish, shimmering exhalation rising from the nitrous pattern toward the yawning fireplace, I spoke to my uncle about the matter. He smiled at this odd conceit, but it seemed that his smile was tinged with reminiscence. Later I heard that a similar notion entered into some of the wild ancient tales of the common folk—a notion likewise alluding to ghoulish, wolfish shapes taken by smoke from the great chimney, and queer contours assumed by certain of the sinuous tree-roots that thrust their way into the cellar through the loose foundation-stones.

II.

Not till my adult years did my uncle set before me the notes and data which he had collected concerning the shunned house. Dr. Whipple was a sane, conservative physician of the old school, and for all his interest in the place was not eager to encourage young thoughts toward the abnormal. His own view, postulating simply a building and location of markedly unsanitary qualities, had nothing to do with abnormality; but he realised that the very picturesqueness which aroused his own interest would in a boy's fanciful mind take on all manner of gruesome imaginative associations.

The doctor was a bachelor; a white-haired, clean-shaven, old-fashioned gentleman, and a local historian of note, who had often broken a lance with such controversial guardians of tradition as Sidney S. Rider and Thomas W. Bicknell. He lived with one manservant in a Georgian homestead with knocker and iron-railed steps, balanced eerily on the steep ascent of North Court Street beside the ancient brick court and colony house where his grandfather—a cousin of that celebrated privateersman, Capt. Whipple, who burnt His Majesty's armed schooner *Gaspee* in 1772—had voted in the legislature[a] on May 4, 1776, for the independence of the Rhode-Island[b] Colony. Around him in the damp, low-ceiled library with the musty white panelling, heavy carved overmantel,[c] and small-paned, vine-shaded windows, were the relics and records of his ancient family, among which were many dubious allusions to the shunned house in Benefit Street. That pest spot lies not far distant—for Benefit runs ledgewise just above the court-house[d] along the precipitous hill up which the first settlement climbed.

When, in the end, my insistent pestering and maturing years evoked from my uncle the hoarded lore I sought, there lay before me a strange enough chronicle. Long-winded, statistical, and drearily genealogical as some of the matter was, there ran through it a continuous thread of brooding, tenacious horror and preternatural malevolence which impressed me even more than it had impressed the good doctor. Separate events fitted together uncannily, and seemingly irrelevant details held mines of hideous possibilities. A new and burning curiosity grew in me, compared to which my boyish curiosity was feeble and inchoate. The first revelation led to an exhaustive

[a] legislature] legialature B
[b] Rhode-Island] Rhode Island B
[c] overmantel,] overmantel A, B
[d] court-house] court house A, B

research, and finally to that shuddering quest which proved so disastrous to myself and mine. For at last my uncle insisted on joining the search I had commenced, and after a certain night in that house he did not come away with me. I am lonely without that gentle soul whose long years were filled only with honour, virtue, good taste, benevolence, and learning. I have reared a marble urn to his memory in St. John's churchyard—the place that Poe loved—the hidden grove of giant willows on the hill, where tombs and headstones huddle quietly between the hoary bulk of the church and the houses and bank walls of Benefit Street.

The history of the house, opening amidst a maze of dates, revealed no trace of the sinister either about its construction or about the prosperous and honourable family who built it. Yet from the first a taint of calamity, soon increased to boding significance, was apparent. My uncle's carefully compiled record began with the building of the structure in 1763, and followed the theme with an unusual amount of detail. The shunned house, it seems, was first inhabited by William Harris and his wife Rhoby Dexter, with their children, Elkanah, born in 1755, Abigail, born in 1757, William, Jr., born in 1759, and Ruth, born in 1761. Harris was a substantial merchant and seaman in the West India trade, connected with the firm of Obadiah Brown and his nephews. After Brown's death in 1761, the new firm of Nicholas Brown & Co. made him master of the brig *Prudence*, Providence-built, of 120 tons, thus enabling him to erect the new homestead he had desired ever since his marriage.

The site he had chosen—a recently straightened part of the new and fashionable Back Street, which ran along the side of the hill above crowded Cheapside—was all that could be wished, and the building did justice to the location. It was the best that moderate means could afford, and Harris hastened to move in before the birth of a fifth child which the family expected. That child, a boy, came in December; but was still-born. Nor was any child to be born alive in that house for a century and a half.

The next April sickness occurred among the children, and Abigail and Ruth died before the month was over. Dr. Job Ives diagnosed the trouble as some infantile fever, though others declared it was more of a mere wasting-away or decline. It seemed, in any event, to be contagious; for Hannah Bowen, one of the two servants, died of it in the following June. Eli Liddeason,[a] the other servant, constantly complained of weakness; and would have returned to his father's farm in Rehoboth but for a sudden attachment for Mehitabel Pierce, who was hired to succeed Hannah. He died the next year—a sad year indeed, since it marked the death of William Harris himself, enfeebled as he was by the climate of Martinique, where his occupation had kept him for considerable periods during the preceding decade.

The widowed Rhoby Harris never recovered from the shock of her husband's death, and the passing of her first-born[b] Elkanah two years later was the final blow to her reason. In 1768 she fell victim to a mild form of insanity, and was thereafter confined to the upper part of the house; her elder maiden sister, Mercy Dexter, having moved in to take charge of the family. Mercy was a plain, raw-boned woman of great strength; but her health visibly declined from the time of her advent. She was greatly devoted to her unfortunate sister, and had an especial affection for her only surviving nephew William, who from a sturdy infant had become a sickly, spindling lad. In this year the servant Mehitabel died, and the other servant, Preserved Smith, left without coherent explanation—or at least, with only some wild tales and a complaint that he disliked the smell of the place. For a time Mercy could secure no more help, since the seven deaths and case of madness, all occurring within five years' space,[c] had begun to set in motion the body of fireside rumour which later became so bizarre. Ultimately, however, she obtained new servants from out of town; Ann White, a morose woman from that part of North Kingstown now set off as the township of Exeter, and a capable Boston man named Zenas Low.

It was Ann White who first gave definite shape to the sinister idle talk. Mercy should have known better than to hire anyone from the Nooseneck Hill country, for that remote bit of backwoods was then, as now, a seat of the most uncomfortable superstitions. As lately as 1892 an Exeter community exhumed a dead body and ceremoniously burnt its heart in order to prevent certain alleged visitations injurious to the

[a] Liddeason,] Lideason, B
[b] first-born] firstborn B
[c] space,] space B

public health and peace, and one may imagine the point of view of the same section in 1768. Ann's tongue was perniciously active, and within a few months Mercy discharged her, filling her place with a faithful and amiable Amazon from Newport, Maria Robbins.

Meanwhile poor Rhoby Harris, in her madness, gave voice to dreams and imaginings of the most hideous sort. At times her screams became insupportable, and for long periods she would utter shrieking horrors which necessitated her son's temporary residence with his cousin, Peleg Harris, in Presbyterian Lane near the new college building. The boy would seem to improve after these visits, and had Mercy been as wise as she was well-meaning, she would have let him live permanently with Peleg. Just what Mrs. Harris cried out in her fits of violence, tradition hesitates to say; or rather, presents such extravagant accounts that they nullify themselves through sheer absurdity. Certainly it sounds absurd to hear that a woman educated only in the rudiments of French often shouted for hours in a coarse and idiomatic form of that language, or that the same person, alone and guarded, complained wildly of a staring thing which bit and chewed at her. In 1772 the servant Zenas died, and when Mrs. Harris heard of it she laughed with a shocking delight utterly foreign to her. The next year she herself died, and was laid to rest in the North Burial Ground beside her husband.

Upon the outbreak of trouble with Great Britain in 1775, William Harris, despite his scant sixteen years and feeble constitution, managed to enlist in the Army of Observation under General Greene; and from that time on enjoyed a steady rise in health and prestige. In 1780, as a Captain in Rhode Island forces in New Jersey under Colonel Angell, he met and married Phebe Hetfield of Elizabethtown, whom he brought to Providence upon his honourable discharge in the following year.

The young soldier's return was not a thing of unmitigated happiness. The house, it is true, was still in good condition; and the street had been widened and changed in name from Back Street to Benefit Street. But Mercy Dexter's once robust frame had undergone a sad[a] and curious decay, so that she was now a stooped and pathetic figure with hollow voice and disconcerting pallor—qualities shared to a singular degree by the one remaining servant Maria. In the autumn of

[a] sad] sag B

1782 Phebe Harris gave birth to a still-born daughter,[a] and on the fifteenth of the next May Mercy Dexter took leave of a useful, austere, and virtuous life.

William Harris, at last thoroughly convinced of the radically unhealthful nature of his abode, now took steps toward quitting it and closing it for ever.[b] Securing temporary quarters for himself and his wife at the newly opened Golden Ball Inn, he arranged for the building of a new and finer house in Westminster Street, in the growing part of the town across the Great Bridge. There, in 1785, his son Dutee was born; and there the family dwelt till the encroachments of commerce drove them back across the river and over the hill to Angell Street, in the newer East Side residence district, where the late Archer Harris built his sumptuous but hideous French-roofed mansion in 1876. William and Phebe both succumbed to the yellow fever epidemic of 1797, but Dutee was brought up by his cousin Rathbone Harris, Peleg's son.

Rathbone was a practical man, and rented the Benefit Street house despite William's wish to keep it vacant. He considered it an obligation to his ward to make the most of all the boy's property, nor did he concern himself with the deaths and illnesses which caused so many changes of tenants, or the steadily growing aversion with which the house was generally regarded. It is likely that he felt only vexation when, in 1804, the town council ordered him to fumigate the place with sulphur, tar,[c] and gum camphor on account of the much-discussed deaths of four persons, presumably caused by the then diminishing fever epidemic. They said the place had a febrile smell.

Dutee himself thought little of the house, for he grew up to be a privateersman, and served with distinction on the *Vigilant* under Capt. Cahoone in the War of 1812. He returned unharmed, married in 1814, and became a father on that memorable night of September 23, 1815, when a great gale drove the waters of the bay over half the town, and floated a tall sloop well up Westminster Street so that its masts almost tapped the Harris windows in symbolic affirmation that the new boy, Welcome, was a seaman's son.

---

[a] daughter,] daughter B
[b] for ever.] forever. A, B
[c] tar,] tar B

Welcome did not survive his father, but lived to perish gloriously at Fredericksburg in 1862. Neither he nor his son Archer knew of the shunned house as other than a nuisance almost impossible to rent—perhaps on account of the mustiness and sickly odour of unkempt old age. Indeed, it never was rented after a series of deaths culminating in 1861, which the excitement of the war tended to throw into obscurity. Carrington Harris, last of the male line, knew it only as a deserted and somewhat picturesque centre[a] of legend until I told him my experience. He had meant to tear it down and build an apartment house on the site, but after my account decided to let it stand, install plumbing, and rent it. Nor has he yet had any difficulty in obtaining tenants. The horror has gone.

III.

It may well be imagined how powerfully I was affected by the annals of the Harrises. In this continuous record there seemed to me to brood a persistent evil beyond anything in Nature[b] as I had known it; an evil clearly connected with the house and not with the family. This impression was confirmed by my uncle's less systematic array of miscellaneous data—legends transcribed from servant gossip, cuttings from the papers, copies of death-certificates[c] by fellow-physicians, and the like. All of this material I cannot hope to give, for my uncle was a tireless antiquarian and very deeply interested in the shunned house; but I may refer to several dominant points which earn notice by their recurrence through many reports from diverse sources. For example, the servant gossip was practically unanimous in attributing to the fungous and malodorous *cellar* of the house a vast supremacy in evil influence. There had been servants—Ann White especially—who would not use the cellar kitchen, and at least three well-defined legends bore upon the queer quasi-human or diabolic outlines assumed by tree-roots and patches of mould in that region. These latter narratives interested me profoundly, on account of what I had seen in my boyhood, but I

---

[a] centre] center B
[b] Nature] nature A, B
[c] death-certificates] death certificates A

felt that most of the significance had in each case been largely obscured by additions from the common stock of local ghost lore.

Ann White, with her Exeter superstition, had promulgated the most extravagant and at the same time most consistent tale; alleging that there must lie buried beneath the house one of those vampires—the dead who retain their bodily form and live on the blood or breath of the living—whose hideous legions send their preying shapes or spirits abroad by night. To destroy a vampire one must, the grandmothers say, exhume it and burn its heart, or at least drive a stake through that organ; and Ann's dogged insistence on a search under the cellar had been prominent in bringing about her discharge.

Her tales, however, commanded a wide audience, and were the more readily accepted because the house indeed stood on land once used for burial purposes. To me their interest depended less on this circumstance than on the peculiarly appropriate way in which they dovetailed with certain other things—the complaint of the departing servant Preserved Smith, who had preceded Ann and never heard of her, that something "sucked his breath" at night; the death-certificates of fever victims of 1804, issued by Dr. Chad Hopkins, and shewing[a] the four deceased persons all unaccountably lacking in blood; and the obscure passages of poor Rhoby Harris's ravings, where she complained of the sharp teeth of a glassy-eyed, half-visible presence.

Free from unwarranted superstition though I am, these things produced in me an odd sensation, which was intensified by a pair of widely separated newspaper cuttings relating to deaths in the shunned house—one from the *Providence Gazette and Country-Journal* of April 12, 1815, and the other from the *Daily Transcript and Chronicle* of October 27, 1845—each of which detailed an appallingly grisly circumstance whose duplication was remarkable. It seems that in both instances the dying person, in 1815 a gentle old lady named Stafford and in 1845 a school-teacher of middle age named Eleazar Durfee, became transfigured in a horrible way; glaring glassily and attempting to bite the throat of the attending physician. Even more puzzling, though, was the final case which put an end to the renting of the house—a series of anaemia deaths preceded by progressive madnesses wherein the patient

[a] shewing] showing A, B

would craftily attempt the lives of his relatives by incisions in the neck or wrist.[a]

This was in 1860 and 1861, when my uncle had just begun his medical practice; and before leaving for the front he heard much of it from his elder professional colleagues. The really inexplicable thing was the way in which the victims—ignorant people, for the ill-smelling and widely shunned house could now be rented to no others—would babble maledictions in French, a language they could not possibly have studied to any extent. It made one think of poor Rhoby Harris nearly a century before, and so moved my uncle that he commenced collecting historical data on the house after listening, some time subsequent to his return from the war, to the first-hand account of Drs. Chase and Whitmarsh. Indeed, I could see that my uncle had thought deeply on the subject, and that he was glad of my own interest—an open-minded and sympathetic interest which enabled him to discuss with me matters at which others would merely have laughed. His fancy had not gone so far as mine, but he felt that the place was rare in its imaginative potentialities, and worthy of note as an inspiration in the field of the grotesque and macabre.

For my part, I was disposed to take the whole subject with profound seriousness, and began at once not only to review the evidence, but to accumulate as much more[b] as I could. I talked with the elderly Archer Harris, then owner of the house, many times before his death in 1916; and obtained from him and his still surviving maiden sister Alice an authentic corroboration of all the family data my uncle had collected. When, however, I asked them what connexion[c] with France or its language the house could have,[d] they confessed themselves as frankly baffled and ignorant as I. Archer knew nothing, and all that Miss Harris could say was that an old allusion her grandfather, Dutee Harris, had heard of might have shed a little light. The old seaman, who had survived his son Welcome's death in battle by two years, had not himself known the legend; but recalled that his

---

[a] wrist.] wrists. B

[b] more] *om.* B

[c] connexion] connection A, B

[d] have,] have; A

earliest nurse, the ancient Maria Robbins, seemed darkly aware of something that might have lent a weird significance to the French ravings of Rhoby Harris, which she had so often heard during the last days of that hapless woman. Maria had been at the shunned house from 1769 till the removal of the family in 1783, and had seen Mercy Dexter die. Once she hinted to the child Dutee of a somewhat peculiar circumstance in Mercy's last moments, but he had soon forgotten all about it save that it was something peculiar. The granddaughter,[a] moreover, recalled even this much with difficulty. She and her brother were not so much interested in the house as was Archer's son Carrington, the present owner, with whom I talked after my experience.

Having exhausted the Harris family of all the information it could furnish, I turned my attention to early town records and deeds with a zeal more penetrating than that which my uncle had occasionally shewn[b] in the same work. What I wished was a comprehensive history of the site from its very settlement in 1636—or even before, if any Narragansett Indian legend could be unearthed to supply the data. I found, at the start, that the land had been part of the long strip of home[c] lot granted originally to John Throckmorton; one of many similar strips beginning at the Town Street beside the river and extending up over the hill to a line roughly corresponding with the modern Hope Street. The Throckmorton lot had later, of course, been much subdivided; and I became very assiduous in tracing that section through which Back or Benefit Street was later run. It had, a rumour indeed said, been the Throckmorton graveyard; but as I examined the records more carefully, I found that the graves had all been transferred at an early date to the North Burial Ground on the Pawtucket West Road.

Then suddenly I came—by a rare piece of chance, since it was not in the main body of records and might easily have been missed—upon something which aroused my keenest eagerness, fitting in as it did with several of the queerest phases of the affair. It was the record of a lease,[d] in 1697, of a small tract of ground to an Etienne Roulet and

---

[a] granddaughter,] grand-daughter, B
[b] shewn] shown A, B
[c] home] the B
[d] lease,] lease B

wife. At last the French element had appeared—that, and another deeper element of horror which the name conjured up from the darkest recesses of my weird and heterogeneous reading—and I feverishly studied the platting of the locality as it had been before the cutting through and partial straightening of Back Street between 1747 and 1758. I found what I had half expected, that where the shunned house now stood the Roulets had laid out their graveyard behind a one-story and attic cottage, and that no record of any transfer of graves existed. The document, indeed, ended in much confusion; and I was forced to ransack both the Rhode Island Historical Society and Shepley Library before I could find a local door which the name Etienne Roulet would unlock. In the end I did find something; something of such vague but monstrous import that I set about at once to examine the cellar of the shunned house itself with a new and excited minuteness.

The Roulets, it seemed, had come in 1696 from East Greenwich, down the west shore of Narragansett Bay. They were Huguenots from Caude, and had encountered much opposition before the Providence selectmen allowed them to settle in the town. Unpopularity had dogged them in East Greenwich, whither they had come in 1686, after the revocation of the Edict of Nantes, and rumour said that the cause of dislike extended beyond mere racial and national prejudice, or the land disputes which involved other French settlers with the English in rivalries which not even Governor Andros could quell. But their ardent Protestantism—too ardent, some whispered—and their evident distress when virtually driven from the village down the bay, had moved the sympathy of the town fathers. Here the strangers[a] had been granted a haven; and the swarthy Etienne Roulet, less apt at agriculture than at reading queer books and drawing queer diagrams, was given a clerical post in the warehouse at Pardon Tillinghast's wharf, far south in Town Street. There had, however, been a riot of some sort later on—perhaps forty years later, after old Roulet's death—and no one seemed to hear of the family after that.

For a century and more, it appeared, the Roulets had been well remembered and frequently discussed as vivid incidents in the quiet life of a New England seaport. Etienne's son Paul, a surly fellow whose

---

[a] down . . . strangers] *om.* B

erratic conduct had probably provoked the riot which wiped out the family, was particularly a source of speculation; and though Providence never shared the witchcraft panics of her Puritan neighbours, it was freely intimated by old wives that his prayers were neither uttered at the proper time nor directed toward the proper object. All this had undoubtedly formed the basis of the legend known by old Maria Robbins. What relation it had to the French ravings of Rhoby Harris and other inhabitants of the shunned house, imagination or future discovery alone could determine. I wondered how many of those who had known the legends realised[a] that additional link with the terrible which my wider reading had given me; that ominous item in the annals of morbid horror which tells of the creature *Jacques Roulet, of Caude,* who in 1598 was condemned to death as a daemoniac but afterward saved from the stake by the Paris parliament and shut in a madhouse. He had been found covered with blood and shreds of flesh in a wood, shortly after the killing and rending of a boy by a pair of wolves. One wolf was seen to lope away unhurt. Surely a pretty hearthside tale, with a queer significance as to name and place; but I decided that the Providence gossips could not have generally known of it. Had they known, the coincidence of names would have brought some drastic and frightened action—indeed, might not its limited whispering have precipitated the final riot which erased the Roulets from the town?

I now visited the accursed place with increased frequency; studying the unwholesome vegetation of the garden, examining all the walls of the building, and poring over every inch of the earthen cellar floor. Finally, with Carrington Harris's permission, I fitted a key to the disused door opening from the cellar directly upon Benefit Street, preferring to have a more immediate access to the outside world than the dark stairs, ground-floor[b] hall, and front door could give. There, where morbidity lurked most thickly, I searched and poked during long afternoons when the sunlight filtered in through the cobwebbed above-ground windows, and a sense of security glowed from the unlocked[c] door which placed me only a few feet from the placid

[a] realised] realized B
[b] ground-floor] ground floor A, B
[c] windows, . . . unlocked] *om.* B

sidewalk outside. Nothing new rewarded my efforts—only the same depressing mustiness and faint suggestions of noxious odours and nitrous outlines on the floor—and I fancy that many pedestrians must have watched me curiously through the broken panes.

At length, upon a suggestion of my uncle's, I decided to try the spot nocturnally; and one stormy midnight ran the beams of an electric torch over the mouldy floor with its uncanny shapes and distorted, half-phosphorescent fungi. The place had dispirited me curiously that evening, and I was almost prepared when I saw—or thought I saw— amidst the whitish deposits a particularly sharp definition of the "huddled form" I had suspected from boyhood. Its clearness was astonishing and unprecedented—and as I watched I seemed to see again the thin, yellowish, shimmering exhalation which had startled me on that rainy afternoon so many years before.

Above the anthropomorphic patch of mould by the fireplace it rose; a subtle, sickish, almost luminous vapour which as it hung trembling in the dampness seemed to develop vague and shocking suggestions of form, gradually trailing off into nebulous decay and passing up into the blackness of the great chimney with a foetor in its wake. It was truly horrible, and the more so to me because of what I knew of the spot. Refusing to flee, I watched it fade—and as I watched I felt that it was in turn watching me greedily with eyes more imaginable than visible. When I told my uncle about it he was greatly aroused; and after a tense hour of reflection, arrived at a definite and drastic decision. Weighing in his mind the importance of the matter, and the significance of our relation to it, he insisted that we both test—and if possible destroy—the horror of the house by a joint night or nights of aggressive vigil in that musty and fungus-cursed cellar.

IV.

On Wednesday, June 25, 1919, after a proper notification of Carrington Harris which did not include surmises as to what we expected to find, my uncle and I conveyed to the shunned house two camp chairs and a folding camp cot, together with some scientific mechanism of greater weight and intricacy. These we placed in the cellar during the day, screening the windows with paper and planning to return in the evening for our first vigil. We had locked the door from the cellar to the ground floor; and having a key to the outside cellar door, we were prepared to leave our expensive and delicate apparatus— which we had obtained secretly and at great cost—as many days as our vigils might need to be protracted. It was our design to sit up together till very late, and then watch singly till dawn in two-hour stretches, myself first and then my companion; the inactive member resting on the cot.

The natural leadership with which my uncle procured the instruments from the laboratories of Brown University and the Cranston Street Armoury,[a] and instinctively assumed direction of our venture, was a marvellous commentary on the potential vitality and resilience of a man of eighty-one. Elihu Whipple had lived according to the hygienic laws he had preached as a physician, and but for what happened later would be here in full vigour today. Only two persons suspect what did happen—Carrington Harris and myself. I had to tell Harris because he owned the house and deserved to know what had gone out of it. Then too, we had spoken to him in advance of our quest; and I felt after my uncle's going that he would understand and assist me in some vitally necessary public explanations. He turned very pale, but agreed to help me, and decided that it would now be safe to rent the house.

To declare that we were not nervous on that rainy night of watching would be an exaggeration both gross and ridiculous. We were not, as I have said, in any sense childishly superstitious, but scientific study and reflection had taught us that the known universe of three dimensions embraces the merest fraction of the whole cosmos of substance and energy. In this case an overwhelming preponderance of evidence from numerous authentic sources pointed to the tenacious existence of certain forces of great power and, so far as the human point of view is concerned, exceptional malignancy. To say that we actually believed in vampires or werewolves would be a carelessly inclusive statement. Rather must it be said that we were not prepared to deny the possibility of certain unfamiliar and unclassified modifications of vital force and attenuated matter; existing very infrequently in three-dimensional space because of its more intimate

[a] Armoury,] Armory, A, B

connexion[a] with other spatial units, yet close enough to the boundary of our own to furnish us occasional manifestations which we, for lack of a proper vantage-point, may never hope to understand.

In short, it seemed to my uncle and me that an incontrovertible array of facts pointed to some lingering influence in the shunned house; traceable to one or another of the ill-favoured French settlers of two centuries before, and still operative through rare and unknown laws of atomic and electronic motion. That the family of Roulet had possessed an abnormal affinity for outer circles of entity—dark spheres which for normal folk hold only repulsion and terror—their recorded history seemed to prove. Had not, then, the riots of those bygone seventeen-thirties set moving certain kinetic patterns in the morbid brain of one or more of them—notably the sinister Paul Roulet—which obscurely survived the bodies murdered and buried by the mob, and[b] continued to function in some multiple-dimensioned space along the original lines of force determined by a frantic hatred of the encroaching community?

Such a thing was surely not a physical or biochemical impossibility in the light of a newer science which includes the theories of relativity and intra-atomic action. One might easily imagine an alien nucleus of substance or energy, formless or otherwise, kept alive by imperceptible or immaterial subtractions from the life-force or bodily tissues and fluids of other and more palpably living things into which it penetrates and with whose fabric it sometimes completely merges itself. It might be actively hostile, or it might be dictated merely by blind motives of self-preservation. In any case such a monster must of necessity be in our scheme of things an anomaly and an intruder, whose extirpation forms a primary duty with every man not an enemy to the world's life, health, and sanity.

What baffled us was our utter ignorance of the aspect in which we might encounter the thing. No sane person had even seen it, and few had ever felt it definitely. It might be pure energy—a form ethereal and outside the realm of substance—or it might be partly material; some unknown and equivocal mass of plasticity, capable of changing at will to nebulous approximations of the solid, liquid, gaseous, or tenuously

[a] connexion] connection A, B
[b] buried . . . and] *om.* B

unparticled states. The anthropomorphic patch of mould on the floor, the form of the yellowish vapour, and the curvature of the tree-roots in some of the old tales, all argued at least a remote and reminiscent connexion[a] with the human shape; but how representative or permanent that similarity might be, none could say with any kind of certainty.

We had devised two weapons to fight it; a large and specially fitted Crookes tube operated by powerful storage batteries and provided with peculiar screens and reflectors, in case it proved intangible and opposable only by vigorously destructive ether radiations, and a pair of military flame-throwers of the sort used in the world-war,[b] in case it proved partly material and susceptible of mechanical destruction—for like the superstitious Exeter rustics, we were prepared to burn the thing's heart out if heart existed to burn. All this aggressive mechanism we set in the cellar in positions carefully arranged with reference to the cot and chairs, and to the spot before the fireplace where the mould had taken strange shapes. That suggestive patch, by the way, was only faintly visible when we placed our furniture and instruments, and when we returned that evening for the actual vigil. For a moment I half doubted[c] that I had ever seen it in the more definitely limned form—but then I thought of the legends.

Our cellar vigil began at 10 p.m.,[d] daylight saving time, and as it continued we found no promise of pertinent developments. A weak, filtered glow from the rain-harassed street-lamps outside, and a feeble phosphorescence from the detestable fungi within, shewed[e] the dripping stone of the walls, from which all traces of whitewash had vanished; the dank, foetid,[f] and mildew-tainted hard earth floor with its obscene fungi; the rotting remains of what had been stools, chairs,[g] and tables, and other more shapeless furniture; the heavy planks and massive beams of the ground floor overhead; the decrepit plank door leading to bins and

---

[a] connexion] connection A, B
[b] world-war,] World War, B
[c] half doubted] half-doubted A, B
[d] p.m.,] p. m., A; PM., B
[e] shewed] showed A, B
[f] foetid,] foetid B
[g] chairs,] chairs B

chambers beneath other parts of the house; the crumbling stone staircase with ruined wooden hand-rail; and the crude and cavernous fireplace of blackened brick where rusted iron fragments revealed the past presence of hooks, andirons, spit, crane, and a door to the Dutch oven—these things, and our austere cot and camp chairs, and the heavy and intricate destructive machinery we had brought.

We had, as in my own former explorations, left the door to the street unlocked; so that a direct and practical path of escape might lie open in case of manifestations beyond our power to deal with. It was our idea that our continued nocturnal presence would call forth whatever malign entity lurked there; and that being prepared, we could dispose of the thing with one or the other of our provided means as soon as we had recognised and observed it sufficiently. How long it might require to evoke and extinguish the thing, we had no notion. It occurred to us, too, that our venture was far from safe; for in what strength the thing might appear no one could tell. But we deemed the game worth the hazard, and embarked on it alone and unhesitatingly; conscious that the seeking of outside aid would only expose us to ridicule and perhaps defeat our entire purpose. Such was our frame of mind as we talked—far into the night, till my uncle's growing drowsiness made me remind him to lie down for his two-hour sleep.

Something like fear chilled me as I sat there in the small hours alone—I say alone, for one who sits by a sleeper is indeed alone; perhaps more alone than he can realise. My uncle breathed heavily, his deep inhalations and exhalations accompanied by the rain outside, and punctuated by another nerve-racking sound of distant dripping water within—for the house was repulsively damp even in dry weather, and in this storm positively swamp-like. I studied the loose, antique masonry[a] of the walls in the fungus-light and the feeble rays which stole in from the street through the screened windows; and once, when the noisome atmosphere of the place seemed about to sicken me, I opened the door and looked up and down the street, feasting my eyes on familiar sights and my nostrils on wholesome air. Still nothing occurred to reward my watching; and I yawned repeatedly, fatigue getting the better of apprehension.

[a] antique masonry] antique-/masonry B

Then the stirring of my uncle in his sleep attracted my notice. He had turned restlessly on the cot several times during the latter half of the first hour, but now he was breathing with unusual irregularity, occasionally heaving a sigh which held more than a few of the qualities of a choking moan. I turned my electric flashlight on him and found his face averted, so rising and crossing to the other side of the cot, I again flashed the light to see if he seemed in any pain. What I saw unnerved me most surprisingly, considering its relative triviality. It must have been merely the association of any[a] odd circumstance with the sinister nature of our location and mission, for surely the circumstance was not in itself frightful or unnatural. It was merely that my uncle's facial expression, disturbed no doubt by the strange dreams which our situation prompted, betrayed considerable agitation, and seemed not at all characteristic of him. His habitual expression was one of kindly and well-bred calm, whereas now a variety of emotions seemed struggling within him. I think, on the whole, that it was this *variety* which chiefly disturbed me. My uncle, as he gasped and tossed in increasing perturbation and with eyes that had now started open, seemed not one but many men, and suggested a curious quality of alienage from himself.

All at once he commenced to mutter, and I did not like the look of his mouth and teeth as he spoke. The words were at first indistinguishable, and then—with a tremendous start—I recognised something about them which filled me with icy fear till I recalled the breadth of my uncle's education and the interminable translations he had made from anthropological and antiquarian articles in the *Revue des Deux Mondes.* For the venerable Elihu Whipple was muttering *in*[b] *French,* and the few phrases I could distinguish seemed connected with the darkest myths he had ever adapted from the famous Paris magazine.

Suddenly a perspiration broke out on the sleeper's forehead, and he leaped abruptly up, half awake. The jumble of French changed to a cry in English, and the hoarse voice shouted excitedly, "My breath, my breath!" Then the awakening became complete, and with a subsidence of facial expression to the normal state my uncle seized my hand and

[a] any] an B
[b] *in*] in B

began to relate a dream whose nucleus of significance I could only surmise with a kind of awe.

He had, he said, floated off from a very ordinary series of dream-pictures into a scene whose strangeness was related to nothing he had ever read. It was of this world, and yet not of it—a shadowy geometrical confusion in which could be seen elements of familiar things in most unfamiliar and perturbing combinations. There was a suggestion of queerly disordered pictures superimposed one upon another; an arrangement in which the essentials of time as well as of space seemed dissolved and mixed in the most illogical fashion. In this kaleidoscopic vortex of phantasmal images were occasional snapshots,[a] if one might use the term, of singular clearness but unaccountable heterogeneity.

Once my uncle thought he lay in a carelessly dug open pit, with a crowd of angry faces framed by straggling locks and three-cornered hats frowning down on him. Again he seemed to be in the interior of a house—an old house, apparently—but the details and inhabitants were constantly changing, and he could never be certain of the faces or the furniture, or even of the room itself, since doors and windows seemed in just as great a state of flux as the more presumably mobile objects. It was queer—damnably queer—and my uncle spoke almost sheepishly, as if half expecting not to be believed, when he declared that of the strange faces many had unmistakably borne the features of the Harris family. And all the while there was a personal sensation of choking, as if some pervasive presence had spread itself through his body and sought to possess itself of his vital processes. I shuddered at the thought of those vital processes, worn as they were by eighty-one years of continuous functioning, in conflict with unknown forces of which the youngest and strongest system might well be afraid; but in another moment reflected that dreams are only dreams, and that these uncomfortable visions could be, at most, no more than my uncle's reaction to the investigations and expectations which had lately filled our minds to the exclusion of all else.

Conversation, also, soon tended to dispel my sense of strangeness; and in time I yielded to my yawns and took my turn at slumber. My uncle seemed now very wakeful, and welcomed his period of watching

[a] snapshots,] shap-shots, A, B

even though the nightmare had aroused him far ahead of his allotted two hours. Sleep seized me quickly, and I was at once haunted with dreams of the most disturbing kind. I felt, in my visions, a cosmic and abysmal loneness; with hostility surging from all sides upon some prison where I lay confined. I seemed bound and gagged, and taunted by the echoing yells of distant multitudes who thirsted for my blood. My uncle's face came to me with less pleasant associations than in waking hours, and I recall many futile struggles and attempts to scream. It was not a pleasant sleep, and for a second I was not sorry for the echoing shriek which clove through the barriers of dream and flung me to a sharp and startled awakeness in which every actual object before my eyes stood out with more than natural clearness and reality.

V.

I had been lying with my face away from my uncle's chair, so that in this sudden flash of awakening I saw only the door to the street, the more northerly window, and the wall and floor and ceiling toward the north of the room, all photographed with morbid vividness on my brain in a light brighter than the glow of the fungi or the rays from the street outside. It was not a strong or even a fairly strong light; certainly not nearly strong enough to read an average book by. But it cast a shadow of myself and the cot on the floor, and had a yellowish, penetrating force that hinted at things more potent than luminosity. This I perceived with unhealthy sharpness despite the fact that two of my other senses were violently assailed. For on my ears rang the reverberations of that shocking scream, while my nostrils revolted at the stench which filled the place. My mind, as alert as my senses, recognised the gravely unusual; and almost automatically I leaped up and turned about to grasp the destructive instruments which we had left trained on the mouldy spot before the fireplace. As I turned, I dreaded what I was to see; for the scream had been in my uncle's voice, and I knew not against what menace I should have to defend him and myself.

Yet after all, the sight was worse than I had dreaded. There are horrors beyond horrors, and this was one of those nuclei of all dreamable hideousness which the cosmos saves to blast an accursed and unhappy few. Out of the fungus-ridden earth steamed up a vaporous corpse-light, yellow and diseased, which bubbled and lapped to a gigantic height in vague outlines half human and half monstrous, through which I could see the chimney and fireplace beyond. It was all eyes—wolfish and mocking—and the rugose insect-like head dissolved at the top to a thin stream of mist which curled putridly about and finally vanished up the chimney. I say that I saw this thing, but it is only in conscious retrospection that I ever definitely traced its damnable approach to form. At the time it was to me only a seething,[a] dimly phosphorescent cloud of fungous loathsomeness, enveloping and dissolving to an abhorrent plasticity the one object to which all my attention was focussed.[b] That object was my uncle—the venerable Elihu Whipple—who with blackening and decaying features leered and gibbered at me, and reached out dripping claws to rend me in the fury which this horror had brought.

It was a sense of routine which kept me from going mad. I had drilled myself in preparation for the crucial moment, and blind training saved me. Recognising the bubbling evil as no substance reachable by matter or material chemistry, and therefore ignoring the flame-thrower which loomed on my left, I threw on the current of the Crookes tube apparatus, and focussed toward that scene of immortal blasphemousness the strongest ether radiations which man's[c] art can arouse from the spaces and fluids of Nature.[d] There was a bluish haze and a frenzied sputtering, and the yellowish phosphorescence grew dimmer to my eyes. But I saw the dimness was only that of contrast, and that the waves from the machine had no effect whatever.

Then, in the midst of that daemoniac spectacle, I saw a fresh horror which brought cries to my lips and sent me fumbling and staggering toward that unlocked door to the quiet street, careless of what abnormal terrors I loosed upon the world, or what thoughts or judgments of men I brought down upon my head. In that dim blend of blue and yellow the form of my uncle had commenced a nauseous liquefaction whose essence eludes all description, and in which there

[a] seething,] seething B
[b] focussed.] focused. B
[c] man's] men's B
[d] Nature.] nature. A, B

played across his vanishing face such changes of identity as only madness can conceive. He was at once a devil and a multitude, a charnel-house and a pageant. Lit by the mixed and uncertain beams, that gelatinous face assumed a dozen—a score—a hundred—aspects; grinning, as it sank to the ground on a body that melted like tallow, in the caricatured likeness of legions strange and yet not strange.

I saw the features of the Harris line, masculine and feminine, adult and infantile, and other features old and young, coarse and refined, familiar and unfamiliar. For a second there flashed a degraded counterfeit of a miniature of poor mad[a] Rhoby Harris that I had seen in the School of Design Museum, and another time I thought I caught the raw-boned image of Mercy Dexter as I recalled her from a painting in Carrington Harris's house. It was frightful beyond conception; toward the last, when a curious blend of servant and baby visages flickered close to the fungous floor where a pool of greenish grease was spreading, it seemed as though the shifting features fought against themselves, and strove to form contours like those of my uncle's kindly face. I like to think that he existed at that moment, and that he tried to bid me farewell. It seems to me I hiccoughed a farewell from my own parched throat as I lurched out into the street; a thin stream of grease following me through the door to the rain-drenched sidewalk.

The rest is shadowy and monstrous. There was no one in the soaking street, and in all the world there was no one I dared tell. I walked aimlessly south past College Hill and the Athenaeum, down Hopkins Street, and over the bridge to the business section where tall buildings seemed to guard me as modern material things guard the world from ancient and unwholesome wonder. Then[b] grey dawn unfolded wetly from the east, silhouetting the archaic hill and its venerable steeples, and beckoning me to the place where my terrible work was still unfinished. And in the end I went, wet, hatless, and dazed in the morning light, and entered that awful door in Benefit Street which I had left ajar, and which still swung cryptically in full sight of the early householders to whom I dared not speak.

[a] mad] *om.* B
[b] Then] Then the B

The grease was gone, for the mouldy floor was porous. And in front of the fireplace was no vestige of the giant doubled-up form in nitre. I looked at the cot, the chairs, the instruments, my neglected hat, and the yellowed straw hat of my uncle. Dazedness was uppermost, and I could scarcely recall what was dream and what was reality. Then thought trickled back, and I knew that I had witnessed things more horrible than I had dreamed. Sitting down, I tried to conjecture as nearly as sanity would let me just what had happened, and how I might end the horror, if indeed it had been real. Matter it seemed not to be, nor ether, nor anything else conceivable by mortal mind. What, then, but some exotic *emanation,*[a] some vampirish vapour such as Exeter rustics tell of as lurking over certain churchyards? This I felt was the clue, and again I looked at the floor before the fireplace where the mould and nitre had taken strange forms. In ten minutes my mind was made up, and taking my hat I set out for home, where I bathed, ate, and gave by telephone an order for a pickaxe, a spade, a military gas-mask, and six carboys of sulphuric acid, all to be delivered the next morning at the cellar door of the shunned house in Benefit Street. After that I tried to sleep; and failing, passed the hours in reading and in the composition of inane verses to counteract my mood.

At 11 a.m.[b] the next day I commenced digging. It was sunny weather, and I was glad of that. I was still alone, for as much as I feared the unknown horror I sought, there was more fear in the thought of telling anybody. Later I told Harris only through sheer necessity, and because he had heard odd tales from old people which disposed him ever so little toward belief. As I turned up the stinking black earth in front of the fireplace, my spade causing a viscous yellow ichor to ooze from the white fungi which it severed, I trembled at the dubious thoughts of what I might uncover. Some secrets of inner earth are not good for mankind, and this seemed to me one of them.

My hand shook perceptibly, but still I delved; after a while standing in the large hole I had made. With the deepening of the hole, which was about six feet square, the evil smell increased; and I lost all doubt of my imminent contact with the hellish thing whose emanations had cursed

[a] *emanation,*] emanation; B
[b] a.m.] a. m. A; A.M. B

the house for over a century and a half. I wondered what it would look like—what its form and substance would be, and how big it might have waxed through long ages of life-sucking. At length I climbed out of the hole and dispersed the heaped-up dirt, then arranging the great carboys of acid around and near two sides, so that when necessary I might empty them all down the aperture in quick succession. After that I dumped earth only along the other two sides; working more slowly and donning my gas-mask as the smell grew. I was nearly unnerved at my proximity to a nameless thing at the bottom of a pit.

Suddenly my spade struck something softer than earth. I shuddered,[a] and made a motion as if to climb out of the hole, which was now as deep as my neck. Then courage returned, and I scraped away more dirt in the light of the electric torch I had provided. The surface I uncovered was fishy and glassy—a kind of semi-putrid congealed jelly with suggestions of translucency. I scraped further, and saw that it had form. There was a rift where a part of the substance was folded over. The exposed area was huge and roughly cylindrical; like a mammoth soft blue-white stovepipe doubled in two, its largest part some two feet in diameter. Still more I scraped, and then abruptly I leaped out of the hole and away from the filthy thing; frantically unstopping and tilting the heavy carboys, and precipitating their corrosive contents one after another down that charnel gulf and upon the[b] unthinkable abnormality whose titan *elbow* I had seen.

The blinding maelstrom of greenish-yellow vapour which surged tempestuously up from that hole as the floods of acid descended, will never leave my memory. All along the hill people tell of the yellow day, when virulent and horrible fumes arose from the factory waste dumped in the Providence River, but I know how mistaken they are as to the source. They tell, too, of the hideous roar which at the same time came from some disordered water-pipe or gas main underground—but again I could correct them if I dared. It was unspeakably shocking, and I do not see how I lived through it. I did faint after emptying the fourth carboy, which I had to handle after the fumes had begun to penetrate my mask; but when I recovered I saw that the hole was emitting no fresh vapours.

[a] shuddered,] shuddered B
[b] the] this B

The two remaining carboys I emptied down without particular result, and after a time I felt it safe to shovel the earth back into the pit. It was twilight before I was done, but fear had gone out of the place. The dampness was less foetid, and all the strange fungi had withered to a kind of harmless greyish powder which blew ash-like[a] along the floor. One of earth's nethermost terrors had perished for ever;[b] and if there be a hell, it had received at last the daemon soul of an unhallowed thing. And as I patted down the last spadeful of mould, I shed the first of the[c] many tears with which I have paid unaffected tribute to my beloved uncle's memory.

The next spring no more pale grass and strange weeds came up in the shunned house's terraced garden, and shortly afterward Carrington Harris rented the place. It is still spectral, but its strangeness fascinates me, and I shall find mixed with my relief a queer regret when it is torn down to make way for a tawdry shop or vulgar apartment building. The barren old trees in the yard have begun to bear small, sweet apples, and last year the birds nested in their gnarled boughs.

[a] ash-like] ashlike A, B
[b] for ever;] forever; B
[c] the] *om.* B

The Horror at Red Hook

"There are sacraments of evil as well as of good about us, and we live and move to my belief in an unknown world, a place where there are caves and shadows and dwellers in twilight. It is possible that man may sometimes return on the track of evolution, and it is my belief that an awful lore is not yet dead."[a]

—*Arthur Machen.*[b]

I.[c]

N ot many weeks ago, on a street corner in the village of Pascoag, Rhode Island, a tall, heavily built, and wholesome-looking pedestrian furnished much speculation by a singular lapse of behaviour.[d] He had, it appears, been descending the hill by the road from Chepachet; and encountering the compact section, had turned to his left into the main thoroughfare where several modest business blocks convey a touch of the urban. At this point, without visible provocation, he committed his astonishing lapse; staring queerly for a second at the tallest of the buildings before him, and then, with a series of terrified, hysterical shrieks, breaking into a frantic run which ended

Editor's Note: The A.Ms. survives in the New York Public Library, but it has not been examined in detail, as HPL himself prepared the surviving T.Ms. This was followed with the usual editorial alterations by *Weird Tales* (January 1927). The other appearances in HPL's lifetime—Christine Campbell Thomson's *You'll Need a Night Light* (London: Selwyn & Blount, 1927) and Herbert Asbury's *Not at Night!* (New York: Macy-Macius/The Vanguard Press, 1928)—are not relevant to the tale's textual history. The Arkham House editions also follow the T.Ms., with some errors.

Texts: A = T.Ms. (JHL); B = *Weird Tales* 9, No. 1 (January 1927): 59–73. C = *Dagon and Other Macabre Tales* (Arkham House, 1965), 240–59. Copy-text: A.

[a] "There . . . dead."] There . . . dead. B; *There . . . dead.* C
[b] —*Arthur Machen.*] *Arthur Machen.* A, B; —ARTHUR MACHEN C
[c] I.] *om.* A, B, C
[d] behaviour.] behavior. B

in a stumble and fall at the next crossing. Picked up and dusted off by ready hands, he was found to be conscious, organically unhurt, and evidently cured of his sudden nervous attack. He muttered some shamefaced explanations involving a strain he had undergone, and with downcast glance turned back up the Chepachet road, trudging out of sight without once looking behind him. It was a strange incident to befall so large, robust, normal-featured, and capable-looking a man, and the strangeness was not lessened by the remarks of a bystander who had recognised[a] him as the boarder of a well-known dairyman on the outskirts of Chepachet.

He was, it developed, a New York police detective named Thomas F. Malone, now on a long leave of absence under medical treatment after some disproportionately arduous work on a gruesome local case which accident had made dramatic. There had been a collapse of several old brick buildings during a raid in which he had shared, and something about the wholesale loss of life, both of prisoners and of his companions, had peculiarly appalled him. As a result, he had acquired an acute and anomalous horror of any buildings even remotely suggesting the ones which had fallen in, so that in the end mental specialists forbade him the sight of such things for an indefinite period. A police surgeon with relatives in Chepachet had put forward that quaint hamlet of wooden colonial[b] houses as an ideal spot for the psychological convalescence; and thither the sufferer had gone, promising never to venture among the brick-lined streets of larger villages till duly advised by the Woonsocket specialist with whom he was put in touch. This walk to Pascoag for magazines had been a mistake, and the patient had paid in fright, bruises, and humiliation for his disobedience.

So much the gossips of Chepachet and Pascoag knew; and so much,[c] also, the most learned specialists believed. But Malone had at first told the specialists much more, ceasing only when he saw that utter incredulity was his portion. Thereafter he held his peace, protesting not at all when it was generally agreed that the collapse of certain squalid brick houses in the Red Hook section of Brooklyn, and the

[a] recognised] recognized B
[b] colonial] Colonial A, B, C
[c] much,] much C

consequent death of many brave officers, had unseated his nervous equilibrium. He had worked too hard, all said, in trying to clean up those nests of disorder and violence; certain features were shocking enough, in all conscience, and the unexpected tragedy was the last straw. This was a simple explanation which everyone could understand, and because Malone was not a simple person he perceived that he had better let it suffice. To hint to unimaginative people of a horror beyond all human conception—a horror of houses and blocks and cities leprous and cancerous with evil dragged from elder worlds— would be merely to invite a padded cell instead of a restful rustication, and Malone was a man of sense despite his mysticism. He had the Celt's far vision of weird and hidden things, but the logician's quick eye for the outwardly unconvincing; an amalgam which had led him far afield in the forty-two years of his life, and set him in strange places for a Dublin University man born in a Georgian villa near Phoenix Park.

And now, as he reviewed the things he had seen and felt and apprehended, Malone was content to keep unshared the secret of what could reduce a dauntless fighter to a quivering neurotic; what could make old brick slums and seas of dark, subtle faces a thing of nightmare and eldritch portent. It would not be the first time his sensations had been forced to bide uninterpreted—for was not his very act of plunging into the polyglot abyss of New York's underworld a freak beyond sensible explanation? What could he tell the prosaic of the antique witcheries and grotesque marvels discernible to sensitive eyes amidst the poison cauldron where all the varied dregs of unwholesome ages mix their venom and perpetuate their obscene terrors? He had seen the hellish green flame of secret wonder in this blatant, evasive welter of outward greed and inward blasphemy, and had smiled gently when all the New-Yorkers he knew scoffed at his experiment in police work. They had been very witty and cynical, deriding his fantastic pursuit of unknowable mysteries and assuring him that in these days New York held nothing but cheapness and vulgarity. One of them had wagered him a heavy sum that he could not—despite many poignant things to his credit in the *Dublin Review*—even write a truly interesting story of New York low life; and now, looking back, he perceived that cosmic irony had justified the prophet's words while secretly confuting their flippant meaning. The horror, as glimpsed at last, could not make a story—for like the book cited by Poe's German authority, *"er lasst*[a] *sich nicht lesen*—it does not permit itself to be read."[b]

II.

To Malone the sense of latent mystery in existence was always present. In youth he had felt the hidden beauty and ecstasy of things, and had been a poet; but poverty and sorrow and exile had turned his gaze in darker directions, and he had thrilled at the imputations of evil in the world around. Daily life had for him come to be a phantasmagoria[c] of macabre shadow-studies; now glittering and leering with concealed rottenness as in[d] Beardsley's best manner, now hinting terrors behind the commonest shapes and objects as in the subtler and less obvious work of Gustave Doré. He would often regard it as merciful that most persons of high intelligence jeer at the inmost mysteries; for, he argued, if superior minds were ever placed in fullest contact with the secrets preserved by ancient and lowly cults, the resultant abnormalities would soon not only wreck the world, but threaten the very integrity of the universe. All this reflection was no doubt morbid, but keen logic and a deep sense of humour[e] ably offset it. Malone was satisfied to let his notions remain as half-spied and forbidden visions to be lightly played with; and hysteria came only when duty flung him into a hell of revelation too sudden and insidious to escape.

He had for some time been detailed to the Butler Street station in Brooklyn when the Red Hook matter came to his notice. Red Hook is a maze of hybrid squalor near the ancient waterfront opposite Governor's Island, with dirty highways climbing the hill from the wharves to that higher ground where the decayed lengths of Clinton and Court Streets lead off toward the Borough Hall. Its houses are mostly of brick, dating from the first quarter to the middle of the nineteenth century,[f] and some

---

[a] *er lasst*] *er lässt* B; *es lasst* C
[b] *lesen*—it . . . read."] *lesen*"—it . . . read. B
[c] phantasmagoria] fantasmagoria B
[d] in] in Aubrey B
[e] humour] humor B
[f] nineteenth century,] Nineteenth Century, B

of the obscurer alleys and byways have that alluring antique flavour[a] which conventional reading leads us to call "Dickensian".[b] The population is a hopeless tangle and enigma; Syrian, Spanish, Italian, and negro elements impinging upon one another, and fragments of Scandinavian and American belts lying not far distant. It is a babel of sound and filth, and sends out strange cries to answer the lapping of oily waves at its grimy piers and the monstrous organ litanies of the harbour[c] whistles. Here long ago a brighter picture dwelt, with clear-eyed mariners on the lower streets and homes of taste and substance where the larger houses line the hill. One can trace the relics of this former happiness in the trim shapes of the buildings, the occasional graceful churches, and the evidences of original art and background in bits of detail here and there—a worn flight of steps, a battered doorway, a wormy pair of decorative columns or[d] pilasters, or a fragment of once green space with bent and rusted iron railing. The houses are generally in solid blocks, and now and then a many-windowed cupola arises to tell of days when the households of captains and ship-owners watched the sea.

From this tangle of material and spiritual putrescence the blasphemies of a[e] hundred dialects assail the sky. Hordes of prowlers reel shouting and singing along the lanes and thoroughfares, occasional furtive hands suddenly extinguish lights and pull down curtains, and swarthy, sin-pitted faces disappear from windows when visitors pick their way through. Policemen despair of order or reform, and seek rather to erect barriers protecting the outside world from the contagion. The clang of the patrol is answered by a kind of spectral silence, and such prisoners as are taken are never communicative. Visible offences are as varied as the local dialects, and run the gamut from the smuggling of rum and prohibited aliens through diverse stages of lawlessness and obscure vice to murder and mutilation in their most abhorrent guises. That these visible affairs are not more frequent is not to the neighbourhood's[f] credit, unless the power of

[a] flavour] flavor B
[b] "Dickensian".] "Dickensian." B, C
[c] harbour] harbor B
[d] or] of C
[e] a] an A, B, C
[f] neighbourhood's] neighborhood's B

concealment be an art demanding credit. More people enter Red Hook than leave it—or at least, than leave it by the landward side[a]—and those who are not loquacious are the likeliest to leave.

Malone found in this state of things a faint stench of secrets more terrible than any of the sins denounced by citizens and bemoaned by priests and philanthropists. He was conscious, as one who united imagination with scientific knowledge, that modern people under lawless conditions tend uncannily to repeat the darkest instinctive patterns of primitive half-ape savagery in their daily life and ritual observances; and he had often viewed with an anthropologist's shudder the chanting, cursing processions of blear-eyed and pockmarked young men which wound their way along in the dark small hours of morning. One saw groups of these youths incessantly; sometimes in leering vigils on street corners, sometimes in doorways playing eerily on cheap instruments of music, sometimes in stupefied dozes or indecent dialogues around cafeteria tables near Borough Hall, and sometimes in whispering converse around dingy taxicabs drawn up at the high stoops of crumbling and closely shuttered old houses. They chilled and fascinated him more than he dared confess to his associates on the force, for he seemed to see in them some monstrous thread of secret continuity; some fiendish, cryptical,[b] and ancient pattern utterly beyond and below the sordid mass of facts and habits and haunts listed with such conscientious technical care by the police. They must be, he felt inwardly, the heirs of some shocking and primordial tradition; the sharers of debased and broken scraps from cults and ceremonies older than mankind. Their coherence and definiteness suggested it, and it shewed[c] in the singular suspicion of order which lurked beneath their squalid disorder. He had not read in vain such treatises as Miss Murray's "Witch-Cult in Western Europe";[d] and knew that up to recent years there had certainly survived among peasants and furtive folk a frightful and clandestine system of assemblies and orgies descended from dark religions antedating the Aryan world, and appearing in

[a] landward side] landward-/side C
[b] cryptical,] cryptical A, B, C
[c] shewed] showed A, B, C
[d] "Witch-Cult . . . Europe";] "Witch Cult . . . Europe"; A; *Witch Cult . . . Europe;* B, C

popular legends as Black Masses and Witches' Sabbaths. That these hellish vestiges of old Turanian-Asiatic magic and fertility-cults were even now wholly dead he could not for a moment suppose, and he frequently wondered how much older and how much blacker than the very worst of the muttered tales some of them might really be.

III.

It was the case of Robert Suydam which took Malone to the heart of things in Red Hook. Suydam was a lettered recluse of ancient Dutch family, possessed originally of barely independent means, and inhabiting the spacious but ill-preserved mansion which his grandfather had built in Flatbush when that village was little more than a pleasant group of colonial[a] cottages surrounding the steepled and ivy-clad Reformed Church with its iron-railed yard of Netherlandish gravestones. In his[b] lonely house, set back from Martense Street amidst a yard of venerable trees, Suydam had read and brooded for some six decades except for a period a generation before, when he had sailed for the Old World[c] and remained there out of sight for eight years. He could afford no servants, and would admit but few visitors to his absolute solitude; eschewing close friendships and receiving his rare acquaintances in one of the three ground-floor rooms which he kept in order—a vast, high-ceiled library[d] whose walls were solidly packed with tattered books of ponderous, archaic, and vaguely repellent aspect. The growth of the town and its final absorption in the Brooklyn district had meant nothing to Suydam, and he had come to mean less and less to the town. Elderly people still pointed him out on the streets, but to most of the recent population he was merely a queer, corpulent old fellow whose unkempt white hair, stubbly beard, shiny black clothes,[e] and gold-headed cane earned him an amused glance and nothing more. Malone did not know him by sight till duty called him to the case, but had heard of him indirectly as a really

[a] colonial] Colonial A, B, C
[b] his] this B
[c] Old World] old world A, C
[d] library] library, C
[e] clothes,] clothes A, B, C

profound authority on mediaeval[a] superstition, and had once idly meant to look up an out-of-print pamphlet of his on the Kabbalah and the Faustus legend, which a friend had quoted from memory.

Suydam became a "case" when his distant and only relatives sought court pronouncements on his sanity. Their action seemed sudden to the outside world, but was really undertaken only after prolonged observation and sorrowful debate. It was based on certain odd changes in his speech and habits; wild references to impending wonders, and unaccountable hauntings of disreputable Brooklyn neighbourhoods.[b] He had been growing shabbier and shabbier with the years, and now prowled about like a veritable mendicant; seen occasionally by humiliated friends in subway stations, or loitering on the benches around Borough Hall in conversation with groups of swarthy, evil-looking strangers. When he spoke it was to babble of unlimited powers almost within his grasp, and to repeat with knowing leers such mystical words or names as "Sephiroth",[c] "Ashmodai",[d] and "Samaël".[e] The court action revealed that he was using up his income and wasting his principal in the purchase of curious tomes imported from London and Paris, and in the maintenance of a squalid basement flat in the Red Hook district where he spent nearly every night, receiving odd delegations of mixed rowdies and foreigners, and apparently conducting some kind of ceremonial service behind the green blinds of secretive windows. Detectives assigned to follow him reported strange cries and chants and prancing of feet filtering out from these nocturnal rites, and shuddered at their peculiar ecstasy and abandon despite the commonness of weird orgies in that sodden section. When, however, the matter came to a hearing, Suydam managed to preserve his liberty. Before the judge his manner grew urbane and reasonable, and he freely admitted the queerness of demeanour[f] and extravagant cast of language into which he had fallen through excessive devotion to study and research. He was, he said,

---

[a] mediaeval] medieval B
[b] neighbourhoods.] neighborhoods. B
[c] "Sephiroth",] "Sephiroth," B, C
[d] "Ashmodai",] "Ashmodai" A, B, C
[e] "Samaël".] "Samaël." B, C
[f] demeanour] demeanor B

engaged in the investigation of certain details of European tradition which required the closest contact with foreign groups and their songs and folk dances. The notion that any low secret society was preying upon him, as hinted by his relatives, was obviously absurd; and shewed[a] how sadly limited was their understanding of him and his work. Triumphing with his calm explanations, he was suffered to depart unhindered; and the paid detectives of the Suydams, Corlears, and Van Brunts were withdrawn in resigned disgust.

It was here that an alliance of Federal inspectors and police, Malone with them, entered the case. The law had watched the Suydam action with interest, and had in many instances been called upon to aid the private detectives. In this work it developed that Suydam's new associates were among the blackest and most vicious criminals of Red Hook's devious lanes, and that at least a third of them were known and repeated offenders in the matter of thievery, disorder, and the importation of illegal immigrants. Indeed, it would not have been too much to say that the old scholar's particular circle coincided almost perfectly with the worst of the organised[b] cliques which smuggled ashore certain nameless and unclassified Asian dregs wisely turned back by Ellis Island. In the teeming rookeries of Parker Place—since renamed—where Suydam had his basement flat, there had grown up a very unusual colony of unclassified slant-eyed folk who used the Arabic alphabet but were eloquently repudiated by the great mass of Syrians in and around Atlantic Avenue. They could all have been deported for lack of credentials, but legalism is slow-moving, and one does not disturb Red Hook unless publicity forces one to.

These creatures attended a tumbledown[c] stone church, used Wednesdays as a dance-hall, which reared its Gothic buttresses near the vilest part of the waterfront. It was nominally Catholic; but priests throughout Brooklyn denied the place all standing and authenticity, and policemen agreed with them when they listened to the noises it emitted at night. Malone used to fancy he heard terrible cracked bass notes from a hidden organ far underground when the church stood empty and

---

[a] shewed] showed A, B, C
[b] organised] organized B
[c] tumbledown] tumble-down A, B, C

unlighted, whilst all observers dreaded the shrieking and drumming which accompanied the visible services. Suydam, when questioned, said he thought the ritual was some remnant of Nestorian Christianity tinctured with the Shamanism of Thibet.[a] Most of the people, he conjectured, were of Mongoloid stock, originating somewhere in or near Kurdistan—and Malone could not help recalling that Kurdistan is the land of the Yezidis,[b] last survivors of the Persian devil-worshippers.[c] However this may have been, the stir of the Suydam investigation made it certain that these unauthorised[d] newcomers were flooding Red Hook in increasing numbers; entering through some marine conspiracy unreached by revenue officers and harbour[e] police, overrunning Parker Place and rapidly spreading up the hill, and welcomed with curious fraternalism by the other assorted denizens of the region. Their squat figures and characteristic squinting physiognomies, grotesquely combined with flashy American clothing, appeared more and more numerously among the loafers and nomad gangsters of the Borough Hall section; till at length it was deemed necessary to compute their number,[f] ascertain their sources and occupations, and find if possible a way to round them up and deliver them to the proper immigration authorities. To this task Malone was assigned by agreement of Federal and city forces, and as he commenced his canvass of Red Hook he felt poised upon the brink of nameless terrors, with the shabby, unkempt figure of Robert Suydam as arch-fiend[g] and adversary.

IV.

Police methods are varied and ingenious. Malone, through unostentatious rambles, carefully casual conversations, well-timed offers of hip-pocket liquor, and judicious dialogues with frightened prisoners, learned many isolated facts about the movement whose

[a] Thibet.] Tibet. B
[b] Yezidis,] Yezidees, B
[c] devil-worshippers.] devil-worshipers. B
[d] unauthorised] unauthorized B
[e] harbour] harbor B
[f] number,] numbers, C
[g] arch-fiend] arch-/fiend A; archfiend B

aspect had become so menacing. The newcomers were indeed Kurds, but of a dialect obscure and puzzling to exact philology. Such of them as worked lived mostly as dock-hands[a] and unlicenced pedlars,[b] though frequently serving in Greek restaurants and tending corner news stands. Most of them, however, had no visible means of support; and were obviously connected with underworld pursuits, of which smuggling and "bootlegging"[c] were the least indescribable. They had come in steamships, apparently tramp freighters, and had been unloaded by stealth on moonless nights in rowboats which stole under a certain wharf and followed a hidden canal to a secret subterranean pool beneath a house. This wharf, canal,[d] and house Malone could not locate, for the memories of his informants were exceedingly confused, while their speech was to a great extent beyond even the ablest interpreters; nor could he gain any real data on the reasons for their systematic importation. They were reticent about the exact spot from which they had come, and were never sufficiently off guard to reveal the agencies which had sought them out and directed their course. Indeed, they developed something like acute fright when asked the reasons[e] for their presence. Gangsters of other breeds were equally taciturn, and the most that could be gathered was that some god or great priesthood had promised them unheard-of powers and supernatural glories and rulerships in a strange land.

The attendance of both newcomers and old gangsters at Suydam's closely guarded nocturnal meetings was very regular, and the police soon learned that the erstwhile recluse had leased additional flats to accommodate[f] such guests as knew his password; at last occupying three entire houses and permanently harbouring[g] many of his queer companions. He spent but little time now at his Flatbush home, apparently going and coming only to obtain and return books; and his face and manner had attained an appalling pitch of wildness. Malone twice

[a] dock-hands] dockhands C
[b] unlicenced pedlars,] unlicensed pedlars, A, C; unlicensed pedlers, B
[c] "bootlegging"] bootlegging B
[d] canal,] canal A, B, C
[e] reasons] reason B
[f] accommodate] accomodate A
[g] harbouring] harboring B

interviewed him, but was each time brusquely[a] repulsed. He knew nothing, he said, of any mysterious plots or movements; and had no idea how the Kurds could have entered or what they wanted. His business was to study undisturbed the folklore[b] of all the immigrants of the district; a business with which policemen had no legitimate concern. Malone mentioned his admiration for Suydam's old brochure on the Kabbalah and other myths, but the old man's softening was only momentary. He sensed an intrusion, and rebuffed his visitor in no uncertain way; till Malone withdrew disgusted, and turned to other channels of information.

What Malone would have unearthed could he have worked continuously on the case, we shall never know. As it was, a stupid conflict between city and Federal authority suspended the investigations[c] for several months, during which the detective was busy with other assignments. But at no time did he lose interest, or fail to stand amazed at what began to happen to Robert Suydam. Just at the time when a wave of kidnappings and disappearances spread its excitement over New York, the unkempt scholar embarked upon a metamorphosis as startling as it was absurd. One day he was seen near Borough Hall with clean-shaved[d] face, well-trimmed hair, and tastefully immaculate attire, and on every day thereafter some obscure improvement was noticed in him. He maintained his new fastidiousness without interruption, added to it an unwonted sparkle of eye and crispness of speech, and began little by little to shed the corpulence which had so long deformed him. Now frequently taken for less than his age, he acquired an elasticity of step and buoyancy of demeanour[e] to match the new tradition, and shewed[f] a curious darkening of the hair which somehow did not suggest dye. As the months passed, he commenced to dress less and less conservatively, and finally astonished his few[g] friends by renovating and redecorating his Flatbush mansion, which he

[a] brusquely] bruskly B
[b] folklore] folk-lore B
[c] investigations] investigation B
[d] clean-shaved] clean-shaven C
[e] demeanour] demeanor B
[f] shewed] showed A, B, C
[g] few] new C

threw open in a series of receptions, summoning all the acquaintances he could remember, and extending a special welcome to the fully forgiven relatives who had so lately sought his restraint. Some attended through curiosity, others through duty; but all were suddenly charmed by the dawning grace and urbanity of the former hermit. He had, he asserted, accomplished most of his allotted work; and having just inherited some property from a half-forgotten European friend, was about to spend his remaining years in a brighter second youth which ease, care, and diet had made possible to him. Less and less was he seen at Red Hook, and more and more did he move in the society to which he was born. Policemen noted a tendency of the gangsters to congregate at the old stone church and dance-hall instead of at the basement flat in Parker Place, though the latter and its recent annexes still overflowed with noxious life.

Then two incidents occurred—wide enough apart, but both of intense interest in the case as Malone envisaged it. One was a quiet announcement in the *Eagle* of Robert Suydam's engagement to Miss Cornelia Gerritsen of Bayside, a young woman of excellent position, and distantly related to the elderly bridegroom-elect; whilst the other was a raid on the dance-hall church by city police, after a report that the face of a kidnapped child had been seen for a second at one of the basement windows. Malone had participated in this raid, and studied the place with much care when inside. Nothing was found—in fact, the building was entirely deserted when visited—but the sensitive Celt was vaguely disturbed by many things about the interior. There were crudely painted panels he did not like—panels which depicted sacred faces with peculiarly worldly and sardonic expressions, and which occasionally took liberties that even a layman's sense of decorum could scarcely countenance. Then, too, he did not relish the Greek inscription on the wall above the pulpit; an ancient incantation which he had once stumbled upon in Dublin college days, and which read, literally translated,[a]

"O friend and companion of night, thou who rejoicest in the baying of dogs and spilt blood, who wanderest in the midst of shades among

[a] translated,] translated: B

the tombs, who longest for blood and bringest terror to mortals, Gorgo, Mormo, thousand-faced moon, look favourably[a] on our sacrifices!"[b]

When[c] he read this he shuddered, and thought vaguely of the cracked bass organ notes[d] he fancied he had heard beneath the church on certain nights. He shuddered again at the rust around the rim of a metal basin which stood on the altar, and paused nervously when his nostrils seemed to detect a curious and ghastly stench from somewhere in the neighbourhood.[e] That organ memory haunted him, and he explored the basement with particular assiduity before he left. The place was very hateful to him; yet after all, were the blasphemous panels and inscriptions more than mere crudities perpetrated by the ignorant?

By the time of Suydam's wedding the kidnapping epidemic had become a popular newspaper scandal. Most of the victims were young children of the lowest classes, but the increasing number of disappearances had worked up a sentiment of the strongest fury. Journals clamoured[f] for action from the police, and once more the Butler Street station sent its men over Red Hook for clues, discoveries, and criminals. Malone was glad to be on the trail again, and took pride in a raid on one of Suydam's Parker Place houses. There, indeed, no stolen child was found, despite the tales of screams and the red sash picked up in the areaway; but the paintings and rough inscriptions on the peeling walls of most of the rooms, and the primitive chemical laboratory in the attic, all helped to convince the detective that he was on the track of something tremendous. The paintings were appalling— hideous monsters of every shape and size, and parodies on human outlines which cannot[g] be described. The writing was in red, and varied from Arabic to Greek, Roman, and Hebrew letters. Malone could not read much of it, but what he did decipher was portentous and cabbalistic[h] enough. One frequently repeated motto was in a sort

[a] favourably] favorably B

[b] "O . . . sacrifices!"] *'O . . . sacrifices!'* C [*not printed as set-off quotation*]

[c] When] ¶ When B, C

[d] organ notes] organ-notes B

[e] neighbourhood.] neighborhood. B

[f] clamoured] clamored B; clam-/moured C

[g] cannot] can not B

[h] cabbalistic] cabalistic A, B, C

of Hebraised[a] Hellenistic Greek, and suggested the most terrible daemon-evocations[b] of the Alexandrian decadence:

"HEL . HELOYM . SOTHER . EMMANVEL . SABAOTH . AGLA . TETRAGRAMMATON . AGYROS . OTHEOS . ISCHYROS . ATHANATOS . IEHOVA . VA . ADONAI . SADAY[c] . HOMOVSION . MESSIAS . ESCHEREHEYE."

Circles[d] and pentagrams loomed on every hand, and told indubitably of the strange beliefs and aspirations of those who dwelt so squalidly here. In the cellar, however, the strangest thing was found—a pile of genuine gold ingots covered carelessly with a piece of burlap, and bearing upon their shining surfaces the same weird hieroglyphics which also adorned the walls. During the raid the police encountered only a passive resistance from the squinting Orientals that swarmed from every door. Finding nothing relevant, they had to leave all as it was; but the precinct captain wrote Suydam a note advising him to look closely to the character of his tenants and protégés[e] in view of the growing public clamour.[f]

V.

Then came the June wedding and the great sensation. Flatbush was gay for the hour about high noon, and pennanted motors thronged the streets near the old Dutch church where an awning stretched from door to highway. No local event ever surpassed the Suydam-Gerritsen nuptials in tone and scale, and the party which escorted[g] bride and groom to the Cunard Pier[h] was, if not exactly the smartest, at least a solid page from the Social Register. At five[i] o'clock adieux were waved, and the ponderous liner edged away from the long pier, slowly turned its nose

[a] Hebraised] Hebraized B
[b] daemon-evocations] daemon evocations B, C
[c] ADONAI . SADAY] ADONAL. SADY. B
[d] Circles] ¶ Circles B
[e] protégés] proteges A, B, C
[f] clamour.] clamor. B
[g] escorted] escorted the A, C [the *crossed out in* A *by* HPL]
[h] Pier] pier B
[i] five] 5 B

seaward, discarded its tug, and headed for the widening water spaces that led to Old World[a] wonders. By night the outer harbour[b] was cleared, and late passengers watched the stars twinkling above an unpolluted ocean.

Whether the tramp steamer or the scream was first to gain attention, no one can say. Probably they were simultaneous, but it is of no use to calculate. The scream came from the Suydam stateroom, and the sailor who broke down the door could perhaps have told frightful things if he had not forthwith gone completely mad—as it is, he shrieked more loudly than the first victims, and thereafter ran simpering about the vessel till caught and put in irons. The ship's doctor who entered the stateroom and turned on the lights a moment later did not go mad, but told nobody what he saw till afterward, when he corresponded with Malone in Chepachet. It was murder—strangulation—but one need not say that the claw-mark on Mrs. Suydam's throat could not have come from her husband's or any other human hand, or that upon the white wall there flickered for an instant in hateful red a legend which, later copied from memory, seems to have been nothing less than the fearsome Chaldee letters of the word "LILITH".[c] One need not mention these things because they vanished so quickly—as for Suydam, one could at least bar others from the room until one knew what to think oneself. The doctor has distinctly assured Malone that he did not see *IT*.[d] The open porthole, just before he turned on the lights, was clouded for a second with a certain phosphorescence, and for a moment there seemed to echo in the night outside the suggestion of a faint and hellish tittering; but no real outline met the eye. As proof, the doctor points to his continued sanity.

Then the tramp steamer claimed all attention. A boat put off, and a horde of swart, insolent ruffians in officers' dress swarmed aboard the temporarily halted Cunarder. They wanted Suydam or his body—they had known of his trip, and for certain reasons were sure he would die. The captain's deck was almost a pandemonium; for at the instant,

---

[a] Old World] old world A, C
[b] harbour] harbor B
[c] "LILITH".] "LILITH." B, C
[d] *IT*.] IT. C

between the doctor's report from the stateroom and the demands of the men from the tramp, not even the wisest and gravest seaman could think what to do. Suddenly the leader of the visiting mariners, an Arab with a hatefully negroid mouth, pulled forth a dirty, crumpled paper and handed it to the captain. It was signed by Robert Suydam, and bore the following odd message:

> "In case of sudden or unexplained accident or death on my part, please deliver me or my body unquestioningly into the hands of the bearer and his associates. Everything, for me, and perhaps for you, depends on absolute compliance. Explanations can come later—do not fail me now.[a]

ROBERT SUYDAM."[b]

Captain and doctor looked at each other, and the latter whispered something to the former. Finally they nodded rather helplessly and led the way to the Suydam stateroom. The doctor directed the captain's glance away as he unlocked the door and admitted the strange seamen, nor did he breathe easily till they filed out with their burden after an unaccountably long period of preparation. It was wrapped in bedding from the berths, and the doctor was glad that the outlines were not very revealing. Somehow the men got the thing over the side and away to their tramp steamer without uncovering it.[c] The Cunarder started again, and the doctor and a ship's undertaker sought out the Suydam stateroom to perform what last services they could. Once more the physician was forced to reticence and even to mendacity, for a hellish thing had happened. When the undertaker asked him why he had drained off all of Mrs. Suydam's blood, he neglected to affirm that he had not done so; nor did he point to the vacant bottle-spaces on the rack, or to the odour[d] in the sink which shewed[e] the hasty disposition of the bottles' original contents. The pockets of those men—if men they were— had bulged damnably when they left the ship. Two hours later, and the world knew by radio all that it ought to know of the horrible affair.

---

[a] "In case . . . now.] In case . . . now. B; *In case . . . now.* C
[b] ROBERT SUYDAM."] ROBERT SUYDAM. B; ROBERT SUYDAM C
[c] it.] it. ¶ B
[d] odour] odor B
[e] shewed] showed A, B, C

VI.

That same June evening, without having heard a word from the sea, Malone was desperately busy among the alleys of Red Hook. A sudden stir seemed to permeate the place, and as if apprised[a] by "grapevine telegraph" of something singular, the denizens clustered expectantly around the dance-hall church and the houses in Parker Place. Three children had just disappeared—blue-eyed[b] Norwegians from the streets toward Gowanus—and there were rumours[c] of a mob forming among the sturdy Vikings[d] of that section. Malone had for weeks been urging his colleagues to attempt a general cleanup; and at last, moved by conditions more obvious to their common sense than the conjectures of a Dublin dreamer, they had agreed upon a final stroke. The unrest and menace of this evening had been the deciding factor, and just about midnight a raiding party recruited from three stations descended upon Parker Place and its environs. Doors were battered in, stragglers arrested, and candle-lighted rooms forced to disgorge unbelievable throngs of mixed foreigners in figured robes, mitres,[e] and other inexplicable devices. Much was lost in the melee,[f] for objects were thrown hastily[g] down unexpected shafts, and betraying odours[h] deadened by the sudden kindling of pungent incense. But spattered blood was everywhere, and Malone shuddered whenever he saw a brazier or altar from which the smoke was still rising.

He wanted to be in several places at once, and decided on Suydam's basement flat only after a messenger had reported the complete emptiness of the dilapidated dance-hall church. The flat, he thought, must hold some clue to a cult of which the occult scholar had so obviously become the centre[i] and leader; and it was with real

---

[a] apprised] apprized B
[b] blue-eyed] blue eyed C
[c] rumours] rumors B
[d] Vikings] vikings B
[e] mitres,] miters, B
[f] melee,] mêlée, B
[g] hastily] hestily A
[h] odours] odors B
[i] centre] center B

expectancy that he ransacked the musty rooms, noted their vaguely charnel odour,[a] and examined the curious books, instruments, gold ingots, and glass-stoppered bottles scattered carelessly here and there. Once a lean, black-and-white cat edged between his feet and tripped him, overturning at the same time a beaker half full of a[b] red liquid. The shock was severe, and to this day Malone is not certain of what he saw; but in dreams he still pictures that cat as it scuttled away with certain monstrous alterations and peculiarities. Then came the locked cellar door, and the search for something to break it down. A heavy stool stood near, and its tough seat was more than enough for the antique panels. A crack formed and enlarged, and the whole door gave way—but from the *other* side;[c] whence poured a howling tumult of ice-cold wind with all the stenches of the bottomless pit, and whence reached a sucking force not of earth or heaven, which, coiling sentiently about the paralysed[d] detective, dragged him through the aperture and down unmeasured spaces filled with whispers and wails, and gusts of mocking laughter.

Of course it was a dream. All the specialists have told him so, and he has nothing to prove the contrary. Indeed, he would rather have it thus; for then the sight of old brick slums and dark foreign faces would not eat so deeply into his soul. But at the time it was all horribly real, and nothing can ever efface the memory of those nighted crypts, those titan arcades, and those half-formed shapes of hell that strode gigantically in silence holding half-eaten things whose still surviving portions screamed for mercy or laughed with madness. Odours[e] of incense and corruption joined in sickening concert, and the black air was alive with the cloudy, semi-visible bulk of shapeless elemental things with eyes. Somewhere dark sticky water was lapping at onyx piers, and once the shivery tinkle of raucous little bells pealed out to greet the insane titter of a naked phosphorescent thing which swam into sight, scrambled ashore, and

---

[a] odour,] odor, B
[b] a] *om.* C
[c] side;] *side;* C
[d] paralysed] paralyzed B
[e] Odours] Odors B

climbed up to squat leeringly on a carved golden pedestal in the background.

Avenues of limitless night seemed to radiate in every direction, till one might fancy that here lay the root of a contagion destined to sicken and swallow cities, and engulf nations in the foetor[a] of hybrid pestilence. Here cosmic sin had entered, and festered by unhallowed rites had commenced the grinning march of death that was to rot us all to fungous abnormalities too hideous for the grave's holding. Satan here held his Babylonish court, and in the blood of stainless childhood the leprous limbs of phosphorescent Lilith were laved. Incubi and succubae howled praise to Hecate, and headless moon-calves[b] bleated to the Magna Mater. Goats leaped to the sound of thin accursed flutes, and Ægipans[c] chased endlessly after misshapen fauns over rocks twisted like swollen toads. Moloch and Ashtaroth were not absent; for in this quintessence of all damnation the bounds of consciousness were let down, and man's fancy lay open to vistas of every realm of horror and every forbidden dimension that evil had power to mould.[d] The world and Nature[e] were helpless against such assaults from unsealed wells of night, nor could any sign or prayer check the Walpurgis-riot of horror which had come when a sage with the hateful key had stumbled on a horde with the locked and brimming coffer of transmitted daemon-lore.[f]

Suddenly a ray of physical light shot through these phantasms,[g] and Malone heard the sound of oars amidst the blasphemies of things that should be dead. A boat with a lantern in its prow darted into sight, made fast to an iron ring in the slimy stone pier, and vomited forth several dark men bearing a long burden swathed in bedding. They took it to the naked phosphorescent thing on the carved golden pedestal, and the thing tittered and pawed at the bedding. Then they unswathed it, and propped upright before the pedestal the gangrenous corpse of a

---

[a] foetor] fetor B
[b] moon-calves] moon-/calves A; mooncalves B
[c] Ægipans] Ægypans C
[d] mould.] mold. B
[e] Nature] nature B
[f] daemon-lore.] demon-lore. B
[g] phantasms,] fantasms, B

corpulent old man with stubbly beard and unkempt white hair. The phosphorescent thing tittered again, and the men produced bottles from their pockets and anointed its feet with red, whilst they afterward gave the bottles to the thing to drink from.

All at once, from an arcaded avenue leading endlessly away, there came the daemoniac[a] rattle and wheeze of a blasphemous organ, choking and rumbling out[b] the mockeries of hell in a cracked, sardonic bass. In an instant every moving entity was electrified; and forming at once into a ceremonial procession, the nightmare horde slithered away in quest of the sound—goat, satyr, and Ægipan,[c] incubus, succuba,[d] and lemur, twisted toad and shapeless elemental, dog-faced howler and silent strutter in darkness—all led by the abominable naked phosphorescent thing that had squatted on the carved golden throne, and that now strode insolently bearing in its arms the glassy-eyed corpse of the corpulent old man. The strange dark men danced in the rear, and the whole column skipped and leaped with Dionysiac fury. Malone staggered after them a few steps, delirious and hazy, and doubtful of his place in this or in any world. Then he turned, faltered, and sank down on the cold damp stone, gasping and shivering as the daemon[e] organ croaked on, and the howling and drumming and tinkling of the mad procession grew fainter and fainter.

Vaguely he was conscious of chanted horrors and shocking croakings afar off. Now and then a wail or whine of ceremonial devotion would float to him through the black arcade, whilst eventually there rose the dreadful Greek incantation whose text he had read above the pulpit of that dance-hall church.

"O friend and companion of night, thou who rejoicest in the baying of dogs (*here a hideous howl burst forth*)[f] and spilt blood (*here nameless sounds*

---

[a] daemoniac] demoniac B

[b] out] out of B

[c] Ægipan,] Ægypan, C

[d] succuba,] succubus, C

[e] daemon] demon B

[f] "O . . . dogs (*here . . . forth*)] "O . . . dogs [*here . . . forth*] B; 'O . . . *dogs* (here . . . forth) C

vied with morbid shriekings),[a] who wanderest in the midst of shades among the tombs (*here a whistling sigh occurred*),[b] who longest for blood and bringest terror to mortals (*short, sharp cries from myriad throats*),[c] Gorgo (*repeated as response*),[d] Mormo (*repeated with ecstasy*),[e] thousand-faced moon (*sighs and flute notes*),[f] look favourably[g] on our sacrifices!"[h]

As the chant closed, a general shout went up, and hissing sounds nearly drowned the croaking of the cracked bass organ. Then a gasp as from many throats, and a babel of barked and bleated words—"Lilith, Great Lilith, behold the Bridegroom!" More cries, a clamour[i] of rioting, and the sharp, clicking footfalls of a running figure. The footfalls approached, and Malone raised himself to his elbow to look.

The luminosity of the crypt, lately diminished, had now slightly increased; and in that devil-light there appeared the fleeing[j] form of that which should not flee or feel or breathe—the glassy-eyed, gangrenous corpse of the corpulent old man, now needing no support, but animated by some infernal sorcery of the rite just closed. After it raced the naked, tittering, phosphorescent thing that belonged on the carven pedestal, and still farther behind panted the dark men, and all the dread crew of sentient loathsomenesses.[k] The corpse was gaining on its pursuers, and seemed bent on a definite object, straining with every rotting muscle toward the carved golden pedestal, whose

[a] and . . . blood (*here . . . shriekings*),] and . . . blood, (*here . . . shriekings*) A; and . . . blood, [*here . . . shriekings*] B; *and . . . blood* (here . . . shriekings) C

[b] who . . . tombs (*here . . . occurred*),] who . . . tombs, (*here . . . occurred*) A; who . . . tombs, [*here . . . occurred*] B; *who . . . tombs,* (here . . . occurred) C

[c] who . . . mortals (*short, . . . throats*),] who . . . mortals, (*short, . . . throats*) A; who . . . mortals, [*short, . . . throats*] B; *who . . . mortals,* (short, . . . throats) C

[d] Gorgo (*repeated as response*),] Gorgo, (*repeated as response*) A; Gorgo, [*repeated as response*] B; *Gorgo,* (repeated as response) C

[e] Mormo (*repeated with ecstasy*),] Mormo, (*repeated with ecstasy*) A; Mormo, [*repeated with ecstasy*] B; *Mormo,* (repeated with ecstasy) C

[f] thousand-faced moon (*sighs . . . notes*),] thousand-faced moon, (*sighs . . . notes*) A; thousand-faced moon, [*sighs . . . notes*] B; *thousand-faced moon,* (sighs . . . notes) C

[g] favourably] favorably B

[h] look . . . sacrifices!"] *look . . . sacrifices!"* C

[i] clamour] clamor B

[j] fleeing] fleeting C

[k] loathsomenesses.] loathsomeness. C

necromantic importance was evidently so great. Another moment and it had reached its goal, whilst the trailing throng laboured[a] on with more frantic speed. But they were too late, for in one final spurt of strength which ripped tendon from tendon and sent its noisome bulk floundering to the floor in a state of jellyish dissolution, the staring corpse which had been Robert Suydam achieved its object and its triumph. The push had been tremendous, but the force had held out; and as the pusher collapsed to a muddy blotch of corruption the pedestal he had pushed tottered, tipped, and finally careened from its onyx base into the thick waters below, sending up a parting gleam of carven gold as it sank heavily to undreamable gulfs of lower Tartarus. In that instant, too, the whole scene of horror faded to nothingness before Malone's eyes; and he fainted amidst a thunderous crash which seemed to blot out all the evil universe.

VII.

Malone's dream, experienced in full before he knew of Suydam's death and transfer at sea, was curiously supplemented by some odd realities of the case; though that is no reason why anyone should believe it. The three old houses in Parker Place, doubtless long rotten with decay in its most insidious form, collapsed without visible cause while half the raiders and most of the prisoners were inside; and of both the greater number were instantly killed. Only in the basements and cellars was there much saving of life, and Malone was lucky to have been deep below the house of Robert Suydam. For he really was there, as no one is disposed to deny. They found him unconscious by the edge of a[b] night-black pool, with a grotesquely horrible jumble of decay and bone, identifiable through dental work as the body of Suydam, a few feet away. The case was plain, for it was hither that the smugglers' underground canal led; and the men who took Suydam from the ship had brought him home. They themselves were never found, or at least never identified; and the ship's doctor is not yet satisfied with the simple certitudes of the police.

[a] laboured] labored B
[b] a] the B

Suydam was evidently a leader in extensive man-smuggling operations, for the canal to his house was but one of several subterranean channels and tunnels in the neighbourhood.[a] There was a tunnel from this house to a crypt beneath the dance-hall church; a crypt accessible from the church only through a narrow secret passage in the north wall, and in whose chambers some singular and terrible things were discovered. The croaking organ was there, as well as a vast arched chapel with wooden benches and a strangely figured altar. The walls were lined with small cells, in seventeen of which—hideous to relate—solitary prisoners in a state of complete idiocy were found chained, including four mothers with infants of disturbingly strange appearance. These infants died soon after exposure to the light; a circumstance which the doctors thought rather merciful. Nobody but Malone, among those who inspected them, remembered the sombre[b] question of old Delrio: *"An sint unquam daemones incubi et succubae, et an ex tali[c] congressu proles nasci[d] queat?"*

Before the canals were filled up they were thoroughly dredged, and yielded forth a sensational array of sawed and split bones of all sizes. The kidnapping epidemic, very clearly, had been traced home; though only two of the surviving prisoners could by any legal thread be connected with it. These men are now in prison, since they failed of conviction as accessories in the actual murders. The carved golden pedestal or throne so often mentioned by Malone as of primary occult importance was never brought to light, though at one place under the Suydam house the canal was observed to sink into a well too deep for dredging. It was choked up at the mouth and cemented over when the cellars of the new houses were made, but Malone often speculates on what lies beneath. The police, satisfied that they had shattered a dangerous gang of maniacs and man-smugglers, turned over to the Federal authorities the unconvicted Kurds, who before their deportation were conclusively found to belong to the Yezidi[e] clan of

[a] neighbourhood.] neighborhood. B
[b] sombre] somber B
[c] *tali*] *tali,* B
[d] *nasci*] *nascia* C
[e] Yezidi] Yezidee B

devil-worshippers.[a] The tramp ship and its crew remain an elusive mystery, though cynical detectives are once more ready to combat its smuggling and rum-running ventures. Malone thinks these detectives shew[b] a sadly limited perspective in their lack of wonder at the myriad unexplainable details, and the suggestive obscurity of the whole case; though he is just as critical of the newspapers, which saw only a morbid sensation and gloated over a minor sadist cult when[c] they might have proclaimed a horror from the universe's very heart. But he is content to rest silent in Chepachet, calming his nervous system and praying that time may gradually transfer his terrible experience from the realm of present reality to that of picturesque and semi-mythical remoteness.

Robert Suydam sleeps beside his bride in Greenwood Cemetery. No funeral was held over the strangely released bones, and relatives are grateful for the swift oblivion which overtook the case as a whole. The scholar's connexion[d] with the Red Hook horrors, indeed, was never emblazoned by legal proof; since his death forestalled the inquiry he would otherwise have faced. His own end is not much mentioned, and the Suydams hope that posterity may recall him only as a gentle recluse who dabbled in harmless magic and folklore.[e]

As for Red Hook—it is always the same. Suydam came and went; a terror gathered and faded; but the evil spirit of darkness and squalor broods on amongst the mongrels in the old brick houses, and prowling bands still parade on unknown errands past windows where lights and twisted faces unaccountably appear and disappear. Age-old horror is a hydra with a thousand heads, and the cults of darkness are rooted in blasphemies deeper than the well of Democritus. The soul of the beast is omnipresent and triumphant, and Red Hook's legions of blear-eyed, pockmarked youths still chant and curse and howl as they file from abyss to abyss, none knows whence or whither, pushed on by blind laws of biology which they may never understand. As of old,[f] more people enter Red Hook than leave it on the landward side, and there

---

[a] devil-worshippers.] devil-worshipers. B
[b] shew] show A, B, C
[c] when] which C
[d] connexion] connection B, C
[e] folklore.] folk-lore. B
[f] old,] old B

are already rumours[a] of new canals running underground to certain centres[b] of traffic in liquor and less mentionable things.

The dance-hall church is now mostly a dance hall,[c] and queer faces have appeared at night at the windows. Lately a policeman expressed the belief that the filled-up crypt has been dug out again, and for no simply[d] explainable purpose. Who are we to combat poisons older than history and mankind? Apes danced in Asia to those horrors, and the cancer lurks secure and spreading where furtiveness hides in rows of decaying brick.

Malone does not shudder without cause—for only the other day an officer overheard a swarthy squinting hag teaching a small child some whispered[e] patois in the shadow of an areaway. He listened, and thought it very strange when he heard her repeat over and over again,[f]

> "O friend and companion of night, thou who rejoicest in the baying of dogs and spilt blood, who wanderest in the midst of shades among the tombs, who longest for blood and bringest terror to mortals, Gorgo, Mormo, thousand-faced moon, look favourably[g] on our sacrifices!"[h]

---

[a] rumours] rumors B
[b] centres] centers B
[c] dance hall,] dance-hall, B
[d] simply] simple C
[e] whispered] whispering B
[f] again,] again: B
[g] favourably] favorably B
[h] "O . . . sacrifices!"] 'O . . . *sacrifices!*" C [*not printed as set-off quotation*]

He

I saw him on a sleepless night when I was walking desperately to save my soul and my vision. My coming to New York had been a mistake; for whereas I had looked for poignant wonder and inspiration in the teeming labyrinths of ancient streets that twist endlessly from forgotten courts and squares and waterfronts to courts and squares and waterfronts equally forgotten, and in the Cyclopean modern towers and pinnacles that rise blackly Babylonian under waning moons, I had found instead only a sense of horror and oppression which threatened to master, paralyse,[a] and annihilate me.

The disillusion had been gradual. Coming for the first time upon the town, I had seen it in the sunset from a bridge, majestic above its waters, its incredible peaks and pyramids rising flower-like[b] and delicate from pools of violet mist to play with the flaming golden[c] clouds and the first stars of evening. Then it had lighted up window by window above the shimmering tides where lanterns nodded and glided and deep horns bayed weird harmonies, and[d] itself become a starry firmament of dream, redolent of faery music, and one with the marvels of Carcassonne and Samarcand and El Dorado and all glorious and half-fabulous cities. Shortly afterward I was taken through those antique ways so dear to my fancy—narrow, curving alleys and passages where rows of red Georgian brick blinked with small-paned dormers

Editor's Note: The surviving T.Ms. was prepared by HPL and sent to *Weird Tales,* where it appeared in the September 1926 issue with the customary editorial alterations. The Arkham House editions made the mistake of following the *Weird Tales* appearance, making additional errors in the process.

Texts: A = T.Ms. (JHL); B = *Weird Tales* 8, No. 3 (September 1926): 373–80; C = *Dagon and Other Macabre Tales* (Arkham House, 1965), 230–39. Copy-text: A.

[a] paralyse,] paralyze, B, C
[b] flower-like] flowerlike A, B, C
[c] golden] *om.* C
[d] and] and had B, C

above pillared doorways that had looked on gilded sedans and panelled[a] coaches—and in the first flush of realisation[b] of these long-wished things I thought I had indeed achieved such treasures as would make me in time a poet.

But success and happiness were not to be. Garish daylight shewed[c] only squalor and alienage and the noxious elephantiasis of climbing, spreading stone where the moon had hinted of loveliness and elder magic; and the throngs of people that seethed through the flume-like[d] streets were squat, swarthy strangers with hardened faces and narrow eyes, shrewd strangers without dreams and without kinship to the scenes about them, who could never mean aught to a blue-eyed man of the old folk, with the love of fair green lanes and white New England village steeples in his heart.

So instead of the poems I had hoped for, there came only a shuddering blankness[e] and ineffable loneliness; and I saw at last a fearful truth which no one had ever dared to breathe before—the unwhisperable secret of secrets—the fact that this city of stone and stridor is not a sentient perpetuation of Old New York as London is of Old London and Paris of Old Paris, but that it is in fact quite dead, its sprawling body imperfectly embalmed and infested with queer animate things which have nothing to do with it as it was in life. Upon making this discovery I ceased to sleep comfortably; though something of resigned tranquillity came back as I gradually formed the habit of keeping off the streets by day and venturing abroad only at night, when darkness calls forth what little of the past still hovers wraith-like[f] about, and old white doorways remember the stalwart forms that once passed through them. With this mode of relief I even wrote a few poems, and still refrained from going home to my people lest I seem to crawl back ignobly in defeat.

Then, on a sleepless night's walk, I met the man. It was in a grotesque hidden courtyard of the Greenwich section, for there in my

[a] panelled] paneled B, C
[b] realisation] realization B, C
[c] shewed] showed A, B, C
[d] flume-like] flumelike B, C
[e] blankness] blackness C
[f] wraith-like] wraithlike A, B, C

ignorance I had settled, having heard of the place as the natural home of poets and artists. The archaic lanes and houses and unexpected bits of square and court had indeed delighted me, and when I found the poets and artists to be loud-voiced pretenders whose quaintness is tinsel and whose lives are a denial of all that pure beauty which is poetry and art, I stayed on for love of these venerable things. I fancied them as they were in their prime, when Greenwich was a placid village not yet engulfed by the town; and in the hours before dawn, when all the revellers had slunk away, I used to wander alone among their cryptical windings and brood upon the curious arcana which generations must have deposited there. This kept my soul alive, and gave me a few of those dreams and visions for which the poet far within me cried out.

The man came upon me at about two[a] one cloudy August morning, as I was threading a series of detached courtyards; now accessible only through the unlighted hallways of intervening buildings, but once forming parts of a continuous network of picturesque alleys. I had heard of them by vague rumour,[b] and realised[c] that they could not be upon any map of today; but the fact that they were forgotten only endeared them to me, so that I had sought them with twice my usual eagerness. Now that I had found them, my eagerness was again redoubled; for something in their arrangement dimly hinted that they might be only a few of many such, with dark, dumb counterparts wedged obscurely betwixt high blank walls and deserted rear tenements, or lurking lamplessly behind archways, unbetrayed by hordes of the foreign-speaking or guarded by furtive and uncommunicative artists whose practices[d] do not invite publicity or the light of day.

He spoke to me without invitation, noting my mood and glances as I studied certain knockered doorways above iron-railed steps, the pallid glow of traceried transoms feebly lighting my face. His own face was in shadow, and he wore a wide-brimmed hat which somehow blended perfectly with the out-of-date cloak he affected; but I was subtly disquieted even before he addressed me. His form was very

[a] two] 2 B, C
[b] rumour,] rumor, B, C
[c] realised] realized B, C
[d] practices] practises B, C

slight,[a] thin almost to cadaverousness; and his voice proved phenomenally soft and hollow, though not particularly deep. He had, he said, noticed me several times at my wanderings; and inferred that I resembled him in loving the vestiges of former years. Would I not like the guidance of one long practiced[b] in these explorations, and possessed of local information profoundly deeper than any which an obvious newcomer could possibly have gained?

As he spoke, I caught a glimpse of his face in the yellow beam from a solitary attic window. It was a noble, even a handsome, elderly countenance; and bore the marks of a lineage and refinement unusual for the age and place. Yet some quality about it disturbed me almost as much as its features pleased me—perhaps it was too white, or too expressionless, or too much out of keeping with the locality, to make me feel easy or comfortable. Nevertheless I followed him; for in those dreary days my quest for antique beauty and mystery was all that I had to keep my soul alive, and I reckoned it a rare favour[c] of Fate to fall in with one whose kindred seekings seemed to have penetrated so much farther than mine.

Something in the night constrained the cloaked man to silence, and for a long hour he led me forward without needless words; making only the briefest of comments concerning ancient names and dates and changes, and directing my progress very largely by gestures as we squeezed through interstices, tiptoed through corridors, clambered over brick walls, and once crawled on hands and knees through a low, arched passage of stone whose immense length and tortuous twistings effaced at last every hint of geographical location I had managed to preserve. The things we saw were very old and marvellous,[d] or at least they seemed so in the few straggling rays of light by which I viewed them, and I shall never forget the tottering Ionic columns and fluted pilasters and urn-headed iron fence-posts and flaring-lintelled[e] windows and decorative fanlights that appeared to grow quainter and

---

[a] slight,] slight; C
[b] practiced] practised B, C
[c] favour] favor B, C
[d] marvellous,] marvelous, B, C
[e] flaring-lintelled] flaring-linteled B, C

stranger the deeper we advanced into this inexhaustible maze of unknown antiquity.

We met no person, and as time passed the lighted windows became fewer and fewer. The street-lights[a] we first encountered had been of oil, and of the ancient lozenge pattern. Later I noticed some with candles; and at last, after traversing a horrible unlighted court where my guide had to lead[b] with his gloved hand through total blackness to a narrow wooden[c] gate in a high wall, we came upon a fragment of alley lit only by lanterns in front of every seventh house—unbelievably colonial[d] tin lanterns with conical tops and holes punched in the sides. This alley led steeply uphill—more steeply than I[e] thought possible in this part of New York—and the upper end was blocked squarely by the ivy-clad wall of a private estate, beyond which I could see a pale cupola, and the tops of trees waving against a vague lightness in the sky. In this wall was a small, low-arched gate of nail-studded black oak, which the man proceeded to unlock with a ponderous key. Leading me within, he steered a course in utter blackness over what seemed to be a gravel path, and finally up a flight of stone steps to the door of the house, which he unlocked and opened for me.

We entered, and as we did so I grew faint from a reek of infinite mustiness which welled out to meet us, and which must have been the fruit of unwholesome centuries of decay. My host appeared not to notice this, and in courtesy I kept silent as he piloted me up a curving stairway, across a hall, and into a room whose door I heard him lock behind us. Then I saw him pull the curtains of the three small-paned windows that barely shewed[f] themselves against the lightening sky; after which he crossed to the mantel, struck flint and steel, lighted two candles of a candelabrum of twelve sconces, and made a gesture enjoining soft-toned speech.

In this feeble radiance I saw that we were in a spacious, well-

---

[a] street-lights] street-/lights B; streetlights C
[b] lead] lead me B
[c] wooden] wooded C
[d] colonial] Colonial A, B, C
[e] I] I had B
[f] shewed] showed A, B, C

furnished,[a] and panelled[b] library dating from the first quarter of the eighteenth century,[c] with splendid doorway pediments, a delightful Doric cornice, and a magnificently carved overmantel with scroll-and-urn top. Above the crowded bookshelves at intervals along the walls were well-wrought family portraits; all tarnished to an enigmatical dimness, and bearing an unmistakable likeness to the man who now motioned me to a chair beside the graceful Chippendale table. Before seating himself across the table from me, my host paused for a moment as if in embarrassment; then, tardily removing his gloves, wide-brimmed hat, and cloak, stood theatrically revealed in full mid-Georgian costume from queued hair and neck ruffles to knee-breeches, silk hose, and the buckled shoes I had not previously noticed. Now slowly sinking into a lyre-back chair, he commenced to eye me intently.

Without his hat he took on an aspect of extreme age which was scarcely visible before, and I wondered if this unperceived mark of singular longevity were not one of the sources of my original[d] disquiet. When he spoke at length, his soft, hollow, and carefully muffled voice not infrequently quavered; and now and then I had great difficulty in following him as I listened with a thrill of amazement and half-disavowed alarm which grew each instant.

"You behold, Sir,"[e] my host began, "a man of very eccentrical habits, for whose costume no apology need be offered to one with your wit and inclinations. Reflecting upon better times, I have not scrupled to ascertain their ways and adopt their dress and manners; an indulgence which offends none if practiced[f] without ostentation. It hath been my good-fortune[g] to retain the rural seat of my ancestors, swallowed though it was by two towns, first Greenwich, which built up hither after 1800, then New-York,[h] which joined on near 1830. There were many reasons for the close keeping of this place in my family,

---

[a] well-furnished,] well-furnished A, B, C
[b] panelled] paneled B, C
[c] eighteenth century,] Eighteenth Century, B, C
[d] original] *om.* C
[e] Sir,"] Sir", A
[f] practiced] practised B, C
[g] good-fortune] good fortune B, C
[h] New-York,] New York, B, C

and I have not been remiss in discharging such obligations. The squire who succeeded to it in 1768 studied sartain arts and made sartain discoveries, all connected with influences residing in this particular plot of ground, and eminently desarving of the strongest guarding. Some curious effects of these arts and discoveries I now purpose to shew[a] you, under the strictest secrecy; and I believe I may rely on my judgment[b] of men enough to have no distrust of either your interest or your fidelity."

He paused, but I could only nod my head. I have said that I was alarmed, yet to my soul nothing was more deadly than the material daylight world of New York, and whether this man were a harmless eccentric or a wielder of dangerous arts I had no choice save to follow him and slake my sense of wonder on whatever he might have to offer. So I listened.

"To—my ancestor—"[c] he softly continued, "there appeared to reside some very remarkable qualities in the will of mankind; qualities having a little-suspected dominance not only over the acts of one's self and of others, but over every variety of force and substance in Nature, and over many elements and dimensions deemed more univarsal[d] than Nature herself. May I say that he flouted the sanctity of things as great as space and time,[e] and that he put to strange uses the rites of sartain half-breed red Indians once encamped upon this hill? These Indians shewed[f] choler when the place was built, and were plaguy[g] pestilent in asking to visit the grounds at the full of the moon. For years they stole over the wall each month when they could, and by stealth performed sartain acts. Then, in '68, the new squire catched them at their doings, and stood still at what he saw. Thereafter he bargained with them and exchanged the free access of his grounds for the exact inwardness of what they did; larning that their grandfathers got part of their custom from red ancestors and part from an old Dutchman in the time of the States-General. And pox on him, I'm afeared the squire must have

[a] shew] show A, B, C
[b] judgment] judgement C
[c] ancestor—"] ancestor," B, C
[d] univarsal] universal C
[e] time,] time B, C
[f] shewed] showed A, B, C
[g] plaguy] plaguey B, C

sarved them monstrous bad rum—whether or not by intent—for a week after he larnt the secret he was the only man living that knew it. You, Sir, are the first outsider to be told there is a secret, and split me if I'd have risked tampering that much with—the powers—had ye not been so hot after bygone things."

I shuddered as the man grew colloquial—and with the familiar speech of another day. He went on.

"But you must know, Sir, that what—the squire—got from those mongrel salvages[a] was but a small part of the larning he came to have. He had not been at Oxford for nothing, nor talked to no account with an ancient chymist and astrologer in Paris. He was, in fine, made sensible that all the world is but the smoke of our intellects; past the bidding of the vulgar, but by the wise to be puffed out and drawn in like any cloud of prime Virginia tobacco. What we want, we may make about us; and what we don't want, we may sweep away. I won't say that all this is wholly true in body, but 'tis sufficient true to furnish a very pretty spectacle now and then. You, I conceive, would be tickled by a better sight of sartain other years than your fancy affords you; so be pleased to hold back any fright at what I design to shew.[b] Come to the window and be quiet."

My host now took my hand to draw me to one of the two windows on the long side of the malodorous room, and at the first touch of his ungloved fingers I turned cold. His flesh, though dry and firm, was of the quality of ice; and I almost shrank away from his pulling. But again I thought of the emptiness and horror of reality, and boldly prepared to follow whithersoever I might be led. Once at the window, the man drew apart the yellow silk curtains and directed my stare into the blackness outside. For a moment I saw nothing save a myriad of tiny dancing lights, far, far before me. Then, as if in response to an insidious motion of my host's hand, a flash of heat-lightning played over the scene, and I looked out upon a sea of luxuriant foliage—foliage unpolluted, and not the sea of roofs to be expected by any normal mind. On my right the Hudson glittered wickedly, and in the distance ahead I saw the unhealthy shimmer of a vast salt marsh

[a] salvages] savages C
[b] shew.] show. A, B, C

constellated with nervous fireflies. The flash died, and an evil smile illumined the waxy face of the aged necromancer.

"That was before my time—before the new squire's time. Pray let us try again."

I was faint, even fainter than the hateful modernity of that accursed city had made me.

"Good God!" I whispered,[a] "can you do that for *any time?*" And as he nodded, and bared the black stumps of what had once been yellow fangs, I clutched at the curtains to prevent myself from falling. But he steadied me with that terrible, ice-cold claw, and once more made his insidious gesture.

Again the lightning flashed—but this time upon a scene not wholly strange. It was Greenwich, the Greenwich that used to be, with here and there a roof or row of houses as we see it now, yet with lovely green lanes and fields and bits of grassy common. The marsh still glittered beyond, but in the farther distance I saw the steeples of what was then all of New York; Trinity and St. Paul's and the Brick Church dominating their sisters, and a faint haze of wood smoke hovering over the whole. I breathed hard, but not so much from the sight itself as from the possibilities my imagination terrifiedly conjured up.

"Can you—dare you—go *far?*"[b] I spoke with awe, and I think he shared it for a second, but the evil grin returned.

"Far?[c] What I have seen would blast ye to a mad statue of stone! Back, back—forward, *forward*—look, ye puling lack-wit!"[d]

And as he snarled the phrase under his breath he gestured anew; bringing to the sky a flash more blinding than either which had come before. For full three seconds I could glimpse that pandaemoniac[e] sight, and in those seconds I saw a vista which will ever afterward torment me in dreams. I saw the heavens verminous with strange flying things, and beneath them a hellish black city of giant stone terraces with impious pyramids flung savagely to the moon, and devil-

[a] whispered,] whispered; B, C
[b] *far?*"] far?" C
[c] *"Far?*] "Far? C
[d] lack-wit!"] lackwit!" C
[e] pandaemoniac] pandemoniac A, B, C

lights burning from unnumbered windows. And swarming loathsomely on aërial[a] galleries I saw the yellow, squint-eyed people of that city, robed horribly in orange and red, and dancing insanely to the pounding of fevered kettle-drums, the clatter of obscene crotala, and the maniacal moaning of muted horns whose ceaseless dirges rose and fell undulantly like the waves of an unhallowed ocean of bitumen.

I saw this vista, I say, and heard as with the mind's ear the blasphemous domdaniel of cacophony which companioned it. It was the shrieking fulfilment of all the horror which that corpse-city had ever stirred in my soul, and forgetting every injunction to silence I screamed and screamed and screamed as my nerves gave way and the walls quivered about me.

Then, as the flash subsided, I saw that my host was trembling too; a look of shocking fear half blotting[b] from his face the serpent distortion of rage which my screams had excited. He tottered, clutched at the curtains as I had done before, and wriggled his head wildly, like a hunted animal. God knows he had cause, for as the echoes of my screaming died away there came another sound so hellishly suggestive that only numbed emotion kept me sane and conscious. It was the steady, stealthy creaking of the stairs beyond the locked door, as with the ascent of a barefoot or skin-shod horde; and at last the cautious, purposeful rattling of the brass latch that glowed in the feeble candlelight. The old man clawed and spat at me through the mouldy[c] air, and barked things in his throat as he swayed with the yellow curtain he clutched.

"The full moon—damn ye—ye . . . ye yelping dog—ye called 'em, and they've come for me! Moccasined feet—dead men—Gad sink ye, ye red devils, but I poisoned no rum o' yours—han't I kept your pox-rotted magic safe?—ye swilled yourselves sick, curse ye, and ye must needs blame the squire—let go, you! Unhand that latch—I've naught for ye here—"

At this point three slow and very deliberate raps shook the panels of the door, and a white foam gathered at the mouth of the frantic magician. His fright, turning to steely despair, left room for a

---

[a] aërial] aerial A, B, C
[b] half blotting] half-blotting A, B, C
[c] mouldy] moldy B, C

resurgence of his rage against me; and he staggered a step toward the table on whose edge I was steadying myself. The curtains, still clutched in his right hand as his left clawed out at me, grew taut and finally crashed down from their lofty fastenings; admitting to the room a flood of that full moonlight which the brightening of the sky had presaged. In those greenish beams the candles paled, and a new semblance of decay spread over the musk-reeking[a] room with its wormy panelling,[b] sagging floor, battered mantel, rickety furniture, and ragged draperies. It spread over the old man, too, whether from the same source or because of his fear and vehemence, and I saw him shrivel and blacken as he lurched near and strove to rend me with vulturine talons. Only his eyes stayed whole, and they glared with a propulsive, dilated incandescence which grew as the face around them charred and dwindled.

The rapping was now repeated with greater insistence, and this time bore a hint of metal. The black thing facing me had become only a head with eyes, impotently trying to wriggle across the sinking floor in my direction, and occasionally emitting feeble little spits of immortal malice. Now swift and splintering blows assailed the sickly panels, and I saw the gleam of a tomahawk as it cleft the rending wood. I did not move, for I could not; but watched dazedly as the door fell in pieces to admit a colossal, shapeless influx of inky substance starred with shining, malevolent eyes. It poured thickly, like a flood of oil bursting a rotten bulkhead, overturned a chair as it spread, and finally flowed under the table and across the room to where the blackened head with the eyes still glared at me. Around that head it closed, totally swallowing it up, and in another moment it had begun to recede; bearing away its invisible burden without touching me, and flowing again out of[c] that black doorway and down the unseen stairs, which creaked as before, though in reverse order.

Then the floor gave way at last, and I slid gaspingly down into the nighted chamber below, choking with cobwebs and half swooning[d]

---

[a] musk-reeking] must-reeking B
[b] panelling,] paneling, B, C
[c] of] *om.* C
[d] half swooning] half-swooning A, B, C

with terror. The green moon, shining through broken windows, shewed[a] me the hall door half open; and as I rose from the plaster-strown[b] floor and twisted myself free from the sagged ceiling, I saw sweep past it an awful torrent of blackness, with scores of baleful eyes glowing in it. It was seeking the door to the cellar, and when it found it, it vanished therein. I now felt the floor of this lower room giving as that of the upper chamber had done, and once a crashing above had been followed by the fall past the west window of something which must have been the cupola. Now liberated for the instant from the wreckage, I rushed through the hall to the front door; and finding myself unable to open it, seized a chair and broke a window, climbing frenziedly out upon the unkempt lawn where moonlight danced over yard-high grass and weeds. The wall was high, and all the gates were locked; but moving a pile of boxes in a corner I managed to gain the top and cling to the great stone urn set there.

About me in my exhaustion I could see only strange walls and windows and old gambrel roofs. The steep street of my approach was nowhere visible, and the little I did see succumbed rapidly to a mist that rolled in from the river despite the glaring moonlight. Suddenly the urn to which I clung began to tremble, as if sharing my own lethal dizziness; and in another instant my body was plunging downward to I knew not what fate.

The man who found me said that I must have crawled a long way despite my broken bones, for a trail of blood stretched off as far as he dared look. The gathering rain soon effaced this link with the scene of my ordeal, and reports could state no more than that I had appeared from a place unknown, at the entrance of[c] a little black court off Perry Street.

I never sought to return to those tenebrous labyrinths, nor would I direct any sane man thither if I could. Of who or what that ancient creature was, I have no idea; but I repeat that the city is dead and full of unsuspected horrors. Whither *he* has gone, I do not know; but I have gone home to the pure New England lanes up which fragrant sea-winds sweep at evening.

[a] shewed] showed A, B, C
[b] plaster-strown] plaster-strewn C
[c] of] to C

In the Vault[a]

There is nothing more absurd, as I view it, than that conventional association of the homely and the wholesome which seems to pervade the psychology of the multitude. Mention a bucolic[b] Yankee setting, a bungling and thick-fibred[c] village[d] undertaker, and a careless mishap in a tomb, and no average reader can be brought to expect more than a hearty albeit grotesque phase of comedy.[e] God

Editor's Note: The surviving T.Ms. was prepared by HPL; it bears some revisions both in pencil and in pen by him, and apparently some marks made by R. H. Barlow and perhaps even August Derleth. HPL sent the T.Ms. (before making the pencil revisions) for publication in the *Tryout* (November 1925), where the story appeared with even more than the usual array of typographical errors; then, as HPL was circulating the ms. to his associates, Derleth decided to type a new draft (see *SL* 4.25) and sent it to *Weird Tales,* where it was published in the issue for April 1932. Derleth apparently typed from the T.Ms. before it was revised in pencil, for the *Weird Tales* text does not include the revisions; moreover, aside from making errors, Derleth may have made wilful alterations in the text. Some of the variations between HPL's T.Ms. and the *Weird Tales* text are more easily accounted for by changes in the Derleth-prepared T.Ms. than by editorial alterations by *Weird Tales.* Barlow's annotations include only elucidations of some of the revisions that HPL had scribbled upon the T.Ms. The Arkham House editions derive from the *Weird Tales* appearance, hence are quite inaccurate. The dedication appears only in the *Tryout* appearance and has been erased from HPL's T.Ms., hence we can assume that HPL wished it to appear only in the *Tryout,* as an acknowledgement that the idea had come from the *Tryout's* editor, C. W. Smith.

Texts: A = T.Ms. (JHL); B = *Tryout* 10, No. 6 (November 1925): [3–17]; C = *Weird Tales* 19, No. 4 (April 1932): 459–65; D = *The Dunwich Horror and Others* (Arkham House, 1963), 10–18. Copy-text: A.

[a] [Dedication following title: "Dedicated to C. W. Smith, from whose suggestion the central situation is taken."] A *[erased]*, B; *om.* C, D
[b] bucolic] bucolitc B
[c] thick-fibred] thick-fibered C, D
[d] village] *om.* B
[e] comedy.] comedy, B

knows, though, that the prosy tale which George Birch's death permits me to tell has in it aspects beside which some of our darkest tragedies[a] are light.

Birch acquired a limitation and changed his business in 1881, yet never discussed the case when he could avoid it. Neither did his old physician Dr.[b] Davis,[c] who died years ago. It was generally stated that the affliction[d] and shock were results of an unlucky slip whereby Birch had locked himself for nine hours in the receiving tomb[e] of Peck Valley Cemetery, escaping only by crude and disastrous mechanical means; but while this much was undoubtedly true, there were other and blacker things which[f] the man used to whisper[g] to me in his drunken delirium toward the last. He confided in me because I was his doctor, and because he probably felt the need of confiding in someone[h] else after Davis died. He was a bachelor, wholly without relatives.

Birch, before 1881, had been the village undertaker of Peck Valley;[i] and was a very calloused and primitive specimen even as such specimens go. The practices[j] I heard attributed to him would be unbelievable[k] today, at least[l] in a city; and even Peck Valley would have shuddered a bit had it known[m] the easy ethics of its mortuary artist in such debatable[n] matters as the ownership of costly "laying-out"[o] apparel invisible beneath the casket's lid, and the degree[p] of dignity to be maintained in posing and adapting the unseen members of lifeless

---

[a] darkest tragedies] darkes tragediest B
[b] physician Dr.] physician, Doctor C, D
[c] Davis,] Davii, B
[d] affliction] affiiction B
[e] receiving tomb] receiving-tomb C, D
[f] which] whieh B
[g] to whisper] towhisper B
[h] someone] some one C, D
[i] Valley;] Valley, C, D
[j] practices] practises C, D
[k] unbelievable] unbeliveable B
[l] least] least, B
[m] known] know B
[n] debatable] *om.* C, D [*written in pencil in A*]
[o] "laying-out"] "laying out" B
[p] degree] degrees C, D

tenants to containers not always calculated with sublimest accuracy. Most distinctly Birch was lax, insensitive, and professionally undesirable; yet I still think he was not an[a] evil man. He was merely crass of fibre[b] and function—thoughtless, careless, and liquorish,[c] as his easily avoidable accident proves, and without that modicum of imagination which holds the average citizen within certain limits fixed by taste.

Just where to begin Birch's story[d] I can hardly decide, since I am no practiced teller[e] of tales. I suppose one should start in the cold December of 1880, when the ground froze and the cemetery delvers found they could dig no more graves till spring. Fortunately the village was small and the death rate low, so that it was possible to give all of Birch's inanimate charges a temporary haven in the single antiquated receiving tomb.[f] The undertaker grew doubly lethargic in the bitter[g] weather, and seemed to outdo even himself in carelessness. Never did he knock together flimsier and ungainlier caskets, or[h] disregard more flagrantly the needs of the rusty lock on the tomb door which he slammed open and shut with such nonchalant[i] abandon.

At last the spring thaw came, and graves were laboriously prepared for the nine silent harvests[j] of the grim reaper which waited in the tomb. Birch, though dreading the bother of removal and interment, began his task of transference one disagreeable April morning, but ceased before noon because of a heavy rain that seemed to irritate his horse, after having laid but one mortal tenement[k] to its permanent rest. That was Darius Peck, the nonagenarian, whose grave was not far from the tomb. Birch[l] decided that he would begin the next day with

[a] an] a B
[b] fibre] fiber C, D
[c] liquorish,] liquerish, B
[d] story] story, B
[e] practiced teller] teller B; practised teller C, D
[f] receiving tomb.] receiving-tomb. C, D
[g] bitter] bitter winter B
[h] or] nor C, D
[i] nonchalant] nonchalent B
[j] harvests] harvest B
[k] mortal tenement] soul A [*revised in pencil*], B; body C, D
[l] Birch] Brich B

little old Matthew Fenner, whose grave was also near by; but actually postponed the matter for three days, not getting to work till[a] Good Friday, the 15th.[b] Being without superstition, he did not heed the day at all; though ever afterward he refused to do anything of importance on that fateful sixth day of the week. Certainly, the events of that evening greatly changed George Birch.

On the afternoon[c] of Friday, April 15th,[d] then,[e] Birch set out for the tomb with horse and wagon to transfer the body of Matthew Fenner.[f] That he was not perfectly sober, he subsequently[g] admitted; though he had not then taken to the wholesale drinking by which he later tried to forget certain things. He was just dizzy and careless enough to annoy his sensitive horse, which as he drew it viciously up at the tomb neighed and[h] pawed and tossed its head,[i] much as on that former occasion[j] when the rain had[k] vexed it. The day was clear, but a high wind had sprung up; and Birch was glad to get to shelter[l] as he unlocked the iron door and entered the side-hill vault. Another might not have relished the damp, odorous chamber with the eight carelessly placed coffins; but Birch in those days was insensitive, and was concerned only[m] in getting the right coffin for the right grave. He had not forgotten the criticism aroused when Hannah Bixby's relatives, wishing to transport her body to the cemetery in the city whither they had moved, found the casket of Judge Capwell beneath her headstone.

The light was dim, but Birch's sight was good,[n] and he did not get Asaph Saywer's coffin by mistake, although it was very similar. He had,

---

[a] till] until C, D

[b] 15th.] fifteenth. A, C, D

[c] afternoon] aftrenoon B

[d] 15th,] fifteenth, A, C, D

[e] then,] when, B

[f] Fenner.] Fenner, B

[g] subsequently] sebsequently B

[h] as he . . . and] *om.* B

[i] head,] head B

[j] that former occasion] former occasions B

[k] had] *om.* B; had seemingly A, C, D [seemingly *erased in A*]

[l] shelter] shelter, C, D

[m] concerned only] only concerned B

[n] good,] good B

indeed, made that coffin for Matthew Fenner; but had cast it aside at last as too awkward and flimsy, in a fit of curious sentimentality aroused by recalling how kindly and generous the little old man had been to him during his bankruptcy five years before. He gave old Matt the very best his skill could produce, but was thrifty enough to save the rejected specimen, and to use it when Asaph Sawyer died of a malignant fever. Sawyer was not a lovable man, and many stories were told of his almost inhuman vindictiveness and tenacious memory for wrongs real or fancied. To him Birch had felt no compunction in assigning the carelessly[a] made coffin which he now pushed out of the way in his quest for the Fenner casket.

It was just as he had recognised[b] old Matt's coffin that the door slammed to in the wind, leaving him in a dusk even deeper than before. The narrow transom admitted[c] only the feeblest of[d] rays, and the overhead[e] ventilation funnel virtually none at all; so that he was reduced to a profane fumbling as he made his halting way among the long boxes toward the latch. In this funereal twilight he rattled the[f] rusty handles, pushed at the iron panels, and wondered why the massive portal[g] had grown so suddenly recalcitrant. In this twilight, too, he began to realise[h] the truth and to shout loudly as if his horse outside could do more than neigh an unsympathetic[i] reply. For the long-neglected latch was obviously broken, leaving the careless undertaker trapped in the vault, a victim of his own oversight.

The[j] thing must have happened at about three-thirty[k] in the afternoon. Birch, being by temperament phlegmatic and practical, did not

---

[a] carelessly] caarelessly B
[b] recognised] recognized C, D
[c] transom admitted] transomadmitted B
[d] of] *om.* C, D
[e] overhead] over-head B
[f] rattled the] rattle dthe B
[g] portal] portals B
[h] realise] realize B, C, D
[i] unsympathetic] unsympathetc B
[j] The] 'This B
[k] three-thirty] 3:30 B

shout long; but[a] proceeded to grope about for some tools which he recalled seeing in a corner of the tomb. It is doubtful whether he was touched at all by the horror and exquisite weirdness of his position, but the bald fact of imprisonment so far from the daily paths of men was enough to exasperate him thoroughly. His day's work was sadly interrupted, and unless chance presently brought some rambler hither,[b] he might have[c] to remain all night or longer. The pile of tools soon reached, and a hammer and chisel selected, Birch returned over the coffins to the door. The air had begun to be exceedingly unwholesome;[d] but to this detail he paid no attention as he toiled, half by feeling, at the heavy and corroded metal of the latch. He would have given much for a lantern or bit of candle; but[e] lacking these, bungled semi-sightlessly as best he might.

When he perceived that the latch was hopelessly unyielding, at least[f] to such meagre[g] tools and under such[h] tenebrous conditions as these, Birch glanced about for other possible points of escape. The vault had been dug from a hillside,[i] so that the narrow ventilation funnel in the top ran through several feet of earth, making this direction utterly useless to consider. Over the door, however, the high, slit-like transom in the brick facade[j] gave promise of possible enlargement to a diligent worker; hence upon this his eyes long rested as[k] he racked his brains for means to reach it. There was nothing like a ladder in the tomb, and the coffin niches on the sides and rear—which Birch seldom took the trouble to use—[l]afforded no ascent to the space above the door. Only the coffins themselves remained as potential

---

[a] but] bnt B
[b] rambler hither,] ramblre hither B
[c] might have] migh thave B
[d] unwholesome;] unwholesome, C, D
[e] candle; but] candle, but B; candle; but, C, D
[f] least] least an B
[g] meagre] meager C, D
[h] under such] under|such B
[i] hillside,] side-hill, A [*revised in pencil*], B, C; sidehill, D
[j] facade] façade C, D
[k] rested as] restedas B
[l] rear—. . . use—] rear, . . . use, C, D

stepping-stones, and as he considered these he speculated on[a] the best mode of arranging them. Three coffin-heights, he reckoned, would permit him to reach the transom; but he could do better with four. The boxes were fairly even, and could be piled[b] up like blocks; so he began to compute how he might most stably use the eight to rear a scalable platform four deep. As he planned, he could not but wish that the units of his contemplated staircase had been more securely made. Whether he had imagination enough to wish they were empty, is strongly to be doubted.

Finally he decided to lay a base of three parallel with the wall, to place upon this two layers of two each, and upon these a single box to serve as the platform. This arrangement could be ascended with a minimum[c] of awkwardness, and would furnish the desired height. Better still, though, he would utilise[d] only two boxes of the base to support the superstructure, leaving one free to be piled on top in case the actual feat of escape required an even greater altitude. And so the prisoner toiled in the twilight, heaving the unresponsive remnants of mortality with little ceremony as his miniature Tower of Babel rose course by course. Several of the coffins began to split under the stress of handling, and he planned to save the stoutly built casket of little Matthew Fenner for the top, in order that his feet might have as certain a surface[e] as possible. In the semi-gloom he trusted mostly to touch to select the right one, and indeed came upon it almost by accident, since it tumbled into his hands as if through some odd volition after he had unwittingly placed it beside another on the third layer.

The tower at length finished, and his aching arms rested by a pause during which he sat on the bottom step of his grim device, Birch cautiously ascended with his tools and stood abreast of the narrow transom. The borders of the space were entirely of brick, and there seemed little doubt but that he could shortly chisel away enough to allow his body to pass. As his hammer blows began to fall, the horse

---

[a] on] no B
[b] piled] piied B
[c] minimum] minimun B
[d] utilise] utilize C, D
[e] surface] surfice B

outside whinnied in a tone which may have been encouraging and may have been mocking. In either case[a] it would have been appropriate;[b] for the unexpected tenacity of the easy-looking brickwork was surely a sardonic commentary on the vanity of mortal hopes, and the source of a task whose performance deserved every possible stimulus.

Dusk fell and found Birch still toiling. He worked largely by feeling now, since newly gathered[c] clouds hid the moon; and though progress was still slow, he felt heartened at the extent of his encroachments on the top and bottom of the aperture. He could, he was sure, get out by midnight—[d]though it is characteristic of him that this thought was untinged with eery[e] implications. Undisturbed by oppressive reflections on the[f] time, the place, and the company beneath his feet, he philosophically[g] chipped away the stony brickwork;[h] cursing when a fragment hit him in the face, and laughing when one struck the increasingly excited horse that pawed near the cypress tree. In time the hole grew so large that he ventured to try his body in it now and then, shifting about so that the coffins beneath him rocked and creaked. He would not, he found, have to pile another on his platform to make the proper height;[i] for the hole was on exactly the right level to use as soon as its size might[j] permit.

It must have been midnight at least when Birch decided he could get through the transom.[k] Tired and perspiring despite many rests, he descended to the floor and sat a while on the bottom box to gather strength[l] for the final wriggle and leap to the ground outside. The hungry horse was neighing repeatedly and almost uncannily, and he

[a] case] case, C, D

[b] appropriate;] appropriate, C, D

[c] newly gathered] newly-gathered A, B, C, D

[d] midnight—] midnight; C, D

[e] eery] evry B

[f] the] he B

[g] philosophically] phllosophically B

[h] brickwork;] brick-/work, C, D

[i] height;] height, C, D

[j] might] would C, D

[k] transom.] trasnom. B

[l] strength] streutgh B

vaguely wished it would stop. He was curiously unelated over his impending escape, and almost dreaded the exertion, for his form had the indolent stoutness of early middle age.[a] As he remounted the splitting coffins he felt his weight very poignantly; especially when, upon reaching the topmost one, he heard that aggravated crackle which bespeaks[b] the wholesale[c] rending of wood. He had, it seems, planned in vain when choosing the stoutest coffin for the platform; for no sooner was his full bulk again upon it than the rotting lid gave way, jouncing him two feet down on a surface which even he did not care to imagine. Maddened by the sound, or by the stench which billowed forth even to the open air, the waiting horse gave a scream that was too frantic for a neigh, and plunged madly off through the night, the wagon rattling crazily behind it.

Birch, in his ghastly situation, was now too low for an easy scramble out of the enlarged transom;[d] but gathered his energies for a determined try. Clutching the edges of the aperture, he sought to pull himself up, when he noticed a queer retardation in the form of an apparent drag on both his ankles. In another moment he knew fear for the first time that night; for struggle as he would, he could not shake clear of the unknown grasp which held his feet in relentless captivity. Horrible pains,[e] as of savage wounds, shot through his calves; and in his mind was a vortex of fright mixed with an unquenchable materialism that suggested splinters, loose nails, or some other attribute of a breaking wooden[f] box. Perhaps he screamed. At any rate[g] he kicked and squirmed frantically and automatically[h] whilst his consciousness was almost eclipsed in a half-swoon.

Instinct guided him in his[i] wriggle through the transom, and in the crawl which followed his jarring thud on the damp ground. He could

---

[a] age.] age. ¶ C
[b] bespeaks] be speaks B
[c] wholesale] wholesnle B
[d] transom;] transom, C, D
[e] pains,] pains B
[f] breaking wooden] break-/wooden B
[g] rate] rate, C, D
[h] automatically] automaticllay B
[i] in his] to B

not walk, it appeared, and the emerging moon must have witnessed a horrible sight as he dragged his bleeding ankles toward the cemetery lodge;[a] his fingers clawing the black mould[b] in brainless haste, and his body responding[c] with that maddening slowness from which one suffers when chased by the phantoms of nightmare. There was evidently, however, no pursuer; for he was alone and alive when Armington, the lodge-keeper, answered[d] his feeble clawing at the door.

Armington helped Birch to the outside of a spare bed and sent his little son Edwin for Dr.[e] Davis. The afflicted man was fully conscious, but would say nothing of any consequence;[f] merely muttering such things as "oh, my ankles!",[g] "let[h] go!",[i] or "shut in the tomb".[j] Then the doctor came with his medicine-case and asked crisp questions, and removed the patient's outer clothing, shoes,[k] and socks. The wounds—for both ankles were frightfully lacerated about the Achilles'[l] tendons—seemed to puzzle the old physician greatly, and finally almost to frighten him. His questioning grew more than medically tense, and his hands shook as he dressed the mangled members;[m] binding them as if he wished to get the wounds out of sight as quickly as possible.

For an impersonal doctor, Davis's ominous and awestruck cross-examination became very strange indeed as he sought to drain from the weakened undertaker every least[n] detail of his horrible experience. He was oddly anxious to know if Birch were sure—absolutely sure—of the identity of that top coffin of the pile;[o] how he had chosen it,

---

[a] lodge;] lodge, C, D
[b] mould] mold C, D
[c] responding] respounding B
[d] answered] responded to A [*revised in pencil*], B, C, D
[e] Dr.] Doctor C, D
[f] consequence;] consequence, C, D
[g] ankles!",] ankles!" B
[h] "oh, . . . "let] "Oh, . . . "Let C, D
[i] go!",] go!" B
[j] "shut . . . tomb".] "shut . . . tomb!" B; ". . . shut . . . tomb." C, D
[k] shoes,] shoes C, D
[l] Achilles'] Achilles C, D
[m] members;] members, C, D
[n] least] last C, D
[o] pile;] pile, C, D

how he had been certain of it as the Fenner coffin in the dusk,[a] and how he had distinguished[b] it from the inferior duplicate coffin of vicious Asaph[c] Sawyer. Would the firm Fenner casket have caved in so readily? Davis, an old-time village practitioner, had of course seen both at the respective funerals, as indeed he had attended both Fenner and[d] Sawyer in their last illnesses. He had even wondered, at Sawyer's funeral,[e] how the vindictive farmer had managed to lie straight in a box so closely akin to that of the diminutive Fenner.

After a full two hours Dr.[f] Davis left, urging Birch to insist at all times that his wounds were caused entirely by[g] loose nails and splintering wood. What else, he added, could ever in any case be proved or believed? But it would be well to say as little as could be said, and to let no other doctor treat the wounds. Birch heeded this advice all the rest of his life till[h] he told me his story;[i] and when I saw the scars—ancient and whitened as they then[j] were—I agreed that he was wise in so doing. He always remained lame, for the great tendons had been severed; but I think the greatest lameness was in his soul. His thinking processes, once so phlegmatic and logical, had become ineffaceably scarred;[k] and it was pitiful to note his response[l] to certain chance allusions such as "Friday", "tomb", "coffin",[m] and words of less obvious concatenation.[n] His frightened horse had gone home, but his frightened wits never quite did that. He changed his[o] business, but

[a] dusk,] dark, C, D
[b] distinguished] disringuished B
[c] Asaph] Asanh B
[d] and] aud B
[e] funeral,] funreal, B
[f] Dr.] Doctor C, D
[g] caused . . . by] due . . . to A [*revised in pencil*], B, C, D
[h] till] until C, D
[i] story;] story, C, D
[j] then] rhen B
[k] scarred;] scarred, C, D
[l] response] reaction A [*revised in pencil*], B, C, D
[m] "Friday", "tomb", "coffin",] "Friday," "tomb," "coffin," B, C, D
[n] concatenation.] contatenation. B
[o] changed his] dhangedh is B

something always preyed upon him.[a] It may have been just fear, and it may have been fear mixed with a queer belated sort of[b] remorse for bygone crudities.[c] His drinking, of course, only aggravated what it was meant[d] to alleviate.

When Dr.[e] Davis left Birch[f] that night[g] he had taken a lantern and gone to the old receiving tomb.[h] The moon was shining on the scattered brick fragments and marred[i] facade,[j] and the latch of the great door yielded readily to a touch from the outside. Steeled by old ordeals in dissecting rooms,[k] the doctor entered and looked about, stifling the nausea of mind and body that everything in sight and smell induced. He cried aloud once,[l] and a little later gave a gasp that was more terrible than a cry. Then he fled back to the lodge and broke all the rules of his calling by rousing and shaking his patient, and hurling at him[m] a succession of shuddering whispers that seared into the bewildered ears like the hissing of vitriol.

"It was Asaph's[n] coffin, Birch, just as I thought! I knew his teeth, with the front ones missing on the upper jaw—never, for God's sake, shew[o] those wounds! The body was pretty badly gone, but if ever I saw vindictiveness on any face—or former face.[p] . . . You know what a fiend he was for revenge—how he ruined old Raymond thirty years after their boundary suit, and how he stepped on the puppy that snapped at him a year ago last August. . . . He was the devil incarnate,

[a] upon him.] uponhim. B

[b] of] o B

[c] crudities.] cruditnes. B

[d] it was meant] it sought A [*revised in pencil*], B; he sought C, D

[e] Dr.] Doctor C, D

[f] Birch] Breib B

[g] night] night, C, D

[h] receiving tomb.] receiving-tomb. C, D

[i] marred] manned B

[j] facade,] façade, C, D

[k] dissecting rooms,] dissecting-rooms, C, D

[l] once,] once B

[m] hurling at him] huring at bim B

[n] Asaph's] Asapha's B

[o] shew] show A, B, C, D

[p] face.] face! C, D

Birch, and I believe his eye-for-an-eye fury could beat old Father Death[a] himself. God, what a rage![b] I'd hate to have it aimed at me!

"Why did you do it, Birch?[c] He was a scoundrel, and I don't blame you for giving him a cast-aside coffin, but you always did go too damned far! Well enough to skimp on the thing[d] some way, but you knew what a little man old Fenner was.

"I'll never get the picture out of my head as long as I live. You kicked hard, for Asaph's coffin was on the floor. His head was broken in, and everything was tumbled about. I've seen sights[e] before, but there was one thing too much here. An eye for an eye! Great heavens,[f] Birch, but you got what you deserved.[g] The skull turned my stomach, but the other was worse—*those ankles cut neatly off to fit Matt Fenner's cast-aside coffin!*"[h]

---

[a] old Father Death himself.] old Father Death himsell, B; time and death! C, D
[b] what a rage!] his rage— C, D
[c] it, Birch?] it Birch, B
[d] thing] thing in C, D
[e] I've seen sights] Iv'e seen sfghts B
[f] heavens,] Heavens, A, B
[g] deserved.] deserved! C, D
[h] *those ... coffin!"*] those ... coffin!" A [*underscore added in pencil*], B [*copy of B in possession of L. W. Currey shows underscore in HPL's handwriting*]

www.ingramcontent.com/pod-product-compliance
Lightning Source LLC
Chambersburg PA
CBHW061026030726
47504CB00002B/264